The Hedgehog Dilemma

Armanis Ar-feinial

Published by Armanis Ar-feinial, 2024.

THE HEDGEHOG DILEMMA

First edition. June 13, 2024.

Copyright © 2024 Armanis Ar-feinial.

ISBN: 979-8990955912

Written by Armanis Ar-feinial.

Dawn of Forest Black

1. A Plagued Elf
2. Two Worlds
3. Siren's Call
4. The Stone of Immortality
5. A Nymph's Love
6. Ranger's Dilemma
7. Blenheim
8. A dark Elf's Snare
9. Temple of Corela
10. A Curse
11. The Death of a King
12. The First Trumpet

The Hidden Fae

1. The Hedgehog
2. The Nihilistic Neverending Nightmare
3. The Tragedy of Ted Anderson
4. Murphy's Law
5. The Thing About Apples

Lira
Keneira
To Tedward

"I loved this book!! The storyline/plot was amazing. The characters were great."

~Emma Reed

"It's a vivid Hell of an opening."

~Marina Tan

"I love the balance in deeper inner character development and the development of the story itself. Definitely a must-read."

~Lia

"Actually clever and so well written"

~Siboniso Mncwabe

". . .it left me fascinated, curious and intrigued."

~Hafsa

"The ending was thoroughly satisfying. . .I also really enjoyed the tie in of real world issues, and weaving storylines in and out to create a pretty wild ride. . ."

~Mel Bell

". . .It has a little bit of everything."

~Victoria

"This book is explosive. Literally."

~Gizelle

"I read this with a positive vibes, although there are many terrible events in it."

~Bear One

"Well crafted supernatural action-thriller filled with anger and bite."

~Prairiesbookreview on Nihilistic Neverending Nightmares

The Hedgehog Dilemma

In the beginning God created the Heavens and the Earth.
In the beginning the Pendragon gave birth to God.
In the beginning the spawn of Pendragon murdered God.

Prologue The Flames of War

~The monsters and demons aren't hiding in my closet or underneath my bed: I'd be fortunate if they were that far away. No, they are all running amuck inside my head, and they're relentless!

***

It was supposed to be a training exercise, nothing more, but on that day, a war hero walked into his own execution. Guns roared, and the engines revved. Bullets fired from all directions, striking metallic debris of crashed helicopters and planes. Blood painted the desert sand of Nevada crimson, and limbs were sprawled over the sand mounds. Iron carriages were blown to pieces. Many of those trucks still had bodies in them, the decaying carcasses were wreathed in flames as their arms hung out the windows, blood dripping down into the sand like oil. Ghost, in his black fatigues, smelled the putrid rotting of flesh, and he heard the buzzing of flies as they roamed above the corpses littering the desert. His limbs were heavy, and his body hot with the oppressive heating wind and pelting of sand.

Ghost ducked behind the bags of sand, his heart pounding. He knew his brain was searing these images into his brain, never to be forgotten should he miraculously make it out alive today, but did he want to? He covered his hand with his mouth as Slithers, Ticker, and Butcher crouched to the side, hiding behind the sandbags. The gunfire finally subsided. Slither's bloody hand covered her mouth as she stifled a cry, knowing that even the slightest sound would give away their position from the Americans. The Americans they swore to protect and fight for! Did they?

Ghost took several measured breaths. His heart pounded, trying to free itself from its fleshy prison, doomed to die. He cursed himself, swearing under his breath, his right hand trembled, with his finger coming dangerously close to the trigger, ready to fire into the scorching hot sand. Words rattled inside his mind like an echo chamber, *Treason.*

He felt the ground around him suddenly tremble, just like his hand did. He stifled a gasp. He jerked his head upwards, still covered by the sandstorm. Military trucks rolled over the dirt of the desert, driving on the roads, and shifting the sand around its line of driving. The vehicles drove past, and he was allowed a moment's rest, just a moment. No telling when the helicopters would soar overhead and ping his location. *What is happening? I don't understand any of this!* He thought to himself.

"Time to go," he said, his eyes scanning the horizon while he peered his head just above the sandbags.

"Ghost." Butcher's face was grave, her hands trembling at her side, her teeth gritted. "Why did we do nothing? They are dead because we did nothing. What did you do?" She turned her head to him, her blood-stained hair swinging in the air as she snarled at him.

"I did nothing. You did nothing. They did nothing," he replied, knowing full well, and bearing the guilt of killing the four that were down there.

That was *his* fault. *He let them die!*

As always, whenever lives were lost, his heart felt weaker, being restrained by those imaginary lines that occasionally, if by accident, rose up to the surface of his skin. The guilt swept over his chest and his heart felt like it was bleeding inside his chest.

"You and I both know, none of us were making it out alive tonight. These last few moments are going to be the most defining moment in our time. We were born to live and die in obscurity. But we need to go. We—we'll see them again before the night is over; on the other side." A tear escaped his eye and he choked on it. "But damn it all, we are blowing up Area 51, and taking every last one of those sons of bitches with us. That will be our legacy, and perhaps they'll learn their lesson to not repeat this mistake ever again." *We were just unlucky. That's all. We were just thirty-two monsters who got the unfortunate short stick.*

"Ghost! That is not enough. We need to do more than just—"
Bang!

Ghost saw a flash in the distance. The bullet howled, whistling in the air. He immediately turned to face Butcher, knowing the trajectory of the bullet, he was filled with a sense of dread and he opened his mouth to scream, but nothing came out. Butcher was next, and then there would be three. He winced as the flashing bullet grazed his cheek. His heart raced as the shot missed him, and his pupil watched the bullet in front of him, spinning as it soared through the air. He was in a daze, not knowing how the sniper knew they were here, watching the firing squad. Or was he watching all along?

The bullet penetrated Butcher's eye. Ghost's brown eyes opened wide as he gasped. Blood sprayed all over the place as she was knocked down with the bullet shards entering out the back of her head. Fortunately for her, though blind in one eye now as she was, and in excruciating pain, all the shards miraculously missed the brain. Ghost blinked as the blood sprayed.

Ticker ducked down immediately, pulling out his Barrett M82, relaxing his grip. His eyes scanned as he aimed down the barrel of his rifle. His rifle swiftly swayed as he surveyed the sandy horizon for the sniper. He found the sniper; the bright reflection of the scope got his attention as the sniper was taking aim again. His trigger finger curled around the trigger. The trigger clicked back, the rifle shot immediately, and flared the end of his barrel. The round reached the sniper's cover, forcing the sniper to pick up his rifle and hide at a different location.

The gunfire was so loud it nearly deafened Slither's ears, who covered them with both of her hands, her face grimaced and tears streamed down her face. Her limbs trembled, and her eyes gaped open. Her brown hair dripped blood on the ground from her sides. Ghost heard the ringing in his ears, just like everything else, hand-me-downs for earplugs.

She cackled a raspy laugh, her voice cracking. "Pain. It hurts. Ghost, it fucking hurts! Isn't it great! I can feel pain." Her tone became soft. Her arms and fingers trembled; her other eye wide open. She set one hand over her wounded eye, and blood seeped through the cracks of her fingers, she took several deep breaths. "Did they—did they feel it too?" She sat up and ripped off a piece of her sleeve and wrapped it around her eye. "I bet I look fucking dashing."

"Damn it all. We can't sneak back there then." Butcher struggled to get to her feet and drew her MK 16. "You said it. We are not getting out of this alive. Not one of us. I'll buy you time. After tonight, we're gonna make sure they know never to mess with Task Force 7 again! After all, there won't be a Task Force 7."

Butcher jumped out from behind the sandbags. Latching onto a flash grenade. Tossing the black cylinder, she closed her eyes. The grenade made a deafening explosion with bright white lights with the soldiers nearby. The noise deafened more ears as she aimed her rifle down, firing at the temporarily blinded soldiers, staggering over their own feet, some stumbling for cover behind sand mounds. Soldiers further away started firing upon her, bullets pelted her limbs. As if on instinct, she pulled out a smoke grenade and dropped it at her feet. "RUN, DAMNIT!"

Ghost, Ticker, and Slithers immediately turned around and sprinted away from the execution zone. He could hear the rapid gunfire from the distance. He could hear the whirring of helicopter blades in the distance with his overly sensitive ears. He must stay focused on the mission, ignore the fact that this was the last time he would see Butcher again.

The remnants of Task Force Seven rushed at their inhuman pace, kicking the sands with their strides, which shrouded behind them. The sand got into their boots, heating their feet. Area 51 was not far from them, the base which kept so many people away successfully would be penetrated and devoured from within with the rage that filled what remained of Task Force 7.

It was at this time, much closer to his objective, Ghost pictured Butcher dead, faced down on the scorching sand, blood streaming out of her body after being pelted with bullets aplenty. He pictured her dead with a defiant smile, a fake one, but perhaps this one in his mind was genuine. He heard the whirring of the helicopters and felt the rumble of the ground with tanks and armored vehicles with heavy machine guns mounted on them driving in this direction. What remained of Task Force Seven departed with such haste they couldn't hide their tracks. *It's okay. It's okay. Nothing is going to change tonight. We are all going to die, and I have accepted it. Butcher, I'll see you soon.* Ghost blinked his eyes and tears streamed down it, and his face cringed as he stifled another childish cry.

"Ghost," Ticker said from the front. "Do we have a plan, or am I just blowing a hole in the front?"

"This was supposed to be training, I don't have time for a briefing. Just get in, kill everyone, blow the hull and we go down into the facility to blow it!" Ghost snapped. "Nothing about any of this is normal! Maybe with this distraction, we can make it."

Slithers never took her eyes off the horizon in front of them. "Don't hide it, Ghost. Don't give us hope where there is none. There never was. That promise was bullshit."

"We can't blow it up if we're dead, now can we." Ghost answered angrily. "Ticker, Slithers, switch. Ticker, while you're running, I need you to prep that bomb. We won't have time to do it when we get there."

Ticker let out a deep sigh as he shook his head, his brown hair dropping crusted blood from his blond hair, slowing down to let Slithers pass him. "If I screw up, we're going to be dead before we start."

"You're the best at it. I trust you." Ghost frowned. "We're dead anyway. What difference does it make?"

Ticker sneered. "Those might be the last words you ever say."

Ghost saw Ticker swing his rifle over his shoulder and pulled up his satchel, and pulled out a large black device, which was just marginally larger than a claymore. The device had blue, green, and red wires of various thickness, attached to numerous knobs. Underneath the device was a metal magnet. Ticker moved some of the knobs and turned them. He shifted the wires around, moving them around the knobs and into various tubes inside the device. Ticker was meticulous, no one knew bombs better than he.

Ghost saw the chain linked fences with guards stationed around, walking back and forth, patrolling the perimeter, the strobing lights swaying in the distance from the sentry tower. The soldiers patrolled in their camouflage gear: their charging American flag patches on their shoulders, something Task Force Seven was forbidden from ever wearing. After all, they were never considered soldiers; their sidearms holstered with single shot rifles aiming down to the ground. There were some unarmored trucks resting about with drivers inside, and other soldiers moving heavily reinforced crates onto trucks. Their eyes seemed to scan the perimeter and the horizon.

Ghost knew area 51. He knew of all the experiments and weapons development, but one thing they never invested in was security. *I guess Task Force Seven was all they ever needed!* Rumors and all that kept the common person out, and quite frankly, the absurd rumors of harboring aliens kept enemy interest in the classified air force base low, surprisingly, but there would be no more wars for a while, Ghost made sure of that.

I can't afford mistakes; however, I can't afford the time necessary to prevent them. But nothing about this damn training exercise would be considered normal. We are all that's left. Ghost thought to himself as he considered his options.

"Slithers. Kill 'em," he ordered from behind, raising his rifle, his eyes barreled down the iron sights.

Ghost noticed, before he looked onward to something else, Slithers sighing heavily and shaking her head. She was exhausted, he knew that. They all were. Fighting these wars for years was finally taking tolls on them, but this battle, or training if they want to call it that, was taking an entire toll on them mentally, killing soldiers with faces they recognized. Ghost heard the sound of her rifle firing several controlled shots. They found their target's heads, blood sprayed out of their bodies as they collapsed onto the ground. The ruckus of gun fire soon followed in front of them as the loud alarms went off.

Ghost lobbed a grenade swiftly out to the fence. It shattered the foundations hidden underneath the gates, forcing them open. Soldiers swarmed out the buildings. Their eyes already aimed down their holographic sights, training their aim on Task Force Seven. Slithers slipped through and made a beeline to the left, dodging behind a building. Ghost moved in front of Ticker as he laid down suppressing fire. His heart jumped as bullets came for him. The temperature dropped, red veins covered his eyes; the bullets fired, they appeared to slow, he could track their trajectory, moving his body to avoid being hit in anything vital. The bullets pelted his arms and legs, but none were of a high enough caliber to sever him. Ghost knew these soldiers never saw *real* war, and their weapons were inadequate to the likes of him, *a monster.*

Ghost felt the wounds, the warm blood trickling down his legs. He felt the lead penetrate his body like needles and tore through the other side, spilling more of his own blood behind him. He felt the temperature drop around him as Ticker finished his calibration behind him, but what he could not feel was pain. Yes, they even took that away from them. From all of them. *Butcher, what does it feel like?*

Slithers rushed behind another building, shooting other soldiers who were distracted with Ghost and Ticker on the entrance. She tossed a flash bang in front of her as she dodged behind the cover of some wooden crates. The crates were not ideal, the bullets could shred the crates, sending debris, splinters, and ballistic fragments; sparks emitted from the crates upon impact.

Bright white lights emitted from the black cylinder as it exploded, blinding the soldiers nearby, some of which ducked, attempting to find some cover. Slithers breathed out, jumping over the crate with her eyes aimed down the barrel of her rifle, swiftly pulling her trigger, gunning down the disoriented soldiers, bullets penetrating their chests as they fell. Reloading, she jumped behind a crate where another soldier was down. He swiftly moved up, and fortunately for Slithers, he was in perfect melee range.

He swung his rifle at her. She blocked the stop with her own arm, hastily pulled out a knife. The blade impaled his throat, she twisted the knife, rending his neck. She ran behind the last line of defense, and up towards the sentry towers, aiming up high, and unloaded into the sentries pushing on the alarms for more soldiers to come up from down below.

Slithers fired upon the last line of defense from behind, the remaining soldiers were immediately killed as bullets penetrated their corpses from numerous directions.

Ghost raised his hand and dropped it, motioning to Ticker to follow him as he ran to Slithers. "Slithers, turn that damn alarm off!"

Slithers went to the sentry towers, climbed up the ladder, and shortly after Ghost saw her in the tower, the alarm stopped.

"Ticker, plant it right here!" Ghost pointed to the ground where there appeared to be an almost unnoticeable crack in the ground, signaling a door for larger vehicles to come in and out of the base.

Ghost noticed a little crack in the ground, with some sand which blew over their feet, the sand itself poured ever so slightly into the crack. He knew this much larger door was for much larger machinery. This would be the best point of entry, after all, every unfortunate soul down there already knew trouble was coming. He glanced over to Ticker and pointed at the crack. Ticker took out the device and attached heavy duty magnets on the bottom, planting it upright over the door. Ticker flicked a switch, and a red light turned on. Ghost exhaled deeply, taking just a moment to reflect on the magnitude of what he was doing, and taking a moment to realize this was going to be the closest thing to a funeral they would ever get.

"We'll wait," Ghost said with panted breath. "We'll wait until they get here."

The remnants of Task Force Seven pulled corpses together behind a building, about fifteen meters from the explosive. Ghost took an arm from one of the corpses and cut it open, pouring the blood over his face. The three of them pulled together some smaller crates in front of the body of corpses. Ticker and Slithers followed his example as they hid underneath the bodies, their eyes open, watching.

They all took measured breaths, allowing their heart rates to finally slow down as they hid underneath the mass of bodies. They had been racing ever since the first shot was fired, and none of them remembered how long ago that was. *Three days? A month?* Neither of them had any sense of time anymore. They hadn't slept since it started.

Time had passed. Ghost couldn't tell how much time, but he knew it was long enough for the *enemy* to regroup from Butcher's efforts, but they took far longer than necessary. Ghost assumed security below was waiting for further orders before coming up from their little foxhole. Perhaps, General Snells assumed that the modest force at Area 51 would hold them off long enough for an appropriate response. One thing was for certain, General Snells was coming for them, and he never left a stone unturned. Ghost knew this from working with him for the last decade and a half.

They certainly took their time getting here. Ghost saw the soldiers walking on the premise, he saw their gazes and their heads turning, looking over the carnage. He saw their eyes always aiming down the barrel of their rifles. Their faces were grimacing and cringing with the stench, but there was one thing different about these soldiers than the rest of them: they had clean faces, as if they weren't out today, or on leave and coming back from leave to see all of their friends dead, and who else to blame for that than them, Task Force Seven. These soldiers had a *black* eagle patch on their shoulders.

Ghost's eyes scanned from underneath the arm resting over his head, trying to get a count of these *black eagle* soldiers, many of them were hiding behind parked, armored vehicles, their sights trained on the corners of the buildings, places where Ghost would normally hide for cover, but not against this foe. He heard the whirring of the helicopter blades coming closer, dusting the sand off the perimeter, and into Ghost's face. He closed his eyes and continued to listen to heavy boots clamor on the metal plates covering the ground. There was that one thing that deeply concerned him. *Where is that damned sniper!*

Ghost had no choice but to carefully listen to the number of footsteps taken, counting with each pace as the rapidly approaching steps were now faster than their beating hearts. It was almost impossible to discern where *precisely* they were. But they likely marched down the middle as he suspected they would, right to the device. He knew too well. He counted their footsteps. Right when he thought them to have passed over the device: "Ticker," he whispered.

Ticker needed no more words. He pulled out the remote in his side pocket and pushed the black button.

The device started whirring. The light blinked red repeatedly. The soldiers who were right in front of the device saw the device, glanced down swiftly, and stepped backwards. "It's a trap!" one called.

Boom!

The explosion was like a small hurricane, blowing flames and debris in all directions. The soldiers immediately caught in the blast were now black, unrecognizable husks. Others were flailed into the nearby buildings and other objects, snapping their bodies, limbs were strewn over the vicinity. Ghost could hear the bones cracking and crushing underneath the tremendous velocity and sudden halting of their respective trajectories. Outside by the armored vehicles, the soldier's eyes gaped open in a daze. Immediately, they retrained their aim at the vicinity, looking for movement for whoever remained from Task Force Seven.

"NOW!" Ghost cried out.

The remnants of Task Force Seven jumped from underneath the bodies, sprinting towards the explosion where the door into the bowels of Area 51 lay. They were more refreshed and confident, firing at the armored vehicles. They were right there, by the hole.

Slithers Jumped down, throwing a dazed soldier off the internal catwalk into a burning heap as molten metal seeped from the opening, melting through to the bottom of Area 51. Ghost was a few steps in front of the hole, and Ticker followed behind him.

Bang!

His heart raced again. His eyes shifted behind the armored vehicles to the flash. *Sniper. You, again.* He could see the bullet flying right towards him. The bullet was too close for him to dodge, being already midair. *Good-bye.* He closed his eyes, welcoming the precisely aimed bullet.

Thwick!

Ghost eyes opened. Blood sprayed across his face. In front of him was an arm, severed by the shot. He swiftly looked to his right, and Ticker was in front of him. The ballistic fragments scattered as they struck Ghost's arms. He now knew the round of the sniper: a .50 Cal. Barret if he had to guess. Ghost saw Ticker pulling out a satchel with his other arm.

"Take this. Quick." He looked at his arm, pouring blood out of his like a faucet, his other arm trembled as his body began to feel the effects of rapid blood loss. Ticker breathed deeply, shaking his head, "I can't get you much time. But damnit! I'll try." Ticker kicked Ghost into the hole, and he charged towards the armored vehicles. It was not long before the roar of gunfire continued, drowning out the screams.

Ghost landed on his feet, following Slithers down the steel grated walkways. His calculations were correct, the damage done here was more than enough to send the soldiers on the upper levels to their untimely demise and sending significant disarray to everyone else.

The guards down here were disheveled, looking in every direction, not going to their battle stations, not knowing where everything was. Many kept their hands on top of their heads, limping to their next location, while others were laying on the ground, covering their wounds with their hands, trying to keep themselves from bleeding out. *Perhaps if they didn't rely on us too much, they might have a chance down here. We carried your burdens, you little shits.* Ghost and Slithers descended to the second level.

Ghost sucked in the air through his teeth, stifling a whimpered cry. *And then there were only two left.* He knew it was time but that didn't make this any easier. He raised his rifle, firing with Slithers the disorganized men below. Their corpses littered the ground, and their blood painted the walls. They made it down three more levels. The stench of gunpowder filled the air.

Red lights from the alarms flared, and the buzzing from said alarm pierced their ears. This level was more open, and the soldiers were more organized, preparing barricades and riot shields.

There was reinforced steel for cover, even Ghost and Slithers' rounds would not pierce them. Soldiers held their ground behind cover.

"Slithers take right!" he pointed right.

She went to the right, firing at the shield walls, keeping the soldiers behind cover as Ghost strode to the left.

Ghost inhaled *essence* from the metal and blood in the ground. This essence passed through his body, and he suddenly felt refreshed as black veins protruded on his skin. He felt the temperature drop, his hair sticking on ends as he *passed through* the barricade, behind their iron defense.

The soldier's eyes stretched open, and their trigger fingers trembled as he opened fire behind them. These soldiers immediately turned around and shot through Ghost. Slithers slipped through the other side, crossing her fire with Ghost's line of sight. The soldiers were in a disorganized mess as they started shooting in random directions. Their fire was immediately suppressed, their bodies strewn behind the reinforced steel cover. Their blood made a large pool at Ghost and Slithers' feet. Ghost's black veins receded back into his body.

"One more level," Ghost said. "One more level, and we're done."

Bang!

A shot came from above. His eyes opened wide before hastily spinning around, aiming his rifle to the top of the catwalk, from which stood a single marksman. Ghost pulled the trigger of his rifle, and he felt an uncontrolled kickback into his shoulder as the bullet ripped through the marksman. The walls were painted with blood. Suddenly, Ghost realized that the shot was not aimed for him. Turning around, he looked at the worst thing he could imagine, Slithers, and suddenly, he knew pain.

She smiled as tears streamed down her face; she covered the wound with her hand. Black blood spilled through the cracks of her hand like the inside of a sinking ship. Ghost had enough medical training to assume the bullet struck the liver. She leaned against a wall, breathing heavily. He bolted over to her, pulling out a med-kit, hoping against hope to save her.

"No. There isn't time." She said, grabbing onto his hand with hers, "They're coming down. I don't have long. You know it's not worth it. You don't have time to waste. With what is left. I will stay behind and *will* myself to buy you what you need."

Ghost didn't want to be alone. He inhaled and exhaled deeply, trying to mask his frustration. He didn't want to cry but couldn't stop a singular tear from rolling down his face. She was the last person he ever wanted to say good-bye too, and now he couldn't even muster the right words. "I understand," was all he managed to say. He turned and sprinted to the set of stairs heading down to the last level.

"Ghost!" she shouted.

She shouldn't be wasting energy talking. Hearing the echoes of military boots descending from above, he snapped at her, "Be quick about it." *If only there was more time.*

"What little time we had in this world, I'm glad I got to spend my last moments with you," she said, "I don't know how to say this, so I'll be blunt. I love you."

He nodded. "I love you too."

"Ghost, if by some miracle you make it through this, promise me this: that you will live. And hold no hatred in your heart for the hell we've been through. Promise me that you will find another light. Even a small fading one should suffice. Now go. There isn't time."

A tear escaped his eye. He could find no words. He nodded to her and turned. *This isn't fair. What did we do to deserve this?* He sprinted down the stairs, down into the next level.

Ghost inhaled the *essence* from the air, and red veins protruded from underneath his skin when he came to a whitely lit room, the metal rods were polished almost, some were rising with sudden changing in the water levels, there were four large bronze tubes connecting these tubes to more volatile parts of the reactor. His eyes scanned the top of the room to locate the command center, his eyes canned downward again for a doorway, red around the hinges.

He moved around the first bronze tube and strapped the bomb to it. He placed the strap close to the bottom, now, if anyone was looking for it then they would find it, but Ghost knew too well that they would not be looking for it. They'd be too busy trying to kill him.

Not more than five minutes passed and the room behind him was roaring with gunfire. It would not be long before he was completely, utterly alone, and they would be on him shortly like flies to a pile of feces. He could not be certain if he had enough time to prime the bomb for explosion. And he still didn't know why any of this was happening. He finished priming the bomb, and he inhaled some of the *essence* from the air, and the veins crawled from his skin, moving themselves from him, and surrounding the bomb.

One of the silver rods ruptured, and steam filled the room. Ghost felt the radiation, and the tremendous heat filled the air. He felt the heat open up patches of his skin, the lightheadedness followed, running towards the exit, tripping over his feet. This continued as the radiation seeped into his body at such a high degree, he vomited on the door, swinging it open, he jumped inside and slammed the door shut behind him, panting, and breathing in more *essence*. There was an explosion in the reactor, followed by several rapid strikes against the door from chunks of radioactive debris.

The bomb was unnecessary. I literally came down here in the middle of a fucking meltdown! Are you serious! Well, that was part of the problem anyway, but that didn't mean they couldn't stop the reactor from blowing. One more thing left.

Glancing up the stairs, he saw the last door leading upwards to the command center. That reactor explosion bought him enough time. He inhaled the *essence* from the air, and the red veins on his skin faded into his body. The veins returned to his body a light cerulean. His strides sent him up the stairs, tackling through the door to an empty command center.

Hastily looking to the monitors, he tracked the soldiers move away from the reactor from where he was going. The soldiers placed iron blockades to the reactor before shifting down other corridors, congregating elsewhere. Ghost shook his head and sighed as he grabbed a chair and logged into the mainframe of the computer, disabling the failsafe procedures.

Locking the console, he took a breath. *Good-bye, Slithers. I love you. And Ticker. And Butcher. And all of you. You're my only friends. I'll see you soon.*

Ghost was fatigued, pushing the chair out from under him, his eyes narrowed towards the door heading out the other end of the corridor, where he assumed the command center evacuated to. He took a deep breath of relief, this last-minute mission was to be a success, but now, he had to pretend to want to make it out, to keep them away from the command center to reset the protocols. *I'll see you soon.*

He breathed in the *essence* from the steel and iron in the room and the blue veins turned grey and opened the door. The corridor was empty but clatter and clamor of heavy boots stamping down the halls. Ghost aimed down his sights as he ran down the hall.

He turned down the hall, sprinting down some stairs, and rushed out the door. Bullets immediately shot past his head. He returned fire against soldiers stationed up in the catwalks. His eyes glanced to the side, and his best friend lay there in a pool of her own black blood.

Slithers was pelted with bullet holes filled her body, and all her limbs were pelted and penetrated that they all severed, being scattered across the room. Blood overflowed from her mouth. As if that wasn't enough, for good measure, someone left a military knife protruding from her heart, impaled blade deep.

One month ago, Slithers and Ghost were laying down in the fields of Paulding Forest, laying down in the empty space, staring at the break in the trees. The moon and stars shone bright this night. Ghost's hands interwoven with Slither's fingers. They were alone, together. They were not off fighting, not with the rest of Task Force Seven, and far away from the U.S. military. They were alone, except for a few crickets singing their songs.

Ghost felt her fingers tightly grip his, and she pulled him to his side, and they locked eyes. Slithers smiled that smile, but bags filled her eyes with exhaustion, the same bags he always wore upon his face. "We'll be free soon." She told him that night.

But she still held that smile, curled upon her lips.

The ground sparked as bullets continued flying towards him. He laid down suppressing fire. He lobbed a smoke grenade on his position and lobbed numerous grenades down the hall and through the catwalks. The halls echoed with gunfire as the smoke obscured his visibility. Taking off his equipment vest he ripped another vest off a corpse. Several more bullets came closer, penetrating him in the limbs and chest. Coughing, he donned on the enemy's armor.

He sprinted through the smoke, firing at soldiers hiding from behind the cover of the other rooms. *Three levels to get to the surface. Just three.* Ghost grimaced, grinding his teeth as the fire from the guns lit up the face around him. His watery eyes glimmered with the bright lights of bullets emitting from their respective rifles. Bullets which struck him in these silver veins sparked around him. He never blinked as he rushed to the stairs.

Clunk! Clunk! Clunk!

A dropped grenade *clinked* against the stairs as it fell, the echo to Ghost was louder to him than the constant gun fire. His attention shifted focus as he was in midstride. The grenade started flashing fire from behind its pineapple-shape, sending shards everywhere. Instinctively, his veins breathed in more *essence* and he felt refreshed as if water coursed through these veins. He knew this was unnatural. The grey light in these veins over his body thickened.

Find the light. Whichever light flickers. Find it! Ghost thought.

The explosion sent the shards piercing through his body, ripping out the out through his back, blood sprayed out. He felt cold as the blood dispelled from his body. The explosion propelled him backwards. He landed on the ground, rolling on his side. He immediately stood up and sprinted back to the stairs. He aimed down his iron sights as he reloaded his rifle with his sleight of hand.

He charged up the stairs, screaming as the grey veins persisted on his body, aiming down the iron sights, shooting everyone in his path. His aim was never faulty, despite the lack of spirit he had. His spirit felt like it was a man, hanging from a noose over the Grand Canyon.

His heart was empty. He stopped caring as the bullets penetrated these monsters' bodies, letting them plop to the ground like empty husks being prepared for their tombs. He stopped caring about the lives he was taking. He stopped caring about the country he fought tooth and nail to protect, but more importantly, he stopped caring about his life.

He ran, leaving his trail of blood behind him as he made it to the next level, which had little more cover than before. He simply jumped over fallen filing cabinets. Bullets sprayed from above as the roaring continued with heavy-machine gunfire. More of that *essence* filled his body and the veins on his body swelled, *clunk*, emitting more grey light in the room. Bullets hit Ghost but they struck the veins, coming to a halt, the bullet shattered, and fragments deflected off his body. He still felt the impact push vibrations through his body.

So much, so much blood. I fought for this? I never would have if I knew this was going to be the futile result! "Peace, is this your idea of some cruel joke? Because this isn't funny and I'm not laughing!" he cried out loud, his voice screaming into the halls, his voice only silenced by the roar of the flames.

He made it through another doorway.

Boom!

A great ball of fire was hurled at him from the other side of this level. He swiftly turned, being hit by a burning filing cabinet. He felt the warmth of the flames, and the immediate thrust bruised his arms. His firm grip was nearly ripped away from his rifle. The filing cabinet pinned him against the wall. The fire burned his clothes as he hastily pushed the incendiary filing cabinet off him. He let the orange air burn as he got up, ignoring its caress on his body. It could only be described as an alien sensation: nothing more. Nothing more.

At last, Ghost made it to the morning, on top of Area 51. Sighing heavily with a pulsating chest, he breathed in more *essence* from the air, and the grey veins receded into his skin, returning to Cerulean. He carefully eyed soldiers training their sights on them from behind the rubble, no doubt thanks to Ticker, whose body was nowhere to be seen. Standing upon the rubbled plains, he stared, knowing full well, a gun fight with his exhaustion was suicide, Hell, why did he care anymore.

He took a long look at the soldiers surrounding him like an animal in a cage. *After all, that is all any of us ever were. Just an animal who needs to be put down. This had better have been worth it.*

His fingers trembled. Scampering with heightened pace, he raised up his rifle like a club, his cerulean veins crawled from his hand to the rifle. Swinging the rifle down, the rifle, and the veins attached to the rifle shattered as it sliced through the soldier's ballistics helmet, and the soldier's skull. He pulled the pin out of a grenade hanging from the soldier's vest as he kicked the corpse, rolling him into the rest of his platoon. He turned to another soldier, who was running at him, using his own rifle as a club. Ghost ducked and swung his foot into the soldier's windpipe.

The grenade exploded, sending the corpse's limbs flying, and metallic debris into the soldiers nearby. Ghost dashed at the group, loosely pulling out his kbar knife, and slit the throat of another soldier. Soldiers screamed out trying to put down this animal before more pin-less grenades fell from the body. Ghost dashed to another group of soldiers: bullets began to impale him again as an explosion sent more debris his way.

Only one platoon left!

Ghost struck the man in the chest with a knife. The soldier, who had some life in him, ripped out a pin of a grenade as he stabbed Ghost in the arm, twisting the blade. Ghost felt the blade twisting in his arm, but pain was just as elusive as ever.

Ghost ripped out the knife in his shoulder and stabbed the man's tendon, ripping himself away before the grenade blew. Shards of fragments of the grenade penetrated Ghost, ripping apart flesh. His fingers trembled again. Swiveled to the side he threw a spinning knife, impaling a soldier between the eyes.

Taking a deep breath as he strode on the scorching hot ground with the blue veins, moving faster than before. As his body felt like a soulless husk, his face became still like it was carved in a mountain.

Ghost pulled a grenade from his own pocket. He trawled the pin out and threw it behind him. He jerked out a second grenade. He tugged the pin out and threw it behind him. He started slashing at these soldier's necks, with the knife, which dulled.

The grenades behind him blew. The roar of the blast was deafening, and the dying gurgling screams of soldiers behind him continued.

Ghost impaled the last soldier with an iron pipe from a plumbing apparatus. The corpse trembled and leaned on him before collapsing at his feet. He heard groans of soldiers who had not yet passed to the other side. He pulled out his sidearm, and pointed at the nearest one, and pulled the trigger. The man's brains splattered on the ground.

Ghost retracted his sidearm to his holster. His eyes were stretched open, and he couldn't bring himself to look at the mound of bodies around him, many of which he killed. The sands were stained in blood, and carcasses were blown away in the wind, and limbs were scattered all over the rubble. His heart sank as he realized again the sanctity of life and how easy it was for him to take it away. Violence, it's all he ever knew, and even then, it succeeded, or was he perhaps the epitome of human failure.

Finally having a moment, memories swept over his mind of his comrades, their faces, and their smiles, as if compelled to remember them not in pain, but of happiness. A life filled with nothing but constant war, and this was the result. He gritted his teeth as he knew not what to fight for, not anymore. He was the last of Task Force Seven, the only survivor. *Damn it all. Why was this happening? This was supposed to be a training exercise!* He felt like a dull stake was being violently hammered into his chest without ceasing, as the guilt swept over him. *I murdered these people. I murdered. Everyone.*

Bang!

He looked up at the flash in the distance. His heart jumped, and then settled back down as he remembered he didn't care anymore. The caliber round penetrated his chest and blood sprayed out of his back. The blue veins retreated back underneath his skin, and he resembled a normal human again. The numerous bullet holes in Ghost's standing corpse were now flowing out of him, almost like he was a strainer. *To live and die in obscurity. A corpse is all I ever was, and all I will be.* He coughed as blood sprayed out of his mouth. He still looked forward at the sniper.

Finish it!

Just as he thought those last words, he heard a loud whistle in the air. His head tilted up as blood drooled from his mouth. Black birds in the morning horizon flew swiftly, their velocity rang in his ears as they came overhead. More whistling came, he looked right above him as the planes swept overhead, and large metallic cylinders dropped out of the tummies of these planes. He smiled, and he let out a chuckle as he grasped onto his elbow with the knife impaled in it. Uncle Sam spared no expense on them. Ghost covered his heart with his hand as he took a deep breath, not making a move. "I pledge allegiance to the flag—"

The bombs struck right beside him, clouding everything in sight. The explosions and flames pushed through him in a torrent of fire. The red air caressed his corpse as sharp debris penetrated him, ripping his flesh apart. Nothing would escape as the fighter jets turned back around and lit the field up with their guns. This continued, until nothing remained.

Area 51 became a crater filled with rubble, limbs and burnt faces, melted dog tags. The smoke was filled with radioactive particles, and the ground became a hazardous wasteland. The buildings were brought to ruin, the remains scattering in the wind. Blood watered the ground. Every. Single. Inch.

Chapter 1 Peace in the Gardens

~Not of my own choice, I became a hero for peace, and I did whatever I was ordered to do. I killed, and I killed, and I killed. I killed without halting. I killed until at last my heart stopped beating. Every life I removed meant I was one step closer to brokering world peace. And then, at last I achieved it. With such an impossible task, you'd think that would make me happy. But that wasn't the reward I acquired 'cause I became unnecessary, and I was framed for treasonous activity not of my own doing, and I was executed. Again, and again, and again!

***

Samantha and Jennifer sat upon their checkered picnic blanket, their cooler onto the side, they were sitting at the Boston Common across the street from Park Street Church. The church overlooked them, the grand church spanned the entirety of the corner of Park Street and Tremont Street, hovering over the opposite side of the common. The red bricks of the church were dotted with two rows of contrastingly white windows, square on the bottom row and grandly arched on the top. There was a clock on all four sides of the brick church leading up to the belfry, and the belfry above pointed upwards like a castle tower, was white, reflecting off the light of the bright sun.

Samantha and Jennifer took great care in getting the creases out of the blanket. Samantha was lying face up, letting the sun beat down on her face, shielded by large sunglasses. She was resting in her t-shirt and gym shorts with her arms resting at her sides. Jennifer was laying right next to her; her face away from the sun as she lay on her belly, her legs bent in the air, shoeless, and buried her face in *Pride and Prejudice*. Samantha heard the birds chirping as they fluttered to the treetops, and the dogs barking at squirrels scampering up the trees. She could hear the annoying sound of some pop music being played by some obnoxious college kid with their boombox. *I thought those were out of style. Those shouldn't even be a thing anymore.* She saw at the corner of her eye, Jennifer twirling her brown hair with her finger.

Samantha glanced at her silver-chained watch wrapped around her right wrist. Her ponytails sprawled to either side of her golden head. "3:27." She read aloud and enclosed her hand to a hard fist. Samantha didn't like being kept waiting. "When are they going to get here? The sandwiches are going to get soggy! They really know how to ruin a good picnic."

"Patience is a virtue." Jennifer snickered, bowing her head deeper into her book before putting a plain bookmark in between the pages before closing the book before turning a playful smile to Samantha, "You know Michael. And Tim is usually only along for the ride. Michael likes to take his time, never in a rush to do anything."

"You'd think he'd be able to keep time better." She was being sarcastic, reflecting on the work Michael does: business consultations. "Maybe he's working."

"On a Saturday? Fat chance." Jennifer cackled out loud, turning on her back and covering her face with her arms, "More likely he is just lounging around waiting to come until the last minute, Michael does as Michael does." Jennifer twirled her left wrist in her air.

"Not like me," Samantha spoke plainly, clicking her tongue. "Consulting and logistics are two completely different things."

"No. But who comes thirty minutes early for everything except you? You are unnecessarily early for everything." Jennifer chuckled, removing her arms from her face, squinting at the afternoon sun. "I swear, you wouldn't be yourself if you didn't get to your own funeral thirty minutes early."

Samantha shot a sharp glare at her. Jennifer wasn't looking, her eyes were closed as her face was focused on the sky. Samantha closed her eyes again and turned her face towards the sun. She looked up into the clouds and started to look at the shapes in the sky. Samantha reflected on this, yes, she was early for everything with anxiety if she wasn't running at least fifteen minutes early but was it really all that necessary. Perhaps she could pray about her anxiety for such a trivial matter.

"I'm not that bad, am I?" Samantha didn't think she was that bad, just punctual. Though, she found more often than not her version of punctual was typically fifteen-minutes early. She was never late.

"Well, yeah," Jennifer told her, rather sarcastically. "I invited you over to my house *after* dinner, which was at five. I invited you at 6:00 p.m. You showed up in the middle of my dinner. You really are funny with time."

"Wait!" Samantha pointed to the sky. "Look right there, it's a cloud. It looks like—"

"What?" Jennifer interrupted, opening her eyes as she shielded them with her eyes. "Don't tell me? No. Don't. Sam. Sam. No. Bad. That's bad! Sam! Don't say it!"

"It's a curtain van!" she exclaimed.

"You really need to stop taking work home with you." Jennifer sighed as she gazed at the cloud which Samantha pointed at. She saw something different. "I see a cloud, an image of condensed gaseous water. Only you would be excited to see some logistic import solutions in the sky." She peered closely at it and rubbed her chin and smiled. "That might be something, now wouldn't it. A very entertaining idea to have freight stuck in the sky somewhere! No wonder my lab supplies never show up on time."

"I'm not sure if that's what clouds are made from. But it's a curtain van!"

"I'm not a meteorologist. I'm a biologist. Something like that is a little out of my realm of expertise." Jennifer shook her head.

"Cloud gazing?" came a voice above them.

"Late as usual, Michael." Samantha scowled at him; his short light brown hair waved as the wind passed through it.

"Hostility is not appreciated on a Saturday, Samantha," Michael said rather nonchalantly, smiling. "Besides, I brought a Tim with me."

"Cloud gazing," Tim repeated and pushed his glasses closer to his face as he looked to the cooler. "I see you brought the sandwiches. Did you get drinks too?"

"Really." Jennifer put her hand defensively on her chest. "Really? You think we would forget such things? Do I hear a sense of distrust from you, Tim?" She stood up with Samantha as they went over to the cooler to open it. Inside the cooler were sandwiches, bottles of water, granola bars, and cans of soda.

"I never knew you to be reliable," Tim directed his joke to Jennifer, wiping some sweat from his forehead.

"Wow!" Samantha exclaimed to Tim. "Rude." She turned her attention to Michael. "So, anyway, why were you so late?"

"Well," Michael sucked his teeth as he scratched his back over his shoulder. "I was with another friend. He needed someone to talk to. Today," he deeply exhaled. "You see, his mother died eight years ago in an accident, I think. Today was the anniversary. She died in Nevada. There was some training accident with the U.S Army that apparently went horribly wrong, killed over two-hundred thousand people. So, he needed a shoulder."

Samantha sucked her teeth in, her eyes stretched open and her chest puffed to take a breath. "You could have invited him to hang out with us, Jennifer and I wouldn't have cared."

"I did but he declined." His smile faded. "He certainly needed a friend, I was there until he was over it, just to make sure he was going to be okay before I left him."

"Well, let's put these grim talks aside for now." Jennifer said, clapping her hands together. "I'm hungry. We've waited long enough!"

Jennifer started pulling out the wrapped sandwiches, tossed one each to Samantha, Michael, and Tim: Then tossed one each to them a bottle of water. They unwrapped their sandwiches and ate.

"What is this?" he almost spat it out. His face cringed as his mouth made obnoxiously loud chewing noises.

"Oh, that's just peanut butter and jelly." Jennifer shot a smile over to him with her eyelid drooped down halfway.

"What! You know this! I am allehgic to freaking peanut buttah!" he cried out.

"Well, well, well." She snickered as she covered her smile with her mouth. "I hope you didn't fehget yeh epi pen."

"Tim, shut up and eat. We all know that's a lie. You just hate peanuts." Michael had some of his sandwich hanging out of his mouth.

Samantha said nothing. Samantha was a little distracted thinking of Michael's friend, and those many people who died. *That's a lot of people.*

"Michael?" she asked.

"Hmm?" he took a bite and was chewing on his sandwich.

"That incident you mentioned," she began.

"Not this again." Jennifer shook her head as she took a drink of water.

"Did you ever hear anything about that incident? I can't imagine something like that happening here," Sam asked.

"I have not. But then again, it was eight years ago. We were all likely still in middle school, except maybe Jennifer here." Michael snapped his fingers to point to her. "Where were you eight years ago? Jennifer, you must have heard something. I mean, that's a lot of people. I find it very hard to believe there wouldn't be a lot of media attention. Maybe Uncle Sam covered it up well. After all, a mistake at that kind of scale would only tell our enemies we're weak."

"The only problem with that theory is that there weren't wars we were involved in back then," Tim argued. He raised his chin up. "However, there always was the possibility they were hiding something they didn't want the general public to know, you know about the rumors on Area 51, aliens, spacecrafts, and so on."

Jennifer took a drink of her water. "Not much. I think I was over in Texas with some family. I did hear something about it. But the news came in very briefly and in spurts. Almost like the news could have been censored, kudos for you Tim." She snickered at him. "News censorship happens doesn't it? We've had the most recent election to tell us that. Besides, with a wealth of information, any number of them can be falsified facts, and if someone reports on fake facts, they could get their butts sued! For the first few days all I remember was that Nevada was a war zone for over eight weeks. That was the only thing consistent regardless if you watched left-wing or right-wing news. U.S government officials finally came out and said it was a training accident. I didn't believe it; still don't."

"A *training* accident killed twenty percent of a million people?" Michael nearly spat out his water. "I don't know if I believe that."

"Well, I don't think many people believed it. But it did happen around Area 51. So, it is believable it could have been an accident, I guess. I mean they hide things pretty well there, and most people who believe in aliens would believe that. An alien laser just went off!" Jennifer waved both her hands excitedly with the last statement. "And it was eight years ago. Most people probably forgot about it by now, well, unfortunately except those who lost someone close to them, and it was in Nevada, so we probably don't know too many people who would have been affected by it. That's not exactly something someone likes sharing. Hey, my parents died in Area 51!" She attempted to sound gleeful. "Nothing. When would that ever come in conversation?"

"Almost never," Samantha commented, she loved Jennifer, but sometimes she can feel cold. She knew Jennifer wasn't a cold person, but with her bubbly and spontaneous personality, the things she says could come off cold. "But they had children who they left behind. It's sad really."

"It is in the past. For some, it is best left there. For others, they will never forget. And the memory will only die when they do," Jennifer replied more calmly.

"Well, it serves no purpose focusing on something like this right now. It is in the past, and apart from Michael, none of us really know anyone directly affected by that, unless they are exceptionally good at hiding it. The only thing we can do is pray for their peace of minds," said Tim. "Hey, I have an idea. Let's throw the pigskin around."

"That's a great idea! I haven't done that since high school!" Samantha jumped up at the suggestion. *I guess it was my fault for keeping up with the subject.* Sam was especially thankful for Tim providing an out of that conversation.

"That wasn't that long ago, it's only been six years," Michael chuckled. "You say that like it's some kind of throwback."

"It is," she replied.

"You were on the football team?" Tim seemed surprised.

"Yes. I was. A little-known fact, I was once a tomboy," she answered.

Samantha proactively packed up the picnic blanket and cooler and then to her car, which was parked not too far away. She opened her trunk and put the picnic in, slamming the trunk shut.

A lone man by the crosswalk caught her attention. His hand was in his shorts' pocket and he stared blankly at the trees over by the common. He seemed happy, with a smile written across his lips, but his eyes told a different story, sunken with lack of sleep and outlined with puffy eyes.

She returned over to her friends, who were already tossing the football. She sprinted in and intercepted a pass intended for Michael.

"Uhm. That's my ball Sam," Michael turned his palms to the sky.

She lobbed the ball to him. Tim seemed extremely focused on the ball. Jennifer seemed to be swaying back and forth as the wind blew. Samantha happy to have the football back in her hands again. It's been too long since she held a ball, too long since she'd tossed the ball and had the feeling of her own enjoyment without the extreme pressure of winning a game.

The first signs of a city at dusk appeared with the streetlights flickered to life, illuminating the sidewalks, which were more hushed, and empty. The light over Park Street's MBTS station lit up the faces of people standing in limbo of the station. Droves of people briskly walked through the station's steel-frame doors to try to catch the train. Some individuals still lounged by the fountain, sitting on benches and chairs, others relaxed on the grass, laying down and looking up at the empty sky with no sense of time or place to be.

"Michael?" Samantha asked as she threw the ball to him.

"Yeah?" He let the ball strike his chest as he caught it.

"It's getting late. I want to walk through the Garden before the sun completely sets." She pointed at the shining streetlights. "Can we?"

"Honestly, that sounds nice," Jennifer exclaimed, letting out a yawn. "We should all go. Isn't that right, Tim?"

"Tim didn't say no," Samantha answered for him.

"Wait, I didn't—" Tim opened his mouth to protest.

"Then it's decided. Come on Tim, I know you don't want to but it's not far. It's not a big garden, man," Michael said. "It's literally on the other end of the street."

Tim sighed. "Fine." He put the ball back into his little traveling bag he kept with him everywhere. "Let's go see *this* Boston Public Gahden."

The four of them walked through the other side of the Common, leading them across the street and into the Boston Public Garden through black gates. They were underneath the covering of trees. Some swans were floating down the body of water to the right side, and on the water was a covering of leaves, hiding something underneath.

Samantha found something peaceful about it. It was quiet, soft, almost like the good Lord's creation. Everything seemed to be in perfect harmony here, nestled away from the city but protected from the loud busy noises of the car horns and alarms, the natural noises of the miscellaneous birds, insects, and squirrels drowned out what little cars drove by. It was a little utopia inside the hustle and bustle of the city, right in the center of Boston! It reminded her of the woods in Vermont, a place she rarely visits anymore now she's left.

Tim and Jennifer were talking amongst each other. Samantha chuckled behind them as Jennifer, the bubbly biologist, had a way of annoying Tim, the introverted events coordinator. One might think that Jennifer should be the events coordinator and Tim the biologist. It was this irony of the personality traits and their respective careers that made Sam chuckle. Of course, one might think they were dating with the way they talked, but Sam knew better.

It was good to just slow down a little. Samantha appreciated that Michael had a similar busyness to their respective work weeks, being able to just simply settle and get drawn back in with the majestic pull of the natural world. They almost had no time just to sit back and relax.

Samantha suddenly noticed that the air suddenly felt wrong, and thin. Exhaling the frost from her breath, she stopped in her tracks with gaping eyes. She felt the cold air fill up her lungs. Her hair stood on ends. The cold air felt like a cold day of winter to her, she rubbed her shoulders to warm herself up.

It shouldn't be this cold. This is spring! She turned her head to see the man from earlier.

His hand was still in his pocket, his smile was still wide, almost too wide. Again, just like before, he wasn't looking at anything specific. His stare was just blank: his eyes sunken in, and overbearingly tired. This man was to the world as his smile is to his face: out of place, like he and it doesn't belong here.

She moved her feet again, catching up to Michael before the man would notice her looking at him. There was something off about the man, but she couldn't place her finger on it, the fact remains, the sudden temperature drop was unnatural. Shortly after returning to Michael's side, the warmth returned to the air, or perhaps she just entered an area where the air was warmer. Perhaps she was feeling things that weren't there.

"That's much better." She felt a little at ease returning to a sense of equilibrium, where the air felt natural, rather than the little pocket of superstitious air she walked through. *Did anyone else notice?*

"What?" Michael asked, turning his head to her but kept walking towards the end of the Gardens.

"Didn't you notice the temperature dropped drastically?" Samantha's eyes narrowed. "The temperature just dropped back there. I hope I'm not experiencing hot flashes."

"I wouldn't worry about it, I mean, I didn't notice," Michael said. "It's New England. We experience four seasons in less than a week."

"That may be, but it shouldn't have dropped that much!"

"I told you, Sam, I'm not a meteorologist," Jennifer called back to her, turning her head.

"I wasn't asking you!" Samantha snapped.

"Well, that was rude," Tim commented, looking back at them over his shoulder as he kept walking. "What's got you all worked up?"

"I just—I just saw a man."

"This is Boston. There's always someone around," Michael chuckled, likely finding Samantha's little episode humorous.

"Not with a blank stare. Not with a smile as wide as his," she replied. "And the temperature."

Jennifer looked around behind them. "I don't see anyone."

"You could just be imagining things," Michael asked.

She shook her head, clenching her fists at her side. "I know what I saw; I know what I felt." She turned to try to catch a glimpse of the man again, only this time, he wasn't there.

"You didn't have a load to pick up, did you?" Michael asked. "You know, one of those Saturday loads that needs to be picked up, but you have no way to confirm if it did or not until Monday, and by that time it's much too late."

"Gosh no! I took care of that one already," Samantha said as they finally exited the garden.

"Aww. Where did the sun go? I still want to be out." Jennifer yawned. "Kong's is not far off from here."

"Cheap beer," Tim commented.

"Not me." Samantha didn't want to go out anyway, the presence and disappearance of this peculiar man made her want to curl up in bed with a book. She also didn't want to spend more time with Jennifer or Tim, they especially didn't seem to believe her. She was a tough girl, but she couldn't help but feel hurt that none of them, especially Michael, believed her. "It's too late for me right now. I'm still recovering from that nightmare those two drivers put me through yesterday."

"What did they do?" Michael asked. Her trucking nightmares were never boring.

"The driver just dropped their trailer in the doors and unhooked their trucks from their trailer and drove off to get breakfast without telling anyone. Back-to-back. Then my customer got frantic because as far as he was concerned, he lost a truck but inherited two trailers he didn't want anything to do with!" she said, letting out a deep sigh. "Oh well, at least he pays well for every other load he gives me. Alright, I'm tired. I'm going home, going to bed. I'll start fresh in the morning. Tuesday?"

"Yes," Michael said. "As long as I don't get caught in one of those overseas conference calls. Those are a pain."

"I hear you. Michael, are you coming?" Tim asked.

"Nah. Next time," he replied.

"Party pooper." Jennifer frowned.

Chapter 2 Terri Nation

~I've been cursed with isolation, you see.

***

Bright headlights beaming into bricks and concrete of the sidewalks on Park Street. The trees' branches swayed in the wind, and so did the leaves, like a ballet dancer, droves of people were scampering into the Park Street MBTA station, entering the metal and glass doors, hastily marching down the stairs. The other buildings on park street had closed their windows, but some had the lights on, to light the sidewalk for other travelers. And for some, a fancy restaurant on the upper end of Park Street, nearly below the street with no clear way on how to get inside. Samantha wondered where the entrance was.

A car drove by, speeding through the red light, honking its horn. The tires squealed as it turned the corner, and Sam covered her ears as the noise scratched her inner lobes.

"I take it you didn't get an overseas conference call." Samantha knew Michael couldn't make it every Tuesday, because his clients' operated in numerous time zones, and sometimes he was forced to stay late.

"No. I got an email that that's not going to be happening for a while, I think. Tensions are rising quickly overseas, with Poland and Ukraine." Michael covered a yawn with his hand.

"What do you mean?" Tim's head immediately jerked, turning to Michael with alarm. The lights from inside the church flashed out as the receptionist flicked the switch off and on.

"Well," he began, his eyes darted back and forth, making sure no one else was listening. "Look, you didn't hear it from me, and I'm not sure the validity of this, but it has a lot of people overseas concerned. We won't be trading anything overseas for a while, or that's what I heard. And this is just a rumor, but apparently NATO is disbanding."

Sam turned her gaze to the ground, kicking some pebbles to the side. Samantha reflected on what that might mean. If NATO disbands, will the U.S.A be protecting anyone anymore, and if not, who are the allies? Will this turn into a world where every country is independent, just waiting for a large superpower to come in, swallow them up? What will keep those superpowers in check? What will that do to diesel fuel prices? Ukraine and Poland, what cause do they have to be tense with one another? All these questions floated in her head. She suspected the rate of fuel might skyrocket, but even that was a guess.

"Wait. What?" Jennifer jerked her head immediately to him, and her jaw dropped. "Why? That's a big development for that to just be a rumor. Michael, you realize it would take fifty liars to even think of spreading a rumor that big!"

"Again. Rumor. That's all I know, and you didn't hear it from me," he explained.

"Dang it. I think I might be fine. I don't know how much my customer takes in imports. I think it's all local though," Samantha said, interlacing her fingers in between her hands. The only thing that would really affect her in the brokerage would be the gas prices. It makes it difficult to find trucks cheaply to deliver truckloads of groceries.

Michael sucked air through his teeth. "Yeah, and I'll likely take a pay cut as many of my associates are over there. But the effects of that are going to change the market considerably. Sam, I think it's only a matter of time before the effects catch up to you; even if this is a rumor."

"If it's only a rumor, what's the harm?" Tim asked.

"The market changes drastically, constantly. There's no way to accurately predict what it will do. Besides, even these rumors will affect the market eventually, creating a great rift in the economic sphere. These rumors, even if they aren't true, will cause an economic collapse eventually, or just a severe recession," Jennifer explained. The doors opened and the rest of the congregation walked outside. Samantha stared at Jennifer, shocked that she put so many coherent business sentences together in a row. She didn't give Jennifer enough credit, apparently. "I'm not an economist. My brother is in stocks. Options specifically. He told me about all of this. The market is impossible to predict, but we can get close; behavioral finance and all that."

"There's your answer. Even if it's false, it's bad." Michael shook his head and patted his pants with one of his hands.

"Well, there goes my 401K flying right out the window," Tim exclaimed, putting a hand through his hair. "Oh well, I suppose I could opt out of it now, I'll just get taxed heavily on it. Thanks for the heads up."

The noise of the rest of the studiers came out to a dull roar. Brian came up to them, he had a thinly shaved beard and mustache, his eyes were wide awake. He was scrawny for his height, built much like a basketball player, only significantly shorter. "Hey, you guys coming to Terri Nation?" He wrapped his arm around Michael like an old friend and had that overbearingly enthusiastic smile on his face.

Samantha rolled her eyes at the mention of Teri Nation, the local pub right around the corner, where they all went out for some dinner, and drinks to continue fellowshipping together after the study. After all, why waste a perfectly good night to play catch up.

"You know it," Michael shook his hand. "Wouldn't miss it."

"Great! I'm going to head back over here now. I need to recruit some of the newbies," Brian disappeared into the small crowd, talking to a few new faces Samantha didn't recognize.

"Well, I suppose it's time," Michael said. "You all coming? We should start leading the cattle."

"Such a specific metaphor," Samantha said.

"Not really," Michael and Tim started walking backwards up Park Street, towards Beacon street, waving their hands towards them, ushering everyone to follow. "Last stop, Teri Nation. Who's coming?"

Michael and Tim started chatting to each other as they briskly walked up the sidewalk towards the City Hall.

Many of the other people around them continued to talk. Others started following in small groups. Jennifer linked arms with Samantha. Erin ran towards them from her group. Her giddiness gave her a child-like aura that was only complemented by the freckles across her cheeks. Samantha braced herself for what she expected to be ten times the amount of Erin's normal bubbliness.

"So, what are you smiling about?" Samantha asked as they walked onwards.

"Well, our office just hired another broker out of nowhere last week. He seems to have already settled in." Erin smiled. "Though he often refers to me as the press."

"The press?" Samantha's eyes stretched open.

"My last name. Gutenberg. The Gutenberg Press," Erin explained.

"Okay, but what does that have to do with you smiling already? Do you like him or something?" Samantha teased.

"Erin's got a crush again." Jennifer chuckled, elbowing Samantha in the side. "Seriously, if it is not one man, then it is an equally terrifying different man, sometimes a stranger."

"I do not!" Erin scolded. Samantha assumed Erin was blushing in the dark. "Jennifer, you always find a way to make something innocent sound so inappropriate. Anyway, he's very smart apparently. He is an excellent resource to go to for help. My job would finally be secure if I went to him for advice."

"How do you know that? He just started the job last week?" Jennifer asked. "No one learns the job that fast."

"He already closed a few hundred-thousand-dollar-deals last week," Erin said. "Either he knows what he's doing or is extremely lucky."

"What?" Samantha couldn't believe it. She herself was working a deal with another customer, but she is not making nearly that much in gross revenue, although it was a different business altogether. "How?"

"I'm going to ask him tomorrow. I'll let you know. Although, I don't know how that will help you. You're in logistics, not in stocks." She snapped her fingers.

"Maybe I'll just invest in a mutual fund," Samantha sneered. She had little interest in stocks to begin with.

"You two go ahead and talk finance if you want. I'm sticking to my germs. Much more interesting," Jennifer said as they turned onto Beacon street.

"So, what's his name?" Samantha leaned into Erin, bumping against her.

"He goes by Ted," Erin answered. "He said he's from Ohio. Not a very social person though, doesn't talk much."

"So, enough about this individual that neither Sam nor I are going to meet. July Fourth. Erin, are you still coming? I need to order the canoes, and I need to have an idea of how many I need to reserve. We plan on meeting at Kendall Square at 6 p.m."

"Yes, I'll go," Erin exclaimed. "I'd love to go, I might be late, I need to skip lunch to leave work early."

"Don't worry about food, there will be plenty. I'll be packing sandwiches again," Jennifer said. They were approaching Terri Nation which was on the corner heading back down towards Tremont Street. The City Hall was staring down at them with the lights behind the gates, and the Joseph Hooker Statue, riding on a horse.

"That's probably not the best thing. You might want to think of something else. Sandwiches don't taste good out in the open sea," Samantha suggested. "Maybe we can get Michael to cook something with his smoker. Or perhaps just bring some vegetables or something."

"But poor dear Erin will be hungry. She's skipping her lunch after all." Jennifer chuckled as she opened the door into Teri Nation. "I mean to be fair, most of us, except me, will not have time to actually eat something after work. I mean, you get out late enough as it is."

"It'll take a few hours, it's fine," Samantha replied.

They walked through the restaurant section of the bar. They walked through the wide hallway and took a left of the statue of a little girl flying a kite at the side. Michael and Tim were already sitting in the back of the upstairs bar, talking to one another about something, while sipping on their own drink. Michael was always trying the weird concoctions that the bartender mixed. He was like the bartender's guinea pig..

Samantha walked up to the bar to talk to Scott, the bartender.

"What's goin' on Sam. What can I get you?" The bartender wore a black vest over a white button up shirt and black slacks behind his bar. Everyone on the wait staff wore the same uniform.

"House Cab is fine," she answered, pulling out her card. "I'll close out."

Scott took the card and went to pour her a quick glass of red cabernet wine. He always had a heavy pour.

"Scott, I'll take your specialty. Whatever that is at this moment," Jennifer asked. Like Michael, she was also an adventurous drinker.

"I'll also take a cider. Bottle please," Erin called out; her hand raised as her other hand reached for her pocketbook.

"Together or separate?" Scott called as he reached behind the bar and undid the cap of a frosted bottle of hard cider.

"Together. I'll buy it," Erin said, nudging Jennifer in the side. "The least I can do if I'm trusting you with my food on the fourth of July."

Erin winked at Jennifer and squeezed her shoulder.

He then made the very odd drink with Bourbon, triple sec, coke, muddle mint and cucumbers. Jennifer frowned curiously as the drink was handed to her. Her eyes skimmed over the physical ingredients, noting this beverage, whatever it might be, should taste refreshing; however, such a taste would likely contrast unwelcomingly with the bourbon. "Well, it is different." She took a sip. And made a puckered face as if filled with something that was too sour. And it did contrast, the way Jennifer expected it to, "Did Michael like this?"

"He liked it," Scott started chuckling. "Do you?"

"It's certainly different, I'll give you ten points for originality." She cringed. "I haven't decided if I'm going to like this or not yet. Give me a few minutes."

"Gotcha," He chuckled, quickly moving back to address the rest of his guests.

Brian came in with his crowd of nearly fifteen different guests. *Looks like he succeeded in inviting the new people here. Well, this certainly is great for the community. They are all new to Boston, or many of them anyways. This isn't a bad spot to be,* Sam thought. Brian's friendliness and his great charisma was what kept Samantha interested in these little late-night gatherings, and surprisingly, kept her going to Park Street Church instead of some local church.

Samantha knew that Scott was going to have a good night. She sipped her wine as she gazed up at the TV screen. Scott generally kept the news on in the back: unless they requested the sports channel. He was always very friendly, though when she first came here, he did seem like a tired and disgruntled man. He couldn't have been more than thirty. He hid a smile underneath that thick beard of his.

Sam looked over to Brian again, noticing he took out a little pen and piece of paper, engaging enthusiastically in conversation with everyone he invited. He spent more time with the new faces than the old ones, nodding as they spoke, showing his elite listening skills.

Sam guessed quite accurately he was offering to buy them a round tonight, by jotting things down on his notepad. Brian leaned over the Bar top, and slapped his hand on it, and looked intently in Scott's eyes as they engaged in some unrelated conversation which Sam couldn't hear.

Brian read off the slip of paper, and Scott immediately punched some buttons on the electronic touch pad and printed out a receipt, handing it to Brian before hastily disappearing behind the bar. Brian immediately returned to the newcomers, turning their hesitant smiles to enthusiastic ones. Samantha thought, *Brian was better at making anyone feel comfortable at home.*

Then she noticed something familiar. The hair on her head felt like they stood on ends, and the chills came over her, cascading like a powerful wind. Goosebumps rose-up from her arms. She looked around, not trying to alarm anyone, hoping this may have been her imagination. Other people around the bar were putting on their sweatshirts or wrapping themselves with their arms. She chose to ignore it. *Someone probably just turned the thermostat down. But damn it's cold!*

Out of the corner of her eye she noticed someone. He was sitting by himself at the other end of the bar, perhaps ten paces from her, drinking a glass of red wine, almost like hers. *Merlot? Or Cab?* It was the same man from Saturday, first at the crosswalk, then inside the Garden. Now here. And it seems the last time the temperature dropped so much and so quickly was with him around. Who was he?

Scott brought this man a plate of mashed potatoes. This man still seemed to be smiling very widely as he thanked Scott for the plate. Scott asked him if he needed anything else, but he declined, and said, "I have more than I require right now. Thank you." She took a closer look as the man took a fork and put it into the mashed potatoes and started eating it. Sam squinted her eyes at the man to see some lined scars on his face. The words barely made it to her ears with the volume of the bar.

Twice she saw the man in a social setting. Twice she saw the man isolated in the social setting. Perhaps he was new to Boston, and looking for friends, perhaps socially inept. *Well, I'm not Brian. But I'll see what I can do. I at least know something to spin off on,* she thought.

She took a sip from her glass, scanning the bar top for Scott when he got a second. She raised her arm and called him over. Scott walked over, drying a beer glass with a towel. Scott leaned over the bar, both palms rested firmly on the bar top after setting the glass down. "What's up Sam?"

"That man over there." She leaned in over the table, pointing a finger to the man in the corner, retracting the finger around her wine glass.

Scott turned his head briefly to look, "That's Ted. He's been coming here lately."

"Do you know what he does?" Sam asked.

"No, he's a polite person, but a man of few words."

"Well, thanks for that. That was it. Thank you!"

She started walking towards him, quietly towards him. He ate silently. She was standing behind him as he was engrossed in his food, scarfing it down quickly. He took a sip of his wine again, turning the glass and looking into it as if he was lost in thought.

"Well, well, well, so a rat sneaks behind me, eh?" said the man. He never bothered to look from his wine. "To what exactly do I owe for the pleasure of such as this?"

Samantha abruptly halted. Her wineglass trembled in her hand as she looked down at the ripples inside the glass. *Did I make a sound? No. Wait. Could he smell my perfume or was it the wine?*

"The scent of Cabernet was coming closer and closer. I could smell it approaching me, and then suddenly the scent just lingered. You can't be more than twenty-three inches behind me." He turned in his stool and looked up to her, and his smile was still wide. "How may I help you?"

"Startling, well I'm not a rat." She chuckled nervously.

"And yet you came to me as silent as a rat."

Well, he's not socially inept, that is certain. He's eloquent and very formal. She found him to be unnerving, yet intriguing all the same, "Rats can be silent nuisances, but I couldn't help but notice that I've seen you before," she commented.

"Well, this is the Heart of Boston. Odds are there are many faces we see again and again, and maybe we recognize a few recurring faces here and there, but we never make a point to meet one of them. I know I certainly don't," he replied. His smile never faded. He stood up and raised his glass to hers. She clinked their glasses together. "Cheers."

Sam found him to be more mysterious, greeting her with a friendly smile, but the words comparing her to a rat were a bit unsettling. He was confident, this was evident, but was there something about her he found to be untrusting? She bit her tongue, fearing she had made some kind of social error. *Brian is better suited for this, but I can't back down now.*

"That is something true you have just said. My name is Samantha Harris," she said. She brought her hand out to meet his other hand to shake it.

He reached out his hand to meet hers to shake it. Samantha could hear the bones in her hand crack: he had a very firm and strong grip. "My name is Ted Anderson."

"It's a pleasure to meet you." She didn't want to make it too obvious she asked about him.

"To be sure, Miss Harris, the pleasure is all mine. Now, I ask again; to what do I owe the pleasure of such an introduction?" There was something different about him though, his brown watery eyes looked right into hers. Ted appeared to her to be in his mid-twenties, but the eyes told a different story, as if they were much older than his body.

"I ran into you twice on Saturday. Right on the corner of Park and Tremont, and then again on the same day at the Garden, towards the end of that night," she admitted, "You seemed to be by yourself, while everyone else was grouped together, or coupled."

"Was that around the time the temperature dropped?" he asked.

Her eyes blinked repeatedly. *So, I'm not crazy.* "Y—you felt that too? I thought I was just imagining things," she stammered as she took another sip from her glass, looking cautiously at Ted. She felt something in her gut, like she should be wary of this man. Numerous people were with her that night, and only she and Ted felt it. And only they acknowledged it. *Why didn't any of them feel anything?*

"Yes, I felt it also," he said, "Well, that's New England for you."

"Yes," she said, lowering her voice a little bit. "Have you been around Boston for very long?"

"A few weeks," he answered.

"What brought you here?" She thought to ask another question, hoping to find something to latch on to. She could hear multiple steps behind her, and the music played from the speakers, and the chatter sounded like white noise.

"Work," he answered.

"Where are you from?" She was dissatisfied with the answer, as simple as it was. Sure, it very well could be true, but there wasn't enough information released from him to pose any meaningful conversation.

"Ohio."

"What part?" *You're like a steel trap.*

"Delaware." He shifted on his stool as he took another bite of his mashed potatoes.

"There's a store I deliver to frequently over there," excitedly, she finally found something.

"Oh, and what is it that you do?" His expression didn't change, but he leaned back against the bar and crossed his hands over his chest.

"I work for a 3PL. I deliver groceries for a major wholesaler. I'm a broker," *Dang it.* She wasn't expecting him to start asking questions, not that she had anything really to hide from him, but she wasn't done trying to figure out who he was.

"As am I. I deal with stocks," he answered. "And options."

It finally hit her. He might work with Erin. "Do you know Erin Gu—"

"The Gutenberg Press? Yes. I work with her." He laughed.

"Yes!" She laughed. "That is exactly what she said you call her. She said something about you today on our way over here."

"Terrible things, I'm sure," He replied, never lessening that smile.

"No, she said she was very good at your job."

"No. I am just very lucky." He got a buzz from his phone. "Excuse me a moment."

He pulled out his phone and opened something up. Samantha assumed it was a work-related email. He read it intently. He shut the screen off from his phone and put it back into his pocket. "Well, on one hand that was terrible. On the other, I'm glad I sold all of those."

"What?"

"Oh, NATO just disbanded, and Russia just declared War on Ukraine," He said nonchalantly. "I just sold most of my foreign assets. Those values are going to drop overnight. I wonder, how will the rest of the European Union fare? Will they follow suit? Will they get involved? Most likely, as they have always done. It's unfortunate that the world came to this."

"How do you know?" she asked. *Well, I guess that confirms the rumor Michael told them, but how exactly are you this calm about it? Ukraine is apparently pissing everyone off!* Samantha knew that national allegiances were trembling as of late, the news told them that much. To her it seemed most everyone was inches away from everyone's throats at any given time, and Russia and Ukraine were now the only confirmed cases of political collapse. *How soon will this uncertainty reach America?* Sam couldn't help but wonder.

"Like I said, I'm very lucky. However, some of the higher ups might think I actually know something when I don't," he let out a brief sigh. "Oh well. I'll cross that bridge when it comes to it."

She turned abruptly, "Michael!" she waved at him as he was now talking with Erin. Samantha noticed that Erin frowned at them with her pouty eyes. She noted that Erin seemed to be boy crazy, she didn't expect that kind of behavior from someone going to church weekly. *But we all have our own shortcomings.*

"Ted, this is my boyfriend, Michael," she introduced them.

Michael walked over with a friendly smile on his face and introduced himself. Michael shook Ted's hand, and Samantha could hear the bones in Michael's hand cracking.

"Firm grip. I like it!" Michael released his hand.

"So, Michael, you know that thing you talked about earlier?"

"I said you didn't hear it from me," He said defensively, abruptly turning to her, frowning.

"It's on the news already," she frowned, knowing that since these rumors were true, global collapse might not be far behind, she guessed this would immediately affect Michael's line of work drastically.

"Wait. What?" Michael asked. "Already? I just found out about it, but I thought those were rumors."

"Rumors have an unfortunate way of being steeped in truth. Odds are, if something is completely unbelievable, it is probably true," Ted said. "I knew of the rumor but thought nothing of it until this morning. Thank God I followed my gut. I can sleep peacefully now."

"Well, it is only a matter of time then. Someone's going to punch someone important," Mike replied.

Ted threw his head back in laughter.

"I think that already happened," Samantha said. "Apparently, Russia's on a warpath again."

The phone vibrated in Ted's pocket again. He pulled it out of his inside pocket and looked at his notification. He read the notification, "That's not the only one on a warpath. Well, I guess it was only inevitable that this would happen."

"What now?" Samantha asked. She was considering how this news was going to affect her. It was clearly going to affect her business. Oil prices are going to rise. Rates for truck drivers are going to rise to reflect that change. Her rates are contracted. Renegotiating her contracted rates are likely to be fruitless. Her individual margins are going to decline. Her profitability is going to plummet. *How soon before this all hits home?*

"Trade deals with China aren't going well apparently," Ted explained. "That being said, it's only a matter of time before someone declares war. It is almost like twenty years ago."

"Those were not good times," Michael said. "Almost every major nation was at everyone's throats."

"Precisely. The global economy was trash then." Ted raised his hand in the air. He dropped it back down. "And just like my hand, we'll probably be freefalling for a while, well, then it starts to decline that's when we'll be freefalling."

"You seem to know a lot about this," Michael said, taking a sip of his exotic, but potentially terrible tasting drink.

"I was in the Army before I came here, China was never too keen on Americans," He kept his smile, but reluctantly gave that answer. "I know too much already."

Samantha knew this would pique Michael's interest. His brother was in the 75th Ranger Regiment, "What was your—"

"My occupation in the Army is classified, above top secret," He said softly. "I can't disclose any information on what I did. I hope you understand."

"I do," Michael said. "My brother is in the Army. He is much the same way. Doesn't give out more information than what is necessary."

Erin finally walked over, her hand resting across her chest. "Ted, did you just get Adam's email?"

"Yes, Gutenberg's Press. I did. I got both of them. Well, if you have any foreign assets, I'd suggest selling them now. The market is still open. You may find a buyer, but if you don't, I'd advise holding onto it and riding it out, or selling it as soon as possible." This was clearly meant for Erin, and he gave her advice to work on, but Samantha picked up on something, noting just how volatile the stock markets are: Sell now, unless you can't, then hold onto it until it rises again. Or just sell later. The window of trading that fast was small.

"Did you already sell yours?" she asked. "How did you know this would happen?"

"I didn't. I just guessed. You should listen to those rumors more closely." He chuckled.

"This is going to be a nightmare," Michael said, ruffling his hand through his hair.

Jennifer popped up with her drink in hand. "Michael, you have terrible taste in this stuff. Why do I let you talk me into these things?"

Samantha felt a weight lift off her chest as her attention was immediately turned away from the horrific events happening with the world to something, albeit random, more pleasant. For that, she was exceedingly thankful for Jennifer's interruption.

"First of all, I didn't say anything." He laughed, nudging her shoulder with his.

"I mean seriously, this is disgusting, why would you drink this?" She turned her gaze to Ted. "So, who is this who is hogging up the party?"

"I mean, you can barely call this a party," Samantha said as Erin was back onto her phone, monitoring her emails.

"I have to go. I'll see you next Tuesday!" Erin walked over to her green purse.

Samantha waved as Erin walked out of the bar, relieved as Erin's constant pining after men was growing tiresome.

"This is Ted. You know; that Ted," Sam clicked her tongue as she pointed to Erin on her way out.

"What Ted—oh! That Ted! Well, I'll say little to compromise anything. I'm Jennifer, and welcome to our little dysfunctional family," she joked. "Never mind me. I'm the crazy one."

Samantha chuckled. *She's never boring.*

"Speaking of, Ted." Jennifer seemed to take over the conversation. She would have made a great executive. "We are going to rent a few canoes over the Charles on the Fourth of July. I know it's two months away. You should totally come with!"

"Fireworks, over a body of water," Ted said. "I appreciate the sentiment, Miss, however, I'm afraid I must decline."

"Oh, well that's too bad. Everyone here is going." She turned her head as if looking for someone. "Now, where is Brian?"

"He drove Tim home," Michael answered. "Tim had an early meeting for an event that's scheduled tomorrow. He couldn't be out too late."

"Such a shame. He really is personable. More fun than I am!" She wrapped her arm around Michael as she smiled.

Samantha and Jennifer's minds were thinking alike. No matter how hesitant one might have been, Brian could always get someone to bend.

"I doubt that very much," Ted commented, making eye contact with her. Jennifer's hazel eyes gleamed in the dim light of the bar.

"Oh, well, I guess you can't come under any circumstances, then, huh? Nothing we can do to persuade you?" Jennifer tried to coax some more amiable responses out of him.

"Unfortunately, no," Ted answered. "But I appreciate the offer, all the same."

"Oh well."

"Well, what about Tuesday next week? Are you doing anything after you get off work?" Samantha pitched in, eager to see more of this mysterious person. She barely struck the surface of who he was, and to her seemed almost one dimensional. She was eager to get the full picture and get the story of those ragged eyes and enthusiastic smile. The contrast didn't sit well with her.

"Um?" He hesitated. Sam briefly noticed his hand shaking as he hid it in his pocket. "Depends, if I decide to leave work or not. I'm a workaholic, and perhaps that depends completely on the rest of the information I know you are inclined to give me."

"We have a Bible Study that we go to on Tuesdays. It starts at seven at Park Street. This next week is tasty Tuesdays so there are snacks before," Samantha continued, linking arms with Michael.

"I think Sarah is making Baklava," Michael said, sipping his who-knows-what-it-tastes-like drink.

"Oh, yes, that's a splendid idea," Jennifer butted in again, clapping her hands together. "Seriously, Ted, you must come. It's much less of a commitment than going canoeing with us in July. Especially if you're new to Boston. It might be nice to have some kind of community that doesn't include drowning yourself in work."

"I'm not going to lie; I do like working," Ted explained, sipping more of his wine. "But with everything else that is going on in the world, I likely won't be able to find anything worth buying in those oversea markets anymore. What's one day going to hurt? Where is it?"

"It's the church on Tremont and Park street. The door is open on the other side of Park Street where the—" Samantha began.

"Freedom Trail?" he asked.

"Yes, that's the one," she answered.

"7:00 p.m.?"

"Yes. But it's tasty Tuesday so you don't have to show up right at seven. You can show up a little after," Samantha answered, suddenly conscientious about how much she'd been speaking. "It is the best time for a newcomer. We'd love to see you there, but no pressure."

"I'll be there," He drank the rest of his wine and grabbed his tab. "I'll see you Tuesday."

Samantha smiled as he left, and she felt a weight being lifted off her chest. *I'm still not Brian. Brian could have gotten him to go out for the fourth for sure.*

"So, how did you meet him?" Michael asked.

"Spill it, Sam, spill it. Details girl!" Jennifer exclaimed. "I need details."

"I saw him twice on Saturday. First at the corner of the church, and then at the garden," she answered.

"Like when you swore the temperature dropped?" Michael inquired. He seemed a little more curious now.

"Yes. He was there when the temperature dropped, and then again when the temperature dropped again in here. Didn't you feel it?"

"Yes," Michael admitted. "But that could have been anything. I wouldn't worry about something so trivial as the temperature dropping, especially here in New England. The temperature and weather changes daily, besides, if it happened here, it was probably just the air conditioning." He glanced at his watch. "And look at the time! It is time to be going. It's closin' time."

Chapter 3 Sverdlovsk

~ This world would look much better on a mantle, covered in flames.

***

Major McCurdy sat in her office, a square grey room with a large thick window of bulletproof glass, and an iron door. Her desk was also grey, but with a brown wooden frame.

It was quiet for sure, as it always was at 0400 MSK. She had all the solitude and privacy she could be afforded to her on the remote Sverdlovsk base. Though the location was above top secret, unknown even to Moscow itself, she still felt the need to be up in her office at 0400 to get an even deeper sense of privacy.

She yawned as she took a sip of her coffee, watched her computer screen, monitored the emails, surveyed vehicles driving by, not suspecting anything at the side of the Ural Mountains. She scanned every single suspicious car. A pang of hurt shot through her each time the framed photo of her uncle caught her eye. She never thought to move it. She only thought of her uncle and what he would have suffered eight years ago. She had to keep his photo up, someone had to be there to remember.

An email popped up on her screen. It was a report from the CBRN team. The radiation at the top of the mountain spiked up again. This time the levels clocked in at 1.294 Sieverts. These levels were three times higher than the last peak. Scrolling through the report she noticed it was isolated, as usual, but substantially higher up than it normally occurred. She skimmed through the rest of the report explaining the abnormality of the event being instantaneous and without currently detectable residue. And again, through the paragraph suggesting closer investigation to find residue. *Radiation. The ruse we created to have a team of regulars monitoring it. If it were a natural occurrence, yes, there'd be residue.* She sighed, knowing she would have to head up this wild goose chase for residue radiation. *But if I went alone, it would only raise unnecessary suspicion.*

She knew that it was only a matter of time before the higher ups would want a full-scale investigation, to find out why the radiation levels are sporadically spiking, but this wasn't radiation: a Fae from someone's administrative branch was operating where they shouldn't be. It's about time to send someone up there. *However, the Administration is going to want to hear about this.* She put her hand on her handset, and breathed in. She marked the handset with an insignia, shaped like a vein, the phone gave off a green aura. No one could trace this call; the wires were now heavily insulated with her mana.

"Admin Colton," the strict voice answered.

"Admin Colton, Major McCurdy here. I just received a report about increasing levels of radiation. I'm reading 1.294 Svs. That's not the odd part. The odd part is that it shortly dissipated with no trace. I think some unknown is operating here. Is this cause for concern for the administration? Location: Devil's Pass."

"Yes. That's not radiation," he answered. "I need you to see to it. Whoever it is, and report back. You know what to do. Admin Colton out."

She returned the phone back to the receiver. She removed her mana from the phone. She immediately went to the radio to call in the CBRN team. "This is Major McCurdy. Report in."

"Yes, Ma'am. Sergeant Nguyen reporting," a voice returned.

"Wake your squad up. Report down in the briefing room. Now!" she ordered.

"Yes, Major." His voice clicked out.

. "And now I have to get people killed that don't need to be involved. There has to be a better way," she said to herself. *We're monsters. We deserve to die for the things we've done. Damn it all to Hell. I'm always in these shadows, getting these men and women killed. They have nothing to do with any of this, but protocol is protocol.* She sighed, breathing heavily as she brushed a hand through her hair. She put her officer's cap on her head.

She printed the most recent report. She put it in a separate file and walked out of her office. She briskly walked down the stairs, and into the now empty briefing room. She went to the desk, in front of the desk and put her folder down, waiting impatiently for the squad to show up.

Just as she was thinking about calling again, they all came in single file. Specialist Adams, Sergeant Nguyen, Captain Gongora, and Warrant Officer Lee. She smiled as they all came in. "At ease," she said, waiting for them to sit down. The familiar but unwelcome lump filled up her chest with guilt.

All fine men. It is unfortunate, really. They are going to see something they are unallowed to see. Sorry, I'd do this myself if I could, but I can't go alone without raising suspicion. I wish you could say your good-byes, but this is how it must be.

I'm sorry.

Chapter 4 Tasty Tuesday

~It was said that Saul killed his thousands and David his tens of thousands: I'd be fortunate if my numbers were nearly that low.

***

Ted's blank stare pointed into the sky. He ignored the hustle and bustle of men, women and children scurrying past him like rats running away from a legion of cats. His right hand was in his pocket as the wind pushed past him. The cars were halted at the intersection of Park and Tremont, halted at the light as the cars drove down Park Street took a right turn, avoiding the numerous street signs and jaded traffic cones. He sighed as he looked at the red bricks leading up the stairs into the side of Park Street Church, and the glass doors.

He looked back at his watch. *6:45*. "Well, now is as good a time as ever," he said to himself. "Let's get this over with."

He pulled the first door into the side entrance open. He went to the second opening, scanned the entire room. He noted there was a fire escape to his left, right next to an elevator, but the only other exit was the door he walked through. The receptionist read a newspaper, his feet atop his desk. He seemed disinterested in anything but the paper. Beyond the threshold of the second glass door was a table, with a banner which read, "Park Street Café". There was a tall man behind it, also very cheery. *I wonder.* There were numerous empty tables behind the other man.

The man smiled at him and waved him in with his large hand. "Welcome to Café," he said, reaching out his hand for a shake. Ted returned in kind, never letting that smile go. "My name is Steve. Is this your first time here? I don't recognize you."

"You could say that." He firmly gripped the man's hand. "Ted."

"You came on the best day for it then! They're still setting up in there, so not everything is ready to get started just yet. They're still setting up the coffee table. How did you hear about Café?"

I'm from Ohio. I'm a stockbroker. Nothing more. You don't need the truth, just the bare essentials. "You could also say a little bird told me. So, tell me, what is the general set up of such a night?" His hand retracted from Steve's, retreating back into his pocket.

"Normally we sing, we pray, then we break up into small groups. There are many small groups here, and there is usually the simple connecting group that works perfectly for newcomers. But we do this once a month to foster some sense of community between small groups," Steve answered.

"Trying to make it impossible for someone to be forgotten I see." Ted smiled, making sure to cheerily bare his teeth, hoping this would pass for genuine enthusiasm. *No one needs to know.* "An exceptionally good system in place I suppose. I guess that is why I received such a warm welcome."

"I'm glad I was able to warm you up to the place." Steve laughed. "Well, that must be them now. I think they're getting the paper plates out."

"I guess I'll head in. It was a pleasure to meet you, Steve."

"You also." Steve immediately turned to the table. "Oops. I almost forgot." He took out one of those sticker name tags. He wrote "Ted" on it before handing it to him. "Just so everyone can know who you are."

"Why thank you so much!" Ted enthusiastically took the nametag and stuck it on the right side of his chest. "Something to identify the body." He chuckled.

Steve stared at him, blinking repeatedly as he jerked his head to the side. "What?"

"Sorry, you'll have to forgive my dry sense of humor." Ted smiled wider. "Oh well, Steve, I'm sure I'll see you again."

Ted turned around and walked into the Fellowship Hall which was brightly lit. The room was a large square, with numerous chairs set up in a circle for everyone to sit down looking at one another, almost like how friends would sit around at a campfire. Ted pictured a small bonfire in the middle of the room. He noticed the wall in the back, appearing to be a sectional leading to the corner of the main entrance of Park Street Church, likely leading to the sanctuary upstairs.

His hand trembled at his side. He became hyper focused on the menial tasks of making a cup of coffee. He focused on the electric coffee maker at the center of the room with small foam cups at the side. He walked over to it and pushed the "on" button. He took out a cup and put it underneath the nozzle of the machine and flipped one of the plastic-coffee-filled-cups waiting for the machine to warm up and heated the water to a boil.

The machine clicked. He opened the top and put his plastic-coffee-filled-cup into the machine, softly pushing the lid down. He pushed another button, and a brown-black liquid filled his cup. He waited patiently for the cup to fill. He opened the top back up. He took out the plastic empty cup and threw it in the nearby trash. He clasped both of his hands around the cup and walked over to one of the nearby white pillars. He leaned up against it and sighed. He scanned the room rapidly, watching carefully for anyone who would come in. So far, only the usual blond-haired girl, who was surprisingly tall for an American, came out to put more plates on the table, which included the honey scented baklava.

He looked back down to his cup of coffee, the ripple circling around his cup, waiting to be halted, waiting to stop and reach perfect stillness within these Styrofoam walls. Peace finally reached the cup, and the ripples were stilled, as his trembling hand was now stilled. He at last brought the cup to his lips and sipped on the hot liquid. He let it settle on his tongue and it immediately swallowed the first sip. *It tastes like—*

"Hey, what's up man? It's great to see you!" came a cheerily familiar voice.

He peered up from his cup. He smiled back at Michael, who had a white button up shirt that was buttoned just below his neck, and khakis. "Hi," he spoke softly. "Just drinking a coffee."

"Yeah, I hear you. With all that's happened lately, I bet you're ripping your hair out," Michael said. "Fortunately, I'll be fine, just my conversations are now being recorded over there. I mean, it's not like I actually have anything to hide. I don't have any national secrets."

"Too bad. I wouldn't mind hearing them." Ted laughed. He couldn't scan the room as well if he was distracted by talking to Michael. "Honestly, it's not that bad. It just greatly affects who I can and can't deal with. I can easily move assets around. It's not that hard. After all, they say that if you look at the nations who rose and fell, you can predict the future. I find the same to be true for wars."

"Yeah. I know you mentioned you were in the Army, that must give you a different perspective on what's going on. Maybe you're seeing what I'm not," he went on. "Do you think it's something I should be worried about?"

"Not really," he replied. "However, economically it'll be a disaster. However, it wouldn't take too long to change and get things back on track once the dust is settled. At least, most likely. That is just a guess. I just so happen to be very good at guessing."

"So, I've heard. And you seem to be very lucky," Michael continued to smile that welcoming smile. Michael's hands were at his side, but not in his pockets.

We were never allowed to have our hands in our pockets, but I don't recognize you. Never mind. You were too young, even if you were, I wouldn't have known you. You are inconsequential.

"Some of my old comrades called me the Amazing Doctor, as it appeared, I could tell the future. I was only ever wrong once," He said dryly, his tone dropping. He hoped Michael didn't notice.

"You don't sound too thrilled." Michael frowned.

"Yeah, you could say that." Ted never abandoned his smile. "Sometimes luck ain't all it's cracked out to be. Sometimes luck is just a little more than a curse. For example, I wished I guessed wrong on one deal, because the profit margin would have been exponentially higher than if I guessed correctly," He explained. *Yeah, that's how I'll explain it.* "But money isn't everything. I have enough of it as it is. I really don't need anymore. I just do it now to keep busy. I really don't have a high cost of living."

"Well then." Michael chuckled.

"Michael, you didn't strike me as the making friends-type." Jennifer snuck up on them, hair was combed, and she had it tied with a red scrunchy. She was wearing a green shirt, paired with some gym shorts, "Seriously, how long have you been here?"

Now that Ted had a better look at her, she looked oddly familiar. Seeing her in the bright light of the Fellowship Hall was both a blessing. And a curse. She appeared uncannily like his fiancée before her passing. The appearance was almost the same, sure, Jennifer was a little taller than her. *Let the dead stay dead.*

"Not long, maybe five minutes." Michael grinned back at her as he wrapped his arm around her shoulders.

"Well then, Ted, welcome back to our dysfunctional family!" She sipped her cup of coffee while she was juggling a plate with baklava. She looked at Ted and then down to both of his hands. "No baklava?"

"No, I haven't had the chance to grab it." Ted smiled at her as he took another sip of the coffee. *Now, what is it you want?*

"What? Michael, hold my things!"

She shoved her cup of coffee, plate, and plastic fork into Michael's hands. He still didn't have his own cup of coffee, and this flustered Michael before regaining his balance with the new items in his hands. Unfortunately, some of her coffee spilled over the side of the cup and onto his hands.

"Well, as you can quite imagine, she can be a handful." Michael chuckled. "She can be overbearing at times, but we love her all the same."

"I can see that," Ted said. His pupils scanned the room almost immediately again as more and more people started pouring into the Fellowship Hall.

"You know, you wouldn't think she would be a social butterfly, or even this vibrant as a scientist, but there's always that one who will be unique among them," Michael said, staring at his coffee covered hand.

"Yes. I've come across those myself," Ted explained. "There's always exceptions if you know where to look."

Jennifer came back with a plate of baklava and a fork. "Ted, this is for you. This stuff is homemade! You can't come here and *not* have it!" She presented it with a smile.

Ted reluctantly released his hand from his cup and grabbed hold of the plate, watching carefully of the people in the room, memorizing every face, every verbal exchange he could see, and he studied each facial expression and their changes. He could tell when they were sad, and when they were happy. The faces had stretched smiles, and the light twinkled in their eyes, the dimples in their cheeks shone brightly, and their smiles didn't seem to have much effort behind them, like these smiles were genuine. Ted wondered, why weren't they miserable? How happy could they actually be?

"Come on. Take a bite!" Jennifer smiled enthusiastically to him, and she looked at him, "You must tell me how it is?"

"Why are you focused entirely on the baklava? You didn't even make it," Michael said. "Come on, let the guy eat it at his pleasure. Sheesh. You'd think you're some raving chef shoving food they're allergic to down their throats. Like Tim."

"Excuuusse me!" Jennifer raised her voice to Michael. "Well, I was clearly talking to Ted. Now, perhaps I wouldn't have to be over the top if you weren't romanticizing your own bromance."

"What?" Michael's jaw dropped and his pupils moved side to side inside his head as they gaped open. Ted guessed Michael was not expecting that comment from Jennifer.

"You've been hogging his attention for five minutes! I want a turn to pry into that little cage trap of a brain he's got."

Ted's heartbeat raced inside his chest. He felt his palm accumulate sweat. *If anyone was going to crack me open, it would be you.*

"I'll let you two have your privacy. I'm sure you'll want to be alone," Michael gave Jennifer her coffee and baklava plate back.

"Thank you." She handed them with care, taking a sip of her coffee.

"Why would I want that?" Ted protested, never losing that tremendous smile of his. He mustn't appear nervous, as nervous as she was making him. *Is she going to trigger me?* He fought his hand's sudden urge to tremble.

"Ah, I'm sure I'll see you around. Come hang out with our group, like Jennifer said, it's a little dysfunctional." He laughed, using this excuse to get away from Jennifer.

"So, I hear you're a scientist?" Ted asked.

"Now, now, eat your baklava first. And tell me how it is. Then we can talk."

He snickered, "You put into a lot of effort in me trying to give baklava a chance."

"You know it." She smiled and waved a finger at him. "Now eat up, mister."

He took a small bite of the baklava. The sticky honey dripped on his tongue, a taste he was certain was supposed to be sweet, but alas, it tasted like nothing. He could also feel the enthusiastic piercing stare coming right in front of him, "So, tell me how it is!"

"It's delicious," He lied to her. "I thoroughly enjoyed it. Thank you." He moved his focus to his coffee.

She looked up to the ceiling. "Well, I suppose you *could* call me a scientist, but I am more of a researcher than anything."

He sipped his coffee, "And what's your area of expertise."

"Biology. I study organisms, virus', bacterium. An old man once said, 'The more germs I get, the happier I am'! I suppose that sums me up pretty nicely, now that I think about it. Oh well, one can't exactly marry a germ, but they keep me plenty of company."

"I can't tell if you're eccentric, or objectively insane," He joked.

"Well, excuuuse me good sir," she said, pressing her forefinger to his lips. "Are you accusing me of being socially ambiguous?"

He retracted his head from her fingers, shaking his head. He paused a moment and smiled back at her. "Absolutely," He retorted, unsure if this little interaction of her touching his mouth was appropriate. He couldn't be certain.

"Well, good." She chuckled, taking a bite out of her own baklava. "That's what I was going for!"

"All right," came a loud booming voice. Ted immediately turned his head to the nearby speaker. He saw man in his thirties, who also looked to be a little tired, not nearly as tired as he was though. He was holding a microphone and speaking into it. "Alright, welcome to Café, my name is. . ."

Ted tuned out the speaker. He had little patience for long monologues. His eyes started scanning the room again: some people like him were not paying attention to the speaker, almost like they didn't need to: as if they'd heard the same thing a million times. Over and over and over again. He looked closely at the exit.

He noticed Samantha chatting with someone else over by the exit towards the main lobby closer to the background. She had a cup of coffee, but not the baklava. *Perhaps she's dieting. Or came in too late to make her way to the food. Doesn't matter.* She was leaning against the doorway.

Ted tuned back in.

"If this is your first time, we'd like to welcome you. Of course, you are most welcome to join any of the open small groups here, but if this is your first time, I recommend joining our connecting group, led by our two leaders there..."

"Is your *family* part of that group?" he asked.

"Oh, yes." She had a playful smile, almost as if she remembered the punch line of some unrelated joke, then she giggled, "Shall we, Mr. Ted?"

"Absolutely," He replied. He walked with her, by her side, eyeing carefully for the trash can, drowned out by the large number of people. *So, people still believe in the faith, despite all the lack of faith in it. I wonder why? Is there something here that can quiet my mind?* He was nearly pushed to the side, and almost missed the last trash can, which was merely on the side of the door. He threw his cup and plate with the rest of the baklava.

Eating is such a chore.

Nearly lost again in the crowd, Jennifer quickly grabbed his hand. He fought the urge to pull it away. Instead, he just let her have it, but he didn't hold her, his hand was limp in her grasp. They walked through the initial doorway back into the main hall, shifting just right past the elevators. He noticed a few people going into the elevators and entered the doorway to the left up some stairs. He followed Jennifer into the back of this part of the church where there were three additional rooms. They moved to the left, although he never took his mind off each individual face that walked into those separate rooms.

The door to the room he entered was the only exit. The tables were arranged to form a boxy circle, creating the similar feeling of the hall having a bonfire in the middle of it. This was a place for friends. *I don't belong here. Why am I here?*

The ceiling stretched for what Ted could reasonably guess without a ruler was approximately fifteen feet high with a second floor. That floor was set up like an internal balcony, looking down on him were rails and bookshelves that layered the room.

Tim waved; he was already sitting at the other end of the corner. Jennifer led Ted to the right corner, closer to the door, and close to Jack. Samantha came in shortly, with another girl, who Ted didn't know. Michael came in, and he waved, trading a smile as he sat down next to Tim and immediately went into a side conversation.

The man leading the discussion looked at the clock in hanging above the white board at the back of the room, and the woman, presumably his wife or other equivalent, wrote something on the board, "Meaningless." Both of them were casually dressed.

Well, I knew that already.

"Alright, so I see some new faces here," The man began, greeting new people as they came in. "So, let's get started while we have some stragglers coming in."

"Icebreaker anyone?" the woman suggested. She looked up to the ceiling, her chin resting on her hand with her index finger resting above her nose.

"Well, I'll start. What's your name? Where are you from? What brings you to Boston? And uh, what do you wish you could see more of?" the man started, addressing the group sitting around the tables. "As you know, my name is Jack. I'm from Houston, Texas. I was brought to Boston through work. I work as a nuclear physicist at your local plant. No, it's not all that local." He chuckled to himself. "So, if there was one thing, I wish I could see more of? Good question, if I do say so myself. I suppose I could stand a little more rain."

Ted listened intently to everyone as they went across the room. They all went across the room, telling their name, their wish, where they were from, and their occupation. With a little more digging he could find out exactly where and what time they worked. This is dangerous information being given so carelessly. They came from numerous states, and numerous countries. He counted that there was at least one from every time zone in America, and every ethnic group.

They for one reason or another, didn't want to see any more from the world, but they desired to see less of something. They wanted less racism, less strife, less hunger, less war, less death, and less conflict. Without adding anything, by just omitting these things could they obtain more peace, an almost perfect peace. *A peace like ten years ago. That bloody peace. If you take one conflict away, you are only enforcing another. It is all meaningless.*

"New guy. Hello? It's your turn. It's not time for bed yet!" He heard Jack's whimsical cry, as he clapped his hands repeatedly.

"My apologies," Ted replied, returning that smile back to his face. *How long was I in that trance? This whatever it is, was taking control again in my mindlessness. I need to be better with it.* "My name is Ted. I'm from Ohio. I came to Boston for a different change in pace. If I could see more of something. . ." his voice trailed off, "I can't think of anything."

"Nothing at all?" the woman asked.

Ted felt Samantha staring at him, and pointed his pupils towards her, seeing her frown as she studied him like he was some kind of rat in a maze. Jennifer nudged him with her elbow. A smile returned to her face. Ted blinked quickly with the sudden pressure assaulting his arm, and he felt the nerves in his fingers want to tremble.

"Come on Ted," Jennifer pulled on his arm. "I know you want to see more. Everyone wants to see more of *something* in the world. What is it?"

"Now, now," he turned to her with his wide child-like smile. "I've seen plenty of the world already. If I saw any more of it, that would be downright selfish of me. I can't take in anymore of the world while the sights can be enjoyed by someone else."

"Well, I suppose that's one way to look at the world," Jack chuckled.

"Well, if Ted doesn't want to say anything, he doesn't have to," the woman replied. "We are an open book, but we don't expect that of anyone here. Now, Ecclesiastes."

"Yes, one of my favorites," Tim commented.

"You would say that," Michael joked.

They studied the first chapter, and all Ted gleamed from this, was that everything is meaningless in life. Every dollar one made, every friend he made, relationship maintained, career goals, life goals, and everything in between, whatever they were was all meaningless. All these things were meaningless. *I already know that.*

Yes, Ted had money, he had a house. It was all pointless, and he knew it. He knew the feeling all too well. And he didn't care for any of it. He doesn't work for money after all, just for something to do, something to keep him busy from his own thoughts. It was all pointless.

His hand started to tremble. *No. Not now! Damnit! You stay still.* He put his trembling hand in his pocket.

"Well, now we don't like to popcorn it up here. We'll split up into smaller groups of three or four and offer prayer requests," Sarah explained.

The chairs started moving rapidly into numerous smaller circles. Ted felt uneasy as his hand wouldn't stop trembling, however, he kept the trembling to a bare minimum. Even a sniper couldn't tell how slow his hand trembled, even though to himself, it felt like a speeding bullet.

Ted was in a circle with Jennifer, and Erin. He looked at them with his bright smile. He was careful, he always was when dealing with circles like this. His ears would be his eyes, and he could sense the room, every movement, every noise, no sound, no matter how little would escape his ears, just like nothing and no one can escape the defense of his mind's eye. He is as he's always been, ever watchful, but no longer by his own choice. He became conditioned to it so much that it just turns on. This is the exact reason he's failed at his one goal, that same goal he gave up on, he keeps failing. Again, and again, and again!

"Well, now this is the part where we wear our emotions on our sleeves," Jennifer explained. "Forgive me if I sound like a tour guide." She turned her head to Erin. "Prayer request?"

Erin frowned. "I—I do." Her voice was solemn, her head was bowed down low. Her eyes were wide open, staring blankly at the floor, as if what she was looking for was buried below the bowels of the church. Her thighs were closed shut, and her elbows met her stomach and one hand wrapped around her other fist, keeping them close to her, as if holding in some secret desire she longed to keep hidden. Her right heel rose from the ground, and then rested back down. Again, and again, and again. "My mother was di—diagnosed with stage four liver cancer." Tears streamed down her face; she began coughing up tears.

Ted tried to look concerned. He noticed something else. He would have thought there would have been others around who would have rushed to console her weeping. But at last, he found that she was not the only one weeping in the room. There was at least one other person in the additional small groups weeping, likely due to some cruel hand fate had given them. *Like the hand I was dealt.* It was also the first time he ever noticed Jennifer not enthused. She wrapped her arm around Erin and pulled her close. She said nothing. She just let Erin cry over her shoulder. That was a prayer in and of itself. Words needed not say more.

Should I really be caring about this right now? No.

Ted did his best to show his concern, however, he retained that smile. He moved his chair a little closer and put his hand on Erin's back.

"Ted," Jennifer began, shedding her own tear. "Before I begin, do you have something to pray for?"

"Nothing that cannot wait. This is more important I think," He answered. *But is she?*

"Okay, then please, but don't feel pressured, bow your head."

Erin's head was already bowed down low, and tears dripped down from those closed eyelids. Jennifer's tears were more controlled, but she bowed her head and was much more composed. Ted bowed down, but he didn't close his eyes. He kept his eyes focused, his pupils continued scanning the room. The rest, as if they all received the order from the same commanding officer had their eyes closed, and heads bowed. Most were holding hands.

He immediately wiped a tear from his face. *Was this genuine? No. It can't be.*

"Amen," Jennifer finished her prayer. Ted tuned out the entire prayer as he was focused on his own individual thoughts, and the behavior of everyone in the room. One by one these prayerful people rose their heads up, opening their eyes. Many of them were happy, almost as if a burden was lifted from their miserable chests. *How?*

The room was filled with chatter again. *Thank God.* The silence irritated him. He could find that he could no longer keep tuning everything out, not in the silence, not like this. Silence was much better when lives were on the line. He looked around the room again, some people were getting up, and putting their chairs right back towards the tables and were leaving. Some of them left in pairs, and others left by themselves after departing amiably with someone they engaged in a good conversation with.

He sought to do the same. He got up before his hand was grabbed by Jennifer. "Hey," she wiped her face clean from tears with her free sleeve. "I told you we wear our feelings on our sleeves here. I hope we didn't scare you off."

"Miss Jennifer, I'm afraid it will take a lot more than that to scare me off," he lied, turning to Erin with a solemn face as she was still weeping and wiping tears from her face with her palms. "I am sorry. Truly. I am."

"I—it's not your fault." She looked to him, "You don't have to be sorry. Buh—but I appreciate it."

"Now," he turned almost without skipping a beat and returning that smile to his face. "I must really be going."

"You're not coming out with us tonight?" Jennifer frowned.

"Not tonight. Maybe next time," he said. He tried to pull away, but Jennifer wouldn't let go.

"Wait. Let me get your phone number," she said.

"As you wish, milady," he spoke dryly.

"My, my, aren't you the romantic." She grabbed a pen and piece of paper from her purse and handed it to him. He immediately wrote down a phone number and handed it back to her. "At least you're honest about it. Unlike some men." She took out a piece of paper and wrote her own phone number on it. "Here, take mine."

"It's a pleasure." He took the phone number and placed it in his wallet.

"Now, now, Tedward." She smiled at him. "I think you know the pleasure is all mine."

"Of course, it is." He smiled back. *You have no idea how true that is.* "Maybe I'll see you next week or around. But I must be going."

"Good night, Ted," Jennifer said.

Samantha transitioned from her seat, pushing it in, briskly walking towards them, trying to catch up to Ted. How good of a host could she be, if she didn't at least make the effort to make sure he was comfortable. After all, it was her who invited Ted to the study; however, he made a beeline for the door, at a brisk pace she knew she couldn't keep up with. She glanced over to Jennifer, who turned to Erin. For a moment, Samantha thought that perhaps Jennifer came on too strongly for Ted's comfort, prompting an exit, or perhaps something else was going on with Ted, something unseen.

"Are you coming out tonight? If you are, I believe it's my turn to buy you one," Jennifer's hand wrapped around Erin's shoulder.

"I think I need a break," Erin said. "I need some rest actually. Maybe next week. I just—I just need to get some sleep. Start fresh in the morning."

"What's wrong?" Samantha turned her gaze towards Erin, noticing wiped tears and reddened eyes. She placed her hand on Erin's back, rubbing it.

"My mother has stage four cancer," Erin said abruptly.

Samantha felt a sudden weight fill up from inside her chest as she covered her mouth with her hand. "I'm so sorry. I'll pray for that, and healing for her."

"Some rest will do you good. I understand Erin," Jennifer said, "I'll put your chair away. Don't worry about it. If you need someone to talk to, you can always text or call me."

"Thanks," Erin stood to leave.

Michael followed and put her chair away. He smiled at Jennifer. "So, how did it go?" he asked.

"My dear, Michael, whatever do you mean?" she snickered as she pushed her chair back in.

"You got him alone," Samantha shuddered as Michael mansplained himself to reiterate the obvious. This was one of her pet peeves. *I'll work on that.*

"Well, I certainly couldn't let you hog him. Besides, I don't think he'd care to listen to more of your business monologue." She gave him a slightly annoyed glare. "I suppose we can finish this up at Teri Nation. Let's be off. I have very important business at Teri's Empire."

"Only you can make is sound so much better than it actually is." Tim chuckled, shaking his head.

Samantha, along with Jennifer, Michael, and Tim followed the crowd out of the room and back towards the lobby where there seemed to be an abundance of people, talking with each other almost like old friends. Samantha always found it interesting that these people seemed so close to catch up weekly, even if they were only a part for a single week, to her, every Tuesday seemed like a reunion. They briskly exited the church, and recruited a few people to go out, not that they needed to do that, Brian would take care of that, as he always did. But it was good to show interest to the newcomers.

Samantha and her immediate friends walked to Teri nation and walked towards the back end of the bar. It was much less crowded than last week. Perhaps there was some foul thing in the air. Samantha did notice four unique individuals by the bar, towards the end of it where she met Ted from last week. Two men, and two women having strong gin.

They were talking to one another in a variety of accents, *that* is what got her attention. Samantha picked one up as Irish, and the other English, and one she could only guess as Russian. The fourth wasn't quite Russian, but it had a similar sound to that of the eastern European countries. It would seem odd since Russia declared war on neighboring countries as of late, and almost as if these individuals were speaking to each other as if there was no animosity between their nations. She found this most peculiar.

Scott made their drinks, Samantha was drinking a dark beer this time, and Tim was held off with a white wine sangria. And of course, Michael and Jennifer got whatever the special was. This one he served in bola glasses.

"So, Scott, what have we the pleasure," Michael began.

"Or displeasure," Jennifer added.

"Of drinking today?" Michael finished. They drank well together. Tim and Samantha were smiling as it was rare that they could get this close together with the two of them. They paired well together, like a fluffernutter sandwich. Their banter bounced off one another almost like they had been friends for years, but truth be told, they've only known one another for a year, and they all met here, at this bar through Café.

"It was some recipe I found on some website," Scott answered as he printed out separate slips. Jennifer already took a sip. Samantha guessed she enjoyed it with the way Jennifer rubbed her buttocks against the stool, "I don't know much about it, but last time it was made a lot of people died." There was silence. Scott turned around. "I'm kidding. Its vodka, chocolate, and seltzer. Nothing too fancy. I may have put some basil in there."

"Oh my God! I am allehgic to freaking basil!" Jennifer joked. Scott's eyes lit up in surprise, almost like he was looking at a dead person.

"Isn't that my line?" Tim laughed as he brought up his glass to sip his sangria.

Jennifer placed two fingers on her lips as she looked Scott in the eye mischievously. "Two can play at that game."

"Okay, cool," Scott laughed it off and went to his other guests as he walked backwards with two thumbs up.

"Alright, you've kept me in enough suspense. Now that you've had him all to yourself, what was he like?" Michael asked.

"Yes. I am dying to know. Spill the beans, Jenn!" Samantha pushed.

"Whoa, whoa, whoa," Tim put his hands up defensively. "You leave my beans out of this. It wasn't my fault."

"No, Tim, it wasn't your fault. And we're certainly not talking about your beans," Michael jeered. "Besides, that was actually some good chili. Jenn. Spill it!"

"Fine." She took another sip. "Really nothing more than what he shared from the rest of the group, during that very questionably boring icebreaker."

Samantha pondered with the fresh liquor to her nose, and then she remembered something which she neglected to mention previously, but perhaps a sensitive question. "Jennifer, did you make note of the scars on his face?"

"I did notice those scars, like lines or streaks across his cheeks. I didn't say anything. That isn't something you want to ask someone who hardly knows you," Jennifer said, trading that playful smile of hers with droopy eyelids. "Your brain is working, what is on that mind."

"I haven't formulated a complete thought. I'll have to get back to you." Sam's gaze shot back to the other end of the bar.

"Did he have something to do? He seemed in a hurry to leave." Tim's smile faded.

"Yeah, I wondered about that too," Samantha commented, turning back to Jennifer.

"Well, he didn't say. I was able to snag his number before his prompt getaway."

"Getaway. Yes, that's the appropriate word for it." Michael poked fun at Jennifer again. "It's hard to escape your clutches."

"I wonder if it had anything to do with the study." Samantha wondered if that was the most appropriate study for someone in a field fueled by money.

"Could be, honestly it isn't the best first book for someone. After all, a wise man once said, 'Meaningless, meaningless, it's all meaningless!'" Jennifer rose her hands in the air as she sat back down on her stool and cross her fingers.

"Well," Samantha said. "Tell us how you really feel."

They all looked at Jennifer, waiting for her whimsical response.

"My thoughts on the matter are all entirely 'meaningless.'" Jennifer smiled.

Michael, Tim, Jennifer, and Samantha all laughed at the joke. It was ironic, and certainly the lesson could be very depressing if taken out of context. After all, not everything was meaningless.

Samantha could feel her hair standing on ends. Her hands remained in place as the ripples in her cup of beer moved towards the end of the glass. She looked closely, and Tim, and Michael didn't seem to notice. Jennifer put on her sweatshirt in response to the chill. *Where is this coming from?*

She looked at the strangers in the bar. She noticed one of them, the taller man, the one with the Irish accent appeared to be flicking his fingers back and forth, violently tapping against a piece of paper on the bar top. She looked back down to her cup and drank some more. She fixed her eyes back on the man and the piece of paper was gone. *I'm not that drunk, am I? I hope not. I barely had a drink.* Was she imagining it? The paper was gone, and the man didn't appear to be tapping anything anymore. This man wore a black suit to match his lengthy black hair tied behind his back.

"You okay there, Sam?" Jennifer glanced at her and she tossed her head back.

"No, yes," she corrected herself. "I just thought I saw something. It's nothing."

"Soooo," Jennifer began.

"Are you okay or not?" Michael asked, putting his hand on his hip disapprovingly. "I'm beginning to worry about you."

Samantha moved her gaze back over to the strangers. "I thought I saw one of them violently tapping a piece of paper. The tall one." This, she whispered.

Michael shifting his attention towards them, hiding his body and face behind Samantha just enough to avoid looking suspicious. "Are you sure it isn't the air conditioning going down again? You've mentioned this numerous times now. I really don't believe a person could be the cause of it. Besides, tapping a piece of paper isn't exactly unusual."

"I—I'm not sure," she replied.

"Well, only one way to find out for sure," Michael said.

He took her hand. "Michael! Wait! What are you doing?"

He ignored her as he pulled her to the strangers. One of the women there looked at them and smiled; she had a very youthful face, her red eyes. Samantha found her eyes to be especially peculiar, unless; was she high? The tall man looked surprised and turned to them, there was an unpleasant scowl on his face.

"Well, well, well, what sort of beast have we ensnared?" he said in his Irish accent.

"Well, we're here every single Tuesday night, and haven't seen you here before. Me and my friend here would like to say hi and introduce ourselves. My name is Michael, this is Samantha, Sam for short." Michael introduced himself and her charmingly.

"Hii!" Samantha introduced herself awkwardly. No matter how hard she tried, she didn't do well in friendly social situations, she was great on the phone though.

"Okay," The man said. "And to what do we owe the unfortunate circumstance for such a forced introduction?"

"Culain, I do not want another repeat from last week's escapade," Said the girl with black hair. She was the one with the Russian accent. "Please, it was a mess. We don't need another one."

"As you wish, Ilya," He replied and returned a sneering smile towards them. "Now, I don't know what it is you think you saw, but you didn't see anything. I don't know what you think you felt, but it was nothing. You don't know anything. Now kindly piss off!"

"Wow!" Michael replied nonchalantly. "I was just being friendly. There was no reason to be rude. And what we—"

"What you think you saw was nothing. Now, before I lose my temper, kindly piss off," The man called Culain said. "The less you know, the better."

"Michael, let's go," Samantha pulled on his arm and shrunk back behind him. She didn't trust them, nor did they seem like people, or at least the man called, *Culain*, she wanted to be friends with. Culain seemed like a man that would sooner hurt you, and then make you apologize for inconveniencing those around you. Michael nodded to her and turned around, pulling her back to their quartet.

He seemed unnecessarily rude and unprovoked. There was so much anger in his voice, despite that smile. There was a raw emotion to his tone, as if they were less than he was. *It is wrong for me to judge the man. I don't know who he is or where he comes from, or what he's going through.*

"There once was a couple in a bar; in life they hoped to get far, thought they were destined, their ankles were nailed in, I needed their love to be marred." Culain mocked them as they retreated.

Chapter 5 Dyatlov's Pass

~I'm honestly not enjoying this.

***

Major McCurdy led her small nuclear specialist platoon up the pass. Rather, she followed behind them, directing them where to walk. Even though it was summer, the weather couldn't be trusted to remain warm. They each had a large bag which had their hazmat gear, the suit with its oxygen tanks and tubes. As they were going into a potentially dangerously radiation infested environment, and every precaution had to be made. McCurdy knew it wasn't natural radiation up here, but even mana was poisonous to the normie.

McCurdy looked down the mountain pass, glancing at the dirt and gravel, crumbs of the mountain rolling down the hill until inevitably coming to a halt when the kinetic energy lost all movement. Just like the radioactive readings this team picked up in the facility. She let out a deep sigh as her ears trained on the four of those with her, listening in on them while they took a break, discussing the fabled incidents of the Dyatlov's pass, infamously called, "Devil's Pass". *Such a fitting name for such a dismal place.*

She wished she could have come here by herself: it would save her from the guilt, save her from the grief of killing these men, or getting them killed. But an officer just simply going off base while on duty was suspect, and she needed a believable ruse, and these men fit the bill perfectly. Just how many more people, close to her, would she have to kill before she became utterly numb to the grief and guilt? How soon until her heart became one large callous?

McCurdy walked over to them as they finished their conversation. Looking down at them from a ledge, she said, "Lee, get the MicroR Meter and start measuring. Breaks over."

73

"Yes, Ma'am," He got into his pack and pulled out a brown box with knobs and a little white screen with readings and a moving needle, he measured the radioactive activity with the device on the terrain.

"Not too far to go now," she said to them. "We're almost to the final destination."

"Is there some kind of bunker up here?" Gongora asked.

"No," McCurdy turned her gaze to him. *Idiot.*

"Major, the readings are picking up again," Lee said. "It's very minimal, 0.83 svs."

"Not terrible," Nguyen said. "However, we still need to be cautious. Let's hope it stays that low."

"Put on your Hazmat," McCurdy ordered.

They slipped in through the yellow material, some were clumsy, but McCurdy put these on thousands of times, and so did Lee, by the looks of it. He was already helping Gongora put on the clumsy black gloves. The face shield fogged up their vision with the breath inside, and nowhere to exhale from, except through the air filter. They put these suits on in the matter of 10 minutes, including the oxygen tank. McCurdy noticed immediately that Adams was fumbling his oxygen tank, and getting the tank attached to the hose. She shook her head as she breathed heavily, walking over to him. Her face's visor fogged up with each breath as she slowly made her way over to him, and grasped the hose, attaching it to the oxygen tank for him.

"I never liked these things anyway. They're stupid, and unnecessarily complex," she commented. *Of course, I would think that, unlike you, I don't need it.* Her vision was fogged by her breath. "Everyone ready?"

"Yes, Ma'am," Lee commented, pulling up his now empty pack to the side of his pocket, his breath began to fog up the inside of his visor. His rifle was at his side. "The svs read higher up."

"Lead on."

Lee led them onward, climbing and following the radiation levels as the svs grew higher on the meter. They climbed up, taking steady breaths along the way. Lee climbed up another ledge which looked like it could be the top of Dyatlov's pass, but the pass sunk back down into a basin.

Around the edges of the basin was a rock labyrinth, leading to a wheel-locked door. It was steel and embedded into the mountain, like a trap door. Lee looked down at his meter, and the radiation stopped reading. He hit the meter a few times. The meter still didn't read any radiation.

McCurdy observed the specialist, Lee, taking his meter to the side. She couldn't make out his facial expression with his fogged visor, but she knew his file, no one knew these old meters better than he did, not in any of her other units, certainly, he knew what he was doing. Lee flipped the microR meter upside down, and unscrewed the back, and took out the batter, and replaced it with a new one, screwing it back together for an updated reading. This is when she knew something was wrong with the machine, those meters can only handle so much.

"What happened?" McCurdy asked, wondering why he stopped. Her eyes scanned the basin, looking for runes scraped on the sides, or mana circles from previous fae, or mana residues, anything to clue her in on the possibility of an enemy here, but so far, found nothing.

"Radiation killed the battery," He replied. He turned the meter back on. "Much better. Only 0.043 svs. Its less than before. Gongora, I think I found your bunker." He turned to McCurdy. "Is this place showing up anywhere on the map? Or even in something classified?"

"No," McCurdy answered. "There is nothing to indicate there was something like this here. Be careful, that radiation can spike back up any minute."

"Do we know why this is happening?" Adams asked.

"That is precisely why we are here," Nguyen said.

"We need to climb down. Keep your eyes peeled. Odds are, I don't think we're alone," McCurdy stated. "Check your fire. I needn't remind you Ukraine Officials could be up here."

"Then why don't we call for backup then? We're not infantry!" Adams exclaimed.

"Don't you get it," Gongora said. "We aren't even supposed to be here. This was a last-minute mission, likely didn't get approved by the higher ups. We're here now, and that's that."

"What do you mean higher ups? She's right here! We're not going to find out bickering," Lee started climbing down and the rest of them followed.

She shook her head in her suit. *You got too comfortable for insubordination.* She kept her thoughts to herself, not wanting to clue them in on the real reason they were there. She didn't need them to know she was sending them to their graves, but she was most of all disappointed. This Army wasn't the Army she once knew, filled with discipline and respect. The unit underneath her was undisciplined, unchecked, and disrespectful. Such men do not belong in the military. *Perhaps this is for the best.*

McCurdy looked to the rocks to her left, and she squinted her eyes as she noticed a glowing circle embedded in the rocks, numerous shapes and designs lay within it. She recognized the ancient language, the ancient runes; runes only a fae would know. To these soldiers, should they see it, would only serve their superstitions. *Another fae is here. Who are you?*

They continued to climb down, carefully to get into the basin of the pass, a rip or tear in their hazmat suit meant almost inevitable death, and they all knew it. McCurdy was the least disturbed by that fact. They observed the basin, carefully monitoring for extra radioactive activity around the basin. McCurdy observed with her hands crossed behind her back, subtly pulling mana out from the rock into her mana veins, hiding inside her hazmat suit.

"Your orders, Major?" Adams said. "Radioactive activity has depleted."

"Affirmative," Lee replied. He turned to the door to the unmarked bunker. "Do we need to go in there?"

"Yes. Lee, I want you up front. Gongora, and Nguyen behind him. Adams, you're with me," she said, "Lee, get that door open."

"Yes ma'am." He stated, walking over to the iron cast door and placed his meter softly on the ground. With his hazmat covered hands, he turned the wheel, unlocking the rusty mechanisms behind the door. He slowly pulled the creaking door on its hinges. Dust came out and clouded his face shield. He wiped the dust from his suit.

He picked his meter up as everyone turned on their flashlights.

The entrance into the bunker was dark and musty, and felt desolate as if it had been abandoned for decades. They entered in, observing the radiation levels, which appeared to have settled down, the clicks of the meters only activated every few seconds, flipping the needle back and forth. They looked to either side of them to see various tables and other rooms with doors that were forced open, dented, and twisted beyond repair.

"What happened here?" Gongora asked, shaking his head as he looked at the carnage. The rooms were completely in disarray. There was coagulated blood on the ground, the gel shimmering crimson on the walls with their flashlights. Some of the blood was smeared like the entrails of a man with his torso ripped open and dragged off further into the dark.

"Silence," McCurdy sternly called. *This is just an illusion. I can tell, damn fae, whoever you are. This was recent.* "Shut up and keep moving. Something's still here."

They followed the entrails, even though Gongora silently protested. It was heard among comrades, sharing the same hellish living conditions. Nguyen was laser focused, his almond-shaped eyes narrowed as he peered into the darkness as they walked forth, scanning the room with every step they took.

This reminded McCurdy of a horror movie, entrails dragging themselves down the hall, the iron doors rusting, and each step she took creaked. She felt unnerved as her fingers in her suit began to tremble, feeling this unnatural place, void of all life, but she knew something more, sieverts did not just start and dissipate naturally. There was a fae here, or perhaps a threcket. She hissed silently at the thought, not keen on fighting one of those down here in close quarters, whatever form the threcket chose to take. She knew this was a false sense of security.

The meters didn't pick up anything new, and almost stopped making its gurgling sounds altogether. The darkness became cold and oppressive, the deeper they adventured into these godforsaken halls, until they came to an end of it all.

They came to a room, no, an altar. Blood smeared all over the place, and many shapes and circles were carved with human blood over the walls. There was no reactor, no working generator, nor was there any viable source of uranium or plutonium anywhere: no radioactive materials.

Lee grimaced as he looked on the altar. He put his meter on the cold metal floor. He turned to McCurdy, and he wasn't smiling. "Major, you have some explaining to do. Do you know something we don't?"

"No," she lied; her heart started to race. *I can't kill a threcket in the middle of a mutiny. Damn it, Lee!* "And don't question me." She stared him down with cold eyes from behind her visor. Her heart started to race, the stakes rising.

"No, I think this is a valid reason for questioning. We've all been here. The radioactive activity died as soon as we came here, and there is no evidence that there was any radioactive activity here minus the readings. Do you know something, we don't?" He pointed a finger directly at her.

"Watch your mindless speculations, Warrant Officer, I don't have time for this," McCurdy snapped at him. "And no, I don't."

McCurdy could tell Lee was scowling behind that fogged mask, rising with a sense of distrust for her, and the distrust would soon spread to the rest of them. *You are right to distrust me. I would.*

"Major, we are soldiers, not exorcists," Adams interjected. "We need a priest for this, or back up. We don't know what is down here. Something is unnatural about this place, and we don't know what we're getting ourselves into. These readings are sporadic enough as it is without us being here!"

"That is precisely why we are here, Sergeant," she said, "We don't know, and we need to know."

"You all came to the worst place," Said a voice in the corner.

All five of them swiftly turned around to see a man, holding a pile of red shlop in his hand: pumping like a heart, but this was no heart, at least, not any heart that McCurdy had seen. He bore a sinister smile upon his face, a man filled with bloodlust that would never be satisfied. The man held himself in high esteem, as if looking down on all of them,

McCurdy could feel the condescension. His pants were ripped in parts, and he had many cuts over them, as if he himself had just fought off a threcket. The man was bare chested, with rippling muscles, and blood dripped down several cuts on his face and chest.

"Onhlidan!" he chanted. "Onhlidan! Onhlidan! Onhlidan!"

A red light emitted from the shlop. The soldiers panicked, drawing their side arms and pointed it at the man. They all aimed down their sights, ready to fire. The light lit up the room, and they found themselves in a room filled with nothing but bones beneath their feet. They glanced below. Bones, human bones, flesh and blood covered their feet.

"What the hell is this shit!" Lee cried out. He stamped his feet on the ground, crushing bones beneath him.

"Who are you?" McCurdy asked. "What are you doing here?"

"I think that not be the question you should be asking, Major." The man said, throwing the beating shlop of mass directly at her. She moved to the side swiftly, letting the mass strike the wall behind her.

"And what question might that be?" She asked.

"Orders! Orders!" Nguyen cried out, his pistol trembling in his hand. "Major! What are your damn orders?!"

"Orders, Major, what are they, Major." The man mimicked Nguyen. He sighed as he moved his bloody hand's palm to the side. "I guess it matters not. Secrets. That is all they are. Secrets."

"What are you talking about?" she ignored Nguyen's cries for an order. Orders were order, but right now was not the time for her to wear her military hat, but as a fae of the administration. "Why are you here."

"I was looking for the Grail. It appears, it is not here. And I don't think it holy. After all, wasn't it the key to pandora's box?"

"I didn't think anyone would tell anyone where the Grail is," she inquired. "And don't speak the Grail. That is on a need-to-know basis, and no one here, yourself included, needs to know."

"Major! What is he talking about?" Gongora interjected.

"That is need to know. You don't need to know." She snapped.

"You, fae of the administration aren't very smart, are you?" the man asked. "It doesn't matter. You are out of time."

McCurdy heard a frightened gasp from Lee. She glanced over to see his fogged mask; she imagined his eyes were stretched as wide open as his skull would allow, assuming, with such a worrisome response from a Warrant Officer only meant one thing: the radiation maxed out the microR meter.

"Five-thousand!" Adams exclaimed. "That is—"

"Not an accurate reading!" Lee shouted. "Our meters only go up that high. It's much higher than that. We need to get the fuck out of here or we'll be fried to a crisp or on our deathbeds with cancer next week!"

"No," said McCurdy. "It's fine."

"Have you lost your damn mind!" Gongora exclaimed. "This is not what we signed up for. We are not getting fried because of whatever the real reason is why we're here! We aren't infantry! We are trained to handle something like this!"

"Look." She pointed.

A gate of fire and ice opened behind the man. He passed through it, and both the gate and he was gone. McCurdy could feel, even with her suit, the temperature dropping in the air, and the hairs stood on ends on her back, as she was certain everyone with her felt the same. Only she knew their hearts were much closer to beating out of their chests. She was certain they were left unaware of these ancient arcane elements kept hidden to them for the last fifteen-hundred years. Just here, they were made aware of everything, magic, fae, portals, illusions, and least of all the Grail, whatever this person was truly after. These were all things that, according to the Caster's Code, must not enter the minds of normies, lest the threads of creation come undone. That is what she was told, anyway.

The microR meters measured back down to zero almost immediately.

None of them needed to be here for this. I hate this code. She let out a sigh.

McCurdy's eyes narrowed behind her mask, the mana still being pulled through the oxygen in the air and through her suit. She backed away from the group of her specialists, who still trembled as they pointed their guns at the precise location from where the portal vanished. She could hear their sporadic breathing over the coms. They were terrified, and why shouldn't they be? No matter how disciplined they were, which they weren't, everything they thought they understood about the world came undone, just like their sanity, as it became unraveled.

They could hear the rapid bubbling from behind them. McCurdy's eyes angled, *it's one of those threckets.* She now knew what the beating shlop was, just a little vessel for the threcket to form from this world. *Whose heart did you take?* "Shit," she swore under her breath. They all turned around them to see a large bubbling red mass forming from the wall. It slowly began to take shape. McCurdy had a better idea of what she was looking at, but even to her, the bull's head protruding from the clicking segments of a centipedal body made her ill. The disgusting creature stood tall on strong horse legs; many arms baring stingers were already flailing towards them.

She let out a sigh of relief. *Well, I don't have to kill them now.*

"What the actual hell is that!" Lee raised his rifle, aiming down the sites to the threcket, pulling the trigger. "To hell with your orders. Damn it!"

Gongora and Nguyen marched to the side as their rifles, firing. The bullets sparked as they struck the threcket. No surprise there, those hides were damn near impenetrable, and needed specific things to pierce it. Weapons of the modern era was completely useless.

The beast roared and smashed into Lee, digging its stingers into him. He cried out in agony as the stingers began to inject him with poison, blood and poison immediately saturated his body. Gongora and Nguyen immediately opened fire. The bullets penetrated the threcket, and the holes in the creature produced purple puss that filled the air. McCurdy walked backwards, leaning against the back wall, waiting patiently for the creature to kill them. After all, she felt that if she personally killed them, it would shatter her spirit. *I'm sorry.*

The creature immediately flung itself into the direction of the gunfire. Nguyen dove to the ground and started shooting at it from below. What should be the blood of this creature came down on him, eating through his suit like acid. The beast impaled Gongora with its venomous stingers and ripped him in several pieces, his limbs twirling in the air spraying his blood in all directions, some of that blood smeared on McCurdy's visor. Nguyen rolled over, ignoring the acid on himself as it ate at him from within. He started running out of the hallway only to be impaled from behind the deadly stingers, and likewise ripped apart. He didn't even have time to let out a final cry for help.

"Well, now that that's over with." McCurdy said. "It is time to send you back."

She pulled the mana from the air into her Mana Veins. She pulled out her knife and blue veins protruded from it as she drew shapes in the air. The beast ran and sprinted to her. She whispered into the air as her body was covered in the blue veins, the same veins she projected onto her knife.

"Deoful Spreot!" She chanted. "Deoful Spreot!"

She pulled the mana from the air, turning the entire room into a vacuum. The mana swirled around her, crafting a red flame, and red spears, fashioned from the mana in the air. The creature barreled into her, but she did not move as her blue veins turned grey, forcing her in place like an irremovable statue. The red spear penetrated the beast, pouring its blood on the floor. It screeched in agony as it flopped on the ground. The mana she pulled in the air protected her feet from being burned.

"Deorfald." She chanted again as she drew another shape in the air, this shape was more square and less elegant than the shape before. Black chains came up from the ground and encapsulated the beast, and it disappeared in a puff of ash. She breathed in the mana of its remains, and the mana from the dead that rested here, until nothing was left except the iron ground, including the remains of Gongora, Lee, Nguyen, and—Adams—he wasn't here.

She shook her head, swearing underneath her breath as she hastily took off the Hazmat Suit. Her veins turned blue again as she bolted out of the room with her flashlight, and the mana spear in her hands. She sprinted through the corridors and exited the bunker. She found him sitting on a rock outside with his helmet off, seemingly not disturbed that the radiation. No, better call it what it is, the concentrated mana could kill him, or cause a normie like him to have severe radiation sickness or cancer that would kill him in the next few weeks.

Adams looked up to her and jolted up, backing away from her. "Major, what the hell was that?"

"You have no right to question me when you left us to die like that," she said, holding the spear in her hand.

He gazed at the spear, "Nothing about today made any sense. A bunker with high radioactivity, with no source to cause said activity, a portal or some shit, and a—a I don't know what to call that, some bubbling goo, and not to mention this illusion or what—"

Adams breathed heavily, his eyes glancing past McCurdy, presumably towards the hatch into the mountain. He lost sight of the spear until he found it in his chest, the blade cut through his chest easily. She ripped it right out of him, spraying blood over the basin of the pass. He coughed blood and placed his hand on his chest while he stepped backwards, tripping over the rock behind him, "Major! What are you doing?"

"I'm sorry kid," she stuttered as a tear dripped from her eye. "You see, normies like you. No, accidents like you aren't supposed to see caster nonsense! It would destroy the very fabric of your beliefs. Trust me, ultimately it is for the best. I had originally planned for whatever it is I found up here to kill you instead, and I would take care of it after, but I didn't plan on you being a little chickenshit and running away. Now, *I* have to kill you, something *I* was trying to avoid!"

Adams' eyes gaped open as he reached for his side arm. She swiftly swung the spear, the elongated red blade slicing right through the hand holding onto the side arm, it flew through the air, spiraling blood through the air. He cried as he turned around and sprinted; his heart racing, beating through his chest like a heavy metal drum solo. He made it to the path where they came from, and tried to climb it, but his stub of a hand was beyond useless.

She walked around to him and pushed him away from the path. He tripped again and crawled backwards as McCurdy stared at him with those teary eyes. "Honestly, I'm not enjoying this either, for the record. Honestly, this is the part about my existence I hate the most. I hate killing people." She felt her heart sinking, and the spear trembled in her hand. *You are all family to me, brothers and sisters in arms.* She firmly grasped the spear in her hand, returning her resolve to do what must be done, despite the singular accepted fact, she didn't want to kill him, but she had no choice. She thrust the spear into his chest, not missing his heart this time. She twisted the spear, tearing his flesh and heart apart.

She looked into his eyes as the life left them, sighing, she took a step back; dropped the spear to the ground. When it hit the ground, it dematerialized in the air, creating little red lights as it faded into nothingness, floating in the air like reversing snowfall.

She leaned against the wall leading upwards. drawing her mana veins to her, absorbing the mana that was the life force of Adams. His flesh began to boil, and it faded away, the muscles and bones were converted to mana, and she imbibed them through her mana veins. His body faded into nothing.

She cried into the air as the guilt constricted her heart as if a sadistic snake slithered its way through her ribs, and wrapped around her heart, suffocating the air and blood out of it. She didn't want to kill him, or get them all killed, but that was the nature of this *cursed administration*.

There has to be a better way, but everything's already been tried. The administration is so cruel. Why does it have to be this way? Why can't these normies know? We would have to kill so much less, she thought.

She remembered something, something important. Her job here was not done, even though the site was now confirmed secure. She had to radio in the Administrator. She pulled out her phone, and planted her veins into the phone, preventing any unwanted listeners. She dialed his number.

"Admin Colton," The voice said on the other line.

"Major McCurdy."

"Status report."

"There was another fae involved. It wasn't anything nuclear on the pass. Someone was using it for experimentation and summoned a threcket here. The fae was looking for the Holy Grail," she replied. "The man seemed to know much. He is skilled enough to open a portal from Pandora, and enough about necromancy and demonic magic to bring demons into this world."

"Appearance?"

"White. Accent was southern United States. Maybe Georgia. Dark hair. Five-eleven. One-hundred-eighty pounds. Muscular. Estimated. No name was given. But he spoke as if he was not a fae himself, and held disdain for the administration, and he seemed to know I was a fae before I did anything."

"Go dark. You are being transferred to London immediately," He said, "Don't worry, you'll have more information on your email in a few hours. Get on the next plane to London. Don't worry about your replacement."

"What's my mission?"

"We can't trust the head administration anymore. Odds are, whoever that is, was a rogue, and a mole sent to spy on us. That is the only logical conclusion, and he may have had a goal in mind that wasn't the Grail, and that was just an excuse to throw you off. You are going to retrieve the Grail from them, diplomatically, covert, choice is yours. We can't leave it in their hands anymore, not when they're so corrupt as it is."

"I understand. If it is the will of U.S.A branch of the Administration, I will see it done."

"See that you don't disappoint. Colton out."

Chapter 6 Crests

~I had a dream once. It was the only thing I was born with. There was compassion in my heart and a drive to strive for peace, to help others. Was that so wrong of me? I helped others and found it to be meaningless. At the end, it was all meaningless, because saving others, means killing someone else.

***

Ilya looked down from the penthouse on Wednesday night. Her arms crossed over her chest as red veins colored her eyes. Her eyes squinted as she studied the now barren streets of Boston. Struggling to keep her eyes open, she rapidly shook her head. These veins allowed her to see traces of elusive mana threads crawling across the streets, pulling apart the creation of the world, and linking Earth to the cursed land of Pandora, a place their kind go when they die, most of them anyway. Some of them might be lucky, and just end up in a hole in the ground. She steadily drank the mana from the air, and the salty perspiration of Culain and Alexander. It was refreshing, and she needed this after her third straight night of no sleep. She twirled her black hair with her finger.

She remembered the previous night, at Teri Nation, their own little hang out spot to make futile attempts to wind down, and of course the girl and boy who approached them out of, presumably curiosity, was then greeted with hostility from Culain. Such a shame, really. A part of the world she could never have, some silence, some peace, and a mind of harmless curiosity. They were curious. That's all. *All I want is a friend, someone to talk to and not have to worry about these damn Threckets! Is that too much to ask! Why was I born this way? And born into an endless war.*

Culain and Alexander held out a map of the state of Massachusetts with multiple red markings on the map, filled with stars. All in all, there were over two-hundred stars on that map. Culain and Alexander were talking amongst themselves. Alexander had dark moppy hair, and was much broader built than Culain, but Culain was not a small man. Blanka was eating a granola bar in the corner, seeming exhausted, they all were. Ilya knew that; it wasn't like she was the only one living in misery. Her thought lingered again on the hostility Culain displayed towards the normie couple.

"Culain, must you be an unbearable ass to everyone we meet?" Ilya rebuked him, glaring at him. Her youthful face grimaced underneath her hateful glare. "They were only being polite, something you could stand to do sometimes."

"People are polite to get close. You know this better than anyone. Besides, Caster's rules. If they saw anything, you know what has to be done. Even a risk is too much," Culain replied, never taking his eyes off the map, his eyes narrowed at the map, he tapped on the table repeatedly with his index finger, "I did what I did to avoid having to enforce that rule. After all, you know how much I just love killing unnecessary normies," he said sarcastically. "I fucking hate it!"

"You and I know you hate it." The white-haired Blanka said, her red eyes looked compassionately to him, and then they narrowed towards him, "You act a tough game, but you're just like them."

"We're not like them, and you know it. They don't know half of what goes on in the world, and they sure as hell don't know half of what's going on within their own hearts," Culain replied. "Blanka, you know as well as I, unlike they, we are forced to wear our masks glued to our fucking faces. They can take that damn mask off, we can't. Because we have a dark job to do. If they get too close, and they see something they're not supposed to see, you know we have to kill them. And let me tell you, that's a lot harder to do when you have a relationship with them."

"None know this better than Culain," Alexander explained. He looked up from the map with his green eyes. "Culain, you need to be better at telling people you work with who you are," he sighed. "Let me explain, because Culain won't: a bunch of orphans saw what happened during an incident thirteen years ago in China. Fortunately, most people died in those flames. The survivors saw the cursed essence falling from the moon. Culain even knew some of them, he shared drinks with them, but he had to kill them all the same. If I'm not mistaken, he underwent some serious therapy afterwards."

"It's a dark job." Culain growled and returned a glare to Blanka.

"What happened?" Ilya asked.

"Some jackass thought it would be funny to take some mana from the Grail and feed it to a normie. The normie grew and bloated up creating this Chasmic rift between the dimensions. Not only did it release the damn creatures from the other side the size of Germany, but the essence multiplied inside the body of the unfortunate normie. That lucky bastard got the short end of the stick. He bloated up and flew up into the sky until his body resembled a giant fucking rock in the sky, and it poured out the essence, killing everyone," Culain explained. "I had to kill all of the survivors. I had to kill so many people, all for what? A prank? Someone's idea of some sick joke is what it was. It was so damn unnecessary, but I had a job to do, and our code doesn't allow any leeway." He slammed his fist against the table. Ilya could see some of the moonlight shimmering in his eyes as they watered, ever so slightly.

"Did any escape?" Blanka asked.

"I wasn't as proficient enough then to kill everyone I saw, there was just too much ground to cover. Likely, if anyone survived talked, they'd be considered insane. Probably ended up in an asylum. No one takes them seriously," He chuckled. "However, those loose ends are fragments of creation coming apart, that is, until they die."

"Yeah, enough of the past. We can talk about that later," Alex turned his gaze to Ilya, pointing his index firmly on the map, "Look, Ilya, are all those portal crests in place? And sufficiently fueled with mana?"

"Yes," she replied, turning to him directly with a scowl on her face, the source of mana was efficient, but in certain place will kill people that don't need to be killed. "I don't like the way I had to do it."

"Will it last?" he asked.

"Yes, there are plenty of them to disperse the energy at any given point; however, the source of mana isn't exactly going to be reliable in such a large area." She walked over to the table with the map and put her finger on a singular location. "Look here, Gosnold, it only has a population of 75 people with an area expanding well over 100 miles.

That is insufficient mana for an area that big," she explained. "I could only afford to make a singular seal there, which acts as a gate towards our one teleportation circle there. However, with a population of that size, the seal itself will not hold. If the seal breaks, the mana used for that will deplete, and if we need to teleport there, the teleportation will exhaust the mana reservoirs there, effactually killing the entire population of that town."

"In other words, God in Heaven Forbid anything happens there, everyone there dies, and there is hardly enough mana to make it back to the mainland. There are a few towns like that in Massachusetts," Blanka simplified the explanation.

Culain smiled to her. "And this is why I'm not an arcane wielder. Because that is way too complex for me to handle. Not to mention I don't think I would even be able to pull something like that off. This is a good thing though, it means you don't have to use your own mana for that, and you can focus your energy on other things."

"Yes, but I still don't adore the idea of having things being done at the expense of humans who know nothing of us. They know nothing of the conflict, and they know nothing of the Hell we've seen. The Hell, the demons and devils are just underneath the ground, and are not far off from wreaking havoc across all the Earth. This—" Ilya brushed her hair behind her ears, tilting her head. *Culain, how can you be so casual about this? People are going to die!*

"These humans who cannot even channel mana are merely expendable assets. They are nobodies. They choose to wear a mask that we are oppressively forced to wear. So, what if they die in the process, if a small amount must be sacrificed along the way to achieve personal victory, that is acceptable. That is the code of a caster," Culain's tone became harsh. "This world is cruel that it would submit us to this fate, but that is not our choice to make. All our decisions were made before we were born, and there is nothing we can do about that. We have a hand, and we need to play that hand as best we can, and hope the other player has a crap hand, or is a shitty card player."

"It is necessary, Ilya," Blanka sided with Culain. "I don't love the idea any more than you do, but what choice do we have? Culain is right. They are tools and resources that we can use. You know the risk, we all do, and you know we have to keep it on the hush hush."

"Last time we were laxed on the policy, we had to start World War Two to cover it up, and we all know that no one in the administration wanted that. They could only let it go so far before Australia was split in quadrants and scattered all over the ocean," Alexander explained. "Are you finished?"

There was silence. Culain waited to speak more.

"Alright, now that that's over with. Ilya, are any seals loosening?" he asked.

"Half a moment." She said as she closed her eyes and folded her hands into fists while resting her chin upon them. She reached out with her spirit, pulling in the mana from the air. Her flesh was crawling with emerald veins, which began to change color from a green, to sea blue, and finally flesh red. She opened her eyes, and the flesh veins entered the whites of her eyes and her pupils turned golden.

She could see darkness, with streams of light cascading over her vision. The many shapes tossed and turned into her sight as the seals remained locked. Her gaze shifted over towards Springfield, and the seals remained in place, and none of the Threckets attempted to unlock the seal, nor tried to attack the barriers from the other side of Pandora.

The veins disappeared from her eyes and body immediately and her pupils returned to their normal color. She took a deep breath as she focused on the door behind them, making sure that no one was listening on the other side. "The Hell remains silent in Massachusetts. They are not moving against seals or the gates."

"Good," Culain sighed. "I can't believe we almost didn't succeed here."

"Yeah, the loss was bad though. I'm certain the Caster's Administrator will call us back to London shortly," Alex said.

"Not likely," Blanka said. "They'll want us monitoring activity here for a while before they declare this project safe and finished. They'll want to make sure the seals and transportation circles are working before sending us back for vacation."

"Vacation sounds nice," Ilya let out a sigh of relief. *A little rest is in order.* "Hopefully, we can make it."

"Yeah," Culain agreed.

Chapter 7 The Empty House

~After all my years of living, I have only one regret: not strangling myself with my own umbilical cord, now I can't even die right.

***

Ted forced a smile, his eyelids getting heavy as he sat with his bag resting on his lap on the subway. At 9:00 PM, the redline was fairly crowded riding towards Alewife. Listening intently, he rested his head back as he sat, watching everyone on this subway, hoping not to see any familiar faces. He noted the diverse population on the subway, white, black, Hispanic, Asian, male, female. There was a significant diversity in the socio economics of the people on the train; some seemed to be struggling families with old purses with the color fading, and others seemed to be well off, dressed professionally with pressed clothes, and the women wore makeup. Some of these people were singular, just monitoring something of no value on their phone as it was glued to their faces. Some were coupled up, talking to one another, and some kids were had their faces lit up by their parents' phones, who, sitting behind their respective children leaned their heads back hoping to get a moment's rest. He saw many isolated single persons curving their lips to a smile. Some of these people wore their smiles genuinely, while the smiles of others were blank, there was no life behind those eyes.

He kept his trembling hand in his right pocket. He smiled as he inconspicuously watched everyone. Many people here had no quarrel with one another; however, many buried their wretched faces into their terribly cursed hands. They had no problem with showing their emotions to such strangers. Perhaps they knew that they would never see anyone on this train ever again. The sense of anonymity was appealing, but something Ted dared not risk.

The next stop came. Many people walked off at Harvard Station. Fewer people walked on. These were students and professors. The professors immediately opened their briefcases as they sat down and worked on grading or additional source material for another class they were teaching, pushing their glasses closer to their face. The students were busy talking, and he noticed one in particular; a girl who looked like she should still be in high school. She put in her headphones and sat at the end, pulling her knees up to her chest and wrapped her arms around them to keep them close. She stared down the train with an empty expression on her face.

He felt like he was looking at someone familiar. The face, the hair, the stance, and that damn blank stare. There was nothing inside her. No happiness, no sadness, no hope. It's like she was tired of sharing her smile, jaded from putting up with the damn façade called life, nor was she particularly open about showing her despair to others, she might not want to inconvenience anyone from her erasing herself from this world. The emptiness, he knew it all too well. The emptiness was hungry, and it ate happiness and hope like a pig. Why bother as hope is only a façade: all it is, is a postponed disappointment. It only ends one way, with despair.

He looked away from her and turned to look out of the window in front of him. The subway started moving again. His forced smile met that of another tired woman, probably in her thirties. Over a decade older than him, he presumed. She also looked tired, brushing away her ragged blond hair out of her face, her eyes like his were sunken in, but she made an effort to smile back at him.

He tried to navigate his gaze away from her and to an inanimate object. He found a convenient advertisement on the pole. It was an ad to a show on broad way. The show looked like people would be entertained, a group of ethnically diverse characters wearing a variety of clothing. Their faces were brightly lit, and smiles painted across their lips, and they even had a twinkle in their eyes, or he imagined they were twinkling at the time of the picture was taken for the advertisement. He only found a handful of people that shared that same twinkle, just a little spark of light in their souls, and yet, with everything moving, he felt trapped in this train. He envied the people in the picture, not their clothes, not their smile, but that little twinkle of light, that happiness or joy, or whatever it is, that was what he was after. He saw the same twinkle in Sam's eye, in Jennifer's and in Michael's, but he couldn't be around them.

He waited patiently as the subway came to Davis Square. The doors opened and he scanned the train again. Almost everyone was laughing as they were walking off, from their jerseys and back packs, some satchels and purses. He assumed these were college kids going to some party or a nearby bar. He followed them out. He walked through the dimly lit, concrete corridors to the escalators to the fresh breeze of Davis square. Cars were honking their horns and buses were dropping people off in droves. He walked through the Square onto College Avenue.

He looked up at the sky. Like the girl on the train, it was empty of clouds and stars. Feeling the oppressive moon mock him, he walked on the sidewalks. His trembling hand remained in his pocket, and he kept his smile bright and wide, as he blankly stared at the sidewalk on which he walked. His heart raced inside his chest and sweat dripped from his palms.

He walked down five kilometers. He came to a blue house with white trims on the door and the windows. He walked up the stairs and put his key into the keyhole. He opened the door as it creaked open. The lights were out, as they should be. He stepped into the house and closed the door. He locked the knob lock. He turned the mechanism for the bolt lock. It clicked shut. He turned and lifted the chain to lock the door with its third lock.

He turned around and leaned against the door. He dropped his bag to the floor, and it sounded like a rock hit the ground. He let out a sigh as he leaned back against the door.

His smile began to fade as his lips curved downwards. He grinded his teeth as he stifled a noise from his mouth. His face cringed as tears streamed down the side of it. He felt his knees giving out, and he felt them tremble; his feet slid from underneath him. His body struck the ground, and both of his hands were in front of him, trembling uncontrollably. He clamped his eyes shut as he cried out. He took one hand over his chest where his heart would be, clenching his shirt.

He took heavy breaths and choked on his sobbing, but the tears never stopped rolling down his face. His weak knees struggled to pull himself back up; however, it is unlike someone from Task Force 7 to allow such an inconvenience to bring him to a halt. He *willed* his knees to be fixated and forced himself to stand up.

He *willed* the first step. He couldn't stop sobbing, his tears dripping from his face to the empty hardwood floor. He felt nerves snapping throughout his body, physically telling his body he was in pain, but he never felt the pain itself. He took regulated interval breaths as the tears came down.

He *willed* his second step, and he pulled out his arm to the wall, leaning against it.

He scanned the room hastily, looking for something to use to walk around. He couldn't do it himself with the constant trembling inside his body like earth tremors. He was in his living room. The floor was empty with no trash on it. There were no bookcases, no tv, no radio, no coffee table, nor other miscellaneous furniture on the ground. There were no pictures on the wall, there were only two things, a display case, and a broken noose.

Inside the display case was where he kept certain items of internal value, half of which would be absolutely useless to everyone else. Otherwise, the room looked like he just moved in today without the moving boxes.

Inside the display case was a spear. The spear he could use. It was the same spear Metal used, quite often was useful. He remembered Metal reaching out for hard-to-reach places with his scrawny little arms when he was just a kid. The red handle of the spear was wood, had some written markings upon it, but since faded, the spearhead was rusted, and Ted couldn't find a way to restore it safely, not without being caught. He was actually surprised to find the spear shortly after the Nuclear meltdown in Area 51 eight years ago.

He *willed* his third step. He cried out as his knees gave out again, as the oppressive mockery of the damned moon light entered his house, beating down on him with its great mocks. The burden of this was too heavy for his knees to bear, even his iron will was not enough to *will* himself back up as he tumbled forward, hitting his head on the ground.

"Why?" he sobbed. He reached out his right hand and pulled himself towards the display case. "Why? Damnit!" He reached out with his left hand and pulled himself closer across the empty living room. "I did everything you told me to!" He reached out his right hand and pulled himself closer, the tears came down so hard, they were missing his face and merely dripping on the floor. His shirt became wet with his tears as he dragged himself across it. "Damnit! I hate you!" his voice was like that of a child, disappointed in their father for mother for bringing him into this cruel world. "Was that not enough? I didn't have much to take anyway. Why did you take them from me?" He continued to grit his teeth together as he pulled himself closer and closer to the display case.

He finally reached to the display case. He pulled himself up, his tears dripping onto the glass. He leaned against the wall and pulled out another key from his pocket. His hand trembled as he tried to get it into the keyhole. The key trembled in his fingers and fell to the ground. It struck the ground with a force; the noise was so heavy he could feel it slipping away from his grasp. He took a heavy breath, and slowly let it out. "Fuck it," He took his free hand and made a fist. He slammed his hand into the display case, cracking the glass. Shards went everywhere and cut his arm. His arm was bleeding, and his knuckles became raw with the impact.

His hand reached for the spear, and his hand froze in place as his hand hovered over it. His tears still streamed down, and his eyes stretched open when he came to the sudden realization, reacting to the shards of glass imbedded in his flesh. He could feel the red, warm blood cascading down his arm. "I—I still can't feel it," He said silently to himself. "Iah—I can't feel anything. I can't feel anything anymore." He grabbed his spear, and it trembled in his hands. He pulled it out of the display case and put the haft of it against the hardwood floor, and rusty spearhead raised up to the ceiling.

The unwanted emotions flooded him again almost as if there was nothing in between them. He struggled as his knees became weak again, as he made his way to the kitchen. He took staggered deep breaths with every step.

He found the wastebasket by the doorway into the kitchen. The wastebasket was filled with empty plastic cups and plastic silverware, and paper plates. He avoided the basket and made it into the kitchen.

The kitchen was almost as bare. The cupboards were disheveled, there was no kitchen table or chairs. The counters were empty apart from a roll of paper towels and napkins. There was nothing like a toaster, toaster oven, or even a coffee maker on his counter. It was bare. The sink was the only thing that had anything else in it. There were dirty pans.

He managed to get himself to the sink. He reluctantly took his hand off his spear and leaned it into one of the empty cupboards. He took out the sponge and put soap on it and ran the hot water. He scrubbed the dirty pans clean, slowly putting everything into it, doing whatever he could to distract him from his thoughts. *Anything!*

Dismayed he was that nothing would empty his mind. He cried even louder, his tears fell into the sink, splashed on the pans. He cleaned the last frying pan and threw it into the wall. It made a loud noise as it stuck into the wall, it just hung there.

He gasped as he suddenly remembered the noose he made for himself in the living room. He hanged there last night, but as if some fluke of nature, he phased through the noose.

Ted firmly tied the noose, hanging it from his ceiling, giving it a strong tug to ensure it would hold him. The rope was thick and sturdy enough, but one can never be too careful to make sure it's done right. After all, this was going to be the last attempt, either a success, or he would just give up trying. Satisfied, he grabbed one of his kitchen chairs, and planted it underneath the noose. Stepping on the chair, he slipped his head through the noose. He used his hands to tighten it around his neck. Exhaling, he kicked the chair out from under him.

He fell, the rope held onto him. He felt the air to his lungs restrict, and he felt that unwelcome refreshment of the essence, yet again fill his body. His arms jerked at his sides as the grey veins protruded over his skin. Air was completely exiled out of his body, and he felt his consciousness wane: if only it was that simple. Another type of essence entered his body, and the veins darkened from gray to black as he phased through the noose. Another failed attempt, and as promised, the last one.

That was the last straw. *I can't even die right!* He angrily thought as he stared at the frying pan, stuck into the wall like a knife. He sighed as he turned and leaned against the sink. His head was raised up as the streams never stopped coming down. He was a slave to his own thoughts, and his master was relentless!

His trembling hands went back into his pockets. He took out his wallet and opened it. He found a picture and took it out. He opened up the folded photo. His hand trembled as he looked on sixteen faces in military uniforms. All of them were of the same height, half of them male, and the other half female. One of the women was wrapping her arms around the waist of someone else. That other individual was himself; his face was scratched out of the picture.

He sucked in some air, clamping his teeth down. The tears rolled down a little faster onto the photo. He choked on some more tears. *This fate is cruel.* He allowed his feet to slowly slip from under him. He looked closely at the photo. Their uniforms all had their number "Seven" on the patch, right above the where the charging American flag would be, that is, if they weren't forbidden from wearing it. He glared up at the ceiling. *You mock me.*

He trembled, pulling himself from the ground. He leaned towards the sink again, glancing at the frying pan stuck in the wall. He took his spear and used it to walk, however shakily, towards the other room. This room was dark. He turned on the light.

This room was large, and square, and just like every other room in this house, this was next to empty. This had only two things in it, a sleeping bag, with no pillow, and a safe. That's it. Even the paint on the walls was bland and passionless.

He walked over to the safe and laid the spear to the side of his sleeping bag. His sleeping bag was wet now with his tears. He turned the knob of the safe to open it. There was no money, and nothing that anyone would find of value to steal. He pulled out a notebook and turned to a blank page. He brought a black inked pen to the page and his pen hand froze in place again as he started to choke up more tears. He gritted his teeth once more, and his face twisted from abstract tormented sadness to nothing short of an ungodlike rage.

At last, he put the pen to the page:

My name. My name. My name. Your name? What were they? Were they as generic as Michael or Samantha? Or were the names on your birth certificate more genuine, and more unique? I never knew your names. I don't even know what was written on mine.

What were we? For years we spent together, and we never even got a proper serial number. We were insignificant. Too insignificant and too much of a burden for the common man to even come up with a name, or even a number. They didn't even care enough about us to assign us a number.

What were we to them? Nothing more than a tool? A valuable all-purpose tool? A tool that only has one use, to strive for that sense of purpose. We obtained that purpose, for even a short while, now it's being ripped apart! Were we too expensive to keep around? Why even bother with us then?

I had but one wish, that this Hell could be undone. But what good of a world is that without conflict? We had no purpose without conflict. And we got rid of the conflict. We shot ourselves in the foot and watched it bleed!

Eight years it's been. Eight long damn years. I loved you. All of you. And I will never be able to tell that to your faces. I will never be presented with that gift, and now I am cursed to live in Hell. Yes, that is fitting for a wretch like me.

Funny, isn't it. I've killed more people than I care to count. It's almost funny how someone like me, can take life so easily. The first one was someone close to me. The first. That was the only one that truly mattered. Every single one after that became nothing but a statistic. Why then? Why? Why do I still see their faces at night? Every single one of them? Can I not rip out my eyes? Then would I stop seeing them? No. I have no hope in that. Because now each face is seared into my brain.

I have no hope in life. I have no hope now in my living death. And I can't kill myself. I've tried too many times to count. Just the sadness of my heart, my heart, if I could rip it out to show the world, it would be filled with scars and bullet holes, but the wretched thing still keeps pumping! It still keeps beating as if it itself is too stubborn to die. Why can't I be like normal people? If they are sick and tired of it, they hang themselves and die. Why must I be cursed with a living death, and cursed to fail every single attempt? Damn it! I can't die right!

This gift I have, I know not how I got it, or why. I don't even know if you had this gift, but I imagine you don't. Not when I saw you being shot to shreds. Why can I fade through reality when you remain solid? I valued this gift enough when you were around because I needed to be alive to protect you, all of you. Now that you're gone, and I failed, why won't this just shut off and let me die?

What were your names? What was mine? We didn't have any. We didn't have any serial numbers. We weren't given any dog tags. We truly were given no identity, only to assume a fake one for the duration of your short lives, and for the rest of my cursed one. How fortunate you are, to be dead right now. You can't feel anything. You have no heart, and I myself am nothing short of a monster filled with ancient regrets. No.

That's not true at all.

After all my years of living, I have only one regret: not strangling myself with my own umbilical cord, now I can't even die right.

He continued to weep, choking on his tears and he closed the notebook. He placed it in the safe and locked it up. This notebook was the only thing keeping him grounded in the world. It was the only thing that allowed him to function every day. These little reminders helped remind him of his own suffering. He got into his sleeping bag and leaned his phone against the safe. He put it on, so the clock was facing him.

There was no need to set an alarm for himself. There never was. Not anymore. His eyes were drifting to sleep, and the clock read: 10:23 PM. *Here we go again. And again. And again!* His eyes closed as he drifted to sleep.

Chapter 8 Reassignment

~It was all a mistake, you see. I adopted a dream that wasn't mine, forced upon me with a promise, the reward for that promise was so great, I didn't care about the risk, however high that might be. That dream was to attain a world without war, and for a time, I succeeded. I suppose they kept their promise to me that I wouldn't have to do any of it again. I was such an idealistic fool to believe them!

***

Sarah McCurdy sat on the plane as it soared through the air. The flight departed early in the morning, the vast majority of the passengers on the plane slept with night masks hanging over their face, or with their caps tipped down over their eyes. The flight attendants were disinterested in the passengers, hanging out in their little cubby area, some of them were on their phones when they thought no one was watching them. She leaned back in her chair, with her hands over her chest, looking out at the black sky, the darkness, she knew it all too well. She knew the night welcomed the threckets, and when darkness came, so did they. For whatever reason, nothing significant ever happened during the day, almost as if darkness can't survive in the light, but then again, can light survive in the dark?

Feeling her phone vibrate in her pocket, she opened it, seeing a notification of an email coming directly from Administrator Colton. She closed the screen and returned the phone back into her pocket, and pulled out her laptop form her carry-on, turning on the laptop to access her email. The email sent to her had multiple attachments, and this was a special email address, exclusive to the Caster's Administration. This email read:

Major Sarah McCurdy,

As per discussed, you already know what your task is. The attachments are to be forwarded to Administrator Sander for reassignment. You start immediately, and do not forget the real reason you are being sent there.

There is only one reason, and only one goal. Do not fail the American Administration. Failure will mean further influence from the outside, and we cannot allow that for obvious reasons. Also, if you can manage to track down whoever it was at Dyatlov's pass and find out what their real goal was. Like I said, odds are, they are working against the Administration, but they must be affiliated with an administrative branch, and not the American one. However, even if he was affiliated with ours, we don't get too many fae from Georgia, like you suggested.

Regards,

Admin. Colton.

She hesitated in opening the attachments, "'Forwarded to Administrator Sander for reassignment,'" she whispered to herself. Releasing a deep sigh, she rested her chin upon her palm. *Colton, what exactly are we doing here? If the UK administration branch finds out–when they find out it was an American who stole the Grail, they will hunt you relentlessly. Just what exactly are you planning? I don't exactly trust the UK branch to do the right thing, don't make me regret this, Colton.*

Finally, she opened the attachments. Just her name, and complete file with the American Branch of the Administration. She immediately forwarded the attachments to the email provided and shut the laptop off, putting it back into her bag.

Adams' face came into her mind. His blood coming out of his mouth as his life left his eyes. Her hand trembled in her seat, because she knew this was guilt, as the anaconda inside her chest squeezed her heart again. She took her one hand and clutched her chest with it, breathing steadily. *Adams, why didn't you stay there to help. I didn't want to have to murder you.* She took control of her own emotions and looked back out of the window. *That damned code. Don't they understand, a little part of us dies when we enforce that code. Silence, it's called. Absolute silence, and then erase the bodies as if they were never there. It's sickening! They're people, not just some mere pawns in a game of chess. It's sick!*

She kept her bags with her inside the taxi as she departed. She noticed the people seemingly cheery, as they always are, ignorant of the Hell that roams the streets at night. The rain was light with greying clouds above, emptying the heavens with dismal tears of the lives lost, especially Adams: Heaven wept for even someone like him, someone so insignificant.

The taxi dropped her off on Newman Street.

The building before her was large, and had numerous windows, with bright chandeliers that could be seen from the outside. She walked up the large marble steps and opened the door. She carefully stepped inside, wiping off her shoes before she entered, walking on the beautiful green carpet, which looked much like a bed of majestic grass. There were many men and women about, talking with one another with pleasant tones, and seemed much more relaxed than they ever were in the American Branch. Many of them wore some semblance of a cloak, while others more subtle attire.

She walked up to the receptionist, and carefully placed her bags on the floor. She leaned over the desk, as the receptionist hung up the phone politely. The receptionist had flaming red hair like McCurdy's, but she was physically smaller, in height and stature than McCurdy. She wore a red ascot over a suit.

"Name?"

"Sarah McCurdy. American Branch. I'm being reassigned to the U.K division," she answered.

The receptionist giggled, "Okay,"

The man behind her laughed at her. "The U.K division? The U.K doesn't have a division. Nope. Nope. Nope! This is Camelot little lady. The Heart of it all. I'd think ye yanks ought to have known that by know."

Well, that was humiliating. She clenched her fist at her side, not appreciating the casual haze at her expense.

"One American transitioning to Camelot!" The receptionist said with a jeer. Her name tag read: Lois. "ID?"

"Sure." She pulled out her purse and pulled out her Caster ID. The card was purple with a spell on it so that to the normal person, it would only look like a generic piece of paper, but to another fae, they can read all the details on the card: ID number, address, name, aliases. She handed it to Lois, "Here it is."

"One moment." She dialed an eight-digit extension. "Sander, I have a Sarah McCurdy from the American Branch who is transferring to

Camelot. Okay. Right away sir." She turned back to Sarah. Follow those halls," she said pointing down a long corridor where the carpet turned from green to blue. The corridor was wide and had several paintings of historic figures hanging on the walls. "You are going to take a right at the end of the corridor and then a left. The door is locked, so you're going to have to knock."

"Understood," she said coldly.

She picked up the bags and about faced, marched through the room to get to the corridor. She could hear the snickering of laughing brits from behind her. She ignored them as she entered the corridor, and slowly admired the paintings of the historic figures. She loved some of the old histories of the legends, which were greatly exaggerated to hide the actual truth behind those myths.

She made it to the end of the hall, where a giant portrait of the founder of the Caster's Administration was. He was a tall man, wearing a blue cape, laced with white fur. He had a mysticism about him, a proud face, a serious one. It was King Arthur who created this administration, and it was he who put the oppressive codes in place. King Arthur, raiser of Camelot, Founder of the Caster's Administration. For many, he was deemed to be a hero, and others, like to Sarah, a symbol for oppression in a fae's world she had no stake in. He had brown hair, and a very scruffy beard.

In this portrait, she gazed upon the scenery, wrought with war and corpses, slain by King Arthur himself, and in his left hand was a depiction of the Holy Grail with divine light emitting from its entrance, filled with crystalline water, and behind him, filled with all its curses, was the Box of Pandora, and it had been opened, never closed.

She passed on, continuing to follow the directions of the receptionist until she eventually came to that door. The door was wood, old fashioned with numerous engravings, including the ancient, outdated creed penned by King Arthur, which was written in Anglo Saxon at the time, but translated, it read: "I solemnly swear, as a Caster of the Administration, to uphold absolute secrecy, for the secrets of the world is not ready for the common person. This I swear, as a knight of this round table, to slay all demons who come crawling out from Hell. This I swear for life, and at the cost of it."

She knocked on the door with a heavy hand. She waited, still holding both of her bags at her side. The door swung open inward. There was a handsome man behind a desk, tall, and physically large, much like a marine, his hair was neatly combed, and it shined through the light. She looked at him as he was penning some paperwork.

"Come in," he said. She walked through the threshold. He tilted his head up with a smile, "Make sure to close the door."

Sarah closed the door tight behind her until she heard it click, and as if some kind of mechanism was in it, she could hear the locks and gears turning inside the door from unwanted ears and eyes from the outside. She came in to sit down on the chair in front of the desk, and there was another woman in the room, her brown hair was let down in front of her as she was looking at a file in front of her. She had a large smile on her face, as Sarah sat down.

"Welcome to Camelot." Sanders smiled, it was an exhausted smile, but he made the effort. "Well, we are much different from you persons down at the American Branch. As you can probably tell, we can be relaxed but don't let that fool you, we can hold our own just fine here, especially at the epicenter of Pandora. So, tell me about this previous incident up in Dyatlov's Pass. It seems highly unusual, but that is usual for us."

"Yes," she began, recounting all the incidents and data she had from the initial incident, detailing names of persons involved, and that most peculiar accent.

Sander turned to the women. "Bridgette, what say you on the matter?"

"Two possibilities. Either he's not one of us, or he is. If he's one of us, he must have gone rogue, and is just saying that to throw you off on the real reason he was there. We all know where the Grail is, so there would be no excuse for him to go *looking* for it there. Trying to get his hands on it is another matter entirely. If he is not one of us, he is probably the husk of some unfortunate soul who now must be put down because he was possessed by a demon from Pandora. He could be an idiot too. That's also a possibility. Anything else?" The woman was leaning against the back window to the courtyard behind the office building. She had blue eyes, and thick brown hair tied behind her. Her arms crossed over one another.

"He did talk to me as if he wasn't one of us," she admitted. "I may have left that out."

"Yes, well, then he's probably possessed. Sucks for him now doesn't it?" Bridgette said sarcastically.

"Yes, well, McCurdy, it isn't like you had a full team at your disposal to actually get enough information on the subject, so we have next to nothing to go on really. We just simply have to wait for him to appear again, whenever and wherever that might be," Said Sanders.

"But if he appears again it could be—" McCurdy objected, swiftly slapping her hands on her thighs.

"Catastrophic. I know. But we don't have enough information. So, if he ends up leveling an entire city with these creatures, that should be big enough to gather enough information." Sanders replied. "Besides, there isn't enough information to go hunting on."

"So, you will sacrifice an entire city of people for him to show up again? You can't be serious!" Her eyes gaped open widely. *You heartless bastards!*

"McCurdy," Bridgette angled her eyes down her like a mother does her child who drew all over the kitchen table. "You really have no one to blame but yourself for this. You have nothing for us to go on. You have a location of where he was. He isn't going to be returning there, that's a fool's move. You really gave us no choice but to wait. So, if you have a problem with it, you can blame yourself for what is to come. It's as simple as that. I couldn't have stopped him alone, most likely, however, I could have at least gathered enough information for us to look into it. We have nothing. If you want to place blame on the Administration for allowing an entire city to die, well, blame yourself for not gathering enough intel for us to start a global manhunt."

"The blame isn't entirely on you. The American Branch should have sent someone out there last minute before they decided to send you up there. I don't know what they were thinking." He scratched his forehead.

"Bridgette, why don't you show her around. She must be tired. After all, it is going to be a long night."

"Understood, Administrator." Bridgette's tone turned cheery. "Well, let us be off then. I need to get my tea."

The locking mechanisms released, and the door slowly swung open. Sarah grabbed her bags immediately as she stood up, walking right behind Bridgette. She took her as a respectfully harsh woman, and one that didn't have a bad figure from behind. Much too tempting, and equally dangerous.

"So, when did you find out about your reassignment?" Bridgette asked her.

"Almost immediately after Dyatlov." She answered. "It was unexpected, but my administrator was quick to find a replacement."

"Ah, Americans, quick to act when it matters the least, but when any important decision is to be made, it seems like the entire world is filled with naught but red tape. Seriously, it is easier getting a corpse to move around."

McCurdy remembered something, that some researching fae, she couldn't remember his name, was trying to do some research into Necromancy. She was curious about the research that went into it, and she knew, just like elemental magic, it was a forbidden craft. Well, that isn't exactly the best explanation, more like a fae was insane if they so much as entertained the idea. A necromancy experiment had a failure rate of over ninety-nine percent. A failed attempt would mean either the death of the one casting the ritual, and destruction and contamination of existing materials for the ritual, or opening a portal into Pandora, allowing the fae in a weakened state to be possessed by a threcket coming out of Pandora; however, with the rumor of someone wanting to do research on the matter, she was curious.

"Bridgette, did anything ever happen with the research into Necromancy?" McCurdy asked.

Bridgette gave her a curious stare, "Oh, we never funded that research, nor are we going to. What on earth would we use it for? Besides, the person who was going to do research into it was given an ultimatum, he could do the research, but he wouldn't be with his unit anymore, because of numerous conflicts involved with it. Trust me, it is for the best no one messes around with it," Bridgette sighed. "Besides, only King Arthur ever succeeded in doing that. Same reason why no one researches elemental magic, while being able to use the elements as tools would push us leagues above those nasty little threckets, it's risky because it's almost impossible to control. Honestly, if someone wanted to do research into making that kind of magic usable, those resources would be better spent."

Well, that answers that. But she knew Bridgette was right, the risk far outweighed the reward, and shouldn't be entertained. *Except in the need to rattle someone.*

Bridget led her into the main room with a boiling tea kettle and some simple teacups. She pulled out a cup and put a bag of tea inside it, filling it with piping hot water and stirring a little sugar in it. She took a sip, sniffing the sweet fragrant aroma. "You want some?"

"I wouldn't mind."

"Help yourself."

Sarah poured herself a cup of tea.

"Okay, onto the tour, if you really want to call it that is all. You're not goin' to want to carry those all day. Let us get you to your quarters."

Sarah followed her with her bags at her right, and the teacup in her left hand, sipping the tea. It was okay, and something about it soothed her. *Maybe I should stop drinking coffee.* She followed her to the back of the main building, and through some large doors.

Bridgette was a talker, that one. She was a talker, and she never stopped walking. Sarah half assumed Bridgette would have kept talking through the sips of her tea had the tea not been delicious. On the way, she noticed some elevators, some went up, but there were those elevators that *only* went down. These elevators were closer to the Archives, which seemed impressive on the outside. *A likely place.*

Brigette took her through a large room, and pulled out her ID card, swiping it on the solid black console on the side. The light turned green, and the door opened. Sarah was amazed as she walked through the threshold of the room, at the pristine condition of the floors, cleaner than glass, and the standards of cleanliness was much higher than any other barracks she has ever been in. The room was filled with numerous beds, some unoccupied, others had some sleeping or studying fae here.

"Let's get you a bed, now. Wouldn't want your precious belongings being stolen, now would we."

"I'm staying here?"

"Yes. I don't care if it's not satisfactory or not. Yes. You sleep here. You live here. You eat here. You make friends or whatever it is you Americans do. We all do, well, most of us. Even I stay here." She escorted her to a triple-bunk. The desk beside it was equally tall and had support on all sides. "You get the top. I'm at the bottom."

"If you say so," she griped, handing Bridgette her tea. She climbed at the top of the bunk and lay her bags there.

"Well, get down now. We have more to see. Come on. I don't have all day you wanker."

"That was rude."

"Who hucking cares! Just get down here."

Sarah climbed back down with haste.

"You know we're all fae here, right? You could have just jumped down. No one would say anything."

Bridgett was right. Sarah knew it, just, her casting abilities were under lock down, subconsciously trying to repress it, constantly denying who she was in front of her peers. Her brothers and sisters in arms were never really her own, isolated by her own birth, from her own inheritance.

"I'm sorry."

"Don't be sorry. Don't do it again. Or in this case, just do it next time. Sheesh. Stupid wanker. Come on! Off to my favorite place. The Archives. Oh, and by the way, you will get your own ID badge at the end of the day. Unfortunately, you're stuck with me until then. We can't just have you go off all willy nilly and just roam around freely, you'll get stuck somewhere."

"Yes, Ma'am."

Bridgette led her out of the room and the door shut behind them. She led her back towards the elevators and opened the door into the archives. The archives were filled with numerous filing cabinets, and shelves filled with innumerable books and tomes.

They went through the vast dusted off shelves in the archives, looking at the many impressive monoliths, portraits, paintings, scrolls, tomes, and of course even the carpet was decorated with many archaic, albeit, but beautiful designs. Whoever funded these archives spared no expense, whatever that may be, a price high enough for even a treasury.

Sarah saw stairs over to the side.

"Bridgette," she said as she drank the last of her tea.

"Hmm?"

"Those stairs. Where do they lead?"

"Well, normally I wouldn't say anything, but it should be common knowledge to fae at this point. We keep the Grail there. It is under protection at all costs, those go down to the vaults where we keep some sacred artifacts, besides the Grail there. It is under lock down, impossible to get down to the lower levels without a key or capsizing the entire building."

Just the information I needed. Now, just an opportunity.

Chapter 9 Area 51

~We were supposed to get married on Saturday, but for her, Saturday never came.

***

Ghost was watching downwind in the arid heat. The day was still young, however, these past eight weeks felt like four decades! The heat was dehydrating them, and he was without sleep. He couldn't afford sleep, and neither could anyone else, not with the overwhelming rattling of gunfire, nor the roaring of engines, and the tremors from the earth underneath the massive weight of the tanks.

This was supposed to be a training exercise, but this was something more than just that. This was no exercise: this was a massacre. His ACR rifle was beginning to jam up. And he was running low on ammunition. He wasn't around any useless bodies he could easily loot for more ammunition. And only God knows how many more there were out there.

Ghost, Ticker, Butcher, and Slithers were hiding in a crater out in the desert. This was no natural crater, for the crater was built by artillery strikes aimed directly at them. The sand was scorching hot, much like what Ghost imagined death would be, not that he knew. His hands held his rifle tight as the noise began to die down.

He could feel the sand pouring down his back from the sides of the crater as numerous trucks were driving by. The trucks were mounted with MGs, and bright flashing lights. His gaze caught the sight of a car, splattered with blood like someone poured a bucket of red paint on it. The windows were smeared in it, and even the wipers were coated in the flesh of someone who blew up nearby, most likely another useless grunt caught in friendly fire. For now, they were safe, and out of sight in the crater, for how much longer, he couldn't only guess.

"Ghost," Butcher whispered. She kept her hand on her rifle while pointed at him with three fingers. "What is going on?"

111

"For once, I don't know," He answered, never letting his gaze move off from the moving caravan. His mind was rattled, still completely in the dark since the first shot, "And keep it down."

"Is everyone dead?" Slithers asked, her hands were burying her face. Her face was smeared with blood, but it wasn't hers.

"Ghost," Butcher's voice trembled. "What did you do? What did you do?" She pointed her rifle at him. He moved rapidly and pointed his at hers while he knelt low to the ground.

Ticker sighed and dropped his rifle to his side. "Look, right now, that doesn't matter," he interrupted their little squabble. "Look, we need to find a way to get away from this all. We were fools."

"What do you fuckin' know, Ticker?" Butcher demanded, she turned abruptly, face cringing as she spat on the ground.

"Don't you see? I pay attention. What are we? Soldiers. All we are, are expendable assets, and nothing more. We are only tools to be used and then discarded. We should have seen this coming!" he answered. "There haven't been any wars lately! Hell, we haven't been deployed in two years!"

Butcher angrily drew her knife and was prepared to throw it.

"No," Ghost replied, his trigger finger hovered over the trigger, careful never to touch it until he intended to fire. "Butcher, that is enough. He's right. We should have—no. I should have seen this coming. I'm sorry."

"Captain," Ticker began. "Think of something, get us out of here."

Suddenly, the radio coughed. "Captain? Are you out there?" The voice of Venom said. Her sweet innocent voice spoke volume and trembled through the radio. "Captain? Captain?"

"Answer that!" Butcher stamped her boot in the hot sand.

"No," Ghost responded, he stood up as he scanned the blackened red horizon. "We can't, if we are going to get out of here."

"Everyone else is dead, damnit!" Butcher snapped again, her hand pointing a trembling finger at him. "How can you leave them to die like this!"

"They are soldiers, just like we are," Ghost told her. "We have to trust that they'll make it out. Besides, all of this is probably bugged, or they're listening at least. If we make it known someone else other than she is still alive, we're only asking for more trouble than we already have."

The radio coughed, "Captain? Is anyone out there? Is anyone there?"

"Then do you have a plan?" Ticker asked.

Ghost put his hand over his mouth as he bowed his head down to the ground, scanning each independent grain of sand almost like each individual grain represented an idea. These ideas were innumerous and almost all bad. He sighed. "Well, we are going to need a distraction."

"God, no," Slithers looked up to him with wide teary eyes. Her hand clenched his tightly. "You can't possibly be considering killing her?"

"What? No. I would never even think about killing her, or any of you for that matter. Something that our dear leader would consider without a second thought. No. We need to get to Area 51. We'll blow up the pillars holding it in place, which will greatly affect the reactor below it."

"There are civilians nearby. Ghost, you are proposing desecrating the nearby cities. If we do this, we would be no worse than them. We would be murderers." Ticker looked at him with stretched eyes. Ghost could tell that despite of it all, he was not keen on getting innocents civilians killed, especially recreating Chernobyl.

"Look around you Ticker, like it or not we are murderers. We are the orphan makers!" Ghost snapped at him. "I don't like it, but that is our one chance out of here. All other chances are gone and will lead to one-hundred percent failure. This has a chance of success, no matter how small."

"What is the success ratio?" Ghost imagined Ticker was skeptical with that hostile glare.

"Half of a percent," Ghost said. "They have us right where they want us. We are out of food and water; we'll be dead before the day is out. Whether by being shot or by natural means. We don't have the luxury of waiting for the perfect moment to strike. That is our only chance, and we need to take it, even if the odds were infinitely worse."

"A lot more people are going to die tonight," Ticker said, bowing his head with a graven face. "Is this what we've become?"

"The monsters and demons aren't hiding in our closets or under our beds. We'd be fortunate if they were that far away. How do you run from them when they're hiding in our heads?" Slithers asked. "We weren't born for this world. We were born with the sole purpose to live and fight for peace, and we've obtained it. Now there's no need for NATO anymore. There's no need for the military or hostile occupations. We've taken that need away. And now, we're meaningless. We were born with the sole purpose to live and die in obscurity." She wept softly. "Even if we did make it out, what would we even do? We have our lives ahead of us, and—and—and then what? We have no identity to stand on. We have no hope. We have no families, they're all gone. It will be impossible for us to integrate into society. We don't even know how they behave! Maybe it will be better if we all just lied down and died."

"Don't say that!" Butcher snarled, but even her harsh tone couldn't keep out the tears from her voice. "Don't you fucking say that again!"

"No," Ticker wept, wiping the tears with his sleeve. "She's right. Can't you see it now? We were damned from the start. We have no friends. We have no family. We have no name and no identity. We lived and trained together for sixteen years, and this is our end. This is a fucking tragedy if ever there was one. Can't you see it, how much better off the world would have been without us in it?"

Ghost caught a glimpse of Slithers as she bowed her head and folded her hands together, touching her forehead and saying one final prayer. She said something so inaudible, he had to pull in the air towards his ears to hear. The soundwaves from her soft voice traveled swiftly into his ears. "Mommy, I never knew you, and the only contact I've ever had was coming out. I never got to hear your voice. I never got to see your face. I never got to see your smiles and laughter and never got to experience the good times with you. I'm sure you're a good person, a much better person than I ever came out to be. I—I'm sure you wouldn't want to see me. Not like this. Not a murderer."

Ghost knew Slithers was talking to her own genetic parents, not the parental units they each were assigned when they first remembered. He was dreadfully assigned the Nakamura's. None of them knew where they came from; what state they were born in. Any identifying records were lost. Ghost knew, he actually looked. There was nothing, as if just a blank slate.

Slithers sniffed her tears and snot back into her nose and she turned to Ghost and smiled. A smile, how cruel of a mask. It could have been like a bandage, a useless tourniquet. It covered up the wound, but the pain still remained. All the emotional baggage was hidden away behind the façade. Her smile was like the whitest bandage, pure, and utterly pointless. It's only a matter of time before nothing will remain of that bandage, except when it's dripping with crimson blood. "Let's go. Let's go and make what's left of our lives count. We'll make it count for something, but for what, I don't know yet."

"To Area 51 it is then," Ghost repeated himself, stone-faced. "If we die tonight, we'll make sure they won't soon forget us. If we die, we'll drag that base and everyone in it down into the depths of the blazing hot sand with us."

"We'll be walking into Hell," Butcher stated, resting her arms at her side. She scanned the opposite side of the crater with her eyes.

"You still don't see. We were born in it, destined to never leave," Ghost replied. His gaze narrowed.

The squad climbed up the blazing hot crater, slowly. Ghost ensured that the radios would be silent. There was no longer a need to use them. The rest of Task Force 7 was dead, dying, or as good as dead.

Helicopters hovered over the air, their blades spinning and dusting the sand, creating a smog. Soldiers in the helicopters aimed their rifles down towards the ground, as the choppers searchlights from the helicopters moved on the sand. The bright light was blinding in the middle of the artificial sandstorms caused by the helicopter's blades. The lights shined on vehicles and blown-up trucks, There was plenty of metallic debris stained with flesh and blood. A small unit of military trucks drove through the sand, windows open, and rifles pointing out of them from behind a masked face.

Ghost signaled them on the ground. The heat was still getting to them, but they knew how to survive in worse conditions. They crawled underneath the sand. They were completely buried underneath the sand, crawling through the sand like worms in the dirt. They proceeded to crawl due south, towards Area 51.

The humming of the trucks grew louder as they scratched their ears. The vibration of the earth pounded against their bodies. They managed to crawl over six kilometers.

Ghost inhaled *essence* around the air, hearing a radio cough in the distance. "Task Force 7 spotted at sector 8." Immediately the vehicles revved up again and many soldiers started whistling. The helicopters shifted direction, flying west. The vehicles started driving faster than before in the same direction.

Ghost waited patiently. The pressure was lifted from their bodies, and all noises became distant. He immediately stood up from the sand, scanning the area with his rifle pointed down towards them. Butcher, Slithers, and Ticker did the same.

"Well, that is lucky," Ticker said.

"That, or insanely misfortunate," Slithers said.

"We need to start running," Ghost replied. "Our luck will eventually run out."

They started running. Ghost turned his radio on so he could listen in on the conversation between soldiers. He refused to say anything. They sprinted swiftly. He knew, he saw nightmares over and over again. No one makes it out without any scars, seen or unseen. Their lives were all fated to be a tragedy, one with no moral, no hope, and fraught with disaster and a never-ending pain. Truly, the world would have been a better place had they never been born.

The radio coughed, "*They moved onto sector six. We need to move now, and corner them there. They can't have much fight in them left.*"

"*How many do you count?*" Another voice came out. Ghost recognized it as General Snells.

"*Four, sir.*"

"*How many bodies are accounted for?*"

"*Eight, sir.*"

"*Ghost?*"

"*Negative.*"

"*His squad is still alive somewhere. Watch your six.*"

"*Roger.*"

That tells me what I need to know, He sighed.

"Ghost!" Butcher exclaimed. "Sector six is on the way."

"I know," Ghost replied. "They're going to be in the way."

"You have to be considering stepp—" Butcher began.

"I reconsidered it. Not worth it," He interrupted. "We need to focus on our own task. Even if there were four more, I have no idea what the numbers on the other side are. Even I can't predict that. Besides, we're all exhausted as they are. Even with four more, we won't last the night."

"But—" Slithers protested.

"No buts. This is final. Look, we need to hide back in the sand. They will be coming here shortly," Ghost snapped.

The four of them buried themselves back under the scorching sand. They waited. Their hearts beat through their chest as the vehicles rolled back over the sand. The helicopters were churning their blades in the air, pushing the sand away as they hovered over Sector six. The soldiers were making their way down the crater towards a large-abandoned building, and hid behind some scattered debris, some were large helicopter doors which were scorching hot with the flames.

Another officer called out on a megaphone.

"Task force 7. I know you're in there. You are surrounded, and we know you can't continue for much longer. Come out, and this won't have to get violent. Just stand trial for your crimes, and no harm will come to you until after the trial."

What crime?

"What crime did we commit?" said another voice. Her name was Viper. "What did we do? Tell us that and then we'll consider coming out! Otherwise, you'll just have to blow us up in here."

A feisty one she was. Ghost remembered her well, she was hard on the outside, but had a little soft spot for Ticker.

Ghost got out from the scorching hot sand. He scanned the area before hiding behind mounded rocks. Ticker, Slithers, and Butcher followed silently, but close behind them. They were concealed from the rest of the U.S soldiers and they could get a better glimpse. The sand was stained red, even here, but the soldiers were still numerous, and too many for Ghost to guess how many there were.

He peered over the rock, down a large basin with a square building. The building was abundantly surrounded, and the soldiers placed claymores around the exits. MGs were stationed around every blockade and protected with a three-inch steel plate. In front of the building were four iron poles, freshly erected for the occasion. *How respectful. They really put a lot of thought into this.*

There was silence for a time. Ghost looked carefully. Task Force 7 needed to make a move, because the good old brothers of arms were willing to wait. After all, they had all the time in the world. Task Force 7 was the one running out of time.

Venom, they can wait. You must do something. You and Viper.

Nothing happened. The soldiers began stretching, still cautiously watching the building. What appeared to be an eternity passed. And then it happened. Glass was broken from the windows. Guns, unprimed grenades, and knives were just tossed out of the window. The front door was kicked down. The soldiers immediately focused their attention on the door with their rifles aimed down, their fingers just above their triggers.

Ghost clutched his chest. *They had given up and had had enough.* He let out deep measured, but silent breaths.

Venom walked out with her hands up. She was weeping tears of anguish, and her face grimaced, shining bright with the flames. "Don't shoot. I'll come in. I just want a fair trial."

Viper hesitantly walked out, her hands behind her back. She glared at all the soldiers, gnashing her teeth at them. She let out a sigh before looking up at the sky. Tears streamed down her face as she grimaced. Her hands made angry fists behind her back.

Wraith came out, his hands atop of his head. He glared at everyone, not letting anyone out of his sight. He knew something, something was not going to go the way they thought. They were utterly alone down here. He stood behind Viper. He never looked to the ground, never to the sky, and he didn't let tears swell his eyes, as if he held some small fragment of hope that there was the faintest chance he could survive, but it was clear that even he was jaded.

Finally, Metal came out. He was a little taller than the rest of them, but he was the youngest of them all. His hands were folded in front of him as he reluctantly walked forward. His steps were small, and his knees trembled beneath him. His head was bowed down low as he came out, grinding his teeth.

"We're out. You damn bastards! What was our crime?" Wraith demanded. "I want answers, and I want them now!"

"You will be tried. Cuff them." Came the officer's voice. He was smoking a cigar and kept his left hand in his pocket.

"Not until we get our answers!"

"You will be cuffed, or I will light you up right here!" General Snells scolded. "With what you did, you're lucky you're getting that much. You've already been tried, traitor!"

This stifled Wraith, the only one who was vocal.

Sixteen soldiers sprinted up to them. They kicked the back of their knees. They cried out in pain as they hit the ground. They were cuffing their ankles and wrists. Knees were pressed into their backs, and they were crying, all except Wraith. Who was scanning the basin for a way out.

Viper cried the loudest. Her screams could be heard from miles like a dying banshee, waiting to be released from this Hell. She, Venom, and Metal were waiting for the sweet release of death, as Death had always been their one true friend.

Ghost couldn't look away, no matter how hard he tried to force his head down. It was as if his body refused to move, like he was stuck in a single time frame while the rest of the world continued to move.

Venom, Viper, Metal, and Wraith were struck in the back of the knees with batons, crying out as they collapsed forward. These batons swung wildly. The tried to move away, but these soldiers swiftly tied them with zip-ties. The soldiers beat them relentlessly, until blood spilled on the ground. These four from Task Force Seven just wept, unable to move. Satisfied, apparently, the soldiers dragged them through the sand, hoisted them up on these erected pillars, and tied them firmly with rope, chains and duct tape. Ghost assumed these soldiers believed them to be monsters, and needed to be as secure as possible, and in order to kill one of them, they needed to be brutalized beyond repair.

General Snells paced back and forth as they watched him with their bleeding and terrified faces. Their faces resembled that of mere dogs trapped in a cage by a master who's beaten them so many times they anticipated the strike. The man was terrifying, and even more terrifying for a dog who was on its last legs.

"You want to know your crimes," he said. "Treason."

"What did we do?" Venom sobbed, her face cringing. "We didn't do anything! What did we do to deserve this? We fought for you so that you could hide behind us! Your Medal of Honor is a disgrace! That belongs to us!"

Truth is the only mistake they ever made was being born. Now they know not to make that mistake again. The more he looked on, the more he saw the events unfold, Ghost felt unnecessary, and his whole life was a lie. One thing he slightly understood now, having Snells confirmed it, the reason this was all happening was because of something Task Force Seven did, and it was labeled as Treason. But what was it? His eyes narrowed as Snells flicked the cigar out of his mouth.

Snells glared at them as he took multiple steps back. "Light them up."

"What?!" Wraith protested. "You said—"

His voice was abruptly drowned out by the road of rapid gunfire. The four of them screamed as their eyes widened at the onslaught, the flashing lights of the guns coming for them. Their bodies were penetrated with bullets, ripping apart their uniforms and flesh. They cried out, but their screams were voiceless.

But one voice reached above the gunfire, only one voice. The voice of Viper, "MAMA!" She cried. Her left arm was completely severed, and blood came out of her mouth. She looked to her left, Venom was already dead, her head bowed down as her waist fell from her torso. Her cries became screeches as she was pelted with more burning bullets into her torso. She turned the other way, and saw Wraith, he was already dead, numerous bullets made it through his skull. Her other arm was finally severed. And then onto Metal, who had it worse of all, his head had finally been sliced from his neck, and his chest was already opened up, his heart and intestines falling out of his torso like a drooling mouth.

"MAMA!" she cried, louder than before. Her eyes were gaped open as her chest started to open with the gun fire. "MAMA!" She could feel her waist coming apart. "MAMA!"

***

Ted immediately woke up, springing himself up from his sleeping bag. His chest was erect. Crossing his arms over his chest, as if trying to hold on to something. A violent scream expelled from his mouth as more tears streamed down his face again. He coughed on his own tears, sucking in his teeth, his eyes wide open, grimacing with his own torment.

He sees this in his sleep, again, and again, and again!

He slowly turned to his phone to look at the time. It read: 10:53 p.m.

Chapter 10 Evasion

~The world is a funny place. You can sacrifice your life and soul for the world, and it will never return your kindness. The world is such a cruel mistress.

***

Samantha Harris was running later than usual. Her heart was pumping in her chest heavily, feeling the sense of anxiety swelling over her like a plague. She sat in the shuttle, anxiously tapping her finger on the cold window as she watched the pedestrians. With every stop, ever moment the shuttle stayed still, she felt like she was going to be late to Park Street. She nervously chuckled, such a silly thing to be concerned about, being late of all things. *Sam, you need to stop bringing work home with you.*

The shuttle dropped off right off at South Station. She walked up the stairs and stepped into the busyness of Downtown Boston. The cars drove by, blasting their music with their windows down. Buses made their stops right next to her, letting numerous people off, she smiled at the people as they came off, either distracted with their phones in their hands, nodding off into some world with their earphones in their ears. Others seemed jaded, as if they were repeating the same routine, again, and again, and again.

She walked west on Summer Street. She paid close attention to the cars, and the streetlights. She waited patiently for the walking sign to turn on with that white light of a person, permitting her access to the other side without harm. Crossing the street, she followed onward towards the narrow street, surrounded by tall skyscrapers looking down with their oppressive magnificence. She crossed the street onto the side of a convenient store. There were several men there, some lively, smoking cigarettes or joints, almost with no care in the world.

But there was someone else there that caught her attention. There was a man, perhaps in his forties with an ungroomed beard with white streaks in it. His eyes looked exhausted and in his mouth was a cigarette, and in his left trembling hand was a paper bag, held in such away where she could tell plainly, there was a bottle in there. Whisky, gin, bourbon, or some other cheap but strong liquor as his breath reeked of it. Hanging around his neck was a pair of dog tags. His coat was tattered, with an American flag on the shoulder, also fading in color.

She sighed as she looked around the area for a bank. *No. That won't help him.* She walked into the convenience store. She looked around, speeding her way into the refrigerated section and pulled out two bottles of water. *I might as well, while I'm here.* She turned around and looked around for something suitable, and nutritious to eat, one where she didn't risk killing him because she didn't know if he was allergic to anything. She found a salad with chicken in it. *Better than nothing.* She didn't bother with any plastic silverware, there likely was none to be found.

She walked to the counter and smiled to the cashier. He scanned her items, and her purchase came up, totaling $17.68. She handed him her credit card. He swiped it immediately, and a receipt popped up. The cashier asked for her signature and she swiftly signed it. She walked out of the convenience store and walked down the side street: Arch Street. The man's eyes were fading out almost into sleep. She went up to him and placed one of the bottles of water next to him and left the salad next to that.

She left him to drift off in his sleep. There wasn't much more she could do, still waiting for her first big commission check from the brokerage. She didn't have her large customer for very long, and she was still eagerly waiting for it. Good part about having that customer is that it allowed her some help in handling all the refrigerated freight she gets from that one account. But this was all she could afford until that check.

She walked up Summer Street. She was in no hurry to get to the Study on time, as the topic was indeed depressing, and she was already late, and she had already decided this was a silly thing to be anxious about. Despite her rise in anxiety, she intended to walk ever so patiently. She walked through the streets, watching the lights light up, and some of the summer performers playing around in the trafficless square that separated coffee shops, clothing stores, and Downtown Crossing over towards Washington Street.

The moon peered out from behind a veil of clouds from on high. She looked up as the blue mystic light shone down on her. She took a deep breath as she kept walking further on the street, Summer turned to Winter real fast and she could no longer see the moonlight, but at the end of this street was Tremont, and at the end of Winter was the international state flower of Massachusetts:(The traffic cones), and parked behind it was a police cruiser, with the police officer leaning against his car, looking at the traffic. His eyes seemed emotionless as she passed by.

She waited with a score of people of diverse origins, waiting at the wide cross walk to cross Tremont Street, the wide street that always had construction here for some reason or another. *It's been the same for years. What are they doing?* She wondered.

The traffic lights turned from green to yellow, and at last red. The cars came to a halt, except the one who was speeding through the yellow light and just missed it. Massachusetts drivers, you can't trust them. They're insane. The cross lights permitted her to cross the street. She ran across diagonally to Park Street, right in front of the Church. On the front steps of the church were people sitting on the marble steps, many with a joint hanging from their lips. Their clothes were tattered and not well kept. There were flies buzzing around, and she wasn't surprised, one of them smelled like they soiled themselves, the rank reaching her nostrils. She assumed they were homeless, and this was the one place they could socialize, seemingly without the police arresting them for loitering. Not wanting to be rude, she briskly walked up Park Street to the glassy entrance of Café.

Her phone buzzed in her pocket. It was buzzing a lot these days, between high alert news, to grocers and reefer trucks going out of business, which was good for her, but terrible for the competition. She felt bad for them, and that was the one part of her job she hated. She had to beat those rates down with the drivers, even if they were desperate to get out of Maryland or California, they'd take almost any rate. Today, the truck driver was beat down so low, she was certain the driver took a $200.00 dollar loss taking the load.

She pulled out her phone and opened an email.

Samantha Harris,

Driver picked up PO 3840172 at Shed Baltimore, MD. 1834 PM. CI 15:34 PM CO 18:34 PM. Groceries. 30 pallets sideways. Outbound to Cincinnati OH.

Regards,

After Call.

She let out a sigh of relief. That was a close one, the load almost never got picked up. But something was in Ohio, enough where the driver was willing to take a steep loss on it. He'll make up for it. She smiled as she walked up the street. Her phone buzzed again.

She looked at it again before turning to the glass doors. It read *breaking news.* She rolled her eyes as she looked down on it. The News was filled with nothing but horror stories these days. Europe seemed to be in flames, and Asia was not far behind it what with all the declarations of wars and last-minute alliances that occurred with the dissolvement of NATO. *What were they thinking?* U.S.A seemed to be out of it for the most part. For that at least she was relieved. She didn't want to think about what a War with U.S.A would be like. As it stood, the U.S.A seemed to be out of everyone's conflict since about ten years ago.

The headline read: *China enters in trade War with U.S.A.* Her eyes gaped open at it. Her hand trembled with the phone. She sat down on the stairs for while she read the article.

According to White House officials, negotiations with important nations which disbanded from NATO are falling through. The world is in shambles right now and the only thing that is certain is uncertainty. U.S.A is trying to maintain relations with nations formerly within NATO after what they call it, "A colossal mistake!" Eastern and Western European countries are at war with another, and many nations in Africa have followed suit. Fortunately, the instability hasn't quite made it to the Americas, but White House Officials state it is only a matter of time.

The world is filled with uncertainty. White officials announced that it has entered a trade war with China, they implied that negotiations went

nowhere, and that China was not amiable with them. When asked further
about the future with China, White House officials stated that the future
is uncertain, and updates will follow. However, they are anticipating a
declaration of War from China.

Opinion: it seems rather unclear why the U.S would enter a trade war
with China. It is even much unclear as to why they're anticipating war,
unless nations are like dominos, next to one another, once one falls, another
falls, tumbling after the one next to it. There is little information being
revealed to us, and our nation's leaders are hiding something from us.

"Well, there's a surprise," she said sarcastically to herself. She looked
up the sky, now empty. She grimaced as she put her phone in her lap. She
lay her head down as she began to pray silently to herself.

After her silent prayer, she looked at her watch. It was 7:27 PM.
Large group was over or ending. She stood up and went inside and went
to the welcome table. The receptionist was still very much disinterested
as he was paying attention to something on his computer screen. She
pulled out a name tag, signed her name on it, and then she placed it on
her suit. She then took out a cup and put it underneath the cheap coffee
machine, placing a coffee cup in the machine and clamped it back down,
waiting for the coffee to drip.

As her coffee finished pouring out, the rest of the members of Café
were walking out of the fellowship hall and into their various small
groups. Samantha followed as Jennifer came out.

"Hiii!" Jennifer called out, running to Sam's side. "Isn't it a little late
for coffee?"

"Too late and coffee should never be in the same sentence," Sam
answered, smiling back at her. Jennifer and Sam were walking side by side
almost like two best friends in middle school.

"Hey, you didn't by chance see Ted out there, did you? On your way
in?" Jennifer asked. She still had that giddy smile on her lips.

"No. I can't say I have," Sam answered, confirming her suspicion that
Jennifer might have a thing for Ted. "Did he not show up?"

"No. Maybe it's nothing. Maybe he'll be here shortly. He did say he
was coming back," Jennifer commented.

"You seemed to get along with him well last Tuesday," Samantha responded.

"Yes, I did. He seems pleasant enough, almost oddly romantic." Jennifer snickered as they turned the corner into the granary room, getting into their corner of the table, waiting for others to start trickling in.

"Well, you did say once you prefer a man in a candlelight setting. Almost like a romantic emphasis from a Jane Austen Novel. Which one did you want? Was it Knightly or Darcy? Is he a keeper?"

"If only I could get those knightly qualities in someone like Darcy." She laughed. "Hard combination to come by. Ted could be Knightly." She joked.

"I get that," Sam replied.

"No Ted tonight?" Tim asked as he sat down next to them.

"Regrettably, no." Jennifer replied, looking at him in the eye. "I was really looking forward to seeing him again."

"Don't you have his number?" Sam asked. "Text him."

"I'm not going to pressure him just yet," Jennifer smiled suspiciously. "You can't just push him to come if he doesn't want to. Look, if he doesn't show up, I'll text him and tell him he's missed."

"Fair enough," Samantha said. *She's totally into him.* She turned to Tim. "Where's Michael."

"He was with me a short while ago, but he said he had to go back to the office to check on emails. He got something breaking news or some bother that he thinks is going to affect him." He replied. "He said he'll meet us at Teri's."

"Did he say what it was about?" Samantha asked.

"Something to do with China." Tim answered.

"I see. He probably has to work another hour to read the room." Sam suggested.

Jack interrupted everyone. "Welcome to Café, welcome to connecting group. I see we still have a few stragglers and new faces. So, that we can all get a sense of one another, I'll start. Say your name, where are you from, what brings you to Boston? And the icebreaker, hmm." He said as he scratched his neck as he looked up to the ceiling. "If you could meet any person, living or dead, real or fictitious, who would it be? My name is Jack, I am from Houston Texas, and I work as a nuclear physicist at a nearby nuclear power plant. I came to Boston for work. If there is someone I would like to meet? Julius Robert Oppenheimer, I'm really interested in his thought process in the Atom Bomb."

They all went down the line, introducing themselves with elation, giving them their background information, and locality. It was routine for everyone, but the differing perspectives always kept things interesting. Even though Sam had known Michael, Tim, and Jennifer the most closely, she couldn't say she knew everything about them.

The line finally made it to Tim. "My name's Tim. I am from Colorado, Denver specifically. I came to Boston for college, and I settled here over in Dorchester. If I could meet anyone, living or dead, I'd have to say Jesus."

"No! No! No!" Jennifer exclaimed, pointing at him. "No. Bad. Tim. Bad. No cop outs! We all want to meet Jesus. No! I *demand* a do-over!"

The room settled with laughter.

"But I really want to—"

"Tim. Bad. Bad Tim. No! No! No!" she exclaimed. "Give us something juicier than that!"

"Fine." Tim chuckled. "Hmm. Come back to me."

"Cheater." She elbowed him. "My name is Jennifer, I am originally from upstate New York, and I moved to Boston for a change in scenery. New York is terrible. I am a biological researcher right around the corner. If there was anyone I wanted to meet, dead or living? Real or fiction? Well, King Arthur. I've always loved his tales as heavily fabricated as they are. He was such the romantic."

"Not Mr. Darcy?" Sam joked.

"Oh, please, Darcy and Arthur, there just isn't any comparison!" she said.

The room was filled with laughter. It was clear that Jennifer was the life of the group, or the class clown. Sam wondered how she behaved at work. She let her own laughter subside.

"Well, my turn! My name is Samantha, I also moved here for work after college. I am moving back. I was from Peabody, went to school down in Virginia, and am relocating back up here when I took a job as an account executive for a Logistics brokerage." She began. "If there is anyone that I want to meet living or dead, and not Jesus since that's off the table," there was another chuckle across the room. "Well, let's go historical shall we, I've always wanted to meet Joan of Arc. Her story sits a special way with me."

"As you can see, we are a very diverse group of people." Jack said. "So, if any of you are new here, and I think there are a few of you, we just started Ecclesiastes. We are going into the second chapter, so without further adieu. . ."

Samantha, Jennifer, Erin, and Tim followed the crowd up through the Park Street, taking a right on Beacon Street, heading back down towards Tremont Street, entering Teri Nation on the left-hand side right before Somerset Street. They entered the pub and walked towards the back, entering an almost empty bar. There was no one except the food runner, and Scott, the beloved Bar tender, who seemed very happy with bright shining eyes and a smile past that thick black beard. Samantha pulled up a stool and sat right down, taking out her wallet. Jennifer and Erin sat on either side of her, and Tim was to the left of Erin, before he saw fit to leave their little quartet and start chatting away with Brian.

"What are we having today and no Michael?" Scott asked.

"Nay—" Jennifer began. "Well, the voluptuous drinker should be coming in rather shortly, or so he said."

"Well, Tim said that. And you know how spontaneous Michael can be. He might just not show up," Sam assured her.

"Who did Tim say wasn't coming?" Came a loud obnoxious voice behind them. Sam, Erin, and Jennifer looked behind to see Michael smiling down on him, his hands resting on Erin and Jennifer's shoulders.

"You," Jennifer said. "Dang it. And here I thought I was going to have a normal drink for once, like some brandy, a glass of wine, a beer or even some rum and coke. Oh well. I guess my dream died early tonight."

"No one's stopping you," Michael laughed, turning to Scott. "Bar Tender's special! Whatever that is!"

"You're stopping me," Jennifer smirked. "Make that two, and for God's sake, don't spit in it like you did three weeks ago."

"That was sweat!" Scott laughed.

"I was joking," Jennifer replied.

"So was I," Scott sneered as he cleaned the bar top and ducked down to get some glasses.

"Just the dark Crellic," Erin asked.

"Cab, for me, please," Sam asked.

"Make that together," Jennifer asked. She slipped her card over to Scott. "Close it out if you would."

Scott hastily went over to pour the wine and simple beer for Erin and Sam. He sliced some cucumbers, mixing in muddled mint and blueberries, poured in some vodka and soda water, and what Sam guessed was simple syrup, and he started shaking them all together. It could be terrible, could be great, it was like playing Russian Roulette, without the dying part of course.

"I don't see Ted. I take it he elected to go home earlier today?" Michael asked.

"No, he didn't show up," Samantha said.

"Erin. You work with him, right?" Michael asked. "How is he?"

"I don't know. He made another big deal again. This was one of those one offs and not likely something he's going to repeat." She said as she sipped her beer. "I don't know how he does it, he must be really lucky or have some insider information, but even if he did, there is no way he can accurately predict when something will just plummet. Even with inside information, he can't make those calls at precisely the right time. Yet, he is making those calls at precisely the right time. He seemed fine though, but when he made the deal, he seemed disappointed."

"How much was the deal worth?" Michael his eyes widened in curiosity.

"Our manager clocked it in at $350K," she said. "I don't care who you are, no one can predict the market the way he does. He is consistently beating it, even with all of the uncertainty in the world."

"But why was he disappointed," Sam asked. "Shouldn't he be happy with that?"

"I don't know. I know I'd love a deal like that! But I am nowhere near to his expertise actually," Erin explained. "He also has the nasty habit of leaving late and arriving early. However, he left earlier today, in the middle of a meeting."

Scott came back with those drinks. They were identical and had a foggy color to them. He slid the drinks on the table to Michael and Jennifer. Jennifer took a sip. She found it beautiful to her lips. She let out a sigh. "Wow, so this is what it's like to be on cloud nine. Tell me, you didn't spit in it did you?"

Michael took a sip of his. He also smiled.

"Just his," Scott answered, laughing because he wasn't serious. Michael almost coughed and spat it out.

"Now, now, Michael, I'm sure he's joshing you," Jennifer sneered.

"Who even says that anymore?" Michael chuckled, and his smile lit up.

"I said what I said!" she took another sip. She licked her lips. "Not bad, this one."

"Hey, Scott?" Sam asked.

He was about to turn to another guest before he turned to her. "Yeah, Sam?"

"That man, that we met two weeks ago, over in the corner. Has he been coming here often?" she asked.

"Yes. He usually just gets a glass of wine and some potatoes," He answered. "He is always pleasant. He didn't show up last week though."

Sam knew that to be true. *Wait a minute.* "Last week? Do you mean he was here earlier?"

"Yes. He left fifteen minutes before you arrived," He answered, turning away to address the rest of his guests around the bar.

"That's not good," Erin said. "I'll try to talk to him tomorrow if I can. I have plenty of reason to."

"I can't say I'm surprised," Michael commented, sipping his drink, whatever it was. "After all, the discussion we had was depressing."

"And to continue it today would have been worse," Sam admitted.

"It is depressing if you don't finish the context," Jennifer commented. "The moral of Ecclesiastes was and always will be, is that if this world is all there is, and God doesn't exist, anything we do is pointless. Our friends are pointless, our family is pointless. Our accomplishments don't mean anything and even our marks on history are pointless as they won't stand forever." She sighed. "But that doesn't mean that we should stop trying to live our lives." She pulled out her phone and scrolled through her contacts. She started texting a message. "I just texted him. Hopefully, he'll say something."

"I'm sure it's nothing," Michael said. "Besides, the world is crazy right now. I wouldn't be surprised if he's just exhausted all of the time and needs a break. I haven't done stocks, but I imagine its exhausting work."

"Yeah, it is!" Erin said, taking a gulp from her beer. "You have to pay attention to everything that's going on in the world. Literally anything could affect the market from good news, bad news, global news, a shipping company goes out of business, or even the materials of certain commodities skyrocket into the air. The more information one has the better, the problem is there is so much information to digest, and not every single thing is going to affect the market. For example, Michael did you read about that Trade War thing?"

"Yeah, that's why I wasn't at Café today," he answered.

"I read the same thing too," said Sam.

"Yeah, well, it's like this. Something like that is undoubtedly going to affect the market, it's probably going to crash, my assumption of course," Erin replied, tilting her arm as if to illustrate a graph, "Now, let's say that Trade War was with China and Russia instead of the U.S. There is a high likelihood that it will affect the market with increased commodity prices since we get a lot of business from China. There is no guarantee that *that* Trade War will directly affect our Market. Its effect on the Market would be indirect to us over here in the U.S. but it will likely affect it, if not immediately. But there is no promise that it will send the market down. Many people will assume that it will, and then sell their assets, hoping to buy them all back when it goes below, this is called shorting a stock, but the way the market works, that kind of behavior may drive the value of the assets up instead of down, causing a lot of people to lose out on money. But since it's us, I'm sure the market is going to crash, it's just a matter of when."

"Well, that is going to make my head hurt. I'll stick to my 401K thank you very much," Jennifer said. "So, what's everyone doing Saturday?"

"I'm free," Michael said without skipping a beat.

Erin and Sam both nodded.

"Excellent. It's decided then. I'll see all of you Saturday, and Tim. Hopefully I can get Ted to come." Jennifer said, clapping her hands.

"What are we doing and where are we going?" Michael asked.

"Why, my house silly." She smiled at him with her bright grin. "Game night of course. I have a little game we play there. It's a great way to get to know your friends."

"Okay. Time?"

"Noon is fine," Jennifer admitted. "I've got the refreshments already arranged!"

Chapter 11 Game night

~It was all a mistake.

***

Jennifer woke up Saturday morning bright and early. She stretched out as the sun beamed down on her face. She yawned and stepped outside of bed and moved over to her nightstand. She picked up her phone to check for her text messages, checking to see if Ted responded. Her texts looked lonely on the screen: *Ted, we're meeting at my house for some games, Samantha, Michael, Tim, and Erin. I did invite a few more that I'm not sure you met or not. Text me later.* The Text message was alone, almost like it didn't want a response. She stared down at it, contemplating what to do with it. She put the phone on the nightstand again and crossed her arms around her chest, violently tapping her arm with an intense index finger. "Tedward!" She finally decided to pick up the phone again and hit the phone icon.

The phone rang, dialing the number that Ted gave her. *I really hope he didn't give me a fake number. If he did, there's nothing I can do.* The phone rang second time. *Come on, Tedward. Wakey wakey!* It rang a third time before forwarding to his voicemail.

"You've reached Ted. I'm sorry I can't get to the phone right now. Please leave your name, phone number, and brief reason for your call and I'll get back to you as soon as possible."

Beep.

"Ted, this is Jennifer, I hope you're not ignoring me. Please get back to me, you're invited to my place for some games and dinner today—"

"Hello?" the voice on the other end of the phone picked up.

Jennifer was surprised and made a very shocked shape with her mouth. Her smile lit up her room, even though only she was in it. "Heeeey there, buddy! This is Jennifer."

"I know." He chuckled. "I memorized your number. How may I help you?"

"So, the reason I'm calling is because I'm hosting a small group of friends, I'm not expecting more than ten of us, for games, drinks and food at my place today. We're starting around noon today, and I want to invite you here for that also." She brought down the excitement in her voice, speaking softly into the phone. "By the way, we missed you this week!"

"I see," he said, his voice went soft over the phone. "This is kind of sudden, to be frank."

"I texted you Tuesday about it. You never answered," she said. "Come on, what better way to get closer to your friends over games and fellowship."

"Uhm. I don't know."

"What? Do you have plans already?" Jennifer asked him.

"No."

"Then come on. Look, if it means that much to you, you can take me shopping next week," she joked.

"I don't recall making an active effort to take you shopping," he replied.

"Well, at least I got a full sentence out of you. Can you do me a favor?" she asked.

He chuckled on the other end of the phone. "What?"

"Do you have a pen and some paper," she asked.

"I do."

"Take my address down. You're coming. I won't take no for an answer."

"What am I, your servant?" he said.

There was some silence on the phone. Jennifer turned her head and then back to the phone as if she was consulting an imaginary friend. She had that sneering smile on her face. "Yes."

He burst out laughing on the other end of the phone. "As you wish, milady."

"There's the romantic Tedward I know." She laughed. She verbally gave him her address as she was sure he was writing it down on the other end of the phone. "Ted, it starts at 12:00 p.m. You can come early or come later. Or on time. That's cool too. Up to you. But you are coming!

Or I'll track you down to the end of the earth and feed you my amazing, boxed macaroni and ketchup."

"Ketchup?" He sounded confused.

"There may or may not be cheese involved in some way shape or form. I don't know. Maybe you don't have to find out, huh? Just come," she joked.

"Do you need me to bring anything?"

"Just yourself," she answered.

"I see," He gave his reserved few-word answer.

"I speak for myself and everyone coming that you should also bring clothes. Yeah, that's a good idea. Don't come naked. That would make for a rude awakening, although a very comical story a year down the road."

He chuckled again, "Okay, I'll see you there. Is there anything else?"

"No. Just give me a time when you'll be here."

"I'll probably make my own lunch, so I'll probably be there around one."

"Okay, we'll see you then!" She exclaimed before hanging up the phone. She immediately started a group chat with Michael, Tim, Erin, and Samantha. *He's coming. He'll be here around 1PM today.*

She hastily went over to her kitchen and poured herself a bowl of cereal and milk. She started cataloguing the games she wanted to have available for them, as well as making the plans to order the pizza. She swiftly ate her cereal before arranging things around the living room, making plenty of space available for the "Acting Game". She didn't have the cards for the physical game, but it was a close substitute.

Hours passed. Jennifer had gotten everything ready, the drinks were in her cooler, and of course the pizza was on its way. She ordered four pies to be safe: Pepperoni, chicken and broccoli, Cheese, margherita pizza. That would satisfy everyone with their dietary restrictions. She didn't think any of them were vegans, god forbid, at least it wasn't clear; however, she did in fact know Tim was a vegetarian.

There was a knock on the door. She quickly glanced at her watch, which read 12:03 PM. She immediately went to the door to answer it. Samantha smiled as the door was opened. She came in with her purse. "Sorry I'm late. There was some problem on the redline today."

Michael was behind her. He lived in the same neighborhood over by Davis Square, the place he calls, "Heaven on Earth".

"What happened? Did it derail or something? I hate that line," she asked.

Michael laughed, "When was the last time you heard someone say they liked the red line? It's like asking if a morbidly obese man likes the tape worm inside his own belly."

"Now that's a specific analogy if ever I heard one," Jennifer said, her face twisted in disgust. "I'm not touching any of the chicken now. By the way, the pizza should be here in about a half hour."

"Great, I'm famished," Michael smirked.

"It's barely noon," Jennifer mocked him. "I swear, where do you put it all?"

"Fast metabolism," He chuckled.

"Wow. I wish I had the ability to eat the things you do and not gain weight." She was about to shut the door.

"Waaiit!" came a familiar cry. Jennifer looked out of the hallway of her apartment to see Tim sprinting down the corridor. "I'm here. Don't start without me."

"Tim!" She smiled at him, and placed her hand defensively on her chest, "I would never!"

"Oh, yes you would!" he shot back as he came bolting down the corridor and stopping him with the ajar door. He panted.

"You're right." She laughed, tossing her hair back. "I'm a monster."

Sam and Michael already took a seat on one of the sofas. Michael's arm was around her shoulder. "Jennifer, did Brian say he was coming?"

"Yes, he did. And you know he'll bring you know who," Jennifer said. She looked at the watch. 12:10 p.m. "But you know him, he probably went to bed seven hours ago, so he'll probably just be waking up, if he's even up already. He probably won't be here 'til closer to three. That's a man that knows how to show up fashionably late." She turned to Tim who was still panting. "Tim, I have some bottled water in the cooler, go get some."

"No thank you." He panted, while making his way to his seat. "You know—"

"Yes, yes, I know. Environmentally friendly and all that," Jennifer sneered. "Well, I have some plastic cups you can get tap—"

"Don't you have real cups?" Tim stared at her blankly.

"Tim! Do I look like some girl who wants to wash her dishes all the time?" she snapped at him. "Of course, I do." She walked over to her cupboard, grabbed a cup and filled it with water to give to Tim.

"So, I want to know," Samantha said to Jennifer. "How did you get Ted to agree to come?"

"Well, I called him this morning. He finally picked up the phone as I was leaving a salty voicemail." She put her fingers to her lips, but her smile never faded. "I talked him into going. He tried to push back but I wouldn't let him get out of his corner."

"Well, that must be—" Michael began.

Ring.

Jennifer took out her phone and looked at the caller ID. *Erin.* She answered the phone. "You've reached the city morgue, you kill 'em, we chill 'em."

Tim spat out the water from his mouth.

"Hey, Tim! Tim! Tim! You clean that up!" Jennifer scolded him.

Erin was chuckling on the other line. "Which door do I enter?"

"It's apartment number 658. I'm on the sixth floor, when you come out of the elevator, take a left. See you soon! Bye-bye now." She hung up the phone. "Tim, who gave you permission to spit water all over my floor?"

Sam was cackling.

"You must have been the class clown," Michael's eyes gaped opened; his pupils opened shifted from side to side as his jaw dropped.

"Oh, dear, dear sweet little carpet," she said. "That wasn't me. That was some guy named David, a terribly dreadful little creature."

"You read Jane Austen last night again, didn't you!" Sam accused, shaking her head.

"You know it! Jane Austen a day keeps depression away." She laughed. "Or was it something to do with apples? I don't know. I'm not a doctor. I'm just a researcher."

There was a knock on the door, "Erin, or Pizza?"

"Erin," Michael answered.

Jennifer went to open the door, and Michael was correct. "Welcome in, excuse the spit, Tim did it. Tim, are you done cleaning?"

"Yes, I am." He was cleaning it with a washcloth. He hated paper towels.

"Good grief. I give you my glorious tap water, and this is how you repay me. Some friend!" The room was filled with laughter as Erin walked in. If no one knew any of them, they would think Jennifer was an unlikable jerk, but the reality was that her sarcasm, while may be over the top, was her love language.

She looked at her watch again; 12:20 p.m.

"Pizza running late?" Michael asked.

"Not yet," Jennifer said.

Jennifer lounged next to Tim on the couch, Michael had his arm wrapped around Samantha's shoulders, and Erin was poking about Jennifer's bookshelves, looking at the impressive Jane Austen collection, in a variety of different editions. Jennifer smiled as Erin pet the spines so casually, especially the leatherbound editions reprinted in '08. "I recommend *Sense and Sensibility,* that's my personal favorite."

"Jennifer?" Erin gazed back at her. "How many times have you re-read this collection? And why do you have so many?"

"I re-read the collection yearly. You might call me the hopeless romantic,"

"Ted bug?" Erin sneered.

Taken aback, Jennifer turned her head to the side, and her cheeks blushed red. "Maybe."

A half hour passed and there was another knock on the door. "That must be it." She went over to the door to open the door. The pizza man came in. She paid him in cash as he walked the pizza pies to the island in her kitchen. There were numerous plates that came with it. Of course, Tim scoffed at them.

Michael went over to get a slice. "Get your frail hands away from that!" she slapped his hand away from the paper plate. "Now, now, my sweet little carpet, we are waiting for Ted. I can reheat the pizza in the oven if I need to. twenty minutes isn't going to kill you."

An hour passed. It was 1:50 PM in the afternoon. There was not another knock at the door. Jennifer felt discouraged, her heart was concerned for Ted, as there wasn't a text message sent to her phone indicating he was going to be later than when he said he was going to be. *I hope he didn't get into an accident.* She sighed, "Well, I guess you all can eat now."

Tim, Erin, and Michael immediately went over to get some pizza. Jennifer was tired of listening to Michael complain anyway. She felt Samantha's hand on her shoulder, "It'll be fine. I'm sure he got caught on something."

"I suppose," Jennifer took out her phone and sent another message to Ted: *where are you?* She put the phone back in her pocket and slouched her shoulders as she walked to get a slice of pizza, and on that dreaded paper plate.

"Hey, Erin, did you ever follow up with Ted the other day?" Michael asked as he took a bite of his Hawaiian pizza. He should really have his taste buds checked.

"Yeah, I did. He only gave me few-word answers," she replied, taking a bite of her chicken alfredo. "He said, he was fine."

"Well, you know when someone answers that way, they're insecure," Sam said. "That's what my boss tells me when I say I'm fine."

"I'm sure it's nothing," Michael said. "As he mentioned before, he works in world markets, I wouldn't be surprised if he was still working and had some remote meeting he forgot to mention."

"Seriously, Michael, how much does he have to be working if he's doing that!" Jennifer exclaimed. Tim's eyes opened as this was the first time in a while that she seemed frustrated, gritting her teeth. "Erin, didn't you say he was one of those come in early leave late kind-of-guys?"

"Yeah," she admitted.

"That isn't unusual for someone in a high-pressure job," Samantha explained. "I do that frequently too."

"So, do I," Michael said, he scratched his chin as he was chewing on his crust. "But if I had to guess, he was probably working close to sixty-hours per week."

"That isn't unusual," Jennifer admitted, "But if he works on the weekends, should he be closer to seventy-hours?"

"Perhaps, and that's a little extreme," Michael admitted. "I would never choose to work that much, unless maybe he has a reason."

"Maybe he just really likes money," Tim said. "I mean, if he's in stocks, that's usually the reason."

"No, that's not it. He admitted that he only does it for something to keep him busy, almost like he enjoys doing it. He said he has more than enough for him to live off," Michael replied.

"Honestly, that's impressive. He doesn't seem to be much older than any of us," Tim said.

Another hour passed. Jennifer received no confirmation from Ted that he was coming or that he was running late. It is almost two hours later than when he said he would show up. Did he lie to her, just to get her off the phone? She couldn't discount that possibility.

There was a knock on the door. Her smile lit back up again. She rushed over to the door to answer it. She opened the door with a grin on her face and when she saw who was on the other side. Her emotions fell heavily upon her heart, almost like she was chained to the ground by large boulders, and she couldn't move, or risk having the weight crush her. Yet, she retained that healthy simper, "It's Brian!"

"Yeah! It's Brian!" he repeated in the third person, shaking his head enthusiastically. "Sorry I'm late."

"Don't fret, my sweet little fox, come on in. The pizza is here. I was just about to pull out the wine," she said, ushering Brian, and Steven, and his little friend, Rosa in. Brian was the oldest of them all, nearing his mid-thirties.

"Oh, excellent, plenty of time for drinking. I brought my own wine actually, it's from the Valley up over in Westford."

"Wait. Really?" Samantha asked. "I love their wine, it's something about their grapes. Their wine is of the best quality."

"Yeah!" he walked over to the island in the kitchen and placed two bottles of wine on it. He put the Corkscrew in one of them and immediately opened it. Brian, Steven, and Rosa went over to the others and started talking about their week. No one brought anything depressing into the conversation.

Jennifer looked at them with a smile, happy that they're able to have such a good time in such a small apartment. The games hadn't started just yet. But she was beginning to lose hope that Ted would be showing up tonight. *You liar. You could have at least told me you just didn't want to come. But maybe I shouldn't have put you in that position, forcing you to either lie or hurt my feelings. I'm sorry.*

She pulled out all her wines out onto the island and started pouring cups of wine into wine glasses and delivered them to her guests, smiling as she handed each one off. She saved Brian's wine for last. He usually bought the expensive wine anyway.

"Hey, whatever happened to that newbie?" Brian asked. "I don't think I ever succeeded in getting him out. I haven't seen him in a while."

"Are you referring to Ted?" Michael's head tilted in response. "The one from two weeks ago?"

"Yeah, that one," Brian took a sip of his Cabernet. "What happened to him? Did someone scare him off?"

"I don't think so. Actually, I heard he was supposed to be coming tonight, but he hasn't shown up yet," Sam replied, the curve on her lips faded.

"Well, I hope nothing bad happened to him," Brian said concerned. "A pity, I wanted to meet him. I never got a chance to say hi to the new guy."

"Maybe you'll get that chance still tonight, or—"

Knock. Knock.

Who was that? Jennifer thought. *It's way too late for it to be Ted.* "I've got it." She walked over to the door; her hand gripped the handle and turned it. She listened carefully as the locks began to remove themselves from the door. She opened the door wide with a smile as she looked to greet whoever stood behind that door.

Her eyes gaped open, and her grin immediately dropped as she saw who it was, Light shimmered in her pupils. Her hands trembled at her side. She grimaced at the man, as his presence suddenly made her angry.

"You know, Tedward, when you tell me you're going to be here around one, I expect you to be here around one, maybe fifteen minutes late or so, but around one. It is four o'clock! I already told everyone you would be here at one. Would you make a liar out of me?" she said with an uplifted tone.

The room filled with laughter went silent.

He simpered and gave her a polite bow. "My apologies, milady. For you see, I just couldn't bring it upon myself to come to some kind of party without bring something of value to my beloved host," He spoke very smoothly, and he was not at all flirtatious, he seemed very sincere. He took out a large bottle of wine, a red wine, and of a fine glass, a fine bottle with the price tag ripped off.

Jennifer's eyes lit up as she immediately grabbed the bottle from his hand and read the label. "This is Colossus' Rome Red Ca'habielli!"

"What?" Brian called over. "Ca'habielli? Jenn put my wine back in the cooler. You can't get much better than that!"

"Ted, that's a $1,200 bottle of wine. Where did you get this? More importantly, why would you give it to me?" Jennifer snatched it from his hands as she looked over the label. She knew the value of such a brand of wine was only reserved for the finest of occasions, and not something easily obtainable in the United States. This was strictly imported from the wineries of Rome.

"Eh, I'm not going to keep it around my house," He replied. "It's much better shared among *friends*." His voice dropped a little at the sound of the word.

"Come on in!" she invited him in, immediately changing her tone from ire to a sense of joy. "There is Pizza, I know you said you ate already, but it's here if you want it."

"I appreciate the sentiment," He answered as he walked through the apartment, scanning the room, as if to read the reaction of each person.

Samantha walked up to him, "I'm glad you came."

"I'm glad I made it," He smiled to her; the bags under his eyes were puffy.

Jennifer took Brian's two bottles of wine and put them back in her cooler. They would be there later. She took out the cork of the bottle of

Ca'habielli. She sniffed it as she allowed it to breathe a little. The fabled wine was such a gracious gift. No one ever made such a purchase on her budget if she didn't think she would like it. Obviously, this should be enjoyed sparingly or with on a special occasion. *With friends, but why did he hesitate?*

The party grabbed their now empty wine glasses and got into a line. Jennifer handed Ted a fresh one, he grinned that impeccable simper; there was something soothing about it. Like the genuine smirk of someone who knew no pain, who knew only the kindness of the world, and was sheltered from the many horrible, physical, psychological traumas from the world. He was always in a safe place.

Jennifer poured the wine into the empty glasses, filling them halfway so she could distribute it equally to everyone in the party. The party stood around in a circle, and Michael raised his glass up.

"A toast, to friends all under one roof, some we have been with since high school, and others are newer than some," He smiled, specifically looking at Ted. "And let us not forget to thank Jennifer for hosting us this evening! For we wouldn't be here without her, and I doubt Ted would have made it without her. Cheers."

"Cheers!" the rest of the party repeating in unison.

They all took a sip for the Ca'habielli. Jennifer let the wine sift through her lips before tasting the sweet and bitter arrays of the beverage. It was without a doubt the finest wine she has ever laid her lips upon. She has spent her years drinking a number of wines, but all paled in comparison to this legendary bottle shipped all the way from Rome. *No wonder this wine is so pristine.*

Chapter 12 Raw Brutality

~Prepare yourselves. You've picked a terrible person to jump. Don't give me that look when I know you don't have the stomach to sit through Raw Brutality.

***

Hours passed. Jennifer couldn't believe it had already passed midnight. None of them were drunk, well, Tim may have been a little buzzed, but that was some good wine. She never had to pull out the reserves of Brian. They played numerous games throughout the course of the night, from social games to the acting games.

Ted had moved around to one of the windows, exhausted, staring out at the window, looking down at the city lights, illumining the empty city streets. He could hear some background talking as Tim, and Brian were leaving Jennifer's Seaport District apartment. Jennifer was engrossed in a conversation with Michael, and they seemed to be getting a long quite famously. This left Samantha in the room.

Samantha walked over to him with another wine glass filled with some of the extra wine. He turned to her and smiled. She joined him, sitting on the wide windowsill. She smirked back to him, and when she was certain she got his attention, she said, "Ted, I have a question, and I hope I don't come off as offish, I hope you don't mind."

"I don't mind at all. The moon is out, the wine is delicious, and any matter of question is allowable," he grinned, and yet he felt exhausted, "But because a question is allowed, it doesn't necessarily mean I'll answer."

"Okay," she said, a little confused by the latter part of his response. "We didn't do anything to offend you two weeks ago, did we? We were concerned that something might have happened to you after we didn't see you. And we were especially concerned when Jenn told us you would be here at one, and still no response when you were late." She let out a nervous laugh. "I think Jenn thought you might have died on the way here."

"Well, as you can see, I am here now, and not dead," he replied. "I don't mean to be of concern, as I did not come to think me to be part of this, how does she put it, part of this 'dysfunctional family'. As such, I didn't think my absence would play a major part in your day's concern as you and I only met three weeks ago."

"Okay." She nodded. "Then, do you consider yourself part of us, then?" She looked at him seriously. "Answer me honestly. You have a hiddenness about you, I'm having a hard time reading you."

He smiled. "I don't intend to keep anything away from you, only that which such information is not required for our *relationship*, and nothing more. I am difficult to read, so you say, and this is the first time I'm hearing of it."

"Because there is some sense of mystery about you. All I really know is what you do and where you are from. I don't know what your likes and dislikes are. Does anyone?" she answered again, pushing for some non-ambiguous answer. She sought to clear the murky water that Ted was swimming in.

"I suppose I like working. I guess that is one thing—" The volume of his voice dropped.

"About that," she interrupted him. "How many hours do you work? From what I hear, you are something of a workaholic."

"I suppose one would say that," He chuckled. He looked up at the ceiling as if searching for an answer. "I work about as much as one-hundred and sixteen hours a week."

Sam's eyes gaped open. "What?" She repeatedly blinked: she couldn't believe her ears. "Can you repeat that?"

"One-hundred and sixteen hours a week," he answered. He was careful to retain that smirk.

"I thought that's what you said. How can you possibly maintain that!" she exclaimed. "Do you even sleep?"

"I sleep enough." He simpered.

She realized something, underneath his eyes were the jaded expression of a man who knew little sleep. "Ted, how much do you sleep?"

"I sleep enough," he replied.

No wonder he can just go out and buy a $1,200 bottle of wine. "Why do you work so much? Do you even have something you would consider fun?"

"I find work fun, and it keeps me occupied," he answered.

"You're avoiding the question," she accused.

"No, I'm answering the question. The truth can be so hairy. Like I said before, I will answer your questions and reveal some of myself as necessary for our relationship." He kept his smile, but his tone lowered an octave.

"That—that's not the same thing!" she exclaimed. "It's not the same thing. You are avoiding the—"

"Miss Harris, I believe you might have had a little much to drink," he suggested. "Might it be time to retire for the night?"

"Perhaps you're right," Sam looked down at her glass, which was now half empty. "I'm sorry, Ted, I shouldn't have said anything. Can you find it in yourself to forgive me?"

"I'm afraid I cannot. There is nothing to forgive. There is no reason to be sorry. Humans are humans." He grinned at her.

"I will leave you to your view then. Will we see you Tuesday?" Sam asked.

"Time, I suppose will tell, assuming I don't have any fires in the market to put out," he answered.

"But look, I know that we just met you, and us going out of our way to make you part of our little group may seem off putting, and for that I apologize. I hope you will see that we mean you no discomfort." She stopped speaking for a moment to allow him a moment for a response. Seeing that there was no response, she said, "That will have to do for now." She took her wine glass and went over to Michael, who wrapped his arm around her shoulder again.

Ted took to the window again and looked at the black, empty sky. The darkness was familiar to him. It was like the murky waters of the

Dead Sea, filled with nothing but hopeless light. His eyes were beginning to droop, and his attention shifted to his hand. His hand was not twitching as was common this time of night.

Why is the emptiness comfortable? Why is the darkness like home? Why does she look like her? Why? Must you really force me to stare back into the past that I am trying to escape, but the only way out is through, and that water is murkier than the Dead Sea. I'd take that wretched sea to this façade you call reality. It is all meaningless, as you say, then why don't we all just lie down and die?

Why are you not trembling? What is different?

The door closed behind him. He turned to see only Jennifer in the room. She smiled to him as she took her glass with her to sit with him and stare emptily out of the window, down to the city lights. She let out a sigh of relief.

"Well, that was fun. Did you enjoy yourself, Tedward?" she asked him.

"Well, it certainly wasn't dull, and I'm sure I have you to thank for that." He grinned back at her. The moon light was oppressively pushing down his spirits.

"So, tell me, Tedward, what is one thing I don't know about you?" she asked him. "Answer, and I will reveal something about myself."

He hesitated.

"So, there is something human about you after all," She laughed, her eyelids dropped down halfway, leaving her smirk. He could have sworn there was something sinister behind her watchful gaze. He knew she didn't miss much.

"Well, I suppose it's been a while since I've played twenty questions, but I can't help but think that's not how it works," He chuckled. "I suppose you'll have to ask me something specific, isn't that how it works?"

"Okay," Jennifer smirked. "So that's how it is, you sly little fox."

"I think I am much closer to a wolf," He joked.

"Perhaps a wolf raised by foxes," She let that sink in. "Well, my dear—"

"So, I'm a deer now?"

"You are whatever your sweet self wants to be. You be a deer, a fox, a wolf, something else of some other cute little characteristic attributed to all animals. So, here's my question, and forgive me if I already asked, but I cannot recall; have you any siblings?"

"There are those that I would have called brother and sister," He answered.

"Well, were they half siblings, full siblings, adopted?"

"I suppose you could say they were adopted siblings," He answered coldly, but he retained his grin.

She smiled, satisfied with the answer. "Now, Tedward, I believe it is your turn to now ask me a question. As reserved as you are, surely you have a question."

"I have many questions," He replied. "Sadly, very few, if any at all involve people."

"Then I beg you to make a question for me. What would pique your interest about me?" She leaned closer to him.

"I suppose this one I can ask, what do you find peace in?" he asked, revealing nothing else, he merely retained that grin as he asked it.

"I suppose I haven't given it much thought. I suppose if I found anything that gave me peace, is that I can be of some help to someone along the way with this very short life I've been given. Like many, I will not live for very long, humans do not live very long lives, as they used to say, what was it, before they all started digesting liquid detergent, 'YOLO', you only live life once," Her face went dark. "I guess I find the opposite to be true, you live and die just as many times as the other, and they equally plague us. Almost like both are a disease that must be vaccinated. But life's vaccination is death, and death's vaccination is life."

"How very, Tao of you," he said.

Her smile returned as she laughed sheepishly. "Then it is my turn then. What do you find peace in?"

"I'm not sure if I like that question," He snickered. "And was it not the same question I asked you?"

"Yes, it is. Is this question a little too revealing, Tedward?" she laughed like a little cat tugging on its yarn of string.

"You could say that, but I also know you will not like the answer," He replied.

Her face went graven again. "Look, Ted, I will decide if I like the answer or not. If I like it, then you would be pleased you were wrong. If I don't like it, I suppose you'll be satisfied knowing you were right all along. But I will accept whatever answer you give me, as it was my question that I asked. The point of this, was to get to know some facet of you that is hidden underneath that shell. They say darkness loves company, but it hates what's on the surface, as the surface is where truth lies."

"Well, they say darkness can't live in the light," he said.

She smirked again. "That is something true you just said," She paused. "Now, might I have my answer?"

"Well, I suppose it doesn't matter if you would like the answer or not, so I don't have a reason to deceive you," His voice dropped.

"Tedward," Her voice dropped, and her neck jerked her head to the side. "I know you may not think that we know you, and you're right, we don't know you as well as we would like, and I suppose you don't have a reason to trust me, but I trust you. I might not reveal all my little secrets just yet, but I trust you."

He let out a sigh, but he kept on smiling. "I suppose I don't find much of anything peaceful. I work a lot, and don't leave myself time for such luxuries," His voice dropped as he broke eye contact with her.

"Ted?"

"Do you know why I chose life as a stockbroker?" he asked. He didn't let her answer. "It is the one job in the world that I can think of that will let me work around the clock. I barely sleep. Maybe, I am lucky if I sleep more than thirty minutes at a time," He paused, looking back into her eyes, trying to analyze her reaction. She patiently waited for him to finish, looking him in the eyes, nodding, "I have no peace within myself, so I drown myself in work hoping to keep my mind occupied."

"Does it work?" she asked.

"Yes," he replied.

"Is it worth it?"

"I don't know," He replied. "I think I've spoken enough of myself for one night. I think it is time for me to go back."

"Home?" she asked.

"That is such a funny word," He said, standing up and leaving his wineglass on the nearby coffee table. "I've been in many countries and moved countless times. I don't think I've ever been to a place I would call home."

She gasped, and her smile completely faded. Her eyes glazed over. "Ted, that is so sad," She went to grab his hand. He pulled it away. "Look, before you go, and I know you must be eager to leave. Perhaps it was wrong for me to push you to come tonight. Perhaps, it is my fault, and this was wrong of me. I didn't know that bringing you here would bring back so many memories, painful, and reminders of what you once had, or never had, and may never get the chance to feel again," She sucked in her teeth as she looked him carefully in the eye. He took a step back. "Iah—I know that I can't imagine what it is you missed, because I don't know you and I'm not going to pretend I do. I will say that I want to know you. Now, I am sorry for pushing you to come, and Iah—I hope you can forgive me. I want to know you more, and I hope that I've made it clear that I want to be your friend, and I'm not going to push you anymore to tell me what you don't want me to know."

"I thank you, Jennifer," He answered. "I must be going."

He turned around and walked to the door. He opened it wide and stepped outside the threshold. He started to softly swing the door closed.

"Ted, will we see you on Tuesday?" she asked, just as the door was still slightly ajar.

"Time will tell," He answered truthfully.

The door clicked behind him. Her hands trembled as she walked over to the door to lock it. She started picking up the paper plates and threw them in the trash, with the now empty pizza boxes. She placed all her cups in the dishwasher before making it to her room.

The room was large, and her bed looked like it was freshly made, and patted down with the utmost care to avoid any wrinkles. She crawled into her bed and lifted her knees to her chest as she stared blankly at her bedroom door. Tears started to stream down her face, because she remembered something, the look in his face was all too familiar. She remembered the same look on her uncle's face, the same over tired look, the baggy and swollen eyes. The one-word answers, and a fake smile while all the same, giving a genuine laugh, laughing at his own misery.

She remembered her uncle being elusive with the truth, not exactly lying, but he wasn't telling the truth either. The man was a hardened veteran, seen his fair share of battle, and the fatigue showed with the lack of interest in anything. The last night she saw him hole, well, he was hanging from a ceiling, his torso stretching. No one knew, or no one made know how long he was hanging there, but if he was stretching, Jennifer knew it was quite some time before anyone made the effort to check in on him. It was long enough anyway, that no one seemed to miss his sudden absence.

Even if just for a moment, she saw the ragged look on her uncle's face to match perfectly Ted's face, and then she knew that Ted was hiding something that he wanted to keep hidden. Some mischief, regret, loss of trauma, but the Ted she knows, is not Ted as he truly is. He wore a fake smile, the social bandage to put on a show, to show everyone he's fine, but it was nothing more than a mask, and underneath that façade was a festering wound, and it hurts. *Damnit. It hurts.* She felt a part of her heart in agonizing pain, and she knew there wasn't anything she could do, but she wanted to do something. But what?

Ted gasped, gritting his teeth as he leaned against the back of the elevator all the way down. He started breathing heavily as the elevator lights blinked from floor to floor. He glared at the lights as if they mocked him. His fist clenched until he reached the bottom. The elevator made a loud bell sound. He took a deep breath and brought that bright smile back to his face. The double doors slid open and he crossed the threshold.

He went down the stairs and opened the last door to enter the empty street of Seaport Blvd. The streetlights were blinking. The cars were empty, and the street was void of all humans. Just the little pieces of trash that flew out of the public trashcans. He parked all the way towards Government Center. It was a long walk to get to his car, but it was a straightaway from Seaport Blvd. He walked west, following the many empty buildings, burger joints, coffee shops, ice cream parlors, and fisheries.

The moon beat down on him, and not a star was in sight. He held that same defeated grin as he walked down the boulevard. He took deep breaths through his nose until he passed the bridge across from the Boston Tea Party Museum. He smelled something foul in the air. He looked behind him, and he could smell the stench of something that was all too familiar to him: blood.

They say that blood doesn't smell like anything. But he's been around too much of it to know better. Someone without a strong sense of smell can't smell it, that's for certain, and those with a good sense of smell might miss it with the other smells in the air. But he can pick it out, because it smells like raw hatred. He turned around in the middle of the bridge and he could see cascading purple, pink, green and blue lights flaring up from the end of Seaport, getting much closer to Black Falcon Avenue. They almost looked like short-fused fireworks without the noise.

He turned around and walked away from the lights. Whatever it was, he wanted no part of it. If someone was getting murdered in an impressive array of fireworks, he didn't care. Besides, even if he did get involved, he'd only end up killing someone, and get caught in an endless loop of violence and murder. That was the last thing he wanted. He continued on in the moonlight, the lights behind him ceasing. He crossed the bridge over the water, walking underneath some trees as he arrived at an intersection, and waited for the crosswalk. There was a large skyscraper in front of him, and a hotel, the dark side of the hotel with the only windows of the tenants. The entrance was on the other side. There were no lights here. The lights in the skyscraper were shut off as there was no one working on it this evening.

He heard the breath coming from some bush, someone with foul intentions. Unfortunately, this wasn't hatred. He sighed and turned to the bush. A man came out of the shadows. He could sense six other men coming out. The one in front of him with the bush pointed a pistol at him, it was a 9mm. The other six others had makeshift melee weapons. One of them a bat, the other a two-by-four. The others carried miscellaneous metal apparatuses such as a crowbar, a pipe, the other two had machetes. *I wonder where they got those from.*

"Empty your pockets!" The man with the pistole said.

Ted raised his eyebrows at him.

"Do you think this is a game! I'm not playin'! Empty your pockets! Or I will shoot you dead!" The man's hand was shaking. Ted knew the man never held a gun before in his life, especially holding it like that, he knew the pressure of the gun would never make their intended target. He said nothing. "Do you think I'm playin'?"

"You're not going to shoot me like that," Ted smiled at him. "Did you really intend on robbing me with such a shaky trigger finger? You're not fooling me, so if you would kindly let me be on my way—"

"Hit him!" the man with the gun said.

He could hear the scurrying footsteps coming from behind him. He laughed as the crowbar hit its mark, hitting Ted in the leg. He never reacted to it. He turned to the man who hit him and grinned at him, mocking the man, just as the moonlight mocks him.

"You see, I don't want to kill you. Don't turn me into that monster," Ted said.

"Again!" The man with the gun ordered, his voice shaking as if this was his first time trying to rob someone, or perhaps this man had robbed many people before—just not with a gun—and this was his first time encountering someone who didn't bother to budge to his demands, and even mocked him.

The man with the bat struck Ted in the side, and it sounded like some ribs were cracked. Ted shrugged it off and stepped forward. It was not his ribs, but the barrel was splintered. The man with the gun got his grip and pointed it at Ted, looking at him with hatred in his eyes.

"Oh, don't even bother looking at me like that." Ted's sneer changed, finally showing his teeth and mania and blood lust in his eyes. His eyes gaped open, "I know you don't have the stomach to handle raw brutality!"

Ted sprinted towards the man with the gun. The man opened fired; the silencer silenced the shots. Ted's eyes scanned the trajectory of the bullets, seeing each 9mm leaving its chamber, hearing the clicks from the gun, precisely knowing the moment each round would leave the barrel. Just like his prediction, the man didn't know how to shoot the gun. Ted followed his bullet lines to avoid being hit, and with a man as experienced as this gunman, there was no need to try to catch any of them. He heard the footsteps of the two running behind him, trying to stop them from getting their ringleader.

The gunman's face grimaced as he missed each shot. His eyes gaped open as his enemy came closer. The gun started clicking, as he tried to shoot a gun with an empty gun. The ejection port was pushed back, and the inside of it was smoking. He dropped the gun and stepped back; his face turned to that of a scared old man.

"I'm sorry. I was jo—"

"Fat chance, and you're too late!" Ted was right in front of him.

The warmth left the air, and everyone could feel it. His left fist and up to his arm revealed blue veins, glowing in the dark as they came to swing a haymaker, and with his right leg, he kicked around to the side. The gunman was spinning in a cartwheel in the air before hitting his head on the sidewalk. With his same leg, the blue veins appeared as he brought it down to the skull of the gunman, crushing it instantly, blood, and bone smeared on his shoe and the sidewalk.

He swiftly jerked to the side, turning around, missing a swing from the crowbar. The man with the bat swung at Ted again. He caught the splintered end with his now glowing hand. He kicked the man's elbow with his right food. *Crack!* The man's forearm broke, letting go of the bat. Ted swiftly moved the bat into his hands, turned it around and stabbed the man in the shin with it.

The crowbar came swinging again. Ted moved to the side to avoid it, and kicked the man hard with his left food, sending him into the street.

The two men with Machetes were close, swinging them in unison to either side of him, to cut him off from dodging to the side. Ted's eyes were still bright as his eyes looked closely at them. He moved off into the side, grabbing the machete from one of the hands, and stabbing the other with it, pulling it down until his guts spilled onto the ground. He took his now bloodied hands and pulled them around the other man's head and twisted it backwards.

He almost missed the other man with the crowbar, running up at him from the street. "You bastard! You killed them!"

He swung the crowbar many directions, furiously. Ted sighed as the man came in grabbing distance, he heard the disturbance in the air, of the crowbar parting it in front of him. Ted thought for, if only a moment, this could kill him, but then why should it? When everything else failed. His heart pumped blood to his head. He snarled at that man. He sidestepped, deflecting the crowbar. He heard the rev of an engine. His eyes scanned the street, seeing a parked car turn its light on. He ignored the car and returned a hateful glare at the man. *Death surrounds everything I touch.*

His left arm lit up with his grey veins. The crowbar swung downward, and Ted blocked it with his arm, and the man's arm was jerked back as the crowbar was vibrating violently in his hand until he dropped it. His eyes gaped open as Ted's hand seized him by the throat and lifted him up. The grey veins turned their color back to blue. The man could feel the strength of his fingers digging into his throat. He clawed at his hands to get free, but Ted's strength was beyond human.

The car's tired screeched. The man's life was fading. Ted's eyes shifted towards the car speeding its way to him. He snickered as the man's arms dropped down, lifelessly. He smiled, snickering at the car. "If you intend to run me over with that, you better be wearing your seatbelt!"

Ted's blue veins glowed from his hands, and into the corpse of the man who he now held. The veins entered the corpse, rapidly until the man was now nothing more than an extension of Ted's glowing hand.

The car sped towards him, the wheels moving round and round as it screeched, staining the pavement with its black rubber tires. He grinned as he thrust the corpse into the front of the car, crunching the hood, blood spattered everywhere. The car came to a screeching halt as the front of the car dented into the axel, sending both front tires spinning off. The crunching metal filled the air as innumerous shards of glass started falling in the air like sweet, bloody snowflakes as the driver, a woman with a brown ponytail ejected through the windshield.

Ted caught her neck with his right hand, now glowing as he let the other man fall from his grasp. The car flipped over him, and crashed into the highway, slowly scrapping and sparking down the pavement, followed by a trail of streaming gasoline.

The woman was still conscious, still out of shock she tried to grab hold of his hands to release herself. There was nothing she could do. The veins entered his right hand again, pushing itself into her neck. He squeezed her neck tighter, she tried to cry out, but her windpipes were crushed, and she could feel the man's grip touch her spine. Her eyes started gaping open as her mouth desperately tried to scream. It was a screamless night.

There was one man left, too scared to scream, too horrified to run. His eyes gaped open as he tried to pull out the splintered bat from his leg. He grunted because he wanted to help his driver, but there was no way to help her, not against *that!*

Crack. Buckle.

Her arms and legs fell lifelessly. He squeezed her neck tighter until her eyes were pushed out of her sockets, hanging on by its retina. He threw her to the side, and she rolled over like a ragdoll. He started laughing, with blood on his hands and feet, he was laughing. Like this was fun for him. Whoever they were, they picked the wrong man to try to rob.

"That was oddly therapeutic," Ted said, smiling up to the empty sky. "I should probably be doing this more often," He turned to look at the petrified survivor. "Whenever you find a man filled with murder in his heart, you stand aside."

Ted's shoes lit up with his veins and he sprinted through Seaport Blvd at an inhumane pace. The man blinked and he was gone.

Chapter 13 Rogue

~Even a corpse is a witness.

***

Ilya sighed in the darkness, hiding behind a shipping container over on Black Falcon Pier. Her hand was on her chest, puffing in and out, inhaling heavily. Her face was cut by the Threckets claws when she got too close. She turned her head right around the corner of the black container, looking at the threcket, which was the size of a house. Its mouth was like that of a boar, and the twisted snout of a deer, its antlers protruding out of its forehead. The four legs were thin, just like a deer's, and had hooves. The arms were the most diverse out of them all, one pair of arms were the paws and claws of a raging dire wolf; another the size and width of a troll, another set of arms had bear arms, and the final set of arms were covered in scales, and the claw was what one might imagine a dragon would have if they existed, but they don't. This threcket also had a tail, long and flexible like a snake, and when it whipped through the air, it summoned lightning in the air.

Ilya looked at one of the other shipping containers, Alexander stood upon it, his bow in hand. His many green arrows pierced the Threcket's hide. The green arrows began to fade, turning into small green ashes as they fell into the sky. Her gaze turned to Culain, who wiped blood from his lip, his black spear impaled the beast. Blanka's mana veins covered her chains as they held down the threcket, keeping the creature still. It was dead, and they were only able to react as quickly to this due to Ilya's teleportation circles. A personal victory, but it would wake people up with the sudden chills to their bodies at night.

"Ilya," Said Culain.

These threckets had a nasty habit of not staying dead.

"Right," She nodded as she came out from behind the container. Taking her knife from her side; the knife glowed a mystic purple. She cut runes into the air, as if she was cutting the flesh of reality itself to create

158

these runes, which hovered in the air until she was finished. Her body was slowly covered in purple veins, and she pushed her mana into the runes, which glided towards the beast.

The bright purple runes covered the beast. The bright lights emitting from the runes forced Alexander, Blanka, and Culain to shield their eyes. "Cu'er na vorgen. Cha. Lathuka prath'haken!" Ilya chanted, closing her eyes as the purple veins entered her pupils. The mana streams from the creature looked like massive multicolored rays of sunlight, the air around her turned crimson. Her mana started streaming out like tentacles, reaching for the mana source for the creature, weaving themselves around the different arrays of light. Her mana streamed into the runes imbedded into the creature. Culain could see the massive concentration of mana being attached to her from the beast.

Ilya was pulling all the life force of this beast into her and harmonized it with her own. The runes, she felt, pushed themselves into the corpse of the hybrid of animals, and the first layer of skin ripped off, and was pulled into the sky, burning away as the source of mana was stripped away from it.

The corpse was being violently stripped away of its mana, the muscles themselves being burned into the air as the mana that held it together was yanked into Ilya. Her eyes glowed as she jerked the mana from the organs and the blood started boiling down to nothing as the mana stream turned crimson. The marrow of the bones was being pulled apart, and the bones cracked like splinters, fading into the ground as the last of its white mana yanked into Ilya.

There was now no evidence the creature was here.

Ilya's mana veins faded into her flesh; her vision returned to normal. Culain picked up his spear from the ground. He looked up at Alexander who nodded, holding his bow that now de-materialized, fading blue lights rose in the air as it became nothing. Blanka's chains faded, and Culain's black spear faded into the darkness.

"Ilya," Culain began. "Did you catch its mana location?"

"No. It faded during all of that. There's no indication of where it came from," she answered, weeping in the moonlight. She took a heavy breath as the mana she absorbed was heavy in her chest, like she was heavily saturated. Absorbing a creation of the dark's mana was almost never a good idea unless a fae could expel the mana. She knew it was like poison to her, "Cutha krevorthen era," The air around her turned black, obscuring her. The black cursed mana faded into the air. Her mana veins bubbled up to the surface. She let out a deep sigh and continued to breath heavily.

Culain sprinted to her. He helped her stand up as the amount of energy needed to expel the demon's mana from her system was significant.

"The—there has to be a better way," She coughed up blood into her hand.

"I wish there was," He said, "But this is it."

Alexander fixed his eyes upon something in the distance.

"What is it?" Blanka asked. She gazed in the same direction.

"Someone's getting robbed," Alexander answered.

"Not our business, not our problem. Let the poor fool die or get mugged. He shouldn't have been out this late anyway," Culain said coldly.

"Wait," Ilya said. Her mana veins turned red, and her vision expanded. Her eyesight went towards Downtown Boston. Her vision looked like it was blurring everything as her mind's eye passed through the streets. She saw a car crash, and now seven dead people. But she could also see red and blue mana streams, just floating into footsteps all over that area, over by intersection, "I see a mana pool."

Alexander's eyebrow raised. "Culain, is there anyone else out of the Boston's Administration supposed to be out tonight?"

"No," Culain admitted. "Let's get over there. Find out what happened. If a fae is involved, he should have cleaned up the mess. Now we have to do it."

Ilya's entire body shivered. *Well, at least I can harvest pure mana instead of that diseased shit.*

Ilya inhaled through her mana veins, now showing on her skin, covering her from head to toe. The mana source from the air, rushed through her body immediately, turning the mana bright blue, and it glimmered in the moonlight. This mana was in its purest form, from the air, without any artificial tampering. Mana from the air strengthened the muscles in her body, allowing her to push off the ground, and sprint off at speeds like a speeding car. Weaving past cars and street signs, her vision blurred. With each step on the street, the impact sounded like a clap of thunder in this silence, but she knew her senses were heightened, and to a normie, they would hear nothing.

They relaxed their mana veins, fading back into their skin as they got to the bridge, briskly walked over the bridge, looking at the carnage before them. Culain was the first one running at a normal pace, getting to the intersection. Ilya was right behind him, and she saw the totaled car, blood streaming on the streets, guts littering the nearby tree, and bone fragments scattered all over the place. *This is brutal. Unnecessarily so.* The rest of her team was not far behind them.

Ilya looked around, and they saw one of the bodies, with a bat still protruding into his leg. The leg was bent out of shape, as if damaged by something else other than the bat. His leg appeared to have three joints, instead of one: one at the knee, the other where the leg impaled his shin, and halfway up his thigh. His body was shaking, and his hands were dropped down. His eyes were opened wide as if he saw a ghost. Ilya went over to him, waving her small hands in front of him to see if his pupils would follow.

He remained silent.

Culain squatted right in front of him and pulled out a badge. BPD. "My name is officer Culain. This is the part where you tell me exactly what you saw. Speak quickly."

The man was quiet.

"What's your name, kid?" Culain said. He turned to Ilya, "Give him some space."

Ilya moved away. Alexander surveyed the carnage. Blanka drew circles filled with triangles in the pavement with a *mana* pen. Ilya knew what Blanka was doing, after all, there was going to be a lot of screaming soon. Once Blanka finished with one shape, she moved to another location to draw another circle. And another. And another. This was going to silence everything around them, as if the air and time itself remained still.

"Ja—Jamal," He stammered.

"Jamal," Culain spoke softly. "What happened here?"

"We were desperate, we were going to rob someone," He began. "I'm sorry. I know it's wrong but, but the man we tried to rob; he was a devil! His eyes glowed like that of some evil faerie! His arms were strong, and he was fast. He was faster than any man I've ever seen. Even—even when he was run over by a car, he left unscathed, almost like he was a boulder. He killed everyone. Everyone."

"What did he look like?"

"He was white, maybe just five-and-a-half feet tall, average build, scars on his face, and moppy brown hair I think," He replied. "He was always smiling."

"I see," Culain said, "Ilya, help me take this bat out of him."

She nodded. She held Jamal's hand as Culain ripped the bat out. The man grinded his teeth together, sucking the air through his teeth as he tried to stifle a cry. Culain pulled the bat out. And dropped it to his side. He stood up and leaned against a tree which had blood smeared on its side. He gazed up at the sky with his stern look as if condemning the moon for its very existence.

"Blanka—" he began.

"Already done. No one can hear us," she said, her silver hair shimmered behind her as she looked towards Jamal. Her blue eyes glazed over.

Culain could see the mana magenta lights creating a box around them, something only a fae would see.

Ilya helped Jamal up to his feet. He was still in a mode of shock, arms trembling at his side, and he blankly stared at the ground with those wide gaping eyes. *Cruel. A world like this, with people like that, wrapped up by people like us.*

"Ilya?" he asked. He never looked to her.

"Yes, Culain?" she replied.

"I need you to find out what our mysterious person looks like. You don't have to kill the kid. I will. I don't want your hands stained more than mine." This he whispered in her ear.

"I understand," She walked to Jamal and smirked to him. "Take my hand."

Jamal, being emotionally rattled by it all, he didn't hear Culain. After all, they've done nothing but help him at this point, take the bat out, help him to his feet. He took her hand.

Jamal felt her warm hands wrapping right over his. She had a beautiful grin, but her eyes were swollen, and watery. She closed her eyes, and with a forced smile, he could tell she didn't want to do this. But what was *this*? His eyes stretched open as the air around him turned ice cold, hair on his arms standing on ends, and goosebumps covered his arms. This woman had veins over her body, black and purple lights flared on his hands. He wanted nothing but to be free of her, but with his leg, he wouldn't get far, and the air around him seemed frozen in place. He physically couldn't move. The veins on her hand crawled on his and crawled their way up his arm to his shoulders. These veins to him, felt like worms crawling on him, and burying themselves in his skin.

The veins burrowed, connecting their nerves to Jamal's circulatory veins, sending messages throughout his body. The veins carried those messages to the brain, connecting Ilya's veins to Jamal's amygdala, feeding Ilya his most recent memories, specifically what caused him to be so frightened. That is where this memory would be.

Jamal felt violated, and insecure. His pupils rattled inside the whites of his eyes, pinning back and forth, feeling the worm-like veins crawl over his entire body, and invaded his internal systems. He felt the veins wiggling through his body and felt sharp pains throughout his body where the veins were: Spine, heart, chest, the bones, neck, and finally his brain, producing a severe migraine. Finally, he was able to scream, and from the look on the woman's face, it seemed the scream was sharply unexpected, and scratched her ears.

Her veins retracted from him, and receded back to her own body, and within a few moments of her heavy breathing, the veins completely faded back into her skin and the warmth returned to the air. Jama's body trembled, leaning heavily against the tree, coughing. Jamal covered his mouth as he felt something coming up from his stomach. Coughing, blood spurted out of the hand he covered his mouth with.

"Do you know what he looks like?" Culain asked.

"Yes," Ilya answered. She looked with a concerned face to Jamal. *It won't be long before mana sickness kicks in. You have one week, and the mana will kill you.*

"Good," Culain sighed.

There was a wind that moved through the air as Culain looked Jamal in the face. Then Ilya looked away from Jamal and towards Culain, whose hand was outstretched to his side as if he was holding something, and in his hand materialized his black spear with the elongated red spearhead. Alexander lit a match and dropped it on the stream of flames, lighting the stream up as it moved rapidly towards the car in the middle of the street.

"Sorry Kid. No witnesses, besides, you don't want to die by radiation sickness," Culain glared at Jamal. "Caster's rules. You aren't permitted to see our shenanigans. Honestly, I wish there was another way."

"Wh—why?" Jamal whimpered, stumbling backwards over the curb. He quickly stood back up, carefully watching Culain, and he looked like a cornered rat without a hole to scurry off in, "Please don't kill me! I'm sorry! Since when was robbing someone an executable offense?"

"You are nothing, but lambs sent to be slaughtered!" Culain's face cringed as his mouth opened. The Spear came at Jamal faster than a speeding train, piercing his heart, and protruding out of his back. Culain retracted the spear back out, tearing through more flesh, blood sprayed everywhere. "Besides, you don't want to be alive when Ilya absorbs your life force. Trust me, that is worse than what you've just been through. Nothing is louder than having the world erase you from existence!"

Jamal's eyes opened as he felt his life coming to a close. His eyes felt heavy, and his vision was blurry before he fell to the ground, clutching his chest where his heart used to be. He bled on the ground. He looked up to the man who brought his life to a close, his vision blurred until only darkness remained.

Ilya grimaced as she pulled out her knife. She drew the purple runes in the air again. Her body was covered yet again in mana veins. "Cu'er na vorgen. Cha. Lathuka prath'haken," She pushed her mana streams out as the normal mana streams of human flesh, organs, blood, and bone was slowly burned away by her own mana. These bodies soon faded away into nothing as their mana entered Ilya's Mana reserves.

She let out a sigh of relief and let out a sneer. She felt refreshed as if she had just drank a nice cold glass of water. She smiled as she clasped her own chest. Blanka removed the shapes she drew around them, and the purple barrier vanished. Time and space returned to normal, and there was not one trace of mana left, no evidence there was a crime, for the oil and gasoline were burned away. Ilya converted the wreckage and glass into mana, which she then drank through her mana veins again.

"They say that dead men tell no tales. That's a boldfaced lie," Culain said to himself. "The reality is this, there is no witness more reliable than a corpse."

Chapter 14 The Holy Grail

~Why do you want my friendship? There isn't a point in a life like mine.

***

Sarah patrolled the empty streets of London with Bridgette. It was early in the morning, where the only people they would see at night, would be the bobbies patrolling the streets or driving around in their ugly cars, or the occasional disgusting mistress of the night, or conman dealing with illegal deals. *Such worthless creatures. They aren't worth saving.*

Bridgette was quiet tonight, a nice change of pace as Sarah was getting rather annoyed with her constant talking and yappering. In many ways, she reminded Sarah of the new girl playing in the little sandbox, trying to make friends with everyone, and everyone returned the felicity; however, they all secretly hated her. In this case, she knew why people hated Bridgette, she was an ass to everyone she encountered. Well, there was no helping it, she was stuck with her until her task was done. She was here for some time, and she knew that it was only a matter of time before someone might catch hold of their ruse, but she couldn't leave without completing the task of stealing the grail, damn brits. But she needed an opportunity to get down to the Archive's basement, and it wasn't like an opportunity would just reveal itself. She had to make one, but how? She turned her attention back to Bridgette. Bridgette's snarled, baring her teeth as she walked.

"You seem quiet tonight. Why? Do you feel uneasy?" Sarah asked, trying to seem sympathetic, but she didn't honestly care.

Bridgette let out a sigh as she gazed at the bare moon, with the few stars to accompany the black sky, filled with nothing but the void inside her heart. The perpetual black stain of the world caused by someone's careless opening of the pandora's box perpetuated the foul stench of humanity, and demonology, nothing sits right in the world. "I'm jaded, I suppose. I am exhausted, much like everyone else, and much like you. I feel like a blanket with too few stitches, there are holes in it, and it easily comes apart. Every fae you see feels the same way, and those that strive to get away with it, by breaking through the code are immediately put down. We put them down, you see, for the fabric of the world would come undone if all this information we held made it to the rest of the world. There was one time where it all came close."

McCurdy knew her history quite well, had to for her job, and to be as efficient as she was in many aspects of her job. There were certain problematic incidents in world history which, if required, the Caster's Administration took no issue with escalating to ensure the proper people were killed. Even if that was to say, a certain artifact was to find themselves in the hands of these dreadful normies. Bastardly creatures. They had no one to blame but themselves for their worthless meaningless existence. This world, she continued to think, was worthless, and all the souls in it. Would it be a horrid thing, really, to contemplate killing God? After all, if He was dead, could His heart break anymore? No. Perhaps maybe, just maybe, it to prevent everyone's hearts from breaking another time, to kill any and all things would be necessary. The world might thank someone for the undertaking; however, there'd be no world left.

"Is it worth it?" McCurdy found herself wondering. The world she knew was abundantly different than the one her classmates from elementary school knew. She began to wonder if unraveling the fabrics of creation would ultimately be a better solution than continue on a living death; in doing so, God's heart would truly be broken.

"I don't know if I think it's worth it or not. I think so, or maybe that's just the lie I keep telling myself. Makes it easier," Bridgette replied. "But I'd be lying. I don't think it is, but I keep doing it. I keep obeying these orders for the hopes of preserving creation, sometimes I think it's better just to let it burn, hell, maybe we should light the match ourselves." McCurdy opened her eyes. She didn't think anyone would openly say that, but even she believed it. "Ah, that's just me talking. Pay it no mind."

"We were never told any of this at the American Branch," she lied.

"Because you are all fools," Bridgette replied, looking back into the distance. "Americans don't spend time learning everything that is important, where you come from. You are all hypocrites."

"I'd say that's hardly fair, and misguided."

"Maybe I'm wrong, or perhaps you're wrong. Be that as it may, we can never accept—"

McCurdy felt the wind abruptly change direction. She felt chills as the temperature around her dropped, her hair standing on ends. She felt the mana in the air being pulled on a singular focal point in front of them. The wind churned again from another direction, spiraling up with heavy winds, McCurdy felt like she was in the eye of the storm. McCurdy turned around swiftly, jumped off to sidewalk, away from the spinning vortex. Bridgette stood by, glaring at the center of the vortex, the wind whistled in the air that the moisture in the air turned into razor sharp ice blades.

Bridgette glared dispassionately as her hand reached out. Her blue mana veins glowed throughout her body, channeling the mana from the air into her hand, materializing a broadsword. The blue veins crawled from her arm, encapsulating the blade she held in the air.

A flash of lightning ripped through the ground, and then a clap of thunder roared. In the ground was now a hole, a chasm opened with freezing wind pushing up from it, pulling Sarah's hair away from her face. She pulled her hat down as she gazed into the abyss. She took a deep breath and pulled all the cold mana from the air into her mana veins. Her body was glowing blue, like Bridgette's, and she held her hand to the left of her, and her spear manifested into her hand.

A second flash of lightning struck the ground they stood upon, followed by another clap of thunder. This lightning was blacker than the hole that seemed to completely empty inside, and with no end in sight. The rocks of the crust of the earth swirled around in the large vortex, making the hole larger with every passing moment.

Sarah investigated the hole, and then back at Bridgette, who seemed still dispassionate. A Third strike of lightning rained down on them, and lightning seemed to be emitting from the hole in the ground, as the bottom of said hole was now producing vast amounts of lightning.

She took a deep breath as there was a loud hissing noise coming in from the hole. She looked down, and she saw a vast mass of shimmering scaley light at the end of the tunnel. She looked closely and it was a large mass of snakes, curled up in a large sphere, rolling down the tunnel as if gravity was working on the other side of it. The hissing continued.

"Get away from the hole!" Bridgette called out.

The sphere picked up momentum, vibrating inside the hole, releasing various rocks and debris from the crust of the earth. Sarah jumped away from the hole, pointing her spear at the epicenter. Bridgette was muttering something underneath her breath. Sarah pulled in the mana into her eyes, observing the mana streams Bridgette was casting. The streams of mana, brown, grey, silver, blue, green wove together like a basket, marking many runes into the air.

The sphere of snakes crossed the threshold of the portal into Pandora, hissing. Sarah pushed her fear behind her, as it came rolling towards her. She firmly planted her spear in the ground, her mana veins turning silver as they started wrapping around her spear. The sphere rolled onto the spear, and she thrust upwards as her mana veins turned silver, pulling the mana from the poor quality of the essence from the minerals in the earth. It wasn't ideal to be using concrete for that, but it was something.

The hissing became like that of a bell tower, and numerous streams of yellow mana from Bridgette's mana source shot out like a beam into the sphere, ripping apart several snakes, casting them aside as they withered like dying plants.

"Don't look into their eyes! That is a Medusa! Don't look into their eyes. The Greeks got that myth right, although only partially. Their gaze will turn you into dust!" Bridgette pointed her sword at her.

Another creature came out of the hole that Sarah could see out of the corner of her eye, and the creature, was a black form with the body of an abnormally large man, and a horse's head. The beast, whatever this one was called was the size of a small house, and certainly very agile. Bridgette struck its arm, and it *clinked*. Her blue mana veins penetrated her sword and struck through the arm, slicing it off, and the beast squealed as its blood sprayed.

Another source of black lightning struck the earth over into the next block. Sarah pushed off from the sphere, ducking behind a street sign. Medusa, the great humanoid snake like creature, completely manifested from slithering serpents threw a small serpent at Sarah, who stabbed it with her spear. She noticed at the corner of her eye, another creature coming out of the hole. She couldn't tell what this one looked like.

"Sarah! Get back to the administration and wake everyone up. We have a Portal Storm on our hands!"

"What about y—"

"I'll be fine, but this is beyond anything you and I can handle by ourselves!" Bridgette asserted. "I can hold the three of them for a time, I can't handle any more than that. I don't know how useful you are yet, but two fae can't handle a Portal Storm!"

Sarah nodded before slicing at the Medusa with her spear, ripping through its flesh, spraying its green blood on the ground. She inhaled the mana from the air through her mana veins, and her entire body was covered in them. With a jump, she landed onto the roof of a building, and started running across the buildings, thinking to herself, *this is strangely convenient.*

Bridgette looked at the blue streams of light moving across the sky. She dropped a stone on the ground and jumped away from the horse beast: the humanoid creature with flesh decayed, and the side of its mouth was exposed. She judged a large hand with a claw, ripping up the concrete, making obnoxiously loud noises as the various rocks and stones struck nearby buildings.

Why such a heavily populated area, and why here of all places! There is no way they can keep this hidden. We're going to have to kill a lot of people tonight.

This other creature flew above her. She penetrated the sword with her blue mana veins as she jumped up, cleaving its left wing. Red blood sprayed as the wing came off, the creature crashed into the building behind her, collapsing the roof, and killed the people inside. Her heart filled with dismay as Medusa came over to her and especially since she started to see lights get turned on. *A lot of people are going to die tonight.*

Medusa tossed a snake at her. She closed her eyes, moving away, and she felt a pinch in her arm. . .

Sarah pushed the door open into the Administration building. There were few people inside the initial threshold into the office, minus the receptionist. There were some others enjoying a cup of tea who immediately turned their heads with alarm as door swung opened violently, nearly pulled off its hinges. The receptionist immediately stood up and glared at her.

"Portal Storm. We have a Portal Storm!" She pointed her spear outside.

The receptionist's eyes gaped open and immediately picked up the phone. She pressed a button and dialed a number. As her phone rang, she opened her drawer. "Administrator," she said. "We have a Portal Storm. Yes. Understood."

The people in the office immediately gulped down their tea, leaving the cups on the tables in the lounge area of the vestibule, and turned, walking to Sarah. "American. Where?" the man asked. He was stern, tall, and menacing, well, to anyone else, but not Sarah. He had scars on his face.

"Corner of Sanford and Edward street," she immediately answered. "Bridgette was there."

Click!

The lights in the room turned red, and a machine in the corner started emitting silent waves of mana, completely undetectable to the normal human, who at this point in history would still see magic as nothing more than a fairytale. There was too much mana interference to communicate through normal means right now, especially during a Portal Storm.

The man took the others in the room and ran out the door, sprinting in the direction of Sanford and Edward Street, London.

She could hear the rattling coming from behind the corridors of the administration building. Administrator Sander came running out, with about fifteen other fae behind him, their mana veins already breathing the air, blue lights flashed as they sprinted down the halls. Sander stopped to look into her eyes as a man who had seen far too many battles. His shoulders were broad, and his eyes angled down his nose as he looked into her. "McCurdy, did you report this in?"

"Yes, administrator," she replied, looking intently into his eyes. "It's at the corner of Sanford and Edward Street."

"Well, one of the portals anyhow. With me. We need to get down to it," He immediately turned to the receptionist. "Melissa, call in help from Cambridge. We need to put a stifle on this immediately. Operation Black Light."

"Lead the way Caster!" shouted one of the irritable women in the back, wiping sleep from her eyes, tied behind her with bangs hanging on either side of her face.

McCurdy nodded her head and sprinted out the door. The Administrator and the fae followed behind her, blue mana veins lit up the streets as they sprinted through them, over buildings and across alleys, keeping eye on the blue shining lights and the lightning Portal Storm looming not far ahead of them. McCurdy thought to herself, *a lot of innocent people are going to die tonight, by accident or demon food, however, more people are going to be killed by the administration itself for witnessing such a thing while the rest of the fae halt time to clean up the mess.* She grimaced at the thought as she led them closer to the Portal Storm. *It is sickening. There must be a better way than to kill those we are made to protect. There must be a better way. But be that as it may, the Casters Administration building is now empty, guarded only by a mere receptionist. Fae from Cambridge are sure to come by and trying to clean up the mess is going to be damn near impossible to do over night. This is far too convenient to my liking. Colton, did you plan this?*

Bridgette was nowhere to be found amidst all the shining lights of blue, green, red and blinding white. There were a handful of fae about, and an innumerous amount of these creatures, pouring through the cracks of the earth. All the lights were on in all the buildings, and some sirens poured out with ambulances, bobby's, and fire trucks, which didn't last long without being torn to shreds.

Sarah saw the carnage. Flames roared, buildings collapsed, bodies crushed and bled out into the sewers.

Children and babies cried as their parents ran with them in their arms, without a moment to think about what they saw. Their flight response moved them away from collapsing buildings, and exploding cars, and flying debris.

To her horror, but not to her surprise, there was an archer, his blond hair was filled with dirt, and his eyes were focused. One might think he was a trained killer, had it not been the tears and hesitation in his eyes. He followed protocol, as only he could, the one archer on the field, taking his mana infused arrows, shining through running men, women, and their children. He sprinted off the buildings he used for his vantage point. One after another, he killed these innocent people. The arrows pierced his targets every time, never missing his shot, and the corpses of the dead bubbled as their life force faded into burning ash. But she noticed it wasn't just this archer killing normies. There were a few more archers patrolling the streets of London, with the sole purpose of killing normies while Sanders and the rest of the fae were dealing with these portals and house-sized threckets.

Their life force was then imbibed by surrounding fae approaching the scene, using the mana to slay these demons, and creatures coming up from these portals from the *other side*.

The fae she was with went on without her. Jumping from the streets to the buildings, summoning their weapons: chains, spears, lances, swords, and axes to their hands as they moved down on the portals. Another class of fae came out, the *Casters* which were few and far between, and exceptionally dangerous. They took their mana infused knives and drew runes at the sides of the portals, screaming incantations.

They left her by herself. *This is too convenient. Or the UK branch is very stupid.*

She drank the mana from the air, and the bright blue veins crawled up her legs as she sprinted back towards the administration building. She looked behind her, saw flares of red, white, green, blue, and black lights. The demons roared, buildings and cars exploded, and more people died. Most of who, she was sure, just got the short end of the stick, as most of them, were not killed by these demons, but of that cursed archer. And there he was again, erasing all proof of their miserable existence. All those fae were far too occupied to be dealing with her, and she knew it, and she was skeptical. Because this was all *too* convenient.

She arrived at the building. She sprinted through the doors. The receptionist looked at her with a surprised look. The receptionist's eyes opened, reaching for a button underneath the counter. Sarah grimaced as she threw her spear into the receptionist's head. She fell silent, dead, her body going as still as a limp fish as she was impaled against the wall behind her. The blade sawed its way through her skull and collapsed to the ground, the blood leaked out of her skull onto the floor.

Sarah yanked the spear from the wall with her hand, she pulled in mana from the air, weaving it with mana from the wood in the table, and the glass from the mugs, and her veins protruded from her flesh, crawling onto her spear as it faded away. She ran down the hall towards the library of archives. She broke right in without ease and ran down the stairs. She ran down several flights of stairs until she came to a large square room, filled with various artifacts, but she came here for one thing only. And she found herself looking at it, the Holy Grail, fused with the purple welding to the box of Pandora. The grail, it was this beautiful object, golden, with silver lettering in the old Anglo-Saxon language, a language that was dead, but there was just something so beautiful about it. The silver writing appeared to glow, as they were carved by the Holy Hand of King Arthur Pendragon himself, or that is how the old stories were truly told. King Arthur, how shamed would he be if he saw the state of the world today, or even the wretched treachery of his Beloved Caster's Administration. But the box, pandora's box, the cursed wretched thing was so infused to the Holy Grail that it was beyond separation. She cautiously walked over to the grail, to touch it, but a searing pain filled her wrist.

She hissed, retracting her hand as she moved to the side, observing the runes implanted in the ceiling above the Holy Grail. *Should've known.* She placed her hand out at the ceiling, her fingertips were spread as she imbibed the mana from the air. She then took another drink of mana, pulling it from the steel and concrete of the floors and foundations. Her arm was covered in concentrated mana of red, violet, and magenta colors swirling around her arms. Colored runes swirled around her body, pulling mana from the room from various sources into her body. Her eyes glowed red, fueled with complete passion, complete hatred as the mana veins penetrated her pupils, "Geinseglian Liesing!"

The light emitting from the ceiling faded, and the contents of the Holy Grail was revealed. The liquid inside should have at one point been golden, but as it was infused with the box of Pandora, the content was filled with purple smoke, filled with nothing but curses. The same force that created this cruel world and all its malformities. She took her hand and grabbed the Holy Grail, and the Box of Pandora and sprinted upstairs.

She ran through the archives and out the main hallway. To her surprise, pleasantly, no one was here. *They should have dealt with the Portal Storm in its entirety by now.* She scoffed as she sprinted to her quarters. She immediately grabbed her bag and put the grail inside it. She strapped it to herself before facing the wall. She drank the mana from the air, the bars, the floor and the foundation as the mana veins flowed through her body again. She approached the back wall and placed her hands on it. The veins glowed black this time as her entire body was covered in black mana, and she phased through the wall.

Three hours later, Bridgette was leaning against a building, her sword dematerialized now that all of the threckets were slain, and portals were closed. She breathed heavily, covering her left eye with her hands. The rest of the administration was searching the now abandoned buildings for surviving normies. If anyone was found, and might be savable, they were killed immediately. All part of the damn dreaded code.

"Still alive?" She heard a voice from above her. He jumped down from the rooftop.

"Unfortunately," she answered. "Did anything happen to McCurdy?"

"I did a brief roll call, and everyone is accounted for, except her," he said. "I went back to the office, and I'm just coming back now. Melissa is dead, and it turns out, someone went into the archives, and the Holy Grail is missing."

"You think she did it, don't you?" Bridgette asked.

"Everyone else is accounted for. The threckets wouldn't dare look for it there," he replied.

Bridgette stared at him like that was the dumbest thing she's heard. "What would she even want with it?"

"What would who want with it would be the better question," Sanders replied. "This was all too convenient. Someone was behind the portal storms, and that someone in all likelihood knew what McCurdy was here—"

Cough. Cough.

Bridgette gasped, gazing over some rubble. Some rocks moved and a little hand stretched out, attached to a little boy. The boy cried, "Help me. Momma! Momma! Papa!" he kept weeping. Bridgette knew the boy's legs were crushed underneath the weight of all that rock, and a weight filled her chest, because this was all too familiar. She knew what needed to happen next.

Sanders placed his hand over the boy's head. Magenta mana veins covered his hand as the boy lay dead, a quiet death, and a simple one. Bridgette looked at the boy, a mop covered head, dirty face, and a face that the worst of mothers would love. She knew he was dead and knew that the way Sanders killed him was painless, and that was a mercy. *But why is this even necessary?*

She started weeping, sliding down to the ground, burying her face in her hands, "Sanders, there has to be another way."

"Do you think all I do is send you all out to fight these threckets and erase evidence? No. I'm researching for a better way. The problem is, I have a theory, and am ultimately disappointed. I end up in dead ends of things that have already been tried," he sat down next to her. "I've ran out of ideas. Everything's been tried already."

Chapter 15 Façade

~As everything fades, the music, the laughter; the smile, the bandage; the makeup and the masks, once it is all removed, we find out for ourselves that we were never okay.

***

Two weeks later, in the middle of June, Samantha, Erin, Jennifer, Tim, and Michael were back at Park Street, on that same Tuesday night, walking upwards of Park Street, taking a right on Beacon street. They all had umbrellas, some were small, and others were wide, colorful, or plain black.

The air was cooler when the breeze passed through their clothes, caressed their bare, exposed skin. The rain was falling down ever so lightly, as if the heavens were undecided if it wanted to rain, the *drip drop* landed into puddles in the sidewalks and streets as cars were driving by, their wheels spinning out water, drenched unsuspecting pedestrians too careless to bring an umbrella.

As Samantha was leading the study this night, she couldn't help but think she might find Ted at Teri Nation. He wasn't there last week, according to Scott, and seemed to avoid them the week before that. She also noticed that Jennifer seemed a little down today, not her usual self. Truth is, Samantha hasn't seen Jennifer at all since the game night she hosted two weeks ago. Samantha looked down to the ground at her feet, her shoes splashed in the small shallow puddles in the sidewalk.

Did something happen between him and Jennifer after we left? She thought.

She hurried up and hooked Jennifer's elbow, who seemed startled. Samantha saw something in Jennifer's eyes that she hadn't seen before, and it filled the air like a stench of regret. She should have known something was off, Jennifer wasn't her usual joking self, not these last two weeks, and the last time she saw Jennifer as herself was at the party, before she left her and Ted alone in the apartment. *He didn't try to hurt her, would he?*

"Hiii!" Jennifer exclaimed. Her face lit up with her bright smile again. "What brings you to my side on such a rainy night?"

Sam needed only to speak to her, and they were far away out of earshot from everyone else following them that night. Their conversation would be kept private.

"Well, I was thinking. I haven't seen Ted in a while. Have you heard of anything?" she asked.

Jennifer sighed through the rain, and sucked the air through her teeth, hissing. "I can't say I've heard from him," she answered, turning her head away from Sam. "I haven't heard from him since that night."

"Have you tried calling him again? Or texting?" Sam was suspicious and couldn't help but fight this feeling that Jennifer was hiding something.

"Yes," she answered. "I started getting abrupt responses again."

"What did he say?" The curve in Samantha's lips became less prominent.

"The last thing he told me, was that he wasn't someone I wanted to get close with. Whatever that means," She exhaled deeply, "Oh, well, nothing we can do about it, right?"

Jennifer's smile returned to her face, and the rain grew heavier, pounding her umbrella with such a tremendous force, as if handing its burden onto her. *Ted.* Samantha followed Jennifer through the bar, waving at Scott as they entered the rear part of the bar.

Jennifer immediately sat at the bar and took out her purse. Sam sat next to her. They were alone for the most part, the rest had yet to catch up to them. They did manage to see the four foreigners drinking to themselves in the corner again. She was not going to bother them tonight.

Scott asked Jennifer, "Having the special?"

"Not today, Scott," she answered, smiling at him. "I'm afraid I'm not in the mood for an adventure tonight. The House bourbon on the rocks is fine by me. Just for tonight."

"Who are you?" Sam asked, joking with her. "I'll take a merlot."

"Big spender, today aren't we?" Jennifer joked with a half-enthused grin.

"You could say that," Sam turned to Scott and slid her card across the table. "I'm buying today," Scott's eyebrows raised as he disappeared behind the bar top. Samantha turned back to Jennifer with a smirk. "I got my commission check last week. And you almost always buy my drinks, it's time I returned the favor."

"Why thank you so much!" Jennifer exclaimed.

Scott came by with the drinks in hand, including the receipt. Samantha immediately took the receipt and wrote in a generous tip. Scott eyes popped. "Thanks, Sam." He sped off to check on the foreigners.

"What's wrong," Sam asked.

Just then, a wave of people came in, flooding the bar. The noise came in like a rushing wave. Out of the corner of her eye, she could see the foreigners getting uncomfortable with the noise. The man called Culain sneered from across the room.

"Iah—" Jennifer began.

"Hey!" Michael's arm reached over Sam's shoulder. He waved down Scott. "I'll take the special."

Scott smiled back at him, "Whatever that is."

Michael looked down, smiling at everyone, until he noticed that Jennifer was *not* drinking a strange concoction, "Not feeling adventurous today?"

"Can't say that I'm up for an adventure," Jennifer smirked back at him as she took a sip from her rocks glass. "Maybe you can use this as an excuse to finally coerce Brian into drinking some of Scott's lovely aromas."

"But I like my drinking buddy," He jested but retained his sneer. "Oh well, maybe next week. I need to catch up with him anyways."

"Ta ta for now!" Jennifer laughed. But it was slightly lower than usual, as if somewhere between a reluctant laugh, or a forced one. Sam couldn't quite tell as Michael scurried off into the unusually larger than normal Tuesday night crowd. *Brian was real busy today.*

"So, Jennifer. What's wrong? I can tell when you're not yourself."

Jennifer grinned at her as she took another sip, "Why, nothing out of the ordinary."

"Jenn. You're laughs are half genuine. I can't tell if you're actually happy right now," she said, placing one of her hands atop hers on the bar top and looked her in the eyes. "You can pretend to borrow Ted's smile, as wide as it is, but they can't hide your laughs. You have unique laughs. I love your laughs. So, out with it, please. What's wrong?"

Jennifer let out a sigh and placed her drink on the counter of the bar. "It's Ted," she said. Her simper began to fade, and her eyes watered. "He showed me a part of him, a part that he kept hidden. He is not what he seems."

"Did he hurt you?" she exclaimed softly. "Don't—"

"What, no!" Jennifer corrected herself, turning abruptly to her, "Don't even mention the idea. He is not like that! He may not be what he seems, but he is far from a monster that would hurt someone in her own apartment!"

"What did he show you?" Sam brought her voice down low.

Sam looked into Jennifer's eyes, those cold, trembling eyes, glimmering in the bar as golden light reflected upon them, almost like the emission of little flames. "I saw nothing but agonizing pain. Just that. Pain, and nothing else. He is restless and suffers from what I can only imagine the most extreme form of insomnia I have ever heard of. He sleeps not more than thirty minutes a night. It's like he's hiding pain that just wants to get screamed out, but when he tries, he can't."

Sam remembered asking him a question that would allude to his insomnia. She recalled he would only give her vague few-worded answers that never really answered the question, rather, it alluded to the idea of an answer to the question that was satisfactory enough to remove any further cause of curiosity. *The man is mysterious, and a tough nut to crack.*

"We talked a little about peace, in our little conversation there. In there, I found that he does not hold any peace in his heart. He has never known a home. Or so he said. He has some siblings, but he talked almost as if they were just part of his past, and nothing of their relationship remained," She took another sip of her cup as it trembled in her hand. "A man like that, can truly exist, but the existence of his life brings nothing but pain to him."

"Do you think he's suicidal? Because if so, we need to get him help!" Her smile was gone.

"Someone once told me, 'The brightest smiles bring us the greatest of joys. The loudest laughter is like a grand orchestra, and the most beautiful faces are covered in makeup, because we are okay, and everything is fine. The brightest smile is like a bandage, it looks okay, but inside the wound still festers, asking to be cut off. They say laughter is the best medicine. And the mask is our way of making ourselves look more beautiful, to reduce our flaws and hide our scars. When the smiles fade away and the bandage is ripped off; when the laughter is silenced and the music stops, when the makeup is washed away, and our mask fades, we find that we were never truly okay.'" She ignored the question.

"Oh my god!" Sam's eyes gaped open wide as she covered her mouth with her hand. In the most obscure way, Jennifer answered the question with an anecdote to depression. She understood the imagery loud and clear, but Jennifer never actually said she believed Ted to be in danger of suicide.

"Iah. I just wished I thought of it sooner." Jenn said, her face went blank, as if staring at something that wasn't there.

"When was the last time you got a response from Ted?" Sam asked.

"Last Friday," she answered. She put the glass down. She buried her face in her hands. "Sam, if you would, leave me alone for a minute. I just can't. I can't." She choked on the last, "I can't".

Sam patted her shoulder. "If ever you need to talk," she found herself choking on her words. "You know I am here, and you know how to get in touch with me. You know this."

Samantha went into the crowd, searching for Erin. If anyone's had contact with Ted, it would be her, although Erin didn't seem to have any kind of relationship with Ted at all, Jennifer seemed to be the only one. *And she wasn't even the first of us to speak to him.*

Samantha caught sight of Erin's straight, brown hair, and walked up beside her, elbowing her. Erin looked at her as she was sipping from her cider. "Well," Erin said to her. "You almost made me spill by drink."

"I'm sorry," Sam hesitated. "I needed to ask you something. Has Ted been showing up at work at all?"

"Yes. Still the workaholic. What is it with you and Ted? Aren't you and Michael dating? And I thought Jenn had the hots for him." She turned in her stool and took another sip of her cider.

"Look, it's just that, it's just that he is new. I'm not romantically invested in him at all. Here he is in Boston, by himself, and doesn't seem to have any network of friends of family here. He comes off as a loner," Samantha replied. "Did *he* seem off to you?"

"I can't say that I have," Erin answered. "I mean, he comes around like clockwork. He moves around the clock always. His behavior doesn't really change."

"What about after Jennifer's apartment the week before?" she said.

"No," Erin scratched her chin.

Sam felt defeated, she was trying to piece who Ted was, and knowing now that Jennifer was emotionally invested in him, she felt a wave of concern fall upon her heart. Ted was like an already drawn on canvas, vibrant in colors, but the artist is unknown, and his strokes of the brush was unknown, hidden upon layers and layers of paint, layers of layers of different personalities, all competing for dominance on one painting.

"Wait," Erin said, her voice dropped a bit. "Actually, I suppose this was a little unusual. On that Monday, he seemed very energetic, more so than usual. It would have almost been like he got a good night sleep or something, or accidently inhaled some speed. That would have been cause for concern, but he immediately went to his typical self the next day. So, there wasn't much need for concern."

"I see."

"Did he disappear again?"

"I suppose you could say that."

"Look, Sam, a man like that sells himself to his work. For him, it's like nothing else matters or exists outside of it. Trust me when I say this, you may see him again, you may not. He may readily move across the country tomorrow if he thought to. He isn't the type of man to keep friends. At least, that's the vibe I get from him."

"That's a sad life to live," Sam's voice dropped.

"He seems satisfied with it, all the same," Erin sighed. "As much as I would love to have his level of success, I mean, that is a ton of money, I wouldn't trade my friends and family for it."

"Satisfied does not mean fulfilled," Sam reasoned, but what if he didn't want to be fulfilled?

"I don't think he wants a fulfilled life," Erin gave her rebuttal. "Look, people get into stocks to make money, and to make a lot of it. Ted, as far as I can tell, has never lost anything so far, his portfolio, and the portfolio of his clients grows exponentially. He doesn't seem happy with it, almost like he goes through the motions," She let out a deep sigh. "It's like, whatever he is going through, that he's just stopped caring. He doesn't seem to care about the money at all, and he's raking it in every single hour. My suggestion, if you don't see him again, is to just let it go. Just let him go."

"I see," Sam didn't feel like talking about this anymore. She was concerned, as if something was pulling at her heart, causing her to choke on a tear. "Thank you for that."

"Look, Sam, I'm sorry," Erin looked her closely in the eyes and put her free hand on her shoulder. "For what good it is worth, I completely agree with you, and I don't think it's a healthy path that he's walking on. And I don't know if this is going to help you get anywhere with him, but I asked him about that last big deal he brokered out, and why he didn't seem satisfied with it. It was because he knew the answer. It's like he wants to be wrong, almost as if there is one mistake in his life that led him to believe was inevitable, almost like being wrong would undo that mistake."

"Thank you for that, Erin. You gave me more than I could have hoped for," She smiled, but she couldn't say she felt happy about the answers she received tonight.

Samantha left Erin there as she continued whatever conversation she was having with Brian. She understood that Erin spoke from a place of matter of fact, and with little empathy. Of course, she meant well, and certainly no malice was ever intended, it didn't always come across that way, especially with this. She certainly was upfront about things, and blunter than Michael. Sam works with truck drivers; she should know how to deal with this by now.

She walked back over to the bar where Jennifer was. Her glass was empty, but her umbrella was still there, leaning just underneath the bar. Jennifer's coat was gone. *Maybe she got a call from Ted. That is highly unlikely at this point,* she sighed.

"So, did you finally make your rounds?" said a very smiling Michael.

"I did," Sam looked up to him. She finished her glass of wine. "I'm worried."

Michael's phone buzzed in his pocket. "Why are you worried?" he asked as he picked up his phone to read something he found enticing on the web.

"Ted. I feel like we made some headway with him, but—"

"You get the feeling he never showed us who he was and are now concerned that something might have happened to him. You are concerned because you feel like he was growing on us to the point where he would consider himself to be one of us?"

"Well, yeah," she said indignantly.

"I wish I could think like that." He laughed, and his face immediately went dark as he read the headline of a news article. "The reality is that we often don't know ourselves well enough to read into others, and we think we can read into others so easily. There are those who protect themselves with an unbreakable wall," He sighed. "Do you remember that philosophical question, 'what happens when an unstoppable lance meets an immovable shield'?"

"I remember the question. I don't remember the outcome," she admitted.

"The shield won. The lance shattered and its rider came tumbling down." He replied. "Look, some shields just can't be broken, and some walls won't come down, no matter how hard you smash against them. There is only one way through, and that is around that shield," he pointed his finger in the air with a half-raised hand and moved it in a circular motion, "hoping there is some kind of crack in there. You can only make it through the crack."

"So, in other words, pain," She came to the sudden realization, that only pain would make it through. She can only talk to Ted through pain, and that is the only thing he utterly understood. Or so she thought. She focused on Michael's phone, "So, what has your eyes so captivated when I'm right here?"

"The suicide rate just spiked up," He answered. "We are beating Japan."

"Great," Sam sighed, *and Ted might become a victim of that.* "As if the world didn't have enough problems. That is not something we need to be beating Japan in."

"I guess, in part it is our fault," Michael said.

"How do you mean?" She looked into his eyes with concern, her smile completely faded again.

"How busy are we? We constantly move and move and move, never slowing down for a second, never checking in on our own mental health. It is inevitable that we will follow the same road, down our own broken-down insanity. How many times do we see the same thing on the streets? How often do we turn our eyes against those who are struggling with their own strife, never lending out a hand?" He locked his phone and put it back in his pocket. "How many times have we seen someone, and not offered to help them? I'm guilty Sam. Every single day. I wish there was more than we could do in the world, you know, something that's more than giving someone a meal, more than giving them our spare change that we know we'll never use. Our spare change, is it really giving it to them? Or are we merely just discarding that which we think is already garbage? Our scraps, we have many, but to those who have nothing, to those born with nothing, those scraps are like mounds of gold, piled up. We, as Christians, need to be doing more than whatever it is we've been doing. Our inactivity is what is killing us inside. It's almost like every single one of us is living off borrowed time and we don't know it."

"Michael," Sam immediately thought of Ted again. "Do you think Ted is—is at risk?"

"I'm afraid I don't know him well enough to answer," He replied, shaking his head and this time his smile faded. "I feel the only one who may have some inkling of an idea of how he feels, is Jennifer. I don't have an answer."

"I'm going to go," she said, her face turned graven at the bar. She put the rest of her wine on the counter and left it.

"Do you need me to walk you to the T?"

"No," she answered. "I'll be fine. I just need to clear my head."

He smirked at her as she turned away, walking out of the back of the bar. She made it down the stairs and walked over the red carpet, being made aware of everyone around her, waitresses with artificial grins walking with empty glasses on their trays. The people in the pub were laughing with their smiles, without a care in the world.

Were they hurting somewhere, deep inside, Sam wondered, were they all patched up with those bandages, and were their laughs singing? Did they remember to wear their masks and put their makeup on?

She turned to ignore them. She continued down the hall, taking a left to the empty host stand and through the glass doors. She opened them and went outside; to her pleasant surprise, it stopped raining. She found the puddles in the ground as she saw Jennifer sitting on the side of the curb, her knees up to her chest and her head was buried in her hands, just like she left her. She was only in a different place not far away.

She sat down next to her; the puddle soaked her bottom as she wrapped her left arm around Jennifer. She said nothing. Jennifer raised her head, looking up at the top of the building in front of her. Her eyes were swollen as tears continued to stream down her face. She leaned into Samantha's shoulder. She tried to stifle her own sobs by intermittently sucking in the air through her teeth.

"Iah—I wish there was more I could do. I can't. I can't do it anymore!" she cried.

Sam's heart became heavy as she leaned her head against Jennifer's. She found herself weeping with her. She sniffed the boogers back into her nose. She offered no words, for she knew that for her friend, she needed not words, only an ear to listen to, a lost art in the world. Most people were quick to console their wounded friends with words, with the best of intent, they only pour salt on the wounds. Not Samantha. She was a listener. She listened, and offered no words of encouragement, for that would be undeniably worse than rubbing salt into a festered wound begging to be cut off. And *she* knew this.

"Why can't I be better?" Jennifer sobbed. "I know I'm not perfect, but I could stand to be a little better. A better person, perhaps if I was more like you, Sam, then perhaps Ted would still find it in his heart to come back to us. I saw—I saw pain, undeniable, unspeakable pain in his eyes. Eyes are like the door into the human heart, his human heart! That isn't something you can easily hide, at least—at least not for very long. Why must I talk so much, without much listening. Why couldn't I have been more like you, Sam?"

Sam rubbed her tears from her own face with her right palms, twisting the tears out. "Because then you wouldn't be you. My gift is listening, but you have something I don't have. Together, we are a complete person, our friendship is something that few can claim. You are a great observer, and you can see pain, where I can't. I just can't," she sobbed with her. "I can listen, but even I can't hear pain. Listening is only good when someone talks to you. But no one can hide from the eyes, no matter how hard they try."

"But if only I—"

"Jennifer. It is possible Ted only spoke to you because he knew you were a talker, and that I am a silent listener. He may not speak to me or open up to me. A man like that doesn't miss anything, not even the smallest detail will slip past him," She sighed. "I must be going, now, Jennifer," She stared at the empty puddles. "Look, God will make a way, even when the gates are completely closed. If God wants him, He will make a path for him to follow, to alleviate his pain."

"And if He doesn't?"

"Then I'm afraid we've done all we can, and all we can ask for," Sam took her hand and pulled Jennifer's head to hers, kissing her forehead. "Good night, Jennifer. We can offer prayer, that's all we can do now. It is out of our hands now. Come, let's get you home."

Home.

Samantha took her hand and pulled her up from the sidewalk. They walked the streets towards Park Street Station. Samantha consoled her as they got on opposite sides of the red line, Samantha taking it towards Alewife, and Jennifer taking her train to Ashmont.

Samantha looked overhead at the announcements of the next train towards Ashmont, while not ignoring Jennifer who was sitting on a bench on the other side. Unlike Samantha, Jennifer's stop was only two stops away before she would transfer to the silver line and be connected to Seaport Blvd. Samantha kept thinking to herself as she waited, and she heard a loud screeching noise coming from the subway, bound for Ashmont. She covered her ears with her hands as she watched Jennifer disappear behind the subway. The subway started off again, and she could see a large number of people exiting the station, and Jennifer was no longer there.

Her thoughts drifted off into emptiness, and couldn't shake Ted's face, and his happy smile that seemed so genuine, but now she wasn't so sure; in fact, she was certain the opposite was true. And another thought plagued her mind, at this moment, he was a man of mystery, of which she knew so little, and yet felt compelled to bring him into their own friendship. Especially when there didn't seem to be any rational reason for it. *He needs help.*

She said a silent prayer to herself.

There were bright lights in the tunnel. She looked down the tunnel for the train that was coming this way. The T was almost never presentable, at least not this late at night. The train screeched as it came to a halt, and the doors slid open. No one came out, but there was an almost full train. She stepped on it, grabbing hold of one of the rubber straps secured to the metal bars at the top.

She stood over a colored woman, maybe in her forties, her right palm implanted firmly on her forehead, her face turning red with the passion of some unknown negative emotion. Sam might not be able to see all pain, but this woman was in dire need of a friend, someone to assure her that everything was going to be all right, just a little more encouragement in the deafening roar of everyday city life in Boston.

If only Jennifer was here. She could be that friend. You were always the talkative one, and the reassuring one. Why can't I be like you too? Perhaps, would things have been much different if yours and my personalities were switched? Would we be asking the same questions?

After each stop on the red line, more and more people got off, and fewer and fewer people boarded to replace them. Eventually, after Harvard Square, she found herself utterly alone on that car. She stared out at the blackened tunnel, with the empty glass and irrelevant ads pasted inside the subway car in various places. She took deep breaths as she was thinking very clearly about Ted.

To her, he was as much a mystery as many unknown things in the world, like Culain, the tall man with a strange name. Ted seemed happy, but she knew now that he was not at all what he seems. To Jennifer, he was more than a blank canvas, waiting to be painted. He was more than a happy person, excited about all things, but she knew something deeper than his skin, some layer he revealed to her when no one else was worthy in his eyes.

The light to Davis Square lit up. She stepped off the subway car and walked up the gray-stone stairs. Samantha stepped underneath the roof of the station, gazing out in front of her, the square filled with bars, and now empty restaurants. The rain picked up again. She was about to step outside when she noticed the luminescent light coming from above; looking upwards, she could see the moon gazing down with its light, shining on the streets, glimmering in the puddles. She sighed, taking a step forward, pulling out her umbrella to shield herself from the torrential rain and oppressive moonlight.

The air. It's different tonight. The moonlight —it is different also, almost alien.

The air was hot and muggy, not cool and refreshing as one might expect during a heavy rainstorm. It was like there was some toxic gas in the air with a nearby leaking oil drums, just ready to be lit on fire and spurting its gasoline all over the place, setting fire to everything around it.

She crossed the cross walk, taking note of the seemingly barren streets. The stop at Davis did not release too many passengers, and she started to feel like the only one. She was alone in the dark street, like a lamb, or sheep drawing in a pack of wolves to devour it.

She walked on the side street, heading up on College Ave, towards her apartment. The rain kept coming down, harder and harder, splashing bigger puddles in the streets. A late-night car was driving down the road. Its wheels turned, splashing Sam with a large puddle of dirty water. The rain felt to her almost as if the Heavens wept, like they held in some inner turmoil and they just couldn't hold it in anymore.

The tears of the heavens were strong. Whatever it had cause for weeping, it kept it in too long, bottled it deep down, never talking to anyone about its problems. The Heavens were silent, keeping and holding all the pain in until finally its flood gates broke open, revealing the insides of its turmoil. The skies poured out its sadness, for it too, was oppressed by the same moonlight tonight.

She walked up to the path to her apartment. Her door looked blue in the peeking moonlight. Out of the corner of her eye, three houses down, she saw a man fumbling through his keys to open a door. She looked down as she creaked her door open. Taking a better look at the man, she recognized him, and that bright, smile. *Ted. You were this close to me all this time?*

The man opened his door. Sam closed and locked hers. She walked over to the sidewalk and made her way to his house. He entered his house; he shut it firmly behind him. She made it to his door and heard the locks.

First, she could hear the tumbler being locked with the knob. The second lock she could hear was the deadbolt. And finally, the third and final lock, was a chain. She knew she needed to be secure in her own apartment, here in Somerville, but three locks seemed too much.

The door shook in front of her. She stifled a gasp, covering her mouth. She placed her hand ever so lightly on the door. The door was stilled, and she heard him cry. His cries started as stifled, and intermittent sobs. Then, as just a little time went by the cries went louder. The cries to her, was like that of a child, higher pitched, like a child who experienced much, or perhaps, that of a child who was about to be given the belt of an abusive father.

Did he have the childhood of grief? Was he exploited or abused? Was he the victim of relational rape? Did he lose his family? Or perhaps was he a child who was born with nothing and wanted nothing more than the experience of children who had even the minimalistic comfort? Was he once a child without innocence, or was that innocence stripped away from him? If so, why did he enlist in the Army, where such things would only break him to the surface, never leaving him.

Samantha took a small, bated breath, and turned away from his stairs. Tears filled her eyes. *Jennifer, if only it was you instead of me. Then, then perhaps it would be different, and maybe there would be a little less pain in the world, and a little more peace. Maybe things would be different.*

She returned to her stoop, bringing her keys back to the door. She unlocked the door and it creaked open. She walked up the stairs and opened the door into her shared apartment. Her roommate was sleeping peacefully naked on the couch.

Her roommate was not Christian like her, and she did not share in the same ideals. She wouldn't say she was particularly fond of her roommate either, as she tended to leave things messy. Especially when she knew Sam wouldn't be home until well into the night.

Samantha walked into her roommate's bedroom, yanked the blanket off the bed to tuck her in on the couch her naked body was laying in. Walking into the kitchen, she pulled out some light cleaning gloves before walking back into the living room to clean up the bowl of half-eaten chips, and collect bottles of bear, which were scattered throughout the room. Now, she wasn't afraid of the beer, but she dared not touch the discarded semen-filled condom on the ground with her bare-hands. Picking it up, she discarded it into the trash.

She pulled her gloves off, discarding them in the trash and went to the sink, and washed her hands immediately. She walked into her room and changed into blue pajamas. Her tears became swollen as she stared up into the ceiling. Her thoughts drifted into an old story, that she now felt she had to contemplate.

It was an old story, and one she'd read numerous times before, and was a case for inspiration for her, especially when things got difficult. The story of *David and Goliath of Gath*. The story was about a child, chosen by God killed a giant when no one else dared to. She re-read the story to herself in her head, told within the First book of *Samuel*. She went over the entire tale, thinking to herself, *why is this coming to me now? And at a time like this? I need action. Not some story about some hope when I live in a world without any.*

And then, it finally came to her. In that story, it was not with man who held victory that day, David was nothing more than a tool. The battle was already won, as was constantly drilled into her brain at Sunday School. But though God never required the assistance of man, He wanted it. God is like a father who asks his six-year-old son to help change the tire of the car on his day off. Of course, He didn't need the help, and with the help of a little boy it would only make the task more difficult, but it was an excuse to spend time with His child, because after all, that tire never needed to be changed. And so sometimes, action was required by humans.

So, Lord, that is what you ask of me.

She pulled her phone off her bedside table. She opened up her calendar and went to this coming Saturday.

10:00 a.m. Saturday, Brunch with Ted.

Just hang in there, Ted. Just a little while longer. Please, just a little while longer.

Chapter 16 Steel Trap

~When Hell's Gates were opened, the friendliest faces are demons and monsters. When Hell's gates were opened, what was left of humanity became nothing more than soulless husks.

***

It's just brunch, Samantha tried to calm herself. Besides, she had to think about any additional questions Ted might ask, like, how did she know where he lived? Perhaps the truth wasn't as creepy as she thought it might be, after all, it was incidental.

She walked down the stairs. She opened the door, and her phone rang. She took it out, looking at the caller ID. It was Tim. She picked up the call. "Hey Tim, it's Sam."

"I know." He laughed. *"I called."*

"Yes. Yes, you did," Samantha wasn't exactly amused. She sucked the air through her teeth, "What's up?"

"Michael, Erin, Jenn and I are going out for brunch in thirty. Wanna come with?"

"I can't. I'm actually in the middle of something," she replied.

"What? Already on a date?"

"No. Michael is with you, that should be obvious it isn't a date," she scolded him, and she shook her head. "Look, I don't have time as I'm in the middle of doing what it *is,* I'm doing. I'll talk to you all about it later. I just can't do it right now."

"Have you considered not doing that and coming with us instead," Tim pushed her. She knew he wasn't serious this time. *"I'm curious though, excuse me while I'm putting my shorts on. This seems important to you. What is it? If you don't mind me asking?"*

"Ted," she answered. "Turns out, he doesn't live far from me."

"Be careful," Tim's tone dropped. *"Remember, if something happens, text us."*

"Don't worry, I'm not going to get into trouble of any sort," she snapped. *At least I hope not.*

"Just be careful."

"You know I will. Okay. I gotta go. B—" she interrupted herself. "Wait, make sure to tell Jennifer. I'm doing this for her."

"I'll pass it along. Bye-bye." Click.

Jennifer, I'm doing this for you. You weren't yourself that night, I can tell, and I have my suspicion it's because of Ted, not because of anything he's done, but what he revealed to you that he showed no one else. He's a man that needs help but is afraid to ask for it.

Sam put the phone back into her pocket, opened the door and crossed the threshold into the warmth array of daylight. She took a deep breath as she closed the door behind her and locked it. She walked down her stoop, and to the sidewalk. Her heart pounded with every step, filled with anxiety, almost like her father glared at her from behind. She stood straight with every walking step, making sure to at least look like she was confident, when the reality was not that, as her heart trembled inside her chest.

She walked three houses down, and up the steps to his door. She took a deep breath. *This is it. Please, let this be the right thing to do.* She knocked three times on the door. She kept silent, listening for any footsteps or movement. She searched the windows to see if anyone would open, or if curtains would move out of the way for whoever lived here, ideally Ted, peeked out to see who knocked on the door. She heard nothing and saw nothing; her eyes stretched open, and her smile faded as she feared the worst . *Don't tell me, Ted. You didn't do it. You didn't do it! Please be alive.* She knocked three more times. She waited again. Just like before, she heard and saw nothing had changed. She waited again, nervously as her gaze trembled on the door. She bowed her head down, letting out a long sigh. She knocked on the door one last time and waited.

At last, she heard the chains from behind the door moving. She returned the smirk to her face and stood up straight. The dead bolt came undone. She let out a sigh of relief. Finally, the tumblers inside the knob's lock became undone. She stared right at the edge of the door where it would open as the knob slowly turned.

Ted opened the door with that bright smile of his, looking at her, and seemed not at all surprised to see her. He was wearing the same cargo shorts she first saw him, and fatigues, "Good to see you, Sam," He said to her in his smooth tone.

She looked at his brown eyes, to see if she could see the same thing Jennifer could see. All she could determine was that he appeared tired, with bags underneath his eyes, as usual. "Yes, it is good to see you also, Ted. It seems that you've become somewhat of a stranger of late. We missed you."

"And I suppose you tracked me down to find out if I would come back?" his eyebrow raised.

"Not exactly. Well, I didn't exactly track you down, I just simply noticed on Tuesday night that you lived here. I saw you this past Tuesday night getting into the door. And I though, since I only live a few houses down, I thought I might invite you out for breakfast," she replied. "I think it might be nice to share a meal with you."

Share a meal? Really? Sam! You're better than this!

"No thanks," He replied, passing through the threshold, closing the door behind him. "I already ate."

"What did you eat?" Sam asked. She managed to peek at the floor behind the closing door, finding it to be bare. *Clearly, he knows I'm not leaving without him, but he's still hesitant. Perhaps this is the closest to asking for help he's going to give. Otherwise, he'd slam the door in front of me.*

"Food," He answered.

Abrupt replies again. "Okay, how about a cup of coffee then. I'll eat breakfast."

"I have coffee, there's literally no reason for me to come out of my house for that," He chuckled.

"Look, Ted," she let out a deep breath. "I'm bad at this. I'm not Jennifer. She is great for this sort of thing, and I'm not her. Sometimes, like right now, I wish I was her, so that I could be better at communicating with friends without making it hopelessly awkward," she looked him in the eye with a stern look. He only grinned at her. She placed her left hand firmly on her hip, "Look, Ted, I'm just going to come out and say it. You need to be more social. Look, I know it's not exactly something you might like or want, but it's something you need. You can't be keeping to yourself all the time. We really appreciated that unnecessarily expensive bottle of wine, and it was a great gift which we all enjoyed, but the reason we enjoyed it was not because it was of high quality, not because it tasted good, but because we shared it with friends, and it was a gift from a friend. You are that friend, Ted. I know you can't see it, and I want to be able to understand you. We all want to understand what's going on in that thick noggin of yours.

"Look, I know you don't want to talk about your feelings because it is like giving a key to your heart. You don't feel like you trust us, and why would you trust us with something so special and private when you've only known us a short while? You wouldn't, but it's also your fault for not putting in the effort to know us either. I know it. You know it. Jennifer knows it, and I saw something, Tuesday night, when I found out where you lived. Her heart was broken, into a number of pieces. I don't know what you said to her a few weeks ago, or what you showed her, but it affected her.

"I don't know if you are afraid of being hurt by us, or if it is the other way around, and you don't want to hurt us. We all have tough skin. We all have emotions that are difficult to process, and this isn't something we need to be doing alone, especially in the crazy world we live."

Ted never once changed his facial expression.

"Look, I can tell I'm not getting through that Steel Trap of yours. You know I'm not great at talking. Jennifer is excellent when it comes to talking. I'm good at listening, but, so help me God, I am not taking no for an answer. I don't care if I need to come into your house to drink a cup of coffee with you, I will. But you and I are having coffee! I said no to brunch to Michael, and Tim *and* Jennifer for the purpose of talking with you today, and I'm hungry!"

"Well, sorry to disappoint but I don't have any food in my house," He opened his palm to his side. "I have coffee, but if you're hungry, I'm afraid I have nothing to offer but an ear."

"And I don't want your ear, I want your words. I'm offering my ear!" She stamped her foot. "Ted!" She grimaced. "Alright, that's it. Give me your hand! I'm taking you to Joe's Bagel Bin. It's a mile this way. At the rotary, you know, where College Ave turns into Broadway!"

Ted shook his head, "Fine, I guess I'll begrudgingly grant your request. After you."

"Chivalrous as ever," She scoffed. "Give me your hand."

"No," he sternly spoke. "I will walk with you to get your breakfast. You may not hold my hand."

"Ted! Why must you be so difficult? Seriously, how am I supposed to know you're not going to just run off when we get to the rotary?"

"You don't," he replied. "Now, Samantha, let's go. The sooner we get there, the sooner I can leave. Upon my *honor*, I will not leave you until I've heard everything you have to say."

"I came here with the sole purpose of listening," She shook her head. "Come!"

She led him along the sidewalk and to the rotary passing underneath many trees from the warmth but overwhelmingly bright rays of sunlight. He spoke not. She spoke not. She just led him with the unrelenting force that was a pissed off woman. Don't ever do it, else you may find that she snuck rat poison into your coffee.

They crossed the cross walk into the rotary and turned around the bend into the coffee shop that looked like a fancy place for breakfast, apart from the large bagel that loomed over the sidewalk, shielding the pedestrians from the oppressive astral rays, whether they be the sun, moon, or even the stars.

The two of them walked through the threshold of the diner, Sam led Ted to a singular table with only two seats. Ted sat across from her. She crossed her hands over the table, and her ankles were also crossed over each other. Ted observed everything in the room, his eyes scanned every moving person, and spectacle. He carefully observed all windows and all ways in and out.

"Are you done?" Sam asked, irritated.

"My apologies," He said as he turned his head to look at her, never losing that smile, nor did it seem to curve even a little less on his face, almost like he really was just a portrait.

"Ted, seriously, sometimes you just need to calm down. You're scanning the room as if there is someone out to get you. All the time. I noticed it at the party when you first came in," she admitted.

"Welcome to Joe's Bagel Bin. How may I help you?" the waitress spoke to them. The waitress had dirty blond hair tied behind her, she was skinny, and had the cheerful grin, probably fake. She held the same fake simper across her face when she waited tables to pay for college.

"Two coffees," she pointed at Ted. "You're not skipping out on this! I'll have two eggs, scrambled, and side of home fries. Ted, what do you want?"

"I'm not hungry. I told you I ate already," He admitted.

"I've never met a man who didn't think with his stomach," she said.

"Surprise me."

The waitress left and returned promptly with two hot mugs of water. The steam poured out of the cups as they were placed in front of the drinkers. Sam took a sip, and returned her gaze to Ted, softening up her irritation. Ted still had that stupid smile on his face.

"Where was I?" she asked.

"I believe you were berating me," He chuckled as he took a sip.

That stupid laughter. It became a part of him, almost genuine but he did it way too much for it to be.

"Yes, now I remember. Do you hate us? Be honest. It would be easier for you, and me, and everyone involved if you spoke the truth. I don't want your riddles, or deflection. I am directly asking you! And I will ask another direct question until I get an answer."

He placed the coffee down and gazed into her eyes, maintaining that sneer. "Someone once asked me a question, her smirk seemed innocent at first. She was a lovely person, or so I thought. She asked me this, 'Tell me some things that you like, some things that you hate'. Well, looking back on it, my answer was very childish when an answer escaped my lips back then, and I guess it's similar to the question you asked. My answer was this, back then, 'I like my friends, but I hate violence'. Such an odd concept, and a childish answer for someone like me, someone who joined the Army, and did things contrary to my nature. If you were to ask me the same question today, I suppose I would answer it like this: there are many things that I hate, and I'd be hard pressed to find anything that I didn't hate. And I don't particularly like anything," He paused and let her think about what he said. "Is that enough to satisfy your curiosity?"

"So, you only hate us because you hate everything," she repeated. "Even though we've done nothing to you."

"Those icebreakers, as Jack calls them, are dangerous things. They reveal personal information, information that one can hold on to, and use, and twist to their own cruel designs. When you give out that information, you're just asking people to stab you in the back."

"You're a man who has no trust in anyone, or anything," she commented. The food arrived in front of her. Ted's plate came by with a heaping portion of scrambled eggs. "What about your family, or friends?"

"I had people that once held my confidence," He answered.

"And?"

"They're all dead," His tone dropped, but he kept the smile.

Sam eyes gaped open, and her fork trembled in between her fingers; she felt there was a great silence at the table, as if the two of them were in soundless bubble where even screams can't escape one's lips. Her expression went from irritation to sorrow, her eyes watered as she took a bite of some of her home fries. "And your siblings?"

"We aren't on a talking basis," His tone dropped.

"I see," she replied. "You said most of the people you held your confidence in were dead. What about the rest of them?"

"None of them can be trusted. I was foolish to trust them. But did thank them for everything they've done for me. It is through them that I knew I only ever had fifteen friends. No more than that. Now I have none." His voice dropped even lower, and his grin faded. His eyes dropped down as if they themselves were exhausted. "Funny thing, really, a soldier, a sailor, a marine, a guardsman, coast or national, they all join the service to sacrifice for the greater good, to fight for honor, to fight for peace, and our freedom. They would like to say that they would lay down their lives for peace, freedom, and honor, but I know the truth. Not one of them will question an order if it comes from the top. Every single one of them will commit genocide and not bat an eye, just because it's an order, they'll do it." He let out a sigh.

Sam continued to listen while she was eating.

"I'll tell you what I told Jennifer, and now I realize it was mistake on my part giving her my number, and exchanging it, I am not someone you want to be close with. I'm not someone anyone *should* be friends with. With everything that I've done, my name will appear in the history books, but not next to Martin Luther King JR, not George Washington. Not even President Lincoln. No, you'll find me in the history books, but not compared to them. The only people you could compare me to, is Hitler and Stalin.

"You asked me the other week why I felt I needed to work so much. Honestly, I want to be working more than I already am. I don't need the money. I don't want it." He waved his hand. "What am I going to spend all that money on? I *need* to work. I need to drown myself in it. It's the o—it's the only thing that's drowning out all of their screams. It is the only thing that is masking all of those faces." He gritted his teeth. "They said that Saul killed his thousands and David his tens of thousands. I on the other hand would be lucky if my numbers were nearly that low. I am the monster and the demon your parents warned me about. I'm nothing but a cold murderer."

She put her fork down to the side of her plate. She looked down with gaping eyes, trying to determine the meaning behind his words. No man, no matter how cruel or sinister, would willingly admit they were a monster. A man who would call himself as such, is a dangerous man. But could there have been something else behind those words? A hidden meaning perhaps? Was this true? Was any of it true? Or was it, just like a mask, a façade to hide the truth? *No. Ted, why are you lying to me, or perhaps do I not completely grasp the situation?*

"Ted," she looked back at him with a seriousness about her, neither angry nor upset. "It would be better if you didn't lie to me. I can't imagine what it is that you're going through, or how it tugs on the strings of the heart. I can't imagine a man would compare himself to Hitler, and yet you've done that. I don't doubt you have done things you regret doing, but that is something we all have done. That is what makes us human. Yes, we lie sometimes. Yes, we betray our friends trust, that is who we are," She sighed. "I have no doubt that you have killed in the service, that is to be expected. I don't believe you killed more than tens of thousands of people. I believe you may feel the rotten stench of regret for the things you've done. I know you must see the nightmares, and every night I'm sure you go to bed screaming and wake up screaming trying to drown those noises out. When I found out where you lived, Ted, I walked up to your door and almost knocked after hearing you lock all three locks. And I heard a man, removing his bandages, removing his laughter, and removing his mask. I heard a child weeping behind that door. You have guilt, I'm sure you suffer from guilt and trauma, but you cannot do this alone, no matter how hard you try," She sucked in air through her teeth as she tried to stifle a cry. "You can't do this alone, Ted. You need friends, and we are offering it to you. There are no conditions attached. All we want is you. That's all we want, that's all Jennifer wants. We don't want your excuses, we don't want your lies, we don't want your laughter or your jokes, or even that smile that you and I both know isn't real. All we want is you and your friendship.

"Maybe, it isn't even fair of me to ask this, but what happened that turned you into this?" She's seen enough war movies to recognize the symptoms of PTSD, and it was clear he suffered from it, but that wasn't all he suffered from. There was more, much more he was hiding underneath the surface. This steel trap was far more complex than she realized, and she couldn't crack it alone. She was the spear, and he was the shield. The shield might crack, but she is at risk of falling off the horse.

"Well, it appears that you have found a way to tug on something that I forgot was there once," He answered. "But I can't tell you what happened. Everything that happened is classified above top secret. I will hold this in, bottle it in forever, and never talk about it to anyone at any time. Because I can't. You don't understand, I want to talk, but I can't. And I can't even tell why I can't talk about it."

"But if you keep doing that, this bottle is going to explode!" she exclaimed.

He let out a deep sigh. "I'm afraid that bottle has already exploded. And it was pieced back together, much to my dismay. That bottle won't stay broken, as much as I want it to."

"What are you talking about?" she didn't understand his analogy.

"In all my years of living, twenty-three regrettable years, I have but one regret: that was not hanging myself with my own umbilical cord, and now I can't even die right."

Sam gasped as the reality finally hit her. *He is suicidal,* but she suspected as much, "Ted, what did you try to do?"

"Everything I can think of," He answered grimly. "And nothing works!"

"If nothing works and you are a living husk, why not try to bring life back into it? Why not try to make friends with what you have? If nothing works, something is trying to keep you alive, or you're not quite ready to go," She waved the waitress down. Ted merely smiled at her, mocking her as if she did fall off her horse, and that shield remains uncracked, and unbroken.

She came by. "I'll take a box for his eggs and the check. I'll pay for it."

The waitress nodded and left for the box and to print out her check.

"You barely touched your eggs," she commented.

"I can't taste anything. I haven't tasted anything in over fifteen years. Not since—not since *that* happened to me," He replied. "Eating for me is like putting fuel in the car, it's tasteless. It's nothing more than a careless chore. There," he sneered again, that façade which he knew wasn't fooling anyone anymore. The smile seemed almost sarcastic. "Now, you know a lot about me. You can believe my tale or not, but that is me. A bitter man filled with nothing but hate and regret. Tell me, then, Sam, would you really want a man like me as a friend, when taking life seemed almost second nature to me? Or am I just a tool to you, a project for you to work on to make yourself feel better?"

Sam pointed a stern finger at him. The box came with the check. She gave the waitress her card. "Ted, I'm going to ignore that, and forgive you for this. Why? Because I know you don't mean it. I think you revealed to me much more than you intended, or you are the best poker player alive. You are making yourself look like the Devil, like I'm sharing breakfast with Satan to make me feel better for breaking a friendship with you or any kind of bond, and that I would be free to do so easily. That doesn't work on me, for the Lord taught me better than that. My friendship, as well as Michael's, Erin's, Tim's, and Jennifer's are still on the table. We want you to be part of us. Now, will you come with us for the Fourth of July Canoa trip?"

"I'll dec—"

"You will accept this invitation."

"I will think about it."

"You will come."

"I said I'll—"

"And I said I'm not taking no for an answer, Ted," she replied. "Unlike before, I now know where you live. I'll drag you on the canoe if I have to."

"Fine. You've got me. Heaven knows even I can't relocate fast enough for that," He snickered.

"You better not even think about that!" she said. "Are you taking your eggs?"

"No."

She packed up his eggs into the box. "Well, I'm not about to let this go to waste. Are you coming on Tuesday?"

"I'll think about it," He replied.

"So, no," she said. She knew what his maybe's or think about its meant. They were the polite way to decline an offer. "I'll see you Saturday. We meet at Kendall Square at 4:30 PM. You will be there then, no. I expect you there at 4PM. If you are not there at 4PM. I am assuming your trying to escape, and I will drive to you and pick you up myself!"

"I see you don't trust me," He said, returning that forsaken smile upon his lips.

"I trust you, but I also trust that you will try to avoid it, using almost any means necessary," she said. "I know you don't trust us, and I'm not going to pry any further," She picked up her purse and stood up. "I will trust that you will be there at 4:00PM. If you are not there, I'm dragging you here myself."

"I understand."

Chapter 17 Ducks

~The unstoppable spear might not be able to penetrate the immovable shield, but it can still make a crack, and a weapon with more force than the spear can break it open.

***

Ted took a short walk, crossing the street and walked into the Nathan Tufts Park. He walked upon the shaded path to the tower. He took a brief look at it, making it look like he was even marginally interested in it. He investigated the blank, empty gate that went into the tower. It was locked. He walked down the path to find an unoccupied bench. Looking around, he made sure that no one else was here, so he could relax a moment. Satisfied, he sat himself down on the bench.

He looked out on towards the empty street. The sun gazed down through the clouds and through the tree line. He leaned back into his seat, crossing his legs and his arms relaxed behind the back of the bench. He deeply sighed before retreating to his thoughts.

"Why?" He whispered softly. "How cruel can you be? You will not let me part from this world, and that is the only thing I want. I don't want friends, and don't want or need a family. I entered in this world with very little, and what little I had was violently ripped from me and left me to ponder the cruelty you left me in, and God, here you are, mocking me, trying to give me hope when I can't see passed the tunnel. You have shown me the light in the tunnel, but as with all good things, I can't trust it. You know I can't trust it. You know I can't trust You. How cruel can you be?

"By some fluke chance, I missed something. I let my guard down once, for just one minute out of a desperation to get in my door, and now *she* knows where I live. Was that—was that your doing? Lord, are you trying to tell me something? Are you really trying to tell me I should be giving this cursed life one last chance before cancelling out a subscription

I never signed up for? This was something I didn't want. I never asked for any of it, and yet You forced me to pay a price higher than any have paid.

"By some fluke, you want my heart when it is garbage. It is filled with scars. You stabbed it. You shot it full of bullet holes. You cast it into the furnace. You crushed it with buildings. My heart is beyond repair and it is dead, and yet, because You stubbornly say so, it keeps beating and powering up this Soulless Husk. I feel just like Frankenstein. I didn't ask for the life my Creator gave me, yet I'm cursed with this cruel existence.

"Even for the very purpose I was thrust in that life. Ten years ago, the wars stopped. Ten years ago, there was no further need for me to kill anyone anymore. You knew that. And yet, forced me to kill nearly two-hundred-thousand men in the blink of an eye, and every single one of them I would have called my brother, or my sister. Now, I know better. What do you want from me? Why won't you just let me go and let me die? Your forgiveness can't reach me, and I am cursed to go to Hell, and with a monster like me, there is no better place for me. Just let me go and let me—"

His train of thought severed when a little flock of ducklings, led by their mother walked in front of him. He counted the flock, and the flock was large for ducklings. There totaled fifteen ducklings, and the mother. There was a duckling in the back that caught his eye. The little duckling had a few black spots on its feathers, and it waddled with a little limp. The little duckling squeaked.

Ted's eye gazed to its little webbed foot, and it appeared that something was not quite connected right, as if the poor little creature was born wrong. This duckling, like Ted, was not born for this world, and lived on simple borrowed time: time that neither of them had any right to. Would it be a mercy killing to put the duckling out of his misery?

He leaned over and placed his hand on the ground, his palm faced the sky. The little duckling turned its little head to him. Almost as if everything stopped, and as if the little duckling knew something, he waddled over to Ted's hand, and climbed on top of it. Ted rose the little duckling to his face and pet the little duck. He smiled as the cute little feet stepped onto his hand like a marching band. Ted investigated the black, empty orbs in its skull.

The mother duck stopped waddling and looked at Ted, as he pet her little duckling. She quacked, flapping her wings erratically, waddling towards Ted who simply traded a gaze, lying even to her. He returned her gaze to her eyes, and he placed the duckling down as he no longer considered killing it. The little duckling returned to its flock and went back in line as the mother duck led the way into whatever paradise awaited them, a paradise *he* was banished from.

"I'm glad you haven't lost your soft spot yet," He heard a familiar voice right next to him. The voice was so nostalgic that he lost his sense of location. The voice of so many memories, the good ones, swept over him. He turned to the left to see a little girl, aged if he remembered right was fifteen. She was the youngest of them all, and she was the closest one to him. She wore torn black Cargo pants, a black long-sleeved shirt with her vest draped over it. Her black hair was down, and one blue eye was hiding behind her hair, while the other one had blood smeared over it. Just below her abdomen was bleeding black blood. She smirked at him, that same playful grin he fell in love with. It was full of energy and hope, and the love to match it.

He frowned.

"Suh—Slithers," He gasped. He didn't mean to. She looked real to him, as if he was looking at an actual person, and not the ghost his mind conjured up.

"Ghost," she answered, smiling as blood dripped down her head. "I miss you. We all do."

"Iah—iah I love you," He choked on his sobs. He knew he was overdue for this, but he didn't expect it to hit him out in the open, exposed.

"Ghost, I love you too. We all do," She smiled back at him. "Tell me, have you lost your tender heart already? I don't think you have."

"Every morning, *every* morning it breaks a little more each passing day. Every single day. I dream these nightmares as they cascade over my insomnia, oppressing me far more than *they* ever could. I am stuck in the past, and I want to leave it behind, but I don't want to leave it behind," He sobbed, tears streamed down his face, and his simper faded, and his face was cringing. "I know when I wake up, I'll never see any of you again. I'll never see any of you again."

"The life we lived was cruel," Said Slithers. "We were all tormented inside, especially with everything that we had to do. We were darkness. We were bitterness. We were hatred. But you taught us all something, before the end. Do you remember what you said to me?"

"I can't remember," He sobbed. "I can't remember."

"That the odds were against us. But if there was a chance, a slither of a chance that we could succeed in doing something good, in leaving some kind of legacy for humanity to follow, just one chance, it was worth it. Whatever it was, even if that chance was infinitely worse, it would be worth it for a chance to get this Hell undone," she answered. "Ghost, we were darkness, and when the darkness was too oppressive, you were our light. You were our Captain, our moral compass. It was through you that we never killed anyone innocent. It was because of you no civies were ever killed on our watch. That was something, wasn't it? Was it worth it for even just that?"

"And everything we fought for is being undone now as we speak," He sobbed. "Our sacrifices were all meaningless."

"Was it, Ghost? Was any of it meaningless?" her hand touched his. He felt the warmth blood touch his hand. She grabbed it and brought it to her cheek, and his hand felt her flesh, as it was, before the last fires raged eight years ago. The flesh was so real in his hands. She took her free hand and pulled out a ring, a scrappy ring at that. The ring was nothing more than a few nails welded together, and embedded in the ring were fragments of bullets, welded together.

He recognized that ring. He looked, but never found it. The ring he made for her over eight years ago. The ring that he made for her was akin to that of a marriage, something he picked up from listening and watching his parental figures, Major and Lieutenant Nakamura, and whatever it was they had together, was what he wanted with Slithers, and he almost had it.

"Was this meaningless?" she said to him.

"No," He sucked in the air through his teeth, gasping as he tried to stifle more sobs. But this was not normal for him, for the tears never stopped like a river dammed up with a cracking dam. The wall was finally chipped. "I—it was worth everything. Almost everything was planned. You and I were to be together that Saturday, but for you, and for them, you never got to see that Saturday."

"I know," she said. "I know. I know our parents wouldn't have wanted to see us like that. But that wasn't for them to decide. No, we were born with a purpose, and our tale ended. But yours still goes on. Ghost, if there is a slither of a chance to undo this Hell, if there is a slither of a chance, and if that chance is infinitely worse than it was back then, it is still worth it. Our time is over. Your time is still moving forward. Time stopped for me, and it kept going for you," She leaned to him and looked at his now sobbing and swelling eyes. "We all lived with a cruel existence, but you gave us light. Who else can you bless with your light?"

"How can I when I see only darkness. The mask faded and it's not all okay. It's not okay anymore," He knew she referred to her biological parents, the one she never met. Ted didn't know who his parents were either, only the dreaded Nakamuras.

Her forehead touched his. His eyes closed. "You say you're not okay. You say that all you see is darkness around you. That's okay. Because that was once my reality. You broke the darkness, and the light forced its way in. The light is there, Ghost. It is right there! You know it is. You must let it in. Just let it in! We can't stand seeing you like this. Just let it in."

He opened his eyes, and he saw Slithers with her hair pulled back in a ponytail. She smiled at him, shading his face with her white sunhat that wasn't there before. She now wore a blue sundress. "Just let it in. You need to let the past stay in the past, Ghost. I know you don't want to forget us, but this pain isn't doing anything good."

"Maybe—"

"Maybe, Ghost, the reason you can't seem to really kill yourself, is because you know that doing that will kill all memory of us." She said: this cut through his heart, and he could feel it bleeding inside his chest. "You gave us hope when there was none. Now, it is time for someone to share that hope with you. I love you. We all do."

She kissed him gently on the lips before her body changed into a wind of flowers, flying away in little pieces, like leaves as they burned away from his hallucination. His hands trembled uncontrollably and the light reflecting upon his eyes shimmered. His body felt weak as he leaned forward.

He curled himself up on the bench, holding his knees tightly to his chest as the tears swelled into his eyes, streaming onto the bench, making a waterfall drip onto the pavement of the path. He felt like a soaked sponge, being twisted and rung dry and then cast carelessly to the side of the sink.

"Juh—Jennifer," He stammered. "Why do you look like her?"

He couldn't deny the similarities between Slithers and Jennifer. Granted, Jenn was older than Ted, by perhaps five years, assuming his estimation of his own age was accurate. They had the same build, the same-colored hair, the same colorful and playful smile and laugh. Even the smell seemed the same, the smell of patience and care. It was something that he didn't smell much of in the world.

Maybe, just maybe it was time to let it go.

Chapter 18 Fireworks

~ To fight for peace, that kind of courage requires a specific type of person. You are not that person: I am that person. And I hate it. Let me tell you something, if you want to truly fight for peace, and if you want to be that kind of person, I'll tell you how: you have to kill yourself, again, and again, and again, until what's left of your humanity is dead and you become nothing more than a murderer. You'll bear the burden of all the hate and discourse of the world, but you'll save the world from itself. Can you bear that burden? I thought I could. No one can.

***

Samantha previously arranged for everyone to be at Kendall Square at 4:00PM sharp, and a little earlier. That would give her enough time to track Ted down in case he bailed, *again!* She looked carefully at her watch as Michael, Tim, Erin, and Jennifer were sitting down on some of the benches, gazing carefully at the stairs, waiting for Ted to pop up.

There were droves of people coming up, and going down the red signs reading, "Kendall Square". There was a large office skyscraper across the street, and on the first floor of the building was a large office, and to either sides of it was the inside of several restaurants and coffee shops, both of which were filled with couples, families, and individuals coming in and out of the glass doors. On the side of the station on which Samantha and the rest remained, was shaded by numerous trees and banners hung over the side of the shops and restaurants on this side of the street with these brick buildings.

Jennifer's smile was written on that lovely face, sincere, as if she had little care in the world. She had a white visor which covered her face in shadows, mixed with a khaki-shorts and a black shirt. Samantha walked over to her as Tim, Erin, Brian, and Michael spoke to each other, about something finance related. Obviously, Michael led most of that conversation, with his confident demeanor, owning that salmon-colored shirt that less secure men would not wear.

"So, what are you feeling right now?" Sam asked Jennifer, sitting down next to her, wrapping her arm around her shoulder.

"Well, I suppose I'm feeling overjoyed, that I might see him again. Thank you, Sam," she said cheerfully, her brown eyes gleamed in the sunlight, "And I'll be relieved if he doesn't show up. I am satisfied either way. Of course, I'd like to see him again, but I will no longer force his friendship with ours. It is—"

"Sometimes, we need a friend to be an enemy," Sam said, looking up at the sky, looking for an answer, and something genuine to say. "Only a true friend will insult us to our face. Only a true friend will call us out on all our shit."

"Sam!" Tim called out. "Language."

"Sorry, Tim!" Sam called back, her blond hair swayed in the breeze, "Look, I can't say what I heard on that night when I forced him to come. " She glanced down at her watch; 3:57 p.m. "But I know what he needs. He doesn't need that soft and passive friend. He needs a stern but active friend. I didn't know that was something I could be, but I think we all need to be part of that. We all need to be active, or else we'll all lose him."

"There are times when we need a stern hand. There are times where we need a motherly caring hand, and the occasional whip up the butt with a wooden spoon." Jennifer chuckled. She took enough beatings with that wooden spoon before. "I read something before, once, many years ago at my undergrad, that a man who grew up in a violent household responds best to order and direction. Such a man is responsive to those who lead them, for fear of being punished. Such a man doesn't respond well to a passive friend because they can't offer that guidance."

"You have no idea how right you are," Sam commented, looking back at her watch. 4:02 p.m. "Can you call Ted. Ask him where he is please. Else, I'm driving to pick him up."

Jennifer took out her phone. She went over to Ted's name in her contact list and pulled his file up on her phone and hovered her thumb over the green dial icon. She hesitated before forcing her thumb violently down on the touch screen. She brought the phone to her ear, listening to the dial tone. Her elbow was propped up over her thigh as she held the phone to her ear, tilting her head and letting her dark hair droop down to her side. The phone rang three times.

"*Hello?*" came that familiar smooth voice.

"Tedward!" She cried out; her face lit up with excitement. "It's me, Jennifer."

"*Oh, I know,*" he chuckled softly into the phone. "*I have your number in my phone, remember?*"

"It's good to hear from you again. Are you coming? Where are you?"

"*Oh, you know, around,*" he joked. It was a very corny joke.

"You've certainly got that Bostonian sarcasm," she jested.

"*Oh, please. Bostonians do it better.*"

"Don't threaten me with a good time."

"*Jennifer! I would never!*"

"So, where are you?"

"*I told you, I'm not threatening you with a good time.*"

"Tedward!"

"*Open your eyes.*"

Jennifer opened her eyes and found an empty subway station. She blinked repeatedly and took one hand to wipe away any sleep from her eyes.

"What am I supposed to be looking at?"

"*An empty subway station.*"

"What?" she turned her head around and found Ted standing on the other side of the street, right in front of the Merlien Building on One Broadway. He waved and bore that smile. "Tedward! What are you doing? Get over here!" Jennifer found herself yelling at him from across the street, but it was apparent her voice carried over his phone as he pushed his phone away from his face.

"Well, that's a relief," Sam said, and took a deep breath as she turned her head towards him. He was wearing his fatigues, wrinkled, and khakis. His hair was still a scruffy mess. "Now I don't have to go chasing him down," She felt a major burden being lifted from her chest. She grinned as Jennifer met Ted at the crosswalk. *Thank you.*

She went over to Erin, and pushed her to the side of her bench, and wrapped her hand around her waist, "So, what do you think?"

"I didn't think you to be much of a matchmaker. I mean, how long did it take for Michael to give you the slip?" she chuckled, elbowing her in the side.

Sam looked at her awkwardly.

"Jennifer would have said it better," Michael laughed.

"Sh! Sh! Sh!" Tim put his finger to his lips. "You don't want her hearing that. Last time someone made that assumption—" he shuddered. "So many accidents."

"That was completely unrelated! The pipe in the room burst!" Samantha knew all too well what he was referring to.

"Yeah, it didn't help we were on the top floor," Michael scratched his chin as he tilted his gaze skywards. "Oh well, not like she caused it."

"So, where's this canoe place?" Erin asked. "Oh, and I suppose I know him a little better, but even I have my hesitations. They seem a good match. Way to be an *Emma*."

"Oh, please, I get enough of that from Jennifer. I don't need that from you, Erin," Samantha scowled at her. "I'm not a fan of Jane Austen personally."

"Before you go off some unnecessary tangent that is likely to make us late—" Michael began.

"You're one to talk." Sam replied sarcastically.

"For the record, I came early today." He shook his head as he pointed an index finger at her chest. "It's about a fifteen-minute walk."

"Michael, I'm sure we'll be fine. We originally planned to be here at 6:00 PM in case something happened. Then Ted happened. And he was on time, contrary to popular belief, it was either on time or not at all. We have plenty of time. Fireworks don't start until later. Which reminds me, food."

"I'll go grab something. Anything in particular we want?" he asked.

"Didn't we plan this—forget it. Go to the store, get some snacks, soda, and anything else you can think of. Fortunately, some of us had a late lunch."

"Come on Tim," Michael grabbed Tim as they went along the opposite side of the street to a nearby convenient store.

"So, you finally came on time, or at least at all," Jennifer said, smiling up to Ted. She heard the constant chatter of people walking by, and she heard the creaking of the opening of the doors, and the clattering of feet against the cement sidewalk. This side of the street was brightly sunny without the shade of the trees. The cars still drove by; some honking because some inconsiderate tourist cut off a driver, ignoring the "no turn on red" sign. "What changed? I didn't think I'd see you today, or at all ever again."

"I hope my sudden surprise was welcome," He smiled, but this grin wasn't as wide as all the other smirks he gave her. There was *something* different about it, but Jennifer couldn't quite place it.

"It most certainly is," She smirked, her eye lids dropping a bit almost like she was planning something. "Honestly though, I was going to be content in whatever happened. Although I would say I wouldn't have liked to have not seen you again, I don't think my sensitive little eyes could take any more of that, and don't dodge my question, you sly fox, you."

"I wasn't planning on it," He let out a small laugh that came out more like a cough. "I know something's changed: I haven't quite determined what yet."

"So, are you going to tell me something pleasant about you? Unlike that dreary excuse of an explanation the last time I saw you?" she asked.

"I—I think I will save that for tonight. I have to think of something that you don't know about me, that is pleasant." He answered, his tone dropping at *pleasant*. Jennifer could tell his simper lessened about a few centimeters. "It is—hard for me to find something pleasant."

"Then, think on it. But don't filter yourself, Tedward. If you must, give me something precious, and I'll give you something precious," She poked him.

He paused, rubbing his chin. "I don't think any of that came from a Jane Austen Novel."

"Nope!" she cackled, pulling her head back and let her hair fall, "I came up with that cheesy line myself, or if it was pulled from some fake crap romantic novel with unrealistic expectations, this was purely coincidental."

"I see. It seemed a little dry for Jane Austen."

"I'm not Jane Austen," she defended herself.

They rented three canoes. Two were originally meant for passengers, and the other was meant to hold their snacks and drinks if they got too hungry. Erin thought that much space was overkill, but they also didn't foresee an additional passenger when they originally planned this. So, almost all the load was dispersed evenly.

The green canoes were tied together with bungee cords, which, of course, Tim thought was dangerous. Ted didn't seem bothered in the least by it. The skies were clear, and the sun was finally setting over the western horizon of Boston, and the darkness was swooping in over the east. The lights were still very widely used, taking away any lights from the stars from above. All of them were wading in the canoe, and Jennifer and Ted shared one.

Samantha looked at her watch. "10:28," she said. "The Pop concert should be ending soon."

"Why did we come out here so early?" Tim complained. "I have to pee."

"Bro." Michael laughed. "You have a whole ocean."

"That's not sanitary, what about the fish? I don't think they'd like that," Tim replied, trying to be sarcastic.

"You do realize they pee in the same water they swim in, right?" Michael said. He reached out to grab an empty coffee can. He tossed it over to Tim. "Use this if you're concerned. My Uncle Jack used to road trip with these things. He'd never stop even to use the bathroom. He just kept driving."

"Uncle Jack," Tim said. "How fitting."

Tim swiftly turned around, using the can as his toilet, hopefully no one would see.

"You better dump that out, Tim!" Erin exclaimed. "If I'm sharing a canoe with you, I don't want to have to smell it the entire time."

"But—" he started to protest.

"Dang it. Just give it to me!" She smiled and laughed at the over-the-top ridiculousness that was someone trying to protect the fish from the toxic waste of the human body. She went over to the bucket and dumped the urine into the water. She rinsed the bucket out with the same water.

There was a loud whistling in the air. They all jerked their heads and pointed at the white shaking stream following the rocket in the air. Sam, Erin and Jennifer leaned back in the canoe and pointed at it. The numerous lights lit up the skies and shimmered in the ripples of the water.

These three seemed to Ted to be the most like children, if that is, how he would expect children to behave. Little did *he* know, many children screamed in terror for the noise that was to follow.

The first one sounded like a distant tank fire, the cannon blowing up, overwhelmed by the enormous pressure of the exploding powder, sending flares and flashes of white. The light reflected upon their eyeballs. The noise was so loud that it sent ripples between the canoes. Ted could feel the weight being shifted in the canoes. Again, and again, and again, the lights would flash, blue, red, green, and white lights, sending debris into the ocean.

His fists clenched at the sides of the canoe. His eyes flared as the beautiful exploding lights lit up the blackened sky. The loud bangs reminded him more of cannons, like a cannon went off right next to his ears, ringing. He took numerous soft, measured breaths as his hands nearly dug into the side of the canoe.

He grinded his teeth as unwanted memories began to assault his mind:

Afghanistan, August 13ᵗʰ, 2012.

The air was dry, the moisture was gone, and the sand scorched.

Ghost sprinted in the sand with Viper behind him. Ticker was to his left, and Butcher to his left, her katana drawn. Her current height made the katana look like a five-foot Nodachi!

Their legs sprinted through the sand, through the whistling howls of the tank fire aimed directly at him. Ghost saw, he jumped to the side, and Viper jumped in the other direction, just missing impact. The sand went everywhere, pelting his body like bullets.

More shells of tank fire followed, the whistling never stopped, as if the tanks themselves were the form of their hated oppression. Ghost took a good look at the line in front of them, the tanks kept firing, and the buzzing of bullet fire came, obscuring their vision.

"Ticker! One hundred-thirty-six meters!" Ghost yelled as two bullets grazed his cheeks. He ignored it. Pain was all too familiar for him to bother with it anymore. "One O'clock!"

"Ten-four," Ticker replied.

He could hear the rapid sprinting of Ticker, the little soldier sprinting faster and harder. Not more than fifteen seconds later did he hear cries, and a loud explosion.

The sound cleared.

Ghost saw the right most tank was nearly toppled, but completely ripped to shreds; Afghan soldiers were dying near the tank, with gunfire, explosive debris, or even the flames themselves.

Ghost, Butcher, and Viper picked up into a full sprint, leaving clouds of sand in their wake. They jumped behind the sandbags. Ticker swiftly blew up another tank. The Afghan soldiers were in complete disarray. It was almost like they were surprised they stood over a foot and a half above their enemy.

Ghost let his Rifle fire; he constantly pulled the single shot trigger numerous times as he aimed down the iron sights. His gun ripped through the second-rate bullet-proof vests the Afghan soldiers were wearing. One of the other men threw his rifle at him. Ghost was briefly distracted as he sidestepped from the man's swing with the scimitar. A second swing was made. Ghost pulled out his knife. He grabbed the man's hand and twisted him down to his height. He thrust his knife into the man's chest, twisting the knife and ripped apart the man's chest.

Ghost watched as the man's corpse collapsed to the ground, and watered the sand with its blood,

More fireworks started firing and whistling in the air. Ted realized he dazed off in an experiential nightmare and attempted to return his smile to his face. He released his grip on the canoe. He stared out at the open sea, and the lights of the city, there were many canoes and other boats with people smiling happily at the bright exploding lights.

His breaths were still short and measured. He needed to control himself, or something worse would happen than these sudden flashbacks. He bowed his head down. *They can't see this.*

He gasped. His eyes were gaped open as he felt something warm touch his hand. His hands started trembling as he was completely nervous but was much too afraid to do anything. His gaze suddenly shifted to his hand and found a warm matter of flesh covering his trembling hand. He looked up at the arm from which the warm, gentle hand was attached. He found himself looking into the concerned eyes of Jennifer, who held his hand firmly. She grinned brightly, with those same concerned eyes.

"Ted," she whispered. She seemed sincere, too sincere for honesty to remain behind those eyes. "You don't have to go at it alone. That's what friends are for. That's what we're here for. You don't have to live life alone."

She crawled him from inside the canoe, still holding his hand over the side. His smirk faded and his eyes trembled in the exploding lights. He leaned back, breathing heavier.

No! Stuh—stay away!

She came closer to him. He leaned into the back of the canoe.

No! Stuh—stay away! You don't know what I've done.

As if reading his thoughts, "No, you don't have to go at it alone. That's what friends are for."

Jennifer, stay away. Please. You don't want any part of this—of this monster. No. I am not a monster. I am something—something so much worse.

She lunged her body softly into his chest and embraced her arms around him, her chin rested on his shoulders. "Ted," she whispered. Her trembling intonation spoke volumes as he felt this alien embrace him.

He felt darkness all around him. Her voice, that *damn* pulsating voice, couldn't be trusted, no matter how much comfort it brought to him. The smiling face of Slithers entered his mind. She smiled at him in the darkness, like, like it was as if Slithers lived on in Jennifer. He closed his eyes as he stifled sobs from within. He took a deep breath with her body leaned so close into his. *How cruel. How cruel can you be, forcing me to look back into memories that I know I can never relive. What would I give to have that again, even just one last time?*

"I can't begin to understand what you're going through, but Ted, I want to understand it. I know you're in pain, and this life, or whatever it is, it can be Hell. But it is like that for everyone. I know you don't exactly wear your feelings on your sleeves, but I know that grin isn't real. I know, those who have larger simpers hold the most pain, and every waking moment is like waking up in a nightmare, and you just can't wait to wake up from it. Those who have the loudest laughs bear the burden of pain and hatred. And those who wear masks, like our smiles, don't want to burden others with their own deficiencies." Her tears streamed down on his shoulder. "I know you want to bear this alone, we all do, but we can't. We just can't. No matter how hard we try; we can't do it alone. Share the load!"

He felt a weight on his chest, almost as if his heart was in his stomach, crawling its way up through his throat, restricting the air he could let in and out. "I—I can't. Because what's on my heart," he began to whisper. "I can't tell anyone. Jennifer, the less you know, the better."

"Then tell me what little you can. Tell me how you feel? If you can't trust any of us, trust me or trust Sam. But you can't grow unless you open up more, or at the least, come out more often. Ted, we consider you a friend. Even if that feeling isn't mutual. I don't know what must have happened to you when you can't trust anyone."

"What I went through is classified," he stammered. "I am not allowed to talk about it, and this would be information that would only place you in harm's way, even if you believed it."

"Then tell me something about you. Something I don't already know. Something precious," she requested. She leaned back from him and looked him in those watery eyes. "Anything. Tell me what makes you happy. If you can't manage that, tell me what makes you hurt: just give me something."

"There used to be a girl. Her hair was black, and her smile lit up the sky, even when there was no sun to illuminate the darkness. She was always happy. You could say, given our circumstances, we were class sweethearts. We were even—what's the word for it: engaged. It was going to be held on Saturday. We were going to invite our little, small group of friends."

"What happened?" she asked, gazing deeper into his eyes. He sensed while they were worlds apart, she understood that, but she was trying to understand him in whatever way was possible, pushing and applying pressure when needed, and releasing him just at the right moment.

"For her, Saturday never came. For them, they never got to see that Saturday either," He answered.

He was vague, using a very subtle and vague metaphor, but he felt she understood what he meant, even if he didn't mean to. "I'm so sorry."

She placed her hand on his shoulder and grasped it firmly to console him as the whistling of the fireworks continued. They continued firing at a much rapid rate, the grand finale filled with innumerable explosions, filling the air with multiple different colors of exploding lights.

"But what bothers me the most about it, is I can't talk about what happened, and that—and that you look so much like her, it's almost uncanny. It's disturbing," he said. He felt he needed to desperately push her away. This was all too familiar, and it only went one place: pain. Either for himself or hers, if he let her into his life, no matter how small of a part she could play to him, he would hurt her, and she would hurt him. It was only inevitable, but he also knew that if there was going to be any shot at providing peace to the turmoil in his heart, it would be through her.

"Well, I hope I can bring back some of her memories if that is what will keep you grounded," she said, leaning back. "Now, it is my turn, but I'll show you."

She leaned back from him and pulled up the sleeve from her left arm. She showed her wrist to him. In the faint light, he could see something all too familiar: scars. There were faint flesh-white scars slitted in x's across her wrist. She smiled at him as tears escaped those fissured lids.

What is she thinking? She's just handing me this information! Jennifer, are you stupid! I could—I could use this to harm you. You know this! But you have no reason to believe I would use this against you. Why? You know how cruel people are, why are you trusting me, a stranger with the scars of your heart?

"Why are you showing me this?" he asked. "This is frail info—"

"Because my dear Tedward." She smirked and looked into his glimmering eyes. "I know you don't trust me, but something tells me that you will never do anything to hurt me."

He let out a sigh. "Perhaps you're wrong. Perhaps you're right."

The fireworks were over. Sam whistled as she saw Jenn and Ted cozying up over in the other canoe. They immediately moved into where they were, hoping no one saw anything. But Sam saw. She saw the whole thing and left with a smile. *I'm glad I was able to do something. Even just a little thing; such a little thing.*

The six of them returned the canoes. They all made it to the Kendal MIT train stop, outbound to Alewife. The subway was crowded, and they all huddled around in the corner of the back end of the large subway car. There was a lot of talking and commotion in the subway car from rolling bottles and cans: it filled the ears of all the listeners.

Michael started engaging in a serious conversation with Ted, asking him about markets. Ted answered those questions in depth, keeping his mind busy from the demons flying around inside his head. Sam said little until they all got off on Davis square. Jennifer and Erin lived closer to Boston, but they were spending the night with Sam, and Tim was planning on crashing at Michael's house, which was not far off from College Ave.

Ted held onto his grin, looking up at the near empty sky, filled with little stars, and that old oppressive moon, beating down on him. The weight of the light was heavy as they walked up towards College Ave. Michael and Tim waved their farewell as they took a right on Morrison Ave. It was now, just Ted, Erin, Jennifer and Sam. Of course, seeing as Ted's house was only three houses further down the road, they might as well have been going to the same place.

Ted's fists clenched at his side, and his right-hand trembled underneath the pressure he put them under. He tried to maintain that fake smile, but now, he knew it became less of a mask now, as there were now two people who could see through it. And they knew it, and he knew it. He felt naked before them.

And yet, the damned majestic moon beat his spirit down as they walked down the sidewalk. *Just a little further, and I can close the door behind me.* He thought to himself. He kept his pace as his heart felt like it was beating through his chest. The breaths became more rapid, he resorted to breathing through his nose to limit his noise as they walked. Erin, Jennifer, and Sam were caught up in some conversation that Ted tuned out. He didn't want to be bothered by anything useless. *What good is it? Everything is pointless.*

At last, he could see his beautiful, peaceful, and empty house. He was close. The three women moved up the stoop to the apartment building. Ted waved good-bye briefly before picking up his pace.

"Tedward!" Jennifer called.

Damn it! "Yes?" He turned his head towards her and greeted her with his smirk.

"I'm sure I'll see you Tuesday?" She brushed her brown hair behind her shoulders.

"I haven't given it much thought," he answered vaguely.

"Will you come?" Her simper faded into a stare much more sincere.

"Time will tell. It always does," he responded.

"Yes or no?" she asked again. "No more dodging the question."

"I don't know if I'll come or not. I'll think about it," he replied, lowering his voice as his hand began to tremble.

"Don't make me text you in the dead of night again."

"I wouldn't dream of it. Good night."

He turned around. He started walking back down the sidewalk at a brisk pace. He could feel visions flashing before his face, the nightmares were not far behind. They never were. He could hear the opening of the apartment building behind him, and Sam, Erin, and Jennifer started walking inside.

Suddenly, he couldn't move another step. It was not as if his legs were heavy, or that he suddenly lost all energy to move, it was like his body lost the will to move. He grunted as he tried to move something, but his body did nothing. Even the will power of Task Force Seven was not enough to move anything. He could feel his knees getting weak again.

Not here. Damnit! Not here! No! No! NO! His knees buckled and he tumbled forward, catching himself from hitting his face on the concrete.

He could feel the darkness coming in around him. The oppression from the moonlight pushed him further into the darkness and deeper into the prison inside his own mind. His whole body trembled.

He gasped, breathing heavily. His eyes closed as he started choking by the pressure inside his own chest. Grief took over him again. And he couldn't hold it anymore. "Yaaah!" he sobbed; his mouth opened wide as tears streamed down steadily at the side of his face. "Aaah! Aaah! Aaah!" His sobs were louder, much like a dull roar.

Jennifer immediately felt the chills come over her, her hair stood on ends, and the goose bumps were raised from her arms. She could hear him and turned from the door before closing it, running outside. She ran towards Ted, and she gasped, never imagining she would ever see Ted on his knees, out in the open least of all. He was on all fours like a beast, sobbing, and choking on the tears of his sadness. Sprinting over to him and tried to place her hand on his back, she gasped as she tripped forward, her hand passed through him like a ghost. Turning around immediately, catching herself. She looked Ted in the face, his eyes open, but swollen with tears. He gazed straight at her, but not to her. Almost like he was in a corner, staring at a wall. His sobs, she recognized them. These were not the sobs of a man, but that of a child.

I—I passed through him? No. I must be imagining it. She walked back over to him while he continued to sob. He didn't move at all. She went to place her hand on his back, and it passed through him again, touching the ground. She gasped, retracting her hand. Her hand trembled, she felt her heart growing heavy, and she found it hard to breathe as the air chilled her throat. *I didn't—I didn't imagine it. What is going on?* Her face cringed. She heard Erin and Sam's footsteps behind her, both with gaping eyes. Tears entered her eyes as fear sank her heart and she grabbed her heart. "Ted?"

There was no answer.

"Ted," he continued to sob, moving from his tones to that of a child, to something even younger.

"Ted!" Sam exclaimed. "What is going on? Answer me!"

"Tedward!" Jennifer cried.

The wind started howling around them. Jennifer peered beyond Ted, looking down the rest of College Ave, seeing nothing out of the ordinary except that the road didn't end. It kept going, and going, and going, as if she found herself in some figment of another reality: a reality of endless despair.

Ted continued to sob. There was a pool of tears below his face.

Samantha went up to Ted and tried to place her hand on him. Her hand passed through him, as if he was nothing more than an empty hologram. She felt the darkness coming in, swirling around her. Her vision saw nothing but blackness, and the temperature dropped drastically, forcing her hairs on ends. Placing her hand in front of her face, and saw all five of her fingers, bright as day, but everything else was dark. She was utterly alone in a black pit.

Erin looked down at Ted as he continued to sob. She noticed that after Sam and Jennifer tried to touch him, they both seemed to stand still.

"Ted! Jenn! Sam! Get up!" she cried out.

She was not about to touch Ted. Not with that.

She reluctantly stepped forward, in the attempt to shake Jenn and Sam up. But she couldn't touch Ted.

Was he some kind of wizard? Why are they like this?

Her heart pounded inside her chest. A flood of thoughts flooded her mind as they turned into innumerous questions. Ted, Sam, and Jennifer appeared to be frozen in place. What she was seeing could only be described as supernatural, which was not part of the reality Erin knew and understood and this mysticism cut something in her faith in God, for a world with magic does *not* exist. Erin touched Sam on the shoulder. She shook her awake until Sam came out, of whatever it is she woke up from, weeping.

"What was that?" Erin looked down at Ted, in his shocked state. Her eyes trembled as she pulled Jennifer away from him. Jennifer was not weeping when she came back to reality.

"I don't—I don't know. It was like—" Sam began.

Ted gasped and his weeping stopped. His arms stopped shaking as his head focused on the end of College Ave.

"Ted! What is going on?" Jennifer went back to him, despite the protests from Erin. "Answer me!"

"Jenn, I don't think—"

The temperature dropped again. "Jenn, get back!" Sam pulled her away from Ted. The three of them took large steps back, keeping their eyes, however trembling, fixed upon Ted, kneeling on the ground. His hands grabbed the sidewalk, and they could see blue veins rose up over his skin, the blue veins crawled over his shoes and clothes, emitting a black light from them. over his body, their eyes opened widely as they had no idea what they were looking at.

Ted? Jenn thought to herself.

Ted pushed himself off the ground in a sprint, and within a singular stride, he landed nearly two-hundred feet away. He sprinted off another stride, and another until they couldn't see him anymore. There was silence in the air, and the summer heat returned.

Sam and Erin started walking back into her apartment, completely flustered and upset. Jennifer could hear them speaking in flustered tones, discussing specifically what it was that they saw, and the sensation of absolute darkness and the sudden chills. Jennifer couldn't hear any more of what they were saying, but she imagined their reaction would be as much the same as hers: confusion. Veins on the skin were not prominent, and she was unaware of any new scientific discoveries about an additional circulatory system. Those were veins, she recognized them, but they're not supposed to be black, or changing color, nor should they even be able to climb and crawl on the skin. She sighed heavily, and clenched her fists at her side, feeling the tears stream down her face.

Tedward, my Tedward, what did they do to you? Is this the source of all your pain? If it is, I don't even think I could forgive it. This is inexcusable. I'll let you go for now, but I will find you again.

Chapter 19 Ghost

~I was destined to live and die in obscurity.

***

Culain sat down in the hotel room. He sat on the bed waiting for a call, his mobile phone rested on the glass coffee table.

He sent Ilya off to London to report to their Headquarters. Blanka and Alexander were sent to scout this late at night. The moon was full, and he knew full well that when the moon was full, the likelihood of a gate being opened was higher. Any number of those Threckets could show up in someone's house or on a rooftop.

But there was another problem here, something that needed his attention. Another fae, unknown or operating underneath someone's radar. He knew full well that whoever did this wasn't supposed to be operating the seaport that night, least of all, killing normies. *Whoever it was didn't even finish the job.* He was waiting on a call from headquarters about any additional information on the man. They had his face through the mana veins of Ilya, who absorbed all the final memories of Jamal, who Culain then executed before Ilya converted their essence into mana that she could use. Whoever this was, he was going to be a problem.

His laptop was out, still locked as he hadn't logged into it yet.

Ring.

He picked up his phone immediately with urgency, fumbling the phone in his hands as he carried it to his ear. "Culain."

"Culain, this is Administrator Sander." Came the voice on the other end of the phone.

"Yes. I take it you got the information you needed?" Culain asked.

"Yes. Ilya is being sent back to you now. She'll be arriving tomorrow. Did you check your email?"

"Not yet." Culain logged into his computer and pulled up his email account, opening a secured email. It had a few attachments from the administrator. He opened it to look at the face of the man in question,

226

of course, Culain never saw him, but this person looked very young, perhaps in his teen years. There was a long document attached as well. He opened it and it was a single one-paged-report. "I have it open."

"That is all of the information that we have on the face that we've been able to come up with."

Culain scanned the page. Atop the page read: *Ghost 19943702940124*. He perplexingly blinked. He scanned through it again. The report wasn't very long. It only gave specific locations in countries, no report on what was done there. No date of birth. No Social. No physical name. "Sander, I don't mean to be rude, but did you forget to leave out his name?"

"No," he answered. *"That is all of the information we were able to locate on this man's face. Granted, it doesn't exactly match the face of the image Ilya provided. Probably due to an old photo."*

"That is what I thought." Culain commented. "How did you come by this information?"

"I had to pull some favors from the American Administration. Unfortunately, even our inside operatives only know so much. That is all they were able find out. American military erased everything."

Culain laughed out loud. "Of fucking course, they did. Damnit. When the fucking American yanks want to keep something a secret, they're almost as good as we are."

"Yes," Sander said. *"Which begs the question: why?"*

Culain shook his head and scratched his chin. "They want to keep something hidden. So, either this person knows something he shouldn't, or he is that something that they wanted hidden. But then, why would they just let him roam free?"

"No idea."

"How old is this photo I'm looking at?"

"Eight years."

"So, the most recent documentation anyone has on this person is from eight years ago." Culain scoffed. "Well, can you have someone look into anything useful that might have involved the U.S. military eight years ago? I'll keep an eye out for this kid. I can't just have him messing around whenever the hell he wants. Besides, I want to keep unnecessary deaths down to a minimum over here. You know how hard that is."

"Yeah, I'll keep you in the loop."

Culain hung up the phone. He looked closely at the features of the man he set his gaze upon. The man had the stern look of a killer. He had broad shoulders, and yet, then stood at a mere 5'6. Culain was certain the man was much taller than that now. Or that was how Ilya put it. Was this a kid?

What were you doing there? And why that night? The thoughts rolled around his head when his laptop *pinged*. He opened another email. It was bcc'd:

Attention all agents,

At approximately 2130 GMT, the Holy Grail and Pandora's Box was stolen. The only known lead we have is Former Major Sarah McCurdy, from the American Administration. All agents are to treat Sarah McCurdy as extremely dangerous. Teams will be sent in to track and locate McCurdy at all costs. Any information you have on McCurdy's whereabouts are to be communicated to Administrator Sander immediately.

It is unknown what she intends to do with the grail. Keep the general population out of this. I don't think I need to remind you what failure to comply will mean. This is of the utmost importance.

~Administrator Sander

He marked the email as unread. He shook his head. "Of fucking course, she did. The dumb white American bitch. For Americans, you especially are intolerable."

He took out his phone. He dialed Alexander's number. Alexander picked up the phone after the first *ring.* "Alexander."

"You, and Blanka, get back here now. There is a code red emergency." *Click.*

Culain started swearing underneath his breath. He made a cup of coffee, probably a bad idea but he needed to stay alert. He knew his history very well, and whenever someone *else* had the grail, bad things tended to escalate. Culain drank his coffee black as he waited for Blanka and Alexander to get back to the hotel.

The door opened. Blanka and Alexander walked in briskly. Culain couldn't have been waiting for more than thirty minutes.

"What's the emergency?" Blanka asked, very concerned because she knew the number of code red emergencies were very few.

"An American stole the grail." Culain answered.

Alexander's eyebrow raised. "What?"

"You heard me right. An American stole the fucking grail." He snarled.

"Why would they do that?" Blanka shook her head rapidly and raised both of her hands up with open palms.

"I don't fucking know!" Culain snapped. "Obviously, we can't exactly do anything about it now. All we know is that Major Sarah McCurdy from the U.S American Army, and the American Administration has the grail; why, I don't know. She succeeded in stealing the grail not that long ago actually. So, it stands to reason it's on its way here. Or somewhere here. Probably DC. We don't have to worry about that now. But everyone needs to know."

"Secondly, we have new orders."

"About?" Alexander kept his fists trembling at his sides.

"What do you mean we don't have to worry about that now? Last time someone else stole the grail, we had to start world war two to cover that mess up!" Blanka pointed a stern finger at Culain.

"Not so loud!" Culain pointed back with gritting teeth. "Walls are thin. Right now, that is going to be another office's problem."

"What if—what if it's a conspiracy? And the American branch is behind it," she asked.

"We'll have to cross the bridge when we get to it," Culain explained. "No need to worry about it now. If that is the case, we're the poster board definition of being irrevocably fucked. Someone else will deal with it, and Sander is good at getting a team together for that purpose."

"World war two was a messy situation to get into," Alexander admitted. "But our new orders."

"Yes, our current order still stands, but we need to be keeping an eye on any unregistered fae activity," he answered. "That kid, whatever, from seaport that night, there is limited information available on this guy, and we need to track him down."

"We tried that night, but his trace disappeared," Alexander said.

"Ilya may have mistakenly absorbed the mana reservoir of what he left behind for us to track him efficiently," Culain explained. "She should be back tomorrow, and we can get some kind of plan in place when she does."

"What do we know about him?" Blanka asked.

"A code name, and he's American. That's it," he answered.

Blanka and Alexander exchanged confused looks with each other. "What?" Blanka broke the silence.

"I said the same thing. His code name is Ghost, and we don't know who he is, identity or otherwise. We need to keep an eye out for him. Besides, if McCurdy is working remotely, she's probably getting help with someone off the grid, and he seems like he's off the grid."

"I find it hard to believe that's all we know." Alexander said. "That is too little information on anyone."

"That's what I said. Sander is looking deeper into it, but this is the only reliable information we have on him that, and he lives somewhere in the Greater Boston Area."

Chapter 20 Hedgehog

~Humans don't take their own lives because they want to die. Every day, every day they wake up in this nightmare. Every single day, I wake up to see the lives of those whom I killed. I see them every waking moment, and in my sleep. I can't escape from them. We take our lives because all we want is for the pain to stop. Is that so much to ask? Is that really so terrible?

***

Four weeks later, Sam and Jennifer lost hope for Ted. He never answered the door. He stopped answering phone calls, and text messages. The mail in his apartment never left the mailbox, just sat there, as if no one ever bothered to take any of it out. Even Erin didn't see him at work anymore. When she inquired, Ted simply left. He was no longer part of that brokerage. His porch grew dust, floating and clouding every time a small gust of wind would blow into the house. He was gone. He packed everything up, and he just left.

Jennifer had high hopes for him. He seemed to have come a long way that night, July fourth, but was it too far? Was he pushed to the brink where the only option for him was total isolation? Did he live in that house anymore? Sam couldn't be sure. But every single Saturday and Sunday morning, she would knock on his door. There was never an answer.

She still didn't understand what she saw that night. Ted showed veins, glowing in the dark in numerous colors, she couldn't even tell how many shades of green she thought she saw on his body *and* his clothes, and not to mention that he made an inhuman stride. She, Erin, and Jennifer all saw the veins and agreed within themselves that they should never mention what they experienced to anyone else, for fear of being labeled as insane.

It was a whole month ago. Perhaps she was just imagining things, but that was the first time he showed his pain openly to them. It was not something to take for granted. *Ted, we tried. We failed you. I'm sorry.* She placed her hand on his door, one last time. *I just hope—I just hope you're alive. If you can't find help from us, find help from somewhere. Please.*

This was the last Sunday she would choose to knock on this door. Perhaps constant badgering him with texts and phone calls did seem rather stalkerish. She should have known, if a man at her office started doing it, she would feel the same way: isolated. A man as alone as he intended to be, perhaps their attempts at friendship finally drove him off, leading him to leave everything behind.

She removed her hand from the door that Saturday, never to knock on that door again.

Tuesday came around. It was the last Tasty Tuesday, and Sam's load was picked up early and without delay. She was enjoying her commission checks but made sure to put plenty of it aside. She walked up to the church and grabbed a cup of coffee in the fellowship hall, nice and early. Granted, the coffee from the coffee machine maker with the pitiful excuse of coffee capsules was disgusting. Still, it was better than nothing.

There were volunteers coming in and out from the side kitchen, bringing in plates of cheese and crackers; some were even gluten-free. She leaned against the pillar, watching as people came by, talking with one another, often with a full mouth or in between bites. She sighed as she bowed her head down, drowned in her own thoughts of isolation.

She felt an arm wrap around her shoulders. "What's got you in a slump?" Michael frowned.

She came to and looked at him. "It's Ted."

"I don't think Jenn or Erin's heard from him either." He took a bite of some sliced cheddar. "I suppose it's time to let go."

"I know, I—I just—I don't even know anymore. I just, from what little he let us in on, I just know he isn't going to get help. Michael, I don't even—I don't even know if he's alive." She started tearing up a little, bringing her hand to her mouth. "Can a man really live with all of that darkness?"

"You and Jenn knew him better than I did. All I could really talk to him about was work. I did my best, but his walls were up around me also." He answered. "But I think that we've done all that we can do. I don't think there's any more we could have done."

"But there must have been something more, something else," she explained. "All it takes is one more good act. All it takes is to know someone is there. You said it yourself, we as Christians need to do better, but how can we if we can't even do this?"

He let out a sigh. "You're right. We can't. We can't do anything. Only God can, and perhaps this is exactly what needed to happen." He let out another deep sigh as he swallowed a cracker, "Have you ever heard of the hedgehog dilemma?"

"No."

"These little creatures that shoot quills outside of their hide as a defense mechanism. Whenever they are cold, they try to huddle with each other for warmth, but fail to do so because whenever they get too close, they hurt each other with their quills, making it painful and dangerous. Effectually, they don't want to get too close for fear of hurting themselves or others. So, none of us know what happened to him because he won't tell us. He seems withdrawn to us, because he's afraid of being hurt. He feels that the closer someone is to his heart, the harder it is going to hurt."

"That makes sense, I think I understand now. He hides behind his mask, the smiles, the laughter because he doesn't want us to know how he actually feels, because he'll be giving a part of himself over to us, or other people. It is easier for him to live in a life of solitude than it is for him to trust others."

"I think, someone, or many, probably many people stepped on his toes and betrayed his trust numerous times where he has no faith in any person. He doesn't trust anyone."

"But Michael, he needs someone to help him carry the load. He needs help."

"He won't accept it. It is a cruel reality. I can't help but wonder exactly what he went through in the military. Maybe, just maybe, inviting him to the fireworks was a bad idea."

"Maybe." she admitted. "But we would never know unless we try."

"You truly are trying to be a new kind of hero aren't you." Michael smirked.

Park Street Church emptied into the street on a dark and dreary night. Fog rolled in. The mist rose from the ground, filling the air with an aura of decaying mud and sadness. Sam felt its oppressive weight fill her lungs. She let Michael lead her up Park Street towards Teri Nation. The group followed behind them, following behind the heavily oppressive fog.

Sam could find in herself, beyond the miscellaneous chatter of everyone around her, she found it difficult to breathe in the fog. Her heart weighed heavily with every passing step. She was missing something. But what was it? What was the one thing she could do, one thing she could have done differently? Or was this opportunity gone? And was Ted lost forever? She knew she had to let it go, but something kept telling her to try, just one more time. She took a deep breath as her thoughts filled her heart again. *If I must knock on that door all day Saturday, Ted, I will. So, help me, God. I will until you answer the door, or my knuckles bleed.*

She held Michael's hand as they entered the threshold of Teri Nation. They walked on the carpet, passing by many smiling faces. The faces smiled genuinely as if there wasn't one less person in the world. So cruel, a world filled with smirks, as if they hide the fact that the world they lived in was filled with Devils that sneered, and kind broken hearts. The broken hearts of the kind souls were damned to die here. The Devils, the cruel smiling devils thrive here.

They turned the corner into the back of the bar. Sam found her eyes scanning the bar, as if hoping against hope that Ted would be here. Scott waved at them with that smiling face hidden behind that glorious beard. Her heart sank as Ted was not here. But why should he be? Something caught her attention, a half-drunk glass of red wine with the beverage nap resting on it. There was no one sitting right in front of it.

Sam let Michael walk her to the bar. Jennifer and Tim were not far behind, still talking amongst themselves. Even Jennifer still seemed depressed, and mildly angry. Her face frowned and her eyes angled emptily at the bar top.

As she walked behind them, tilting side to side, she looked downward at the ground. She wasn't mad at Ted, how could she when she didn't know the whole story. She wanted, out of her own scientific curiosity to know the whole story, tucked away in a steel trap, but she now knew that she would never get an answer, and would never see Ted again; however, whatever the story was, whoever or whatever did it to him, was so horrible, it led him to his perpetually hollow existence.

"Are we having the special again?" Scott asked.

"You know it," Michael said, also not feeling enthused enough to give a vibrant answer.

"Same. Scott. Same," Jennifer answered. She didn't smile.

"I'll take a cider," Tim answered, his usual answer. He was the only one of the four of them who was in a *normal* mood, if normal was the right word for it. He never had much of a relationship or interaction with Ted.

"Merlot," Sam answered. She almost didn't make it to the "lot".

Scott pointed his index finger back and forth between the four of them. "Together, or separate?"

"Together." Michael nodded his head as his hand reached his back pocket for his black wallet. "I've got this one."

They stood in silence for a minute, waiting for the bar to fill. Moments later, the ruckus started. Scott quickly returned with their drinks, a cider, merlot, and some mystery drinks that Sam didn't pay much attention to. Sam twirled her cup dispassionately, staring down at the ripples inside her glass.

"Well now, let us not let the drear and gloom get our spirits down, shall we?" Jenn forced a cheerful smirk. "After all, in the end we all die anyway. Our life is frail and fleeting. Let us not remain in the bitter pit of despair, and then let us remember what we were able to do for those not us, while we are here. That is all we can rely on, is what we are able to do with what little time we have before we're called to death." She raised her glass, her hand trembling with tears streaming down her face. "To my dear sweet Tedward. May you find some hope in this fragile world."

"To Ted." Tim raised his glass. He looked at her closely, thinking this felt like a toast to a funeral, and of course, he knew to Jennifer, this seemed to be. He couldn't help but feel this was rehearsed, and here she was trying to bring closure on herself.

"To Ted." Michael raised his glass; he frowned as his cup was lifted.

Samantha felt it surreal to be raising a glass to someone they didn't know if they were going to see again. She felt like she was saying good-bye as she raised her glass in the air. "To Ted." *Good-bye Ted. Until next time, if there is a next time.*

They all took a sip of their dismal toast, inside a bar which was filled with many happy smiles. Any normal human person would find this to be an odd venue to mourn the loss of a friend or family, or acquaintance.

Sam leaned into Jennifer. She knew that out of all of them, Jennifer would take it the hardest. She was not Ted, who seemed to have Jennifer under some spell, intentional or not, she couldn't tell. She slowly wrapped her arm around her shoulder and swayed with her back and forth as they drank. They offered little words. They only drank, waiting for this period of mourning for their friend's departure, however long ago it was.

Sam looked through the bar again. Seeing friendly faces, those not aware of the pain around them. They don't care. They don't care about anything or anyone. Those sneers, those faces, merely simple contracts of agreement of respect, giving the impression that they truly cared. None of them did. Only through this, and only through Ted, did she understand this sudden truth. Even if Ted was no longer here, she would find him teaching them all something about the frailty of the human mind, and of mortality. *Who could actually be trusted?*

"Scott, I'll take another." Came a loud voice from across the other end of the bar.

It seemed familiar somehow. Sam looked in the direction from which it came. She excused herself, walking in the direction of the crowd. She passed through the clumps of people. She followed Scott as he brought another glass of red wine to the other end of the bar. She followed him until he made his delivery at the end. She made it to the end of the bar.

"Ted! You're here!" she exclaimed as the man took the cup of wine and looked down at her.

"You again! What the fuck do you want? Get out of my face! No one wants you here." He said.

"I'm sorry. I thought you were someone else." She said, bowing her head as she turned around. "My mistake."

"Yeah, keep better control of your friends, Bitch. I don't want to talk to you again." Culain snapped at her.

She scurried through the crowd and saw a lone man sitting behind a menu. He had his arms crossed as he carefully scanned the room. He had a smile on his face but didn't appear to notice her staring at him. He looked like Ted. She stopped walking and took a deep breath. She moved around the other bar top, into the little cove with the table with the man. Drinking a glass of wine and had some mashed on a plate, with only a singular bite taken out of it.

"Ted?" she asked.

"Hmm?" he looked up to her and grinned. "Oh, it's you. How have you been?"

"That is a painful question, and not one that I need to answer right now. Where have you been? We thought you were dead! Your mail, it's still sitting there!" she exclaimed, taking a seat next to him. She pointed a finger at him to emphasize the rage she had in her facial grimace, "Are you okay?"

"I'm about as okay as I'll ever be." He answered." I'll not get any better than this. I'll only get worse."

"How much worse can you get?" she said. "Look, I'm still not sure what I saw, and I'm not going to make you tell me. I'm not. If you want to talk, I'll listen. But Damnit Ted, you need help."

"I know I need help." He continued with that accursed fake simper.

"You know!" She was angrily sarcastic. "If you know, why don't you get help?"

"Because there is no one living that can understand how I feel, and there is no one living I can trust. Sure, some people experience emotional pain," his grin faded. "Some deal with grief, or depression, some deal with loss, and others deal with lack of trust, others feel guilty. But it is rare that they must put up with more than two or three of those at a time, and not near to the extent that I feel. My heart is always heavy, my heart is broken and it's nothing more than a ball to be played with, filled with scars and bullet holes. This heart is broken, and the body hasn't caught up yet."

"The only way for someone to understand is for you to talk about it. You don't let anyone try to understand. You keep pushing us away by your little disappearing acts." Her tone became soft. "Look, Erin isn't here. Michael, Tim, Jennifer and I just did a little toast because we thought you were dead, or at the very least none of us will see you again."

"I've told you before," his voice dropped down to the whisper, his eyes angled to her eyes. "I'm a murderer. I see the faces of the dead around me when I'm awake. The faces come back full throttle in my dreams. I hate sleeping because of this. I have nightmares, every single night, and I wake up in the same condition you saw me in that night. What you saw is me every single night. Every. Single. Night. There is not a day that goes by. I don't take vacations because of it. I don't rest because of it. My only hope is to work myself to death until I can no longer see these things."

"It's hard to imagine that you're still alive if your life is as tragic as all that." she asked.

He showed his wrists. There were no scars. "There should be scars here from me cutting. They're gone. I've tried drowning, driving a car and locking myself in while driving into the ocean. I failed that. I tried hanging myself, and all I did was hang there until the damned rope snapped."

"Why don't you ask for help? Ted, you need it!"

"You don't understand! I'm not human!" he gritted his teeth. "I don't deserve help, besides, in the end who would want to help a monster like me?"

Sam's eyes gaped open.

"What I told you that day, and you thought I was exaggerating, was the truth. Yeah, sure, I believe in God, a God of forgiveness and mercy, but so does the devil. I have killed too many people for Him to even consider forgiving."

"Te—"

"No!" he jabbed her in the chest with his finger. He grabbed his wallet and dropped a c-note on the table. "No Sam! You know something, they told me the first one was the only one that mattered. And it fucking broke me! And they lied! They all fucking lied!" His knuckles struck the table, "The first one wasn't the only one that mattered. Every single one mattered. I remember every single face. Every face! And I was never given a choice. Not one! Sam, I know the monsters and demons aren't hiding in the closets or underneath our beds. I'd be lucky if they were that far away. No, they're running amuck in our heads. And they are restless." He stood up and started walking away.

"Ted!" Sam called, trying to grab his hand.

He pulled his hand away. "No Sam! I'm not—I'm not worth saving." Tears streamed down his face. The ruckus of the bar ceased, and everyone turned. Jennifer put her drink on the bar and stood up, keeping her hands to her side. "I would like to believe," he choked on his tears. "That a person like me would be welcome into Heaven, because that's where I believe them to be. But I can't. I have too much blood on my hands. I'm not welcome there, and why should I be? I only have a handful of good memories, and what I wouldn't give to have that again, but the nightmares never stop. It haunts me when I'm awake, it haunts me when I'm asleep.

"I came into this world with nothing. I still have nothing. Everyone I have ever loved is dead. Everyone I ever trusted is either dead, dying, or betrayed me, and those that betrayed me I killed. And I would do it all over again. I came into this world with nothing, and what little I had accumulated was ripped from me. I will die with nothing. I'm not even going to get a tombstone. None of them ever got a tombstone. They served their country better and with more honor than anyone flashing that damn flag ever has and ever will and they were all thrown away for something they didn't do. If I could go back in time, I would, and I would get into those hospitals and strangle each of us so we wouldn't have to live and face the cruelty of this world. It would have been—it would have been better had the thirty-two of us never been born.

"There. Are you happy now? There's my heart. It's out in the open. Now why don't you do with it what you want and dissect it like a science project. I'm done!"

He went to turn away. Gunfire and screams filled his ears. He could feel the hot gun in his hands, ready to fire. The faces assaulted his mind again, the bleeding, and desecrated faces. He couldn't hear the swift footsteps of a weeping woman, sprinting behind him. He felt pressure on his chest as the woman wrapped her arms around him and held him as tight as she could.

Ted gasped, and he came to, realizing he was crying all this time inside the back bar of Teri Nation. There was no sound, except the deafening sobbing of this woman in front of him. He reluctantly scanned the room, sobbing, still. All eyes were on him, many people who had seen him in passing, many whom he didn't know, nor did he care to know. He looked down, and it was Jennifer who was holding him.

"Ha—how were we to know the pain you were in? The guilt, the shame, the hateful regret, despair and utter isolation. Any one of them can be as heavy as a mountain. And you bear all of them, your spirit is crushing underneath all of that weight!" Jenn sobbed. "Why do you do this to yourself? Why? You can't—you can't keep living like this. You just can't! One mountain is enough to kill a man, crush his spirit. And you bear all of it. There's no need, none, to go at it alone. You need to stop not wanting to burden yourself to others. I know you feel like we won't understand, because we don't know what you're going through. I know you feel like we would sooner stab you than help you. You can't keep living like this, Ted. Not when you have—you have friends to help. You may not see it, and you may not accept us as your friends, but here we are, trying to help you." His body was still, and firm like a petrified dead fish. She buried her face against his chest. "We want to help. You can't go through life like this alone. Let us help you!"

His eyes gaped open straight at the bar, as if filled with some traumatic memory he found himself trapped inside. His eyes watered and his pupils trembled inside those bulbs as if he saw something absolutely terrifying.

"I know you don't trust us, but we trust you to make the right decision."

"The—the last person who put trust in me died in my arms." He sobbed.

She looked up to him with sobbing, swollen eyes, and she smiled through the pain. "Then let us be a light that your darkness so desperately needs. Let us fill that empty hole. I will help you bear this burden, Ted. We all will. I will be your light and I mean that." She rubbed her tears on his chest again. "I will—I will help carry that pain. You don't need to do it alone anymore. You say you've lost everyone you cared about, but we're here. And you may not care about us, but that feeling isn't mutual. Even in the handful of times we've gotten the chance to hang out with you, your absence will not go unnoticed. You say you no longer have a family. Let us be your family. I know you're in pain, and hate yourself for living, but damnit all Ted, life is too short to be bitter about the past, give yourself a fighting chance to enjoy what little life you have left. Give yourself a fighting chance, if—if not for your sake, then for mine!"

She sobbed into his chest, still held onto it tightly. He tried to move his arms up to push her off him, but then the most peculiar thing happened. Even his will was not enough to move his arms, no matter how hard he tried. They just wouldn't move as if his very being refused to let go of this woman, who provided something to him.

She released him, only to wrap her arms around his neck. "This is—this is what you forgot: the world is filled with so much uncertainty. The world is filled with darkness, and is contaminated by the utter rot of humanity, and at times we may think that life is not worth living. But what is certain, is that while the darkness of the world may be like murky waters, and impossible to see through, behind the veil of darkness is light."

"But the darkness has a way of snuffing out the light. I don't want to do that to you." He stammered.

"If that is what it takes, I will gladly take that risk."

"No—"

"At the cost of my own light." She repeated.

Why does she talk like her? Damn it, why is she so much like her. I don't want this. Why can't I just die in peace? Why must I be flooded into ancient memories of the past that must be buried, and buried properly? Jenn, if I let you in, I can never let go. Do I—do I even want to let it go? Slithers, you were always there. Slither's face crossed his mind. He could see her smiling at him with the sun radiating behind her, and that beautiful meadow with the ducklings crossing in the lake. *So cruel, forcing me to look into the past as real today as it was, but it is only a mask. It's not real, but does it—does it really matter?*

Immediately, he burst out in tears, weeping as the strength of his arms returned him and embraced Jennifer. He wept into her shoulders, berating her with all his pain, all his trauma, all his grief, all his depression, and all his isolation. Lord knew he had those in no short supply.

Sam's tears streamed down her face as she approached him from the side and hugged them both, her head was buried on Jenn's shoulder. No one could hear the steps of Michael and Tim who made it to the other side. Tim hugged Ted from behind as Michael placed his hand on his back. Tim was much more emotional than Michael.

The bar began to empty. The citizens of the bar left, one by one, leaving the huddled mass of people just there, moving around like water on rocks. Some glanced at the crying mass but gave it no more thought than that of curiosity, not sharing a shred of care in the world for the broken man, the man who wanted nothing more than to die, but could never follow through with it, or else risk killing what remained of his squad's memory, his only true friends and family.

Jennifer rubbed her face against his chest again. "Ted, will you come with us on Tuesday?"

"Ye—yes." Was his reply. "I'll come. I'll come. You don't need to find me. I'll be there. You don't need to call or text. I will be there."

Chapter 21 The Hunger

~Innocence was murdered that day. A true friend will kill his friend, because only a true friend would bear the burden for him. A true friend wouldn't let another friend live in rotting regret.

***

It was a long year. He waited in the bright white room. He sat in a grey steel chair, watching the room with his ever-watchful eyes, listening with those sensitive ears. There was a large speaker in the ceiling, and a large one-way window. He sat at a white table, pristine, and without flaws. The door creaked open, and another child, his age, came into the room, escorted by a soldier, dressed in his camouflage uniform, proud and mighty, like a hero.

This kid seemed friendly. He didn't have a name yet. He was sat right in front of him. He was happily sitting down, turning his head and marveling at the bright lights with a large smile and gaping beautiful brown eyes. He waved his feet forward and backwards, just waiting for whatever surprise they had next for them. They were all good kids. They earned some kind of reward. He looked at the boy's shirt, which had merely the number "2" written on it, not a name. He turned down to his, looking for something to identify himself with: "7".

"This is exciting!" Two said, clapping his hands with elation, like a child who knew without a doubt something good would happen. He could barely restrain his excitement. "Seven, what you think they gonna gif us?"

"I dunno." The boy called Seven shrugged, leaning forward, looking at the room suspiciously.

"Maybe ah, ah, ah, one of those thick brown things the rest of 'em eat. That looks good!" Said Two, who began drooling.

"Or maybe a glass of that white stuff," Seven replied.

243

Two's blue eyes glistened with elation, and his blond hair matched as it glimmered in the light. "Somethin' nice and sweet to wash it down!" he continued to clap his hands erratically.

Another soldier opened the door and came in. Seven read her name tag, J. Nakamura. She had the gold-bar insignia. Seven paid attention to this. She came in with a plate, a single plate and on that plate was a piece of a bread, just a slice, and the most unappetizing one they could find, it would seem. The white bread was browning, with green mold growing at the side of it, the bread was crumbling on the plate. Nakamura placed it in the middle of the table, directly in between the two.

Number too looked down at it and was immediately disappointed. He turned around in his chair. "Ma'am. Is this it?"

"Yes, it is." She smiled at him.

"You dun feed us a week and this all we get?" his head was downtrodden.

"Affirmative. Now, do be good, sweet little boys and don't touch it until we say so." She answered. She closed the door behind her, locking the locks from the other side.

"Well, sucks this!" Two cried out, slamming both of his fists on the table. The reinforced table trembled. His face grimaced and tears streamed down his face, his hands were grabbing his hair as he leaned forward on the table. "I hungry." His stomach growled.

Number Seven joined in, staring at the food. Even the mold looked good enough to eat. They were all hungry, he couldn't think how much longer he could wait. They were starving to the point where Seven, at least, would gladly eat dirt. He was not so sure of number Two.

The bright light went out. Both leaped from their chairs and backed into the walls. The red lights came on, flashing the room in that twirling bulb in the ceiling. They were both startled, their hearts pounding against their chest. They huddled close to the wall. The intercom came on, and the loud alarm went off, scratching the inside of their ears. They both screamed, tears streamed down as their eyes remained gaped open, covering their ears tightly with their hands. Even their hands were not enough. The oppressive sound pushed them to the ground as their back slid down. They wept, crying, "Momma!"

The alarm stopped, and the white lights were turned back on. The intercom clicked on again. "I think it's time we play a little game. How's that sound?" said the voice of Lieutenant Nakamura. "That sounds like fun."

Two and Seven were still stunned on the ground. They panted heavily.

"Don't be like that. Do I have to sound the alarm again?"

They immediately crawled to their chairs again, crawling like little children out of their pen. They crawled up to their chairs, which to them seemed tall enough for a giant. They pulled themselves up with relative ease. They sat straight in their chair, both scanning the room.

"So, do you want to play a game."

"Yes!" As if he nearly forgot about the alarm, Two sounded elated yet again. *Why?*

"You see, the door is locked and will only open from the outside. You have a plate with one slice of bread on it. Only one of you can leave. Decide for it yourselves. You can both starve or fight for the bread. This is a winner take all game. You've got this!" she exclaimed rather enthusiastically.

They both looked at each other in disbelief. "Se—seven, are they—are they makin' us fight?"

"I don't wanna." Seven protested. He crossed his arms and turned his body away from the bread. "I don't wanna!"

"That's the name of the game." Nakamura said over the intercom. "You live or you die."

Seven stared at the wall, pushing his legs back and forth in the chair, ignoring his hunger. He ignored the growling in his stomach. "Seven. I'm not doing it. I'm not."

"I'm not doing it either. Cross my heart hope to die." Seven replied. "Then decided."

Two went into the other corner of the room and sat there. Seven moved from his seat and sat in the opposite corner. They smiled at each other from across the room.

Hours passed. Neither of them moved. The hunger from inside their tummies was growing, eating away at their life like a tapeworm. They both grimaced, breathed deeply by sucking through their teeth as they both kept their hands on their tummies, applying pressure in the hope that it would alleviate some of their discomfort.

They both were in so much pain, they couldn't fall asleep. All they could think about, was not fighting, and not eating that disgusting moldy bread. They both toppled to the side, curling themselves up with their knees to their chest: grimacing, and crying.

The intercom turned on. "Congratulations!" Nakamura exclaimed from the other end of the mirror. "You've passed. You both can leave. Just make sure to finish the bread first."

They both felt a new energy sweep over them. They crawled got up and crawled to the chair. They both sat in, and number Two excitedly took the piece of bread and ripped it in half. He held both pieces in his hand and told Seven, "It be okay! I knew we do it. Here."

Seven smirked at him, taking the smaller piece. They both simpered and nodded as they ate the moldy bread. It was bitter, dry, and almost unbearable, but it was food. They could hear the door mechanisms come free. "Seven! We can leave!" They both got up from the table together, and went together, walking side by side. They reached for the handle of the door, smiling.

Click.

Two's eyes opened wide, as he sucked air through his teeth. The handle turned but the door wouldn't open. He grinded his teeth. "Hey! Lady! What gives? You said we can go!" he pounded on the door with both fists. "Let out!"

"You both are going to leave." Nakamura explained, in her sweet voice. "You didn't think we'd just leave a body in there did you? Only one of you leaves alive. You can't leave at all until one of you is standing. Good luck!"

"Sucks this." Two said.

Number Seven moved away from the larger boy. He cowered in fear as he leaned against the wall. Number Two sighed, and turned to number Seven, raising his fists. "I need out." He sobbed. "Come here! I can't do dis anymore!"

Number Two charged at Number Seven. Number Seven raised his arms over his head to protect himself from the much larger boy who struck him with fists like rocks. He was kicked in the side; his face was slammed into the wall. Number Two grabbed the hair of number Seven and repeatedly knocked his face into the wall. He tripped number Seven and started swinging his feet until number Seven stopped moving. He took his free foot and kicked the head into the ground, hoping for certain number Seven was dead.

Number Two cried as he walked back to the door. He went to open it, and there was no click. He looked back to the mirror. "Lady! Open up. He dead, just like you wanted. He dead. Let me out!" he sobbed, moving his fists to his side. "LET ME OUT!"

"I said, only one of you leaves alive."

"I already fucking told you! He dead!" he cried out. He cried into the camera monitoring the room, pointing with open hands where he thought Seven was laying.

"N—no. I not." Said Seven. His face was bruised and swollen. He put his hands up, in defense position. "I do dis arr day. I can do dis arr day."

"Let me out!" Two cried as he swung at Seven.

There was a blue flash as the temperature dropped in the room. Blue veins lit up Seven's arms, lighting up the room. Seven's output of his Mana Veins was so much that he was surrounded by blue cackling light, burning parts of his own flesh. Seven punched Two repeatedly with lightning-fast jabs, the impact made a sound so large, that the window cracked. Seven grabbed hold of Two's throat with his hand. His face grimaced as he squeezed the air out of Two's lungs. The larger boy tried his hardest to rip himself free, but to no avail as the blue light burned at his throat.

Crack!

Two's arms dropped down. Seven let him go, and the corpse fell to the floor, blood filling his mouth and his eyes seemed empty. Seven gasped as the mana veins receded into his body, and his hands stood still. He slowly, mechanically moved his head to look at Two, dead on the floor. His eyes gaped open with his mouth as he let out a screamless cry.

The lock from the door came undone. The door creaked open. Seven looked to it, looking at Lieutenant Nakamura coming in with a smile on her face, and a plastic zippy bag. She walked over to him, and kneeled, meeting him at eye level. She had a pleasant soft smirked on her face as she stroked the side of his face with a soft caress. "Good job, number Seven. You are my sweet little boy. Good job. As a job well done, here." She pulled out a black pill from the zippy bag and a bottle of water from one of her pockets, handing them both to him. "Eat."

Hungrily, Seven took the Pill, and washed it down with some water.

"Good boy." She said, taking his hand in hers. "Come with me."

Seven followed her silently, coming out of the oppressive white room. He walked with her down empty corridors, with the occasional soldiers looking down on him with disgust. They exchanged no empty simpered to him. They just glared in passing.

His right hand started to tremble. He began to realize the value of life, and its mortality. Life is not something one just takes away, it ought to be cherished and valued higher than a meal to a starving orphan, and he had just taken the life of his friend.

He let that sink in as he came to a large vertical door. The gears and mechanisms in the door started to move, causing the metal to creak as it scraped against itself. Slowly it let in the welcomed array of moonlight, where he saw many of the other children outside, in a chain linked fenced. Nakamura brought Seven to the fence and opened the door. She ushered him in and locked the door behind him.

He stifled a cry as his heart grew very heavy, turning around to look Nakamura in the eye. She smiled back at him. "I'll play with you later, my sweet little boy. Good job tonight. I knew you had it in you, Seven."

He watched her walk backwards, behind the vertical door as it closed in front of her. He looked up at the moon, and he could have sworn there were less stars in the sky. He looked down at the children in front of him. He counted them. One. Two. Three. Their faces were bruised, and he could have sworn the smaller red-headed girl had a black-eye. Four. Five. Six. They were nursing broken limbs: arms, legs, fingers. Seven. Eight. Nine. These three were coughing up red blood. The larger black—haired boy, coughed up some baby teeth. He breathed heavily. Ten. Eleven.

Twelve. These three had blood, not their own, smeared over their faces. Thirteen. Fourteen. Fifteen. These three were huddled in a corner, staring and clawing at the fence. And Seven made sixteen. This morning, there was thirty-two of them. Tonight, they were reduced by half.

He bit his bottom lip and clenched his fists at his side. He started wailing with tears streaming down his face, the guilt of his first kill took hold of him. It felt like someone was inside his chest, punching his heart repeatedly. His knees buckled and he caught himself with his arms, kneeling on all fours like the dirty dog he was. His hand was covered in the sand, and his tears made mud in front of him. He looked at the rest of them, as if they waited for someone to start, they all wailed in the air. Tears streamed down their faces.

Number twenty-seven, the thirteenth he counted, her glasses tilted down on her face, with blood smeared over both lenses. She raised her gaze over the sky, her mouth opened as something resembling drool came out of her mouth.

Next to her was a crying girl, brown hair tied up in a ponytail, with bangs on either side of her face. Her face grimaced, and her teeth grinded. She let out one squeal before she silenced herself, closing her mouth and letting her eyes scream with rolling tears into the ground like a puddle. She was number thirty-one.

Number thirteen, cried out loud, covering his mouth with one hand, and wiping an eye with a closed first. His short dark hair was almost invisible in the darkness of the night. The blood got into his eyes as he collapsed to the ground, curling in the fetal position and held his hands together in a tight ball, cutting off his own circulation in his hands. He brought that ball to his face.

Not one of them had names. These three would be part of Seven's personal squad in the future: Ticker, Butcher, and Slithers. All of them wept hard that night, and before the sun rose, nearly every foot had a puddle of nothing but tears.

Chapter 22 That is Enough

~After it all, I'm falling apart and I don't want to be put back together, but you're putting me back together anyway.

***

Jennifer woke up in the early morning, gasping for breath. She sweat profusely. She mechanically turned her head to her alarm clock, which read 7:21 AM. She coughed, covering her mouth with her hand as she slowly rolled out of bed, striking the ground. She slowly pulled herself up, using her side table to support herself. Her joints trembled, filled with searing pain. Her bones to her felt as frail as thin glass. She pulled herself back on her bed and leaned forward, taking deep breaths. She felt like her chest was caving inside her chest, the lungs bursting out at the seams of her ribs. She took numerous measured breaths.

She now felt at equilibrium. She leaned backwards, still breathing heavily with her hands rested on her chest. She looked up to the sky outside her window, the sun beamed down on her, glimmering with shadowy clouds slowly rolling in. She eased up on her breathing, and she felt her shortness of breath was stable, but her bones still felt like glass. She pulled out her cell phone, and immediately opened her email. Her fingers trembled as she rapidly typed with both fingers:

Good Morning Serine Galino,

I regret to inform you I cannot make it in today. I have some symptoms and need to get checked out by my Doctor.

Jennifer Miller.

She went into her contacts. She scrolled down to DR. Korowitz, her thumb trembled. She clicked the green call icon. She clicked speaker as the phone rang. She placed her phone on the side table. It rang and was answered quickly,

"Doctor Nicolai Korowitz's office. This is John, how may I help you?"

"Hi John. This is Jennifer Miller. I am one of Korowitz's patients. I woke up with a shortness of breath and I feel exhausted, and my joints are in searing pain. I woke up like this, in the morning. It was sudden. Is there anyway Doctor Korowitz can see me today?"

"Half a moment Jennifer." Jennifer could hear the rapid typing away rapidly. *"What is your date of birth?"*

"Eight. Second. Eighty-nine." She answered. *Click. Clack. Click. Clack.*

"He has an opening at nine o'clock."

"Please." She spoke with bated breath.

"See you at nine o'clock."

Jennifer sat in the waiting room in the medical office. The office was empty this morning, apart from a man sitting in the corner, waiting for his turn to get into the office. John, the receptionist was typing away on his computer, making notes and appointments for the doctors in the office. She waited patiently, still feeling weak in the legs. She crossed her arms over her lap as she stared ahead, concerned with whatever was going on with her body. It was all sudden. She had shortness of breath before, but not with this severity.

"Jennifer?"

Jennifer looked up and smiled at DR. Korowitz. The doctor had a thick Russian accent, and bright brown hair in his full lab coat. "Yes?"

"I will see you now."

Jennifer trembled as she stood up from the ground. She grimaced as the pain seeped into her legs, and she put on a smirk as she stood up. She walked quickly, but carefully towards DR. Korowitz. Korowitz frowned as he looked at her. He took her hand as she approached him, and he led her firmly to his patient room. She took a seat on the bed and he took a seat on the stool, logging into his computer.

"How are you feeling?" he asked in a soft voice.

"I'm in pain. This morning, I woke up with a shortness of breath. By itself, it isn't unusual; however, this wasn't usual. It was far worse, and it hurts my chest. I felt like my chest was going to collapse. I barely made it back to my bed after I fell off. My bones, particularly my legs feel like glass." She grimaced, letting her tears stream down either side of her eyes. "I've never felt this way, at least, not with this severity."

He started to take her blood pressure. "Is this the first time you woke up like this?"

"Yes." Was all she managed to say.

"Ease up on that arm." He instructed. His eyes angled at the machine, as if trying to piece together an age-old mystery. He wrote down the blood pressure. "Blood pressure is fine. Nothing to worry about there." He took a needle out and he drew her blood. "I'll be back." He placed a bandage on the spot where he drew blood. He left her inside the empty room.

She wiped her tears with her hand. She took deep breaths. She felt a vibration in her pocket. She took her phone out of her pocket. And she received a text from Ted. *Tedward. I wonder how you're doing. That was a serious breakdown, or breakthrough last night. I don't know what kind of pain you're going through, but it seems you and I will suffer together. Perhaps I'm being overdramatic. Yeah. That's it. I'm fine.*

She opened the text message:

Good morning, Jennifer. Words cannot express my feelings, sometimes I don't understand them myself. Do you want to come and feed ducks with me by the Gardens?

She sniffled, smiling at the text. She returned it quickly, *I don't know yet, Tedward. I would certainly love to. Can you do me a favor and call me later? Whenever you get off work tonight. I'd really appreciate it.*

Almost immediately, he returned the text. *I'll call you after 6 pm.*

She smiled. He was certainly quick to return a text, a swift response, and a response with utmost certainty. She had no doubts within her heart that he would call her at that time. She wiped more tears from her face as she put her phone back into her pocket.

The door swung open. Korowitz took out a medical document and handed it to her. She looked over it, while much of it was a lot of medical jargon, there were some things she did recognize. These were the results of her blood test; her CBC was alarming: three. Her eyes opened wide as the document trembled in her hand.

"We need to get you to the hospital. Did you drive here?"

"Yuh—yes." She stammered.

"We'll get the necessary call in place. You may be developing Leukemia." Korowitz took her hand. "Are you okay to walk right now?"

"Yes." Was all she could say. *Leukemia?*

He took her hand. He led her out of the patient room and led her down the hall, leading her through the vestibule and down to a chair in the waiting room. He went back behind the door. Korowitz went behind John, saying something to him inaudibly, who started typing away, and sent something to the printer.

She sat down, her hands trembled in front of her. She held back her tears, but her hands betrayed her feelings, for even John could notice the anxiety fueled her: her eyes gaped open as the pupils trembled inside her head, streaming down reluctant tears and her uncontrollable trembling. She leaned forward, frowning into her trembling hand.

She took another deep breath and buried her face in her hands, and spoke into her hands, muffling her words to God, "Lord. Forgive me. I don't think I've faltered. I don't think I have, but perhaps I've been caught up with Ted, and paid too much attention to him, and not enough of you. An innocent mistake by our standards down here below, but you are a perfect God, and our standards are not yours, and by yours I've made a fatal error. I'm sorry. I've escaped death before, twice. If it is your will, it would be a third time, but if not, I understand. I've had one too many second chances already. If it is your will, I accept. But please, let this not be my time. Just, please let me have a little while longer. Perhaps, I haven't been as faithful as I think I have. Perhaps that is my fatal error. Lord, remove the callouses from my heart. Please. Please. Please."

Jennifer woke up from the anesthesia, finding herself in a white room while sitting up. She looked out the window, the sun was setting. She looked around herself, seeing the nurses and physician assistants walking back and forth, attending to various patients. She looked around, to see if she could find her own pants and her phone. She looked carefully, trying to find something to tell the time. She knew she wouldn't have the results from the biopsy for another seven to ten days. There was no use trying to worry about it.

She found her brown purse sitting by the side of her bed. She couldn't reach it. She looked back up and moved her braided brown ponytail off to her left shoulder. She looked for a free nurse and waved her down. The red-headed woman moved over to her swiftly and gave her a warm smile. Jennifer looked at the women's name tag, catching only the last name: McCurdy.

"Hi. Miss. Could you tell me what time it is?"

McCurdy looked at her watch. "Five-forty-seven." She answered.

"Oh, really. I guess I woke up just in time. Could you hand me my purse, I can't reach it, and I'm not sure if I should be moving around much yet, but I'm expecting an important call."

McCurdy reached for the side of Jennifer's brown purse to her. "Thank you very much. Would you happen to know when I am to be discharged?"

"Let me find out for you. Do you have someone to pick you up?"

"Not yet."

The nurse walked from her into the other halls. Jennifer looked at her phone and saw no notifications just yet. It wasn't like she received texts very often, especially not on a Wednesday. She scrolled through her contacts. She went to Sam's number and started to text: *Please pray for me. I woke up ill. I'm being tested. Pray that it's negative.*

There was silence, except the constant walking of nurses, the rolling of wheelchairs, and the constant stamping of crutches and walkers. There was constant rolling of various machines filled with oxygen, and other medical accessories. She waited as the time passed by, waiting for that call. She was still certain he would call, despite the constant efforts of distancing he kept putting between them. She was certain that *he* really wanted to talk to her, even to discuss something mundane. Perhaps, he'll finally reveal something else, not traumatic, about himself. She heard the imaginary clock ticking inside her head, like a little lost dwarf hammering away at her cranium.

She looked down at her phone, still waiting for any kind of response from Sam, while she still waited for Ted's call, her notifications remained empty, and silent as the sounds of the hospital drowned out the ticking of her internal clock. She looked back out the window, staring at the streetlights outside, illumined the streets, which was still filled with lots of pedestrians, walking around with their phones to their ears, or their faces bowed down and typing or reading away aimlessly in the streets. Many others, children, seemed happy to be skipping along in the street with their parents, skipping away like little children. Many of those children were tugging on their parents' arms for attention. All of this she could see, and she couldn't help but smile.

She looked back to the end of the bed and looked at her feet. She wanted to know and feel if her bones still felt like breaking glass as they did this morning. She sucked in the air through her teeth as she lifted her left leg up, taking the cover underneath them. Her left leg trembled as it rose, but not so much from the pain, but rather with anticipation. Her leg was growing defiant of her condition, however severe it may be. She put left leg down and rose her right leg, which trembled as it rose, just as much as the left, and with just as much anticipation and defiance. She smirked as she put her leg back down.

Buzz.

She looked down at her phone, grinning as Ted's name shone across the screen. She swiftly answered the call and brought it to her ear. "Tedward." Her tone was filled with excitement as her mouth rose from ear to ear.

"Jennifer," he spoke. His tone was not cheerful, nor did it seem grim or depressing. It was just there, empty.

"Tedward!" she exclaimed yet again. She simpered through the phone, not because of the empty monotone, but simply because his tone wasn't cheery. This time, he wasn't trying to hide anything. "Are you feeling okay? I mean, the other night, that was a lot to process. It couldn't have been easy."

"Well, I suppose I've seen worse." He replied. *"It is hard to say I've seen much better times in my life, but perhaps that was for the best. There's just only so much I can say."*

"I think we've all had our trials and faults. I think that it is not all you." She said, dropping her smirk as she saw the nurse walking over to her. "I think part of it is on me, and Samantha. We did push hard on you when we had no right knowing anything, but we didn't want to see you alone. I recognize a fake smile, and while some fake simpers fade well into the crowd, yours stood out to me."

"I don't blame you. I don't. I find it difficult to express myself, even when you annoy me."

"Well, it was bound to happen. I annoy a lot of people. It is one of my quirks."

"You mean charms, don't you?" his tone was playful.

"You can be discharged if you have a way to get home." The nurse said to her.

Jennifer nodded. "I suppose it is one of my charms. You haven't ditched me yet, have you?"

"Discharged?" his tone became monotonous.

"I'm in the hospital for a biopsy. I'm about to go home, somehow." She explained. "Nothing serious." *I hope.*

"Did you drive?"

"No." she answered. "I was delivered here by ambulance. My car is still at the doctor's office."

"Are you okay?" he said, his voice was still monotonously apathetic.

"I'm sure I'll be fine. Hey, here's an idea. Why don't you pick me up and take me home? Sam's not getting back to me."

"Where are you?"

"The diseased manor." She answered.

There was silence on the other line. And then he laughed. *"There is no hospital with that name."*

"We can make it one." She joked, smirking with one curve of her lip rising higher than the other.

"Sure, so where am I picking you up?"

"Jameson's Hospital. Thirty second Broadway, Brookline. I think I'm on the fourth floor." She replied.

"Okay. I'll drive over. Give me about a half hour. I'm coming from Dedham."

"I'll see you soon!"

Click.

She looked back down at her phone, seeing a text message from Sam: *I will pray. Sorry for getting back so late. Work troubles. I hope you're doing well. Brunch on Saturday? Michael and Tim will be there. I don't want to invite Ted back just yet. I think he needs some time.*

She smiled down at the text, feeling accomplished. Not that she had Ted all to herself for the night, but the fact alone that he spoke to her without masking his emotions much. For tonight, maybe he will completely remove that mask. Perhaps finally, the iron heart *was* being softened, capable of being malleable by a hard mallet.

She texted back: *I think I'll pass on brunch this week. I'll see you Sunday.*

Jennifer leaned back and looked up to the ceiling, placed both hands beneath her head and she let out a deep breath. She let out a deep breath, sighing into the air as an indescribably heavy burden was violently lifted from her chest.

"Lord, be with me." She prayed; she closed her eyes and crossed her hands over her chest. "Lord, thank you for the gift of modern medicine, and thank you for Doctor Nicolai Korowitz and his insight in catching this disease. I am content. Thank you for pushing me through my limits, through my dreams and aspirations. Forgive me Father, for even though I fall constantly, and fail to follow your laws. Please humble me when I am consumed by arrogance and pride." She opened her eyes at the room. She took a deep breath and tried to move her legs again. This time, she could move both legs up and down, and she did so, taking turns, not grimacing with any discomfort, for it seemed to have subsided, and she smiled. "Thank you for everything. Truly, I am grateful. I have more than enough, and more than I need. Thank you. Amen."

***

Ted walked through the doors into the hospital. He smiled as he walked in. No one here needed to know his *true* condition, or his *true* hatred. He noticed many people in wheelchairs, some amputees, many who's faces were void with sunken eyes, long and skinny faces, devoid of all personality, just like they were completely dead inside, much like himself, only they stopped caring enough to hide it from anyone. He grinned at the thought, being dead inside, if only his heart would stop beating. He went to the receptionist, waiting in line, still scanning the busy hallways, and the busy white floors, smeared with feces, and urine, just waiting to be cleaned up.

"Sir. Sir. Hello! Is anybody home?" the annoyed receptionist called out. Her spectacles were hanging by her chest with grey beads.

Ted jerked his head to her, catching a very unforgiving but friendly face out of the corner of his eyes. His fist clenched at his side as he hid a grimace with a bright smirk to the much older woman. "Sorry about that. My mind seemed to have slipped."

"Careful, or you'll end up slipping too. How can I help?"

"I'm sure. I'm actually here to pick up a patient. Jennifer Miller."

"What's your name?"

"Ted Anderson."

"I don't see your name here."

"Embarrassing." He chuckled nervously, as he was sure was the appropriate response. "I just got the call to pick her up. She does know me if you want to call her down, I'll take a seat somewhere."

The older woman motioned him to sit in a chair which was vacant.

"Thank you."

Ted went and took a seat on the chair, waiting, and scanned the room. He continued to scan for the man he saw, the unforgivable man. The man still had that buzz cut, that sinister smile with his dog tags hiding underneath his lab coat. The man looked like a seriously joyful man, smiling cutely at other women who happened to walk by, as if encouraging niceties.

DR. Adams. Are you really a medical doctor? It sickens me to think that you could actually care about people. I certainly never received such treatment from you. Not after you strapped me to that damn chair in leather straps, sending electrical currents all through my body until my pain receptors no longer worked. Adams, if I wasn't trying so damn hard to live a normal life, as normal as I can despite my own psychological deficiencies that you caused, I wouldn't hesitate to kill you.

Doctor Adams disappeared as he continued to walk down the end of the hall.

Ted's hands relaxed as he pressed them against his pants, still scanning the hospital. He didn't feel safe here, not when there was a familiar face present, well, one that wasn't Jennifer's. For of all the things he knew, and it pained his heart, her smile, the least of all was genuine. He took a deep breath as he stared down the vestibule with a little nurse pushing a wheelchair, and in that wheelchair was Jennifer, holding her purse on her lap. She grinned as she waved her arm at him. She had a light blue medical gown over her clothes.

He smirked at her, breathing deeply as he got up from his chair, almost forgetting that he had just had a brief encounter, however one sided, with an old friend. *If that is the word for it.* He focused his attention on her as he walked over to meet the nurse.

"Hi, Tedward!" She simpered that foxlike smirk of hers, there was something suspicious, but beautiful about. As always, like she was playful, her eyes were half opened.

"Elizabeth." He returned the gesture.

"Well, is Mr. Darcy reading up on his Jane Austen for me? How romantic."

The nurse giggle behind her. "You got her?"

"I'll take her." Ted went into the back of the wheelchair to push her along.

"Onward! The Chariot awaits!" She rose both her hands and kicked her feet out. "Weeee!"

"Well, I can't say I've had to be in a hospital before. But I don't think I would be in good spirits." Ted chuckled, pushing her out the door.

"Tedward," She leaned back into her seat as she looked up at him from below, admiring his sharp jaw, and his near stern gaze, scanning at everything with those ever-watchful eyes. "You need to learn to live a little. Life is too short to be miserable." She paused a moment. "I'm sorry. I know I can be overbearing at times." She sat back, all snugged in her little chair and hospital gown as Ted rolled her over the board walk, and carefully into the parking lot.

He awkwardly grinned down at her. "I see. Well, I suppose I've lived long enough to know how short life can be. Some lives may be long; others tragically short." His tone dropped.

"Ted." She looked back at him as he rolled her to his car. "I'm sorry. This isn't my way of trying to pry anything out of you. I just want your company."

"I understand." He wheeled her to the side of his black car. He opened the car door.

"Of course, what kind of friend would I be if I didn't desire to know something else about you?" she said, sneering at him. She wobbled out of her seat and sat herself into the car. She smiled as she moved her feet into it.

"Is the chair yours or do I need to put it back into the hospital?"

"It goes back into the hospital. There should be a little depot right by the front doors, if I remember right." She gestured back to the hospital. "It's okay. I'll be here, waiting while you return it, Mr. Darcy."

"As you wish, Emma, " he replied.

"Wrong Jane Austen novel! Emma was Mr. Knightly!" she snapped at him, pointing fingers at his chest. "Don't disrespect Jane!"

He snickered as he shut the door, and rolled the wheelchair back to the hospital, leaving Jennifer alone as she stared out the windshield. She fastened her seatbelt as she adjusted the seat, the bones inside her fragile legs trembled as she applied pressure to the floor of the car to push her seat back. She grimaced as the chair locked into place at a more comfortable position. She leaned her head against the window to her left as she scanned the skies, the dark clouds reigning in overhead.

"Ted. I hope you find it soon. The storm is coming." A shiver went up her spine as the temperature appeared to drastically drop; she could still feel it from within the car. She started rubbing her shoulders and gazed back out the window and saw a woman, walking through the street, with crimson eyes, silver hair, and a youthful face as she skipped along. She seemed familiar of a sort, someone looking for adventure, or so she thought.

The girl disappeared behind a crowd, and then she was gone like a wisp.

The door on the other side opened. She sharply turned her head as Ted moved into the car, buckling his seatbelt. "Alright, Jennifer, let's get you home. Where did you leave your car?"

"It was at the doctor's office."

"I'll pick it up for you." He put his key into the ignition and started the engine. Jennifer could feel the vibration with the car rev up.

Ted drove out of the parking lot, into the street, and started driving through the heavily congested roads of Boston as they moved towards the Seaport District. Jennifer moved in her seat, thinking about the tears Ted shared that night, on the night she would remember, the Fourth of July. He opened a piece of his heart to them that night, although she was sure he never meant to. She was certain he had every intention of wearing that mask, living in the façade of his own life, forgetting everything else that was important to him. *But does he really have anything important to him?* Then an image flashed through the back of her mind, walking in the darkness of the night, the quiet stillness of College Ave when he broke down on all fours, weeping, crying, letting all of the pain leave his body. But truly, there wasn't an outlet big enough to house all that pain to let it out at once.

The temperature dropped drastically that night, and light emitted in the air. An unnatural light that shouldn't have been shining, the light came directly from his body. Maybe it was something small enough, small enough to pry that he would remove a brick from that wall he keeps up.

"Ted?"

"Yes?" he replied, never taking his eyes off the road.

"That night, when you ran off," she began. She noticed he shifted uncomfortably in his seat. "I'm not going to ask your feelings or what you are going through, I'm not going to pry, but perhaps you can explain something to me that I am having a hard time trying to understand. I saw these lights coming from your body. What was that?"

His smile faded, and he let out a deep sigh, keeping his eyes on the road, maintaining his laser focus on the busy road. "I am the only person I know that has ever had them. I don't know what they are, but they are regrettably a part of me. I can't get rid of it. I've tried, but nothing works. I don't know what they are, nor do I truly understand what they do. All I know, is that when I use this organ, the temperature drops. It's really hard to describe. I've never had to describe it before. I first noticed it was a part of me during an especially difficult time in my life that I don't care to discuss right now."

"That is enough Ted." She replied.

"Hmm?" he turned to her slightly.

"That is enough." She smirked to him, twiddling the loose ends in her braided ponytail with her right index finger. "Just to admit that, is enough. You don't have to explain any more than that. The fact alone that you trust me enough with that, is warming to my little frail heart. I want you to know, that even while it may be unnatural, I do not judge you for it, nor will I condemn you. I just want you to know that."

"Thanks." He gave her a one-word answer before turning his head back to the road, his eyes angled at the road with a sharp frown like he made a fatal mistake.

The streetlights shined brightly on the sidewalks. He parked his car in the back of the Seaport, a short walk away from her apartment. He turned the key off. "I don't think I asked, but maybe we can talk in your place. Do you need help getting up?"

"If you don't mind, Tedward." She smiled at him as she opened the door. "My legs are still a little weak."

"Hang on." He took the key out of the ignition. Opened his car door swiftly, and briskly walked out of it, shutting his door. He walked hastily around the front of the car to get to Jennifer on the other side. He took her hand and carefully helped her out of the car. She moved to the side, leaning against the side of the car for support. He closed the door and locked it.

He pulled her arm over his shoulders, pulling her closer to him. He held her close to him as they walked, using his strength so that she felt almost weightless, light, like a feather. He walked her across the street and into her big apartment building. He took her up the elevator and walked her down the hall. She breathed heavily with each breath, especially reaching for her keys in her purse. She opened the door, and it creaked open. Ted walked her in and brought her to her couch.

"Thank you." She said, smiling up at him.

"You're welcome. I've been meaning to ask you, and I don't know why I waited this long. Why were you in the hospital?" he asked empathetically.

She let out a sigh and patted the cushion next to her. "Take a seat." He looked suspiciously at the cushion before cautiously sitting down next to her. She looked up to the ceiling as if the answer to some unknown question was written on it. "Life, it is so fragile and ought to be protected. No matter how worthless it might seem, no matter how useless. All life has value, and I think sometimes I feel I take the life I have for granted sometimes. It became apparent to me today, when I woke up, gasping for breath like some devil was inside my chest. I am a survivor, Ted. I've survived a lot, and perhaps that is why I seem to be overbearing at times, so full of life because I have already been on my deathbed. I called the doctor's office and had a blood test, and my doctor seems to think I have a high chance of having Leukemia. I went to the hospital for a biopsy, and I did have some treatment to deal with the pain. I don't know if I have been confirmed for Leukemia, that is what the biopsy is for, and if I have it, it will determine the type of Leukemia I have."

"You seem to be in good spirits for someone who has potentially received her death sentence." He said grimly, turning his head away from her, not wanting to look into her eyes.

She took her hands and clasped them around his cheeks and turned them to her, so she could smile that faithful grin, filled with cheer. Despite the cruelty of her uncertain condition, she was full of cheer. "This world can be a dark place. It is filled with despair and hopelessness. It is filled with tragedy and loneliness. It is filled with gloom; however, I know where I will go. If it is my time, I will gladly accept my deliverance from this world, and be all the gladder because of it. I don't know where your faith lies, or if you have any in the Lord, but I wholeheartedly believe, and He gives me peace in all of this. I may be cheery now, but like many others, I will cry, but not yet."

"I didn't grow up in a church, I've heard telltale mentions of a God who is loving and good." He replied. "However, I find it hard to justify a loving and just God created this world with so much tragedy."

"I thought the same thing once. Many years ago." She sighed. "But no point in dwelling on this now, if you don't want to. I'm hungry."

"You're not in any condition to cook," he said.

"I don't want to cook, silly." She giggled as she released her grip from his face. "What do you like to eat?"

"I can't taste anything. I can't taste anything. I haven't been able to taste anything in over eight years."

"Well, that's boring." She sighed as she leaned back in the cushion. "So then, the baklava?"

"I couldn't taste it. I tried it and tossed the rest that night."

"Ted," her tone dropped. "I appreciate you being honest and showing me a part of you. It's almost like meeting a new person."

"You're welcome." He said flatly.

"I want Chinese food." She pointed to a brochure on her TV stand. "There is a menu right there. Can you grab that for me?"

"As you wish." He replied, getting up from his cushion to grab the menu. He brought it back to her. She looked at it. "Ted, I know you said you can't taste anything, but are you hungry?"

"I barely eat." He replied. "Only when necessary."

"I'll order you something." She dialed a number on her phone as she stared at the menu.

About an hour passed, and they sat at her dining room table, with the brown crunchy paper bags, and the sturdy white boxes with aluminum handles sprawled around with some paper plates. They were filled with fried rice, chicken fingers, and teriyaki. It smelled delicious as the steam from the steamed vegetables assaulted their noses with their sweet and delicate fragrances. Ted ate sparingly.

"Ted?"

"Yes?"

"Last night, at Teri Nation, you came back there, and hid away on a Tuesday night around the time we would have been there, which we were of course. Why did you come? I don't entirely understand why, if you were hell bent on avoiding us."

"I guess, you could say I was running away. I quit my job, fortunately I can still do that with my computer and not have to worry." His voice trailed off as soon as he realized how stupid that was. "I don't worry for money; I have plenty of it. It's much rather I worried about not having something to keep my mind occupied. I knew you all would be there. I wanted to say goodbye, to give that courtesy, but when the time came, I couldn't muster it up within myself to do it. So, I tried to leave, only, something else happened instead. Sam managed to find me there as I was finishing up some potatoes. Unfortunately, I am very good at hiding my own thoughts, my feelings."

"I know you don't wear your heart on your sleeves, but they came out bursting at the seams last night. Ted, forgive me, I know I said I wasn't going to pry, and I guess I won't, but I do want to know a little more about what happened to you. Would you be willing to share something?"

"I would be willing, but the question is what? A lot happened to me, and so much of it wasn't exactly legal." He let out a deep sigh as his eyes scanned the ceiling as if to study it. "I suppose this I can be vague enough on it, and it would be fine, but please understand, much of what I did was completely confidential, above Top Secret. I doubt even our current President even knows of how easy his administration was because of me, and because of them.

"You see, Jennifer, I was part of this group that was part of the U.S Army but the program itself was headed up by the CIA. They chose Thirty-two men and women to be part of this program, of which, I was one of them. I almost didn't make the cut due to an early heart attack. We were all physically fit, and battle hardened by the time we started our series of deployments, lasting a total of four years. We barely slept. We barely ate at all during that time. For four years, we were up before the sun, and didn't sleep until the moon was almost asleep. One morning, we'd end up in Iraq, and fight a two-week fire fight. After we were done raising hell, we would go back to the Forward Operating base to resupply. We wouldn't get a chance to go into our barracks, of course we had none, we didn't need them. We'd be on the next flight immediately to North Korea the following day. Repeat. Fly to Russia. Repeat. Fly to China. Repeat.

"The nations began to fear us, and rightly so. We learned their tactics and killed them in their sleep. Whenever there was a fight between

America and any other opposing force, once it was known we were on the battlefield, the battle was already over. It didn't matter how many people they took with them; it was a matter of how fast they could arrange an organized retreat." He let out a deep sigh.

"I too value life to the highest degree, and yet my job consisted of taking life away. You'd think that after doing it so much I would become numb to it. I never did. I still see the blood on my hands, and I still see the light leave their eyes. I still see their faces and I feel they never leave me, always staring at me like a murderer. Why shouldn't they look at me like that?" he choked up as he shed tears from both eyes, his heart was on the table, and it was opened. But this time it wasn't something that needed to be pried open, he willingly gave her the key. "I didn't have a choice. I didn't have a choice." He wiped his eyes with two fists, twisting them about.

She looked into his eyes, or rather his fists. Her smile faded as she reached out to him, resting her hand in front of him with her palm facing up. "We always have a choice. At times there may not seem to be any good options, but there is always a choice."

He looked down at her hand as it beaconed for him to hold it. He reluctantly took it in his. He squeezed it firmly, as he clenched his teeth. His eyes met her as they shimmered from the ceiling's light, reflecting the tears. Jennifer gasped as she looked into those eyes, the grimace on his face, and conflict inside him. *If only he could bring it upon himself to seek help, and yet, as if some cruel fate or curse was laid upon his birth, he is compelled to do nothing and carry the burden of guilt alone. Ted, you didn't tell me everything, and I don't mean you to.*

He took a deep breath, sucking the air through his teeth, and let the air out through measured breath through his clenched teeth. "You're wrong." He spoke silently. "And I can't tell you why."

"Can you tell me why you can't tell me?" she asked.

There was a silence. Jennifer gripped onto his wrist a little more tightly. Finally, Ted slowly shook his head. She slowly nodded, never once letting her gaze escape his as she finally clasped his hand with her second free hand. "What you've said already, is enough. Like a shaken-up soda bottle, you need to release some of that built up tension before you can open it properly without it getting messy and blowing up all over the place. You have told me what I have asked, and I will ask for nothing more tonight, and Tedward, I want you to know that what you've told me is not going to leave my mouth, nor my lips tonight, tomorrow, or ever. I hope you believe me."

He nodded.

She scarfed down the rest of her food. "I could use a shower, but tonight has been a rough one. I think I'm going to turn in early."

"Good night."

She turned to get up, and her legs wobbled before she gained full composure of her legs. "Okay. It isn't that bad." She started walking back towards the couch. "Ted, you are still in your house, right?"

"No. I sold it as soon as Sam started getting too close to me. I have an apartment somewhere in Waltham."

"Ted, I wouldn't normally do this," she said. "But I do have an extra blanket if you want to spend the night here. The couch isn't all that big, but it does pull out into a spare bed. I don't want you to be alone tonight."

"I'll stay."

She smiled and tilted her head down as her eyelids drooped halfway down. "Now, Ted, does this mean I'll see you in the morning then?"

"Yes." He said slowly, and his volume dropped to a whisper.

She smirked as she went into the other room. Ted watched her, carefully monitoring her every step. He watched as each leg shifted, and her feet turned with each passing step. They were disorganized, likely due to her current disposition. Tonight, he felt an incredible weight lifted from upon him. It's been eight long years, at least, that is how he remembered it. Too bad. The memories won't go away. The nightmares won't stop.

She came back out of the room with a large blanket already folded up. She came into the living room and placed the blanket on the coffee table. She moved the cushions off the couch and moved them to the side as she pulled out the folded bed from the couch. She set the blanket on top of the bed and started to tuck in the sheets.

"There you go." She said.

"Thank you." He spoke softly.

"Good night, Ted."

He nodded to her as she slowly closed the door to her room and walked to the futon.

He looked down at the bed, soft as it seemed, he let his arms drop to his sides. It was made for him, specifically him, and it was wrinkle free, devoid of all imperfections. His hand went to reach for the blanket, and his hand trembled as it got close to it. He glared at his hand as his reality pulled his nightmares into it.

His hand was covered in crimson blood, lit by the light of burning flames out of control. He saw the iron and stone rubble in front of him, and the roar of the flames drowned everything else out. He grimaced as the nightmare turned into reality, and he could smell the unwanted stench, the stench that was all too familiar—burning flesh, and he could hear the buzzing flies flying around the corpses. He covered his nose and mouth with his hands as he moved forward, reaching for the bed that was no longer there.

He tripped into the bed, hitting his shin as he came down to the blazing hot ground. His head hit the pillow as he let out a small gasp, coming back into reality, and leaving the flames of regret behind him. He let out deep breaths as he finally removed his shoes. He laid on his back, staring at the blank, empty ceiling, he sprawled his limbs on the unnatural comfort of the bed. He took deep breaths as he tried to lay himself to sleep.

"We trusted you, you know." Came a voice out of the corner. Ted immediately sat up and scanned the room. To the corner of his eye, he found an all too familiar face, someone he forgot. She had glasses on her face, and her black bangs framed it as the rest of her hair was tied back in a ponytail. To him she was wearing black pants and the green fatigues. Her arms crossed over each other.

"Roach." He said.

"Ghost." She said, disapprovingly. "Why are you here?"

"The same could be said of you."

"You know why I'm here. Why are you here, trying to make a life for yourself? It was what you always wanted, wasn't it? To live as a normal man, with a wife, maybe have some kids, a job, get a house, and yet, here you are just as miserable as you were when you were with us." She dropped her hands and tilted her head as she took two steps forward to him. She sneered at him, showing him her teeth. "You should be sacking Uncle Sam right now."

"You know how I feel about that."

"Ghost don't give me that!" she snapped at him. "Everything we fought for was a lie. Everything we died for, was nothing more than a sham. There is no point in lives like ours! If you don't sack Uncle Sam, then there is no point in a life like yours!"

"I don't want to." His eyes angled to hers, and he frowned, clenching his fists at his side.

"You don't want to, but you need to, Ghost. Do you want to finally lay us to rest?" her tone softened.

"More than anything."

"Then you need to sack Uncle Sam. You know what all of us sacrificed for that! Do you want your nightmares to go away? Do you want to stop seeing these vivid dreams? Do you want to end it all? I know you do, and if you do, you need to sack Uncle Sam!" she aggressively pointed a finger at him.

"There is no point." His voice was stern. "Roach, even if I did, I know that the nightmares will only get worse. There is no closure for a monster like me. It won't mean a damn thing." He gritted his teeth.

"Then you've given up."

"You don't understand, Roach. The difference between you and me, is that your nightmare ended eight years ago. I wish mine ended that day. I go to sleep, and I experience it all over again, and my nightmares refuse to end!"

"Ghost," she sighed as she took a step back and leaned against the back wall. "I know. I know. We all know that you don't have the damn guts to do it, and you're the only one of us who can." She sighed as she stared at the ceiling. "Well, I've got to go. This was useless. You're useless. Oh, and Ghost, don't blame yourself with what happened to us. It's not your fault. It's not your fault."

Ted's eyes glimmered as they were coated in tears again. He wept softly as he rolled his fists in his eyes.

"It's not your fault I died." Roach said coldly. Ted looked at her and he saw her as he left her. Her left arm was severed in her black uniform. Her right leg was completely torn off, and the stumps bled profusely on the floor. She removed her uniform with her one hand, revealing the cavity that was inside her chest: the bones were shattered inside. The right side of her face completely burned: the oil on her face still burned and he could smell the burning flesh. He could smell the soot of blowing gun powder. "The fault was entirely mine, for trusting my life in the hands of a wretch like you! I can't believe I trusted you to be able to protect me. You can't save anyone. How could you when you can't even save yourself."

He gasped as she shook her head in disappointment. The color in her body and blood began to slowly fade into transparency. The silence to him was deafening, but he knew it wasn't over. The demons and monsters were about to come out. He slowly went to lay back down as he started to choke on more tears. He grabbed one of the cushions an brought it closer to his head as his ears were filled with the unrelenting agonizing screams of men and women. It drowned out his thoughts completely as the room around him turned into a prison made from flesh and arms, and the tiles of the walls were faces, dead and dying with eyes still lively, seeking out his face.

Servicemen and women surrounded him, aiming their weapons, the screams of agony outweighed the sudden bursts of gunfire. He felt the vibrations in the air as bullets passed over his head. He silently wept, his eyes filled with tears and terror as he tried to drown out the noise by squeezing his ears with the cushion to no avail. He could still hear them as plain as day. These men swore in the languages of all the people he killed: English, French, German, Chinese, Russian, Polish, Italian, and Korean. He can see every last detail in all their faces, the scars, the malformities, every last one of them.

Because of him, he thought, he made countless widows and orphans. Because of him, there are families going without food. Because of him, there is going to be an emptiness in their lives, and those kids the parents left behind are going to think ill of him, and should they know who he was, for certain, they would seek his head. And who could blame them? If only, he thought, there was a way to achieve world peace without needless bloodshed, he could have found a purpose for his miserable existence. Roach was right. There really wasn't a point in a life like his.

Jennifer's eyes came open with a start, and they were wide as her ears were ringing with a loud tormented scream. The temperature dropped drastically, and she pulled the covers off and hopped off her bed. She opened the door into the other room, peering behind from it. The room was filled with a light of rainbows. *Tedward.* She investigated the bed where Ted should be, and she found the cushions ripped from the sofa, laying to the side, and the blanket was disheveled. *Ted.* She moved out from her room, dragging her blanket with her. She put her hand out in front of her to shield her from the blinding light and she found Ted in a corner, huddled up with his knees to his chest with multiple-colored lights emitting from his body. These lights looked like human veins, and they covered his entire flesh from his fingertips to the top of his skull. The lights were beautiful like a rotating rainbow.

She looked at him carefully, tears streamed down his face and he looked dead ahead, at nothing in particular, but as if he was in one of those horror movies and a monster just killed everyone he was with and he was next, and the monster was not far behind. He looked terrified as his hands clasped both sides of his face to cover his ears.

She sighed as she walked slowly towards him. She kept her eyes on his, and they didn't seem to react to her presence as the temperature continued to drop. She took each step with care, knowing full well her condition, albeit, maybe not as severe yet, but one can never be too careful. Her heart felt some strain on it, but not because of her condition, but merely because it hurt her inside to see anyone like this. *Ted, it is good you stayed. This was what worried me.*

She took another step beside him and leaned against the wall with him. She wrapped her arm around his shoulders and leaned into him. He jerked away as he stared into her eyes as if he didn't know her. She moved in front of him and placed her hands on his wrists ever so gently and removed his hands away from his ears. She cried tears with him, and they streamed off her face and into his lap as the strings of her heart were pulled.

"Ted. I can't hear what you hear. I can't see what you're seeing right now." She spoke softly and his hands dropped to her wrists. "I know you don't want to talk about it, and I'm not going to force you to. But at some point, you will need to talk about it, or you'll explode. I'm here when you want to talk about it."

She moved to the side of him and leaned into him again and wrapped the blanket around them. He started to take deep breaths as he wiped the tears from his eyes with his fists again, turning them in his eye sockets. The temperature began to warm up again and the lights from his face and arms faded and these veins appeared to coagulate into his flesh.

"Why?" he breathed.

"'Why'?" she replied, turning her face to his.

"Why are you and Sam so focused on me? I am filled with regret and guilt. I try so hard to function in the real world, but I just can't. These nightmares and phantoms simply won't let me. My nightmares don't end when I wake up. Every night. Every night when I try to sleep, I wake up screaming because I see ghosts. These ghosts are people I've killed. I remember their faces, every single one of them. I see those who I fought with and fought for. They're all dead, because of me. I couldn't save them. I can't save anyone. I couldn't save any of them because I just couldn't muster the strength in me to kill anyone anymore. I couldn't save anyone. Perhaps they were all right, and there really isn't a point in a life like mine."

She nodded. "You may feel that way. It is human, to believe in the sanctity of life, and while there are those that like to undermine it by defining life on their own terms, the truth remains the same, we all value life and when we take it away, we feel guilt and regret. We are told to value life at a young age, or at least I'd like to think so, and taking that life is enough to break us. Ted, even when we are not the one taking something away, we feel heartbroken by it. I can't say I've lost anyone close to me, yet, but I know there are plenty around me that have. As to why Sam and I are focused on you so much, well we care. I know Sam can be blunt at times but that is who she is. She is a great listener when she wants to be, but sometimes she can be as subtle as a jackhammer. She means well, even when she is bulldozing through walls trying to get them to say something. Many things she says may be harsh, but she has the best of intentions. As far as myself? I mean well. I know I can be overbearing sometimes, and annoying but that is what makes me, me.

"Life can be hard, and like I said to you on Independence Day, life can be Hell. It's like that for everyone. We go through rough patches, and sometimes we feel like the light at the end of the tunnel is nothing more than where the last traveler fell, and what is left of his hope is burning in a lamp, stationary in a dead end. And sometimes we get to dance in the meadows and see the fireworks.

"It is no mistake to say I've become fond of you, even if I seem to know next to nothing about you. I know where you're from and that's about it. I know you served to protect our nation, and that whatever happened to you there is unforgiveable, whatever it was. It sounds like what you went through was nothing short of betrayal and regret."

She was right. She knew nothing about him but was able to ascertain that much that everything that happened to him should never have happened to begin with. Could he trust her?

"Ted, do you trust me with your heart? I will never say anything to anyone that you don't want spoken aloud. But do you trust me?"

"No." he hesitated. "I don't trust you." He paused as he looked at her again. "But I am willing to try."

"That is enough."

Chapter 23 The Garden

~ There was something I tried to run away from. But it won't leave me alone.

***

Jennifer woke up with the sun beaming on her face. She stretched out and yawned over the back of her bed. She looked at the clock, 9:32. *A tad early. No matter.* She leaped out of bed and put the covers back on to it. She looked at her phone, no messages yet, except there was a voicemail. She saw that it came from Doctor Korowitz's office. *Must be the test results.* She stared down at her phone and her hand trembled with anticipation. She felt much better these last few days, and even now, the pain in her bones had completely subsided. She took a deep breath as she opened her voicemail to listen:

Jennifer. This is Doctor Nicolai Korowitz calling. It is important that you call the office when you get a minute. Thanks.

She erased the voicemail and sat back down on her bed. She looked up at the sky, as if looking up to the Lord for her guidance. "Give me strength, Father. This is hard, but, not my will, but yours be done." She smiled with certainty. She scrolled through her phone to find the number for the Doctor's office. She dialed it.

"Korowitz's office. This is John, how may I help you?"

"Hi, John, this is Jennifer Miller. I'm returning a call from Doctor Korowitz." She replied.

"Sure thing. One moment."

She was immediately placed on hold and she danced to the annoying hold music with the obnoxiously loud saxophone. The music stopped, and Nicolai's thick Russian accent filled the silence, *"Jennifer, are you feeling okay?"*

"I'm doing fine. The meds are keeping the pain down. I can walk without wobbling, and I don't feel dizzy."

"That's good. So, your test results came back. Fortunately, we caught it in time where it's not necessarily going to be fatal. So, you are positive with

chronic lymphocytic leukemia or CLL for short. When can you come in for an appointment?"

"Monday?" she asked.

"Let me see." Jennifer could hear him typing heavily on the computer on the other end of the line, his heavy fingers hammering the keys. *"2:30 PM work for you?"*

"Yes. I'll put it on my calendar."

"I'll see you then." Click.

She brushed her hand through her thick brown hair. She took a deep breath. *It's not serious, not yet. No point in worrying about it right now.* She exhaled deeply, letting the air decompress her lungs. Her hands relaxed as she held her phone. She went back into her phone and scrolled through to Ted's phone number. She dialed it.

"Jennifer?" he immediately picked up. If Jennifer didn't know any better, she would have thought he was staring at the phone waiting for her to call him, not that there was any reason she would.

"Tedward." She smiled into the phone, filled with an overwhelming sense of felicity. "Hey, so I am feeling much better. Are you still up to go feeding the ducks today?"

"Yes." He grinned through the phone. *"Do you need me to pick you up?"*

"Ted, you're farther than me. Let's just meet outside the T at Park Street station. We can walk to the Gardens after and feed the ducks there."

"Sounds like a plan. What time?"

"I was thinking noonish."

"I'll be there."

"Do you play Chess?"

"I used to play it frequently." His tone went low.

"I'll bring my mini chess board. I'll see you at noon!" *click.*

Jennifer walked down on the boardwalk, walking all the way from Seaport Boulevard, with her purse hanging from her side. She had her hair held back with a green headband and wore a modest yellow sundress and white sneakers. She walked briskly through the boardwalk, over the bridge, and crossed the sidewalk. She welcomed the warm gentle breeze caressing her hair as she made her way to the Boston Common. Of course, she could have just taken the T, but it was such a nice day outside with the bright sun shining down on her.

There were many people about at this hour, after all, tourist season was upon them, and there were many tourists, domestic and foreign walking the Freedom Trail, and exploring many small domestic shops and antique bookstores. She walked up through Winter Street, ignoring the heavy traffic of pedestrians and street performers in the street.

Winter street was dark as it had parallel to each other, tall skyscrapers. She welcomed the warm breeze of the sunlight again as she walked across Tremont Street, welcoming the lovely view of Park Street Church on the right. She walked towards the T stop which was behind a concession stand ran by a woman, handing out cans of soda and bottles of water with the exchange of cash.

She looked around her, and found many people happily tossing frisbee, or playing with their dogs on the grounds. She saw the gathering area filled with many round tables and folding chairs which surrounded the big fountain there, still streaming water out of its various holes and into the makeshift pool at its base. She saw the many birds of the air chirping around her, fluttering their little wings about.

She heard the doors behind the T stop open and out came flooded people as they pushed themselves almost carelessly out the door, excited to see the lovely Boston Common, and all things of which it had to offer. And out of that same crowd came a man, modestly dressed in shorts, and dark hair with a plan T-shirt, holding a paper bag which had a large roll of bread.

She giggled and hid her smile behind a hand. With her other hand she waved at him. "Oh, Tedward, that's a rather big roll you have there. I think that might be too much bread for our little ducks."

"One never knows." He grinned.

She reached out with her free hand. "Come on. We have ducks to see!"

Ted took her hand in his and she led him away from the hustle and bustle of the gathering area and down a path, leading upwards closer to some more of the dogs and frisbees. She led him enthusiastically down the path, almost skipping with her feet as they watched the squirrels scurrying up the trees with their acorns.

"Tedward," she said to him. "You have shared a lot with me, during the Fourth of July, and this week, I think it is time I tell you a little more." She smirked as he turned his head to look at her while they continued their little stroll. "You see, I got off the phone with my doctor this morning. I do have leukemia, but it isn't the aggressive kind. Of course, that little incident I had the other day may have just been an isolated incident, or perhaps altogether it wasn't even related at all, but by God's grace, because of it, I was able to find out that I had something serious. Fortunately, I don't need to get treatment right away, but I will be starting more in-depth treatment, as necessary. I just wanted you to know."

"Information can be a dangerous thing, and so is trust. This was something I regrettably learned the hard way and thank you for sharing that with me." He said as he turned his face to something else that moved behind a tree, like eyes were watching him. "I'll try my best to not betray your trust in me."

"A paradox wouldn't you say," her eyes dropped to cover half of her eyeball as they walked, and finally reached the end of the common, to the entrance to the Boston Public Garden. The black gate was open and the pathway on the other side of the street was pleasantly shaded by trees. "You can trust me, but you don't."

"And you can't trust me, but you do." His eyes continued to scan the pathway.

"I knew you'd say something like that, but if that was the case you wouldn't have warned me of the potentially harmful nature of giving part of myself to you. Of course, I feel I know you much better after this week, and quite frankly, I don't think we've seen more of each other than this week at all. Seriously, Tedward, it is like pulling your teeth out to get you to hang out with me. Well, I must say, I am pleasantly surprised that you actually started this. Although, I did talk you into picking me up at the hospital."

"Yes, I am sorry. I'm trying to be better." He stared down at the ground.

"Don't try to be better, Tedward, try to be you. That's really all we can be, is ourselves."

"Right." His tone dropped.

"Tedward, I heard that." She snapped at him as the light changed and they proceeded to walk across the crosswalk.

"Hmm?" He turned his head towards her.

"Your tone dropped. What's wrong? You know what, Ted, I'm sorry. I shouldn't have asked. Eh. I take it back. I should be asking that question, but *please* don't feel pressured to answer."

He sighed as they entered through the gate. "No. You're right. I appreciate you asking. Just, that particular thing is something I struggle with, because I don't really know who I am. Part of my job was espionage. If you put me in Russia, Italy, or almost any other country, I have been able to assume identities."

"You know, you seem to be very experienced for being so young. How old did you say you were?"

"Twenty-five." He replied softly.

"Sam thought you might be twenty-three." She squeezed his hand tighter.

"Sorry. The truth is, I don't know how old I am. It's complicated. I don't know when I was born, or where. That is really all I can say about it."

"I see." She spoke softly as she tightened her grip on his hand. "How is the sleep?"

"Still the same. Only thirty minutes." He replied as they continued to walk through the gardens, watching the trees and the beautiful lake with flocks of ducks paddling about in the waters. "I still see the nightmares, and they aren't going away. I don't expect them to."

"They will. They will." She assured him as she drew him closer to the lake.

She found a bench and pulled him down to it so they could be closer to the water. He ripped off a piece of the bread roll and handed it to her. She sniffed the bread and started pulling a little piece off and tossed it on the ground. A small flock of ducks started waddling out of the lake. Ted ripped off a piece and tossed it to the flock.

"Did you have friends? In the service I mean." She ripped off a little piece and placed it in her hand and leaned down to some brown ducklings to feed off of.

"Really only that of my squad. I grew to trust and rely on them, and they on me. I didn't see much of anyone else. My squad was filled with a total of fifteen of us." He sighed as he ripped another piece off, tossing it a little closer to the bench as more ducklings flocked towards them. "That was it. One I got really close with, and I proposed. I think I spoke to you of her during the fireworks. She died. They're all dead."

"Did you ever have closure with them and their families?" She exhaled heavily as she tore off little pieces of bread and littered over the ground.

"No. The only family any of us had was one another. I suppose you could say we were all picked up from the same cloth. We were never on speaking terms with our families, for good or ill." He picked kept tossing more bread to the ducks. "In many ways, we were the only family we ever had."

"And are you on speaking terms with your family now?" she turned to him as she continued to rip bread up in little pieces.

"No." his tone dropped.

"I'm sorry for probing." She placed her free hand on his shoulder.

She took her pieces and tossed it in the air and let them fall down like snow to the ducks. The flocks of ducks became larger around them. There were white ducks, brown ducks, mallards with their green heads as they picked up the bread from the ground and quacked, and waited for the next one.

"Why did you join?"

He sighed as he tossed aside his last piece of bread. "I suppose you could say I was forced into it. I was groomed you see, to fight and was pushed to pursue a career in the military. That's all I wish to say about that, but what I will say is why I continued to fight. I continued to fight, despite knowing full well what it was doing to me, with every life I took brought pain and regret as if my heart was being torn to pieces inside my chest. But I kept fighting because I was promised that if I kept doing it, the world would be safer once the foreign powers were left at bay. I killed, and I killed, and I killed. I killed without halting. I killed until at last, I stopped caring and became an empty hollow husk. And at last, my hope came true, there was peace for a time. Now, that doesn't seem to matter anymore with NATO disbanding and all that."

"The world will be a darker place now because of it. That's certain." Jennifer replied. "But no one man should ever have to bear that burden alone. Not you, not anyone. No one should carry it by themselves. You should not have been held responsible for that, as you can see, that peace was very short lived. Don't get me wrong, the peace was great while it lasted, and I think you might be closer to my age, if not older than me, Ted. My entire adult life I've lived in world peace, and it is now crumbling, but knowing what I know now, no one man should be forced to carry that burden alone."

"Yeah. You're right, but unfortunately that doesn't change the past." His voice became barely audible.

"No, but we can move forward, and you aren't serving anymore. It's not your problem, nor your responsibility." She tossed her last piece of bread on the ground and leaned into his shoulder. "Tedward, who am I to you?"

He leaned his head atop hers. "My friend."

Chapter 24 Ted Anderson

~No matter what good you accomplish, there is no point in helping others. In the end, you will find that humans are selfish conniving little dastardly creatures that aren't worth saving.

***

Ted Anderson looked up into the sky, the red ashes floating up like reverse snowfall. His left arm had a sharp piece of metal impaled in it, and his warm blood streamed down his arm and into the hot Nevada sand. He pulled the knife out and let it drop through his fingers onto the ground. He breathed deeply as he walked away from the carnage, avoiding the stench of dead bodies piled up high in the sand. His right arm dragged his AR15 into the sand, and his trigger finger rested on the side of his rifle, away from the trigger. His eyes drooped down, and his mouth was open wide as if to say something, but he couldn't muster up the courage to speak. He walked towards the FOB.

He could smell the burned-out oil and fuel; the rotting flesh assaulted his nose as flies buzzed around the dead. The Nevada sand was filled with blood after all of this. There were many other soldiers walking around with stretchers, trying to get the wounded out of the way, before starting the long arduous process of identifying the dead. The burning gunpowder still filled the air, and he could still hear the loud revving of truck engines, and the movement of the tanks as they were being driven away.

He looked at the desert sand and was haunted with the sight that would never leave his mind. Bodies littered the desert, so many, one wouldn't think there was a desert out there. Limbs were strewn all over the place, the uniforms torn to shreds, and even helicopter parts were on fire, blown up out of the sky. There were numerous failed parts from missiles that littered the flaming sands.

He stepped over the bodies, looking at the numerous dog tags on the necks of his fallen comrades, many of which, their faces were unrecognizable. Many of them no longer had faces, and some missed their dog tags. Identifying this many was going to be damn near impossible without DNA testing for identity. And then, he found something most peculiar about many of them, not all of them had an American Flag on their emblem patch. Some wore the patch of Russia, Ukraine, France, Italy, and China.

What were they all doing here? He thought.

"Sergeant Anderson." Said a soft but ragged voice.

He turned swiftly and saw none other than Lieutenant Nakamura. "Go get some rest. You need it."

"Yes, Ma'am." He walked over the corpses of the unnamed soldiers.

He continued to cover his mouth as the flies were beginning to buzz around him as they began to think him to be dead. He found an angry platoon, dragging severed limbs and corpses, a small number of corpses into a pit. He watched them, and he was able to identify most of these individuals, man and woman alike. These were the corpses of Task Force 7: every single one of them.

Two masked soldiers came from behind him holding large red plastic oil containers. They made it down to the pit with the bodies and dismembered limbs. Behind him was another man, an ensign, Ensign Malcom. He looked down angrily at the bodies as the two soldiers poured gasoline on them. The ensign took out a match and lit them aflame. There was one still alive, her fair but dirty face began to scream in agony as her face caught on fire. Her fists barely clenched. "I'll kill you! I'll kill you! I'll kill you! I'll kill all of you!"

"Sir?" One of the masked men pointed his pistole at her screaming head.

"Negative. She'll be dead soon enough. No use in wasting another round. We've already used enough of those as it is."

"What did they do?" Anderson asked. "They didn't deserve this."

"Evidence was found on Ghost that he was colluding with Germany to stage a coup. They are traitors." The ensign answered. "Now, don't get yourself in too deep in all of this, Anderson. Much of this is need to know, and you don't need to know any more than you do now."

"Yes, sir." He about-faced.

Anderson left it at that and continued dragging his weapon in the sand as bodies were being counted and collected, being sent to the coroners for examination and identification. The amount was staggering. He continued walking to the FOB. *Didn't we just broker international peace? Ghost, why would you do this? At least I, at least I can finally go home.*

The entire firefight was completely endless and overly exhausting. Ted knew he had been sleepless for nearly two weeks, and he wasn't even present for half of it. His legs were heavy, his arms were weak, and his spirit felt like it was being shackled inside his chest as he took heavy breaths, his lungs expanding. "It's over." He said under his breath. "I don't know what this was all about, and I don't care anymore. At least, the world will be a little safer."

Sergeant Ted Anderson never questioned any of the orders given to him over the last two weeks.

***

Six months later, Ted went on leave for a full week before returning back to active duty. No new wars were declared, no recent terrorist activity, in the middle east, nor here in the United States. It looks like the military was about to do some downsizing or pushing people out of the service. There was now next to no need for an over abundant military force. The army was going to be cut first.

Ted was on base in Fort Bennington, Georgia. He was running his half marathon in the oppressive heat. He stopped towards the end, leaning against a Humvee, sweating profusely and inhaled the fresh scent of his own body odor. He went to the barracks and showered before heading back into his office to finish off some paperwork. He planned to resign today.

He was in his office, on the computer and printing out some paperwork for his discharge. There was a knock on the door. He looked up; it was Private Hernandez. "Sergeant, you're wanted with Lieutenant Nakamura, immediately."

"Copy." He sighed as he got up from his chair. He followed the private down some lengthy halls through Georgia. He moved around and listened very closely to the conversations around the hallway, some small talk, others were more political in nature. He didn't care. *Today's the day.*

He was ushered into Nakamura's office. She held a clipboard and pointed to a chair. "Have a seat."

Hernandez closed the door behind him as he took the seat in the black chair.

"Anderson, you're being reassigned." She said, looking him in the eye with a soft glare, "Effective immediately, you are being shipped out to Germany."

Fantastic.

"How are you holding up over that little incident?" she leaned back in her chair, crossing her arms over her chest.

"All things considered, could be worse." He said. *You crazy bitch.*

"It was Hell on all of us. We're not going to recover from that." She sighed. "Many good men and women died."

"It's behind us. Are we done?"

"Yes. If you're psychologically fit, you are flying out at 0600 tomorrow."

"Thanks." Ted got up from his chair and went to the door, his hand touched the doorknob. He turned to her as she filed the paperwork away. "Nakamura."

"Anderson." She looked back at him from her desk.

"I'd tell you to go to Hell, but I think they would spit you back out." He told her coldly as his eyes angled down his nose.

"Excuse me?!" she looked up suspiciously to his face.

"Hell is too good a place for you."

He swiftly jumped over her desk and tackled her to the ground before she could scream. The various items from her desk slid off to the floor. His hands clasped around her neck and pulled her up from the ground. She was striking him with her hand and tried to release his grip. "Hell is too good a place for you! What the hell were you thinking! What's wrong with you? They were just kids damnit! They were just

kids! You know full well as I do, they did nothing to deserve any of it."
Crack! Her arms immediately dropped down. He released her corpse to
the floor as it tumbled.

He opened the door and briskly walked out of the room, closing it
behind him. *Good riddance.*

The Hedgehog Dilemma: The Nihilistic Neverending Nightmare

Prologue This World Is Truly a Hell

Two years since the initial assault on our US borders on both the east and west coasts from Russian and Chinese forces, engineering specialists provided by Black Eagle have continued to rebuild. Debris removed and replaced with high-rises allowed the continuing of jobs to return back to their offices, stabilizing the economy. Today, Americans from around the region remember what was lost, and the sacrifices made, and many are paying homage to the relatives and friends that were lost.

***

Samantha Harris prepared scrambled eggs for her husband. Cracked them flawlessly, poured the milk in, and whisked, careful not to spill any out of her glass bowl. Her frying pan heated with butter slowly melted all over the surface. Just the finest butter for her husband, and only the finest eggs. The bacon sizzled on another pan. Brown and wavy, on its way to crispy, smelling savory on this fine morning. The sun was just rising through the windows, white curtains pulled back.

"Well, that smells heavenly." Michael walked right through the door, closing it behind him with his beaming smile, she loved his smile. The most beautiful thing about it wasn't his perfect teeth, or that carefully trimmed beard, but that it was genuine. He was genuinely happy to smell the food, regardless of who was cooking it, but she knew, above all else, her husband was pleased to see her. And as usual, even with all the horrible things in the world, that was something that made her feel warm and fuzzy inside, like little birds were flapping around inside her chest.

He turned on the coffee pot to prepare a few cups of pour-over coffee—none of that industrialized nonsense. Coffee these days was almost impossible to find, especially in the supermarkets. The war with Russia and China made things very difficult for shipping coffee internationally, however, in their little community, there were a few greenhouses with coffee plants, and produced no small amount. However, still due to basic economics, the price for coffee in these greenhouses were higher than the supermarkets when they were stocked. This was often the last resort for most people to make a decent cup of coffee. All things considered; she was happy they had that much.

Samantha swirled the now fully melted butter this way and that inside the scorching iron bowl; it ran down the edges like waves on the shore, simmering and spitting.

A vibrant squealing tire sounded from across the street, scratching at the innards of her ears, and it was all too familiar.

A large Humvee was right in front of her. A whistle in the air. A sonic boom pushed her to the ground. Warm blood trickled down her palms; glass shards sliced into her. Another sonic boom brushed her hair with warm air. The jagged metal that was part of the Humvee's door crashed around her, and crimson water dripping down her face.

"Get down!" Canine cried out, pushing her into a ditch, laying atop her. Canine, in that fair face, turned her head briefly, her muscles tensing up, ready to move. "Get up! It's do or die!"

Canine pulled Sam up from the ground. Sam heard gunfire roaring overhead, and the screeching tires chasing them, and watched as the vehicles nearly flipped themselves over the rubble of what used to be Massachusetts. But the rubble, broken glass, and shattered wood made it all but recognizable.

"Sergeant! RPG!"

"GET DOWN!"

Her grasp slipped, and she flipped the frying pan over the stove, eggs sputtering all over the sizzling bacon, and the rest of the counter.

Her body froze, her eyes rattling inside her head, and her body gave, caving onto the floor, screaming. Her legs pushed her away from the stove hastily underneath cover, and yet, still dirt debris splashed all over her face.

The flames cackled, roaring, and sputtering underneath the rage of blown-up vehicles, piping hot metal, and shattered glass, carving at her face. Her own blood painted her face, and the crimson water was boiling hot.

A noise, muffled.

"Get it away from me!" she cried, bringing her hands over her ears, looking straight forward. "Get it away!"

"SAM!" she turned, and looking into her face, was that red head, that beautiful redhead with freckles.

"Erin! Get me out of here! Get me out! I'm scared!"

A hand firmly grabbed her shoulder.

"SAM!" A firm tone called her name. Her hands jolted right in front of her, feeling warm tears down her face, and she was looking right at Michael, not in a flaming rubble, but here she was, holding herself firmly in the fetal position, underneath the table. Cover. It's safe. It's safe here, under the table. Nothing can hurt here.

Except on that night when it all happened, the kitchen table was the first to go, shattered. It wasn't the only thing that shattered that night.

"SAM!" Michael's soft hand caressed hers, grasping it firmly, yet with a soft embrace. Real and warm, it was. Not hot. Not like that night when even the touch of snowflakes was boiling. He gently grabbed her wrist, pulling her out from the table.

The strength of her legs returned, now standing, she stumbled into him; his arms wrapping around her shoulders, hugging her tightly, firmly, and yet, in the way that only he could, softly. His breath matched hers, unable to see anything but the flames, but she felt the warm, stiff brush of his rustic beard, scratching her neck. "It's a flashback. It's a flashback. It isn't real. Breathe with me."

The warmth of the kitchen surrounded her, penetrating flames, slowly dying out, but the exploding debris continued, the dirt, iron hot on her bare legs. She inhaled. And the scent of the bacon reached her nose. She exhaled. Again. And again. And again!

"Tell me what you see," tenderly he spoke.

Her head moved back and forth, looking at her kitchen, and the sun shining from outside. She saw the stove, the pans on the ground, bacon, and uncooked eggs over the floor. The stove was off. No flames rising from it, no smoke. "I see, I see the stove. It's off. The pans and breakfast are on the floor. "Oh, Michael, I'm so sorry!"

"Don't be sorry," he said. "I don't care about the brunch. I care about you."

She took several deeper breaths before turning her gaze to the paper towels. "I have to clean that up." Now she understood why Ted Anderson worked so much. Keeps the mind busy. *Must stay busy.*

She broke from his embrace and clumsily walked over to grab the paper towels. Michael's hand touched her wrist gingerly, and without any sudden movements. She looked back to him. "Let go, Michael, I have to clean this up. I'll make a new breakfast."

"Are you okay?" he asked.

"Yes, I'm fine," she answered, turning back to the towel, and pulled some of the soft fabric off the sanded brown roll.

"Are you okay?" he repeated.

"Yes, I said I'm fine," she said, and knelt to pull the pans off the floor, walking them carefully to the sink. She turned around with the paper towels, and Michael was right in front of her, frowning. His eyes were glazed over; he was crying. *Why are you crying? Is brunch really that important to you? I said I was going to make more.*

"Are you okay?" he repeated himself a third time.

A third time. Why does he keep asking? She didn't know, but she knew one thing. She felt a large hole in the center of her chest. She looked down, seeing that there was no such hole in her chest, but her hand touched it to ensure her brain wasn't fooling her. And then it hit her, the hole grew heavier. She felt a lump growing inside, and she looked to him again, eyes laser focused into his, daring and discerning gaze. Again, she found it hard to breathe, the windpipes in her throat tightening up.

"No, I'm not," she answered, and she felt warm tears falling down her face. "I'm not okay, Michael, I'm not!" He slowly approached her. "These flashbacks always come. They're there when I'm awake. They're there when I'm asleep. They're there when you're away. I keep seeing things, and the one thing that haunts me the most, is the trigger I pulled."

"Sam, you didn't kill anyone," he replied, hugging her tightly. "You saved someone. You saved me."

"But was it the right thing to do? I see his face as clear and vivid as I see yours, and there are times when I'm looking at you, and I see his face, and whenever I see his face, I feel the urge to clean my blood-soaked arms when there's nothing to clean!"

She wept into him, dropping her paper towels on the floor.

"I know. I know," he said.

"Do you think, what I'm seeing, what I'm going through was what Ted was going through?"

"I'm afraid he's no longer with us to answer that, Sam. You know that," he answered. "But he gave us a chance at life now, and he'd want us to live the best lives we can."

Ted. Even after all this time, you and I are seeing the very same thing. I can see it now. Truly, this world is the Hell we've made. We made this Hell, we chose it willingly, and after we've chosen it, there's no hope to fix it.

Chapter 1 Touchdown

Anonymous reports suggest the Russian Navy is removing its shipyards.

We don't know why Russia is moving toward the west, but the Eastern Front seems a likely vantage point for them if hostilities grow. The ships appear to be mostly carriers, with some destroyers. Among these carriers, there are a number of super carriers, the likes of which dwarf our USS Carl Vinson. At this time, we don't know what kind of equipment is on these vessels, Secretary of Defense Brown reports.

***

Ted Anderson, the man with an unknown past best left buried. Jennifer knew this as she watched him, finger hastily tapping on her arm as she waited for him to finish making himself at least somewhat presentable. After much fuss, he was finally—himself, if that was the appropriate word for such a man. He at last had his jacket and some pressed khakis and donned his gloves. Typical. She knew much more of him after speaking to him over the last several months.

To bring up the past only brings pain to him. She knew that all too well, but she didn't even need to bring it up. His nightmares did that, and he came running to her, calling to her when they do. She's the first person he speaks to. The only person really. He had to be treated with the care he never knew, to overbalance the amount of instability that was forced into his past, instability he didn't ask for nor wanted.

But the reason Ted was in her Seaport apartment today, was because Michael's brother was coming into town. Flying in from deployment from overseas, or so that's what Michael told her. They would be picking them up by Michael and Samantha shortly, to go greet his brother at the airport. She previously arranged for Ted to be here for that very purpose. But of course, whenever it would be a bad day for Ted, it would be a good day for Jennifer. And like so, she noted especially, she was having a particularly good day.

Ted carefully put a hat on his head, while Jennifer tied up her hair wrapping it in a black scrunchy. She looked at him closely, still trying to piece together all his little intricacies. After all, he was a very complex person with multiple layers that she knew even he wasn't aware of. She noticed his hand trembled as he hastily retracted it into his pocket.

"Tedward," she walked over to him briskly, clasped his trembling hand with hers and pulled it out of his pocket. She gazed down at him as he tilted his head up. No smirk upon his face, for which she was exceedingly thankful, for this meant he did not feel the need to lie to her. She was grateful for that. Truly. That alone was progress. "What's wrong?"

"What is—what is the name of the man we're picking up?" he asked.

"Jeff Clemens, I think," she said. "He's Michael's older brother. By a lot, I hear. Nearly fifteen years or so."

"That name sounds too familiar," he said. "What does he do?"

"Army. Like you," she said. "Tedward, I understand if you don't want to come. You can just hang out in my apartment until I get back. Would you like that?"

Tedward appeared to be deep in thought, his eyes watering ever so slightly as he blankly stared at her blue fall dress. She knew enough not to interrupt him during these moments. Whenever he did this, he was considering all possibilities which laid before him. Carefully thinking. Considering all possible consequences of his actions to come. What would happen if he came? How many different scenarios could he piece together? To him, maybe it seemed safer for him to not do anything. But what about the possibilities down the road? A week from now, a month, and so on. Of course, Jennifer only speculated this.

Jennifer squeezed his hand tighter, waiting for him to finish. He exhaled heavily before returning his attention to her. He wiped the tears away with his fists. "I think, it is best that I come."

"Okay." She nodded.

Her phone rang. *It must be Sam. Outside already, but we've just decided Ted would come. Dear Tedward, my sweet Tedward, why do I feel filled with a certain kind of dread?* "Hello."

"I'm outside. Is Ted coming?" Sam replied on the other end.

"Yes," she answered. "We'll be right out."

Jennifer led Ted by the hand. She covered her eyes as the sun shone into them but noticed that Ted bothered not to shield himself from the harmful rays.

She found Michael's SUV was in the parking lot.

Sam rolled down her window, "Hey, you two, come on, we don't want to be late. Michael already has lunch reservations!"

Jennifer sighed, sighing with Ted following behind her, trying to prepare herself for whatever manner of dread was to follow. "Hi!" she said, drawing out her friendly greeting; she glanced back over to Ted, she saw his hands shaking to adjust his seatbelt before it finally clicked locked. *Just another layer to unravel, dear Tedward. I have my reservations about this. Is this, okay?*

"Hey, man, how's it going?" Michael turned to his seat to offer a hand to him.

Ted's lips stretched into a fake grin, even if they all knew it wasn't real. "I'm doing well, Michael, and yourself?"

"Great! I'm excited to see my brother for the first time in a while. Military type. I'm sure you understand."

Ted chuckled, "that I do."

Careful Michael. Be careful of the words you say, we don't want to start all over again, Jennifer thought.

Jeff Clemens looked out the window as the plane landed. Restlessly, his eyes scanned the ground level of all the personnel, the equipment, and of course, the open doors. There were many open doors. *TSA will have fit over that.* He sighed, waiting for the plane to dock. The lights flickered on, and he stood to remove his carry-on from the overhead bin.

The hallway out into the airport was gray, boring, and unsurprising, the way he preferred it; honestly, didn't want any surprises. Exiting the terminal, and into the airport, he checked his corners, looking swiftly to the left and to the right. Carefully watching people and all their activities as he walked down the escalators, and into the baggage claim. Military personnel stood upright by the baggage carousel: heads jerked left and right as they checked each corner they passed, just like his does. Every corner must be checked, and every stone turned. Never know when a suicide bomber might come in and blow everything to shit. Especially with those open doors.

He stood out by pickup, his luggage on the ground. He held a piece of paper as he read the address of the hotel he would be staying at for a few weeks before he redeployed written upon it. Folding the piece of paper, he forced it to retreat into his wallet. He peered to the overhead pass, hearing the number of vehicles honking their horns. It was nice and chilly here, made up for the balm and sweat on the cursed plane with other military corps returning to their loved ones. *Those troops really know how to perspire on a plane.*

Bored, he cracked his fingers with his thumbs on each hand, feeling the strain on his fingers. It reminded him of the single-most irrefutable fact—he is getting too old for this shit, in his late thirties. He was already beginning to feel it, but that didn't mean he wasn't in great physical condition. After all, he had to be to continue fighting for Black Eagle.

Much plagued his mind, thinking ahead of himself, the news, which was never good these days. Hell, it was never great to begin with, everyone lying by omission, no one knew what fact or fiction was anymore. He stopped listening because it was the same day after day, just a different player on the field as global lines crossed from between nations, and last minute alliances were made.

Although he stopped listening to the news, he could never escape it. His colleagues always made a point to remind him by sending him unwanted emails. War loomed over his notifications everywhere, reminding him he wanted to get out, but of course, getting out with a pension was ideal.

Only three years left. And he was done. Forever, and hopefully to escape forever the chains that bound him, the orders he followed which led everyone he fought with to a certain Hell.

His hands weren't clean either. They never would be. He knew this, accepted it as part of his history, should the world find out about everything he's done, the general populace would march right on beacon hill, calling for him to be hanged.

His vision barreled down his.50 cal, aimed down the desert plains. Soldiers around the vicinity of Area 51 pushed themselves further into the collapsed building, tripping over dead carcasses of other soldiers, trying to finalize the execution of Task Force Seven for their collaboration with Germany to overthrow the US government. A single man, swiftly dispatching soldier's left and right, sweat beading down his face, and dripping on his blood-stained uniform. The man he recognized as Ghost, arguably the most dangerous person who ever walked this earth.

Ghost, lit up by blue veins, struck, shot, and stabbed, until even the vehicles were nothing more than skeletons of their former selves. Ghost entered his sights, and finally stopped moving. Jeff took a deep breath, exhaled, and squeezed the trigger. The recoil pushed against his shoulder as the bullet left the barrel, bearing down on its target. The bullet struck Ghost in the chest, pushing him back a step, and blood sprayed out his back still drooling out of him like molasses from a strainer. The blue veins all over Ghost's body faded, but the body still stood defiant.

Ghost, of course, had the audacity to place his hand over his chest as he glared directly at him. He saw those words form on those accursed lips; that traitorous bastard recited the Pledge of Allegiance.

The bomb's dropped, and the corpses were scattered. Smoke encapsulated the top of Area 51, and flames rose from the ground. When the dust settled, before he could confirm if Ghost was truly dead, his radio coughed: "Exit the vicinity now," Malcolm called. "Area 51 is about to go nuclear, evacuate now!"

Shit!

Jeff turned his back on the carnage, running away from the devil, and the bodies left behind. It wasn't long until he was picked up and transported safely away by another Humvee before an even larger explosion shook the ground, gas pumping out of the earth like an erupting volcano and casting nuclear ash across the skies. It poisoned the air, and anyone within ten kilometers had their life cut drastically short.

And to think, we've managed only two years after achieving world peace. Funny how fragile it can be.

Jeff bit his lip, gazing over to the many people getting picked up by other passenger vehicles, and others jumping into larger shuttles, driving off to go rent a car. He patiently waited for his brother Michael to pick him up. Considering the exorbitant costs involved with achieving peace, it was a worthy price tag. That transaction, the lives spent, the funerals, it was all worth the cost. *And there shouldn't be anything stopping us from doing it again.*

A seven-passenger car drove by and parked in front of him. It honked obnoxiously, and the window rolled down. A beautiful blond-haired woman with a ponytail smiled at him, waving, Michael was on the other side pressing a button releasing the trunk door. The windows were tinted, but there were outlines of two more people in the back. The doors opened, and a woman pushed herself inward to make room for him, and another man, head downcast crawled out of the vehicle.

"Jeff," Michael called out from the driver's seat. "Hurry up and get your bags in the trunk. Ted will help you."

"Thanks. Late as usual, Mike." Jeff shrugged, turning his attention to the overpass, cars honking like tuba players.

"Yeah, well, especially now, come on, we don't have much more time before we lose the reservation!" Michael shot him a smile.

Jeff turned to grab his bags and didn't notice the other man climbing out of the SUV, until he stood right in front of him. He saw scars on his face and slight burns on his arms. He knew this man, and this man was supposed to be dead. His heart rate shot up immensely. Exhaling thickly through his nose. The man smirked at him with a gleam in his eyes. Jeff, finding himself trapped with nowhere to run, traded a grin.

Ghost!

"Sergeant Jeffrey Clemens, I remember you. How the hell are you?" said the other man enthusiastically.

"Fine, forgive me." *How the hell are you still alive? I blew a hole through your damned chest. A bomb landed on you. There's no way in Hell you outran a nuclear meltdown.* "I can't seem to remember your name." *Play dumb. He doesn't know you know yet.*

"Sorry. Ted Anderson. 75th Ranger Regiment," he replied, stretching out his hand for a firm handshake. "Now, you remember?"

You know he's dead right? You're not fooling me. "Ah, yes, now I remember. I seem to remember you falling off the grid after the little *accident*," Jeff shook his hand firmly, and he felt the hand, a firm shake with inhuman bone cracking strength. *He's gonna fucking kill me.* "How have you been?" *Shit!*

"Fine as I can be, after you know what happened. I would like to chat about that some time, whenever you have a minute. It would be nice to catch up with an old war buddy," Ghost had a grin on his face, ear to ear it was.

Why'd you take his name of all people? He was the real hero in all that mess, as unbearable of an ass he was. "Sure, but not right now. Not the best place around it, and besides, you ought to know much of what happened was classified."

"Not talking about the operation, itself. Shall I?" he flashed a grin, but this was no normal grin. Jeff knew it. He's seen this grin far too many times to not know better. This was his little way of saying, 'I know you're not buying my little act, and I know you're acting yourself.'

"Please," he yawned, covering his mouth. "It was a very long and irritable flight."

"I don't need specifics," said the man masquerading around as Ted Anderson. He reached around him to grab his last duffle bag and moved it around to the back.

I'm going to die! I guess I can't put this off any longer now.

Jeff walked around to the other end of the SUV, and he sat in the back. The trunk door shut. Ted stepped into the SUV, closing the door, and secured his seatbelt. He carefully scanned Ted for any kind of weapon. *Who am I kidding? It's Ghost. He doesn't need one.*

Jeff's heart was pounding inside his chest, his heartbeat pumping behind his ears. *Michael, how do you know him? Do you know how dangerous your position is right now? And now that I'm here, it only makes the situation that much worse.*

Jeff retracted his hand into his pocket, trembling profusely.

"What time is the reservation?" The woman in the front asked before interrupting herself with a raised finger pointed to the roof of the car. "Hold that thought," she turned to look him in the eyes with a warm smile. "Sorry. I'm Samantha. Nice to meet you, Jeff. I've heard so much about you."

Jeff chuckled. "Probably nothing worth noting, I'm sure. I'm barely around." He smirked to her before focusing his gaze back to Ted, who without a doubt, already knew he was being watched.

"We're going to the Grendel's pub. We are just on time to be late," Michael smirked through the rearview mirror at his brother, and they drove off.

Jeff bit his lip at that one. Late to pick him up. Late to lunch. *Will you be late to my funeral too?*

Ted and Jennifer spoke, while Jeff pretended to doze off in the back, keeping a close eye on anything Ted might do. After all, *he* was the dangerous one here.

The SUV stopped at a parking garage. *Great.* He yawned again, hoping to force Ted to let his guard down, because that was the only way to beat a man like him. He did it once. He can do it again. However, something tugged at him. There wasn't anything remarkable about Ghost this time, nor did he do anything suspicious. He merely spoke and laughed with Jennifer, almost like they'd been dating for years, and he might pop the question at any moment. But Ghost was a liar of all liars, and none of those feelings were true. How could they be when he didn't give her his real name? *But you don't have a name. Do you?*

The trees were bare, planted along the sidewalks, and people walked about, careless and happy with one another. Meanwhile, Jeffrey checked every corner of every building they walked by. *Can't be too careful—overseas or back here.*

"Ted," he didn't force a yawn this time. "How did you come to meet Michael?"

"Well, you better talk to Samantha about that one, really," Michael interjected, turning his head to him. "After all, he is really only a part of our—"

"Dysfunctional little family," Jennifer finished, turning her head back to face him, grinning politely.

"Right, our dysfunctional little family here because of her," Michael continued. "But more on that later. We are almost too late for it to be fashionable anymore."

"You need to get better with time, Michael," Jeff said, turning his head back to Ted, who offered a generic ass smile. *Go to Hell, you lying sack of shit. Malcolm would know what to do.*

"Hey. I'm early for business, not personal or family matters. I thought you'd have known this by now." Michael led the way down the slanted pavement into the warm array of sunlight, beaming down on them. "Come on before we lose our reservation."

Jeff shook his head. They crossed the walkway and descended the brick stairs into the dark lit place.

"Reservation for five," Michael announced to the smiling hostess at the wooden stand.

"Good of you to show up. I was about to give away your table."

"I like to be fashionable." Michael jeered, elbowing Sam in the side. "Isn't that right."

"Can you be normal for once?" Sam rolled her eyes.

"Right this way."

The hostess led them to a table in the back of the room. A dangling chandelier overhead cast an orange light over the space. Jeff sat on a cushioned seat, followed by the others. A server placed five glasses of water in front of them. On either side of Jeff was Jennifer and Michael. He scanned the room, careful to watch for anything, looking for an out to call Malcolm. He would want to know about Ghost being alive, after all this time.

"So, Sam, do you care to explain?" Michael asked.

"Hmm?" she sipped some water. "Oh, right. How do we know Ted? Several months ago, I saw him in the Boston Public Garden during one of our little picnics, and at the time I thought nothing of it. Something weird was going on with the weather."

"It *is* New England," Jeff replied.

"You see!" Jennifer said, pointing across the table. "That's exactly what I said."

"Well, anyway, it wasn't until the following Tuesday that I formally introduced myself to him as we all happened to be at the same bar at the same time. I started talking to him about that strange weather occurrence, and the rest of us, Jenn, Michael, and Erin, huddled around him. The rest was rather," Samantha's voice trailed off.

"It was rather turbulent," Jennifer finished. "Really, I don't think we need to say any more than that."

"Only a few months huh?" Jeff turned to Ted. *Well, you always were the convincing liar, but what are you planning here? Sabotage the Federal Bank? No.* "So, Ted, how long have you been in the area then."

"What Sam said was the long and short of it. I haven't been in Boston for very long." *Or so you tell everyone.*

The waitress came by, refilled their water glasses, dropped off two pitchers of water, took all their orders and scurried off to give the orders to the kitchen.

The bathroom. Perfect.

"So, how long are you going to be around?" Ted asked from across the table, giving him an amiable yet fake smile.

Bullshitter. You and I both know you aren't happy to see me. "I'm only going to be around for about a week before I get deployed again." *Of course, the fact that you're here complicates matters exponentially.*

"Well, you two seem to know one another quite well," Sam commented as she brought her glass to her lips. "Same regiment?"

"Not exactly," Jeff swiftly replied, scanning everyone around the table. *Ghost, how will you reply?*

"I suppose one could say we were," Ghost answered.

Shit! Jeff tilted his head and forced his lips to raise in a smile. "Often times we found ourselves on the same battlefield. But never within the same unit." *Still as sharp as ever.*

"Jeff, have you heard anything from Mom at all?" Michael asked.

Jeff turned his attention to his brother. He didn't want to take his attention off from Ghost, who sat too close for comfort, yet he knew in maintaining such attention, eyebrows would be raised; he didn't need that. He sucked in the air through his teeth. "Unfortunately, no. I've been way too busy with planning for—future efforts."

"Are you referring to the Collapse?" Michael asked.

"Is that what they're calling it?" Jeff thought his brother was referring to almost all of Europe, Africa, and Asia being engulfed in flames of war. He didn't even know why this was all happening. It hasn't reached the Western Hemisphere though. *Yet. It's coming far sooner than anyone thinks.*

"Yeah."

"Well, yes," he waved his hand palm up. "Classified."

"Yeah, too bad we weren't able to repeat what we did last time for that, wouldn't you agree?" said Ghost.

What do you want me to say? "Well, whatever it was, the price was worth it, and we should do it all over again. It was deemed necessary. The price wasn't too high."

"Really?" Michael asked incredulously. "I'm certain that's classified too."

"Yup," Ghost and Jeff replied simultaneously.

Not a moment too soon, and the waitress came by, and asked them if they needed anything. *Perfect.*

"Where's the bathroom?" he asked. She directed him down the hall and to the left at the brick sign.

"Thank you."

"I have to go too actually. Great idea!" Ghost said, putting his napkin on the table to stand up.

Damn it! That isn't something men do. Is he—going to kill me in the bathroom? A convenient enough place. Perhaps feign that I slipped, struck my head hard against the sink to break my neck in half. But I—but I shouldn't be surprised. He is The Ghost after all, always seventeen steps ahead of everyone, minus that one little incident. He's like a virus, and a very adaptable one at that.

"Great, I wouldn't want to get myself lost along the way. You've always had a better sense of direction than I ever had," Jeff said.

Jennifer removed herself from the booth to allow Jeff up. He followed Ted, scowling the entire time; he carefully monitored Ted's hands, both of which were in his pockets. *He has a pocket-knife tucked in there doesn't he? Just my luck.*

The door into the bathroom was a swinging-door on hinges, swung both ways. The two entered the bathroom together, and much to Jeff's dismay, it was empty.

"Good to know you haven't lost your edge, you dirty little bastard." Ghost said to him, and he wasn't smiling. This manikin of a man frowned, and his eyebrows tilted upward. *There's the Ghost I know.*

Any hope of reporting this to Malcolm was destroyed with Ghost looming over him. *Probably thinking I'd do exactly that.* He sighed. "What do you want me to say, Ghost? What's done is done, and we can't take back what happened."

"You have no idea what you did to us, do you?" Ghost asked. "Do you know what was in my mind these last several years?"

"I don't care to know. You were never a soldier, not a brother in arms to me."

"What were we to you except monsters? The fact is you being here is a bit of a problem for me."

"And you being alive is a problem for everyone. I'm not going to ask how you survived all that. You wouldn't tell me anyway." Jeff scowled and walked to the urinal. "You're right. You're a monster. A dog like one who lost control, you deserved to be put down, and yet here you are." *You all were.*

"Well, the truth is partially out. Some of it, anyway. Tell me, why?" Ghost stood to the adjacent urinal. "Why were we executed? All these years, I still can't figure out why. All the codes of conduct, I obeyed them all to the letter."

"Classified," Jeff said.

"So, that's how it is then. You won't tell me why, so I guess I'll go on returning back to my nightmares."

"Nightmares? What are you talking about?" Jeff flushed the urinal.

"I supposed a cold-hearted son of a bitch like yourself wouldn't experience it. Never mind. Forget I said it," Ghost replied.

Jeff turned the faucet on, put soap on his hands as he washed them underneath the hot water, and he saw Ghost looking at him through the mirror. "What now?"

"One more thing. If you so much as think of doing something that is going to force me to start over, I will rip your fucking limbs off." Ghost scowled at him through the mirror.

Those eyes. Those fucking eyes! I've seen those before, but they weren't in your head. Butcher's, was it? She went on a killing spree last I saw those eyes in her. You really expect me not to do anything? Forget it.

He looked down, and his hands, both trembled erratically as they bathed in the faucet's waterfall. Knowing entirely who Ghost was, only added many questions, some he already asked, others, well, they'd be bubbled up to the surface soon enough. Death was certain, almost like taxes, but here, death was more important taxes, and his poor little brother now attached to the moral quagmire. Michael had no business in this. It was for the better really.

He finally heard the door creaking behind him, and then he was alone. But he couldn't stop shaking. His heartbeat raced. *Michael, you're in the middle of this.*

Chapter 2 Brothers

Russian trade reports state that the commodity tariffs are unjust, leading to a hike in transportation costs for the following imports to the US: mineral fuels, metal, stone, steel, iron, fertilizers, and inorganic chemicals.

Press Secretary Jenna Walters reports: The tariffs are in place to bring in revenue to move the country in a more stable direction for the economy and combat climate change effectively. These tariffs will reduce the supply and demand for such commodities, and we will resort to more home-grown materials to further employ Americans.

***

Jeffrey sat on his couch. The one person he didn't want to get any closer to, was the one person he needed to always stay within earshot. The consequences of someone loose in Task Force Seven was a calamity waiting to happen. Even still, for a monster, a killer, he seemed to be fitting in quite nicely.

This reminded him ostensibly of the common witticism for getting someone out for Halloween who didn't want to dress up, or who hated it; 'Just go as a serial killer, they look like everyone else.' And Ghost fit the bill perfectly, behaving like everyone else.

Meanwhile, alliances were crumbling to dust all over the world, and the world was nowhere near safer. What did ten years of relative peace mean when it crumbled apart so easily? The lives lost. The tragedy meaningless, and of course, the needless blackmail from that bitch, Nakamura.

J. Nakamura.

Of course, Jeff knew Ghost had no clean slate. He wasn't a good boy, as she would often refer to him. 'Good little boy,' she would say, and for what? Blowing up an orphanage? Though, if he was being honest, Ghost only ever did those things because the creepy bastard only watched him do it. Blackmailed by the bitch of course. Jeff would go down in history as a murderer and a baby killer. Hell, even a rapist if the world knew the truth, all because of that dreadful bitch. *Hell is too good a place for you, but you better be burning there all the same!*

She's dead though, strangled in her office. No one really knew who did it, but no one bothered to send word to the authorities. Perhaps they should have, because it wasn't much longer until her husband was found, chopped up in pieces, no doubt in a fit of rage. Likely by the same person, whoever that was. They did suspect Sergeant Ted Anderson to be the culprit, but after they went searching for him for answers, they only found him hanging from a noose, strategically swinging on creaking rope over a kicked over chair. The trail went cold after that. The military was filled with murderers these days, all with something important to lose, and would do anything, even stage a coup, to hide the truth.

Jeffrey was no exception to that. He knew. His crimes swept underneath the rug, and it needed to stay that way. His parents and *especially* Michael would never forgive him for all he did in Area 51, or over in Bagdad. Sure, the great of the cause, but what of the cost to others? His family valued certain things above their own freedom. They would never truly understand what was at stake here, or why he did the things he did. It was all in the name of America's freedom, and if that freedom cost the lives of some reluctant animals, so be it. In this case, it was a traitor, anyway.

But onto more necessary and urgent matters. The fact was that if Ghost was still alive, there was a possibility, no, a certainty that the truth would come out. And Jeff had to protect it, no matter what cost, even at the cost of his brother.

A simple call should suffice. That's all he needed. Questions he needed answered before anything else. How long has Michael known this fake Ted Anderson, how does he know him, and what other connections does he have? He must push for this information to even think about being in the same room with him, which now seemed all but inevitable.

He took his phone out of his pocket, exhaling and dialed Michael. By *your phone always. How convenient.*

"Hey, Jeff, what's up?" Michael's voice sounded hurried.

"It seems I got you at a bad time,"

"No, you didn't wake me. I'm just on my way to drop Samantha off. What's up?"

"I have a few questions about some things as they are alarming to me." He spoke coldly. "I hope you have a moment to answer them."

"Rather unusual timing, but sure,"

"How did you come to know Ted Anderson?"

"Sam already told—"

"I need to hear it from you," he pushed.

"Fine. Sam was experiencing some hot flashes when she started noticing him, and as it happened, we just happened to be at the same place at the same time," Michael answered.

I don't know why he would go out of his way to find you—not when he wouldn't have known our relation. Maybe I'm just paranoid.

"Anyway, he had just moved here a few weeks ago at that point, so it's been several months now."

"Uh huh," Jeff replied. *Two questions answered in one.* "Does he meet up with anyone, like from his army days? Anything like that?"

"Jeff, what's this about?"

"Nothing at all, just curious,"

"Well, if you really want anything more specific than what I told you, you're gonna wanna talk to Jennifer. He's closest to her. Not that we aren't friends, but there are things he only tells her, so even if he was meeting someone other than her, I wouldn't know."

So, I must step in the Lion's Den, eh? Shit. "Okay, thanks Michael."

"No problem," he replied. "Anything else?"

Yeah. "Oh, and one more thing. Do know you someone renting an apartment?"

Chapter 3 New Orders

Opinion: Janica Williams of the Houston Press.

President Samuel Snells is a joke of a president. Repeating mistakes that the nation made years ago during the first and second world wars, remaining at ease, and not stepping in to help allies overseas during the struggles. With tensions around the world at an all-time high, it remains likely that President Snells, true to form, will sit back until one of the hostiles reaches our borders here in the USA, effectively, bringing a conflict directly to us: War.

It's a tale as old as time, and this time, the USA is not a world power anymore. Russia and China have grown their influence within global markets and military prowess over the last ten years with research, development, and innovation. Our conservative president will not change for the sake of balancing the budget as his highest priority.

The American people don't need a balanced budget right now. They need services, and action. The likes of which our president refuses to give us.

***

Jeff peered outside the transparent glass of his hotel room, gazing downward into the empty 2:00 a.m. streets. The raindrops on his window blurred images of puddles and parked cars under the streetlights. He drew the curtains closed.

He went over to his bedroom door and listened. No footsteps. No breathing. *Good. He didn't follow me here.* But then, Ghost sat close to him the entire time; he could have planted a bug on him.

Jeffrey checked his coat pockets, pants pockets, took them off, shook them until all the lint poured out, and no bug. No wires, no other electrical devices. On to his briefcase. Jeffrey took to his luggage, poured everything out of it, checking all the pockets, the surface area, combing it with his hands to look for anything out of place. Grabbing hold of all his clothes, shaking each one of them. Same thing. Nothing. He checked his keys, and wallet, opened them out, inspected each card and crevice before taking to his phone. Same thing: nothing.

Wow. I'm honestly disappointed.

He took his phone into his room, the furthest place from the door on the off chance, and presumably unlikelihood, of Ghost listening in to the other side of the door. *Don't be hasty. Be thoughtful and stay ten steps ahead. That's you Ghost, always telling me those things, and yet here you are dropping the steps like they're flies. Even the best makes mistakes, eh?*

For good measure, he got on all fours, looking at the carpet floor, ensuring there were no tears. Nothing to indicate this room was tampered with. Of course, how would Ghost know which room he was staying in? *But it's Ghost. He knows everything.* Seeing nothing of note, he sighed, sat on his bed, and took out his phone to finally dial Malcolm.

It rang a few times.

"Come on, pick up! Pick up!" he tapped his shoulder repeatedly with his index fingers, one of his many nervous habits.

"Clemens, you have any idea what time it is?" said Malcolm.

"Yes, but you're going to want to hear this,"

"Spit it out!"

"Ghost is alive,"

There was silence on the other line.

"You don't mean, Task Force Seven Ghost, do you?" he said.

"Yes," he answered. "He's living as Ted Anderson. *The* Ted Anderson."

"How is that even possible? That Ted Anderson is dead. He hanged himself."

"I don't know. But he is. And I saw him today. I'm sure the grimy little bastard had to stop himself from killing me out in the open."

"Shit. How positive are you?"

"One hundred percent."

"He's like a cockroach," he hissed. "New orders. You don't have vacation. Stay there, talk to me if you need funds for procurement of any supplies. Big players afoot, and we're getting real friendly with Russia, but we can't have Ghost on the loose. Stay close but stay reasonable. Don't provoke him. Periodically, check in with me, and no one else. Nakamura better be burning in Hell for this."

Chapter 4 Senseless Insanity

Suicide rates have spiked more than 200 percent in the last year, says expert magazine, Psychology Analysts. Among those within the population, teens suicide rate spiked, as did the following demographics: Veteran, Black, and Hispanic American. Meanwhile, the Caucasian suicide rate dipped by 3 percent.

Mental health professionals need help. They are over booked, and the US may see a decline when it comes to the mental health of psychological professionals as they are over worked. Additional experts argue that the rise in the suicide rates is related to the lack of government assistance related to health care, pulling funding from Medicare and Medicaid services across the US to reduce the amount of coverage to professionals, and related to higher co-pays for individuals, again, spiking up since 2023. These issues extrapolate the effects of undiagnosed mental illness among Americans.

***

After saying goodbye to Jennifer this evening, Ted closed the door behind him so she could rest. She was doing lots of resting these days. He didn't know much about the treatment for leukemia, but whatever it was, whatever chemical she was being induced with was taking a toll on her. She was bursting with energy before, but now, while still having sprints of that energy, by the end of any given day, she was left exhausted utterly.

His feet took him down the hall, and he pressed the elevator button. He exhaled as the doors opened, and he stepped into the threshold of this metal box, this prison, before selecting the main lobby button. Leaning back, his hands retreated into his pockets. His anxiety escalated, body shaking amid the stress Jeffrey now put him under.

His eyes narrowed and he gritted his teeth, scowling at nothing in particular.

He wanted to kill him. No. That's putting it lightly. He wanted to break every bone in his body. Make him squeal and bleed out black blood and watch him suffer till the lights in his eyes fade. See how he likes it, the son of a bitch. He deserves nothing better, and yet he'll be buried, family will miss him. Better than he deserves.

I could kill Michael and make Jeff watch him bleed out. No, Sam would never forgive me. Just calm down. It won't solve anything.

The doors for that claustrophobia-inducing container opened its doors and he passed through the threshold, and left the building, running to the parking lot to his car yet again, pushing past the street, and avoiding oncoming traffic, as only he could, nearly getting side swiped by the car as he inhaled a mixture of *essence*. That alien form of matter coursed through his veins, black veins forming as the part of the car that *would* have hit him but instead just passed right through him. He was a *Ghost* after all. Nothing about him made him inherently human.

Finally, he arrived at his car. He jumped inside, fastened his seatbelt, and revved the engine a few times. Funny, he knew how machines worked, just as he himself was nothing more than a machine, a tool created for the sole purpose of taking lives, but he didn't understand people as well as he wanted to. Sure, he could masquerade as one to play the part of one's identity for a day, but that was the limit.

He pressed the gas pedal, edging forward and onto the street. Driving through the oncoming traffic of Boston before taking a number of different turns through various streetlights, tunnels, and one-way streets which made Boston, as a general rule, one of the worst places to drive in the world. As they say here, if you can drive in Boston, you can drive anywhere. Boston drivers were an aggressive bunch, able to drive through the worst of calamities. Pothole? No problem. Detour? Yeah right. One-way? Drivers only ever drove one-way.

One day to masquerade as a person. That was his limit. But here he was, completely lost in the identity he chose to make his own; polite, patient, and calm. Of course, inside, he was none of those things. Patient, maybe. Not calm—his nervous anxiety told him that. He was not polite, not with the expletives that roam around his mind, especially not since earlier today; he threated to rip someone's fucking arms off.

No matter. He'll continue to play this part. It's the part that Jennifer knew, rather, she was aware of the façade all too well, and Sam, too.

They knew him to not be the polite person, but the crude individual who had a questionable past on which he could speak nothing of. Not because of the confidentiality of it, but for their own safety. If President Sam Snells knew he was still alive, he would send the entire military down on his head, which, undoubtedly, would put Jennifer and Samantha in harm's way. Those were the two he truly cared about. They went out of their way to save him from his own darkness, and because of that, they were worth protecting. No matter what the cost.

He arrived at the relative safety of his place of residence. He pushed the door shut, and one by one, locked each lock to the door, including the chain lock, the bolt, and the knob.

No one's getting through that.

He knew that was a lie. All it would take was a damn battering ram to shatter the wooden door, finely painted white. He leaned against the back of it, hands trembling. He exhaled, stepping forward into the room toward the display case that held Ticker's spear and Slither's bow. Unharmed.

"You had your chance!" A voice cried out from the corner.

He jolted, turning toward it. *Roach.* She was in her BDUs, of course, still whole, no loss of limbs—not yet anyway. She scowled, teeth gritting, and her fists trembled at her side.

"You had your chance. Why didn't you take it?" She shouted. "He was right there." She pointed an angry finger at him, tears glazing over her eyes. "After everything he did to us, all of us, why did you let him live? You should have ripped his fucking arms off."

He sighed and walked into the kitchen. *The nightmares again.*

"Don't you ignore me!"

Steps hastened behind him. Her arm grabbed him, pulling him firmly to the ground. The wrench was like an old burn. "Don't walk away from this. You need to kill him. Kill. Him."

He looked into her eyes; the hair that was once tied back now framed her face. His hand grew cold, trembling in her grip, her firm grip. Tears glazed over, streaming down her face as she was crying. "You have to do this. Who else can?"

"No," he replied, feeling a weight of regret on his chest. *She's right. Only I can do this, but—*

"Ghost, we can't rest right. No one knows who we are. Who we were," she pleaded. Her free arm fell off, bleeding on the floor. A gash in her chest opened, her snake-like intestines pouring out, staining his shoes. "No one knows what we did for them. Our badges of honor, the ones we earned, wrongfully given to others who dared not lift a finger. What became of the lives we gave? Buried? No. We were burned and not a physical trace of our existence remains. Just you. *You* have to do this. Who else can? Who else is capable?"

"She's right, Ghost," another voice in the corner.

He gasped, turning his head. Another girl, red hair tied back, and that familiar hilt at her side, a rifle strapped to her back, and her unforgettable side arm. She tilted her head to him; a disappointed face staring down at him. *Butcher.*

"No. You're wrong," he shook his head, closed his eyes tightly. *Go away. Go away! Get out of my head.*

The cool air warmed in the room, caressing his skin. He looked forward and the walls faded. The sand coursed the earth, stained crimson underneath the scorching sun, and whirling winds pelted against his face. The sound of a gun firing a large caliber entered his ears. He fell backward, the hot sand shredded his clothes. The bullet soared and struck Butcher in the face, blood spraying out the back of her head.

He panted heavily, with warm tears glazing over his eyes. Looking down at his arms, they shook, rapidly. His heart raced with each breath he took. The shakes tore through his body, rattling his bones and boiling his sanguine fluids.

Butcher looked at him, eyeless, and crimson, thick liquid pouring down the side of her cheek.

"Do you see it now?" Butcher asked.

Roach was next to her, bowing down, vomiting with her intestines on the floor.

"Get out of here." He cried. "Get out. Leave me alone."

"Do you want this to happen again? To someone else? Is that it?" Butcher asked, her hand firmly resting on his shoulders. Her gloves were torn with red water poured out her hands, glistening.

"No!" His hands reached over his head. He covered his ears, and his warm tears streamed down his face. "I can't. I can't do it. I have something here, and if I do that, I'll be forced to leave it all behind. I don't want to lose—"

"So what?" Roach turned her head. One leg separated at her knee, and more blood leaked out over the sand. She hopped forward. "We don't mean anything to you anymore. Is that it?"

"No. That's not it at all." He closed his ears, but that didn't stop them from talking to him, and it didn't stop him from hearing this nightmare.

"All of a sudden, Ghost has a house again. A roof over his head. A job, a life, like the good little civie you are," she said, condescendingly. "You have friends, a family even. Just because you have those, we don't mean anything. You hear this Butcher? You listening to this?"

"Yeah." Butcher leaned back again; arms crossed over her chest. "Fine," she breathed lightly. "Ghost, or Ted, whichever lie you want to believe, just let the children die again. Snells did it before, he'll do it again unless you do something. You're just a tool. I mean, look at you. You can't even function right now, crying in this little dipshit of a corner. I guess we never meant anything to you. And you were the closest thing we ever had to a father, a proper father, not one with uniforms raping us to see how many times until we finally snap."

"That's not—" he dropped his hands into the blazing hot sand.

"The only thing we ever had was each other. The closest thing to siblings and a family was us. And you're happy to throw it all away!" Roach cried. "Does none of that mean anything anymore? Were we a joke to you? Or were we just tools?"

"Ghost," Butcher closed her one eye. "If there's part of you alive in there, and you truly care about us, you'll kill them all. Every last one of them."

He breathed heavily as his flashback faded, returning him to his home, crying like he imagined a baby would after seeing these things. He pulled his knees to his chest, back against the wall as he rested his chin on his kneecaps, rocking back and forth.

Chapter 5 Favors

Several high-profile military personnel reported missing in the DC Metropolitan area as their service has ties to the 75th Ranger Regiment.

Detective Hernandez claims they're "doing everything [they] can to locate the suspect." Detective Hernandez rejected further questioning.

***

John Spadero stood outside the night street; raindrops rippled in the puddles of the empty street. A black unmarked van with tinted windows drove in front of him. The driver's side rolled down the window, and a tanned woman with raven hair and blood red eyes glared at him. "Your bargaining chip is in the back."

"Thanks." He replied grimly with sunken eyes. He walked to the back of the van; his trench coat swayed in the wind. His pocket vibrated, drawing the phone out of it, checking the caller ID: Sander. His hand swiped the phone to his ear, "Spadero here."

"Do you have an update for me? I need additional information on the target. I don't need to tell you how urgent it is," Sander said in a rushed tone.

John sighed as he leaned against the van, implanting his handprint onto the tinted glass. "Not yet. Some of these soldiers, former or not are tough as nails. Though, I have one in hand, and I just got my bargaining chip. I'll break this one."

"Report to me with an update."

"What is this about?" John asked, his eyes focused on the ripples in the puddles. "You'll tell me that much, won't you?"

"Possibly a rogue. We have one for sure, being Sarah McCurdy. This other one is an unidentified individual. This person doesn't cover his mana trail," Sander replied. "After all, things will get suspicious should they pick up on trails and heightened levels of mana, which they think is radiation. Excellent cover, really. Get to it and get back to me."

"On it," John hung up the phone and placed it back in his pocket. He swung the two doors open, revealing a woman in her late thirties, clutching onto a little sleeping child. The woman trembled as her eyes stretched open and stared into John's eyes. He felt like he was looking at a trapped animal in a cage, trying to forestall its execution. *Fitting.*

"Out."

He stepped away, keeping a trained eye on the two of them. The boy stirred, rubbing his little eyes with fisted hands.

"Momma, where are we?" The boy sleepily turned his gaze to John.

I gotta dirty my hands again, just to learn the truth, and only with the truth can the world become a little cleaner. Such a shame this is even necessary. You should have spoken; else I wouldn't have to resort to this.

"I don't know sweetheart." The woman tried to sooth the boy and feign a mask of confidence, but her sweat and quivering body told a different tale. Her hand brushed the boy's hair. "I'm just going to answer some questions. Then we'll be free to go home."

"Precisely right." John placed his boot on the edge of the van's threshold; this time John faked a smile. "Just a few questions and we're done. Then you can go back home." *Six feet under, that is.*

"Don't you dare touch him." She snapped as John approached.

John scowled at her, "Madam, get out of the van. The sooner we finish here, the sooner we can leave."

The woman had a snarl which softened as she pulled the boy down next to her. She started to climb out of the van. John immediately snapped his fingers at her. "I can't hold the van. He comes too." He pointed his finger at him.

"Gerald, come on, dear." She reached her hand back into the van. The boy took it, and she pulled him out, easing him on the wet street.

John led them to the building. The high-rise was near empty, and the windows were boarded up. Glass from shattered windows littered the ground, crunching as they stepped on the shards. John opened the door and guided the two down the iron grooved stairs, further into the dark. Gerald clutched his mother's arms as she walked down the metallic steps. John closed the final door behind them, and they were in a large room filled with yellow flickering lamps, some swayed with the sudden movement in the room.

"Jack. I brought something for you." John called out, sneering as he held the boy and his mother close to him.

"I'll never talk, you monster." The man called from the other room.

"We'll see just how far your resolve is. How long will you let the truth lay silent? I am determined to get the truth out somehow, and you are my last stop." John called back. "You wanted this. I gave you an out."

John kicked the wooden door down into the other room, and there was Jack exactly how he left him; beat up, bloodied, tied in numerous ropes and duct tape. There were photos sitting on the table in front of him. The man tilted his head up toward them. His swollen eyes couldn't open, but John imagined they would be wide indeed.

"Jack! Jack! What happened to you?" The woman cried out, running out to the man. She embraced him and looked in his eyes as John shut and locked the door with its numerous tumblers.

John walked to the corner of the room, hoisted a metal chair, and slammed it on the ground at the table. He pulled the woman away from Jack. She shrieked. He pushed her to the chair. The boy leaned against the locked door, arms quivering, retracted to his chin, staring at the table with gaping eyes.

"Jack," said John. "Talk. I want answers, and I want them now."
"No."

John abruptly grabbed the woman's arm and slammed her wrist on the table. He pulled out a knife and stabbed the table with it. "I've been patient enough with you. Speak. This can be easy, or difficult. Take your pick."

"Babe, what is he talking about? Just give him what he wants!" she sobbed.

"Dadda! What—"

"Silence, boy." John snapped, turning to him briefly and scowled. "The adults are talking."

The boy gasped, pushing himself against the locked door. His teeth grinded together, hands down, clutching at the door.

"Nothing," said Jack.

John assumed Jack was scowling behind the blood and swelling.

"Fuck it,"

John pulled the knife out of the table. He firmly held her hand in place and kept her pinky nail firmly pinned down. He squeezed her nail until the color began to fade. He placed the blade of the knife just underneath the manicured nail.

"Just don't hurt my son," she pleaded.

"That all depends on Jack," John explained. "What's it gonna be?"

"What are you doing?" Jack's chair budged as he struggled against the restraints. "Leave her alone. She has nothing to do with this. I don't—I don't even know what this is."

"Bullshit. Give me something better than that." Jack pushed the blade into the nailbed and pried off the nail. She wailed. Blood dripped off to the sides, the tender skin exposed. *Don't you dare make me pry off toenails.*

The screech scratched John's ears. He grimaced as he pinned down the next finger on the table. She squirmed, trying to rip herself away to no avail.

"MOMMA." The small child's strangled scream came from behind him.

"Just tell me what I want, and this stops," John scowled to Jack.

"MAKE IT STOP." The woman shrieked.

Her wrist tensed, and with her free palm, she slapped John across the face. He turned, and with his hand grabbed the other wrist, breathing in the mana from the air, blue veins climbing on his fingers, and with a reinforced thumb, sprained her wrist, and slammed it again on the table. She sucked in air through her teeth, closing her eyes tight.

"Time's wasting." John didn't give Jack a moment to reply. He stabbed the nailbed of the next finger and pried the nail off. The blood started to drip onto the table, her shriek scratched his ears. The floor squealed as the iron legs scrapped across it as her futile attempt to pull herself away . "Now, talk."

"Fine. I'll talk." Jack's chair stopped moving as he bowed his head down. "Just stop."

"Who is Ghost?" John asked. He pinned her middle finger on the table.

"Ghost," Jack gazed up at the ceiling, presumably to jog his memory. "Why do you care about a dead man?"

"Wrong answer!" John slipped the blade of the knife underneath another nailbed, prying the third fingernail off. He pinned her index finger on the table as she screamed, trying to get out of his grasp. John breathed in the mana from the air, and bright blue veins were risen on his skin, his hands. "Answer the damn question."

"I told you. He's dead." Jack cried. "Stop it."

"I have been asking you this question all day, with the same damn answer." Jack stabbed the other nailbed and pried off her fingernail. He pinned her thumb on the table. "I don't care if he is dead or not. I want to know who he is. Who is he, Jack?"

"He's dead and meaningless, what possible thing do you have to gain in me telling—"

"DAMNIT." John swore and stabbed his knife through her thumb. The thumb severed and was pushed off the table, blood splattered on it. The woman screamed, her eyes tearing. "You should know this, I would not be asking about Ghost if he was dead, now, would I?"

Jack finally went silent. He looked up to John with a grim face, a face even darker than when Jack cut his wife's thumb off. "That's impossible."

"Now, we're getting somewhere. Why is it impossible?" John moved to the other side of Jack's wife and pinned her other hand on the table, ready to start over. He shot a scowl over to the boy in the corner. *If I can get that answered at least, I deduce something else from this.*

"He's dead. KIA in Area 51. Training exercise," Jack replied.

"Was there a body?"

"No."

"Then how do you know he's dead?" John asked, "And don't tempt me. I have five more fingernails. And ten more toenails. Don't make me add your son to this."

"He was last confirmed at the base of Area 51. The base itself was blown to shreds, never mind the nuclear reactor that blew up. Where he was, is now filled with radioactive waste. No one would dare touch his body even if there was one to recover."

"So, the military falsely claimed him as KIA, and not MIA?" John inquired.

"So, it would seem."

"And he was last seen on Area 51, which was blown to bits, and then was the epicenter for a nuclear meltdown. Correct?"

"Correct."

"How did Area 51 blow up?" John asked, knowing full well what radiation really was. Enough of it would cause cellular damage to normies, and might blow up persons' mana veins, which, if Ghost was a fae, it would have still killed him.

"The same way they all do. There wasn't enough water in the reactors at that moment in time, and the failsafe systems in place didn't work," Jack replied.

"That's a highly classified base. You mean to tell me they were sufficiently primed for failure?" John asked.

"What do you want me to say? I wasn't stationed at Area 51. I was leading the 75th Ranger Regiment."

"What the hell was an entire calvary doing at a training exercise at Area 51?" John didn't believe that Ghost was KIA. Not like this.

Jack didn't answer.

"No matter, we'll come back to this, and I expect an answer," said John. "Now, who is Ghost?"

"Ghost was the captain of Task Force Seven," he answered. His wife quietened down, her screams now a whimper.

"Who is Task Force Seven?"

"An elite division on the Army. They were well hidden and trained alongside with the special forces."

"What did they do?" John cataloged this information in his head. He would write it down later and report this to Sander, and of course, the four fae assigned to this manhunt in Boston. So many pieces adding up, none of them made sense without the common missing link.

"They infiltrated high valued military bases from across the world. They led counter strikes, and often held execute authority, including overriding commands from the colonels, and answered to General Snells alone. They assassinated high level targets, forcing our enemies in a constant state of disarray."

"They gave a captain rank equal to that of a general and answered to only one person in the US Army?" Spadero raised his eyebrow, staring into the muddled eyes of the man sitting across from him, blood dripping out of his nose into neat puddles.

"Sounds surreal, but it's true. Even my rank by the time I retired, I would answer to Ghost if he and I shared the same battlefield," Jack spoke solemnly.

John recapped. "Is that the long and short of it?"

"Yes."

John sighed heavily. His finger tapped against the iron table, warm blood sputtering underneath, dripping on the floor. He heard the dripping of thick coagulating fluid on the floor as the room felt eerily quiet. He even stopped hearing the whimpering of the brat in the corner.

"Good. What does the official record say about that incident at Area 51?" John pressed further.

"I can't give you the full report. Reports were collected and submitted to Lieutenant Nakamura, and then finalized underneath General Snells. Lieutenant Nakamura is deceased, killed in her office in Georgia, and you know General Snells, the president."

"What happened to the rest of Task Force Seven?"

"Falsely documented as KIA in the training accident at Area 51."

"Who else was in Task Force Seven?"

"I only dealt with Ghost. The last reported dead were Slithers, Ticker, and Butcher, and Ghost was the final one."

What the hell is all this mess? None of this makes sense, and if all of this was true, it would be impossible to cover it up as well as it's been covered. And still, nobody knows anything.

"Now, I did my own digging, and like I said, you're my last stop," said John. "Do you care to explain to me exactly why there are no records of Task Force Seven? All I found was a few faces and codenames." He noticed a drop of blood on his slacks. *Shit.*

"I couldn't tell you. Like I said, all our reports concerning Task Force Seven were submitted to Lieutenant Nakamura. Presumably, she submitted all the reports to Snells, who drafted the final report."

"So, people were aware of them, but there was no official record proving their existence. Is that correct?" John asked.

"Yes."

John let go of Jack's wife's hand, and his blue veins retreated underneath his skin. *A dangerous force, as it were. No official records of them existing, minus this little conversation, and that is the only thing I have on this Ghost. I'm not done yet. I have two names, one of which is impossible to get, but perhaps...* "You said Nakamura was dead. How did she die?"

Jack surrendered the information. "I don't have all the details, but the reports say she was found dead, strangled by someone on a Georgia base."

"Suspect?" Jack asked. *This is a lead!*

"There were a few, but only one was ever a serious suspect. His name was Sergeant Ted Anderson," Jack replied.

"Where is he now? To the best of your recollection." *Ted Anderson. The missing link. You know something.*

"Memory serves right," Jack hesitated. "Ted Anderson was in the 75th Ranger Regiment. He was heavily involved with the secret projects with the CIA, of which Snells and Nakamura were deeply invested in for some reason. He's reported dead."

John leaned over the table, and covered his forehead with his hand, rubbing his temples. *Damnit.* "Killed in action?"

"Negative," Jack replied like a soldier. "He was hanged."

"He was executed?" John looked back at the swollen face.

"I don't know."

"Yeah, why would you," John replied. *No loose ends were left untied. Snells. Ted Anderson. I suppose I'll need to make another trip.* John smiled. "No further questions, your honor."

John took himself away from the table and shifted his body to the door. The woman rushed over to her husband. Watching the boy scramble and embracing his father, John reached out of his back pocket, and retrieved a Glock nine-millimeter pistol and aimed it at the grouping. "No witnesses." Jack and his family screamed as John pulled the trigger in rapid succession. The muffled nozzle produced bright lights as each round was evacuated from its chamber striking each target in the head. He returned the Glock to his holster.

A look, he took, one final look. The man was useless, he had no respect for the likes of him. Utterly useless. His swollen head had a hole in it, one eye lightly opened, and his head bowed down as if to pray. His wife, now on the floor, blood pooling out of her head, and who could forget the boy whose sensitive cranium shattered. *Jack. Why did you make this necessary?*

He let out a deep sigh, pulling out his knife again, and he drew runes in the air. The purple veins were pulled from his body and concentrated into the sigils. The shapes were pushed out and placed themselves carefully on the bodies. The bodies slowly turned to ash, burning away. He felt their bodies becoming mana, and he imbibed them through the runes. The runes faded away; the veins fleeting into his body.

***

Sander picked up the phone immediately as if he expected the call. *I'll never get used to that.*

"What information did you gleam?"

"Almost nothing to go off of," John started before he went into the details of the interrogation, line by line, almost verbatim. John was twiddling his thumb with his other hand. "The loose ends over here have been tied."

"Good," Sander replied. "Spadero, you seem to be hiding something from me."

"I wouldn't say hiding," he chuckled nervously. "More like, I have an idea that has not been able to formulate a complete thought yet."

"Shoot it at me. I'll make sense of it."

"Ghost, whoever that is, is alive, so, he somehow survived being at the epicenter of a nuclear meltdown. What if, it was not Ted Anderson who killed Lieutenant Nakamura, but Ghost masquerading as Ted Anderson?" John reasoned. "This is the only conclusion I can come up with, and mind you, all speculation. No solid proof. Evidence is completely circumstantial."

"Are you suggesting that Ghost, who happens to be in Boston, is not using his own name? Perhaps using the papers and effects of Ted Anderson as an alias?"

"Affirmative," said John. "The only other lead I have is President Snells. All other ends are tied. And I can't get close enough to Snells without causing a scene. You know how dangerous that is."

"We'll assume this Ghost is Ted Anderson then."

John hung up the phone.

***

Sarah McCurdy walked into the office, Administrator Colton stared at her with wide eyes, heavy bags underneath them. He folded his hands and propped up his elbows. She closed the door behind her and waited for it to click shut.

"Well, where is it?" He spoke coldly.

"Here," she walked forward with her bag.

She carefully placed the bag on the floor, opened it up, and pulled out the Grail, placing it firmly on his desk. The golden Grail had numerous ancient Anglo-Saxon engravings, elegantly embedded into the outer rim of the cup. Other runes were carved down to the bottom, layers upon layers of them shifting around in circular motions. The bottom of the Grail was fused into the bottom of the Box, which was dark purple and made of an unknown metallic alloy, not of the same material of the Grail. The runes over the Box and the Grail were illegibly overlapped with intricate polygons.

Additionally, she at least didn't know the original language the engravings from the Box depicted. The crimson liquid inside the Grail rippled constantly, and dark black smoke emitted from the Box.

"It was encumbering to get it here unnoticed," Sarah continued. "But what was the point of all that? What are we to do with it?"

"You don't need to know that. All you need to know is the head Administrator has been withholding information from everyone as of late, and can't be trusted with such an important artifact," he said coldly. "I don't have use for you right at this moment so you may leave."

"Where?" she snapped. "There isn't anywhere for me to go. Fae are still looking for me."

"I don't have the time to deal with—"

The phone rang.

"Hold on," he picked up the phone. "Colton."

Sarah watched the numerous contorted facial expressions of Colton on the phone.

"Okay. I'll ask around to get you information. I'll get you something within seventy-two hours. Colton out." He hung up the phone. "Hang on. I need to make a call. I may have somewhere to send you after all."

Sarah nodded, feeling uneasy with the Administrator as he dialed a set of numbers.

He looked up as he brought the handset to his ear. "Go wait outside. I'll call you in, in a minute."

***

Samuel Snells looked out the window of the Oval Office at green lawn lit up by spotlights. The sky was starless. He let out a sigh, and pulled his hands behind him, his left hand massaging his wrist.

Making those promises to the people, doing all the things he did was to ensure world peace. Not for himself, or any promotion, rather, desiring it for his children's sake. But the report he had just read told him that all was meaningless; it was only a matter of time. Russia and China would be on their doorstep, and those were both forces he was not fond of.

He about-faced and walked back to his chair. A file lay on his desk, and on that file was the "Black Eagle" emblem. Something he started, and something and someones he didn't want to resort to as frequently as he did. The military isn't what it used to be, that was certain. *But what went wrong?*

The phone rang, disturbing his thoughts.

He exhaled deeply, not knowing who it was. A call at 1:00 a.m. was never a good sign.

"Snells' office," he swiftly pulled the phone off the received and brought it to his ears.

"Snells. It's Colton."

His heart skipped a beat, and his hand trembled with the phone in his ear. This was the only thing worse than the threat of global war reaching his shores. "Colton. To what do I owe the—"

"Enough with the fucking niceties! You were supposed to do something. You remember what it was?"

"I need a little more information than that."

"The deal we made that landed you in the White House. Do you remember what it was?"

"That I am supposed to erase all involvement with your Administration. And furthermore, I am a dog to you, and will obey your orders."

"That was the memo, wasn't it? Now, what didn't you do?"

"I don't have any active ties with your organization," Snells replied, perplexed.

"I told you how to do it. Why didn't you erase everything and everyone related to Task Force Seven, like you were supposed to?"

His eyes blinked. Another skeleton in his closet. A project that required the creation of Black Eagle Company. If a loose end remained, and word got out, all Hell would break loose. A World War would pale in comparison. "What are you talking about?"

"Don't play the village idiot with me." Snells pulled the receiver away from his ear so the yelling wouldn't pierce his ears so much. "One of them still lives."

"That's impossible," Snells interjected.

"Is it? Is it? How many bodies were accounted for?"

Snells no longer had the record. The record was supposed to have been deleted along with everything else, especially with Nakamura's sudden murder, a few months after Task Force Seven was exterminated. "I don't have access to that report anymore. It's gone since it was part of the arrangement."

"Fucking damnit. You do it just to piss me off don't you?" The voice on the other end of the phone was filled with ire. He never again wanted to see this man in person. He only ever met him in person once, and that was one too many times. "Get all information and reports you have and send them all to me. I don't care how you do it; I don't care how long it takes, get it to me within two days."

"Those reports are all gone," Snells said roughly, hand firmly clasping on the phone.

"That's not all true, now, is it? You will do this; I don't care who or what you must do to get it done. If you don't do it, I'll kill you and replace you with someone who will!"

The call dropped.

He covered his face in his hands as he leaned over the desk, his dark thinning hair now messy. *All I wanted was a world without war, and in creating that peace, I have only made it worse. Well, I am a soldier, and orders are orders.*

***

Colton put his phone down and stared at the wall. His face cringed thinking of all the wasted effort. Of course, Snells would do what he asked, but he had much on his plate. Not that Colton particularly cared. It needed to be done.

Colton bit his lip, exhaling heavily, pondering just the problem that lied before him. Sander was getting close to this Ghost. Should Sander get Ghost, so many questions will be asked, and many of them ultimately lead straight to himself.

You've got Culain and his team there searching for him, without a doubt to take him to Camelot. Use that to somehow find McCurdy, or even link me to the Holy Grail. I thought I had everything figured out. And Congressman Spadero, here, also, he's one of your players too, isn't he? Loyal as he ever was to Camelot, the blind fool! He tapped his fingers violently on his wooden desk. *Now, I can't just assign someone to look for Ghost: that would be too obvious, and we don't know what kind of guise this man is wearing.* And of course, using McCurdy will create a whole slew of problems and connections he didn't want created. *He's in Boston. Perhaps if he was killed by the tensions we've been seeing lately. But the battlefield is messy, there's not a guarantee it will work out the way I want it to.*

"It's the best worst option right now," he exhaled deeply as he picked up the phone again and dialed another number. It rang in his ears.

"Good morning, Colton," answered the man on the other end.

"Oh, piss off. It's 1:00 a.m., Mikhail," Colton said. "I need a favor."

"You Americans always are so polite first thing in the morning. I haven't had my cup of coffee. You have a hostile way of asking for favors," Mikhail replied with a thick Russian accent.

"I have a big problem." Colton sighed.

"What is it the great Colton cannot do himself?"

"I need a war."

There was a pause. "Why?" Mikhail was no longer playful.

"Nothing fancy. What is it going to take to shut you up about it?" He ignored the concerned question.

"No! Your tricks will not work on me, not like last time," Mikhail replied. "Why do you need a war? And with who specifically?"

"The Cold War will suffice," Colton continued. "But if you must know, there are complications, and I need someone killed. And I can't just do it; in fact, someone in the Administration cannot be directly involved in this individual's death."

"Who is it?"

"You see, this is why you don't ask questions. I don't have a name yet, I just know a relative location, and I would hope a war with Russia might resolve that problem."

"No. I'm not giving you a war, my friend," he replied.

"Mikhail, you owe me one, and I've never gotten payment for that favor I did for you. Are we not friends?"

Mikhail chuckled on the other line. "What friend tells his friend to fuck off at one in the morning?"

"Look, if you don't want to do it for me, then fine," Colton replied. "Do it for Mother Russia. Russia has been wanting to punch Uncle Sam in the face for quite some time, has she not?"

"That's a lot of people you are asking me to kill. Does this serve our Administration's purpose? This person's death I mean."

"Look, I'm trying to stop another World War here. I'm trying to prevent that from being necessary," he lied.

Mikhail was silent for a moment. "Are you being serious?"

"Yes," he answered.

"And Sander, does he know?" Mikhail returned a serious tone.

"Yes," he answered. "So, can I get that war then?"

"Yes, for the Administration."

"For the Administration, may whatever God holds dominion over our lives forgive us," Colton said.

He hung up the phone.

Gwen is becoming a problem.

"McCurdy! Get your ass back in here!" he called.

McCurdy walked back to her seat as he shuffled some documents into his file below his desk.

"It turns out, I do have a job for you. I can only trust you with this. Gwen is aware of our little arrangement. You will be safer there. I need you to monitor her. Do whatever she asks, and report back to me. I want to know what she knows, and what she's researching. *Especially* what she's researching."

"Why not just ask?" Sarah held her hand out to the side. "She reports to you, doesn't she?"

"Don't get smart with me." He snapped. "Just do what I ask. Don't get on her bad side, and for god's sake, don't get caught."

She rolled her eyes as she hastily walked to exit the room.

Gwen Swan. What exactly are you keeping from me?

Chapter 6 Loose Ends

The thoughts of one with a conscience:

I was awarded the congressional Medal of Honor today. Me, along with Lieutenant Nakamura, for being so instrumental in the brokering of world peace. It sickens me. The ends justify the means they say. Do they though? I'm not so sure. Not after everything we've done. Especially this medal. It doesn't belong to me. It belongs to them. It belongs to those that earned it. This medal is trash. How can anyone accept this with a straight face? It's disgustingly sick. Our forefathers would be ashamed. The world would be sick, and we declared public enemy number one if anyone found the truth.

***

Snells sat down in his chair after the call with Colton, hands folded with interlaced fingers, leaning over his desk at the Oval Office, still reeling from his call with Colton. The threat was plain and simple, and he knew Colton was good on threats. He had crossed Snells before to prove a point, which was loud and clear as a whistle. Who'd ever think, the most powerful man in the world was nothing more than a lap dog for some shady organization he didn't understand. And yet, here he was. Shaking like a scared puppy.

And yet, there was something else at stake here. Creating Task Force Seven was no small feat, and red tape was ripped apart to make that happen. Nothing about Task Force Seven, their creation, their operations, or even their trainings were legal or ethical.

All of them were supposed to be dead. Sure, some bodies weren't recovered, but those that were unrecoverable were right at the epicenter of the meltdown almost nine years ago. No possible way anyone could survive that. Colton told him that one of them survived. That isn't possible. Just can't be.

But say it was. And there was a person born who could survive a nuclear meltdown, fat chance of that for certain, and if someone survived, why would they stay silent after all this time? Was there a purpose?

The carcasses stunk as the flames died down, ashes rising in the early morning desert sun. Thirteen bodies, black, charred, unrecognizable. Malcolm stood there with that disgusted scowl upon his lips. He shot Snells a hardened snarl, the likes of which was seen only among the worst of people. But Snells always liked his results.

Task Force Seven colluded with Germany to stage a coup. That was the lie he cooked up to tell their comrades. Evidence planted on Ghost's computer system to prove that. Malcolm planted it underneath Nakamura's directive, which ultimately came from him.

Of course, there was a reason to that madness.

This was all necessary. An end to justify the means. Leading to what nations would call the greatest brokering of world peace the world had ever seen. All it took was to create a common enemy fiercer than anything. Banded together, the world took it upon themselves to stop fighting one another: provided Task Force Seven was eliminated.

All sixteen of them became devils. And this was to be their end. No one would know the truth. But the truth is, he came in like a thief in the night, ripping children away from their parents, telling no one, stifling the cries of the media for thirty-two children who went missing.

The truth is, the reason he chose to have them all killed at the end of it was not because the world required them to be disbanded, but he knew these children would never be able to integrate into normal lives, especially without any family support. It was inevitable that they were end up behind bars, and of course no prison could hold any one of them.

Snells retracted his hands to grab the receiver of his phone. His hands trembled with the weight of the falsehood he had chosen to believe. He killed them. Their blood was on *his* hands. Their slavery was on *his* hands. The childless parents were on *his* hands. It was all *his* doing.

But suppose Colton was right, and one of them managed to survive, living among them all. And that person had plenty of time to stage a coup and rip apart the world that created what they were. It meant they *chose* not to. Whoever it was *chose* not to lash out with vengeance. Whoever it was *chose* not to seek justice. And that meant Snells was wrong, all those years ago. And there was a chance for them to integrate out into the world. And he murdered them for no reason.

He turned to a portrait of his family. His little girl, Jacqueline, her dress swayed in the wind outside their family home in North Dakota. "If I was anyone else. It could have been you out there, burning."

And yet, all that to say, the truth could come out, and if it did. He's finished. The peace he built will come crumbling down as a sham, regardless that the world was burning in flames, and he had nothing to do with it. But he will still shoulder the blame, and all those with Black Eagle. They trusted him when he led them, and to think of their lives being chained underneath the oppressive weight of guilt, and blackmail.

He shook his head. His guilt doesn't matter anymore. What does, is getting those files and records off to Colton, or else, who knows what Colton will do to him. There was no telling with him. And there was this Administration, this grand syndicate which seemed untouchable. God, he felt like he was playing around with the mafia, and since he's played, he has no choice but to continue to play, trapped. *Payback's a bitch, ain't it.*

He removed his hand from the receiver. He secured the line before dialing.

"Snells, do you have any idea what time it is?" Malcolm said on the other line.

"I have a favor to ask," Snells replied. "You remember Task Force Seven, don't you?"

No response.

"Malcolm?"

"Yes, I remember. What of it?"

"I need all files and records sent to me immediately, it is vitally important."

"Okay. I'll send it discreetly. Expect it tomorrow."

Snells hung up the phone. *Receive it. Send it to Colton. Wipe my hands clean of it. Call it a day.*

***

"Who was that at this hour?" Malcolm's wife Alexandra asked.

He yawned as he rested his head back on his pillow. The heavy comforter laying upon his body. The bed shifted and squeaked as she turned to him, wiping the sleep from her eyes. She was a light sleeper. Surprised him most of the time. He couldn't even rollover without her noticing.

"Snells." He turned his body to hers, brushing her sleek hair, gazing into those eyes, moonlight shimmering.

"Are you deploying yourself again?" she asked, caressing his cheek. Her touch was like a warm pillow. It was too comforting for a world shrouded in darkness.

"Well, not related to this. No. Unlikely," he pecked her on the lips. "I just have a busier day tomorrow."

Suspicious. A call from the President regarding Task Force Seven. Shortly after a similar call from Master Sergeant Clemens. Ghost. What we did to you was inexcusable. But what have you been doing all this time? Revenge would be understandable, but if you wanted revenge, you would have fought back by now.

Thinking back on the coincidences: *Snells. What the hell did you get us into?*

Chapter 7 Bittersweetness

Removal of funding from the behavioral health coverage from Medicare and Medicaid services has led to an exponential increase to the suicide of Americans and resulted in a number of undocumented and undiagnosed mental illness.

Press Secretary Jenna Walters had this to say about these reports, "it wasn't a priority when funding the rapid expenditure funds into the health care system. People with mental health needs can still work and contribute to society in a healthy way and are in no way at risk. Concerning the rise in the suicide rate, who are we to tell them what not to do? It's their choice. No one decided to do that for them. They chose that. Their bodies. Their choice. Who are we to take that from them?"

***

"Ted?" Jennifer asked as they were walking through the Boston Public Gardens; this place was special to her. To her, he confided his trust in, and admitting for once that she was his friend, and that he trusted her. She knew that. The sun set behind the dark clouds, and her stomach started to growl. That, and the added pain to her bones made this much more unbearable. She'd elected to wait and have it looked at later. "I'm hungry. Do you need to eat something?"

His hand rubbed his stomach, rubbing it like a pregnant woman does with a baby growing inside her, "I think it might be time to fill it."

Of course, that was about as much of a straight answer he would give. Jennifer was relieved that this wasn't completely life threatening, so she shrugged it off, and took his hand and jerked it downward. "Good. I'm in the mood for something specific."

She turned her head around, carefully looking for anyone who she might think Ted would find to be suspicious. The snow glistened in the moonlight on the ground, lightly coating the sidewalks, the streets, even the cars. Men, women, and children clad in their thick winter coats, pants, and gloves walked in and out of the subway station, talking away. Nothing out of the ordinary, no one was standing idly by. No one was watching. It was safe here, if safe was the appropriate word for such an evening. "I'll let you decide if you want to eat it here or come back to my place. I have work in the morning."

"I don't—I don't think I can manage dining right now," he stammered.

She felt his hand tremble in her own, and his hand was cold. A natural cold, not influenced by his *special* veins. But her own scientific curiosity caused her to question what it was, even if she would never be able to study it in depth.

"I understand. Then we'll go, order, and leave. Simple," she answered and shot him that foxlike smile of hers. "We'll take it back to my place."

She guided him down the streets. The winter coat clad people walked to and fro, darting through the busy Boston traffic which navigated the many-laned one-way streets. They scurried like rats, kicking up snow as they avoided being run down by industrialized horses. Of course, the drivers of these horses didn't find it funny, nearly weaving into poles, honking their horn to play the urban symphony.

There were so many things she wanted to ask him, but she knew better than anyone else not to really ask those questions, or rather, to push for an answer. He was the type of person that wouldn't say anything, and just merely disappear, avoiding all human contact until he took up another name, and went to another play, bought another house, and lived in solitude till the end of his days. She knew he wanted to do that last time they pushed him, and they had pushed hard.

But there was one question, as it involved Jeff Clemens' sudden arrival. Not the arrival itself, but it stirred something inside Ted—she knew it. It was apparent in his demeanor, and Ted even went out of his way to guide the man to the bathroom just a few months ago, which she had to admit, was well out of character for him, regardless of the persona he chose to adopt at that moment in time. The other thing remained: Jeff never left Boston like she was led to believe.

But of course, leaves get extended sometimes, but there was no firm answer from Jeff as the reason why his leave was extended, and until further notice. And of course, all these things changed when Jeff met Ted like war buddies, but she was certain they were anything but. Jeff seemed to know Ted, and while she didn't know the whole story, she knew much more than any of her friends. But why would he pretend to know who he was?

And then there was the reality that Ted wasn't Ted's real name. She knew that and accepted it, and that he couldn't share his real identity for something he didn't commit.

Previously, he alluded to the fact he was framed for something that he didn't do and was still paying the price for. That was reason enough to hide. That was all the reason she needed. But was it possible Jeff knew Ted wasn't who he said he was? If so, why did he play along?

Or was he merely stupid?

Yes, that's it. Jeffrey knows something's awry. This would more than explain Tedward's recent behavior, and his anxiety soaring. She learned to catch those things, primarily in the shaking of his hands, and if they weren't visible, he hid them.

She took her other arm and hooked it around his, pulling herself closely to him, sharing the body heat during the cold late November nights. The heavy dark clouds oppressed the moon from the other side. They walked further away from the Government Center MBTA station, down the stairs, and crossed the four-lane highway to the Quincy Market. It was very quiet. Some people strode around the various shops, but not to where Jennifer and Ted were going. Making their way over the cobbled pathways, they entered the back building, where the walls were glass, and further in, taking a right turn into the shop. There was a man standing behind a podium, operating the phone and he greeted them.

"Table for two?" He said as he finished with the phone.

"Take-out actually." She smiled at the man, pulling one of the paper menus from the desk, and handed it to Ted.

Ted scanned the menu. She preferred that he didn't pick something at random. He still didn't taste anything, after all. *Is this okay? Ted, I can't read your mind, so it's okay, you can tell me that much can't you?*

"Chicken ramen," he said.

That was fast. "I'll take the same, but I want the spicy one," she replied, and took out her card, presenting it to the host. "It's under Jennifer."

"You didn't have to pay for it. I could have done it," Ted said.

"Hush, my Tedward. I will not hear it." She pushed her fingers to his lips. He smiled a fake grin, and while at one time those simpers would have been old and unforgiving, this one she didn't mind. At least she thought it was feigned. He gave her a lot of deceptive smirks, and barely one that wasn't deceiving. *He's still wearing a mask, but it isn't for me. It's for himself, at least, I think.* "It's a gift. If you want to give me something, make me something. Put some of your soul into it."

"I understand."

She took his hand and led him to the light brown, polished bench for guests to sit at while waiting for their food.

Surprisingly, the food didn't take very long. She was presented with one large bag with two carefully wrapped bowls, and some wooden chop sticks.

"Time to go." She assured.

***

Jennifer's living room was brightly lit with Christmas Decor. There was even a nice Christmas Tree decorated with all the cute little bulbs, tinsel, and red and green lights, all of which Ted helped put together. Ted brought the takeout to the little island and took the bowls out, placing the chili ramen in front of her place, and his regular ramen right next to it. Jennifer danced around, grabbed some matches, and lit her pine-scented candle and brought it carefully to the island.

She smiled at him and reached for his hand from across the island. He frowned as he reached for hers. "Are you okay with this?" she asked.

He nodded, looking cautiously into those eyes. His eyes were slightly glazed over with chronic anxiety of course, fear of the great unknown that was undoubtedly coming. "Yes," closing his eyes as she showed him to do in prayer many times.

"Father, thank you for this meal, and the hands that prepared it. Please use it to nourish our bodies. Thank you for this opportunity to share in this together and thank you Father for our provision. While others may go without, we have plenty, and we have You. Please forgive us when we go astray, and please be with all those that need you, and be with those who live in the dark. Amen," she prayed.

She opened her eyes and released his palm. She noticed him studying her hands. She took the pair of wooden chop sticks and broke them apart. Her clumsy fingers took the top one, held it like a pen, while rested her ring finger below the other one and stirred her ramen, before wrapping some of the noodles with the chicken and rings of red chili. She took a bite.

The taste was spicy and had a slight ginger and lime taste to it, along with its unique spice. It wasn't too spicy, nor was it mild. "Thank you for the meal!"

"I didn't buy it," he said, copying her movements perfectly and without deviance to eat from his own bowl.

"Sh!" She slurped the noodles into her mouth, chewing and gulping. "Don't ruin this for me. Let me pretend. Have you used chopsticks before?"

"No," he said.

So, even with no direction you can learn something and master it almost instantly. Tedward, you must a very high IQ. Such a shame that your mind went to waste, and your true personality was burned away.

The broth dripped from his noodles. He never broke eye contact with her. He waited patiently as he took the noodles to his lips and slurped the noodles down. His mouth closed and he chewed slowly.

His fingers trembled uncontrollably, dropping the chopsticks which rattled on the island's surface.

"Tedward?" Deeply concerned, she looked at his hands and moved her gaze to his face. His face contorted. His hand retracted to his mouth, as if stifling some kind of cry. He didn't answer.

She hopped down from her chair, and stood by his side, wrapping her arm around him, and resting her chin upon his shoulder. "Tedward?" She asked again, and she feeling his chest taking stagnant gasps for breath.

"I can—I can taste it," his voice muffled into his hands.

"Are you going to be okay, Tedward?" she asked, petting his arm.

"I'll be—I'll be fine." He stammered.

Eight years is a long time to go without any taste.

"Why don't you take another bite?" she offered. *Is this really the right thing to do?*

His hands reached for the chopsticks once again, poked the ramen, pulling the noodles up from the broth and brought them back to his lips; inhaling, sucking the noodles down swiftly into his mouth, the hot ramen spitting on her face.

She closed her eyes, wiping the broth from her face with a napkin, and when she opened her eyes, she noticed the most peculiar thing. People who didn't know him wouldn't have taken notice of such a thing, but his brown eyes glimmered in the light for what seemed to be the first time, and his lips curved upward naturally. Even some color returned to his cheeks. Lips were pulled back revealing his teeth. She never was too close to notice his teeth though; he had white, healthy teeth. Even his eyes closed ever so slightly, revealing a smiling face.

Not the nasty, deceitful smiles that lie to the beholder. This was a genuine grin. Tears streamed down his face, but of course; he was just reacquainted with an old friend. *Happiness, or some equivalent, however brief it would be.*

He chuckled. Another feature that he overused frequently, but it was fake then. Not this time. It sounded so much different, and not something that was rehearsed a thousand times.

She felt a burden lifted from her chest, and her lips naturally curved into a bright simper. "Well, how is it?"

"It's—" he stammered. "What's the word for it?"

It was a genuine question.

"Delicious if you like it. Disgusting if you hate it." She guided him to an answer.

"Delicious," he replied.

"Well, if you like it so much, we can have more tasty food. Just promise me you'll enjoy it." She smirked, returning to her seat so she could look into the eyes of a very happy Tedward, who enjoyed the meal for once.

"As long as I can still taste something, I'll enjoy it. I promise. Disgusting or otherwise," he answered.

"Well, don't enjoy the disgusting food." She pointed one of her chopsticks at him, winking. "That's not how you enjoy food."

Chapter 8 Identification

Leading economics researchers state the tariffs are leading to the rise of a trade war within China. What effect will this have on America? These tariffs are both placed on building materials and gasses, and agricultural supplies and food, such as tea, rice, spices, fruits, and vegetables, of which, previously 50 percent of American imports are from China.

That import dropped 13.4 percent from last year, and researchers say the imports from China are only going to drop down lower.

An anonymous tip from China said the government is actively seeking to change their supply chain to exclude American business and grocers, and trade more directly with neighboring nations, to reduce the need to supply chain to the Americas.

***

Culain sat at the end of the bar inside Teri Nation. His long fingers constantly tapped the blank piece of paper in front of him. The bar tender served him his glass of red wine. Looking down, he rolled it circularly so the dark liquid inside sloshed around. He sniffed the glass, just like those pompous pricks do at those fancy shmancy balls. Honestly, he never understood why they smelled the wine. Something to do with flavor he guessed, or quality? He sniffed his beverages for a more practical reason, to see if someone would be dumb enough to try to poison him.

"Lighten up. You're so damn serious all the time."

Culain sneered as he tilted his head back. Ilya glared at him, her hands on her hips, tapping. "You took your sweet ass time gettin' here."

"Yeah, well no one bothered to pick me up from the airport." She scuffled around him, sitting at the stool next to him, smiling at Scott as he hurried over. She planted her buttocks on the stool. "Besides, I had some family business I needed to tie up first. I had to fly over to Moscow to take care of that before returning here."

"What will it be tonight?" Scott asked.

"I'll take your house brandy, please!" She hid her accent well.

"Right away." Scott moved behind the bar to pour her drink before handing it to her.

She took it from him. "Thank you, dearest."

"Careful, or I might take her from you," Scott joked while casting a glance at Culain.

"Go ahead, take the bitch. I don't care. More trouble than what she's worth," he shot back. Culain scowled as Scott moved over to the other end of the bar to start taking care of a large group of people that just came in. It was almost always like this on Tuesday, for some reason he didn't quite understand, but he didn't care. He just hoped it wasn't important. Of course, Scott was accustomed to Culain's rash behavior by now.

"So, where's Alex and Blanka?" Ilya sipped from her glass, scanning her red-rimmed eyes over the countertop.

"I gave them the day off. The congressman finally came back, so he'll be helping us a little more directly moving forward." He sipped his drink as he turned to her, elbow propping his chin off the bar top.

"Spadero?" she asked.

"Yeah. So, Sander has his hands tied. What did he report regarding our little, 'Ghost'?"

"I don't know any more than you do." She sipped her drink again, wrapping her left arm around his torso. "Well, would it be the worst thing?"

"Uh, yeah, it would." He brought his voice low.

"Yeah, you're probably—" she nearly brought her glass to the bar top as her fingers trembled around it, ice clattering inside. She smiled as she turned her head mechanically to the right side of the bar as if she sensed something... *off.*

Culain looked behind her, trying to figure out what had her in such alarm. The only thing he noticed was a couple of people. Nothing out of the ordinary there, but what would really have Ilya in such ire? And then, he noticed a man. This man was shorter than those around him and had a very sturdy body in his suit. There were scars on his face. Culain looked closer, and he saw a striking resemblance to the kid that showed up in his email.

"Ilya," his hand reached to her collar and pulled her close, whispering softly in her ear. She turned to him. "Is that him?" *Please don't be him, because this just became damn near impossible if it is.*

"Yes," she whispered back, her teeth clenched as she scowled. "You son of a bitch. You burned the bridge we need to cross, you Irish cunt."

He sighed, covering his face with one hand as he brushed his hair with his fingers. "What?"

"You need to be nicer, you piece of potato cabbage! The people he's with. You threatened with that shitty limerick!"

She jabbed his chest with her finger. The tip of her finger was warm, and his eyes glanced down to see the numerous shapes of mana veins at the tip. The temperature in the room dropped. He swiftly grabbed her finger, squeezing it tightly. "Not here," he shook his head. His eyes scanned the bar and he rose his hand in the air. "Check, please!"

Scott brought the check over. Culain pulled out some cash and slipped it into with the checkbook.

"Come on, we need to head back." He stood from the stool and walked, briskly passing by the group who seemed to be having a joyous time. He glanced over, catching a glimpse of the man they were looking for, and for a moment, things seemed to slow down as he sensed Ilya scurrying behind him.

He collected all the information he received from this *Ghost.* The man's eyes filled with a look that was all too recognizable. A man filled with guilt, regret, and a cancerous despair. And those bags underneath those eyes were familiar.

Damnit. So close, but yet, so far away.

He turned the corner and they moved and evaded numerous people and their drinks.

"This complicates things," Ilya said from behind him as they exited Teri Nation. The snow fell softly on the pavement, and the two walked several blocks before arriving at their hotel.

They took their keys and moved up to the elevator to the upper floors. The elevator was full, and Culain and Ilya stood shoulder to shoulder, silently staring at nothing in particular as the elevator emptied, and then ascended to the top floor. Culain scratched his chin as the door opened and they departed the box, moving down the hall several doors and rapped resoundingly on door number 76.

Footsteps shuffled from behind it. The door creaked open, and a bright light shined in his face. He pushed his way through the doorway and went into the living room.

"If it isn't one thing, it's something else. What happened?" Alexander brushed off Culain's rash behavior. He was used to it by now.

Blanka yawned, covering her mouth, drinking a cup of hot chocolate, leaning against the window. "Break over?"

"Well, Culain done fucked up. Shame on you." Ilya slapped the back of his head.

"How were we to know?" he snapped back at her, flicking her forehead.

She winced, rubbing the spot he flicked with her palm. "Tell them."

"We found him," he answered.

Alexander let out a deep sigh, crossing his arms and looked at the ground. "And what stopped you from calling us so we can put an end to this manhunt?"

"There were people there." Culain glanced over to Blanka who looked down, tilting her cup at the ground. It was empty.

She stood, glaring at the ground. She wound up and threw the empty mug. Culain sucked in the mana from the air through his mana veins in his hands, and the room lit up blue. The temperature dropped; his hand swung and struck the mug, shattering it to dust, and particles of glass spread through the room.

"What is the real reason? Surely, that wouldn't have stopped you of all people," Alexander continued to push him for an answer.

"Really?" Culain snapped, pointing a trembling finger as he scowled at her. "I'm not about to k—"

"Culain!" Ilya snapped her fingers repeatedly in his ears.

He hated that, and he turned back and slapped her hand out of his face.

"Keep it down!"

He closed his eyes, exhaled deeply as his mana veins receded back into his flesh.

"Culain, what happened?" Alexander asked softly, rubbing the sleep from his eyes.

"This was at our own usual spot. Remember those people that tried to speak to us several months ago?"

"You mean the ones you threatened?" Blanka asked. "What about them?"

"He's all buddy buddy with them," Culain answered.

"We had one job." Alexander kicked the coffee table. It flipped over sending the coasters flying to the ground. One shattered underneath the couch. "How do you manage to screw it up *before* we get the assignment?"

"We need to get someone from Boston involved in this," Ilya suggested. "Now, we can't do it, because the couple that Culain threatened to murder will start asking questions they don't need to know the answers to."

"Do you have someone in mind?" Alexander asked.

"Spadero has been trying to get more information on him, but he still comes up empty," Culain softened his tone.

"I want to go home." Blanka stamped her foot on the ground. Her eyebrows pointing downward with creases over her face.

Ilya tilted her head, her silver hair dropping over one side of her shoulders. She walked briskly to her, wrapping her arms around her. "I do too." She scowled at Culain. "Get Spadero on the phone and fix this."

Culain shook his head as he shifted to the other room to call Spadero.

"What is it, Culain?" Spadero voiced coldly.

"Do you happen to have any additional information on our Ghost?" he asked, keeping it abrupt.

"Not really. I'm still sifting through this bullshit report Snells gave Colton. It's a bunch of nonsense, and nothing we can reasonably use. The only thing that really puts anything to use, is the fact that Ghost seemed at one point friendly with a Sergeant Ted Anderson, deceased. I just got this the other day. We still have no information."

"I think we've identified him. Still no name though," Culain replied.

"How inconvenient."

"But I think we've established some kind of pattern. He is real close with some people who frequent a local bar on Tuesdays," Culain continued. "It would appear we may continue to see him, but we can't get close enough."

"Why?" he drew out the question.

"I may have threatened his friends' lives before I know who they were." His finger tapped the back of his phone.

"God fucking damnit! What bar?" The voice was so loud Culain had to pull it away from his ear.

"Teri Nation," he replied.

"What time on Tuesdays?"

"They get there between 9:45 and 10:00 p.m."

"Don't you, or anyone else in there go there! I'll handle it. I'll feed you intel as I find it."

Chapter 9 On the Mend

Oil spills in Saudi Arabia leads to an estimated fifteen tons of crude oil lost from the supply chain. Saudi Arabia has reported this year, they will be reducing their crude oil shipments to other nations by 15 percent.

According to a report by the largest logistics brokerage, Perfect Transportation Solutions, diesel is to go up by more than 15 percent to match the change in the supply of fuel. Skyrocketing those solutions, according to one broker, will make transporting goods from the ports to the warehouses and stores even further. This broker said she pays for one load, $850.00 from Upper Marlboro, MD to Delaware, OH for 40,000 pounds of dry groceries, and up to $950.00 for refrigerated goods for the same lane. She expects once the market catches up to the change in fuel prices, she is expecting to add nearly $200.00 to both of those lanes.

***

Erin was in the waiting room, in line at the reception desk of the Memorial Hospital in Worcester. *Was it Wooster? Worchester? Woostah? Worchestah? Woosteshire?* One of the towns it was in, the unpronounceable town because the locals made it so with their numerous dialects. She shook her head at the name, stepping forward. The receptionist was a young man, perhaps just out of high school, and on his way to college. He wasn't a teenager; she knew that much. He had a bit of a scruff.

"Appointment?" He looked up to her.

"Yes, I'm here for visiting hours, actually." She smiled down to him. "Emily Gutenberg," she wrote down her mother's DOB, and slid it into the boy's hand, who took it down, typed it into the computer to look for her appointment. She turned her head up to the ceiling.

"Here you are," he said, pulling out a visitors' pass and handed it to her.

"Thank you." She took the pass in her hand, pulled it over her neck as she followed his instructions down the hall, walking over the tiled floors, squinting at the bright lights emitting from the ceiling, and the white coat doctor's and the various nurses in their scrubs helping patients attached to life-maintaining devices.

This was a very versatile hospital, she found out. Not many like it. At least, not any from Bridgeton, Maine. That's why her mother was here in the first place, to get the best possible care she could. But it was expensive. Even the insurance couldn't pay for everything. The medical out of pocket expenses had skyrocketed over the years as the insurance providers were willing to pay more and more, effectually inflating the cost of medical care.

She hissed at the cost of the medical care. She was not poor by any means, and neither was her family, and yet, even now, the cost of the medicine to deal with the cancer treatment was eating a hole through even her wallet. She was better off than the rest of the family, she had to care for her mother in any way she could, and this was the best way, though, not ideal.

She knocked on the door to her mother's room. Her mother, laying down on the hospital bed resting, had sensors attached to her skin to measure her vitals. They showed she was still healthy enough, but still in need of the various treatments and medicine to help manage the tumor before an appropriate procedure could be scheduled to have the tumor removed, or most of it anyway.

"Yes, Erin, come in," her mother, in her thinning hair, turned, smiling her bright smile, and the sun shone in all the clearer. "Be a dear and shut the door behind you, will you?"

"Yes," she said, crossing the threshold, gently shutting the door behind her. And she pulled up a stool next to her mother, and placed both her hands on her Emily's hands, gently squeezing them. "How are you feeling?"

"I'm well, now that you're here," she replied, her hand squeezing Erin's fingers. The strength in her hand still had not faded.

"I'm glad, but what if I wasn't here?" She asked, leaning closer.

"Well, the pain would be a little less bearable," she answered.

"How's the treatment going?"

"It's going well. Not ideal, but no one ever wants to be here. Erin, don't get cancer. It's not fun," she replied.

"If that was something you could avoid, you wouldn't have it," she answered.

"True." Her face turned, facing the ceiling. "The tumor is receding though, according to my doctor."

"That's great news."

"Now, now, I'm not out of the woods yet," she said. "I still have it, and I'm sure it could swell up any minute if it isn't taken care of properly."

Erin nodded. She knew they wouldn't schedule the removal of the tumor until they've been paid in full. Getting the finances for something like that wasn't easy. Scheduling it was difficult with the health care insurance provider still saying it wasn't 'Medically Necessary.' Since they consider it not essential, regardless of how far the tumor went without the proper treatment, the plan won't cover a cent of it. The hospital was requiring over $50,000 dollars out of pocket to schedule it, and because the surgery would not have been approved, the insurance wouldn't pay for any of the other services she needs to recover from that. More unknown out of pocket expenses. God only knows how much any of that would cost.

She leaned forward, tears glazing over her eyes. "Do you think they'll accept a payment plan?"

"I don't know. I never asked," she said. "But, I think Erin, it's safe to say that without that surgery, what I'm resting on is my deathbed."

"I'm sorry." She exhaled.

"Don't be sorry." Her mother's other hand reached over the side, placing it firmly on both of Erin's. "It isn't your fault, and it may very well be my time."

"But—"

"Erin," she interrupted. "If the Lord calls me, I'm ready to go. It's the world we live in really, I may get placed on a waiting list even if the hospital has what they want, or what they need to perform the procedure. There isn't anything I can do about that.

"You know, I see people here, and I hear them. Scared out of their minds. Because for them, this life is all they know, and it's the only thing keeping them going, a false hope that they will be healed, and that the last chance of their hope is a life changing procedure that they're fortunate enough to meet all the *requirements* to have their services covered in full. They're terrified, and they hinge on the fact that they need to live life as long as they can. Do you know why they're scared, Erin?"

"No." She spoke softly, looking carefully at her mother's weak, but smiling face; her mother's eyes glazed over.

"Because for them, they've accepted that there is nothing beyond this world. For someone like me, and perhaps even the Catholic priest in the other room," she continued. "We accept that there is a life beyond the one we know, and that we'll go to whatever it is. I want you to know, that if tonight, the Lord calls me, I don't want you to be sad, because I'll be happy. And I'll be sure to keep watch over you."

"Thanks, Mom." She bit her lip, squeezing her mother's hands tighter.

There was a brief moment of silence as they stared into one another's eyes, and Emily's fingers caressed her daughter's knuckles.

"There's something else that's bothering you," she said. "I can tell. What's wrong?"

Erin pursed her lips. "Mom," not knowing where to start with her own convictions. *But I made a promise not to say anything about it. I don't even know what it was I saw, or if I'm crazy.* "Something happened a number of months ago, and I can't say what it was because I promised I wouldn't talk about who or what to anyone. But what I saw, and what

I experienced that day made me question God. I'm having a problem reconciling what I saw, and the God I thought I knew, but now, I don't even know anymore."

"Erin," she said. "We're not meant to understand everything. I've told you this a thousand times. The Bible isn't a textbook. A very vague roadmap at times, sure, but that's it. Don't turn it into a textbook. It won't make sense logically. Those who do end up being confused use the contradictions inside to disprove anything of the supernatural, but the supernatural exists."

Supernatural. Yeah, that's what I saw.

"As you know, the country is hopelessly divided right now, and our brothers and sisters in Christ are partially to blame for that," Emily wiped her forehead as if there was sweat on it. "And the reason, because they think God to be above reprieve, and therefore, should never be questioned. I disagree with that wholeheartedly, and you should always question. You may not like the answer, but that's okay. But always question."

Erin let out a sigh of relief. Still unsure of what to make of Ted's colored veins over his body that one night still bothered her, since it wasn't part of the natural human anatomy. But with that, she chose to chalk that up as the supernatural, which in turn, was not outside the realm of possibilities, that she was aware of, and could accept it as such.

"Thanks, Mom."

Knock.

"Who's that?" she asked.

"I'm not sure," Emily said, frowning. "Come in!"

The door creaked open, and her care manager came in.

"Mrs. Okofa," Emily said. "Whatever you have to say, you can say it with my daughter in the room."

"Sure." She smiled as he closed the door. She sat down and looked both of them in the eye. "So, when are we scheduling this procedure?"

Erin jerked her head. "Mrs. Okofa, we haven't paid for it yet. We can't schedule it."

Mrs. Okofa looked down in her chart, frowning in confusion. "Well, someone authorized the procedure. So, when are we scheduling it?"

What?

"What do you mean someone authorized it?"

"There is nothing in the way from scheduling it," she replied. "Someone authorized the procedure, and I would not be in this room right now otherwise."

"When was this authorized for?"

"Fifteen minutes ago."

"Well," *who paid for it?* "Mom, you want to schedule it?"

"Do we know who paid it?" Emily asked. "I'd like to thank them; this was no small thing."

"If that was what prevented us from scheduling it before, I can't really tell you. I don't know that information." Mrs. Okofa replied. "Just give me a few dates and I'll work on scheduling it for you with the administrative staff."

Ah, yes. Mr. Anderson. Was this you? If it was, thank you.

Chapter 10 Summit

Critical commodities dwindle from the supply chain as demand is on the rise. Imports to the US suffer. President Snells is still holding onto the tariffs despite Congress and the Senate's plea to remove them. There is complete bipartisan support behind this.

Senate majority leader Tran of TX stated: These imports are reducing efficiency in dealing with world leaders around the country. Much of what is affecting us right now has to deal with the lack of insight coming from the President. These imports are increasing productivity of supplies that frankly, we don't even use. I half suspect we'll be building cars out of vinyl within the next year if we keep using our own supplies. I don't think I need to explain why that's a bad idea.

***

Adam was in the archive, one of the main rooms to be precise, where there was a green screen. The room filled to the brim with wide mahogany bookcases, with dusted off red spines on a variety of different books, written by many different authors throughout the history of Camelot. Of course, there was a great fire long ago, 300 years after the death of King Arthur, and someone re-transcribed all these texts and reprinted them. It was an arduous task that was done by hand. Of course, they take better care of their buildings now to avoid this from happening again, and a mass digitization project was underway.

Adam pulled out a book carefully; this one had a green spine with a blue and red stripe down the middle. This was by far the oldest account, and it detailed the account of the reign of King Arthur when he took everything and made the Administration to protect all of creation from unraveling itself. He read it a thousand times, but this time, he placed it on the table and opened to the end of it. Just to see if there was something, something he missed.

For years, he toiled, scanning pages, new and old, much like the pages of the book he had in front of him. Searching for an answer to the question, a solution rather to defuse the curse his kind was plagued with. He was sick of it. He knew all those under him was sick of it. Needlessly killing normies and the like for being innocent spectators, controlling the very world they inhabited. And all he had for a lead was this book detailing some obscure prophecy that didn't make sense because there was something about it that just felt incomplete. Not just that the ending was missing, and of course the ending was in fact missing, but also the middle seemed to be gone. This was a short section detailing the return of King Arthur and how salvation for Fae might be achieved, but of course, it was missing vital information: How? When? Where? All he could gather is that when King Arthur would return, he might be flying on the back or wings, or even talons of some metal bird. Whatever that meant.

The prophecy was vague. The details were vague, and the solution was still out of his reach. The piece of the one puzzle he wanted an answer to, above all else. This answer, to him, was monumentally more important, in his eyes, than the missing Holy Grail and Pandora's Box. There were two unknowns. Two strangers. Both seemed nearly impossible to track down, though one might be easier than the other. Not by much.

He slowly closed the book shut and sat back, folding his hands on his chest. "Fifteen hundred years since your proposed solution to all this mess, and it only leads us down a rabbit hole none of us want any part of. Fate. God. Death. It's all the same," he leaned back in his chair, waiting for his screen to light up with faces; the summit had begun. "Your solution is not wrong, but there has to be a better way than killing the innocent. How much longer can we continue like this? It's only a matter of time before one of us embraces nihilism, and who would blame them?"

His eyes shot to the door. It creaked open and Bridgette stood behind it.

"What is your report?" he asked.

"We still haven't a word from Culain on this Ghost, nor have any new leads come about as to the whereabouts of Sarah McCurdy or the Grail," Bridgette sighed. "I thought you might like to know that."

"Any other unwarranted Portal Storms? As the traitor she is, I still think there's some merit as to that individual on Dyatlov's Pass, and something tells me they may be connected in some way."

"No."

He leaned forward, propping his chin up as he bent over the table. "Three vital pieces of information. Three unknown motivations. Three individuals. Almost all of which we know absolutely nothing about, and I fear they may be connected somehow. If I can get my hands on one of them, that may be the key I need. But I need someone who can pull something out of a hat just to get one of them." He exhaled heavily as the first face popped up on the screen, followed by another, until ten faces were on the screen. "Stick around, Bridgette. I need to bounce a few ideas off you after this."

When he turned his attention to the screen all the usual faces were there, ready and waiting. There was only one woman among them, Claire from France. They all reported in promptly, all revealing their faces, some smiling, others jaded. All of which, different walks of life, different demeanors, and of course, differing objectives. He couldn't discount the possibility of someone being a traitor, as minimal that reality might be, it is still a possibility.

Well, time to get started.

"You all know why I called for this summit," Sander said, addressing them on the screen, tapping his finger on the table with his left hand. A pad of paper was in front of him, and he turned a clicking pen in his right hand. "Now, this has been an issue for several months, and we are nowhere closer to solving any of the problems. Obviously, one of them can wait. Secondly, we have a rogue somewhere in the Boston area of the United States," he looked specifically to Colton, "He's not cleaning up any mana residue, which is a problem for reasons I don't need to dwell on. The other, is the biggest problem of all. The Holy Grail is still missing, and we are nowhere closer to finding it. Stolen by Sarah McCurdy, who is also nowhere to be found."

"I don't have any new information on either of those two," Colton began. "I have been actively working with Spadero, who is in communication with Culain to try to find this Ghost. I don't have a reason to suspect he is a fae, nor have I heard from McCurdy."

"Could be a possessed normie," Hector offered, the fae who was assigned the territory south of the Rio Grande.

Shit. That won't do. That won't do at all. He shifted uncomfortably in his chair, looking carefully at Colton, who was the first to speak. The first to speak usually hides something. But not always.

"That is a little too optimistic, Hector," Claire puffed out smoke. "Especially for someone about whom so little is known. Honestly, it is far more likely that he is this *Devil's Pass* character that was reported. Ukraine, was it?"

"Why do you assume this Ghost was under my domain? We don't know that," Mikhail said.

"We don't know anything." Elias exclaimed. "We need concrete information, not speculation."

"But without an idea of where to start, we are hopelessly speculating," Claire continued. "We have a goal, but no foreseeable way to achieve that goal here. The report McCurdy gave us on the individual was lacking in detail."

"But can we trust that report? After all, that report came from a traitor," Wang interjected. "Quite frankly, what if we cannot trust Colton."

"Enough of that." Sander spoke sternly, glaring at the Chinese Administrator. "We don't have time for any of that. You all know, just like all of you, I appointed him in his role. He can be trusted." *Though I cannot completely disregard that possibility.*

"I think we're asking all the wrong questions here, Sander Bucho," Daiki said. "I think we need to know just how urgent this is. What are the stakes involved?"

"Excuse me?" Sander replied.

"Well, the Holy Grail, which is fused with Pandora's Box, has been greatly unused since it's fusion, thanks to King Arthur," Daiki continued.

"That was a horrible idea," Hector spoke sternly. "Look at where it got us. A history of murders on our conscience. But do continue."

"If we knew why someone would want the Grail to begin with, perhaps that can give us more of a firm foundation as to where to locate it. That is the pressing issue," Daiki finished.

There was silence in the room. The faces turned their heads up as if to think heavily on the subject. Most of the faces told Sander they were thinking earnestly on the subject, getting all the cogs turning, as it were. But so much time has passed, how much more time before whatever leads they have run cold.

"Sander, Arjun speaking," said the Indian. "What function did the Holy Grail serve prior to King Arthur fusing it as a lid to Pandora's Box?"

"Nobody knows. I've scoured documents and history books prior to King Arthur's reign, and there is nothing to signify that it's ever been used as anything but this lid. Clearly, if someone removed the Grail from the Box, a direct link to Pandora and Earth would be formed. Which is why it's the lid. No one's been able to study it since," Sander answered.

"So perhaps this person wants to remove the Grail from the Box to find out what it does. So they separate the Box from the Grail—"

"That is no small feat. The fusion is paired with magical weaves no one understands," Sander interrupted Mikhail. "It is beyond anything I've seen or studied, and I'll dare not touch those weaves."

"And if the fusion was bypassed by force, what do you suppose would happen?" Colton asked.

"I'd assume the force needed to make that happen would rip the Box open and shatter the Grail. And with it, the Threads of Creation would come undone," Sander answered.

"You assume, so, you don't know?" Claire asked, tapping her cigarette to an ashtray.

Before Adam could answer, Obi said, "Why would someone want to do that? That is a fool's errand. Unless there is some kind of benefit to doing that, there would be no real motivation to even have the Grail or the Box."

"Yes, but that would just be too evil of a problem for one of the fae of our ranks to do, not to mention trying to clean that up would lead to—" Oliver trailed off.

He might be on to something then. But what are you thinking precisely. You certainly don't have anything to hide here, and no connection to any of the mysteries we're unfolding.

There was some silence in the room as Oliver gathered his thoughts.

"Yes?" Mikhail urged him. "Don't keep me and the motherland waiting in suspense. What's going on in that head of yours?"

"The problem is we don't know exactly how the Box was fused to the Grail, so even entertaining that idea would be pointless," Oliver dropped his head to his computer screen as he casually yawned. "Forget I said anything."

"No, I think you might be on to something. Go on," Claire replied.

"Fusions are like locks. Mana veins intricately woven in between objects and left there. We don't know what those patters are like as they are invisible after some time, and we ourselves can't sense the intricate patterns. My assumption is that the pattern used was so incredibly complex we don't use it anymore, and if someone was to attempt to undo that pattern, they may not only sever the Grail from the Box, but in so doing, might break the Grail. There is no easy solution for anyone to try to sever the connection from both artifacts."

Daiki tapped his finger on his desk, and it was loud enough for everyone to hear it. "Sander Bucho, what might happen if someone attempted this, and the Grail was destroyed?"

"The Holy Grail is what holds creation together. We fae, our souls essentially started there, or something like it. If that was destroyed, we, and all life, all creation would cease to be. If someone broke the Grail, and it is impossible, they would do the impossible and destroy everything: Hells, Heavens, and Earths," Sander answered. *The worst possible outcome.* He already felt his heart rate skip a beat just thinking of the idea.

"So, in short, it would not benefit anyone for even trying," Claire replied.

"Unless they were a true nihilist," Mikhail commented.

"Or believed they had sufficient enough power to destroy the Box once it was removed from the Grail," Colton said.

"We all know it's impossible," Wang said.

"That won't stop someone from trying," Obi said. "And if it happens, they might weaken the connection between the Box and the Grail, and the dark spirits from the other side will start inhabiting this side of creation."

"We've seen this before," Adam replied gravely. He knew where the history books repeated something like this.

"No." Elias spoke sternly as if to read his mind. "None of this. I will not do it. We solve this before it gets to that."

"We need to start making preparations if we need to repeat it again," Mikhail sighed.

"But if we accept that we're going to do this, again, and kill millions, if not *billions* of people, *again*, we won't solve the problem. And when it gets out of control, we won't be equipped to deal with any of these mysteries that have now fallen on our laps." Elias said, his face rejuvenated, and his voice filled with passion. Of course, Adam knew the German was none too proud of his nation's history. Why would he be? They have two world wars under their belt, and to think to add another one, but on who's soil would this start?

"Colton, Hector, work together to track down and find McCurdy immediately. I will have Culain and Spadero continue their investigation of the Ghost. He, whoever he is, likely poses the least possible threat. Mikhail, I need you to pair up with Claire to find out what happened over at Devil's Pass. Get me something. Anything. I want to find out who this person is, and I think that whoever it is, has his hands in more than one of our administrations. This person needs to be ousted. Meeting adjourned."

Sander pulled himself out of the conference call. Exhaling heavily, he turned to Bridgette, who looked at him disapprovingly.

"Really? Another World War? Are you serious? Look, maybe one of the fae is sick and tired of all this unnecessary killing and wants to destroy the Grail. Maybe they think a universe that doesn't exist is better than the universe we live in. Damnit, Adam."

He knew she was spouting off nonsense. She didn't truly believe that, or at least he didn't think so, but there was something there. "We created these circumstances, have continued to these last fifteen hundred years. We've been cultivating a world where nihilism may be the best alternative, and our worst nightmare. Dear god! Bridgette, you're a genius."

He pulled up his email and started typing away.

"Why?" She looked at him, confused.

"You may have offered us the very information we needed to find a motive," he replied. "Yet a problem remains. Where is it?"

***

No doubt Hector will call me within the next few days to arrange a meeting to locate McCurdy. Fool. I already know where she is, and I'm not telling him.

Colton shut his monitor off. He glanced over to his safe, locked with gray mana veins protecting it from damage from the inside. The safe itself rested above an arcane circle he drew to keep the mana and the curses inside, preventing spilling. No one except he and Sarah knew where the Grail was, and he intended to keep it that way, at least until further study could be made to remove the Grail from this Box and rid this conflict once and for all.

He turned forward, looking at all his recent files, pulling one up, with a younger woman, late 20s with silver hair and red pupils. *Gwen Swan*, the file read. It was easily a hundred pages long, containing every accolade the woman had under her belt. He knew she was hiding something, but the question was what?

She couldn't be trusted, but she was far too valuable to attempt to discard, assuming that was even possible.

He scratched his head, evaluating the world map for all possible scenarios.

"I have the Grail. Sarah is in Alaska with Swan. Gwen is hiding something. Hector will likely call me tomorrow to start looking for Sarah. I must think of something for that little scenario. Mikhail will be sending troops to the East Coast to get rid of this Ghost. I need to kill Snells. Still waiting on the other file." He kicked his desk. "Some pompous bastard was out and about, supposedly with some Georgian accent in Devil's Pass. I doubt that's related to any of this."

"But Gwen is dangerous." He tapped his fingers firmly against the wooden desk, weighing his options and all the intricacies of all his plotting.

Three unknowns he counted. The first, was this Ghost character. Still no good information was sent his way pertaining to his precise location or identity. The man should be dead. Of course, if he was a normal man, he certainly would be. He may have been one of the few who belonged to a fae's family, perhaps the Old Blood. This unknown man over by Devil's Pass. Why was he looking for the Grail there? It made no sense, unless to purposely throw everyone off. And Gwen. A dangerous manipulator if ever there was one. Of course, she had her uses, and wasn't someone he could easily dispose of. She made that abundantly clear. The main problem with her was she would never do anything without knowing the reason why, and she also knew she was the only fae willing to do any of those things, leveraging that fact to her advantage with negotiations. He couldn't lie to her, or else risk her wrath. Gwen was a problem. She knew too much. And if he attempted to dispose of her, it must be all or nothing, because after a failed attempt, who would she tell other than Sander?

Chapter 11 Boston Duck Tour

Hostilities continue to rise across the sea. While Russia is underneath acquisition of bordering nations, the tensions appear to be reaching their arms overseas with Russian and Chinese fleets sailing from across the seas.

Chief Commanding Officer Malcolm is not concerned with the military forces overseas. He stated he has divisions in space monitoring would be enemies of the state, and would harp on them quickly should, "[They] so much as think about firing a missile."

***

Jeff sat on his couch in his little studio apartment he arranged with Malcolm, his direct Superior Officer with Black Eagle. After all, he was to remain there to keep an eye on this *Ted Anderson*. Of course, Jeff knew who it was. Stood and walked to the window, opening it to allow the gentle air to fill the small space. The cool breeze moved by him and brought a chill when it pressed his damp shirt. He scanned the surrounding streets.

Gazing toward each trash can down Summer Ave right in Dorchester, he wiped the sweat from his brow before he returned to the couch, flicking through the channels until he found the news station.

Tensions are rising with the US and Russia. According to sources inside the White House. Russia has halted all trading to the US President Snells declined to speak further on the matter, but did tell us that he is, 'working on speaking with the

Russian President to open up trading again.'

"We saw that coming. Damnit," he said to himself. "Steel, fuel, and iron." He turned off the TV. "Those are imports we desperately need. I suppose Snells could strong arm him, but is he trying to avoid conflict?"

Jeff couldn't help but consider the idea that Snells grew too soft. Of course, peace often did that. *What was the saying again? Great men make great times; great times produce weak men, and weak men create bad times.* It doesn't solve anything—it just makes things a little more tolerable.

His phone rang.

"Michael, what is it?" he answered it.

"Hey, we're going on the Boston Duck Tours this afternoon. Wanna come with?" Michael replied.

His hand trembled, remembering precisely why he was kept here instead of redeploying. Not that it made any of this any easier. *Mr. Anderson. Ghost. What or whoever you are. You aren't bombing shit on my watch.*

"Is Ted going to be there?" he asked.

"No, I invited him, but he declined. Said he was busy, and all that." His tone dropped ever so slightly.

Jeff knew Michael well enough to understand that there was sympathy in his voice. As if this little errand Ted went on was something passionate or filled with tragedy. Ted Anderson or Ghost was the source of so much tragedy. *What did he have to be sorry about?*

"Sure. I'll come over. Where are you meeting?"

"At the Prudential Center on Huntington Ave. You remember, it's right off the Green Line."

"I'll be there."

***

Jeff stood outside the Prudential Center. His eyes scanned the streets, the trash cans, anything that might have something hidden inside it. One can't be too careful. He waited for Michael as he eyed numerous pedestrians jolting by, some in the hurry to get somewhere. Hands briskly wiping their pants hastily back and forth, slipping into the snow. Others were much less worrisome, loitering around, their hands in their pockets to shield them from the winds, icy winds they were. Though the clouds appeared ready to drop some snow, it was a clear day.

The sound of patterned speeches and footsteps clapped behind him. Jolting, he turned, eyes gaped open as he saw people coming out of the Prudential Center, many chatting away with little silent jeers, eager for this Duck Tour.

"Jeff!" a hand waved higher than the rest.

It was a small hand, a soft one. He settled down, feeling his heart rate rise underneath all the stress of sudden noise. One can't be too careful. *Especially when someone like Ghost could be around.*

"Michael," he said, reaching for his wallet. "I'm about ready."

Michael squirmed his way through the crowd of people pushing their way to the ticket booth for the Duck Tour. His other hand held Samantha's. She wore a winter jacket over some jeans. Behind her was a man, much taller than Michael, and he pushed himself forward adjusting his glasses. He followed closely behind Jennifer.

This man shook his hand firmly when he got close, introduced himself bluntly as Tim. He should have known. Any man who introduces himself in such away is always named Tim. Almost like all the Tims in the world have their own little convention on how to introduce themselves to strangers. *Fucking Tims!* Maybe that's why he didn't remember seeing him before. Now that he thinks of it, he remembered Tim at the bar, though, barely tried to talk to him, as Ghost was always nearby. Always watching.

Jennifer had a soft demeanor, a gentle voice, and yet, with all those fluffy traits, he could tell when he looked at her, and the sharp glare she gave him, despite that smile. She told him without saying anything, that there was one thought that connected her to him: Hatred.

What do you know, Jennifer? What did he tell you?

Of course, he knew he would never get an answer to either of those questions, but perhaps he could get some clues. He was certain she didn't know he knew she lied to him, or that he saw right through her ruse. Despite the fact he caught on this little sharp gaze, like a fish on a hook.

Forcing himself to breathe, ignoring the fact that his throat tightened with anxiety, he found this to be a precarious situation to be in. After all, Jennifer might be the bait, and he the fish, and Ghost could very well just string him along. Jennifer might not realize this, but Ghost was using her.

Ghost, always scheming, getting civies caught up in your web of lies. What are you plotting? If you aren't blowing up orphanages, you're always planning some coup. Who are you trying to overrun?

Jennifer moved past them, and they eased up toward the Duck Tour.

The five of them purchased their tickets, and moved onto the amphibious boat, the wheels on the ground, ready to start driving, and the tour of Boston to commence. He didn't care for Boston all that much. Too much noise. Too many people, and of course, the stench of regrets as he saw a man, with the BDU jacket, smoking a joint around the corner. There was a patch on that BDU: Airborne. Homeless. Of course. The same fate that they all shared. It was inevitable. At least, so he thought. It wasn't a fate he wanted to share. *That doesn't suit me at all.*

He took a seat next to Michael, and Tim on his other side. And then, his duty tugged at him, and he turned to Jennifer. "So, no Ted today?"

She turned a grin toward him. *She's good at faking a smile.* "No. He had some things to take care of."

"What things would those be?"

"Oh," Jeffrey felt Michael's arm around his shoulders. "You don't know. He's in stocks."

"On a Saturday?" he raised his eyebrow, turning abruptly to him.

"Yeah, well, he's somewhat of a workaholic now," Sam chuckled. "He was working 120 hours a week I think, that's what he said, right Jennifer?"

"Just about. Fortunately, he takes time out of his busy schedule for me," she said, twiddling her braid with her fingers. Jeffrey saw her smile, gleaming toward Samantha as if to trade a few silent words he wasn't a part of. Without context, he knew he'd never be able to listen in on *that* conversation.

"Yeah, tough one to crack, that one," Tim replied. "Sam, I want to say, you did the right thing. Skipping out on brunch that day."

Is this the context I'm missing? Jeff thought to himself as he resolved to merely listen, and almost entirely remove his mouth from the equation.

"Yeah," her curved lips flattened. "Well, sometimes I'm not so sure, but I think we have Jennifer to thank."

"Perhaps," Jennifer said, her voice dropped low. He noticed she stared daggers into his eyes. "It is best not to talk about him right now, after all, the tour is about to begin!"

The boat drove into the water, splashing on both sides. It reminded him of the many people at sea, lost. Memories and dreams became useless once drowned out at sea. No one would ever notice them gone. Not the dreams anyway. His own dream vanished; just like theirs. Just like the many he killed, stealing, and murdering their dreams. After all, one's dreams stop at their deaths.

They say Russians die in war just to die, and the French once died for love, while the English die for honor, and Americans die for freedom. Yes, he willingly gave up his freedom to give it to others, but now, he found the poison inside his mind pulling the nerves in his brain apart, his guilt for stealing the freedom of others. Yes, that's precisely what he did. And now, he was enslaved to the reminder that was his curse. He deserved to die, but even he can never admit to all the crimes he committed. How could he when all he wished was for the guilt to numb?

"Hello! Are you listening?"

He shook his head, turned to Michael, who was trying to get his attention. "What?" His brother showed some concern, and even a warm squeeze on the shoulder. His shoulder tensed up.

"Are you okay?"

"Yeah, I'm fine," he ignored the lady speaking about the tour.

"Okay, so, I was trying to figure out how long you've known Ted. He doesn't seem to try to get out with us nearly as much since you ended up staying." Michael said.

"I'm quite fond of an answer myself," Sam added. "I'd love to know why you aren't out there. I mean, war is picking back up. Not that I'm not happy you're safe, but I feel like the government isn't taking the overseas conflict seriously."

"The government hasn't had need to take anything seriously in over a decade," Jeff answered. "I still have some leave time here, and my CO decided it was time for me to take a little break, get some R&R. The functionality of our military doesn't rest solely on me." *Damn civies. Never understand anything beyond the only world they've known. Toss them in fire, and they'll sing a completely different tune.*

"But what about your relationship to Ted? He seems to want to distance himself from you. Even I've noticed that," Tim said. "I was under the impression that bonds of military brothers and arms were unbreakable."

They're supposed to be. But considering Ghost, that makes it impossible. Considering who I am, and what I'm forced to be, that camaraderie is forever out of our reach. This dynamic forced Jeff's heart to race, insulted, irate, and of course, humiliated that people such as these, who know nothing of the Hell he's seen, forcing him to think back as to why he can't enjoy a moment's rest. Maybe they meant well. Or maybe, using him as a tool to further understand their 'Ted'. A tool. A disgusting truth.

"Ted and I had a complicated relationship. We ran into one another a few times, both in the briefing environment, and in the grit of the battlefield. To say we were in constant disagreement on solutions was an understatement. I swear," he chuckled, "sometimes we were close to just throwing fists at one another." *That's true enough.*

"Siblings often throw punches at one another. It's what we do," Jennifer smiled. "But my Tedward isn't the confrontational type."

Liar.

"Of course," Jennifer said, as if to answer his sudden thought. "He can be abrasive at times, but more so to himself than anyone else. It was almost as if someone close to him hurt him."

What did he tell you?

He wanted to scowl. No. He wanted to punch her in the face. Just for knowing. Whatever it was Ghost told her could get him shot. *Ghost, I hope you know that by not being here, you can't defend yourself.*

"He's very abrasive to others, from what I remembered. Wasn't always the ethical soldier, after all. But the higherups always did like his results," he responded. *Jennifer, I can play this game too.*

"How do you mean?" Tim asked, pushing his glasses up closer to his face.

Wait. How old do they think he is?

"I can't get into any specifics, but he did many questionable things, as no one at war is ever presented with a moral choice," Jeff answered.

With closed eyes, Jennifer shook her head. She turned to Sam, "So, sad of me to ask this, me being the romantic one, but I do want him to come out more with us. I can't be the only one to help him."

"Still no therapist, right?" Samantha asked, picking up on what he guessed were Jennifer's subtleties.

"Hush." Jennifer snapped.

"Perhaps," Tim interjected, leaning back into the seat, looking at the rippling waters at the side. "It would be good to get him to do something. Like these tours, or perhaps something else. Help ease his mind into something a little more public, make him feel like a real human being for once. Yeah?"

"He doesn't do anything." Jennifer scolded him. *Oh, he's doing something all right. I don't know what, but that shit's gotta stop!* "It's like pulling teeth just to get him out, but I must admit he's been more open. After all, I managed to get him to order out with me for once."

"Didn't you do that when you were, uh, you know?" Sam asked, as if hiding something just because Jeff was right there. *I need context!*

"No, that was take-out. We went to this noodle shop and ordered some ramen. Like, he ordered it. I didn't do it for him," she smiled, seemingly forgetting Jeffrey was there. "Sam, I forgot to tell you. He said it was delicious."

Sam blinked. "He did? Like, you didn't beat it out of him, did you?"

Michael. Why did you invite me here? At least present me with a situation I can actually use. I can't use this. I'm like the spare wheel here on a bus. Let's hope one of those tires don't pop.

"No. And that was the best part." She was vibrant; her personality was shining all the clearer, like someone who knew some despair, but above all, someone filled with a certain type of joy found in so little people. A joy that, regardless of circumstances, nothing could take that away.

I could. I can do it so easily. But why the attention on taste?

"I don't get it. Explain it to me," Jeff requested.

"He can't taste anything. Or at least, he couldn't. Not until just now," Sam replied.

"Sam, I saw him smile," Jennifer continued.

"He's always smil—"

"No, Michael dearest," she waved her finger at him. "Not like that. I could tell. It was plain that this smile was more than just a mask. He cried over noodles."

"Jennifer, I'm going to invite Ted to come get some coffee with me downtown next week." Michael shifted in his seat, pulled out two slips of paper, and reached over to Jennifer, who extended her arm to meet his. "I'll give you the details when and where, but why don't you come by, crash our little coffee bromance, as it were," the two of them chuckled, as if they both knew of some joke shared only between the two of them. "I got these from work. Take him to it."

"The Boston Symphony Orchestra. It's been some time since I've been to a show there. Do you know what's playing?" She pursed them, not bothering to look at them.

"You could read the tickets you know," Michael snickered.

"Michael," Tim interjected. "If you knew Jennifer, you *would* know she never reads anything. Other than Jane Austen."

"Hey." She poked him in the chest. "I read!"

"What was the last thing you read?" Tim asked.

"'Sense and Sensibility.'"

Jeff took a mental note of the information being discussed here. The love of literature, a romance novelist in particular seemed odd. Not in the context of them talking about it, but rather associating this with a dangerous man, Ghost, who by all accounts of who knew him, would say there wasn't a single romantic thing about the man, nor amiable. He bit his lip, contemplating the different personality this Ghost showed them, his brother of all included. He continued to listen as the bystander, knowing who *this* Ghost was.

"Point made. Ha!" Tim pulled his arms behind his head.

"So, anyway. It's some anime soundtracks by a string quartet, a choir, and I think there's a brass section. I don't watch anime, so I'm not all that interested in going. I got these from work. I don't know why they chose this of all things to give us, but hey, it's free."

You all, Ghost has you all wrapped around his finger. Doing whatever he wants you to do, telling you whatever sob story he can come up with. If you knew the damn truth, you'd know the monster he is. Blowing up orphanages in Bagdad. I still can't fathom why he'd do that, of all things.

***

A loud alarm.

Clemens bolted upright, the red lights shining brightly. Swiftly pulling himself out of his barracks bed, he darted toward his gear. The rest of his platoon followed as they rapidly marched down the hallways, with their equipment fastened to their bodies, side arms, long-ranged hunting rifles, grenades, and flashbangs. Overkill for a base like this, considering no one knew where they were.

"Prisoner escape. Task Force members: Seven, Nine, Eleven, Thirteen, Twenty-seven, and Thirty-one, are on the run. Send out the hounds now." Nakamura's voice, stern as ever.

The howling of the canines echoed down the halls. Footsteps clamoring. Rifles engaged, safeties off, and the dark night was none too favorable against these people. But of course Seven would know that, the creepy little bastard.

Pushing through the door, his eyes scanned some scrappy work for hiding tracks, "Eleven o'clock."

His platoon pushed past the dirt, scouring the tracks. His company found themselves in a desert storm, hiding just north of Area 51. Any tracks were now erased in the storm, almost like Seven would know that a storm was coming, predicting the impossible. He was filled with surprises.

The dust obscured his vision, pelting him, hot and scorching. It crawled their way into his BDUs, searing and marking his skin underneath. The uncomfortable sensation was irritable. He grimaced as the sand scratched his face.

What are the other little shits doing?

Surely, they'd all be missing, yet the rest of them are just hiding in their bunks or sleeping. Not even a peep. They found nothing.

Little shit. Of course, what the hell was I thinking. Seven ain't an idiot. He'd thrown us off into a different direction. Damnit.

"Target sighted. Target picked up, returning to base," Sergeant Ted Anderson.

Of course, Ted would've known that we went the other direction, took a gamble in any other direction and happened to find them.

"You find all of them?" Nakamura's voice choked in.

"Affirmative."

"Everyone, return to base."

Seven, you son of a bitch!

***

The missing members of Task Force Seven were thrown out of a Humvee, operated by Ted Anderson, who gave him a mirthless smile. The sneer was one of contempt, but oddly, not one at Clemens. It was just easier to justify against someone like Clemens. After all, he himself knew he was unlikeable. By anyone really.

Clemens averted his gaze to scowl at the little devils on the ground, their hands zip tied, kneeling on the dirt. Nakamura, in her exhausted agony came walking out of the facility, her hands behind her back, her black hair tied firmly into a bun as she frowned. It was never good when she frowned. No. Not like last time.

And his worst nightmare. She scowled at him. *She's going to chew me out.*

"Clemens. Where were you?"

"The locks were fastened before I was relieved from my post, Lieutenant," he answered. It was the truth.

"So, you didn't kill, Smith?"

"No, ma'am."

She shook her head, clearly disapproving his answer. It was the truth, but here, at Area 51, truth didn't matter. Just orders. Nothing else. Fall in line just like everyone else or be hammered down. Or find oneself hanging from the tree the next morning. It wouldn't be the first time.

He remembered what happened to the last soldier who refused to fall in line, asked one too many questions. Ted Anderson asked questions too, riding that small, thin line, but never more than what was necessary. Clemens never asked questions. Not his business. Just follow orders, or be just like Gunnery Sergeant Ramirez, hanging for all to see. Set as an example by Nakamura, and no one questioned anything since. Don't cross her. A lesson he learned early with this new reforming company: Black Eagle.

Her hands came to her sides as she looked at the demons, all with bruised and bleeding faces. *Ted Anderson wasn't kind to them.*

Seven's eyes were swollen; one was left open. She knelt in front of him, her hand caressing his swollen cheek. He hissed, jerking his neck back. "D—don't touch me!"

"Aww," she said. "My sweet little boy. Don't be like that. I'm trying to protect you. Why'd you run?"

He didn't answer. She pulled out a handkerchief, and spat into it, wiping the boy's face like he was her child.

But you're not a child. You're a murderer.

She turned, whistling, "Anderson, have Seven tied up behind a post."

"Ma'am," he scowled, pulling Seven up from the ground.

"No! No! No!" Seven squirmed, but to no avail; the zip ties did their job. Anderson dropped the monster on the ground, took the rifle off his back, and struck him in the head with the butt of it. He was knocked out, blood staining the sand covered floor.

The rest of the shits remained silent; those little arms clung close to their chests. The girls had their hair covering part of their faces, turning their head in sudden movements, terrified as their bodies quivered.

Nakamura turned to Clemens with a devilish smile. And when she smirked like that, one must be prepared for the worst, and no amount of preparation was ever sufficient.

"Clemens, get in my office while I tidy things up, I've got a favor to ask."

Favors. More like death threats.

"Yes, ma'am."

***

Clemens sat in a chair in Nakamura's office. The room was brightly lit, and it had a wooden desk, and of course, pictures on the wall which showed a part of who she was outside the uniform. A family woman, married to the Colonel—a prick just like her. The door creaked behind her.

He jolted.

"Oh." The door slammed shut. "Don't even bother standing up."

Her voice, cold when she was in here, at least to him. Seriously, one might think she didn't like him.

"Now, clearly, Smith is dead. I need to write a report on what happened, and he was to relieve you." She sat at her desk, a clipboard in hand. "Tell me what happened."

"zero hundred hours, he came, relieved me as per protocol. And I left to my barracks. He was alive when I left," he answered. His hands were in front of him, and his thumbs were shaking.

"Now, he was murdered. His head twisted back like a Russian doll," she replied. "Are you telling me you didn't do it?"

"No, I didn't."

"It would be best if you didn't lie to me," she snapped. Her eyes narrowed, staring into his.

"That's a lie. I didn't do it. There are cameras you can look at to confirm who did it." *She's trying to frame me.*

"Honestly, I could check. But I'm not going to." She jerked her head to the side and sneered. "Why can't you be more like Sergeant Anderson? He plays the game we play just as well, follows the rules."

"You can't get away with that. There has to be an investigat—"

"Clemens. Do you see any military police?" She was right. None here in Area 51. "I arranged that. Go ahead and try to test my patience again. Seven is tied to a post out in the back."

"And?"

"You're going to beat him to a pulp."

"No."

She frowned. "Let me remind you. You're expendable. They aren't. When I decide to hang you, you're not going to stop me from slandering your name to your family." She leaned over the desk, her chin over her folded hands. "I told you I'd keep quiet after your little incident, but if you don't play along, I'll hang you for the jeers."

His heart sank, and it became painful to even breathe; jaw dropped open. The one terrible thing he did, causing him to grow cold with all the horrible things he would continue to do. But this was something even the Devil would be ashamed of, for devils don't do this. Only humans do, and they are far worse. But then again, orders are orders. His entire palms shook, sweat dripping down in angst.

"You ordered me to do it," he attempted to stare her down.

She tilted her head to the other side. "Now, that's not true, is it?" She sneered.

He sucked in the air through his teeth.

"Do we understand one another?"

"If you want him beaten up, why don't you do it?"

"Because I don't hit quite as hard as you," she answered, pointing out the window. "Now, he's out there. If I find he can walk tomorrow, you'll be hanged."

Clemens nodded.

"Dismissed, and make sure not to disappoint."

"Yes, ma'am." He frowned, clenching his teeth and his fists at his side.

"Good doggie."

He dashed out of the room, slamming the door behind him as he made his way, furious, stamping his feet with every step, scowling with a cringing face. *Ted Anderson. You son of a bitch. Seven, if it wouldn't get me killed, I'd fucking kill you.*

He rushed out of the facility, marching past the chain-linked gates.

There he was, dark hair over his swollen face, blood dripping on his side, chained behind a wooden post. The little demon coughed, his legs sprawled right in front of him. The boy's face averted his gaze from the ground, staring wide eyed, tears glimmering in the moonlight. *What did he have to be sad about? Nothing.*

Clemens grimaced as he bolted toward the boy.

"NO," he cried.

Clemens grabbed him by the hair, lifting his body from the ground, legs dangling down.

"NO! NO! NO!" the boy's cries were akin to that of a baby, high pitched screaming.

Clemens squinted; ears pierced. His hand formed a fist at his side, thrashing at the demon, tied, defenseless against the post. His fist made contact, striking it hard in the face.

"MOMMA! HELP!" it cried.

"You have no Momma!" Clemens thrust forward, his knee striking Seven in the chest. Ribs cracked. He pulled Seven's hair back, punching again. And again. And again. Until the screams stopped, and just raspy breathing sounded. Seven hung by its wrists, face swollen, blood drooling from its mouth.

Clemens grimaced, kicking it hard in the stomach until Seven spat out shattered molars.

Seven coughed, tears dripping off his cheeks into the sand.

Clemens took his fists again, striking Seven in the face, blood lining his eye lids, dripping down. He pulled his feet up, kicking its shins.

"Momma," the devil cried.

Faker.

"Help me. Please. I'll be a good boy."

He kicked its shins again.

Crack.

"MOMMA! Help me, please. I'll do whatever you want. Please!"

He kicked the unbroken shin.

"Ah! Momma!" it cried, taking a back hand across the face. More blood drooled to the ground.

Clemens pulled its hair, shoving it to the post.

Thud.

"Momma, please."

Clemens tightened his fist again, punching it in the jaw.

Cough. Again. *Cough.* Again. *Crack.*

It breathed. Whatever this thing was, it breathed. It can't scream anymore, blood drooling out of its open mouth, unable to close. Broken jaw. Broken shins. Fractured ribs. This ought to be enough.

Good riddance.

"Good job."

Clemens turned around to Nakamura holding a cam recorder, undoubtedly recording the entire incident. She was escorted by Ted Anderson, and two other armed guards. "I'll save this for later. At ease."

She walked toward Seven and knelt in front of him. The devil panted, unable to speak, but turned its ugly head toward her.

"How's my little boy?"

Clemens looked down, uncomfortable as he stood at attention. In that moment, he wanted nothing more than to strangle her, but he would be shot before he got his hands around her filthy neck. She looked, bringing her hand near its puffy cheek. It jerked its head away from the hand, touched carefully by her other hand.

"There, there. Did he hurt you?"

Again, it didn't say anything, just drooled, but its head nodded. Her head reached forward, touching its bloody, swollen head.

"Ahl. Ahl," it said.

"Are you going to run again?" she asked.

"Nol. Nol." It coughed.

She patted her hand on his cheek. "Good boy. Don't do it again, okay?"

It nodded.

Chapter 12 Coffee

As exports drastically slow down, along with the hostile interactions coming from overseas by way of the east and the west, and asked about the disruptions in the supply chain for supplies, Chief Commanding Officer Malcolm had this to say:

I'm not worried. I get my supplies direct. Our acquisition team gets holds of their due of the supplies before Uncle Sam does, so our operations remain undisrupted. It gets harder, sure, but for us, business is as usual. Now, that doesn't mean it doesn't affect us, so we have research and development on a couple of projects, and with them, we've been able to produce some significant tech. Currently, foreseeing some issues rising with the supply chain disruption, we are slowly working our way back to steam powered and electric technology. Currently, we have a tank in development that is strictly electric. We expect once it's done, it can fully operate for three weeks without a full recharge.

***

Ted Anderson stood over the edge of a roof staring down at a large apartment complex, with curved windows where he knew Jeff Clemens was assigned. This bothered him. Not that he could trust Clemens. He didn't. He could throw him far but trusted him no further than where his eyes could see him.

He peered down, eyes scanning past the particles of falling snowflakes, shining brightly in the streetlights as they coated the ground, chilling his bones. He rubbed his hands together, exhaling into them to bring them warmth. Physically, it didn't bother him, but he knew that should he force himself to violence, he would want to be as nimble as a fox. And he couldn't do that when his bones were rattling, now, could he?

What bothered him the most was the fact that Jeff knew his identity. Or, rather whatever identity was known to anyone inside of Task Force Seven and Black Eagle. The fact he was still here and had not returned to duty was cause for concern too.

Who owns it now? The damned group of mercenaries with execute authority, and arguably better discipline than the rest. You told them, didn't you.

His lips curled into a scowl.

I told you, didn't I? I told you if you forced me to leave the life I've built, I'd rip your arms off. But he couldn't prove anything. No evidence, just a history of very lucky guesses, but that wouldn't be just. It wouldn't be right. But why did he care for right or wrong? Nothing has ever gone right for him. Except *Jennifer.* He could at least try for her. He could try to do the right thing and hear Clemens out.

Jennifer's face flashed across his mind. Her hair, her smile, not toiled or corrupted like his were. The smile, and gleam she shared with him time and time again was just enough to make him forget, however briefly, his chronic torment. She made him feel like something. Like part of him rekindled, not work down as he constantly was. Her patience with him fueled the husk he once was and turned it into something a little more human. Ted Anderson now had something to lose.

Is this really that much to ask? Maybe you could at least tell me why you tried to kill us. You owe me that much.

His phone rang. Michael Clemens.

What does he want at this hour? Unfortunate timing, I was about to pay your brother a visit. He answered it. The wind whistled behind him. "It's Ted."

"Hey, Tedward!"

Ted stifled a chuckle. He found the pet-name funny, coming from Michael, who knew just enough about him, more or less, and understood what was fundamentally true: Ted's mental state not being healthy. And it was a name specifically usually Jennifer called him.

"Michael, what can I do you for today, at such a late hour," he asked.

"It can't be too late if the wind is whistling in the back. You're wearing winter gear, right?" He chuckled in the background.

Ted imagined Michael grinning on the other end of the phone.

"Well, anyway, back to why I called. I wanted to get some coffee with you tomorrow if that would be okay. I hear you like chess?"

He sighed. "I've played it. I don't particularly like anything. But you know that."

"That's not what I heard," he cackled on the other end of the phone, audibly too loud, that Ted pulled the phone from his ear. "I heard you like ramen."

Jennifer.

"Well, joking aside, everyone likes something. The trouble is, finding out what that something is, and having the passion and energy to enjoy it. So, I wanted to do something with you. Just you. Just me. Now, normally I'd ask if there's something you want to do, but well, you know. You claim to not like anything, so we'll do something I want to do. I'll play chess with you. Let's grab a sandwich or breakfast or whatever, and some coffee. How's that sound?"

"And you think I'd enjoy that?" Ted laughed in near hysteria.

"Glad I got a laugh out of you. I'll assume that was real," he chuckled back. "But to answer your question, who knows. You don't know if you like anything or not, so at least one of us will be happy. So, how about it? You know what? I'll pull a Sam. You don't have a choice. I won't take no for an answer. I know someone who knows where you live, and so help me, I'll get Jennifer to get you to come out with me."

"That is something Sam would do?"

"She rubs off on me. How about the café shop on Washington Street. Right by Lafayette Ave?"

"You mean the Gremlin Café?"

"Ah, you know the one?"

"Yes,"

"10:00 a.m. tomorrow. I'll meet you there!"

Hanging up the phone, he shook his head as he gazed down on the time. *2:00 a.m. Shit.*

He exhaled white air from his lips as he turned back into the building. *Another day, Jeff. You better be thankful; I still have half a mind to murder you.*

***

Ted walked off the subway car early the next morning. Not early for a man who only sleeps for half an hour, and every single nap was an existential crisis waiting to happen. He really should seek therapy, he knew that. He knew he needs *something* to keep his nightmares under some control. After all, these nightmares had a nasty habit of seeping into his reality, and he couldn't fully comprehend what was real, what was a memory, or what was a nightmare. He didn't have problems with his dreams. He didn't have any. Only nightmares.

Ted walked up the escalators into the street, filled with an abundance of trash pouring out of the trashcans strategically placed on the sidewalks. He heard the squeaking wheels of a skeletal cart to his left. He knew what it was. Just another thing casually discarded with a pulse as something less than human.

He turned his feet, shifting away from one end of Washington Street leading down toward the old Town Hall, and averted his gaze down the street leading to Chinatown. The pedestrian-only street was lined in carefully placed gray bricks. This street wasn't designed for vehicles. As he took his first step in this direction, people rushed past him in their winter garbs, some simple, others more extravagant as if others were dressing to impress someone. Men and women alike, careless, not a care in the world, none at all. Sure. It wasn't like war was on their doorstep. But then again, most of these people have no memory of war. Not like him. Implanted in his brain, never to forget it, only death would grant him that luxury. *All because of the sacrifice we made. All because of the weight of those sacrifices was thrust upon our shoulders.*

The wind picked up as he emerged from the building's overhead. The crunch of the snow on the ground underneath his boot filled his ears. The snow was compact, perfect for, what was the word—

A little child ran in front of him, as the large menacing tree with green and red lights loomed over him atop the store on the opposite side of the street. The little boy in his hat, his clothes, grabbed some snow in his hand, clumping it together, firmly molding it into a grenade, and took it, handling it as if it was one, before hurling it across the street, striking another child in the shoulder. The cluster of snow dispersed into dust, brushing into the face of the other child, who cried out, laughing with an open mouth, and two missing teeth, one on the maxillary, the other on the mandibular jaws. The smile was cute, authentic even, filled with a joy that Ted could never have. Something that was stolen from him. No matter what money could bring him, no matter what glee Jennifer brought to him, and any hope that is neither here nor there. Nothing could ever return childhood, and no number of apologies could ever return friends, that ought to have been buried in the ground, not shot up to pieces like a witch during the Danvers' Witch Trials.

He walked on, taking a left on Washington Street. His laptop was resting at his side, holding his portfolio and all his notes. The streets were still fairly empty at this time. The cool breeze kept bringing him chills. Not typical. After spending some time in the northern parts of Russia, he didn't think he'd feel chills again, and yet here he was, walking through the bristling weather, chafing his cheek.

He found the café, the sign hanging out of it, just inside a hotel of which he didn't care to find the name of. The sidewalk was lightly trampled on as he walked by the snow-covered trashcan, a black steel canister turned pale with flakes white. He exhaled, stepping forward as the white breath churned. He took another step, and suddenly, just like many times before, the temperature dropped yet again. Bones rattling inside. Exhaling heavily, he rubbed his arms, clinging to the friction for a piece of warmth.

He realized something: he wasn't breathing in that cursed *essence*. Whatever it was, it wasn't him doing it. Turning behind him, eyes scanning past the people flooding outside the subway tunnels, and turning corners up on Lafayette Ave, he couldn't shake the feeling he was being watched. Something he was good at picking up, but he couldn't quite gather the intent of such a person sneaking about on a late Saturday morning.

He hissed as the air warmed up slightly, and brushing the snowflakes off his hair, he turned inside the glass door, pushing it open. The smell of freshly baked bread assaulted his nostrils. There was something about it, something familiar...

"Ghost! Ghost!"

He awoke abruptly, eyes forward, scanning the darkened room. A sweet aroma filled it as he rubbed his eyes. He turned, pulling his legs over his cot, standing up. Door creaking open, and shutting silently, a girl coming closer, with a roll running to him, the steam coming up from it.

"Ghost! Look!" Slithers said, smiling at it as she held it in both hands to his face, gazing hungrily, and as if she was looking at salvation in her hands. Her hands were coated in patters of white lines for the innumerous scars she had, from debris, glass, rusting iron and bullets. He reached for her arms, seeing similar scars on his arms.

"Slithers," he stammered, hands trembling uncontrollably. "You shouldn't have taken this. If they find out—"

"So, what if they do. I want them to find out. I don't—I don't care anymore. We're animals. We should behave like animals! Trapped in cages are we." She ripped it in half and brought it to him. "Listen. You don't care either."

"How did you get this?" He shook his head. "You couldn't have made it to the pantry on your own," he said, reluctantly grabbing his half, and bringing it to his nose. He squeezed it gently, it was so soft, softer than his pillow.

"Ted Anderson gave it to me."

"Ted Anderson," he repeated, taking bite out of the bread. Tasting sour and tangy, chewing softly. "Ted Anderson."

"Ted Anderson," they repeated together.

The walls closed in around them, fading everything to black, suffocating him as the air grew heavier, and the temperature, standing on ends was worse than Northern Russia. His eyes closed, and opened, consumed the horror of the flames filling the room, rattling of metal shells dropping down the cold hard metal grates above.

And there, Slithers lay in a pool of her own blood on the ground. Knife protruding out of her chest, limbs scattered on it. Black blood. Black blood. Black blood.

He turned, and the vest on his chest weighed heavily as his vision faded, blood pouring out of the walls, and covering him completely.

He looked around himself, feeling a fog sweep over him. Lightheaded, almost non-existence fueling his angst. He felt his heart beating faster and faster. Lost. He swept his hands in front of him, trying to find something that was physically real. Something he could touch. Something he could use to pull himself out. But all that was there was nothingness.

He exhaled heavily, white breath coming out of his mouth, pouring into the café. He opened his palms, his eyes opened wide staring blankly at the sign in front of him. Unable to process the words he was reading, he clenched his fists, and unfolded them repeatedly.

"Hey, man!" a firm hand clenched his shoulder.

Exhaling heavily, palms sweating at his side. Heart racing as the panic poisoned his veins. He turned abruptly, arms raised, and his teeth grinded.

"Whoa!" Michael put his hands up nonchalantly, a slight smirk on his face. "It's just me."

Damnit.

He sucked in a deep breath through his teeth and let out a brief sigh of relief and returned that dreadfully fake smile. "Michael, don't do that again."

"You got it." Michael's grin brightened. "Hey, why don't you grab a spot. I'll get us something. What do you want?"

"Coffee," he answered, looking back into the café, scanning for a place to sit.

"And to eat?"

"I smell fresh bread. Whatever just came out of the oven,"

"That's it?"

"Yes," he sighed, taking himself away from Michael. He walked briskly to a seat next to a window. It was cozy, and this table in particular was near a fireplace, crackling wood, burning coals. This place was filled with familiar scents, some pleasant, and others horrible. Never before did he come to a place both beautiful and terrifying simultaneously. He chose to tough it out, but how long could his mind take it?

The leather seat was rich and comforting. He had never sat in one of these before. Even in his day jobs, he only ever had the office chairs. Nothing like this brown, cushy, leather chair. It squeaked under his weight, and he looked at the table in front of him: wooden, lightly sanded on the edges, polished dark. He wiped some crumbs off the table and onto the floor, feeling it's smooth, flawless texture under his rough, defective hands.

He snarled out the window as the snowflakes fell again, dancing carelessly in the wind, just like everyone else: careless. He felt the unwavering suspicion of someone watching him. Just him. Why would he have drawn attention, but because he did have that little episode at the entry way. No. Everyone was watching him, sitting by himself in the corner.

They bit down on their food. Sandwiches, eggs, sausage, all those aromas hurled toward his nose, and unwanted attentions presented themselves, looking at him not as a person. He knew better. It was the same stare he received from other soldiers, marines, and sailors when they found out who he was with, or what he was. A monster.

Oh. Yes. They'd run if they knew the truth, and the police would be here in ballistic gear followed by the National Guard to put me down. Especially if they knew I was still alive. Black Eagle would not be far behind, but why aren't you moving? You definitely know. Why haven't you done anything or moved on me unless—

That's it. You have a spy here. Don't you? But who is at the top this time? It isn't Snells.

"Here we are," Michael interrupted his insanity as he set a bowl of fresh rolls, steam rising from them. Michael placed some butter and jam to the side and a butter knife clattered on the table. *Dangerous thing here.*

Michael placed his cup of black coffee on the table in front of him, swirling restless ripples inside the cup, just itching to pour over.

Michael sat down, his breakfast sandwich was resting peacefully alone on a plate, steaming in front of him. Bacon, eggs, and a toasted English muffin, with undoubtedly melted butter.

Ted gazed back over to his bowl of rolls and pulled one out, squeezing the soft roll in his hands. He brought it to his mouth, biting onto it, inhaling the delicious yeasty aroma, tasting the soft, sweet roll onto his tongue. Another thing he remembered, another thing he forgot. Something he was forced to forget, as his memory of Slithers passed through his mind, warm tears streamed down his cheeks, taking small savory bites. He finished the first roll and reached for another, eyes glancing to Michael who's eyes were closed and lips were moving but no words came out. Michael's hand stopped moving.

"Don't stop eating on account of me," Michael chuckled as he placed his coffee back down and took a large bite of his breakfast sandwich. "Ah, eggs. Can't beat those first thing in the morning!"

"What were you doing?" Ted asked, curious as to why the man wouldn't just take a bite first. "Just now. What were you doing?"

"I'm surprised Jennifer didn't tell you." An eyebrow raised. "Praying. I always pray for my meal. I'm always thankful."

"You did that silently though," he questioned further. His hands retracted from the table, folding over themselves underneath the table, clenching firmly.

"Yes, I don't have to speak loudly. He hears me. I know He hears me. He grants me my requests just as easily as He denies them."

"And what did you pray for just now?" Anxiety filled Ted's hands, shaking underneath the table. His heel lifted and struck the ground repeatedly. He almost forgot someone else was tracking him. Just as he was reminded, a cold draft pushed through the café; the door opened and a singular woman walked through the room, shot a smiling glance at him, with the same tired look inscribed in her face as he knew he shared with her. He didn't know her. Didn't care to know her, as elegantly as she walked through the line to order her own cup of coffee.

He almost forgot Jeff, but he found himself growing fond of Michael, and this relationship they were developing. But it was complicated with Jeff in the picture. Far too complicated for his liking, and it would have been better if Ted left in the summer, just like he planned. It would have been better.

Yet, here we are.

"I thanked Him for my food," Michael answered plainly. He looked Ted in the eye, the curve on his lips straightened, and his eyelid dropped halfway down both eyes, much like Jennifer's very playful gaze. But for Michael, it was something entirely different. "And I prayed for you. Your health and wellbeing." He sipped on his coffee cup as Ted gasped softly from across the table.

Why?

Michael tapped his cup with his finger as he rested it on the table. "Look, I know I haven't exactly been around you much. So, I suppose you might say you don't know me, and what I know about you I get from either Jennifer or Sam. And I know you aren't well. And please," he said as Ted shifted uncomfortably in his chair, "do not blame Jennifer. What you don't want the rest of us to know is still with Jennifer. What Samantha, specifically, knows, I know. That's it. I know you can't seek conventional help. I don't know why, but that's all I really need to know. In fact, I don't need to know any more than that until you're ready to talk."

"What did she—"

"What she said doesn't matter," Michael interrupted. "You know, I don't know if Sam ever told you this, but she thought you to be heading off the deep end, like a-blade-becoming-a-little-too-friendly-with-your-wrist deep end." His voice dropped down low so only Ted could hear him. "When she first thought of it, I read something in the news. It was interestingly horrifying enough, but who would ever think that America would finally beat Japan with the world's highest suicide rate? One thing we don't need to be beating them in. But I guess, what brought me to that was my acknowledgment that we aren't doing enough for others. Of course, it doesn't help that when you needed it most, the government stopped funding suicide prevention services. And police aren't going to get involved in something like that, for God only knows what reason."

Ted listened carefully, not breaking eye contact, maintaining his composure, but on the inside, he was screaming. He brought the coffee to his lips; the bitter taste brought some satisfaction to him. He wasn't sure why, but he didn't like it too much. But he drank it to seem like he needed it to stay awake during the global stock markets. Which he didn't. The nightmares made sure he was awake.

"But here I am, talking to you, someone who needs help, and someone that the government thinks is better off dead, just like everyone else. And I want you to know that despite it all, we are going to be here with you. But, I think the real tragedy here, is that war has a habit of killing the living. And not just literally. Personalities are burned away. And it saddens me we will never know who Ted Anderson was meant to be. Just who he's become, a man diverged from the path he was originally designed to follow.

"Ted. Whatever you need, Sam and I, and of course Jennifer are only a phone call away. Call us at 3:00 a.m. I don't care. Neither do they. I mean, Sam might. You don't want to get in the way of her beauty sleep," he laughed, finishing his sandwich. "She'll rip you a new one."

The words stung deep, a lump was crawling up his throat like he was going to vomit. The heart sank, growing heavier with every breath. Placing the cup down, he raised another roll to his lips. Warm tears still. The memories. Few good ones remained, and he was confident there would be a day where he would forget the good ones and forget what his friends looked like. After all, he didn't have much to remember them by. Just the spear, the bow, and a fading picture. That's it. Nothing more. He felt Michael's eyes looking at him. Not down on him, but at him, trying to figure out how to help, but he chose not to say anything.

Michael made it known; he was there. And he wasn't going anywhere. While Ted couldn't trust him entirely, Michael trusted him enough to offer him help, even if it was just another person to call.

"Ted, if you don't believe me," he offered again, sipping down the rest of his coffee. "If you find yourself in Alaska, for whatever reason, and you need someone to be there. Call us. And we're on the next plane out there. I don't care. Just call us."

Ted's eyes gaped open, bringing another roll to his lips, blindly eating it. The lump growing inside his chest seem to lessen, slowly wiggling itself down into the abyss of his stomach. *But Jeff is going to make this relationship of ours exceedingly difficult. Michael, how can you say any of this when I* "Thank you," *want nothing more than to bury your brother in the ground?*

"No problem, man," Michael replied, pulling out a little box, which slid open to a checkered board. He opened two small brown boxes underneath the board and started pegging all but two pieces in it. He placed the two pieces into his hands, and behind his back.

Ted's heart raced.

Michael pulled his hands out, closed, palmed facing the ground. "Pick one."

Ted gazed carefully at each hand, wondering which hand held which piece. Chess was a game of strategy, of which, no one knew battle strategy than he did. He could play distracted, and it wouldn't make a difference.

"This isn't the stock market, Tedward, it's okay. Money isn't on the line," Michael chuckled.

He shook his head and pointed at the left one. Michael flipped his hand over, opened his fist to reveal the black pawn. *I suppose you need to get every break you can get. Or maybe you're the lucky one.*

"Hey, maybe you'll get your bad luck after all," Michael joked.

Of course, when they first met, they had a conversation about luck, and the farce of luck was that good luck wasn't all that lucky, and it was better to have bad luck, since at the very least, you could be better prepared should things take a turn for the worst. Consistent good luck leads to complacency, risking being easily fooled. *I don't want to hear that right now. Not when everything else is coming down to the ground around me. Your brother is a wild nuisance.*

"Shall we begin, Tedward?"

Ted flipped the board, so he was black, and pegged his piece in. "Yes. Let's."

"May the best man win."

They played a few rounds across the table as Ted ate his sourdough rolls. Of course, he wasn't going to let those sweet memories get out of place. Michael wasn't a bad player, not at all.

"You're very good at this," Ted remarked.

"Chess President of my college's chess club!" Michael moved a pawn forward, replacing it with a knight, and puffed his chest out with great pride.

Bold move. But that won't save you.

Ted moved his queen right in front of the King. The queen sat with the King locked in place. The only move for the King was to take the queen, however, what queen remains unprotected by her loyal knight. Michael didn't see this coming, clearly, as the pawns were arranged in such a way that allowed his larger pieces to advance down the center. This bold strategy would work much like Blitzkrieg, with one fatal flaw: should something with enough sense go behind the front lines into enemy territory, well, that always invited disaster.

"Checkmate," Ted declared himself victorious, however bittersweet it was.

"Again?" Michael wiped his brow. "Never have I had a chess game end like this before, least of all, not on me. You, Tedward, I announce my defeat and my undying support to your throne."

Ted blinked as he looked down on the chess set. He glanced upward, unsure if this was meant to be a joke. He couldn't quite tell, and Michael was hard to read sometimes. Sometimes he could figure out his motives, but not today, he seemed a little more off than usual.

Ted's phone rang in his pocket.

And who might this be?

"Excuse me." Ted said politely as he took out his phone. Erin. *What does she want?* "Gutenberg Press?"

"Funny Ted, funny," she replied over the phone. "Seriously though, I have a question for you, that you I can trust will answer me honestly."

"Whatever it is, sell it," he answered.

"Wait, what? You don't even know what I was asking about it,"

"I guessed you were going to ask me some stock related question, weren't you?"

"Clever as ever, Mr. Anderson," she cackled over the other end of the phone. "But who would want this? It's Gernazation USA."

"Definitely sell that. That's worthless," he replied.

"Okay, thanks. I was planning on it,"

"Out of curiosity, why did you even buy it?"

"It looked good. Now that that's out of the way, I wanted to thank you," she said over the phone. *Thank me?* "I don't know how I'll ever pay you back."

"For what exactly?" He asked. "Forgive me, Gutenberg Press, I don't remember what I did for you."

"You saved me from a terrible trade for one," she answered rather sarcastically. "But onto the actual reason for my call today: someone paid that hospital bill for chemo. Who else could it be? Someone who has lots of money, and not a want for it. You may never acknowledge you did this, but I know. And I won't tell anyone else. But I wanted you to know I'm thankful for it."

"You're welcome," he replied.

"Well, I'm sure you're busy, I'll let you go. Talk to you soon!"

"Bye,"

Ted hung up the phone and withdrew it to his pocket.

"Well, that sounded like an obviously boring conversation. Michael, what did I tell you about bromancing?"

"Dear God. Why now?" Michael chuckled, turning his head around.

Jennifer walked with her own coffee cup, wrapping her arm around Ted's shoulders. Ted noticed she wiped her nose with a napkin, blowing it hard before swiftly discarding it to the trash. He didn't see the color dilation from the napkin.

Ted's heart felt uplifted, rising from the pit of despair that was caused by the smell of freshly baked bread. But Jennifer was here, whole, and unspoiled by the traumas of war, though she did have her own experience with people who saw war. Those in her family who, like Michael said, had their personalities burned away. But Jennifer reminded him of what he was. The good and the bad would continue to plague his mind, but now with her, it was at least somehow bearable.

"So, tell me." Bringing a spare chair, Jennifer brought her face close to his, cheeks rubbing together, invasive in her own Jennifer-like brand as she was. She was excitable, her hand squeezing his shoulder. "You didn't beat him too bad, did you Michael?"

"I'm afraid I couldn't beat him at chess if he was blindfolded," he chuckled.

"Tedward," she turned her face toward him, gazing into his eyes.

"Hey, hey, hey." Michael exclaimed. "I can't bromance him, but you're practically romancing him. Why can't I have a bromance?"

"Because," she averted her gaze back to Michael. "You're not *bromantic*. Where's the candle lights?"

"I've got a fireplace behind me. What do I need candles for?" He retorted.

Ted chuckled lightly, his gut reacting in rhythmic vibrations.

"This is why you deserve no bromances, amateur." She threw her hair back and laughed. "Anyway, Tedward, I've got some tickets for tomorrow to go to the Boston Symphony Orchestra. I like music."

"What's playing?" he asked, as a polite nicety. He didn't truly understand music at all. He knew there was a military band, but it was all white noise to him. It didn't really mean anything. The only thing he could say he enjoyed was reading, and even then, that reminded him of the numerous different briefings he'd had and orders he'd read when he was deployed. Nothing was ever for enjoyment. Though, he could say he found this engagement today was fruitful.

"Looks like some local orchestra for some miscellaneous soundtracks from various anime."

Ted blinked, "What's anime?"

"Oh, it's some Japanese medium for movies or shows. It's densely animated, some heavily rely on absurdism. I'm not a fan, but great music though." Michael snapped both his fingers and stood up. "I've gotta get going, I'll leave you two alone together."

Jennifer sneered at him. "Yes, Michael, I really, really want this."

"You can have him." He turned away, walking briskly out of the café, waving on his way out.

"So," She held his cheeks firmly her warm and soft hands. Warmth spread through him, his breath caught in his throat. At that moment, it was the only thing he could think about. "How about it? You get to come out, it's just you and me, and of course a hall filled with people you don't know, most likely."

"Sure, I'll come along. What time?"

Chapter 13 Breaking Down

Snells initiated a peaceful draft that is expected to inflate armed forces by 30 percent from draftees alone.

This is the first Peaceful Draft since 1940 when FDR first signed the Peaceful Draft during WWII. The draft still excludes woman from registering for selective service, and men between the ages of 18-23 are being called up from the local recruiter's office to sign, imposing them to service.

Press Secretary Jenna Walters claims, "It is up to us to decide the fate of our world. We cannot trust the allies from overseas to help us in this conflict. Russia and China have declared war on us. It is the position of the government than everyone must do their part to ensure the survival of this democratic republic."

***

Ted looked up at the black night sky, snowflakes drifting down endlessly from the heavens, a place he was forbidden from entering when he died. The beauty of the snowflakes was unfettered; they fell different shapes, different sizes, coalescing onto the ground where he stood. It covered his shoes and soaked his pants and coat as he waited outside the Boston Symphony Orchestra Hall. The lights outside shone brightly, both the streetlights loomed over him, and the golden yellow lights shone from inside the hall.

Snow dusted the ground, being kicked through the scattered and disorganized steps of those around him. He turned around, scanning those coming out of the Green Line station. He didn't remember the name of the stop; the Green Line was still confusing with its number of different routes to all different parts of Downtown Boston.

Then, at last, she came up the stairs, walking in her blue dress, the top tucked away in a winter coat, a hat, and some earmuffs. He carefully looked at her nose, still skeptical. That napkin, he had a hard time forgetting about it. Up the nostril, as he stole a quick glance as to not be rude, was not bleeding. She approached him, and clumsily, with her leather gloves, she pulled out the tickets. "Dear Tedward, art thou ready?"

He raised an eyebrow. "As ready as I'll ever be, William Shakespeare."

She cackled as she took his hand in hers, the soft flesh sent warmth to his palms. Never really had cause to hold someone's hands before. Not even Slithers. This hand, smooth all around, curved, and a faint pulse he felt beating into his. There was nothing of note on the hand, like a blank canvas with nothing but the future to mark it. She led him up the stairs as he marveled at the building itself. The marble rimmed pillars welcomed them into an exquisite red backdrop, filled with carved frames and windows. He sighed as they walked into the vestibule to the ticket window, and through the halls.

Jennifer led him inside the main hall where the instrumentalists were preparing their tools for the main event, the golden statues and other various decorum lined up on what looked like mini balconies for spirits atop them, looming over, watching them as they walked through the crowd to get a spot.

Another thing that was flung into his attention was the dress. Jennifer dressed the part, sure. He didn't. He had a collared shirt, and some slacks, with no tie to go with it. The belt was passable at least. He was hopelessly underdressed and that was an understatement. How did a man like him end up coming to a place like this, and a woman like her? He was so unrefined.

As he sat down next to her, something else came to his mind: why did he care about how he was dressed? He wasn't in the military anymore. He didn't need to play a part, but he felt like he needed to, now everyone was going to be watching him. And not paying attention to the orchestra, not that this was his concern, but he didn't want to be the center of attention. Not here.

His heart beat faster as more people showed up, taking their seats, glancing over him. Why wouldn't they? He stuck out like a sore thumb. There was no lie here. No need for it. He just needed to calm down. He took measured breaths.

A cool gentle touch caressed the top of his hand. Startled, he opened his palms. The touch remained, but firmly pressed his hand to the arm of the seat. Turning his head, Jennifer was there, finally sat down, and her hand rested atop his, and her fingers, gentle, delicate, saw fit, it seemed by their own accord, to interweave themselves into his fingers like a basket, damned to fall apart. Slowly, his heart rate slowed down, and his fingers relaxed again on the arm of the chair.

He leaned into her, mouth breathing into her ears, "Thank you."

"You're welcome, Tedward," she whispered back.

The lights dimmed as the instrumentalists took their places, picking up a variety of stringed instruments, drums of various kinds, and trombones, and trumpets, and tubas, and other various brass instruments he didn't recognize. *This was much more than a quartet.*

The chatter dulled down as the choir came out. They took their spot and the lights fell upon them.

And then, the music began to play. It was soft at first, soothing with the backdrop of the choir singing different parts of differing tones, and slightly altered tempos, this much he could tell, but why was the choir so disorganized? The violinists started to strum their strings with carefully precise movements of the bow, moving back and forth, scratching his ears as the high pitches started to scream. And the brass. Nothing was worse. The brass was horrible. Sounded like the horn of a ship sending out an SOS.

He wasn't sure what it was like to feel enjoyment, but he was certain this wasn't it. But he continued to listen, until the music stopped again, coming abruptly. Started again. Stopped with the violins ringing in their last note, like the last gasp of breath before a corpse's soul was released to either Heaven or to Hell. *Shit.* His other hand started to tremble as visions of flashing gunfire and grenades coursed over his mind, clearly paving the way for room for more nightmares, and this was something he didn't need.

Just tough it out. It's not real. It's not real.

He exhaled rhythmically again, heavily as the air in his lungs felt compressed and restrained, pushing the air out of his air sacks. He wanted to throw up. He took his other hand as he covered his mouth. Tears slid down his face.

Ticker's arm flung right in front of him. Warm blood coalesced on his face, dripping down as he felt a foot kicking hard in his side, a rib cracking.

Ticker. Ticker. Ticker.

His hand reached out for something, and the room was clapping for the intercession. He felt Jennifer's hand squeezing him tightly. The lights came back, lighting everything in the room, and everyone stood up, chatting again as others made their way out to the bathroom.

"Ted," she whispered, her hands framing his face. "Are you okay?"

He ignored everyone else around him. The only thing that mattered was the warm hands on his face, and the person they were attached to. His hands reached up, holding onto her wrists gently, almost like a dead fish. He didn't want to break her. He didn't want to scar her. He didn't want to fill her with the same poison that plagued his brain. She was precious to him.

Exhaling into her face, she frowned as he slowly, mechanically shook his head. "Can we—can we go? *Please.*"

"Yeah. Let's go. Why don't we come back to my place first?"

***

Ted was seething, teeth sputtering, clashing against one another like halved coconuts. The door opened. She ushered him forward, his body shaking, but not because of the cold, but because of something else. "Ted. Sit down. Couch." She said, slowly closing the creaking door, hearing the latch lock behind it. She secured the deadbolt just in case Ted felt unsafe without all the bonds latched.

Ted took a seat, shaking, hands trembling in front of him as he exhaled heavily, hyperventilating uncontrollably. His eyes focused forward, looking at her TV stand. He leaned forward and his shoulders rolled. She walked over to the kitchen, turned the tea pot on.

Feeling some moisture swell up in her nose, she took a napkin, and wiped it. Blood stained the napkin red. *Not now. Please.* She discarded the napkin into the trash, washing her hands waiting for the water.

When the kettle whistled, she pulled out two mugs, placing teabags inside, poured hot water into the cup, and steeped. She then removed the teabags, removed them to the trash, and poured the milk in. She brought the tea over to the coffee table where Ted was having an episode.

It won't be long now, and the lights are going to start going haywire again.

"Tedward, take off your coat," she said, sitting next to him. He didn't respond, still breathing heavily, eyes still locked on her TV stand. She looked to the stand, and his eyes seemed focused on a collection of Blu-ray sets. Nothing of any real importance. Her hands reached out to his, separating them, and then to his coat zipper, pulling it down. Her hands reached into his jacket to pull the sleeves off. Still no reaction. Nothingness.

She sighed as she took a sip of her tea. *Well, it's coming. Just. When? There it is.*

She felt her bones chill. Her hands shivered as it reached for the cup, and its temperature was dropping. The lights in the living room dimmed and shut off, but the room was lit with another light, rainbow-colored veins on Ted, dear Tedward, lighting up the room, and shutting nearly every electrical appliance off in her apartment. It was almost colder in here, than it was out there.

It wasn't long before the temperature returned to homeostasis, and the steam from the tea floated from the cup. She stretched out her hand as the light faded, grabbing the ceramic handle. It was warm to the touch. *Odd.* She brought it to her lips, sipping cautiously. *Also hot. As it should be?* She turned to Ted, her arm around him as she leaned into his shoulder.

"Tedward, if you can hear me, please grab that tea," she pleaded. "It's right in front of you. None of this is real."

His breathing steadied as he leaned forward, his hand fumbling around in the dark, grabbed hold of a cup clattering atop the table before bringing it to his lips, pushing it forward until the liquid poured into his mouth.

"Ted, do you want to talk about it?" she asked.

His head turned slowly to face her; eyes gaped open. Fear in his eyes, like a little puppy, awaiting punishment from its master, or that of a little baby boy, gentle spirit, and a want of nothing but safety, but all he ever got was abuse. Yes. Those were the eyes she saw. She couldn't see much of anything else. The only light now in the room was the shimmering moonlight, reflecting through the snow-filled clouds.

"No," he said, turning his head back to the table. "And yes."

She placed her head on his shoulder. "I'm right here. I'll listen when you're ready to talk, but right now, just drink."

Ted took another sip and placed the cup, clamoring as it struck the table. He took a large gulp of air, and choked on it, drawing in another breath, and did the same, choking on it. She felt his body shake, not just with the sudden movements of the breath, but his shoulders were trembling as he stared at another living nightmare.

Another tragic symptom of his condition she didn't understand how to deal with. But over the last several months now, she knew when he was experiencing a nightmare in the real world, where he can't tell the past from the present. The nightmares were so vivid, no one could tell the difference, and perhaps only someone who dealt with something similar to him would be able to pull him up from this living Hell.

Of course, it didn't help that he didn't sleep more than half an hour a night. That alone can't be healthy and was most likely only making it worse. She saw his shirt breathing in and out, as he coughed. She held herself away from him to see that his hands covered his face. *Tears.* He was crying.

"Hush," she spoke softly. She wrapped her arm around him, pulling his body into hers, his head resting on her shoulder. His moist tears wet her dress. "There, there. Tell me what's on your mind when you're ready to." Her hand brushed through his hair as he continued to sob.

"It's hopeless," he whimpered. "It's hopeless."

"What's hopeless?" she asked.

"Everything was pointless," he sobbed.

"What's pointless?" she asked.

"War is coming. It's inevitable," he sobbed. "I don't—" he choked. "I don't want to fight again."

"No one's forcing you to fight, Tedward. I won't ask that of you," she spoke softly. "You've done enough for us already. You don't need to fight anymore."

"But what if—but what if—" he couldn't bring himself to finish the question.

"If it comes here, it will come here," she replied. "Such is the nature of the world we live in. We can buy peace for a time. And war will return once that season of peace is over. There is no cure for war. It will come when it's time. It's inevitable."

Ted gasped for air, silently holding her tightly. "Then does that mean—" his voice trailed off again.

"What are you thinking Ted?" She knew he was going to start asking tough questions. Questions she had only a cursory knowledge of how to deal with.

"There was a man once," he began. "He gave me something. Something dear, and something I long to forget was ever a gift, and here I am, throwing that gift aside."

"What did he give you?" she asked of him. A probing question, and a question that needed some elaboration. Over this past year, he spoke of horrors, of his friends now lost, but never before was there a mention of a man, and on so vague. Another layer, another mask, another façade to his personality slowly coming undone. It's a shame really that this was even necessary. Sadness. Bitterness. Isolation. Hopelessness.

It reminded her of a short story, one that held merit, for one born into a world of Hell. Filled with so much violence and grit:

The soldier stood at the gate of heaven, and his head was downcast at the gate. Said he to the Lord, "Sir, do you have room enough for me? I don't need much. Just a space. I understand if your house is full, but I thought I'd ask all the same."

The gate didn't open.

"Sir," he spoke again unto the Lord. "There isn't much food elsewhere. Nor shelter. Nor good company. If there isn't enough in your house, would you just say so. I'd hate to keep bothering you like this."

The soldier's head remained downcast. Unable to bring himself to face whatever should open that gate. He was not worthy. He was not good. He was not good company. He was not even worth mentioning. He knew this. But he thought to ask all the same. What harm was that? But the fact remained, that there wasn't one good thing about this soldier.

Knowing all the dead he left in his wake. Knowing all the crimes, and pillaging he'd done to accomplish the mission, and to make it home, who would dare open their home to him. The history would follow him, to the end of his days.

He was tormented by grief. One might even suggest that he was in a living Hell. The war was no longer on the field, and his weapon wasn't a gun. The war was now within the confines of his own mind, and this time, he had nothing to defend himself with.

"Sir. I will leave you now, and never return. I'm so sorry to bother you."

The soldier never looked up, only did what soldier's do, about-faced, and turned. Walking slowly, defeated as the man was not fond Hell's gates, and whatever guarded those gates would gladly receive him, regardless of what his past had done.

And the gate opened behind him. He dared not turn, dared not look. Only bad things would happen should he even think about looking upon the face of the Lord.

The gate slammed shut behind him, and footsteps drew near, and said, "Turn and look upon my face."

The soldier turned, and slowly, reluctantly dared to look upon the face of the Lord. "Sorry to bother you," the solder said.

And the Lord replied, "Come here, will you, there is plenty enough to eat inside, plenty of room. You've already paid your due to Hell."

"I don't know what it was he gave me, all those years ago, after the fires, and after he—" he trailed off, weeping harder into her shoulder. "After he died."

His body slid forward onto her lap, crying like a little child. Her hand rubbed his back as he wept. "There, there. Tell me what you want to tell me, and here it will stay. It will not leave my lips. Whatever you say will stay in this room. Ted, do you trust me?"

"You're the only one, the only one living I trust," he answered.

"Then tell me, what happened to those you did trust?"

He turned, she could feel his body reluctantly turning to face her, and her hand rested on his belly as he stared coldly at the ceiling. His arm swayed on the ground, and the other now covered his eyes, hiding tears, but there was no hiding it from her. She already knew.

"It was supposed to be a training exercise. Nothing more," he breathed heavily. "They were my friends. I learned everything from them. Everything was supposed to be a dud, blanks, nothing that would kill anybody, but I knew when one of my friends stepped on a claymore, which was supposed to have a laser to sensor failure, but no. They didn't care at all. They set off real claymores." She saw his fingernails scratching his forehead, drawing blood. "They hunted us like dogs, sending us scattering in all directions. At the end of it, I still remember my squad hanging in there with me to the end. And she, she told me to find the light. She told me to live.

"But is this really living? I barely sleep. Still, I can't sleep. Still, I have nightmares pushing in through my senses, triggering these flashbacks that I can't tell are real or—" he trailed back into weeping yet again. "Yesterday, at the café, it happened again. I saw her face, one last time with a smile, one of the few smiles we ever shared, before we realized we were born in Hell, and our parents were demons and devils. And demons and devils can only spawn devils and devils worse than they were."

Jennifer's hand stretched over his as he continued, softly resting. She felt it; empathy, the absolute despair he was born in. She remembered what he said: *I didn't have a choice*, and the only choice she knew now that he ever had, was *who* to kill.

"And again, at the orchestra, I saw his arm, severed right in front of me. Saved me. And he's gone. Dead. Their remains are gone, nothing left of them, not even the records. I know. I've looked. There isn't a trace of where we came from, who our real parents were. Just tools of war.

"And what pisses me off the most is that we sacrificed everything, not by our own choice. Everything. We fought for peace, and they held on to it for what? Ten years? They couldn't even manage ten years without pissing on it." His hand on the ground tensed as did his body on her lap. "And Jeff Clemens is here, alive, and doing well, reminding me of the piece of shit he is!"

Her other hand rested on his skin, and his shirt lifted, allowing her to touch his belly. She didn't know exactly why she wanted to touch it, but out of the sake of old curiosity; this part of him was never exposed to her, and yet, her fingers touched wounds, hardened scars underneath the surface. Scars like gashes, malformed healing underneath with previously broken bones which were forced to mend incorrectly. Dots of scars, which she imagined were bullet holes. To think he survived even that, was astonishing.

"He shot her, and him, and me," he rambled on. His sobs subsided, and he continued to rest on her lap.

"Does he know who you are?" She breathed heavily, hoping against hope that Jeffrey didn't recognize him, for at this point, she was certain she was looking at someone who believed himself to be better off dead. He had no family, and she knew isolation, he was like an orphan, lost and alone.

But you're with me now. I won't leave you. I'm sorry.

"Yes."

And that was that. Nothing could truly be done about it now.

"And he recognizes that you are—you?"

"Yes," he spoke softly. "And it terrifies me. More than the nightmares because I know Hell isn't far behind. I don't know when, and I can't predict it. I am going insane. I want to—I want to—"

"As I said, nothing leaves this room." She already knew how horrifying the truth was, and that whatever Uncle Sam did was unforgiveable. She remembered a quote from her uncle, 'Patriotism is supporting your country when it deserves it,' *and I am certain it never did.*

"I want to kill him so much. He took them from me. He took their futures. We were promised we'd go home."

"Tedward," she leaned forward, removing his hand from his bleeding forehead, and sat him up. "Stay here," he held her hand as she rose from the couch. She walked over to the kitchen; his hand didn't let go.

"Don't leave me. *Please*," he pleaded. She could tell he desperately tried to hang on to something; something worth holding on to.

"I'm not leaving you," she promised, smiling back at him. "Trust me."

His hand slipped out of her hands as she walked away, turning into her kitchen, and pulled out a washcloth, soaking it in hot water. She wringed it over the sink, walking back to him. *He needs something much more than reality, he needs God. But how can a man like this accept a God like mine? Or perhaps, did You curse him? Or is he like the blind man, and You made him live this way so that all may know?*

Extending her hand over to him, she wiped the blood off his forehead. She leaned forward, taking her hand behind his head, nudging him to bend down, and she planted a soft kiss upon his forehead. "Tedward. You're mine. Do you hear me? Don't forget that. And I am yours. Don't forget that, for I won't. Whatever you see coming for you, I'll bear it with you. I'll be right by your side. Do you hear me? Where you go, my heart will be also. Do you hear me?"

"And when you die?" he asked, and she felt his arms around her, holding her close as he breathed heavily.

"Did I misspeak? Where you are, my heart will be also. Even if my body dies, my heart lives on, and it will be with you. Just as God is with me, so too am I with you."

He became flustered like a child. Averting his eyes away from her. She imagined Ted felt much like that soldier did when faced with the prospect facing the divine, or the accursed.

"Now, do you understand?"

His body trembled into her, whimpering, crying, more tears he had to cry, and with recent developments, his angst must be through the roof.

He barely managed, "I do."

Chapter 14 Two Front War

It's been a month now. Since my last fight, that is. As I pen this, I still hear their screams scratching like nails on the chalkboard. They refuse to stop screeching in my ears in the night. I take my meds. I go to therapy, but even that isn't quite enough, now, is it? I can't even look my wife in the face anymore. It's times like these I feel completely, utterly alone. My body is a disgrace and is better off floating upriver somewhere. If my wife found out all the things I did, she'd leave me. And who could blame her? I'm a terribly rotten person. I'm defective. Always have been. And the messed-up part about it, is I let them take the blame.

***

Sam Snells walked into the briefing room, escorted by his Press Secretary. The dark room was filled with chatter at the Pentagon. Secretary of Defense Johnson, and the General of the Armies, Admiral of the Navy, as well as many intelligence officers of both branches stood at attention at the table.

"At ease," he said, glancing at the files on the table.

Everyone sat down promptly as he walked over to his seat.

"Johnson, give me the situation straight," he demanded, tapping his pen on the table. The secretary stood behind him.

"Admiral Smith?"

"Russian fleets have stalled three-thousand knots east of our borders. Carriers, including mega carriers in the rear, destroyers up front. No submarines detected," Smith stood up. He could hardly be seen with his dark skin. "Chinese fleets are still advancing. Similar makeup to the Russians. Again, no submarines."

The admiral adjusted the ships on the map, indicating where the fleets were.

"Flight capacity?" Snells replied.

Not one to show his feelings, but the truth was, he was terrified. Russia or China was not someone to be trifled with. But to add both together was to invite catastrophe. There wasn't going to be much opportunity for defense if they're working together. China, he understood. He didn't negotiate well with China. That was on him. But Russia? Why were they converging on him?

"Intelligence suggests they have lots of fuel to run a long war. Each carrier is sufficiently supplied with Chengdu-j20s and Su-57s," Smith explained. "Intelligence suggests China will attack the West Coast first. It also suggests that Russia will wait for an opportunity."

"What kind of opportunity?" Snells asked.

"For us to abandon the East Coast," General Gernardt answered.

"What options do we have at our disposal?"

"Well, we can't just assault Russia, despite knowing their intentions," Johnson said. "And just an outright air bombing over waters to halt China's fleets is problematic without advancing our own fleets."

"We could advance with our own fleets and marines, fighter pilots on standby for refueling with strategically anchored carriers," Gernardt suggested.

"Submarines," Snells adjusted his tie. "Why aren't there submarines?"

"Neither radar nor sonar detected any," Smith answered.

"I don't like this," Snells stared at the map of ships circling around the United States.

It was possible to mask the existence of submarines especially hiding underneath fleets that size. But there was someone researching technology that would make submarines impossible to detect, regardless of how close they were. Radar and sonar wouldn't be able to pick that up, even without interference with other vessels. And now that research developer was MIA. MIA and location narrowed down to Boston where he could be doing God knows what. That research developer was Ghost. *And if China and Russia both had it, it could mean only one thing. Ghost was behind all of this.* He sighed. *So, you're not as innocent as it would seem.*

"Did your intelligence officers ask why there were no submarines?"

"Negative," Smith replied.

Shit. I was too thorough, and discipline of our troops shot out the window.

"We have to assume they have submarines," he leaned back in his chair. "I didn't want to have to do this again, but we may need to call on Black Eagle."

"I would advise against that," Johnson said. "Not a good look to be using mercenaries to do our bidding, fight our wars on our territory. Mr. President, you have the election coming up to think about. Using Black Eagle is going to come across as weak, and your opposing party will use that against you."

Why is that the thing you zeroed in on? Ah. Because if I don't win, he risks losing his job.

"Then what do you suggest?" Snells asked.

"Reinforce the borders, call upon the reserves. Push training for the new recruits and get them out in the field stat," he answered. "Prepare the defenses and swing back with a counter strike with stealth bombers once they reach the border."

"You're suggesting we leave the door open?"

"What can I say, I have an open-door policy,"

Snells frowned, tapping his finger on the table.

A phone rang. The secretary stepped outside as Snells was considering his options.

"Either option is not good for publicity," Snells replied. "But that's not what's important."

Gernardt frowned at him, shaking his head. Smith did much the same. "Either way, it can't be good, and there is no good option here. For if we advance, and we make good on their bluff, there's a chance those submarines are hidden well, and God only knows what kind of arms they have. We might as well be walking into a—"

"Mr. President," the secretary said from the door. Snells turned his head to her. "The First Lady is here to speak with you."

He sighed, putting his hands on his thighs to stand. "Five mikes."

He stepped into the brightly lit hall and his wife stood giddily with her clipboard. "How does the planning go?"

"Fine," he shook his head. "What is it? I don't have time for whatever this is."

Andrea looked around the halls, ensuring no one else was within earshot. "Now dear, that's no way to talk to me, now, is it?" She frowned. Grabbing him firmly by the collar, pulling him down. Her warm breath caressed his ear. "Now, you are going to do precisely as Johnson says. Or else Colton comes knocking down our bedroom door tonight. You understand what that means don't you?"

What?

He looked her in the eye. Not knowing the purpose for such an intrusion was bothersome, and now, here she was telling him how to do the job he was elected for. *How does she know who Colton is?*

"Oh, don't give me that!" She berated him. "Go in there, be a good little boy."

His heart raced. Here he was, forced to think on the fly. Colton. He was a rabid dog that bit onto his arm, and refused to let go, and called all the other dogs to roost, biting and twisting his arm until he chose the play catch. But now, the ball was in his hand, and he didn't throw it, he may end up like Jezebel, feasted on dogs right below the window of the White House. It was generally assumed the president of the United States of America was the most powerful man on the planet, and now, Snells was certain that couldn't be farther from the truth.

"So that means—"

"Yes. Johnson is one of us, so Colton will know. It is part of his plan. Now, do as you're told, or you won't live to see tomorrow." She smirked as if she didn't just threaten him. "Now, you're a busy man. I won't hold you up anymore my dearest."

A couple of officers walked past them, talking among one another in hushed tones. Andrea walked down the other end of the hall.

It was this moment he realized he was nothing but a puppet. And there was no room for personal agency. He simply had to do what he was told. When he was told.

Chapter 15 Mommy

Outraged parents show up in droves at the CA State Court House after Sandra Mills (38), was accused of alleged sexual assault of her child, Mark Mills (13) after she gave birth to another child. Picket signs requesting justice, shouting obscenities as Sandra Mills was seen entering the courthouse. After several months of deliberations, the Grand Jury is reportingly giving the verdict.

***

Several months passed into the early summer winds, and Ted found himself walking again through the park of his town, Waltham. The trees shaded him from the oppressive heat, wavy heat waves wiggling up from the stone slabs in the ground. His sneakers kicked forward as his hands were resting in his pockets, defying the rule they told him all those years ago. There were couples coming out, holding hands, and he paid special attention to the children at their sides, all joyous smiles, closed eyes, and bright teeth, despite the deformities of missing teeth.

Remembering the day Clemens knocked all his molars out, and they weren't ready to come out. *What did I ever do to him?*

He strode off the path, taking off his shoes, and folding his socks into them, holding them carefully as he attempted to settle down. Finding a trunk, he leaned down against it, back against the rough exterior. There were couples, families, children, dogs barking—oh, that gave him a new kind of thrill. *Damn dogs.*

His hand rested on the moist blades of grass underneath him, furling his hands through them like Jennifer did to his hair during his last emotional break down. *Been a few months. Nothing triggered it. Not yet. It's bound to happen soon. Should I be here?* Thoughts rattled his fatigued mind, eyelids drooping down, slowly over his eyes as he faded out of consciousness...

***

The night was dark. The moon was out, crickets, roaches scurrying across the floor, rats clawing at the dreaded walls. He bent his back forward.

A pain jolted in his wrist. Metal restraints. "I see. I can feel pain here. This must be the time before they stuck me in that damned electric chair!"

"Now, now," said a calm, familiar, and caring voice. If anything at all could be said about that woman, Nakamura, those definitely weren't it. He still couldn't see anything, couldn't feel anything except the steel cuff around his wrist, and his—his ankles. "A good little boy doesn't use foul language like that."

He gasped, heart pounding. "I can't—I can't breathe." He exhaled heavily, rattling the chains tied to the cuff around his wrist, and the bedframe. He kicked up, the muscles tensed, cracking the bone in his ankle. "No! No! No! Get away!"

The mattress beneath him squealed as added weight pressed down on it. A firm weight. Next to him. He can't tell what it is. A monster. Yes. A fitting word for one such as her.

"But why would I do that, baby boy?" She asked.

More pressure weighed in on his other side, and tentacles for hair framed his face, black, horrid things, scratching and cutting the sides of him. His body tensed up, blood cooling down rapidly, restricting his movement. Rapid breaths, exhaling and puffing his chest. Sweat covered his wrists, and it felt like the air left the room, none to breathe in, and suffocate. With wide open eyes, he saw nothing. Total darkness. Absolute emptiness. He felt tears streaming down his face, gritting them as her warm breath, came to him, breathing that horrid stench of rotten air, like a monster trapped in their own cave, unable to come out.

Clenching his teeth. Gasping for breath. Muscles frozen in place like petrified wood. No. It would be no mistake to say, in this moment, his body finally gave way to the horror inside his mind, and he too was empty. But why did any of this happen?

Slithers' familiar, tormented scream echoed in his ears, the nails scratching inside him, like nails on a chalkboard.

"Shut up! Shut up! Shut up, Demon Bitch!" came another familiar voice, a voice he hated, almost more than he hated the woman breathing down his neck, drooling over him. Clemens.

"Hush little baby, don't you cry," Nakamura sang.

"No! Stop it! Get away!" the damned nursery rhyme was supposed to bring calmness to them, but it only presented sheer terror for what followed.

The monster's ice-cold hands touched his belly, lifting his shirt as she continued to sing.

"Please. Don't touch me!"

He heard Slither's howling in agonizing pain. "Don't touch me. No. No. No!" It was like nails on a chalkboard.

Another voice. But not the voice he recognized resting above him. Clemens. "Shut. Up."

He heard a slap in the corner. And Slithers was silent. Another monster. An evil person. A wretched being beyond saving.

"Shush," she coddled him, and he felt the weight of her body on his. He couldn't move, not with her on him, not with the cuffs around his wrists and ankles. Even if his muscles were allowed to move, the terror freezing everything in place as he felt her cold hand touching his cheek, turning his frozen neck, and he gazed into this monster's eyes, cold dead eyes, almond shaped. "I'll make you feel good, baby boy."

No.

The drool coated him, coalescing around him as a barbed tongue scratched his lips.

***

He jolted up right, head sweating, arms forward to protect himself. He gazed forward, and the rest of the people enjoying their day like they should, like good little boys and girls. He folded his hands together, and pulled his knees to his chest, looking down at the space between his legs. So long had it been since that night. That horrible, wretched night. He felt chills running up his spine as if he was there, in that moment. But the dream, it hadn't been as vivid as the rest. It faded, almost.

He noticed the marching footsteps of runs. He turned his head to the left of the common, and a large group, say two-scores of people, men and women in ROTC shirts running in between groups of people, marines, it looked like, with that boring beige hat, rimming in a perfect circle as if everything was all fine, and it was an honor to serve one's country. He studied each individual.

You're all gonna die. And what good will it do anyone really?

They were of different body shapes, sizes, ethnic groups, all running in with one another, but there was one woman who was above the rest, it seemed. Very fit for her age, and quite frankly, it would seem, faster than everyone else. She was an Asian woman, paler than the rest by a margin, and those—

"So," an unfamiliar, but calm voice behind his tree interrupted his thoughts. He turned abruptly, and he saw that same woman at the café in the winter. "I've seen you before." *Yes, I know.* "What brings you to this neck of the woods?"

He looked up to the woman, suspicious of her. This would be the second time he's seen this woman, and the second time both people seemed aware of one another's existence. The only difference last time was he was not out in the open. Alone. He could run from whatever he suspected this person wanted of him, but that would only raise questions that had no answer.

"Good enough spot just to sit. Does one have to have a reason to sit in one particular place, or must he have a reason for every little thing that he does?"

"A sharp mind, just like mine, do you care if I have a seat?" she asked, flipping her black braid behind her. She had an accent. It wasn't one he was around recently, so he couldn't quite remember where he heard it from.

"Don't let me stop you, I was just leaving anyway. You can have it," he said, unrolling his socks over his feet.

"Now, I didn't mean to pull you up from your spot. You seemed so peaceful,"

Ha! No, I wasn't.

"It's quite all right. As I said, I was just leaving."

The constant questions and polite nagging of this woman was bothersome. She didn't at all appear to be someone worth mentioning, but here she is, clearly very important, but to what degree, and to whom. Who was she to take such interest in the likes of him?

"Come on, have a chat with me."

"Why? I don't know you, nor you me." *What is your purpose here? This is no chance meeting.* He smiled softly.

"Why, how do you get to know someone without chatting with them? If you want to know someone, you introduce yourself, and you talk to them. Find out what makes them click, and if amiable, offer the same in return." She grinned back, offering a handshake, almost like a business transaction. "I'm Blanka, nice to meet you. And you are?"

"Ted." He reluctantly shook her hand.

A dangerous place to be, out in the public. Trouble is, you simply just can't run, especially when someone has your attention like this.

"Ted, pleasure is all mine, I'm sure."

You have no idea how right you are. Now, what do you want?

"I have a few questions for you," *there it is.* "You see, there was an incident out in the edge of the financial District in Downtown Boston about a year ago. A number of people died, and a car was totaled."

He vaguely remembered. They tried to mug him. Wrong person to try to do that with.

"Do you know anything about that?"

Shit. It's the police. But why are they asking me?

"I know nothing about the incident, Blanka," he lied.

"Oh, but surely you would have seen it on the news,"

You are a god-awful interrogator. If it was anyone else, the trail is cold. No one would remember the exact details. Let alone a news story from over a year ago. Damn you. "No offense, detective,"

"Oh, I'm not a detective."

You lying sack of shit.

"Well, the news is dated if anything else, but I have no memory of it. Fairly, the news is saturated with doomsday conspirators and world leaders pissing on everyone."

"Sadly, you are correct. And what pray tell, are your thoughts on that?" She finally sat down.

Good. You're making me nervous. "Everyone's gonna die. We all do someday, right? Better sooner than later, I'd wager."

"I take it you're a betting man?"

"I'm not betting on anything right now, but curiosity has gotten the better of me, dear," he turned to her eyes, gazing into them, looking for a hint of deception, but he couldn't find any. Either, she is an exceptionally good liar, or not one at all, which means, she might not be the police.

"Why ask a stranger about a criminal act of which occurred over a year ago that anyone not involved would have no memory of?"

"You never know what someone might say about something so obscurely meaningless, wouldn't you agree?" She chuckled, sharing the trunk. "You seem terribly formal, or is this just the way you hold yourself, *Ted*?"

The way she said his name sent a shiver up his spine.

"Very formal indeed, I'd not be a shrewd businessman if I was anything but formal," he replied. "But I doubt that is the real answer behind your motive for asking me such a, as you put, meaningless scenario."

"Perhaps you are right, and yet, perhaps you are a horrible gambler," she smiled, tapping on the tree behind them. "You see, I'm a bit of a betting gal myself. I bet a lot of things, sometimes I wager money, other times I wager people and their independent relationships with one another. Children especially." *You're one of those people.* "But then again, lives are affected by the games I play, and perhaps in the same game of business you play, enriching some and pissing on others."

I'm glad I'm not the only one who is not entirely formal.

"And what is your point in all this? Come on, you're leaving me in suspense." *Why are you coming to me specifically with these inquiries?*

"I suppose you'll have your answer at the proper time," she removed herself from the tree, standing up tall. He put his shoes back on before standing up, looking up at her chin. *You are standing far too close to me.*

"And how will you present to me my answer to your inane inquiries?"

"I'll present to them at such a time fitting for the occasion. Until then, farewell, Ted," she said before turning away.

"And if you have no way of finding me, what then?" he asked.

"Let's just say a little birdie told me our paths will cross again, real soon. Much sooner than you'd like, and it will be, how do you say it here, *tragic*."

Damn you.

He watched her walk away, her skirt swaying in the wind like feathers, and head back to the path. Her pace was brisk, faster than he walked, even. And he was not a slow walker.

Who are you? You don't remind me of someone I'd met at Black Eagle all those years ago? Is it you I sensed watching me?

Chapter 16 Suspicions

Numerous power outages have been reported throughout the community of Boston. Engineers have been working on the issue, and stated, "The breakers are short circuiting." Still, there is no reported reasons as to why the circuit breakers are short circuiting, and this has the engineers perplexed. The engineers have replaced the circuits with each instance, but no long-term solution has been proposed. These shortages leave Boston in the dark at night.

Crime rates have not been affected by the shortages; however, Detective Henny with the Boston Police Department stated there is a correlation between the short circuit breaking and missing person reports. Since the problem remains unidentifiable and there are no suspects, Detective Henny advised to travel in the dark in groups, supervised.

***

Spadero gazed at the sky, his suit and shirt tucked tightly, pants firmly pressed, wrinkle free. *Fucking congressmen!* Allow some of them to be elected, they said, it'll be fun they said.

Yeah, right. Making the nights longer just to hear themselves speak. What might they say, if I told them their opinions don't actually mean anything, and we just let them talk to make themselves feel like they have any sway? Yeah, even Sander wouldn't let that slide. As laid back as he is.

The night sky was brimming with excitement, for once. Someone finally paid the electricians to do their damned jobs and fix the power circuits that keep getting shorted out. Generators were still running, so that's a good sign, but times are tough in the empire, and still, he had this little rat to deal with, and he hadn't been able to find time to get to it.

It's almost like these damn Threckets know he's a piece of the puzzle. I really should just let Culain deal with it so I can get on with this manhunt and put it to rest. And finally, the mystery can go die for all I care. Where was that bar again? When did they frequent it?

He remembered Tuesdays, but he didn't remember the name of the bar. Foolish of him for not writing it down.

He walked down the streets, into the hotel lobby, yawning of course, got to make it look good. Briskly walking up the vestibule, pressing the button to open the elevator, as his other hand remained in his pocket. He needed to plan further details with them, now that, supposedly, he had more time to capture this damn rat.

Stepping inside the elevator, he leaned back as he watched the doors shut. No one entered on the way up. *Good. Let's keep it this way. Don't want to accidently make a corpse in here, now do I?*

The elevator took him all the way to the top in silence. Just what he needed after that fraud of a congressman.

He walked down the hall after being released from the horizontally challenged canister, to Culain's door, knocking on it firmly with his fist.

The door opened to an irate Culain. *Good. Keep him angry. Keep him waiting.*

"Come in," he snarled.

He didn't need to be asked. Spadero pushed past him, and took a spot on the couch, resting his arms nonchalantly around it.

"I can't really wait any longer for this, Ilya," he said to the white-haired Russian. "I really need you to pay attention to those alarms and warn Culain promptly. I need you four to—" he scanned the room. Alexander was opening a beer, Ilya was staring out the window for a long-lost answer to a question she didn't realize she had, and Culain was shutting the door. "Where's Blanka?"

"She'll be running in shortly. Heaven knows from where," Alexander burped.

"So unrefined," Ilya replied to the question designed specifically for her. "Yes, I got it, but we can't be everywhere at once."

"You all are going to owe me after this," Spadero shook his head. "Do you have any idea how difficult it is taking orders form two heads of Administration? Do you? In my case, it's actually three, and I must manage everything and everyone else, and I'm about to blow a gasket."

Culain shook his head as if he didn't understand. "Pissant. Don't you think we're doing everything we can to give you the time to get to our target? And what do you mean, multiple heads of Administration? This should only be coming from Sander."

"I have my orders from both Admin Colton Cancer, and orders from Adam Sander, and of course the Head of the House," he scoffed. "What else would I be talking about, you potato munchin' bastard?"

"At least the insult was original," Culain shook his head. "You Americans always want something. You will get what the Administration says is due, nothing more. We serve the Administration of Camelot. You are no different." He scowled, tapping his arm with an impatient index finger.

"My point is, I'm going out of my way to help you with this missing piece of the puzzle, which isn't my problem," he snapped.

"The Holy Grail is missing along with Pandora's Box. It is everyone's problem," Ilya scolded. "I will do what I can on my end, just make sure you do your damned job."

"Who are you to give me orders? You're in my territory." He tilted his head back and faced her.

"We are of the British branch; you are of the American. We outrank you, anyway. The fact that you're taking orders from Sander is a sign that he trusts you of all Americans to get the job done, and report to him, and to us alone." She turned and walked to him. The room grew cold, ice-like veins protruded from her arms and face, poking him in the chest with her icy finger.

Few can play with elements. Flexing much, Ilya?

"The only reason we now trust you is because Culain ballsed it up, and," she pointed her finger at him, "fuck you, too!" She returned her finger to Spadero's chest. "And we have no choice, but we all serve the same cause, or are you likened to a traitor?"

He didn't need to hold on to it for long, but this was a stressful situation when the threads of the world could come undone. What did the world ever do for him? Just force him to work twenty-hour days, and he really only needed one job. And he was forced to work two jobs to put up a front for the Administration, and make sure the appropriate bills were passed and shut down to keep the normies in their place. Oh, the things the normies would go off about if they knew what really happened behind these closed doors.

The door bolted open. Blanka was giddy, smiling from ear to ear. She was the only one of the four that smiled. She closed the door behind her and took off her jacket, kicking off her shoes, bolting to the refrigerator, pulled out a can of beer. She cracked it open, taking a sip. "Ah, much, much better."

"And where were you coming from?" Culain snapped, locking the door.

"Off in a little charming place north of here, actually. Waltham. Ever hear of it?" She leaned against the counter, her beer off to the side as she placed one leg over the other.

"What were you doing there?" Spadero asked, turning his attention away from Ilya and her icy finger.

"Piss off, peasant!" Culain snapped, grabbing a cup off the table and walking it to the sink.

"Oh, Spadero, when did you get here?" Blanka chugged the can of beer, crushed it with her fingers and tossed it to the waste basket. She opened the door to grab another.

"I've been here." His eyes narrowed as he leaned forward, hands folded atop each other.

"I see, well, I didn't see you when I came in, so, might as well have just surprised me," she replied.

"So, it would seem," he said, rather rudely.

"Hey! Mind your own business!"

"No, Culain, I wasn't done scolding him for his blatant disregard for the importance of this mission," Ilya replied softly. *There's a codeswitch if ever there was one.*

Blanka chuckled, one arm resting over her belly as she flipped her hair behind her, the open can, the beer sloshing around inside.

"What's so funny?" Spadero asked.

"Never mind that. Blanka, what were you doing?" Culain asked.

"Spadero, you are so easy to poke fun at. Forgive our little clan here." She swayed back and forth, sipping. "Ah. That is some good beer, if I do say so myself. So, anyway, what was I doing? Oh," she snapped her finger before slamming the can on the counter. "Culain, fuck you very much, by the way,"

"Oh, piss off!" He retorted, cleaning the cup.

"I swear, Culain, how do you manage to piss everyone off within a matter of minutes," Alexander shook his head, leaning against one of the bedroom doors.

"How was I supposed to know?" He threw a fork at Alexander, who caught it in one hand.

"Can we get back on topic please?" Spadero shook his hand, slamming a fist on his knee. "You animals."

"The only animal here, is you. Surely, even our little rat out there has a little more humanity than you," Blanka stated. "Our rat, one little rat hunted by five large cats for reasons we ought not know, but do cats have any other reason for playing around with their yarn at all? Not this cat. I find not the joy. But, since I can't go home, I'll find some enjoyment out of it."

"What are you babbling on about?" Culain interjected.

"I was in a rather bumbling city today, lots of ROTC guys showing up, running their rounds, no doubt. Mother Russia will have their fun with them. Isn't that right, Ilya?" Blanka sneered.

It wasn't a question, and clearly it was in reference to the events unfolding overseas, lots of which wasn't public knowledge, or rather, wasn't supposed to be. Spadero was thinking about the scope of the prospect of WWIII. Something so large involving so many pieces to fall in line could only be the work of the Caster's Administration, and yet, no one thought to tell him. A simple oversight like this was bound to go unnoticed, unless there was a faint possibility someone else was pulling strings *outside* the Administration.

"Waltham it was, and from what I remembered, a man with some scars on his face, and resting back against a tree trunk, resting before bolting upright like someone was going to attack him, and yet, there I was minding my own business when I invited myself to sit next to him."

"What?" Alexander breathed out.

"I'm sorry, I don't understand babble," Culain said, turning to Alex. "Get that beer away from her."

"No." She turned to hide her beer. She chugged it again, crushed it, and gave Alexander the empty can. "Get your own beer." *Two?* "I want another."

"Finish your story in English, and then you can get blackout drunk," said Culain.

"Our little Ghost. A handsome man. Ilya, why didn't you say he was handsome?" she burped.

"She's drunk. And now useless. Get her to bed," Spadero exclaimed.

"Hey. Hey. Hey," Ilya scolded him yet again with the icy finger. "Shut yer American trap mouth!" She turned to Culain. "Take her to bed. And don't be...Irish."

"I don't wanna go to bed." She burped again. "I'm fine."

"What is that supposed to mean?" he grabbed Blanka before she stumbled back into the refrigerator for another beer. "Seriously, you're such a light weight. It was only two beers. What did you have before you came here?"

"She's drunk off something else, clearly," Alexander snorted.

"Clearly if she took all this time to get here," Ilya sighed as she sat. "We need her sobered," she turned a glaring eye to Spadero as Culain walked the drunk into her room. *Don't be Irish? What does that even mean?* "What did you come here for anyway?"

"Things may have changed since Blanka ran into the Ghost, but I was coming here with a plan on how to reach him and get him alone. Too bad Blanka ran into him first because it might complicate things a little bit," he replied.

"We know that," she said, condescendingly. "That's why we asked for your help, to uncomplicate it, but right now, that seems like it's a little out of your wheelhouse. Look, what we need is more information about where he's coming from, and possibly, at nighttime, get him alone. That is what we need. We don't need to involve his friends if we can help it. What they don't know won't kill them."

Shaking his head, he stood. "Well, this was a waste of time. Tell me what she says when she's sober will you? I might need that information. I need to know exactly what she said, and what he said, so I can come up with a good ruse to get him alone or invite him over for drinks."

He briskly strode his long legs out to the door, unlocking it to depart.

"We will feed you information but be kind when you talk with her again. I'll have her call you," Alexander said.

"Sure thing." Spadero slammed the door behind him.

Chapter 17 Sakura Riley

China is taking a page out of Russia's book and acquiring other countries along their borders, expanding to include Vietnam, Cambodia, and Thailand. Sources remain unclear as to why these nations were allowed to be purchased through Chinese influence and alter their state lines.

When asked, Press Secretary Jenna Walters said: It is concerning that these acquisitions are happening as supplies dwindle within our country. We assure the American people, we are being prepared to the highest degree to ensure our nation's survival, and to reopen trade with Russia and China.

***

It was a nice hot summer day, a day to be outside, and muggy, yes, that is what she was used to down in the southern ramparts of Atlanta, but here she was, inside, in the cold room, with her roommate for whom she didn't really much care for, having the AC on full blast, chilling the room. Not nice at all.

Inside, she sat at this desk, looking out the window, left one slightly ajar, despite Keisha's protests, who was very loud. She had a squeaky voice that one. Unfortunately for Sakura, she also had a loathing for high pitched noises. After constant nagging, she reluctantly shut the window, allowing the last warmth of the sun to scatter. *Really, the nerve of these liberal northerners.*

Her English textbook was placed meaningfully atop her desk. She was reading it in preparation for class the following morning, but something was eating at her. She wasn't quite sure what it was. Her raven hair wasn't properly pulled back, as a respectable future officer should, just like her mother, her birth mother, that is, not like her adopted mother. Of course, she didn't complain about the Rileys; she was truly thankful for them taking her in and allowing her to follow in her birth mother's footsteps. Truly.

Sakura loved her mother and her father, what little memory she had of them. They departed from this world at least a decade ago. Shortly in their projects from securing some semblance of world peace that she had the opportunity to enjoy, but now, it was not the time to be comfortable, but to secure it. It had to be defended at all costs, whatever cost it was.

Whatever was paid to secure peace last time, she would be proud to pay such a thing again. Whatever it took, so her children and their children could prosper, just like the USA had the opportunity to do for these last ten years.

Her dreaded roommate turned on the news. Again. She was now subject to a non-update update. Always the same with the same old news story repeating over and over again. These days, everyone harping on the Russians for wanting to expand their borders, but the reality was, when didn't Russia want to expand their borders. One country sets sanctions, while others refuse, no matter how loud the populace cried. It was all more of the same.

"How can you listen to this? Do you really think anything new could be gleaned from this?" Sakura turned, her arm resting on the back end of her chair, frowning.

"Sakura." Keisha shook her head. "Of course, I know. How can I not know? But as a citizen, I need to know as much information as I can, when it comes available. That's how you avoid ignorance."

"It's the same thing, and it's everywhere."

"And you think that to be any less of a threat to us now?" Keisha challenged. "Anyway, I have to get to class."

Sakura's hands clenched at her side as she watched Keisha leave the room, shutting the door behind her. Keisha was infuriating. Sakura had to turn the tv off, getting rid of the pessimistic, nihilistic news coming her way. It reinforced the thought that she should do something, but while she was here, she could do nothing but study, especially with the sun setting.

World peace. It almost seemed like a distant memory now. Peace was a sort of calm before and after storms, but even the unsettling of the news source, and the content of said news in a world where news was biased. No matter who you listened to, someone was lying right to your face, and laughing as you chose to believe them, or someone else. Who cares who gets hurt? No one died from a lie, right? Not like those harm anyone.

But she remembered something, something from long ago, something her mother said to her, prior to her departure from this world:

"My cutie. Stay young, will you? Peace, it is such a wonderful thing really. Once obtained, it is so precious, and it must be safeguarded, whatever the cost. You can't make an omelet without breaking a few eggs, isn't that what they say? Whatever gets broken gets broken, but you can fix that, should you choose to. When the time comes, you will be expected break a lot of eggs to preserve peace. Can you do that?"

"Yes, Mom. I'll break all the eggs. As many as it takes," Sakura said to herself.

She yawned, putting her textbook back in her backpack for tomorrow. Peering out to the sunset, she decided now was as good a time as ever to go for a nice long run through Boston before the university's curfew.

She peered outside the window, hoping it was a little less muggy outside for her run. Feeling the cool breeze, she hurried outside with her wallet, water, and her phone, just in case. Hurrying down the stairs of the university, she strode off the grounds and into the cross walks, running through the heart of Boston. Her body dashed toward the center really, where many interesting things happened, well, interesting to her at least. For someone living in Boston all of this may very well just be the mundane things for the day to day. After all, she admitted, while interesting to her, these things were of a regular occurrence here.

She ran with long strides, feeling the sweat cake her shirt to her chest, as she came up to the grand church building, she saw a lot of people milling about. She'd never been to a church before. Not where she's from, and the Riley's weren't the religious type, no, not at all. Seemed like interesting things were happening, but she thought it was something or somewhere you went to in the mornings, specifically, very specifically on Sundays. Why Tuesday? Why at night?

She stopped, panting, drinking her water, carefully taking each step as it came, the lactic acid building up in her legs, stiffening them up. *Perhaps now would be a good time to come in, rest. I can leave soon, right? Not like one of those cults.*

"Hello," said a bright man, a little heavy set situated behind a table.

In front of him was a little banner, reading: *Café*. It was decorated with elegant letters, and on the table, markers, and name tags.

"First time?"

"You could say that," she said.

"Oh, you sound just like that other fellow,"

She tilted her head curiously. "Other fellow?"

"Someone who's been coming here. When I first met the guy, Ted's his name, he always said that. 'You could say that,' I mean, it doesn't mean anything really. I just noticed."

The man motioned for her to take a name tag, and so she did, signing her name, *Sakura*, in large letters, large enough to be read, and placed it carefully on her sweat covered shirt. "How did you hear about café?"

She glanced over to the crowd of people heading into a side room, a large open area filled with people intermingling with one another.

"I didn't," she said, gulping down another mouthful of water. "I was just running, and this looked interesting, caught my eye. What is this exactly?"

"It's a Young Adult ministry with Park Street Church, catering to the 20s and 30s. We get a lot of new people around here," he said, pointing inside. "You actually came on a good day. There are refreshments in the fellowship hall, where everyone else is."

"Thanks, I guess I'll let myself in,"

Just as she said that a firm hand grabbed her shoulder from behind.

"Hi, Brian," said the man behind the table.

She turned abruptly, twisting her hand body around and stepped away.

"Whoa," said the man with black hair and a rustic beard, whom she assumed was Brian, as he took and printed his name on his nametag. "Easy, we're all friends here. Newbie?"

"You could say that," she repeated.

As part of some cruel joke she was on the outside of, and wanted desperately to find out, Brian threw his head back in laughter. "You sound just like Ted. What's your name?"

"Sa—Sakura," she pointed at her nametag, barely hiding her stammer. "Just what it says here."

"Where are you from?" he asked, stepping toward her, but not touching. She was allowed to turn on her own as she walked side by side with him into this *fellowship hall*. Nervous, her breathing became shallower as she crossed the threshold.

"I'm from Georgia." She tried to ensure her southern accent was not apparent, especially up here; however, the movies never really got those right.

"What brings you to Boston?" he guided her to the coffee table, and the plastic coffee containers for instant coffee. *Disgusting.* He poured himself a cup, and walked over to the long table, grabbed a plate in his free hand and filled it up with cheese and crackers.

Delicious.

Grabbing a plate herself, and a napkin. *Mustn't appear to be a slob after all.* "I just started at BU, and I am getting ready for an entrance exam. I'm considering ROTC."

"Oh," he said, a smile beaming on his face. Several people walked in, and it wasn't long before some additional chatter came about, assaulting her ears with a few different vocal frequencies. "You may actually want to talk to Ted. He was in the Army himself."

Brian turned his head this way and that, as if looking for someone. No. He definitely was looking for someone. His eyes narrowed, homing in on something. She glanced that direction, and a man, shorter than the woman standing next to him.

"Hey, Ted!" Brian called over the crowd of people.

Both the man and woman turned to them, but the man seemed to take special interest in her, making it a point to make eye contact, and he frowned. Such eye contact, fierce, and unreasonably intense. He looked like she expected she looked while staring at Keisha, irate. Now that she got a look at his face, eyes sunken in as if with no sleep. She didn't see that often, but she did know enough to understand insomnia. There were scars on his face, some parting where his eyebrows were. This was a man who had seen some shit.

The woman had a concerned look on her face, not nearly with the amount of ire the man had, for whatever reason was still a mystery. Sakura could only assume that she would find out, but hopefully when she does, it won't end up a tragedy. She couldn't envision what kind of tragedy he was imagining, but it couldn't be enviable. Such a shame if it ended like that, really.

"Come on, let me introduce you," Brian said rather enthusiastically.

She followed him through the crowd of people, and the closer they got to them, the more anxious it made her. She felt no motivation or desire to be in conversation with this woman, she wasn't the important one; she didn't have any answers to questions she had, but this *Ted* fellow would have interesting answers to some questions, being in the thick of it all at one point or another. Each step was heavier than the last with the weight of anxiety, or lactic acid. She couldn't rightly tell which.

"Ted, this is Sakura. I thought you two should meet," Brian said.

The woman sighed and shook her head rather disapprovingly, like they knew the content of questions for which, none of them had any reason to suspect. But these people, whoever they were, had keen eyes and minds, keener perhaps than her own.

"And what, pray tell Brian, would be the reason to bring Sakura to me, rather than anyone else of this entirely fine event you have scheduled and brought me to?" Ted said. He had a way with words of telling someone rather verbosely, 'Why would I want to talk to this person?' Verbose and formal. "Well, rather, you have this lady to thank for making sure I'm here every week, and not in some ditch elsewhere. One might be fearful that I might be infested with rats eating on my insides. Terribly tasting meal I'm afraid."

Sakura coughed up some water, bowing her head, covering her mouth.

"Well, you speak from the heart, it seems like, good grief," Brian exclaimed, patting Sakura on the back.

"Funny, I thought I was speaking from my lips, but regrettably, that shows you I know nothing about the human anatomy," Sakura looked up to see a sneer across his lips.

"Hi Sakura, please forgive my Tedward, he has a certain habit of words. One might say he often quotes Jane Austen, or even the great Shakespeare." The woman reached down to shake her hand. She clasped both her hands around her free hand, which now had spit all over it. "I'm Jennifer. Pleased to meet you. So, what business have you with my Tedward?"

"Oh, I should mention, she's up here for school for ROTC. I thought Ted would be a good person to talk to about that, no?"

Silence.

Jennifer's eyes drooped down low, shaking her head, obviously disappointed. "Brian, text me next time you want to introduce someone to Tedward. He's very sensitive."

She pointed a finger at Brian. Clearly, she was overprotective of Ted. If he didn't look so war beaten, he would be so cute standing next to a woman so tall. Of course, not in the romantic way but more like a mother protecting her teenaged son from the horrors of the world. But regrettably, coddling someone was far worse than allowing them to make the mistakes themselves.

Jennifer turned her gaze back to Sakura. "Mind what you say." She then turned to the man called Ted, and her mouth approached his ear, whispering something specifically for him to hear. *More coddling.* Jennifer turned over to Brian again. "Come, knave! Let me explain to you why you don't just introduce people to Ted."

She took Brian's hand with force, pulling him away from the conversation, leaving Ted and Sakura alone. Ted's sneer on his lips never faded, watching as Jennifer as she disappeared with Brian into the crowd. If bones could rattle, they'd be rattling inside her.

"So, as you rightly guessed, I am Ted. You, are Sakura, presumably, unless Brian is playing his games again and I need to play twenty-questions to figure out the answer."

"Yes, no games here, no lies here," she said.

"If I had a dollar for every time someone told me that, and lied to my face, I'd be rich." He chuckled, as if it were true.

"Well, I guess, I do have one question. I'm heading into ROTC, and the Army officer training after that. I already have good referrals, but what does being a patriot mean to you? I want to follow in my parent's footsteps as patriots, and they passed before they could tell me what that means."

"A patriot?" he asked, standing up straight, ignoring the fact she mentioned both her parents were dead.

"My mother once told me," She watched his lips curved into a scowl. *Struck a nerve, did I? Sorry?* "That it is my duty to serve as a *patriot*, and I guess there are certain things I can't reconcile with what's going on."

"How do you mean? I know the world is falling apart, and that itself is a cruel joke," he replied.

"Well, can a country fight for freedom without being patriots, or is the mere act of serving one's country an act of patriotism itself?" she asked.

"Well, that's ambiguous, and I personally think that anyone who wears the charging flag on their shoulder is nothing short of a traitor."

She crinkled her nose. *Shameful to even say something like that.*

"When I was in," Ted continued, "you didn't question the orders you took, the lives you took. You didn't ask what became of the people who fell in your place. You'd get your comfort knowing that all the horrible things you did were for the *greater good,* or so they told you anyway. Sometimes, it becomes a, 'I'm going home, so the others can't' and trying to reconcile that is impossible. I'd be lying if I said it was easy. I'd be lying if I told you it ever got better.

"The truth is, patriotism is a flawed concept, and shouldn't even be in your vocabulary. Because in the end, patriotism is hinged on the fact that you are right, and everything else is wrong. And free thought is plagued, both in the civilian world, and the military. There is no exception to this rule. The military is big on 'orders, are orders,' and you follow that rule to the letter on which it is stated and written. No questions. Don't question your superiors and you'll be fine. You'll fall in line with the rest of them. They don't want innovation, just obedience. Mindless drones."

He stepped forward, finger pointing at her chest. She didn't know why, but she felt insecure with this man, as if he knew something she didn't.

"The other facet of this formulaic relationship that you'll form is the illusion that you are a person. You are not. You are nothing more than a number, a statistic, with a set amount of uses, carefully cataloged somewhere by your superiors who assign you a specific value, which, just like the stocks, adjust over time. Your use will deteriorate as your body deteriorates, and you will be useless, and like so many before you, they will find the most efficient way to dispose of trash. Discharge? Is it beneficial or cost effective? Or is an accident much more effective? So many ways to go." He spoke with the demeanor of a villain of sorts, one of those ones with a lot of experience manipulating people, almost like he planned to push her away from either him, or the military. But she couldn't disappoint her mother.

"You didn't answer my question," she pouted, crossing her arms, looking down to him.

"But I did, and you simply weren't paying attention," he chided, retracting his hand into his pocket. "So, what else is on the docket for today?"

"Why don't you tell me about the events unfolding. What are your thoughts on—"

"An inevitable tragedy," he answered, completing her thought for her. "What's the point of it all, really? You fight, you die, repeat, over and over again. There was peace for ten years."

Because of my mother.

"And here we are, World War Three is on our doorstep, and it was all but unavoidable. What became of the hearts of those who died for the peace? It was pointless. So, what if we offer up monuments? Doesn't mean anything when they're knocked down, shattered by way of a nuclear bomb. The question you need to ask yourself, is what is the price you're willing to pay? What is the price you will accept from others? Or will you be like my CO and be a rat, and not pay anything for the cost involved, but lay that cost on others to pay? And in the end, with it all being worthless because when you die, regardless of you succeeding or not, will you find satisfaction knowing that in a generation yet to come, this world will be scattered, shattered, and covered in ash? If the answer is yes to that last question, by all means, waste your life."

She exhaled through her pursed lips, looking down on a bitter old man. Her fist clenched her bottled water. *Be kind. Be respectful. Hard to do that with someone by the likes of him.*

She turned her frown upside down, making eye contact. It's only respectful after all. *You don't like him or anything. How could you?* "Thank you so much for taking the time to talk to me, and your intriguing input."

"Glad I could help," he smiled, teeth shining in that creepy way a villain does in a movie.

About-faced, she walked to get some more cheese and crackers. *Free for the taking, right?* She pops a cracker in her mouth, and a woman walked right by her.

"Oh, didn't see you there," the woman reached over to grab a plate.

"No problem," Sakura smirked brightly, fighting those negative emotions of extreme ire toward someone who clearly hates his country, and his countrymen. The blatant disregard of sacrifice, and lack of willingness to move on, to do what needs to be done. *We don't need men like him.*

She made eye contact with her, the blond-haired woman with bangs hanging to frame her face, and the rest neatly tied back.

"New here? I don't think we've met," she stretched out a hand.

Sakura took it in hers. It's only polite after all.

"Samantha Harris."

"Sakura," she answered.

"Oh." Samantha exclaimed, "feel free to just call me Sam, everyone does. Forgive me if this is too personal, but are you a second generation or third generation? Just, your name, isn't typical for an American, and you speak perfect English. So, I'm just assuming, I don't mean any offense if you are actually from Japan."

"What?" she chuckled. "No, none at all. Our family's been here since the concentration camps, unfortunately." *Always with the concentration camps. I get why that was done, but still. It pushed my family into* *generations of service, whether we wanted to or not.* And so, she silently thought to herself if she was continuing on that path or wanting to striver for it for her own reasons. Was the future hers? Or had it already been decided?

"I'm sorry to hear that," Samantha said, taking a bite of some cheese.

"It's okay. We've been in the military since then, serving in what way we could. It was our way of saying, 'we forgive what happened.'"

"That's very big of you, and your family, and you still share those ideals, so it's nice the fast-paced American culture hasn't changed that in your family history," Sam continued. "But what brings you here? Sorry, I know you've probably been asked that already, but I'm interested in you."

"What?" Sakura was taken aback, heart racing as she shot a glare.

"No." Sam said, waving her hands nonchalantly. "Not in a romantic way, I have a boyfriend, if that's what you were thinking. No, as a person. So, what brings you here?"

"Er. Well," her glare softened. "I was just passing by. I was on a run, taking a break from my studies."

"Oh, what are you studying?"

"I'm going to school for ROTC, but I actually just finished talking with Ted, the—"

"Were you kind to him?" She asked.

"As kind as a Sakura Tree," Sakura said, chewing on another piece of cheese.

Samantha let out a sigh of relief. "Good,"

Good? Why is everyone coddling him? What makes him so special. "He's special," as if to answer the unasked question. "It was hard for him, for more ways than one. It's kind of hard to come back from all that."

"From what?"

"Trauma," she said. "But, we'll not talk about that. That would be for him to tell. Honestly, even I don't know everything, but the one other person who would know close to everything would be Jennifer."

"I see." It was all beginning to make sense. Jennifer and Ted had some kind of relationship, and she said something specifically to him, what was it?

"Anyway, are you going to stick around for the study?"

"Study?"

"This is a Bible Study, every Tuesday night."

Sakura gazed outside, watching the streetlights turn on. "I suppose I have time to spare, I'm all caught up. But, it shames me to say I've never opened a Bible."

"For many people, it's their first time. Sometimes it's also their last, but sometimes they continue to read it," she smiled.

Another man came tumbling in, tripping over his feet, wearing BDUs. He tumbled in; his eyes glazed over as he saw the cheese.

Cheese. Everyone here likes cheese for some reason. I like it too, but not enough to go goo-goo over.

"Hey, you made it back." Sam called him over, waving her hand.

"That I did. Didn't want to forget."

Samantha eyed his BDUs. "You know, you really should think about civie attire."

"I still think it's funny you know that's what I call you," he chuckled, filling his plate.

"I have Ted to thank for that," she laughed.

Sakura noticed him rolling his eyes. "That man needs some serious down time," he turned to Sakura. "Who's this?"

"Oh, she's joining us this evening. Sakura, this is Lamar." Samantha introduced.

He stretched out his hand to shake hers. "Pleasure."

"We don't use BDUs anymore," Sakura commented.

He threw his head back, chuckling as some crumbs escaped his dental prison, and onto his beard. "Nope. Not in the service anymore, discharged." He wiped his face clean. "But you're right, everyone uses the ACUs now. I don't have those. No reason to."

"So, Sakura is going to school for ROTC,"

"Is that right?" he asked. "Well, we better start calling you ma'am."

Samantha laughed at that.

"What? No." she said, turning away. She knew her cheeks were turning red.

"Lieutenant Sakura, uh." Lamar chuckled.

"Riley."

"Lieutenant Sakura Riley." He smiled, nodded, and turned to Sam. "That has a nice ring to it actually. Well, any man or woman would be proud to serve under someone like you, I'm sure."

The people around them started walking into streams, heading back out the door. Sakura shook her head this way and that, peering through the people, seeing Jennifer and Ted holding hands, and he didn't waste a moment to shoot a glare at Sakura as they passed by.

"Time to go. Come on," Samantha said. "Sakura, follow me and Lamar, we're going to a small group. There will be some fun after. There always is."

Sakura followed behind Lamar and Samantha, growing ever conscious on how she smelled, not that anyone said anything with her BO perforating the room. She followed, blending in with the crowd into the lobby, heading up a few stairs before exiting the lobby, following down another set of stairs, very small, as if to bypass some rubble in between buildings, and in another room. She followed into some chairs, pushed into some long gray tables, and around this room, which had windows overlooking the side of the street, were bookcases filled with books, and books above them, which could only be accessed through other rooms above them, much like balconies.

She sat next to Samantha, and Lamar was on Sam's other side. Another man came in and sat next to Sakura.

"Sam, you didn't save me a seat?" he asked.

"Michael, you didn't meet Sakura."

The man snickered as if he didn't mean the sarcastic remark toward her. "Michael, nice to meet you. Newcomer?"

"Yes," she said, dumbfounded that she's answered this question effectually an inexhaustible number of times, and she didn't want to answer the question again. "Sakura. Riley."

"Michael Clemens."

"Now, like usual, we have a number of new faces here, and we don't know you," said a man in the corner.

She noticed Ted out of the corner of her eye, and he shot another glare at her. *What's his problem?*

"So, we'll go around, state your name, where you're from, what brings you to Boston, and the icebreaker, hmm, if you could be remembered for one thing before you die, what would it be?"

She took note of all the monotonous answers, and the general overview of the demographics of people in the room; several different ethnicities, many local to the United States, and of course from around the world. Many of these people didn't fail to mention their concern with the tensions rising everywhere toward everyone, and no hope in sight. Despite that blatant concern, none of them wanted to be do bodies, no action, none of them wanted to be remembered for doing anything remotely worth mentioning. Clearly, none of them had the state of the country at the forefronts of their minds. *Why?*

"I'm Michael, I came here for work, and never left really, I'm from Vermont. Remembered? I want to be remembered as the last one laughing!"

The room was fueled with awkward laughter, but none from Ted, who leaned back in his chair, hands folded over his chest as he scanned the room.

"I'm Sakura. I'm from Atlanta," she began, nervous about exposing her roots. "I study at BU for the ROTC program, and to be remembered, I want to follow my parents' footsteps and keep serving, so I want to be remembered as someone with unwavering commitment in service to my country."

"How very patriotic of you," Sam said.

Ted would clearly disagree with you. Ted's the real traitor, isn't he?

"I'm Sam, and I'm also from Vermont, came here for work, and mostly to follow and stalk Michael." More laughter. Even Jennifer lightened up, cackling with her hair hanging over the back of her seat at the other end of the room. "Remembered for anything, I don't want to make it in the history books. Something always unpleasant pops up, but if anything, perhaps that I could do one good deed worth remembering for the little guy."

"I'm Lamar," he said. "I'm still adjusting to civie life, came here for a job after the marines, and I guess I'm from all over, ha! I can't think of something to be remembered by, but there is someone who's memory I'd like to remember."

Sakura turned her head, and Ted, also out the corner of her eye, glared at Lamar. *You hate him too, huh?*

"There was a man once, never wore a patch or anything like that, but he saved my life a number of times, but ten years ago, he just vanished. I'd honestly like to thank him for saving my life. He taught me the value of it. Don't remember his name or anything."

Interesting.

She listened to everyone, one by one they shared their answers, and who they were. Then her blood boiled, and her left hand retracted into a gentle fist, and released pressure. The man she grew to hate in such a short time: Ted.

"Ted Anderson, I've been in Boston, for about a year now. Came here for work, and someone decided I should stay here, so I stayed here." He let out a sigh, placing his hands behind his head, averting his gaze to the ceiling. "What do I want to be remembered for?"

There was a silence in the room, all waiting for an answer from Ted, as if he was going to say something absolutely profound and that it was worth listening to. "I don't."

That's it? She frowned. *That's seriously it?*

Shaking her head. She didn't care if he saw her disapproving answer. Simple enough really, but all that to say, she got no useful information from him at all, and that he's just an unbearable ass.

The study of the Bible commenced, but truth be told, Sakura was too fuming to understand any of it, and all of it went over her head. Not that she considered herself dumb by any means, but rather, Ted managed to piss her off by setting these expectations, and failing all of them, much like wrapping a noose around someone's neck, taking him out to a cliff, and attaching the other end of the noose to a number of cinderblocks, and tossing them out to sea, watching their souls depart from this world in a last effort of defiance. Soldiers were supposed to be patriots. It was who they were. Who she understood them to be, disciplined and self-sacrificing, proud to have served. All of these, he failed to meet.

But regarding anything she read that night, she couldn't tell someone what she read. In fact, she couldn't recall any of it, not even the name of the individual book.

Despite everything with Ted, she was glad to have stumbled onto an event tonight. It was good for her to take an extended break but, damn that man. The man should just go and jump off a damn cliff with all his nihilistic tendencies. The experience was good, but Ted pissed her off so much she couldn't enjoy all the good things about it.

Lamar touched her shoulder as she grabbed hold of the parking sign. "So, did you enjoy yourself here?"

"Yes, I'd say it was enjoyable."

"Sakura, do you want to hang out with us tonight?" Sam walked over with Michael; hands interlaced.

Sam swiftly turned to Jennifer. "Jennifer, Teri's?"

"Not tonight." Jennifer called back, guiding Ted off into the street toward the subway station. *Good.*

"Next time, then." Sam turned back to her. "How about it? You don't actually have to drink or even order anything. We just go there to hang out."

"Since Ted's not going," she was not going to be subtle about her distaste toward him, "Sure."

Sam frowned.

"Well, considering his history," Lamar began, "I still don't fully understand him myself. I figured I of all people here would."

"What do you mean?" Sakura asked.

"How do I explain this?" He tapped his chin. "Ah, if I were to go to the store, and wait in line at check out, and there's another person behind me, who also served, but I've never met them before. All it takes is one word, and we're talking like we've known each other all our lives, because no one understands a veteran like another. It's a brotherly bond that can't be broken. Ted is the exception. Someone in his unit, or his past, or multiple people must have screwed him over real good to make him not trust anybody."

Chapter 18 Uncertainty

World report: The US fleets remain ocean bound at our harbors, fully manned and gunned, both on the East and West Coast. Destroyers, Cruisers, and Carriers were recommissioned.

Russian fleets sail further in, closing in across the Atlantic Ocean. Submarines were reported scouting. The Russian Atlantic fleet is on standby. Chinese fleets sailing in from the west, carriers, destroyers, and Cruisers recommissioned with heavy artillery rounds. The Chinese Pacific Fleet is on standby.

Passenger flights have not been canceled from overseas.

***

Bridgette sat down in the main hall, her legs hovering over the carpet with her knees bent. In her left hand, she held a cup, steaming hot tea. The way it should be, steeped nice and proper. Not like horrible people make a habit of ruining a perfect cup of tea. Americans. They don't know how to make tea, or enjoy them, truly awful people. Like McCurdy, the blond-haired wanker.

Bridgette exhaled deeply, sipping her tea before placing it back down on the table, set very finely with green embroidery. Ancient Anglo-Saxon symbols woven into the old world to this one, intertwined relations, corrupting the Threads of Creation in an irreparable way. It was only a matter of time before creation undid itself.

And yet, she thought, one hand dangling over the side of her arm rest, the idea that one of them would be so fatalistic to make the choice for everyone else, that life was meaningless; moral and religious principles were null and void and held no value. Of course, one who truly believed that didn't hate the world, they just hated the people in it. Earth, so tragically beautiful, filled with love, but the despair was ever growing, ripping hearts to shreds before their time was up.

It was all over the news. Oddly enough, Camelot wasn't responsible for these wars, for once. Humans managed to wage war and focus on killing one another all themselves at a mass scale. Shouldn't be a surprise, really, for humans were only good at breaking things. Even most of their creations were shams, not worth mentioning, and the things worth mentioning were horrible. Fae didn't build weapons of mass destruction. They didn't need to. With enough planning, humans managed to do that all on their own.

"You okay there, Bridgette?"

She looked up, and Adam briefly smiled, but that same tired expression on his face remained. She knew why, another sleepless night. He took a seat across from her, steam rising from his cup.

"As fine as I'll ever be." She frowned, tapping her toe on the ground, her hand warming up to the cup of tea.

She closed her eyes, breathing in mana from the air, and the chair on which she sat, weaving them inside her mana veins like little cyclones of storms inside her body. Red veins protruded on her palms, heating the cup. *Gotta keep it hot after all.*

"You know, sometimes I wonder if these gifts of ours were designed for war, like we so often use them," said Adam, pulled out his palm and absorbed mana from multiple sources, showing his mastery of castery, and snobbery. Temperature changed to a draft, cooling down just a little, but not enough inside Camelot's lobby to draw attention. Truly, a master at snobbery. A little black western jackdaw chirped in his hand, fluttering its wings for the first time, and dove from his hands, fluttering as it flew up, and out the nearest window on this fine occasion.

"Was there a point to that? Don't keep me in suspense." Bridgette frowned.

"No." He forced a laugh. "I found something—"

"ADAM." She cried. "What in God's name is going on? I'm in the dark. I want to know what's going on, and these goose chases are taking us nowhere."

There was silence in the lobby, and many fae inside, male and female of equal ratio trained their eyes on her, clicking their tongues as they ignored the outburst. Adam's lips curled downward into a disapproving frown.

"I'm sorry," she said, picking up her tea again.

"It's fine." He replied.

Ha, no, it isn't.

"I've told you everything I know. I have you in meetings with me, discussing these matters. Because you speak your mind, and without restraint do I trust you, and that you are no stranger to tough decisions. We own the whole world, and yet, here we are, clueless about any of this, which implies someone on the inside wants something, but what? There's no way anyone, no matter how hopeless would go through with the desecration of creation."

"But it isn't outside the realm of possibilities," she said, calming her nerves. "That's what scares me most. You know, some days, I go about, getting some tea, reading a book to get me out of this Hell I've been thrust into. And the people of creation, the ones we share no faith in—the ones who can't know what we are, or what goes on in the grim darkness of the night—who say the world is better off dead, and the people in it. That is what terrifies me. The darkness of humanity mixed in with our own darkness, is far worse than dealing with these Threckets, demons, and devils. Humans are far worse."

"I know." Adam pursed his lips, leaned back, and brushed a hand through his hair. "And we're nowhere near finding a solution. I've tried everything, and everything I haven't tried has been tried by someone else. I'm beginning to think there isn't a solution to this curse."

"Maybe this was a curse without the possibility for atonement," she said. "Why would there be? What grace is there for someone who fused Pandora's Box to the Holy Grail? God banned us from those gates. We live in a Hell, and what makes it worse is we still serve Him; knowing that we'll only ever see Hell, and at best, nothingness. And just end up in a hole in the ground, six feet under, forgotten."

He nodded. "Indeed, there are days I wake up where I think death might have been easier, except that little promise of prophecy."

"What prophecy?" she jerked her head, scowling. "The one where King Arthur will rise from the dead again, and guide us all to Avalon? That prophecy? A land we thought was promised to us, only to end up being a mirage."

"It's a hope, a possibility," he replied.

"Adam, it's a false hope, with nothing to back it up." She took her palm into her mouth, biting it firmly. "The moment that we, whatever we are, are born, we are born into the throes of death, and only through the sense of duty to protect a world, a creation we don't have any stake in."

She felt tears coming down her cheeks, and Adam leaned forward, eyes locked in with hers, listening intently. "What's the point? If King Arthur comes, what about those who came and died before? Those who were lucky enough to just have the worms eating their corpse? And those not good enough for that? We live in this nightmare everlasting, for what?"

"Bridgette," he spoke softly.

"You said it yourself, 'Death might have been easier.' Then let us be done with it." She waited for a response from him, to allow him the faintest notion of a chance. There was nothing out of Adam's lips.

"Is it really our fault that we were cursed so? And thus, submitted to a life of torment without any hope of it getting better. What hope is there? *Tell me.*"

Her hands firmly gripped the table. The rest of the Administration inside the lobby looked at her, and Adam, eagerly waiting for his response. This told her: they were thinking the very same thing. They were suffering the same thing. They were living the same thing. What was the point of all this?

"Bridgette," he began, softly as only Adam could, "The only thing that is certain, is uncertainty, and with that uncertainty, we can be certain that not everything is lost, and that there's a chance, no matter how infinitely small, that this Hell can be undone, and we can go home.

I am banking my last guess, my last chance at this unknown and the mystery of both men, the Ghost, and whoever was at Devil's Pass. Maybe then, they can provide some certainty, and make things a little less uncertain."

"Administrator Sander," came a shy petite voice scurrying around like a detestable rat. A woman held a manilla folder with loose documents, her auburn hair not quite tied down, swaying back and forth as she approached them.

"For God's sake, just Adam." He turned away, breaking away this dramatic discussion, and what better way to make her forget her cynical tendencies and thoughts than a disruption like this? But, it must be important—"

"Out with it, Rebecca," he snarled.

"Sorry," she bowed her head. "I was doing the research you asked me to correlate it to Devil's Pass, and all I really found was, well, missing pages."

"What?" he asked.

Missing people. Missing Holy Grails. Missing Pandora's Box. Missing answers. Missing pages. What else will go missing? Sooner or later our minds will be mush, and thus, missing also. Great. Sarah McCurdy. Fuck you. We will find you. We will take back this Grail. I will fucking kill you and feed your carcass to the rats! You cunt!

"Pages in the archives. They're missing,"

"Yes, I heard you the first time."

"Out with it!" Bridgette threw her teacup across the room, shattering it on the wall.

"Like did someone rip out the pages or...?" Adam surmised in that mocking tone that told her enough. He was through with a bunch of other crap no one wanted to deal with.

"No, like, when the monks of old rewrote everything, pages weren't documented,"

Adam bit his lip, probably trying to keep his composure, and clearly failing, though Bridgette knew it prevented him from swearing most of the time. "Get me a detailed report. I want the name of the book, the volume, where the page, or pages are missing, and if it is the same typographical error throughout like volumes. I want the history of those books also in that report. Work on it with haste. I want it tomorrow. Get as many hands on it as possible." He turned to Bridgette. "I'm going to bed. I must deal with this tomorrow. I suggest you do the same."

She watched Adam walk off, moving down the corridors into the Administrator's room. She lived here with the fae, well, the fae inside this facility designed as an emergency response unit to combat Threckets at a moment's notice. Rest was often in short supply, but yes, rest sounded nice. Hell, who knows. Maybe she could finally get a full four hours.

Chapter 19 Firing Range

It is clear now more than ever that the Russian and Chinese fleets are working with each other to assault the US borders, with fleets on both sides. The US fleets remain harbored, and there is no word from Press Secretary or the Secretary of Defense. We'll take you now to Chief Commanding Officer of Black Eagle Company was available for questioning, and had this to say:

It's a crying shame is what it is. I have my fleets. I have my soldiers and my technology. We're ready to fight, I just need a funding source. I have solicited Snells himself for funding, yet he seems to be avoiding my calls. It might be time for him to retire, assuming there's an America left to retire in. We're a company, not affiliated with the government. We don't risk our lives for free.

***

Sakura laid in her bed, still had her pajamas on, the camo style that she loved. For whatever reason, she liked the idea of various shades of green and brown molding together in various shapes. When she found out the military transitioned to pixelated gear, though, for good reason, she was none too impressed. She would keep these until they started fading out, color, threads, and all. The Saturday morning sun was beaming down on her face, and she covered her eyes, yawning as the sun irritated her nose, forcing her to a violent sneeze.

Her roommate, someone tolerable at least when she was sleeping, snoring far louder than any alarm clock. She imagined the military alarms when horrible things were happening were exponentially louder than everything and everyone else, drowning out even these obnoxious snores.

Her phone rang.

Who could that be at this hour? The sun was just rising. Her roommate stirred, and she took her phone. *Lamar. God why did I give him my phone number?* It was polite to give something someone asked for. That's why. She took off to the outside hall, closing the door to avoid Lamar hearing the obnoxious woman in her dorm.

"Sakura," she said, leaning back against the wall, one leg crossing over the other.

"How'd you sleep?"

"Fine."

"Hey, question. Do you like guns?" Lamar asked on the other end of the phone.

Why, of course I do. I shot them all the time, until that is, I came here, where the guns I shoot aren't allowed.

"Yes, why do you ask?"

"I've been dying to go shooting with someone, and no one around wants to, I know a place in Dorchester. You interested?"

She spent months up here already, rarely went home down in Georgia, and she had to assume her touch with the trigger finger was getting rusty. Few places to go around shooting here, and not like she could hunt here either.

"Sure, why not. Where?"

He gave her the location of where the closest T-stop was. *These people really need to learn to drive.* Upon giving her the detailed instructions on how to get there, she walked back into her room, pulled up her laptop and grabbed the driving instructions online, and dressed in her jeans, and grabbed a plain t-shirt before driving out.

She drove out with her truck onto I-90, heading eastward toward the ocean, before traversing through the tunnel. It would be crowded, and dangerous if one doesn't pay attention to the signs. Impromptu drivers cutting you off for no apparent reason except to dangerously merge across three lanes into oncoming traffic to turn into a tunnel just too sharp for their turn. She thought she should hear screeching or crunching metal coming from the other end of the tunnel. *These Boston Drivers are insane!*

Continuing driving and avoiding all manner of calamity, (which was the minefield of caffeine, sleep depravity, and the recklessness and probably suicidal drivers inside this city, filled with nothing but disdain for their own existence). Upon arriving, she parked safely at the driving range, and there Lamar was, in civie attire, standing outside the range, which was inside a large and tall building.

She shuddered.

Not her favorite. A controlled environment for which anyone could feign to be an expert in marksmanship because they don't have to account for longer distances, velocity of the round and the type of rifle used, the lack of moving targets, wind resistance, and the temperature outside causing rounds to go haywire off course if too hot or cold. Firing guns wasn't a science, it was an art that few truly understood. Of course, an art that no one in Boston would understand, since they only allowed certain types of firearms in the hands of civilians, herself included. Hell, she couldn't even bring her AR15 here.

"You drove?" He asked.

"Yeah," she replied, slamming the door shut, locking it with her key. "All right, let's go."

"Eager?" He smiled as he turned to head into the door.

She smirked back. "Well, I can't exactly go out in the backyard and start shooting, now, can I? Someone will call the police and have me arrested. I can't have that."

"No, especially if your aim is to be a commissioned officer. You need to have a clean record, but here," he led her to some shelves. The instructor was inside the shooting range, observing one round of individuals, eyes and ears covered. "You can go crazy. What type of rifle do you prefer shooting with?"

"Bolt-action," she replied. "I prefer a Forthington."

"It's all they got here for bolt-action, actually," he replied, picking out a box of rounds specific to the Forthington design. There was no worse way to blow out a barrel and have one's face blown up with shrapnel than to fire any gun with the wrong kind of ammunition.

"Did you say you served in the marines?"

"Yes," he said as he pulled out his wallet. He brought the rounds to the cashier, "Two lanes, please."

"Sure thing." The cashier took the card, ran the transaction through, and Lamar left with the boxes of ammunition. "When was the last time you shot anything?"

"Six months ago. I was out huntin' with my AR15," She gasped, letting her accent slip.

"The good old AR," he said stiffly walking, one legged staggered over the other toward the firing range.

"War wound?" she asked.

"Hmm?" He said as he pushed the door open into the firing range. It was much more secluded than the other one, with a separate instructor handing them the goggles and earmuffs.

"Your leg?" She spoke louder.

"Oh, that." He shouted, going onto his lane. "Yeah, remember the other day I talked about someone who saved my life?"

"Yeah,"

"Well, the truck I was in exploded, and a large part of it landed on my leg. I had to take an extended leave of absence to heal it back up. The man who saved me secured the position before pulling the entire front end of the burning truck off me," he replied. "Truth is, just being in the truck when it blew should have killed me. Luck was on my side that day."

She tried to envision what this looked like as the instructor was going over safety protocol and measures. Nothing she hasn't already heard over a thousand times. The instructor cleared the floor to start firing. Her target was a small dot, resting far down range, on the backboard as it connected to some concrete behind it.

Holding and pressing the stock to her shoulder, loading the rifle's cartridges, and her trigger finger just above the trigger, she breathed steadily, lining up the sights with the target, dead center. Exhaling, she squeezed the trigger. *Bang!* The rifle kicked back into her shoulder, pushing her back half a step. The bullet traversed, spinning through the air, striking what she thought was the target, as the paper rippled. She fell into a rhythm. Pulling the bolt-action lever. Reloading the round from the cartridge back into the chamber. Aiming down the sight.

"All right, that's enough!"

She didn't realize she had shot that much already; the box was completely empty. She sighed with disappointment.

She wheeled her target up to her, and when it reached her, she pulled it off the stables and looked at her results. *Dead center. Same as always.* Indoor ranges never gave her the variety she craved in a shooting range, one of the many reasons she preferred hunting over shooting cans.

"How'd you do?" Lamar peered over his corner.

"Take a look for yourself!" She said excitedly, waving her results right in front of him.

"Dead center. You're a good shot, much better than I am." He pulled out his sheet, and she noticed one hit dead center, but the other ones were much more focused around the edges toward the white. Clearly, he was out of practice.

She followed Lamar back out of to the parking lot while many people came in and out of the firing range. "I wanted to ask, since I couldn't get any information out of Ted. It's been bothering me, since I don't have a clear way on how to answer it..."

"Yeah, you're not going to get much out of Ted, like I said."

"You wouldn't be talking about Ted Anderson, would you?" Said a man, largely built, and a serious face. "Sorry to interrupt, I know the guy, how's he been?"

"Honestly, I don't know," Lamar answered, scanning the man up and down. "Did you serve?"

"Yeah," he said. "Still do. 75th Ranger Regiment back in the day, with Sergeant Ted Anderson."

"My man. Bring it here." Lamar and the man hugged each other. Clearly, they didn't know each other as they talked almost like old war buddies, almost as if to catch up on their lives. This was the brotherhood Lamar mentioned. 75th Ranger Regiment was no joke, and yet Ted seemed to be of a different cloth altogether, rejecting this same brotherhood which she was witnessing now.

"Sorry to interrupt your reunion, but my question," she said to them.

Lamar turned to her. She got the other man's name out of the small talk: Jeffrey Clemens.

"Sorry, Sakura, what was the question again?" Lamar asked.

"How would you define patriotism?" She asked. "Like I said, Ted wasn't helpful."

"He always was a nihilist," Jeff explained.

"Supporting your country. Giving life and liberty to a higher goal, protecting the Constitution we serve, the democratic republic we serve, and the people who reside here," Lamar said. "Well, that's what it means to me."

Lamar bit his lip. "Hey, Jeff, whatever happened to your unit after the wars?"

"Our unit was ultimately disbanded. Not the 75th, but our unit was merged into Black Eagle."

"I didn't realize that was your unit," Lamar said.

"Black Eagle?" Sakura had heard of them before. She didn't know who they were or their purpose, but it seemed evidently odd to her that the Ranger Regiment would rename themselves to Black Eagle. Unless even now, she didn't fully understand the entirety of the scenario.

"Never heard of them?" Jeff asked.

"No," she replied.

Jeff raised an eyebrow as if he didn't believe her. "Really?"

She was silent.

"It's mostly out in the open now. I'm surprised. Black Eagle was inducted twenty-five years ago under the directive of General Snells at the time," he answered. "It ultimately turned out to be a mercenary group, which didn't hire themselves out to the highest bidder, but only to the US There are things we do and can get away with, that Lamar could never. It grew exponentially, especially after these last few years as they took applications from other servicemen from around the world. It is effectively one large governmental branch, with its own funds and resources. Currently, it's about as large as the US military, all six branches, and a much better research and development division. Think of it like the French Foreign Legion."

"That sounds like a colossally bad idea," she said. *Hiring out mercenaries? Rules of Engagement? Lack thereof? What couldn't go wrong?*

"Very efficient actually," he answered. "Without restraints, it is very easy to take out key personnel when needed. It takes a specific type of person to be in Black Eagle."

"And someone with lots of mud on their boots," Lamar agreed.

"Welcome to a moral quagmire. That's what you get with war."

"Sounds like something that Ted said," she said.

"Well, say nothing at all for Ted Anderson. He was the best at his job. No one could ever take that away from him, but he was always a prick," Jeff said. "Well, see you around. I've got places to be."

Chapter 20 Reassignment

Long Beach Washington was struck with cannon fire from a nearby destroyer. Chinese fighter jets are soaring over Seattle, dropping bombs on civilian targets. Cruiser ships pulled in, deploying amphibious vehicles, dropping off and securing the coastal state of Washington, allowing envoys to deploy infantry on the shorelines.

No response from the Military personnel led to drastic preparations by Chinese forces, deploying heavy calvary units.

Chief Commanding Officer Malcolm in a report: It's a tragedy. There is literally no reason that had to happen. I can't do anything. My hands are tied by the bureaucracy.

***

Sarah leaned forward, sniffling as she gazed into the mirror of the brightly lit bathroom of the airport; gazing deep into her green eyes, watering, and her red hair shriveled, combed, and tied back. Her button up shirt wrinkled, a loose button at the top, and her black slacks pressed. The only thing neat on her person, or it would have been if someone didn't vomit their lunch on her shoes, still polished, shiny enough for her to see her reflection, not that she ever wanted to, unless to find herself deep in thought.

Deep in thought. Such a state she often found herself in, not bothering to negotiate or talk with other people.

Her glazed eyes reminded her of the curse she'd been born with, just to live in this world, along with everyone else with this damned

Caster's Administration, and who could forget the crimes, historically they committed to cover up the truth. Where do these lies end? Where does the truth start? She was certain even now, the head of this organization didn't even know what was going on. Falling in line, just like everyone else.

The truth was lost somewhere; she was certain of it. If she wasn't, she wouldn't have even gone through the hassle of listening to Colton in the first place, and conducting a heist to steal the Holy Grail, golden rim. For something half cursed, fused with Pandora's Box, it was pretty. Other than that, it was the painful reminder that she necessarily killed humans she got close with. Humans—*normies*, people who can't use the radiation through their veins, because it would kill them. Of course, that wasn't the only thing that separated them from the normies.

What else but that curse come down from God that they would never enter the Kingdom of Heaven in their own deaths, but at best, just merely die, with their souls brushed away like a vapor of the wind. Nothing. Emptiness. In the end, no one would truly miss them for attaining such a high standard of living, of killing, and of protecting the truth everyone wanted hidden, even from them. The grand prize of this life was just that—death, and it almost unattainable, and those that failed, which was almost everyone, was certainly cast into the number of different Hells based on how many innocent lives they let die. Never mind the amount of innocent lives they killed, of which, Sarah could number herself in the hundreds.

Of course, killing people was necessary. It came with the territory. She expected no less, but she never chose to do any of it, just born cast running, provided she knew exactly who her birth parents were. She didn't. Just tossed to an aunt and uncle who was accused of some shady dealings before their lives were ultimately snuffed out and consumed. Fed to the Threckets in their last deal, sent to their graves, and early deaths, if you will, fed to beasts by none other than Adam Sander, the English Swine. But could she fault him for that? He was just doing his job after all.

That's what she kept telling herself anyway. She kept repeating it to herself in the hopes that one day she might believe it. It would be a lie to say even if she accepted it, that it would get easier.

This obscure reference to things, texts, and events that none of them truly understood led them down a dark path of nothing but horrible deeds, tragedies, and murder. Yes. Murderers are fitting of a murderer's death, and she was one of them. Deserving of it from the moment they were born, and they should accept that. They were not of this world; they should stop pretending like they belonged to it, fitting in as one of them as if they didn't have their own jobs to do, working to put on a show, working to hide the truth, the moral quagmire of the world they lived in. This world filled with political machinations, all of which were controlled by the British Empire. Sure, the world thinks it was dead, and gone, but the truth was, the British Empire was alive and well by way of the Caster's Administration, who had their hands in every treasury in the world, and a mole in every politician's house, pulling every single string.

She brushed her hair back one last time, straightening it out, walking briskly into the overcrowded airport terminals, taking her luggage with her, her one duffle bag with some clothes: just a few sets of clothes before she would be reimbursed with some unimaginably thick down coats. Until such time, onward to the next task, the next person to royally screw over, and murder. No shortage of murders on her hands these days. What's a few more to add to that damned list?

She sat down in one of the seats, watching the clouds in the night sky roam by, other aerial crafts outside, and of course, paying close attention to every face. One of them might recognize her. Thanks to this, the whole world was after her, a manhunt, to scour every single stone to look for her. Fortunately, she was in Colton's territory, and he planned the whole thing. She would be lying if she said she wasn't curious about the Grail, or Colton's intentions with it.

She exhaled heavily as she leaned forward, hands folded over one another, patiently waiting for her terminal to be called forward. Eager to be done with it. Eager to get to the next step. Eager to do God knows what.

Her terminal was finally called, and she stood, bag in hand. She walked with everyone else, blending in like the habitual liar she was. Standing up front, she walked onto the crowded plane, shoving her duffle bag into the upper shelving units and sat in her spot, next to the window, where she could watch the darkness swallow up the plane. Swallow the light and snuffing out their lives like little flickering candles representing what little hope their arrogance held over them. Fools. That is what they were. They all were, given so much, and yet, with a blink of an eye, they could die, and who would be to blame but themselves?

Truth be told about humans, they're conniving dastardly creatures who aren't worth saving, really. They're stupid. They're smelly. They're cruel. Anything to be said about the sake of human ingenuity or innovation, cultivation was not produced by the hands of man, but by the help of the Caster's Administration, but they'd never admit to something as good hearted as all that. Let them think they own the world, and you'll have them believe they have the power, and therefore, with untrained minds, they'll make foolish decisions that will lead them down the path of death. And here she was, along for the ride, to watch them die.

Sighing, she pulled out the manilla folder Colton gave her. She couldn't have electronics on her person: too trackable.

She slipped it open with her light on as the plane took flight. She opened it, and on it was her target. No specific instructions on eliminating her, just to observe, as if Colton didn't trust her to do the job right, or was there something else hidden from her? Even Colton, just like the rest of them, was known to be a liar.

Gwen Swan was a woman, tall with silver hair, it would seem, and quite a résumé even as fae were concerned. Holding the governor's office. *Hard to do a lot of activities while in that position.* She was the head Administrator for the Alaskan district. *No small feat there, either.* Sarah skimmed the line that brought some light upon her accolades, which again, was impressive.

She was younger than Sarah was, but not by much. Even so, she studied underneath the wing of Sander, and, by the looks of it, must have had a death wish. She had slayed nearly four hundred Threckets herself and had an affinity for elemental magic of various kinds.

As much as Bridgette would insist, elemental casting was not forbidden like necromancy was, but it was strongly discouraged. It required an impressive amount of control from the various sources of mana coming in from certain objects, and not only that—it required a specific amount. Trying to cast a specific kind of spell, pulling mana from an inappropriate source was a great way to get oneself killed. And adding in the scientific requirements of elemental magic, well, it would be almost impossible, since no one has been able to develop any system where mana usage could be measured.

This reason alone made Gwen extremely volatile and supremely dangerous.

Moving around her wasn't going to be easy, and quite frankly, any and all support for her task was unavailable. No one from the Caster's branch in Alaska would ever undermine their own Administrator. But then again, this led to another question, which would only lead down a further line of questioning into the larger picture of what all else was going on? No doubt, Gwen would not be giving out information, even if she had any of the faintest of clues as to who or what the man from Devil's Pass was.

She was flying back into murky waters, the thickest of weeds, and the only thing that was certain, was uncertainty. No. That's not true. There was a certainty that she was safe from the rest of the Administration while she was there, and it would be in her keenest of interests to not screwup any part of her objective.

Going there tired would be a colossally poor decision on her part, so the only logical solution was to go to sleep. Resting her redhead on the window, next to a snoring fat man with foul breath, which smelled like rotten fish—not that fresh fish smelled any better.

Approximately eighteen hours later, as far as her watch could tell, she arrived in the dark hours of the night. Early night that is, that wasn't to say there wasn't the possibility of Threckets roaming around in the foggy chilled winter air, coalescing outside and feeding on the poor mundane souls that were the inhabitants of Juneau. She followed everyone out of the pit, grabbing her bag, which was the only thing she brought with her, there was no need to wait for anything else at the terminal.

She smelled the freshly baked and fried food pouring out from the kitchens on either side of her as she walked the brightly lit tiled floor with black marks as if someone shat all over them. She didn't care. She wasn't washing them, stupid fat janitors taking their sweet time, not a care in the world that little rat-sized Threckets come about, poking about in their little heads to gnaw on their brains.

She shook her head, then looked dead ahead. Her eyes gazed this way and that into the blackness of the night through the windows. She made her way down the escalators with lazy people without the need to go anywhere any time fast. People the world would be better off without really. No hurry? No spring in their step? However, they were excellent food for some Threckets out there, and nice distractions for a quick getaway, if need be, even the children, yes, foul little creatures who knew nothing better than their own imagination. Innocent.

If only we were all like little children. If only we kept our innocence. Perhaps the world would be a much simpler, happier place. But here we are, forcing them to adult. Forcing them to grow up in this Hell we created for them, and told them to shoot for the stars, telling them if only they made it would their miserable existences be worth a damn. And when they fail, and they will fail, they'll succumb to despair and their own mental illness, while those that succeed in the farce of a dream, lost everything just to get there, because their naivety grew was so high, they never bothered to count the cost of such a silly dream. In the end, it's all worthless.

Sarah walked down through the rest of the lobby, walking past the threshold of glass doors where the wind whistled through her clothes. It would have swung a lesser woman's arm, but Sarah's grasp was firm, firmer than anyone else's. Even normie men. She exhaled chilled breath.

A black government vehicle turned its lights on, driving toward her. She gazed through the tinted windows, unable to see the driver, or the contents of inside. Her hand gripped an invisible shaft by her side, ready to cause a ruckus should it be one of those pesky fae looking for her. Just then, did she finally question the validity of Colton's promises, and that she might not be as safe here as she once presumed. Her heart raced.

The car slowed down, and the windows opened. The driver was a woman in a cap, her black hair pulled behind in a bun, and she didn't once take her eyes off the road, a coldness about her. But unlike the stiff coldness of the wind, this was the coldness of a heart; the dear dreaded heart of Alaska was one seemingly without warmth, the same despair held within her presence was the same that plagued her own mind. The back windows opened as the car rolled to a stop, and a woman, vibrant, wearing a black petticoat opened her door, stretching out onto the side, looking at Sarah with a curious eye.

Undoubtedly, this was Ms. Gwen Swan. Lead fae of the Alaska's branch of America's Administration. Elegant was her face, and her silver hair glimmered in the moonlight. Her face held a sneer that made Sarah's skin crawl, and underneath her skin where she felt like there were rotting worms growing, scouring her insides. Gwen stepped out of the car, slamming the door shut. Sarah saw those pupils investigating her body.

"Y'aren't as tall as I reckoned ye to be," she said, her hand reaching up, caressing her face with the back of her hand, ever so softly, yet, those hands were colder than snow. "Sarah McCurdy, I've heard some good things about you." Her nose crinkled at the touch, as soft as it was, it was unwelcomed, but she had little choice in the matter than to endure this gross invasion of personal space. It was almost like she was being treated like a dog.

The governor took the duffel bag from Sarah's hand and tossed it in the trunk. "Get inside, we've lots to discuss back at my office. Take a look at the lay of the land on your way there."

Sarah nodded, and took a seat, while Gwen sat next to her, paying attention to other things, talking to the driver, or even playing a game on her phone.

Shouldn't be on your phone. Threckets are out at night. You need to be alert.

To say anything about Sarah, anything at all, she was alert and aware as the car started to drive off to an unfamiliar destination. But she was in the military for a decade and a half and moved constantly. So she was used to constant change after all.

The winds outside were whistling, the temperature, while rather cold, was much more due to Alaska's climate, and not due to the mana pockets. Which was unusual; these mana pockets didn't seem to be here in abundance. She didn't sense any in the mountains, the airports, or even the wintery plains.

They drove by some old ports, unloading large drayage shipping containers on a cargo ship, that appeared to be disembarking, heading further up north, if she guessed right. Impossible to tell without the sun to direct the position of the shadows cast on the buildings, and the people underneath those lights, trading paperwork, and signing off on the shipments. However, they must have had something to guide their way, the stars were obscured by the clouds.

But all of this, was what normies would call *normal* human behavior. Nothing related to Threckets, fae, or the like, keeping them forever sheltered from the lies they were told, and led to believe. This is the kind of thing she wasn't used to.

"So, you notice anything different?" Gwen asked.

"It's safe here," Sarah answered, turning back to the governor.

"In a way yes, but is anywhere safe when trust is always a concern?"

Trust. She suspects something.

"Yes, I always do," Gwen answered.

Sarah's eyes gaped open. Her heart skipped a beat, racing it was as she came to the sudden realization, even her thoughts were no longer hers.

"Oh, don't act surprised, there isn't anything outside the realm of capabilities. Not for me anyways. You can remain silent all you want, but I think it's best that we defuse this little misunderstanding we have with one another," Gwen said, leaning in closer, flicking her finger back and forth. "I know why you're here, and it isn't for your personal protection for the crime you committed against the Administration."

Sarah gawked, turning to the driver.

"Don't be alarmed and bothered. All of Alaska knows,"

"Then why haven't you killed me?" Sarah glared at her. Her eyes scanned the car, now more invested in precisely where she was heading. Administration building, or was she to be disposed of?

"Honestly, even if Colton wanted you dead, it would be a hassle I could do without" She smiled, eyes drooping low, plotting something, but the woman was almost unreadable. She couldn't read her. "So, back to business, you are here to spy on me. More specifically, to find out what information have I been keeping from Colton. Well, you'll get what information I choose to give you, and it will come with a cost. And those costs you will pay up front. Do I make myself clear?"

"Yes, Administrator Swan," Sarah gritted her teeth, feeling like her lungs were going to collapse. She realized how easy one can be an animal, and she was no less. She remembered those nuclear soldiers she led up to die. Was this how they felt in their final moments? Betrayed with nowhere to go, locked in a cage, trapped in a corner, doomed to die, and without a final moment to say their goodbyes.

"You intrigue me, you know, or else I wouldn't have agreed to let Colton send another realm of emissaries here to spy and trap me. The last four did a fantastic job on trying to get to my secrets. They found out, but they were all killed before they could even think of reporting back to Colton, I trust you're smart enough to not make that same mistake." Gwen frowned. "Answer me."

"I will not cross you." She exhaled, her heart racing hastily.

"What you'll notice is there are no Threckets here—not this part of Alaska. The Portal Storms are up in the north, way up in the north, unsettling wouldn't you agree," Gwen said. "This I will give you, there's an army of Threckets amassing at the North Pole. I am doing nothing to them, and they've stayed put. Can you hazard a guess why?"

"Because they have hearts," Sarah said, making it sound like this was a genuine answer, but it wasn't. Of course, it wasn't. They have no hearts, they're mere demonic creatures and manifestations arising from Pandora.

Gwen thought it funny, throwing her head back against the window, grinded her teeth as she laughed, and rubbed the spot where it struck the glass. "Funny, but no. Because it is simply impassable. I can get people there, I can't get people out, so let the Threckets have their fun, and their own little patch of creation, something of which was denied to them."

Sarah relaxed, knowing full well the predicament she was in was paramount to understanding how to deal with it. She admitted she had rarely been in a situation like this before, but as Gwen said, her thoughts weren't her own, and they could be accessed at any such time Gwen saw fit; however, Sarah was nothing if not an admirable liar. She made it leagues this way and that, sending people to their deaths on whims. The lies she played was always the military elite, an officer who was trusted, and one of the few who could actually read a map and lead them in the right direction. Well, if she wasn't hell bent on her own mission, which always resulted in killing others.

She did it before, she can damn well do it again.

Chapter 21 Not All Brothers

Status Report: Military units were deployed to secure Oregon's borders. Fleets secured, deployed to combat the Chinese fleet. The Airforce pilots sent overhead to keep the airships off the borders. Northern California was bombarded by planes. National Guard and Active Army infantry deployed to push back. Fighting against an impressive display of artillery and air bombs, the front lines were forced to retreat. North California was fortified by Chinese forces on display, importing heavy machinery from their carriers.

Chinese Destroyer ships sailed into Southern California, bombarding San Diego's ports. FOB built and stationed in Los Angeles, filled with Marine and Army Personnel. Fighter pilots discharged to Southern San Diego to assault the destroyers.

***

Spadero listened to the director of this grand café, or so it said on the banner when he came in. This was a church. Chairs were set in rows, and a number of different people sat among them, all gathered in this room, quietly whispering to one another about their days, or so he guessed, hard to tell with so much chatter, and the director of this event spoke through the microphone. He had some concerns being here of course, being a congressman.

Fortunately, not too many people paid attention to him. Not that he needed the additional publicity. He sipped the coffee in his Styrofoam cup. Of course, tasteless, just like everything else in the world, and without taste, there was no sustenance. The only purpose of drinking coffee was to stay alert. His eyes scanned the room, vigorously looking for this *Ghost*. And yet, here he was, talking like a normal person, standing next to a couple, who, he was certain, were the victims of Culain threatening, or some other bother that prevented them from even coming here to begin with.

He shook his head, thinking just about how this wasn't his job. *Damn Irish bastard, quick on his wits, but hasn't the faintiest clue on how to be tact. Yes, treat this with tact, and all will be fine, and I can get the information I need without rousing too much suspicion. Ghost. Scars on your face.*

Spadero chuckled. Clearly, this Ghost didn't think anything of him being there, and didn't raise suspicion. By the individual accounts given to him by Culain, this Ghost is a fae. Whether he knew himself to be one or not, or even what a fae was, well, that's an entirely different matter.

The director ceased talking, and almost immediately, Spadero found the man walking with the rest of the crowd like ocean waves, or specifically of molasses: slow deplorable molasses. He followed him, but at a distance. Laser focused. That was the key. He was so close. And yet, Ghost was a smart man to hide in plain sight, but then, perhaps the poor little dickhead didn't know he was on the fae's most watched list.

***

Sakura, against her better judgment, begrudgingly accepted another request for her to come to the café, on Tuesday. There was something that drew her, but she couldn't quite tell what exactly. It certainly wasn't that pissant Ted Anderson. The man—she only ever met him once—was insufferable, and left a detestable taste in her mouth, more bitter than the Saltiest Sailor, home brewed, of course, and something specific to Atlanta. No one else had it.

The night sky lit up, regrettably, unlike Georgia, lights everywhere, and polluted the sky, hiding all the distant stars. The majestic sky was forever out of everyone's reach, and she wondered to herself, if people from Boston knew what laid beyond the pollution of the night. Sure, they knew of the existence of stars, which might be treated more like a dying fairy tale than anything else.

Of course, coming out of the street at night, she found the disparity to be an annoyance, especially the little group of people. They had worn out cargo pants, holey t-shirts, and backpacks with more to wear down on, and holes in the straps like locusts fed on them like leaves, or termites in wood, now rotting.

And just like she suspected: she remembered none of the details of the Bible Study, but this wasn't the reason she was going. Nor did she remember answering questions, truth be told, all of it went inside one ear and out the other. *How much could one college student handle?* Surely, she wasn't seriously considering new information that wouldn't do her much good in the future, and that's what this was: useless information. The friendships were fun though.

Samantha and Michael were amiable enough, and she couldn't count Lamar Cooper as useless either. The rest of the group came waltzing down the steps, resting and taking a deep breath of that fuel infested air. A hand grabbed her shoulder. "So, are you coming with us tonight?"

"I'm not doing anything, so, sure," Sakura smiled back at Sam who laugh giddily as she attached herself back to Michael, breaking into a conversation that flew over her head, something about finance? Sam clung like an overprotective woman to her boyfriend, declaring, 'He's mine, and no one else's.' Not that it involved her at all. Not in the least.

She noticed Ted, scowling at her with his scarred face, and clearly, her assessment matched up with whatever that man at the shooting range, and Lamar knew about him; he had seen some semblance of Hell, and a certain disdain for people in the military, coming out of the military, or even desiring to join the military. He hated all of them. That was certain, but that prompted a particular question: *why?*

A mystery to be sure, and one that she might not find easily, not without specific details or breadcrumbs to follow, and only with breadcrumbs could someone come close to an answer. The trouble was, nowhere near Ted was there a crumb, or a trail to lead to him, or at least connect anything to his disdain. Nothing at all. Granted, she only knew about him for a short while, and there was nothing particularly useful about him, but there was something that disturbed her.

He seemed to make an active effort to scowl at her, and while he wasn't particularly kind to Lamar, he rarely scowled at him. Sexist maybe. Maybe that's his problem.

As if the stars above sought to make Ted's life a little more miserable, a man in a nice suit, walked in front of Ted, forcing him to break eye contact with her. He spoke to Ted. *Thank God.*

Sakura turned, and a woman with a red head and freckles was chatting away with Samantha. Something finance related, still. Something she didn't have a remote interest in. It didn't make sense to bother one outside the natural cycle of things. Such as using currency to make more currency, which seemed like an oxymoron to her.

Samantha glanced her way. "Come on, you don't need to be by yourself." She ushered her into their little circle, and there was Brian, the most social and likable person of the whole bunch. He was very confident in his demeanor, loud, respectful, but always teetered on the fine line of being too pushy, but how close to the line could he toe without getting into trouble.

"Sakura, this is Erin."

Samantha introduced her to the red-haired woman, who turned with a bright smile on her face, and reached out her hand.

"Erin. Pleasure to meet you. New here?"

"You could say that," she answered.

"Okay, Ted," Erin chuckled. Samantha and Michael didn't seem to find that funny and frowned toward Erin, who's chuckle immediately died. "I'm sorry, that was in poor taste, I shouldn't have said that."

Coddling, again. The man is a jerk. You shouldn't be coddling him!

"Well, come on, what was it that Jennifer always said: 'Very important business at the empire,' or something like that." Michael seemed to want to lighten up the mood to start ushering people up the sidewalk toward the elegantly designed city hall. "Let's go, come around little children."

Sakura shook her head as she followed them up the street. It's where she went last week, but the most notable thing that happened last week was that Ted wasn't there, and she shared her phone number with people she enjoyed talking to. Now, she had no need to share her number, and Ted was there. And then there was this man who took a special interest in him for some reason. In fact, she noticed the man try more than once to get Ted into conversation, and now, there didn't seem to be a place for Ted to deflect to something else.

Ted smiled amiably at this man who had tried numerous times to get him to talk, just walking up from the church and around the corner to their little spot, he said, "And I don't quite understand what that has to do with any part of me, so I implore you, sir, why come to me with this?" Ted asked the man, Spadero. John Spadero, Congressman of Massachusetts. He wondered why the congressman had any interest in him, and of course, all high and mighty, as the higher ups always were, giving orders this way and that. This only led people to their graves, early or well timed, it was always based solely on the circumstances of one's death should they have found anything worth mentioning in their obituaries.

"You were a man of war, were you not?" Spadero replied, seemingly trying to butter him up, as the young men did the older ones. Thinking any of those compliments had any value to anyone other than themselves. *Idiot.* "I'd think a man of your history would have keen insight as we move on toward the future, attempting to avoid further war, the likes of which we've seen on the West Coast already. You'd agree with me, won't you, that further war is better off avoided?"

"I suppose if you want to spend money on saving lives, then sure, spend the money to save lives, but you're only costing people in the future. War is inevitable, and unstoppable. It will happen sooner rather than later, and I think you'll find it is far more costly to avoid war, than to jump head in," Ted answered.

But something tells me, Congressman, that this is not the conversation you mean to have with me. What are you after?

"It was Sergeant, right? Sergeant Ted Anderson of the 75th? Or am I mistaken?" Spadero urged on.

What exactly are you getting at? Don't you dare remind me; I'll make sure you won't be around to get re-elected. "One and the same."

"I read your record. It was a very impressive accolade."

"Please, tell me, what has become of the military, and of myself that my records aren't sealed shut?" *He's dead. What do you know? You dirty little bastard.* "And what business does a congressman have going into my file?"

"Let's call the information I received divinely inspired, shall we?" He sneered.

Ted shook his head. "You're a terrible liar."

"Well, I'm a congressman; I shouldn't be lying at all."

"Well, how's this for divinely inspired. You have had this cozy little experiment for ten years called world peace."

They turned the corner, crossing into the threshold of Teri Nation.

"All thanks to a unit which never existed, and quite frankly came out of nowhere, and it was that unit in particular who ripped the world to shreds, forcing the rest of the great nations to cower, sucking their thumbs like little babies."

"Interesting. I don't remember any of that," Spadero said, following him like a rat scurrying into a little hole right behind him.

Ted was suspicious of this man. This was no coincidence. This man didn't just walk in on a random Tuesday. He came here, looking for something. But what would that be? Ted couldn't help but wonder that this man was up to no good, but what was certain, Spadero was out for something only Ted Anderson would know.

"You wouldn't," he scoffed, sitting at the bar.

Scott, oh Scott, you're about to see me in one of my moods. Unfortunately, this jackass has my nerves up. Ted scanned the rest of the bar top, and the crowd blocked his vision of where the foreigners used to be sitting, but regrettably, he didn't see them. *Very curious.* "Anyway, like I said, there are no records of such a unit anymore, it was all erased."

"Let me buy you a drink."

"Hell, no." He snapped. "A gift from a politician is a gift to cast off into the trash, no matter what the intent is. It never leads anywhere good."

"Point taken."

"Scott, Cab please," the bar tender came over abruptly.

"Sure thing."

"I'll just have your house bourbon," Spadero ordered. "On the rocks is fine." He sat.

Ted shook his head as Scott swiftly came by with the drinks. Ted's hand was shaking visibly on the table, heart racing. He stared down at the glass, observing the sweat from his palms dripping from it. *Just like those rich people do. Just like those rich people do. Just like those rich people do. Come on, you can do this. Play the part of a rich man. You've done it before. Don't let this man, whoever he is get under the skin.* But his hand trembled, all the same.

"Yes, I remember reading about such a unit, but their accolades and their existence remains a mystery. Do you care to shed any light about that?" Spadero's eyes fixed upon the trembling hand.

"Look, Spadero, all of that is classified information, even to you. I don't know what clearance you have as a congressman, but I doubt it permits you to go snooping around files of confidential information like that," Ted replied. "Even if I knew why, I couldn't tell you." He took a sip after swirling his glass. *Honestly, I'd like to know the answer to that myself.*

"Oh, Ted. What are you doing all the way over here?" Sam called, cheerily twirling that Cabernet, as only she can.

Thank God! Sam, get me as far away from him as possible. Please!

"Is he being kind to you?" she asked Spadero.

Fantastic.

"Polite and blunt," Spadero chuckled, his hand over his rocks glass, bringing it carefully to his lips. His pupils shifted back and forth scanning the bar.

Hyperalert too, huh? You're disciplined for a bureaucrat.

"So, Ted, how is Jennifer doing?" Sam asked, her hand resting softly on his shoulder. His shoulder jerked ever so slightly, still highly alert with this new *Spadero* right here, interrogating him about information a normal person couldn't be reasonably assured to know.

"She is okay." He smiled at her. *Thank you, Sam.* "She's recovering, resting rather."

"It's been scary," Sam replied.

She's been on and off, some days were much better than others, but sometimes the bad days were really bad. Ted understood what the reality was, and as much as he's faced it before, he didn't want to have to face it again. Not with a woman of which he grew fond of, someone who helped him taste food again. "Yeah." *Again, thank you.*

"Who's this?" Spadero asked.

"Why, none other than our flamboyant biologist, researcher, whatever it is she does," Samantha said, leaning in toward Ted's ear. "Anyway, the reason I came, Spadero, was it?"

"Yes,"

"Apple picking," she replied, pointing at both with fingers, three fingers tucked in, and thumbs resting on the pointing index finger like pistols. "Saturday, noon. Coming?"

"I'll think about it," Ted answered. *Now, Spadero, will you go, or won't you?*

"I'll come. Where?"

Ted looked at him suspiciously, not bothering to hide a frown. This man reminded him of someone cold, and calculating, someone with a lot to gain, but not so much to lose. *Well, Spadero, congratulations. You intrigue me, but don't think I won't kill you if you get too close to the truth. Not that I don't want the truth uncovered of course, but the truth jeopardizes what I have here, and I don't want to lose it. I've already lost everything. Let me have this. Please.*

Chapter 22 Cesspool

President Snells' popularity rating has plummeted to below 10 percent in polls of both conservative and liberal voters.

Opinion: Such a low score reflects the poor handling of the West Coast invasion: the US is clearly losing, losing nearly all the West Coast population, pushing evacuation efforts further into secondary state lines. It is impossible to get the Executive Administration office to do anything of action, despite its efforts to draft.

Chief Commanding Officer Malcolm seems to be the only one remotely concerned and available for questioning.

***

Still no answers, only more questions. Of course, nothing was ever easy, but this mystery raised way too many questions. At least he knew what the Ghost looked like, physically, his scars made him stick out like a sore thumb. Wounds all over the place. Clearly, this man had seen some semblance of war, but he didn't seem that old and there hadn't been many skirmishes recently with the US forces. At the very least, nothing that would cause a man to look like that, and he didn't seem old enough to be in the armed forces when there was conflict, fifteen to twenty years ago.

The man has a strategic mind, even when presented with external stimulus of which he had no reason to suspect the unexpected, and he wasn't a food. He chooses his words carefully, but what of his friends? Can I use them to get closer to him, to get him to trust me to get him alone? Just for a chat. There are too many additional questions. Spadero had to stop himself, crossing the street. His mind was asking questions. Something it was good at. Many of these questions didn't get him closer to a solution, closer to the problem, or implementing any sort of solution should there be one. He was a tough nut to crack and grabbing hold of him could be like sticking a hand in the open mouth of a crocodile.

He stared up at the blank and empty sky. The lights were on. *Finally, the poor pissant of a congressman can go die in a hole.* He stepped inside the hotel again, walking through the neatly swept lobby, a change from last time. It was storming last time, and the lights were out, and yet, he found a speck of dust, resting on the marble tile. Shaking his head in disappointment, he walked to the elevator, slid through the doors, and then a couple came in behind him.

"Which floor?"

"Fourth," the woman answered.

He pressed the button which lit up before he reached forward for his floor; the tenth. He smiled back, leaning against the metal bar behind him. His ears perked up when they identified him as a congressman. *Great. I wonder what scandal they'll have about me spreading. Someone ends up dead, I get blamed for it? Foul play perhaps? Or Spadero, the great visitor of ladies? No. That title was already taken by John Dunn. No such luck here. Honestly, I wish it was that exciting.*

The doors opened, and he was all alone. Just the way he liked it; silence for his thoughts when he had the energy to meditate on them, but he didn't have a single lick of energy left. All of it, dealing with Culain, his short temper, and the possibility of Blanka's drunk ass waltzing in late at night doing God knows what. For heaven's sake, Ilya and Alexander were the only reasonable ones around, and Ilya just recently returned from a leave of absence for a while, collecting and refining data for their manhunt of this Ghost, along with some personal errand in Russia.

He walked and knocked on the door heavily, and like always, Culain opened the door. Scowling no reason other than to make the world know he's angry. Always angry. Everyone's angry these days. Even himself.

Spadero pushed his way into the hotel room, and the bastard slammed the door shut, locking it behind him. Seeing a spot with his name on it, he jumped over the coffee table into the couch, nearly tipping it over, and crossed his arms. "I hope you don't mind, but I'm staying the night here."

"Don't you have a house?" Culain moved into the kitchen and pulled out two cans of generic beer. He tossed one to Spadero, who caught it firmly with his sweaty palms. The can hissed violently at him as he pulled the ring up, pushing into the tear line.

Spadero sipped it. "Yes, but I had to deal with an annoyance, and I work a stone's throw away. I'll be outta yer potato head in the morning."

Ilya walked in. "You know how to make an entrance, or rather an impolite disturbance. Have some tact, will you?" She didn't scowl at him, she only glanced, and turned away as she went into the kitchen, pulled out some cheese from the drawer, sliced cheddar by the looks of it, and started eating. "Well, what news have you?"

He didn't answer at first, just bit his lip before opening his mouth. "Only more questions, no answers."

"Did you talk to—"

"Irish cunt!" Ilya slammed her fist on the counter. "I'll handle this. You'll only fuck it up," she scowled at Culain. *My God.* Ilya watched him skimp off, shaking his head, and muttering what he only guessed could be Irish insults. "Spadero, tell me, did you talk to him?"

"Yes, I did. A shrewd man, for certain," he said, leaning forward. "Only more questions."

Ilya sat across from him, leaning back in her seat, cozying up in her jacket as if she was freezing. She looked downward to his knees. A wetness seemed to shimmer on her eyeballs, which were redder than usual.

"All right." She bit her lip, crossing her arms over her chest, slouching into the couch. "What questions?"

"All the answers I have are that he is masquerading about as this Ted Anderson, who was a sergeant of the 75th Ranger Regiment before his particular unit merged with Black Eagle. After which, Ted Anderson and his unit went completely off the grid. There are no records. Why aren't there any records? Even he admitted to not knowing why there aren't any records, and I believe he told me the truth in that regard." He took another sip of beer. "Scars stain his face. All over. My guess is shrapnel from explosions, so he's been in war time, which dates his time of service to when Ted Anderson's unit disappeared. But this Ghost doesn't appear very old, I'd guess early twenties at the latest. College aged."

Ilya didn't look up, but she pursed her lips before speaking, "And what are you getting at here?"

He tapped the coffee table repeatedly with a firm middle finger. "I could be off here, but say he's twenty-four. Virtually all conflict would have stopped around nine to eleven years ago, placing him between the ages of thirteen to fifteen at the time. Sergeant Ted Anderson has been dead for about nine years now, hanged in his own apartment. Ruled a suicide. Now, this kid stole this dead man's identity, has been masquerading as him since then. These assumptions are purely circumstantial. I don't have any hard evidence of this. Whatever training he'd—"

"You're hinging these assumptions based on circumstantial evidence which cannot be verified," she said. "You're taking me down a rabbit hole I have no business being in, Spadero. We need additional details on how we can get him alone."

"I'm getting to that, or rather, the complications of doing just that," he said, his voice growing raspy. "But this man never had a childhood. Likely never knew his parents. And Black Eagle must have stolen him like a thief in the night."

"I fail to see how any of that matters. Get on with it," she said, making eye contact, and tears streamed down her face, as if she suspected this all along.

Spadero remembered Jack, and his family, left dead and absorbed. One of the many acts of violence he conducted to get answers to one problem. There were many problems, and so many innocent bystanders, their blood was on his hands. Add a few more fae to the mix, and that number rose exponentially. Sometimes children were involved as a last resort, needfully. *We would never needlessly involve children. And this was needless. There's a special place in Hell for you, whoever you are.* "I'm simply saying, if the wrong person knows of his existence, and I assume they do, then we aren't the only person looking for Ghost. I'm getting close with his friends. If need be, I'll use one of them as a hostage."

"Be careful of what you do, Spadero, or else you become the Devil you hate," she said, wiping the tears from her eyes.

He knew it. She knew it. There was something foul, and another hole to dig, just getting the right shovel to dig it was what made it worse, and whatever else is going on in the world. He couldn't be sure it was connected, much like just grabbing at straws and hope an idea sticks long enough to dissect it, and hope the truth makes sense. If it doesn't, just grab another straw; one must find the one that makes sense.

But she was right. He was already in a moral bog. He was at risk, he knew, of digging a hole so deep and dark that he may be swallowed up entirely, and forget why he did the things he did. Already, just to get a grasp of this man's pseudo identity, he killed several different contacts, and half of them, who he didn't kill, went missing after the fact, and their families. No one will ever know why they died, or what tied them to the marsh of the states. Surely, if there be any true patriots among anyone in the states, they'd be disgusted to find their country was nothing more than a toxic cesspool.

"We should get Sander on the phone," John said.

"Yes, if we can." She pulled out her cell phone, dialed it, and threw it on the table.

"Adam here, Ilya, you better have some good news for me," he said over the phone.

"Yes." She smiled. A very fake smile, and it made her sound a little more cheerful. "We have a positive ID, but origin remains unknown. He is going by the name of Ted Anderson, and we think specifically—Ted Anderson of the 75th Ranger Regiment, prior to his unit disappearing off the face of the planet."

"I take it you have yet to acquire him?"

"Correct. But we have been able to plant a congressman right next to him, and his friends, should drastic measures be necessary," she continued.

"And you said there is still no known origin. Did I hear right?"

"Correct. All we have on origin is speculation which won't do us any good. We need Ghost to find his origin, and to tie him to any such activity relating to the Grail, or McCurdy. But, in any case, we can at least get him to clean up his mana messes," Ilya replied. "Which was the reason we were looking for him to begin with. Honestly, Sander, do you really think he's tied to this Devil's Pass man, and McCurdy?"

"No, but I can't let the possibility slide. Too many things happening all at once. Ta ta."

The phone hung up.

"I don't want to go apple picking." He leaned back into his seat.

"Apple picking?"

"Ghost's friends are going apple picking. Ghost didn't commit to it. He's a shrewd man."

"You mean a shrewd child?" she corrected.

"Yeah."

Chapter 23 Confrontation

Status Report:

Washington Chinese heavy cavalry, and Northern California Chinese California uproot Oregon's defenses in a pincer attack. With American resistance uprooted and forced to retreat east, Chinese Forces take root into Oregon.

Chinese scouts north of Washington inch forward. The Chinese fleet closes in on Los Angeles, forcing Air Force pilots and personnel to remain stationed at the FOB. The Chinese forces in Southern California inch forward with their heavy cavalry units into Arizona.

***

Jennifer yawned, waking up from her nap, the moon shining in her room. The covers were nice and cozy, comfortable, but that was all the comfort that was present. She peered out the window, and most of the lights of the city were off. The ones that remained were the streetlights.

The darkness inside her room was comforting, but one thing couldn't be overlooked, she might have her time cut short, but she mustn't let the dreary reality get to her, no. Many times, she read of the cynical passages of Ecclesiastes, and some parts entering into Revelation, and while it talked about thieves coming in at night, Revelation especially, there was a hope of rest, and peace, and painlessness.

She spent more time on these passages lately with her diagnosis, and sometimes she felt like it came as a thief in the night with nothing else to do but to cut her time short, and to give her menial tasks she'd rather not be doing. It stole her time from her. She'd much rather spend her time hanging out with her friends, drinking, though, say one thing for leukemia: it didn't stop her from re-reading Jane Austen. The charming writer if ever there was one. Most others were secluded and plagued with naught but simple prose the common person could not understand.

But was that the point for such simple prose? To reduce flowery language and an abundance of adverbs for which Jane Austen was filled with? To make such excellent stories worth knowing in such a simple way, that anyone, if they could read, could read this book? Or a series of novels. The biggest crime really, was taking away one's ability to read.

She pulled the blanket off and swung her legs over the side of the bed, her toes gently touching the furry carpet, slowly resting down as the joints in her toes moved in place for easy transition to standing. Her hands rested with the utmost care on her knees, which, though not inflamed, were stiff, and bending it didn't cause her pain, but it removed a small amount of comfort.

"Move your knee," she said. "Come on, you can do it. Just move."

It was no small thing, peering out the window. Glass. Easily breakable. If someone was in here with her, they could easily push her out, shattering the glass, screaming out the window, plummeting all the way down until eventually struck the ground, shattering her bones, especially as fragile as they were. She was still waiting on a donor for her blood type, the appropriate stem cells for her treatment, but they were in short supply. They always were. *Well, the bleeding would stop.*

She grunted, forcing herself forward. The discomfort entered her knees as she staggered forward, catching herself on her nightstand, standing strong. *I probably shouldn't have done that.* "Oh, well." She stretched her arms and leaned back and forth, loosening the joints of her body till she adjusted her comfort to the discomfort provided to her. She glanced back over to the window, her breath against it, one open hand touching as she looked outside again.

The sky shined all the clearer today, and she was by herself, alone in her apartment. Not that she minded, of course. Sometimes it was good to be in a silent place, away from all distractions. She became accustomed to the silence. She had to. Because that's what Ted needed. He needed someone who he could confide his trust to, portraying it in such a way of a child. He needed these things because he never knew them, and she, and Sam to a degree was able to provide that to him.

Yet so much about him remained a mystery, and though he never said why, she finally picked the pieces together. Quite frankly, it was the reason for him not seeing a therapist. Provided those were in short supply these days, and new patients were always immediately waitlisted for nine to twelve months.

The phone rang.

I like company. Sounds nice.

She turned to her phone, picking it up, not bothering to read which devilish fiend called her at this hour, not bothering to check. "Samantha, dearest."

"Jennifer," Sam squeaked into her ear.

"Yes, Sam, my adorable little carpet," she replied.

"Yes, I am your adorable little carpet." She laughed on the other line. "Speaking of carpets, how do you feel about apple picking this Saturday?"

Honestly, it did sound nice, despite the discomfort she currently found in her kneecaps, which may or may not subside entirely by Saturday. However, there was the risk that it would be inflamed with heightened physical activity, of which apple picking required. But then there was the matter of Ted.

"And Ted? Did you invite him?" she asked.

"Yes, he didn't commit to it yet," Sam replied.

"And Sakura?" She sighed.

"Yes, she's coming," she answered.

Oh, dear. "And Michael's brother?"

"Yes, he's—"

"Samantha Harris," Jennifer screamed over the phone. "I told you, those two can't be within the same vicinity with one another. There's—there's bad blood between them. On the outside, pleasant for all of us to see, but inside, they hate each other." Jennifer knew Sam was better than this. She felt her own blood boil with her hand gripping the phone tighter at Sam's blatant disregard to what was developing between Ted and Jeff.

"I'm sorry, Jennifer, I forgot," she apologized.

"I'll be there if Ted goes. Wherever Ted is, that is where I'll be," she said. "I'm sorry for snapping, but—"

"I understand," she interrupted. "How is chemo?"

"Hard sometimes," she answered softly. "It still hurts. All this time, waiting for a donor, but every day, some days are harder than others, and there are days that I hardly notice it at all."

"Well, I hope you feel better, get some rest. I'll pray for you,"

"Thanks, Sam," she replied.

The phone went silent.

Chapter 24 Enter Sergeant Emily Miller

Rioters are on capitol Hill.

Picket signs are asking for the removal of President Snells for his inaction of the West Coast, and inability to address the public. The Press Secretary is nowhere to be seen, and the staff remain at the White House. The security is out at force with security fences and riot gear.

***

Emily Miller walked up to her front porch just as the sun was rising. Her brown hair, her brown fatigues, and her shorts were soaked with her sweat. Why wouldn't they be after running a marathon first thing in the morning? She opened the screen porch door, kicked off her shoes as she went into her kitchen, filling up her bottle with water, and started chugging it.

Her husband just turned on the early morning news. He was exceedingly concerned about the events on the world, but if *you'd heard it once, you've heard it a thousand times, as the saying goes.*

She finished her water, tuning out the horrible news of what she imagined was all but inevitable, and coming to her husband, wrapping her sweaty arms around him as he sat on the couch, her lips kissing his cheek ever softly.

"Babe, it's not worth it to give yourself another stress induced anxiety attack over things you have no control over." She looked at the screen, glancing briefly. An anchorman was reporting with a bulletproof vest, illustrating the decimation of what she guessed was Moscow, blown up vehicles, shattered glass over the place. This channel didn't even have the tact to censor the corpse bent over backward out the shattered remains of the windshield.

You're not the one who must go running into that, I am.

"I know but, our daughter has to live in—"

"There's nothing you can do about it," she said, stretching her neck to rest on his shoulders, feeling his black scruff scratching across her cheek. "Come on, I'm hungry. Make me something to eat."

"Yes, dear," he said.

He moved around the couch and hugged her. "Shower first."

She smiled back at him, hugged him closely, wrapping her arms around his waist, holding her hands tightly.

"Hey, enough of that." His hands tried to pull her grip off him, but she was far stronger than he was. She had to be, with all the equipment she had to carry for her job, which she told him little about. Most of which was classified information anyway.

"I was planning on it," she said.

"Baby, you're sweaty. I just changed this shirt."

She snickered, releasing her grasp and patting his cheek. "Breakfast is the most important meal of the day."

She turned and walked down the hallway.

"Next to lunch and dinner," her husband called.

Opening the door to her room, the early morning sun rays cascaded into her chamber. She walked over to her closet, pulling out a new set of clothes before briskly walking to her bathroom, locking the door, and turning the water on. Undressing, she immediately stepped into the ice-cold water as it slowly warmed up, steaming up the glass walls inside her showering bathtub.

Feeling the hot water cascade over her body, washing herself, her extremities, her hair. Each droplet of water felt like a needle, and she cringed as she brushed her hand through her hair, looking out into the steamy glass walls around her, and muffled sounds penetrated her ears, and slowly, became clearer.

"Sergeant Miller! Get me out!"

Her hand stretched out into the burning Humvee. A soldier, an infantryman stuck, pinned to the ground. Her hand reached his, the warm, thick blood forced her grip to slip. Gunfire raged in the distance, the sand pelting her from the night sky, the whirring of helicopter blades rising above her.

Steps came out from behind the truck. She dropped the man's hand, drew her side arm, aimed to fire. Russian Patches. She fired a shot, and the Russian soldier's head burst like a water balloon. Bone fragments and blood sprayed over the side of the truck.

Another soldier climbed on the truck, aiming a rifle at her. She turned, firing an aimed shot down his throat, and the same, blood sprayed, pushed back. The corpse folded back over the other end of the truck. She heard the body slam onto the ground.

"Sergeant Miller! What the hell are you doing!"

She gasped. Her hand touched the glass. *Oh. It was them or me. That's it.* She shook her head, stepping out of the shower. *Him or me. All for the prize of freedom.*

She dried herself off, dressed herself, and threw her smelly clothes into the hamper. It may be one of the first things Jessica smells, and that was the best sort of love anyone could ask for. Really, she should be honored, taking a dump first thing in the morning, smelling her mother's morning odor. She chuckled at that last bit. *It doesn't smell like blood, so there's that.*

She opened the door, and walked back down the hall, and when she got to Jessica's room, she rested her ear on it. There was no sound, not one. She slowly and sneakily pushed it open, and her daughter, who was just entering high school, was sleeping soundly this morning, her curly dark hair making a mess over her face.

Can't have that. Not my daughter.

She sat on the bed next to her, and carefully pushed the frazzled hair out of her face, tucking it neatly behind her ear. *Much better. Sweet dreams.*

Standing over the bed, she left. Timidly and sneakily shutting the door behind her, leaving with not a sound.

Briskly walking back down the hall to freshly cooked bacon, eggs, and pancakes, she found the table set for three. Of course, Jessica would be joining shortly after. The large cups filled to the brim with orange juice. But her eyes peered disappointingly at Kevin, who was on the landline.

He covered the mouthpiece and brought it to his shirt. "It's Malcolm again."

"Kevin, if I told you once, I told you a thousand times never entertain calls with him." She firmly struck the hand with her table, the silverware clattering. Her husband jolted and was bringing the phone to his face. "No, you don't."

She sprinted over to him, hopping over the couch, and ripped the receiver from his hand, hanging up the phone. "Don't, talk to him. I mean it."

"What does he want?" he asked.

The phone rang.

"Don't answer it. Let it go to voicemail. He wants me to apply for Black Eagle, that's all, and he won't leave me alone. I swear, I'm getting him processed as processed salted ham."

The phone stopped ringing. She was hoping he would just leave a voicemail for her to ignore. She didn't want to bother with a call from Malcolm. Besides, didn't he have any better things to do than act like a recruiter?

"There, now I can enjoy my meal." She took her husband's hand. *That son of a bitch.*

Just as they were sitting down, "MOM! MOM! You stank up the toilet!"

"I love you too!" she called, digging into the eggs.

Jessica came scurrying out the hall, sitting at the table, her brown braided hair tucked behind her. She started eating. "Jessica, you going out with your friends later?"

"Yes, we're going to the—"

The phone rang again.

Damnit, Malcom.

"Let it ring." Emily spoke softly and politely as she continued cutting into her pancakes.

The ringing stopped. *Don't call again.*

"So, Jessica, you were saying, dear?" she asked.

"Oh, yes, sorry," she replied. "We're going to the mall later. Jack is picking me up."

"Make sure to stay—"

The phone rang again.

You son of a bitch. You're not gonna stop until I answer the damn phone, are you?

"Babe." She calmly put down her fork. Her rage was getting the better of her, and the last thing she wanted Jessica to hear was her cursing someone out over the phone. Not very respectable, but it was something that needed to be done.

"Hmm?" he asked with his mouth full.

"Can you take Jessica outside for a minute?"

"But Mom, I barely touched my food,"

"Outside please," she said, smiling at her precious daughter. *You don't need to hear this.*

"Come on." Kevin put his fork down, and grabbed Jessica's hand, pulling her gently from the table, and walking her outside, closing the door firmly behind them.

Emily wiped her mouth clean, stood, and took herself to the phone, ripping it from the receiver from the base. "What do you want?"

"Well, Emily, as you know we're starting applications again, and we'd like you to—"

"Piss off. I'm not interested," she said.

"You might not be, but war is coming to the East Coast," he said.

"It's America! War is always coming. All because of bureaucrats like yourself who can't get their fingers out of their asses. Stop calling me," she gritted over the phone.

"Pays much better,"

"I don't care if you're offering six figures. You can't buy honor. You can only purchase freedom with blood, and the lives of those willing to put their life on the line."

"And none know that better than Black Eagle."

"No. The difference between you and me, is that I work for freedom, and you work for a goddamned paycheck. I've told you to stop calling me, so stop," she replied.

"Well, I was hoping to not have to resort to this, but your skills are completely invaluable. I don't know how invaluable you think you are, but it is priceless,"

"I'm not interested in anything you have to offer. Your organization is shadier than the fucking Gestapo!" She slammed the phone on the base.

He's a fucking Nazi is what he is. Who would ever think that America, of all places, would become a breeding ground for Nazis?

The phone rang immediately.

She picked up the receiver, hanging up.

It rang again.

She hung up the phone.

And again.

"I told you to—"

"Since you don't want to, I think it would be beneficial for me to send a recruiter over to the high school," he interrupted her.

"You wouldn't dare." Her eyes narrowed, teeth gritting, palms sweating.

"I think you and I both know I would,"

"If I so much as smell a recruiter walking those halls, I will hunt them down, and hang them upside down from their balls, and watch the crows eat him alive!"

She hung up the receiver and went behind the phone.

And like clockwork, it rang again.

She ripped the mtg cord out, and the ringing stopped.

If you did your homework, you would know, I don't respond to black mail well.

"Come in," she called. Kevin and Jessica walked back in.

They took their seats and resumed eating.

"I'll be over here. I'm a little worked up." Emily turned, taking herself into the living room.

"Mom?" Jessica asked.

"Yes, dear?" Emily sat herself on the couch, leaning back.

"Who was that on the phone?"

"Nobody important. Speaking of..." She turned her head to peer over the couch. "If you see someone at school, recruiting for *Black Eagle,* don't talk to them. And you tell me immediately. Do not talk with them unless I am present. Do you understand me?"

"Yes, Mom. I won't talk to them." She continued eating.

Good.

Chapter 25 Puppets

I was about to cut ties with Black Eagle once and for all. Leave the military behind me. I was about to send my papers in today when I was called into her office to be deployed to Germany. I leapt across Nakamura's desk and broke her neck. I can't tell you enough how satisfying that sound was. My hands are still marked with her nails trying to scratch her way free from my grasp. Killing her was so satisfying. To be rid of her, privately. It's only a matter of time before they find me. I'll be dead before then. Slander me all you want. I don't care anymore.

***

Malcolm combed his hands through his hair as he looked at his strategy board. His office was small with his large table, holding world maps. He worked with advanced technology and a large grid was in front of him with various elevations. This vertical board showed him where all the planes might by at the present time.

The ships on the horizontal board were all over the place. Ships along the West Coast was in disarray, and from what his intelligence officers were telling him, the US Armed Forces weren't faring any better with artillery strikes cascading their position. He was standing by, waiting for the funding source from Snells, but there was no such luck.

Not these days. Luck was in short supply. He moved black ships to the board of the map sailing from the Arctic. His ships. Not American. His ships. Operated by Black Eagle alone, and their armed forces were on standby as he commanded. But the funding source was paramount. Without it, he couldn't do anything.

Damn bureaucracy. Snells. This isn't like you.

Truth was, he was hard to get a hold of. He was the president. He should be hard to get ahold of. But to be absent in the state of affairs of war, especially with how poorly the war efforts were going was a travesty. As if just waiting for the Russians to invade the Eastern Shores. That was a certainty. A guess. But he was certain the guess was correct.

Malcolm was tutored by the greatest military mind that he ever had the privilege and dishonor of knowing. *Stay six steps ahead.* Easier said than done, especially when he can't move his pieces across the board without the green light.

He huffed out a sigh before collapsing back into his chair, staring at his ceiling. His hands wove across his chest. Pondering what the next best course of action was. Still, he came up short.

"Flanked by Russia and China. Russia is doing me a grand favor by just staying put, but they won't stay idle forever. Still got that little problem of Ghost being over somewhere in Boston. Clemens called me to confirm that specific information. Only for me to be called by Snells about all reports pertaining to his unit. Around that time, former comrades close enough to our units started disappearing. No explanation. No investigation. Just simply vanished without a trace. Like Ghosts. Higher intelligence officers within the US military might be aware that Ghost is still alive. But why aren't they tracking him? Doesn't make any sense. So then, is someone else looking for Ghost? Who would that be? And what would be the reason for it?"

He kept thinking about all the scenarios, but one thing kept bugging him. More than anything else. Snells was nowhere to be found. Almost dropped off the face of the earth. But then, why hasn't the next in line of the change in command taken the reins?

Puppet? But then who is pulling all the strings? Assuming there is a puppet master in all of this, why doesn't it allow Snells to make big picture decisions like this? Where is this puppet master? Must be close. The question is how close, and how close am I allowed to get to this puppeteer? Sadly, it is the only thing that makes a fraction of the sense I need it to make. Especially since no one is at all concerned.

If there is some syndicate, it suggests that is who is looking for Ghost. It also stands that the possibility is there, that they are behind the world burning to the ground. It also stands to suggest that Snells is in their pocket and can't do jack about it.

He looked back to his horizontal maps with all the ships. He turned his gaze toward the East Shores.

"As soon as I move my forces from the Arctic into the Pacific, it is guaranteed that Russia will invade on the Eastern Front. I'm not going to be able to coordinate a two front war. But Ghost is in Boston. If he's directly pushed, he will fight. If it's to protect something. I'm going to have to count on you, Ghost. As much as you're a problem. I'm going to have to use you, for old time's sake."

And there's this problem with this syndicate. I don't know where you are. I don't know how many of you there are. I will uproot you and smoke you out. Once you've been made public, I will hang you. Just as Nakamura would have it.

Well, welcome to World War III.

Chapter 26 Apples

Report from the Front Lines:

Another pincer attack from North and South
California closed in on Los Angeles, demolishing
the FOB, forcing the last of US forces off the West
Coast. Chinese forces push further into the US
into Nevada and Idaho. Army and Air National
Guard was immediately deployed and holding the
front lines into these states, also with the assistance
of Army and Air National Guard units from
Colorado, Wyoming, New Mexico, Montana and
Texas.

Speaker of the House Samuel Monabello has been
in contact with the COO of Black Eagle Company.
He believes that 'the President and his Vice are not
eligible to serve under the current condition.' The
nature of his contact with BEC is not confirmed.

***

The brisk fall air reminded Sakura very much of the nature of life,
fleeting and oh so temporary, changing color with age until it withered
and finally died. But there was a certain beauty in that, especially out
here, with the apples in the trees, low hanging branches for them all.
This orchard up north in Andover, a place she never thought she'd find
herself, least of all with this small group of Christians of a variety of
personalities. Again, no talk of faith here, but perhaps that was
intentional.

She was surprised to learn that Jeffrey was Michael's brother and that
he showed up, and of all the people here, he was who she could relate to.

He appeared not to be a man of faith, but a man of grit, deeply rooted. Not some far off distant goal that for all she knew, was just a lie, which made certain people feel better, and some worse depending on their own individual walks of life.

She went to pluck an apple from the low hanging branch. It shook, and the red apple was knocked off, falling down onto the ground, rolling to a stop not far from the tree. A red lady, she called it. She bent down, picked it from the ground, wiped it on her shirt and dropped it into her paper bag with all the others, and then there was another one. A large green man she called these, the sour ones were her favorite apples, but she was eager to grab *that* one. It was large, and likely succulent upon sinking her teeth into it. She pushed herself into the trees, the branches rough against her clothes, and the leaves caressing her skin like her mother used to do before she got too old, and the red apples below, bobbed against her for attention. No apple gets left behind.

Her foot pressed against the trunk, and her loose arm wrapped around the tree, firmly grabbing hold of the bark, and lifted herself up to stretch to get that apple.

"Oh, you'll never reach that apple," a voice came from behind her, and a large hand wrapped its grimy unwelcomed hands on her beautiful apple. *Her* beautiful apple.

"Hey." She turned around, tumbling down, smacking her face against the bed of soil. The bitter taste forced her to cough it out. She wiped her face with her sleeve and stood, facing Jeffrey, who wiped the apple clean before offering it to her. "I didn't need your help."

"You are too short for that branch. I don't care how good a climber you are," he chuckled.

She took the apple, inspecting it for malformities. Pleased that there was none, she placed it in with the rest of her apples. "So, uh, when do you go back on duty?"

"I don't actually know," he answered, turning back to the path. "China on the west shore, and Russia threatening us from the East. They're probably figuring out where to put me before they deploy. So, I was told to stay put, and here I am, staying right where I need to be, until I'm called."

"How exactly did it come to this?" she asked. "Couldn't it have been avoided?"

"'Wars can be prevented just as easily as they are provoked, and we who fail to prevent them must share the guilt of the dead,'" he replied. "Unfortunately, Omar Bradly didn't have mercenaries in mind when he said that. He was a good General; anyone would have been lucky to serve under him. But I guess you must first know what created the peace to begin with, and that was a weapon."

"A weapon?" She turned to him. *One weapon begot world peace? How?*

"Details are classified, but that weapon kept everything at peace, and it wasn't until now that all the major players in the world knew of its decommissioning," he continued. "Now that the threat of using that weapon is null and void, it makes threatening nations far easier."

"Why'd they decommission—"

"Classified, and building a weapon like that takes a decade," he interrupted. He looked down to her, "Look, I know you have a need for patriotism, but there isn't any of that in war. Freedom can be bought, but not with anything less than a massacre. I urge you to chase that impossibility, and trust no one else to make the determinations for you. Follow your orders, and place orders when need to. The military is a cesspool, and you'll be asked to do things that disgust you."

She continued to walk with him, clutching her bag close to her chest. Lines get crossed and with a world like this where the actions made are irrevocable, how could she reconcile the horrible things her family did—the horrible things she would do. Where does it get drawn, and how far was too far?

"Where do you draw the line?"

He sighed heavily. "If you want to go home, or if you want to move up in rank, there is no line."

He sped off ahead of her, catching up to Michael and Sam. They were a cute couple. Such a wholesome view should have eased her nerves. But it didn't. Jeffrey filled her with an existential dread, forbearing the future actions which may inevitably give her nightmares and fill her with regrets, or so she thought. So then, it would take a monster to complete the tasks she has set on her own shoulders, or quite possibly, imposed upon her by her lineage, her proud Japanese American lineage. Could she be that monster?

Jennifer held Ted's warm hand, silently off to the side, with their own collection of apples. Ted was very good at picking apples, getting into places where she couldn't, and wouldn't since she wouldn't tear up her dress; the twigs and thorns might get in the way. Curse her for deciding to do this last minute, but what she did find a certain felicity in, was the fact that Ted continued to smile, and his eyes lit up brightly like a child. A child finally allowed to play, cheeks puffy like a chipmunk with nuts stuffed in its mouth.

Something like this was taken from him, and he never got the chance to have fun, and here he was, climbing trees efficiently. She supposed he had his fair share of tree climbing, marks on his face, but he didn't seem to mind the minor scratches from the branches or thorns on his hand. She wondered if he felt pain. Fearless, he had to be for something like this, and something like this was so casual, so playful considering everything else he was forced to go through. What's one tree to an exploding car?

She noticed his head turned to gaze at a top branch. *Oh no.* He placed his bag on the ground, and she looked up. "Tedward, be careful, that doesn't look too stable!" she said as he scurried up the tree, almost like a squirrel. The thought was cute, until she got a much better look at the top, a cluster of green apples atop the tree, and of course, where all things were considered, it was thin, and easily breakable. "TED! Not those apples!"

But she was much too late. The wind came in, pushing the top of the tree, having the tree wave at her as Ted was reaching for it, and his hand stretched to pull the apples off. The wind whistled as it brushed through the leaves. *Honestly, how is he even going to get back down?*

The top of the tree creaked.

"TED! GET DOWN!" she cried.

Ted slowly picked off the apples, rolling them on his sleeves, and placed them in his pants pocket. He slowly climbed back down, hopping from branch to branch, and came down safely, minus a few bumps and scratches from earlier. She placed her hands all over him.

"Are you okay?"

"Yes," he said, pulling the apples out of his pockets and putting them in the paper bags. "I'm fine. Nothing at all to worry about."

She took a closer look at him. There was one scratch that wasn't there, on his cheek, red and dripping.

"You're bleeding," she said, reaching for her purse to grab a napkin, and spat on it, rubbing his cut clean, and took another look.

Ted didn't flinch. As his history with hand trembling became all too constant, his hands stopped whenever she was near. She felt honored that he should trust her, with such frailty, she knew she could never betray his trust in her. This bleeding was natural, she turned away from him briefly, feeling the warm blood in her nose, and wiped it into the napkin, and withdrew it to a waste bag.

She turned her gaze back up to the tree, still swaying in the wind, whistling as it picked up, brushing her hair over her shoulders. She placed her hand on her sun hat to stop it from blowing off. The tree still creaked, but the top remained there, as if it didn't just deal with another man grabbing apples it clearly didn't want pulled.

She sighed, shaking her head. "Well, I suppose we should go meet with the others. With all the apples you got, we can make an apple pie, or maybe a delicious apple crisp." She peered into his bag. "Have you ever had an apple before?"

"No," he answered.

Opportunity knocks for those that open the door. "Well, when we get back and have these apples washed, I'll have you try one of mine."

"Why—"

"Pesticides, germicides, and all matter of other cides to keep the critters and bugs out of these apples," she replied. *He wouldn't have known about this. At least, I don't think he would.*

She heard snapping twigs. She abruptly turned, and that congressman showed up, neatly dressed as if he wasn't important. He came in his own car of course, and she exchanged niceties. He wasn't the regular politician; this she could tell. There was something about the way he carried himself which she found to be suspicious. She caught him following them.

She shrugged the feeling off. Probably just not very good at picking apples.

One as important as John Spadero taking an interest in her dear Tedward. No one but her needed to know Ted's past, and the source of all his despair. In fact, she might even say no one ought to ever know, unless they wanted to violently rip open an old wound, voraciously rubbing salt with lemon juice all over it. Listening to them scream for help in the most eloquent way.

Spadero placed a few green apples in his bag before walking to another tree. The poor man. He didn't know how to pick apples. He always followed behind everyone, getting whichever apples they chose to leave behind, as if to say, 'you forgot some, but I didn't.'

He turned to look at both her and Ted. Smiled at her, and she traded the grin. *Ill placed suspicions. Nothing more. He is harmless. A nice change in pace.*

Upon leaving the orchard, Michael proposed that Sakura should stay a while longer for a little campfire. She didn't have any plans, so why not? A nice crackling fire with the ashes of burning wood assaulting her nostrils with those wonderful smoky scents.

Michael and Jeffrey went off in the brush somewhere to get wood. The clearing was nice, fall autumn leaves decorated the forest floor, the crickets sang, and the owls hooted their lovely songs, and of course, who could forget the stars, and the moon shining up high in the sky.

The lovely forest air was refreshing to her nose, leaning back, and propping herself up with straightened arms. Sam sat down next to her, pulling out some bottled water.

Michael planned this already. What other explanation would there be for coolers, I suppose to keep the apples nice and fresh on the way. She did hear talk of some apple crisp. Oh, what she wouldn't do for some of her mom's home-made apple crisp, with the sweet aromas, the lovely taste sweetened just with the right amount of cinnamon sugar. Nothing too fancy, nothing too bland. Just right.

She took the bottle. "Thank you."

"No problem," she said. "So, are you having fun?"

"Yes," she replied. "Thank you, for being a friend. And inviting me out like this. I don't really get involved too much at the university."

"Uni life," Sam elbowed her. "I barely remember it."

"Yeah, gotta do it though," Sakura said.

"Do we, though? I mean, you're going to be an officer, aren't you? So yeah, you might. I have my BS, and I learned a bit. But do you know how much I use the information I learned there? None." Sam laughed, taking a gulp of her own water, and then tucked her knees to her chest.

Michael and Jeffrey lit the fire, and the logs were burning, red ash floating into the sky, and the smoky scent filled her nose as the smoke rose. Ted and Jennifer's face glowed orange on the other side of the fire.

"Well, I don't actually need a degree to even be hired for my job. You just need to know how to think."

"Doesn't college teach you how to think?"

"Hun, I have met some of the dumbest people who have PHDs, and some of the smartest people who never completed high school. All college really does is prove that you know how to think and write, and that's all anyone wants. Officer candidate school is probably the same. Not that I would know of course," Sam argued. "And take Ted, over there."

Sakura scowled and Sam waved her hands down to the ground.

"I know, he's unbearable at times. He is the epitome of what it means to attain success, by American standards. He's rich to the point where he doesn't need a job anymore."

"What did he do, steal from a bank?"

She laughed nervously. "Stockbroker. He did a lot with that job before, then he started doing it all himself, and now he just works from home. Granted, he did put in an unnecessary number of hours. So, if you want success, whatever you do, don't do what he did. It wasn't good for his mental health, although one could make the argument it was the best thing for his mental health at the time."

"A contradiction if ever there was one,"

Sam threw her head up in laughter. "Humans are funny creatures, aren't we? Say one thing, and upon further reflecting realize the opposite might be true. But I think that you might find he is a valuable source of information—"

"I didn't get that from him," she said, taking a drink.

"Well, he doesn't just talk to anyone either. I'm curious as to how your conversation with him went," Sam asked.

"He said it was all meaningless."

"You know, we were studying Ecclesiastes when we first met him." She chuckled.

Sakura raised her eyebrow, not understanding what was so funny between the words meaningless, and Ecclesiastes. She's never read it, but she had a feeling there was a bit of sarcastic irony there. The fire continued to crackle as Michael moved some wood around with a stick.

An orange leaf fell in her hair. She brushed it aside. "So, naturally I'd find that funny." Sam faced the fire, and her lips curled downward to a frown. "The thing is, we weren't designed to take human life. Ted knows that better than anyone. As someone whose job it was to take human life, again and again, and again." She turned and smiled at her, a halfhearted one. "So, forgive him, please. I know he's unbearable, and he has a nasty taste in his mouth for anything related to the military."

Sakura found this oxymoron troublesome, as the man didn't seem to be much older than she was. *Who was he killing? Something isn't right. Okay. Fine, let's have at it a second time.*

Sakura turned the cap on the water bottle. "Thank you for that. I'll try to forgive him." She stood, before walking closer to the flame, the heat caressing her skin. Ted made eye contact with her, and that scarred face and its deadly scowl turned its hideous gaze toward her. Jennifer grinned, but another halfhearted smirk. It appeared that even her presence made her nervous.

"Ted," Sakura began.

"What do you want?" he asked.

"Tedward, please be nice. She doesn't know," Jennifer said, leaning her back into Ted, keeping a careful eye on Sakura.

"It's best she doesn't."

"Look, I don't know why you hate me, I didn't do anything to you."

"You're throwing your life in the trash, is what you're doing," Ted replied. "Look, I don't care what rank you are, what rank you end up being. Become a four-star general or admiral for all I care. You are nothing but a tool and a statistic. Do you know what a statistic is?"

She shook her head. "I bet you're going to tell me." She sighed.

"A statistic is a variable with a numerical value. That numerical value changes. It starts at an infinite value, representing the potential someone has, and over time when their bodies start to decay, or they get their limbs blown off, it depletes. Once that numerical value becomes zero, you're just baggage, the first thing they do is dispose of you in the most efficient and least problematic way possible. I already told you that. It happened to me, it happened to—"

"What about those who came back? They have value. Otherwise, we wouldn't have invested in the funds for the VA." Ted was having that effect on her again, like a pit growing in her stomach, trying to throw itself up. As if those that died didn't have value for simply having the audacity to die for their beloved country.

"Are you ready for something real?" He looked at her, chuckling, as if he knew something of some cruel joke. "The VA gets great pride at 'giving our troops another chance to die for their country.' Your mind blown yet? Not that I care, because I can't even use the VA even if I wanted to. No. You can't ask me why."

He still had that wretched smile on his face. As if he delighted in mocking her, calling her goals stupid, and by way of that, insulting her lineage, and her birth mother specifically. What would she say if she let this slide?

"You came to me twice now, and I said the same thing," Ted continued. "You've met Jeff, an active member of Black Eagle, who undoubtedly told you his way of things, and of course, Lamar Cooper, a discharged gunnery sergeant, which, out of the three, has the most normal experience out of all of us, and didn't bother himself, wisely, with anything classified. I see you've talked to him more than once now, so why come to me? I'm not going to tell you what you want to hear."

She crinkled her nose, exhaling heavily through the cracks of her teeth. She was angry, and it showed, but anger never solved anything, it only added fuel to the fire, so she closed her hands in fists repeatedly opening them up until she calmed down so she could ponder, thinking just that, after all, what did he offer her? Nothing really except the promise of regret. Well, that was his answer anyway.

"Because Sam said I should give you a second chance to—"

"Sakura," Jennifer smiled, and this one seemed genuine. "Ted's experience is...unique. And you don't want to share in his experience, trust me. Samantha doesn't know everything, neither do I, but I don't need to know."

Odd choice of words for someone who's supposed to be a couple.

"You're talking about war time, which, I'm sure you know, you can expect things to go wrong, and you're talking to a man, who, in his entire life. Nothing has ever gone right. He's a flower, with plenty of scars, but it still stands tall."

Sakura shook her head, turning back to Ted. "There's one last thing I'd like to ask you. The other week, I spoke with Lamar who touched on the common bond of having a brotherhood, and which he seemed to share when he met Jeff for the first time. But like me, he told me that you don't share that kind of brotherly bond. Why?"

Ted scoffed. "Doesn't the fact that I don't share that bond tell you anything? Jennifer just told you nothing has ever gone right in my life. *Nothing.*" He snarled at the ground. "Not a single. Damned. Thing." He turned his snarl back at her, smiling with a menacing smile. "Where were my brothers? Where were my sisters when I needed help most? Nowhere to be seen. 'Leave no man behind' was the biggest crock of shit I've ever heard."

"Sorry I asked." Sakura turned away, clenching her fists at her side, walking back to the other end of the fire. The man was insufferable. Honestly, what did Jennifer see in a man like that? The man was a dick if ever there was one, who carelessly shits on heroes for fighting for their personal freedom so he can do God knows what behind closed doors. Ted, you got some sketchy things going on in your basement, don't you? Does Jennifer know? Or is she also hiding something neither of you want out?

But that still didn't answer the question about who he was killing. He was killing people, but the answer was just as elusive as his nihilistic nonsense. But the question was an important one. Deductively speaking, he shouldn't have been killing people from overseas with the peace treaties in place.

Unless that was part of the initial agreement, or were there other forces at play that remained hidden underneath the veil of world peace, and those forces were the same forces he was fighting, people he was killing? But then, what were these forces?

There must have been something else going on in the world, otherwise, he would have been fighting overseas, and the last time the US should have been abroad fighting wars was well over a decade ago, which meant that *Ted* was a lot older than he looked.

Sakura glanced over at the congressman, tired as he was, bags underneath his eyes. He sat by himself, and he smiled at her, taking a large bite from his red lady. A sweet apple, crunchy even, but not sour. He gnawed on the skin before he tossed the core into the blazing fire. There was something about him that separated him from everyone else, apart from the fact that he was an important man in Massachusetts. He was reserved here, but his eyes were ever watchful, scheming by the looks of it.

She took out an apple from her bag, the green one by the looks of it. She looked at it carefully, the stem, elegant, the peel was shimmering with the flames light, and it was still firm. She took the rest of her water and poured it over, using her shirt to dry it off.

Something about an apple. It was so sour when she bit into it, the delightful crunch in her teeth. Part of a peel got stuck, she pulled it out, swallowed it, and slowly sucked some of the apple juice from the exposed flesh from the surface. *Apples.* She took another delicious bite from it. They never fall far from the tree.

Chapter 27 Dyatlov's Pass

President and Vice President's whereabouts are still unknown.

"The US Armed Forces are working with Black Eagle Company to secure the West Coast. We assure you, the American people, everything is under control...we strive to take back our borders and remove China from our midst...We will push back the Chinese and send them back home," Press Secretary Jenna Walters stated, responding to the negative questions regarding the West Coast Conflicts.

***

Claire shuddered in her coat and thick pants, waiting for Mikhail to come outside from one of his glory *Atavasta* as it were. Whatever that meant. She waited carefully, her eyes scanning the oncoming cars in this little village, which was secluded from the rest of the world, but not yet isolated. There were some main roads on which postal carriers drove by, braving the harsh Ukrainian blizzard with thick, wet snow coalescing the ground.

She'd been outside this little pub for his *Atavasta* for not more than fifteen minutes, and yet, her entire boot was already covered in snow. She exhaled heavily into her gloves, feeling her warm breath blow back on her face.

The door creaked open, and Mikhail spoke something in Russian she didn't understand. Must have been a joke, because the people inside the pub, just regular normies most likely, laughed at it. He proceeded to wave as if saying goodbye to an old friend before shutting the door behind him.

"Nice day for a walk, isn't it?" he spoke in his thick accent.

"Of course, and what better way to spend our last days together freezing our tush off, freezing to the bone." She glanced up at the path, a notable elevation.

"You got everything you need? We go on foot from here," he said, hoisting his travel pack over his shoulders.

"Yes, and I could say the same of you. You may be Russian, but you're terribly slow," she said.

"Hey, at least my people win wars," he snorted. "Let's go."

Her journey up the slope began, fighting against the elements, the snow chilling her bones with each step.

***

After hiking for hours, the sun finally began to set, and she was freezing. Mikhail didn't seem to be near bothered by it, the brute, but he was useful, carrying additional supplies when he didn't need to. Claire was knee high in snow, breathing in mana from the air, melting some of the snow with the additional heat her body produced to make walking a bit easier.

"Hey," Mikhail turned around. "You can't do that here!"

"Why not?"

"Well, you have some jests." He shook his head. "There are still tourists that come this way. It's a pain to try to shoot down a helicopter when all I've got is a spear."

"And what do you propose we do then? I'm not freezing anymore," Claire said as a gust of wind blew snow across her face.

"Look, there's a plateau just up there, it's well off the tourist trail, and we can camp there for the night," he said, leading her. He slowed his steps so she would have steps to walk into, to reduce the lag in her own feet, and thus keep up with him. Mikhail at times was a little much, but he had his uses.

She breathed heavily, frost breath getting in her way from the flash's light, and she saw Mikhail's hand in the snow ahead of him, grabbing hold of an unknown item: a torch maybe? A rock? Perhaps a lever to get out from the elements? That was a little optimistic, she had to admit, but the possibilities were endless.

His foot raised up, and with his other hand, he appeared to be grabbing rocks, or crevices inside the pass itself, climbing up.

Fantastic, my wee little fingers won't freeze off.

She followed him, her hand cold underneath the snow, and colder even with the surface of the rock, clearly iced over. She gripped it firmly and peered down for a crevice to put her feet into another crevice for her to reach. She pulled herself up, grabbing hold of the other slit, and pulled up her feet to grab another spot before leaping upward again, catching up to Mikhail. The muscles in her arms and legs were stiffening like shards of glass, fragile, ready to shatter if she moved anything wrong. She wasn't weak, but as far as fae were concerned, she wasn't going to the Olympics anytime soon.

Finally, the last of the snow fell from Mikhail's boot onto her face. She shook her head, tossing the snow off. She reached for the ledge, but it was slippery. He reached down, grabbing her wrist firmly with his blue mana veins, lifting her up with ease. "There, hard part is over, now—"

She pushed past him. "You said this was well off the tourist trail, right?"

"Yes." He turned back, a smirk on his lips like he wasn't enjoying himself.

A man in his thirties, all alone with a beautiful damsel in distress. *Yeah, right. Thanks for ruining all the good fairy tales my ancestors wrote.*

"Good. Don't stop me." She shivered, pulling out a knife from her boot. The curvature edge shimmered in her hand with the light. She inhaled the mana from the air, and the moisture of the snow, combined within the hard ore-like mana from the rock. Her mana veins glowed brightly, covering her skin, and penetrated her gloves as they touched the knife, imbuing it with the mana source she created, carefully blending the mixture inside.

She cleared some snow, until the surface of the rock was visible. With a forward motion, she stabbed the rock, penetrating it with ease. Fragments raised up, striking her face, and the wind around her rose from the hole in the ground, blowing the snow away around her. Writing the old runes down, from the language of the ancestors, she wrote: *Snâw Wèohsteall.*

Around the perimeter, bright yellow vein-like lines appeared from the hole, crawling like caterpillars, crafting a box around both her and Mikhail, and rising, creating a golden light fixture and the temperature within this box rose.

"Ah, the little woman does it again, protecting old me from the cold." Mikhail knelt to the ground, pulling out his bedroll, laying it down. He pulled out some small twigs he had hidden, obtained from God only knows where, and set them up before putting some larger pieces of burnable materials. "Lîgbryne," he said as a spark lit the flame from his lips, and there was a fire. "Now, how about some nice brandy."

"You Russians. All you ever think about is spirits," she said, pulling out some beef jerky, chilled to the touch, but not for much longer as the heat rose to room-temperature

"And you like to stick to your sweet rolls and cheese." He pulled out his metal flask, unscrewed it, brought it to his lips to take a swig.

"It's jerky. *Va te faire foutre,*" she cried out.

"Well." He chuckled again, closing the flask. "Someone's got a mouth. Here."

He threw the flask toward her. She caught it and sealed her container of jerky before throwing it over. She took a swig, and it was bitter as always. Nasty brandy. Not like her fine wine, her favorite, Ca'habielli.

"I suppose you and I never got the chance to discuss in detail what we're doing here," Mikhail said.

"What is there to talk about? We were already told what we need to be doing before assembling a team together." She took another sip, watching Mikhail eat a piece of her salty jerky. The saltiest of jerky. But it didn't seem to bother him much.

"Well, yes, and I suppose we know the why—"

"Do we, Mikhail? Do we know the why? This happened under your nose, somehow flew across radar, heading deeper into the heart of London. Under Adam's snout, all the while, under someone else's directive?" She interrupted him. "You," she snapped her fingers. "Adam," she snapped a second time. "McCurdy, Sarah McCurdy underneath the wing of Colton. America, *Mother* Russia, and London, the heart of our operations, and yet, the most valuable thing in the world disappeared. A mysterious man, possibly two mysterious men, one in America for certain, the other, the last known location is where we're going. Don't you find this to be at least a little odd?"

"Well, distrust is alive and well, I see." He shrugged, hand to the side, palm facing the sky while the other one firmly gripped the jerky, almost like his life depended on it. "Look, Mademoiselle, we can spout off distrust with one another all we like, but it won't get us anywhere, and it will make the trip up and down this pass all the more treacherous." His lips curled downward.

"Fine." She spoke softly, eyes facing the rock, and laid down in her bedroll. "How's your family?"

"Very well, very well, thank you," he said, zipping up the jerky and tossing it back. She caught it and placed it in her travel pack. "Children are just about to get Mother's first arcane lesson. Teaching them the Anglo-Saxon after all."

"The old language is important," she said, pulling her arms behind her head like a pillow, gazing at the night sky. The clouds were thick.

"And how is your family?"

Her eyes were getting sleepy, but she remembered all the same, her two little children: Juliette and Jean. Young children, taken care of by her husband Hugo. Of course, they'd be about the same age as Mikhail's children, playing with what little time they had left before starting the vigorous training to become a fae, just like her. They all had to do it. Have fun until eight, and then delve into the pits of training from sunup to sundown, with just enough time for a few hours of sleep before getting to school. Nothing short of straight 20s will suffice for her children. Though, right now, they'd be sleeping. "Nothing beyond the usual. They haven't started learning Anglo-Saxon yet, just French and English. Soon, and very soon, they'll be ready."

***

Several nights passed just like this one, blizzards one day, and turbulent winds the next, the kind that were so fast, and so brisk, it could rip one's face off. Terribly horrible for one's complexion, especially one so fine as Claire's. She'd have to dress the wounds later, feeling the warmth of her skin receding into her face. Of course, avoiding any possible interested parties, they finally made it to the top of the summit.

She climbed down with Mikhail, taking care with every step along the jagged rocks, and to the smooth surface. There was no dead body here, not where McCurdy said there would be, but she was no new fae—that much was abundantly clear; McCurdy would have known to erase all evidence of mana residue. *Let's just hope she wasn't too efficient.*

Mikhail walked forward, exhaled, and red mana veins formed over his body, generating heat, melting the snow around his feet.

Claire inhaled mana coming from the rocks, and the generated heat, and she felt the creepy crawly mana veins veiling her eyes. Peering around, a red tint covered her vision, and she saw some traces of blue going into the iron door into the mountain, which was closed. The trace was faint, fading into nothing as she peered into it.

"Mikhail," she pointed at the door. "Right there, that's where she was. We need to get inside. Looks like the Major wasn't overly thorough."

"Seems that way," he replied, releasing the mana from his veins, fading back into his skin. "I was personally never fond of bunkers, but this place was made a gem for artistic expression."

He walked over to the door, turning the wheel knob, pulling the iron door open. Dust poured out of it, fogging her view as she made the unfortunate error of standing right behind him. She covered her mouth, coughing.

What foul remains lie dormant behind this dreaded door?

Claire turned her eyes toward the pitch blackness of the bunker, iron rust fueled the scent, and of course, a very familiar, and very, unwelcomed stench: blood.

"You smell that?" Claire asked.

"Yes." Mikhail frowned, coughed and covered his mouth. His hand reached for a flashlight. "You remembered to pack one of these, right?"

As if on cue, she pulled one out, and they crossed the streams of light into the abyss.

"Well," he said, eyes narrowing into the deep dark dank of the bunker, "we won't find out one part of this mystery just standing outside, now, will we?"

Claire's heart raced as she stepped a delicate foot inside. Heart pumping inside her chest, and it was places like this, unexplored places with the dark unknowns that she feared the most. She hated not knowing, her teeth clattering against one another. "Let's—"

A screeching door slammed shut in the distance, echoing across the halls like nails against chalkboard. A truly deplorable sound, filled with nothing but the regrettable ear drums which then requested to be ripped out viscerally, never to be of use again.

"Well, something's here." Mikhail sighed and turned off his flashlight. "These probably aren't going to do us much good here."

"Agreed. Let's find what we need." She breathed in the mana from the iron, and the stone in the pass. Her eyes veiled red with it, and she could see clearly, busted doors, creaking cockroaches moving across the halls with nothing to eat: a small trail of blood leading further into the place. "And get out."

Mikhail did much the same—she could tell.

"Agreed but let us take a look at what's on this level first." He reached in the air, and swirls enveloped his hand, and a green spear manifested in it, and he grabbed hold of it like an Amazonian warrior. Truth be told, the Amazonians only learned that from the Fae.

Sighing heavily, her hands up right, she pulled her knife out, just in case. But she was more accustomed to the arcane than most of the other administrators. She just hoped she wouldn't have to prove it today. A terrible business.

She moved into one of the other rooms, climbing over sharpened iron in the crevice. The room around her was filled with dust and other particles but was otherwise undisturbed. She suspected McCurdy never opened the door, but then, there is the possibility this was all an illusion. However, she sensed no trace of that here. She found a desk with a drawer, partially caved in. She pulled it out, and it struck the ground, the noise echoing in the room.

"You know they heard that, right?" Mikhail called from another room across the hall.

"Mikhail." She knelt to grab the manilla folders which dropped out. "They've known we were here since we got here. Let's just let them think we don't know that, eh?"

"I found something here. You might want to come look," he said.

She placed the folders into her traveling pack and climbed out to reach him in the other room, almost identical, except a few broken lockers, which seemingly just had some old skeletons with Soviet Union uniforms stuffed in the side violently. "Friends of yours?"

"Ha. No." He chuckled loudly. So obnoxiously loud, that he made it clear they were here by whatever roamed the halls yet, sending the same lie to whoever was stupid enough to believe them, that they didn't know they weren't alone.

He laid out some paperwork. "I've got these files here, now. They were written in Polish, by two different hands, it would seem."

"So, what's it say?" she asked.

"I speak Japanese, English, and Russian, and Ukrainian. I don't know Polish," he replied.

"What makes you think I know Polish?" she replied.

"So, let's just grab all the files we can, and we'll worry about getting this translated later," he said.

"What we'll do is find out what's down there." She pointed to the blood stains. "And do what needs to be done and get out. We'll send someone else here to grab everything."

"I can't risk that," he shook his head. "If we miss something, odds are they're going to take the files with them. We need to scour over every little thing while we're here."

She shook her hands. "Gah! You are so thorough."

"No wonder your people haven't won any wars since, uh, well, not in recent memory."

"Shameful." She shook her head as she scoured around for files, which, in all likelihood, had nothing to do with the reason they were here. However, there was something that bothered her immensely, with the certainty that this was Ukrainian territory. These documents should be written in at least Ukrainian, not Polish; in fact, Polish is one language it shouldn't be written in, unless of course Mikhail was lying, but now was not the time for cynicism.

"All right," Mikhail sighed, after bleeding the last of the rooms dry of all files.

"Find anything new?"

"You mean apart from these files being written in every other language when it should be Ukrainian? Or Russian? No. Not at all. I can't read any of this," he said, eyes narrowing down the hall, following the blood.

"No one ever accused you of literacy." She smiled, and turned a death's snarl toward the black abyss, further into the dark, the iron walls coated in dry crimson dust.

"Funny," he said. "We'll get this to Sander, and he'll put together a coalition of linguists to decipher all this nonsense."

"Well, first, we must leave," she said. "Let's be done with it. I want to get out of this bunker."

"Agreed."

The two walked side by side, their steps echoing in the corridor as drops fell—God only knows what was leaking from the bunker's ceiling. The smell didn't get any better, just wafting in. Coming without some kind of hazmat suit was a mistake. Not for the radiation—just to filter out this accursed smell, whatever it was, for it was no longer blood she was smelling, it was something else. She smelled it once before, but she couldn't remember where.

They walked down some steps, grabbing hold of the railing. The steps were wet, soiled with something, blood perhaps. She was too disgusted to even think of looking down. The noise of the repugnant splashing of her own boots in this foul liquid was becoming squishier, and she only assumed she was stepping in *shit*. Actual shit.

A door was ahead of them, an arch door, and another wheel like crank, and above it, was nothing. There was a grate as if on one side, there was going to be someone kind enough to greet them in and give them the good old welcome of Ukrainian hospitality. But the grate was checkered, and an ominous red light shone from behind it, shining upward.

"You ready for another waft of adventure?" Mikhail asked, grabbing hold of it, and turned the wheel.

She breathed heavily with each turn he made, slowly creaking the locks. She pulled her knife out again, eyes focused, narrowed at whatever was behind this door. This is part of the report that didn't make it in, or perhaps McCurdy just failed to tell them about this in the report.

Whatever the reason, they were going to find out, and put a stop to one part of the puzzle, which didn't seem to be doing anything since they only found more questions, and not even a path to an answer yet.

The door creaked slowly open, and there was an altar, candles burning brightly, wicks smoldered, and the tiles around the altar were shattered. Mikhail shook his head as he walked in. "Satanic cultists! Satanic cultists."

"The worst kind of cultists," she whispered, walking through the threshold.

"There is no worst kind of cultists. All cultists are the worst cultists." Mikhail stood over the candles, "I'm honestly quite disappointed."

"Don't be that way," she said, tracing mana around the room. She found this room itself was like a heart; mana veins were faint, but pulsating, the thrums drumming in her ears. "Something isn't right here."

The door slammed shut behind them.

She gasped, turning around, taking her knife to draw symbols in the air.

The wind swirled around them, freezing the flames of the candles in place, and the room became like an ice prison. Stalactites and stalagmites formed spears from the ceiling and floor respectively. *Damn it. It's so cold.*

Mikhail screamed something in Russian. His spear shattered some of the stalagmites coming for him. He focused his eyes on the door, and his spear lit up, a spire, a purple spire thrust, screeching like a plane, shattering the ice in front of her, blowing the entire wall out. The vibrant action of his spear shook the foundations of the bunker, many bolts coming loose, clinking against the floor they landed upon.

The ice melted, and the temperature rose considerably.

Claire panted, looking at Mikhail, who breathed heavily, sweat coming from his brow.

I see. Immediately bringing out the artillery, huh? She went over to him, letting him rest on her shoulder. She scanned the room again, and the mana veins completely faded.

"Are you—"

There was a large tearing sound behind her. She turned her head around to see a rip in the flesh of creation, protruding against the wall. Of which, there was now a hole, and she beheld bright blue flames in front of an iron furnace. A little creature sprinted out. This looked like a little goblin, a Threcket one with large claws, and did anyone ever tell him? Spiked hair is out of style.

The Threcket bolted past them, stretching an elongated claw. Mikhail thrust his body into Claire's before the claw could reach her, and the nails shredded the flesh in his left arm. Leaving them on the floor, the Threcket dashed up the stairs, scurrying like the little ugly, wretch it was.

"*Mais quelles conneries,*" she swore.

"*Cush' sobach'ya!*" he agreed, before turning to the gaping hole in creation. "You go track it down. I'll close this portal."

Mikhail grunted, drawing his own knife, and already, purple mana veins protruded from his epidermis, crawling onto the blade.

Don't need to ask me twice. She inhaled the mana from the air, and her mana veins manifested on her skin, including her legs as she leapt off one foot, tracking down this dreaded Threcket. Clearly, this place only prompted more questions than answers. For a Threcket's heart was in this world, manifested inside Devil's Pass. Such a fitting name for such a dreadful heart.

Chapter 28 Threads of Creation Undone

Status Report:

Communications are online. Armed Forces, heavy and light infantry and cavalry are deployed to the front line. FOB and Air Bases operating at full capacities in Arizona, Nevada, and Idaho. The Chinese forces have come to a halt and the USA are at a standstill.

Black Eagle Company has deployed fleets to the Pacific Coast, sailing in from the Arctic. Fleets have engaged in ship-to-ship combat, while the fighter jets take to the skies in dog fights.

Additional reinforcements expected from China: none.

***

Claire panted, following this Threcket through the dark, coldness of a Ukrainian winter, following its little footsteps. But when she made it to the base, toward Sverdlovsk, her worst nightmare happened. Their failure here meant a lot of things, and a lot of calls were to be made to cover this up. How the hell was she to explain the disappearance of a large city to the world?

The Threcket blasted through the snow, kicking it up, obscuring her vision, but she could see the larger things at play: the cars squealing, women, children screaming, and men shouting things as they jumped atop their cars, not knowing what this thing was. A natural reaction, really, after all, they never did see anything like it. And such a shame, really, they didn't prepare for this, and now, cars were squealing off, driving away from this base of operations, and they would have to be hunted down, else the Threads of Creation come undone.

"*Merde,*" she swore, pulling her knife, bolting back toward the Threcket, melting the snow around her. She sprinted faster than the truck, trying to escape, but, "*Forðeon!*"

Mana veins seared the truck; glass shattered. Legs and arms of those inside tried to immediately pull themselves out, severed as the truck crunched, gnawing at them inside. She grimaced, the white snow stained with crimson and flesh as the screams from inside the truck died down, but the screams outside only amplified.

The Threcket thrashed a normie, sending the limbs at her. She ducked and wove herself to avoid a direct strike and sprinted forward, warm blood splattering on her face. The Threcket looked terrified of her, as it should be. "*Je vais te défoncer!*"

The Threcket scurried off again, kicking some more snow. As small as this Threcket was, it was far more annoying chasing it down the damn mountain pass to get here, and now, there were places to hide. And so it did, immediately scurrying underneath the foundation of a house. *Damn it.* "*Nieðdearf!*"

The house in front of her was uprooted, flying upward. The wooden pieces rose, splintering in the air, the wood rotten, blasted apart, the furnishing falling to the ground, and the people still inside, falling out of their house. *Thud.* A body splattered over the ground, bones shattering. The Threcket, in all its cursed demeanor, whimpered like a child.

How dare you! "T'es pas un gamin! Onbryrdan sôl!"

The clouds above dispersed, and the moon glimmered all the clearer. Like a beam from the heavens, it blasted the area right in front of her, melting the snow. She shielded her eyes. More screams followed, piercing her ears. *I'm sorry.*

***

Crunching metal. Screeching tires. Lots of sunlight. All signs that none of this was going too well. Mikhail panted along the way, just getting down to the base.

She certainly knows how to make an entrance, but it can't be helped.

Shit. He took out his phone and dialed, and the other end was immediately picked up,

"Dimitry, Sverdlovsk, now. Bring all able-bodied Fae."

"What's this about?" he spoke.

"Let's call it Operation We're Gonna Kill Everyone and Cover It Up. Send a team to track down some strays heading..." he glanced back at the road. Luck smiled upon him. "...mostly south."

"Got it. Be there in a few hours,"

He hung up the phone.

Shaking his head, his hand reached out, and his spear formed into his hand. His eyes narrowed toward the convoy. The spire around his spear lit up. Hurling the spear, much like a missile that would make Mother Russia proud of her little boy; it threw itself at the convoy. It struck the earth behind it with such velocity, and distorting the mana around creation, which undoubtedly would compromise the way to Pandora significantly, it did its job. The earth shattered, debris shooting ahead, striking, impaling the steal as it popped tires. Squealing, the trucks flipped over, glass shattered as the people inside died, but for good measure, he ran to the massacre.

Dashing through the snow and the debris, he saw men, women, and children here. Only one was barely clinging to life, sitting down, feet sprawled in front of him, hand clutching his chest, back leaning against a flaming truck, without the will to move. He was a beautiful boy. He couldn't have been more than five years of age. Still had his life ahead of him. But this mess, this accursed mess forced his life to be cut short.

"Zakroy glaza," said Mikhail, summoning another spear in his hand.

The boy obediently closed his eyes. "Ya napugnan," said the boy.

Mikhail looked at him, his hands firmly gripped on his spear, ready to thrust. Of course, he's scared. But Mikhail knew what needed to be done to spare the boy of further pain and fear. "U tebya yest' polnoye parvo byt', no eto ne dlya tebya, a dlya menya."

The boy panted, closing his eyes, leaning his back against the truck firmly. *I'll try to make this easy for you. I'm sorry. All Hell. I'm sorry.* He thrust the spear again, the boy's heart was thrust outside the back of his chest as the car was pushed back, and the boy just rested there. He didn't make a sound, but his own blood now dripped from the sides of his lips, his life now gone. *And this is how the Administration designed it. A cursed existence to be sure. I'm sorry boy, but Mother Russia cannot save you this time.*

***

The damned Threcket didn't die, and Mikhail wasn't there yet to help track it down. *Who am I kidding, the poor man is probably out trying to mitigate the mess; however he's going to handle this, a lot more people are going to die.*

She pushed past some more people, her mana veins giving them a slight shock as she brushed up against them, but she didn't care. With the amount of mana being expended here, not only was she abundantly aware she would summon a Threcket, by accident of course. But the people she brushed against would be dead soon after.

The little goblin of a Threcket found its way into a horrible place, a place with children. Ukrainian children. Orphans. Fantastic, as if there wasn't more tragedy in the world.

Sorry your parents died. You'll join them soon. Or perhaps parental irresponsibility created these poor orphans. Who knows? Not her problem, and soon, neither theirs.

She pushed through the wooden doors, thrusting herself against the Threcket, pushing it into a wall. Framed pictures fell down, shattering glass with the collision. She breathed mana from the air, and her left hand emitted a strong blue aura, striking her hand into the ribcage of the Threcket. With a penetrating force, her hand reached out from inside, grabbing hold of an organ. The screams were enough to make her crazy, piercing at high decibels as its blood poured onto the floor.

She peered forward as she was getting to know this Threcket so intimately. Just when her husband proposed to her, she had to think about the genetics, make sure the heart was a strong one, and just so, her hand *knew* every part of this Threcket. Children, however horrified, covered their ears, wailing in their own petite death throes of an orchestra. Sure, to an untrained ear, it sounded like nothing short of a banshee wailing its last screech.

Finding the heart, a frail little thing, fragile as glass, her hand gripped around it, feeling it's veins and other musculature constructs inside, she inhaled more mana from the air, and her blue mana veins lit her body up like a beacon, burning the external extremities of the Threcket, and ripped its heart out. It wailed on the ground, like a dead fish trying for water, its claws striking every which way.

Only one last thing to do here, make sure this little critter doesn't form his heart again. She crushed the heart with her hand, and with her knife, drew runes in the air. Light shone back at her as she cut the air like flesh.

"Cu'ernavorgen. Cha. Lathukaprath'haken." Purple veins flowed from her body, replacing the blue ones, shining toward the body, restraining the Threcket to the ground. She burned it, turning it to little more than yellow lights, and with those purple veins, like tentacles, they reached for the light, drinking the remains of the Threcket, taking it into her body.

Feeling the toxin fill her, she leaned back against the wall, the children staring back at her. Too so, to move with all that toxin coagulating in her veins. Her purple tentacles grabbed hold of the children, who wailed as they too were absorbed into her being, and they became like little lights, shining all the clearer, but their clothes remained, and nothing short of their scent in their wrinkled clothes remained as evidence of their unnecessary existence.

She inhaled and exhaled. Staring in front of her, the fragments of the souls of the children roaming around her, never able to see the world for themselves, but rather, given a hand so cruel only forcing themselves to climb up a social ladder.

"All things considered," Mikhail walked through the door.

Nice of you to finally show up.

"It could be worse," he said.

Don't count your blessings yet.

"Dimitry will be here shortly. Organizing the disappearance of this place and pulling people off the roads. This is one hell of a mess." He opened his flask and offered it to her.

She took it and took one large mouthful of that piss water. It was refreshing, but even urine was tastier than drinking the soul of a Threcket. Lucky those kids were here, or she would have vomited. "I suppose that's some good news, then. Let's take a moment then, and recap what we learned."

"I learned nothing," he chuckled, trying to lighten the mood.

But how can this mood be light? We're going to kill nearly two million people, make it look like nothing happened, and move on. Not to mention it's a great pass, lots of traffic through here. This will undoubtedly raise unwanted questions.

"Yes, let's call Adam up, tell him the two of us went up the pass, found nothing, oh, and by the way, Adam, get this, get this Adam, a major city went missing!"

"Sarcasm doesn't suit you, my friend. I get that enough from Colton." She glared at him.

Colton. That damned American yank can go rot in hell.

"Well," she said. "To condense this report before we get linguistics involved for all the damn unreadable reports, there's a heart in Devil's Pass. Threckets are forming in weakened spots around the world, most notably, Devil's Pass. The existence of reports in Ukraine, in neither Russian nor Ukrainian. What the hell is going on?"

"This may boil to knowing an expert code breaker who knows all these languages. You know anyone?" he asked.

"You're talking about fifteen different languages. What you're asking for doesn't exist," she scowled.

"We can always hope, now, can't we?"

Chapter 29 Not Right Now

Status Report:

US Armed Forces push back the front line into Washington. Attack Choppers fly into Los Angeles from Delta Force under the directive of CCO Malcolm's demands. Delta Force deployed directly into China's FOB in Los Angeles under confusion, disabling communication systems.

Chinese Navy fleet has been sunk. Fighter pilots remaining retreat to carriers to the Southern Pacific. Black Eagle Company's destroyers fire their heavy machinery into the sky, shooting most of the remaining jets before they were out of range. The fleet proceeds to sail south.

***

Colton stood over his desk, a large map of the United States atop it, some lights shining over all the pieces. Staring down, looking at all the pieces. By himself, as always, gazing over all the different scenarios a situation like this could create. *Snells. You may be stupid, but good job where it's due.*

His finger touched the West Coast, tapping it with his finger. "China's navy is pushing along the West Coast. Granted, I didn't need that, but it does protect McCurdy from prying eyes," he said, turning another index finger to DC "And Russia is moving their fleet to the East Coast. Finally. Thanks, Mikhail, I'm gonna need to buy you drinks after this, assuming there's a world where drinks exist after all this is done." He pointed his finger up toward Boston. "And then there's this pesky Ghost here. You should have been killed."

Ping.

522

Turning his gaze to his computer, a report came in from the President himself. *Good boy.* He briskly ran to his computer, and opened the email, subject header: Status Report. It was a lengthy report, but no stone was to be left unturned. That was how mistakes were made, and undoubtedly, that's how this Ghost has remained alive all this time.

Concerning the procurement of Task Force Seven:

Stem cells were studied from a group of anonymous donors. Testing these cells and samples, a selection of thirty-two promising couples were located. The sample size exceeded a total of 3,000 couples across all demographics, high socioeconomic status and low, white, Black, Hispanic, Asian, ect. Those thirty-two couples chosen for Task Force Seven gave birth that year.

CIA was charged with creating Task Force Seven, sponsored by Lieutenant General Snells. Addresses of the hospitals where the births would be taking place were immediately placed into the custody of the CIA. All the while, Lieutenant General Snells was given execute authority to create a habitation for such individuals, given temporary family units in an undisclosed location, that location ultimately being Area 51.

Upon the births, CIA operatives were immediately dispatched into the hospitals, taking the selected children out of the units, and bringing them to a CIA undisclosed location, DC underground. Files of the birth were erased from the hospital within that same day, and no notice was ever submitted to the news, apart from thirty-two missing persons reports.

At this time, it is unknown which set of parents belonged to which child. Details of parents are disclosed below:

Colton skimmed the list of parents and siphoned them off to look at later. Eyes scanning the report downward to:

Execution: Area 51

Per your request, Task Force Seven was to be eliminated. They were advised to expect a training exercise, of which they were given dummy guns and blanks. They were split up into four parties. Party four consisting of Clubs, Spearhead, Apple, and Mist were immediately dispatched, bodies removed from the scene. No casualties.

Operatives Roach, Ivy, Winters, and Summers were dispatched by the following day, buried themselves in the sand. Casualties: 26,329.

Operatives Metal, Viper, Venom, and Wraith were brought down, buried in an old bunker. The four dropped their weapons, came out willingly, tied to posts before being executed. Casualties: 33,297.

Operatives Ghost, Slithers, Butcher and Ticker.

Butcher was found dead right at the execution site of the previous operatives. Estimated casualties before deceased: 9,000.

Ticker's Body was found well above the skirmish. Body unrecognizable, cause of death, ruled to be blood loss. Body unrecognizable due to radiation poisoning. Estimated casualties: 10,300.

Slithers and Ghost's bodies could not be identified. It is assumed that Slithers died below ground. As evidenced in a report by one Sergeant Jeffrey Clemens of now Black Eagle Company, it is confirmed Ghost was the last one atop Area 51. Bombs dropped by aircraft, leveling the facility before the nuclear meltdown, causing any and all bodies remaining there to be unrecognizable.

Jeffrey Clemens stated in his initial report, Ghost took one final .50

caliber to the chest before the bombs dropped. The meltdown killed a total of 200,000 people, more than half of them were civilians.

This concludes any and all information I have regarding Task Force Seven.

Colton leaned back in his chair. Suppose a fae could survive all that, he'd be scarred for life, but there's no way one of those couples would have been a fae. No chance in Hell.

The phone rang.

Damnit Garcia, not now!

He answered it. "I'm busy right now, what do you want?"

"Someone's touchy. So, what are we going to do about McCurdy?" Garcia's flamboyant voice echoed in his ears.

"I told you, right now, I don't know where she is," he lied.

"Yeah, and how are we going to find out, hmm?"

"Let me check the air itineraries and get back to you," he said.

"Why wouldn't you have done that already?"

Because I'm hiding her from you, you dumb shit. "Garcia, in case you haven't noticed, my jurisdiction is about to be assaulted by two fronts."

"That has nothing to do with this,"

Oh, it has everything to do with this. "How about the fact that I'm moving pieces right now to make this more manageable for myself. I haven't had a chance to dissect every last itinerary. I still don't have time for this. Is this all?"

"You need to get on this. You know how important the Grail is."

Oh, I know. I know exactly how important it is. You don't. "Look, give me a week, till I know what's going on with Mikhail and why he sent a Russian mob here, and then I'll give you all the time in the world. I'll fly down and you can throw your disgusting tequila down my throat. How's that sound?"

"Rude."

"Bye!"

He hung up the phone.

He shook his head, biting his lip, eyes narrowed, scrolling back up through the couples, looking over their names, faces and background. The screen was about to make him tear his eyes out of their sockets when he was done with this menial task. With each group of parents, he cross referenced their information with the web, identifying where they gave birth to such individuals, and of course, most of these parents were dead, or incapacitated. No reason why. Unless they all were suicide victims, but he didn't care about that. What they did with their own lives was up to them, and them alone.

But these two in particular caught his eye. In fact, they were screaming at him. Sam and Elena Romanov-McCurdy. *Sarah. How the hell are you involved in this?* He sighed, staring at the computer. Same surname didn't necessarily mean anything, but the possibility was still there. One suspicion leads to another, and further questions down a line that is so far off from the truth. It was almost like there was another invisible hand working that he didn't see. Such cruelty couldn't be by the hand of God, but perhaps the Devil instead. But why and who? *Well, if nothing else it does confirm my suspicion. Ghost. One cog in a grand machine and we don't even know what it does. You clearly don't, and yet, you're in the center of it all. Britain is especially looking for you. I'm looking for you, and Uncle Sam, the good old Malevolent Uncle is going to have an intriguing interest when they confirm for themselves that you are alive, and this little war from Russia is that catalyst.*

But a nuclear meltdown, and to be at the center of it. Though Mana was, by normies, radioactive, (and caused all sorts of calamities because they failed to fully grasp it's danger in their hands,) was something that Fae inhaled through their veins to perform all kinds of magic, and of course may open up portals to Pandora. But there were limits to how much one could breathe at any given time. It was not limitless. And to be in the epicenter of one of these is a sure way to blow out all mana veins. It was almost guaranteed. This could even kill a fae, but could this Ghost be part of McCurdy's line? That would explain some things. He should make a call.

He reached for his phone, dialing it rapidly.

"Yes, Colton?" she asked as if expecting the call. Efficient as ever.

"What do you know about a Sam and Elena Romanov-McCurdy?"

"Why the sudden interest?"

"McCurdy, right now, I don't need you pestering m—"

"Colton, you're on speaker phone, and I want to know. I have no reason to want to know, I just want to know,"

Swan. You silver-haired bitch!

"I should have you know that I am well aware of your ploy against me, Colton, and I don't appreciate it. What's this, two times now?" She cackled on the other end of her phone. His eyes narrowed, gritting his teeth.

"I wonder what Sander might think when you had his pupil the target of political machinations, poorly planned, I might add, killed. I might even add that you seem to be losing your grip."

"Get off the phone," Colton demanded.

"No. I'm not going to do that. Now, either you tell me what I want, or you don't get the information you need. You should keep your toys a little closer to you, because I like to play, and I play for keeps. Isn't that right, Sarah?"

"Yes," she said reluctantly.

He hissed over the phone. "Their names popped up in an investigation and I need to know who they are, that's it."

"Now, was that really that hard, Colton. That's all I wanted. Now you can talk to her without my influence. Ta Ta!"

He heard doors slamming in the background. "Take me off speaker!"

"You got it," she sighed. "Who are they? Yes. My uncle and aunt. They've been dead for well over twenty years."

"Okay. Do you feel safe there?" He asked. He may have a need for her to come back to him. Especially when a relative is involved, and it is most definitely a relative. Cousins, it seems like.

"Not safer than any other part of the world. There don't seem to be Threckets here."

"And what of the task I gave you?"

"I'm not permitted any access to any additional information until such time as Gwen sees fit. No access to facilities. I am really little more than a glorified secretary. I don't need to tell you how hard this is," she answered shrewdly.

Damn you, Gwen.

"Okay, keep me in the know if anything unusual happens, and without Gwen in the room!"

He disconnected his phone from the call.

A moving machine. That's what Colton found himself in the middle of. Just one Administrator trying to navigate so many pieces and more and more pieces just pop up out of nowhere, unplanned. Other administrators are moving their own pieces and he was finding it damn near impossible to predict where all of them were going. And now, Gwen, is by his account acting of her own volition, planning her own plots for what he could only guess.

She's gonna bite me in the ass, isn't she? And she is going to enjoy every minute of it.

He sighed, staring at the safe, and walked over to it. His hand touched it, mana veins, emerald, lighting up his skin as they crawled onto the safe, and into the crevices. The safe's own mana source lit up, red veins to contrast. He squinted as his mana veins wove around the red veins, the light beaming in his face. The veins canceled one another out finally, and he touched the dial to manually unlock the safe, *16, 42, 8.*

The door opened, and purple smoke blew out of it. He focused the mana from the room into his eyes as he saw the artifact, the one holding everything all together, regardless of how hopelessly shattered the world was. He reached into it, pulling the Box out, and bringing it to his table, setting it down.

It was a purple box, bones of various animals, and people, and of course, Threckets, demons of old, a time much simpler than today, engraved into the edges. His hand touched the exterior, bone fragments slicing his hand, his warm blood dripped down the sides.

He funneled mana from the metal nails in the walls, silver veins protruded on his hand, and the bones retreated back into the surface of the Box. The Box was filled with runes and symbols of the old Anglo-Saxon tongue, interweaving themselves with another language, unknown to him, but it didn't look like any known human language he was aware of.

It wasn't runed like the Saxons or the Vikings, nor were they filled with symbols or lines like Kanji, or the eastern languages, nor the scribbles of the Middle Eastern Languages, nor Romanized.

And the surface of the Grail, golden metal, where the Anglo-Saxon runes started, shimmering in the light. Smoke protruded from the bottom of the Grail. He blew into it, waving the smoke away, and at the bottom of the Grail was a hole in the shape of a human heart, but not a regular heart; one of the Old Blood. And deeper into that crevice was a slot. His hand reached inside, the smoke pushing at him. He caressed the edges of the slot, gauging at its length and width. *A sword goes in here, and a heart. First, before anything else, this all needs to be translated, but to get a linguist with this kind of talent is nothing short of impossible.*

Chapter 30 Another Tuesday

Status Report:

US heavy cavalry rolls into central California into Los Angeles. Chinese forces lose morale, forcing a retreat to the shoreline. Los Angeles was retaken, forcing the Chinese fleet to resort to Artillery strikes on the mainland.

Black Eagle Company deploys heavy infantry and cavalry units on the shoreline of Washington. Flanking with the US Armed Forces in Northern Idaho, Washington is retaken. Forces mobilize and march Southward to Oregon.

***

Spadero followed the crowd again in the snow. His hands jittering in his peacoat, following, eyes and ears focused on Ted talking very intently with Jennifer, who he assumed was his girlfriend, with how close they seemed. He didn't see her the previous time he was there, but there were other things he picked up, her overwhelming positivity, and while she was flamboyant, she was not healthy, though very good at hiding her medical condition from others.

Well, don't offer to buy him a drink. Just ask him questions. What's one question he would know a great deal about? I could ask him about Ted Anderson, but he is Ted Anderson, or masquerading around as him. But that would only blow his cover if he's careful and alienating him is something I'm not trying to do. We need him as willing as possible, but if I can't even get my foot in the door...

He crossed the threshold again into Teri Nation, walking with the smiling faces and the drink trays carried by the waitstaff, professionally dressed like some high-end place. He smiled back, careful not to lose sight of the reason he was here to begin with, Ghost. He was so close, and yet still so very far away.

He followed up some stairs around the back, just like last time, and Scott, that smirk on his face hidden behind that thick black beard of his, welcomed them honestly.

"Welcome back." He spoke. Jennifer and Michael hurried to the bar, to their seat. "What are we having today?"

"Oh, you know I'll have the special, whatever that is," Michael said, pulling out his wallet and grabbing a card. "I'm buying today," he turned. "Ted, what do you want?"

"I'll take whatever you're having," he replied.

Spadero felt more people coming in, rushing past him. He pushed himself to the side as the roar of laughter pierced his ears.

"Whoa," Michael grinned widely, and more genuine than ever. *He's a good person. I thought you were a myth.* "Another special that is."

"Hey, hey, hey," Jennifer said, slamming her palm down on the table. "What am I? A joke to you? Make that three." She held up three fingers to the bartender.

Michael laughed at that. "You can close me out too."

Lively bunch.

A strong hand reached his shoulder. "You made it again," Sam said to him, with a bright smile, a genuine one, almost as completely genuine as Michael's. *There's something about this crowd. There can't be any good people here, not in this great number in one location. But then there's Ted and myself, and together, we make up for all the hostility that's required to balance that out.*

"Scott, I'll be boring. Just a Cab."

"Boring indeed," Sam called back. "Merlot for me, please and thank you."

"Together or separate."

"Separate," she said.

He disappeared behind the bar, and he pulled out two bottles of red wine and poured them over two glasses. His attention averted to the crowd, around the bar, many smiling faces, and whimsy laughter.

Spadero picked his up promptly just after paying, looking down into the glass, staring at Ted: who seemed to have a good old time with his *concoction of whatever.*

Another man popped up in the bar. Grabbing Michael's shoulder, talking about a good old time playing video games and a first-person shooter. Wasn't sure who he was, but whoever it was clearly made Ted uncomfortable, shifting uncomfortably in his seat, rolling his shoulders forward.

That man, largely built, a large fatigue and some jeans came laughing away when he drank something even more boring than this glass of Cabernet, a damned Boston Lager, is what it was. A boring, bitter, poor person's beer. At least go for something a little more exotic. The man hurried off to the other end of the bar.

He walked closely, noticing a red-haired woman with freckles picking up a conversation with Michael.

"So, about our Christmas party? You in? You all in?" She asked.

He couldn't remember her name.

"Yes," Michael answered. "Secret Santa or Yankee Swap?"

"Secret Santa!"

"Erin, that's a fine idea. Your place in Sudbury? It's big enough," Jennifer asked.

"Yes, that would be fine," she said, sipping on her cider. Not as boring as a Boston Lager. She turned to Spadero. "Hey, new guy, you can come, too. John, was it?"

"Yes," he grinned back. He traded phone numbers with her, and she sent him a spreadsheet. It went to a lot of different people, and he could see names of people being claimed anonymously. "Cap?"

"Fifty bucks," Michael said. "That way, we don't end up with another $2,000 bottle of wine."

Everyone but Spadero laughed. *Clearly, an inside joke.*

"December 18th," Erin said, "The address and the time is in there. I'll see you next week!"

He nodded and turned his attention toward Ted. The man of the hour, the man who would have all the answers, or at least more unanswerable questions to be deciphered by no one.

"So, Ted," he said.

"Here we go again," all but Jennifer and Ted went to the other side of the bar, leaving just the three of them.

"You know China nearly massacred the West Coast," he began. "What says an old veteran about what we can do better?"

"I don't care," he replied, frowning into his glass. "Empires Fall and here we are, they're all gone. It might be time for America to set. Rise and fall they say. Doomed to die they say. What point is there, really? Spadero, you're a congressman who has an unhealthy interest in my opinions."

"And yet, you swore to defend the Constitution—"

"'Against all enemies foreign, and domestic,'" he interrupted, turning his head, and sneering. "That's what it says."

Jennifer gazed up at Spadero, a concerned look on her face, eyes watering as if *he* was violently opening a wound.

"Why do I really care? Generals and politicians, not exclusively America, but *especially* America created the rise of the circumstances which led to these wars on our doorsteps. Russian and Chinese navies are floating by, and because of the bureaucratic nature of our government, we didn't mobilize our navy? Why is that? I wonder.

"Let me ask you something, John. You want my opinion, but I'll ask yours on something. If there was a group of people who gave their all for their country, dying in the line of duty, and their bodies recovered, should those bodies have been given a proper military funeral?"

What is he referring to? Task Force Seven? That's a dangerous question, particularly for you. "Yes, without a doubt."

"And if certain individuals were accused of high treason," he peered into his eyes, a scowl of only the ugliest of Threckets. "Should there be a trial before execution?"

"Undoubtedly," he answered.

"And what if I were to tell you that some individuals accused of high treason were executed without a trial? What should happen to the accused?"

"They're dead in this scenario?" he asked. *Clearly, Task Force Seven.*

"Yes, they all are." He snickered. "They all are dead in this fictitious scenario."

"They deserved a trial. They didn't get one, and now they're dead. I think you and I can agree that was a gross miscarriage of due process. But if they're dead, what does us bickering about it do? What difference does it make?" he asked.

"You're right," he laughed again. "No number of apologies can bring back the dead. Now, what should happen to the system itself that authorized their execution before a trial?"

"The system should be abolished," he replied.

"There, you and I agree on something," he replied, taking another sip. Spadero noticed Ted's hand shaking with the glass, ice berating the edges. "Now, what if I was to tell you that the accused never committed treason?"

"Then the system itself is flawed and should be dismantled. The system is the real traitor here."

"Exactly!" He pointed an excited finger. "The US Army put a lot of resources on thirty-two unique individuals. Sixteen were killed early during the training process. No one notified their families; they received no burials. I watched them cremated. Sixteen other individuals were wasted, all killed by the tragedy that was the nuclear meltdown at Area 51, which, I might add, was no accident.

"They gave their lives, all of them. Not one funeral. Not one family was notified. Not even the general public would ever know of the lives they had, or the hearts they gave. On that day, we remembered the oath, to protect that damned piece of paper that's supposed to mean something. It doesn't, from enemies foreign and domestic, and on that day did I realize the only enemy we ever had was domestic."

He placed the drink on the bar top. Bringing his arms to his chest, bowing his head down so low, and all he did was cackle.

"Tedward," Jennifer turned to him, interlacing her fingers with his, and her free hand on his shoulder. And hanging from her fingers behind him, was one of her napkins, and he saw that the stain, just over the shoulder, was red.

"Do you know what the funniest part about all that is?"

"I can't imagine anyone finding any of this funny," Spadero frowned. *He just accused the government of treason.*

"Those thirty-two people I mentioned, never swore to uphold that oath." He turned his face back to Spadero, tears streaming down his cheeks, teeth gritting. His other hand started shaking, squeezing Jennifer's hand firmly like a stress ball. "And they followed that oath to the letter."

Ted's eyes glazed over, and his gaze averted to looking right past him. A scowl, no. Not a scowl. There isn't a word for the kind of face he made. If Satan stood before him, he would get out of the way. That is the amount of malintent that filled that scowl.

"The only difference between them," he lifted his other hand and pointed across the bar. "And that mother fucker over there, is he took that oath and wiped his ass with it. They obeyed that oath, and they weren't even allowed to take it. Bottom line, any man or woman who wears those patches, wears those tags or flags, is no friend of mine, nor will they ever be. I'd kill all of you if I wasn't trying to be a good little boy."

Damn. The plot thickens. And answers a question.

There was silence all around. The shouting and laughter stopped as the patrons of the bar turned, gazing at the disgruntled veteran at the bar, the one unique to them all, and the one hiding in plain sight.

Spadero managed to lock eyes with him.

Ghost. You and I are seeing the very same thing. "Sorry I asked, Ted. I won't ask again." He turned to walk down the vestibule, out the bar. "Ted, I don't know what happened, but I will find out. I'll see justice for them. Whoever they are."

"How can you when they don't even have names," he scowled.

"Tedward, let's go," Jennifer pulled on his arm.

Sakura watched as Jennifer and Ted exited the bar, following after John. She chewed some gum, watching them go by. She had her Coke in hand. It was the only thing she could drink here that had some flavor to it. She wasn't of the drinking age after all. She turned, wondering exactly what kind of conversation they would have had that prompted Ted to call Jeffrey a "Mother Fucker" all the way from across the bar.

Of course, she still had her own hesitations with Jeffrey Clemens, mainly because he was a mercenary, and she didn't appreciate that. Wasn't an honorable thing to fight and kill for the sake of money. Clearly, more now than ever before, she knew there was bad blood between Ted and him. She walked over to Sam, talking closely with Michael.

"Sam?"

"Yes?" She sipped her wine, winking at her.

"What kind of history does Ted have with Jeffrey?"

"They served together," Michael answered. "Both in the 75th Ranger Regiment. Both secretive and good at keeping secrets,"

"But is that—"

"I watched a video once. I wasn't huge into shows, I still am not," Michael explained, smiling to her. "But this one I found absolutely intriguing, and it gave some excellent insight. Though, as you can rightly tell, Ted is a unique case and the normal rules, even applicable to Veterans' with mental health needs, don't apply to Ted."

"That's a good way to put it," Sam said, her simper fading.

"So, you know something about him that I don't?" Sakura asked.

"Sakura," Sam said. "You just met him."

"That didn't stop either you or Jennifer," Michael laughed softly.

"No, you're right, but then, I saw a veteran on the corner, homeless. I didn't want Ted to end up like him," she replied. "Anyway, I've said this a number of times already, talk to Jennifer."

"Hey!" The little redhead woman came between Michael and Samantha, her arms around their shoulders. "Sakura, right? You want to come to our Christmas party next week?"

"Sure? Where is it?" She nodded.

The redhead grinned brightly. "Sudbury," she released her shoulder grip and shook Sakura's hand. "Erin, nice to meet you. Anyway, let me get your number."

Chapter 31 A Worthy Gift

Status Report:

Black Eagle Company's fleets engage with forces in the Oregon part of the Pacific. Pilots refuel and re-engage in dogfighting over the Pacific.

In a conjoined effort between air and national guards coming in from Idaho, fueled with the technology of Black Eagle Company, the heavy cavalry units roll south, invading the Chinese company in Oregon. In what amounted to not more than a few days, Oregon was completely overrun by US Armed Forces and Black Eagle Company.

US Armed Forces from Los Angeles and Arizona roll forward into the southern parts of California, pushing the Chinese Heavy Cavalry units out to sea. The Chinese Navy bombards Southern California with artillery shells.

***

Ted walked down the streets of Boston. A nice change of scenery to Waltham, always busy, and especially with the sneaking suspicion that he was being watched. John happened out of nowhere, and he only showed up twice to café, which wasn't terribly unusual, but he asked him questions which he found to be an odd icebreaker of all sorts of things, things he wouldn't have any information on.

The snow was slick, his boots slipping this way and that sometimes. He grabbed hold of street signs to avoid slipping in the street. They didn't salt the streets yet this Saturday morning, or the sidewalk for that matter. Heaven forbid he slipped and crushed his skull into the mailbox. Not that that would kill him of course or cause any serious harm. He'd hate to have to inconvenience the city staff for replacing such an item.

The white clouds were especially thick this morning as he looked up, gazing just over Summer Street, the large highway leading to south station, a beautiful building if his opinion mattered. It didn't.

The Christmas party was coming up. He knew he was going to pick Jennifer up, some apple pie, her idea, and drive all the way to Sudbury, but something about this overwhelmed him with an aura of unnatural dread, leading him further and further away from the contentment he had grown accustomed to. He saw a large pillar just outside a building, holding another building hovering over it, the shade provided some dry measure from the snow and ice. He leaned up against it, dropping down low, sitting on the ground.

He reached for his back pocket, and pulled out his wallet, opening it and pulled out a picture. A picture that reminded him of the past, which was both a blessing that he still had it, and a curse. Sometimes he wished he would burn it. Hell knows he tried. But he could never bring himself to part from his mistakes, to part from the friends he used to have. Not the nasty friends, wearing masks masquerading around someone one might want to be with for the rest of one's unnaturally short life, but the friends one knew would stick around through thick and thin. They'd still stick around had they been alive, if they weren't unjustly executed for crimes they didn't commit. Ted still didn't know the reason.

Slithers with her beautiful hair hugged him. He sometimes still felt it, a ghost symptom of something he lost. But this time, this time he didn't feel his heart growing heavy. He looked at all sixteen of them. All scarred faces. All dead. No. That wasn't true. He was still alive.

"So," said a familiar voice. He heard the crunching of snow, and someone sitting down next to him. He turned. Slithers. Her hair tied back, and she was in the BDUs. "Ghost, did you finally find the light that flickers?"

"Yes, Slithers," he smiled, leaning back against the pillar, eyes to the sky, watching the snowflakes fall.

"Good," she said, tearing up, leaning her head against his shoulders. "That's good."

Wind blew, and Slithers blew with it, dusting into ice crystals, fading into oblivion with the rest of the snow. His heart grew heavy, feeling a lump inside his chest that she was there one minute, and gone the next. But part of him was able to leave that where it lay, part of him able to move on, and that's the part that mattered.

That part of him that led him to Boston on this particular day was right there with him, urging him not to forget the past, but accept that it couldn't be changed, and he can only move forward to the end of it all. He remembered when Slithers asked him to find the light that flickers, no matter how dim.

"Find it," she said. And he found it.

Jennifer.

He stood, rising against the pillar, moving back to Summer Street, walking up to where it turned to Winter, and the hub of Boston started to liven up a bit. People poured back out of the subway stations as if Ted didn't just finally say goodbye to his best friend. But he was asked to find the light, and so he did. It was Jennifer, and she was what drove him off here to begin with. To buy her a present. Nothing too fancy.

Walking down the streets of shops and stores, he found a jewelry store. He didn't have much experience here, but he could learn. Even the promise ring he gave to Slithers was little more than a bullet and welded metal. A laughable attempt.

Stepping inside, the store was bright, filled with some men looking for a gift for their significant other, and women who undoubtedly were shopping for the very same thing. He walked on the tiles, searching the store for anything that he could imagine Jennifer would have any interest in. Specifically, something for wearing.

Sighing and gazing at some shiny necklaces and then a peculiar feeling came to him. He jumped as an unknown hand touched his shoulder, and he twisted, pushing himself away from her.

"Just here to help." She smiled brightly. Those over abundant fake grin from overly happy simpers from retail staff, who, one was almost certain were on speed. Or some other drug to keep them happy to deal with all the nonsense.

"Sorry, nobody does that," he panted, heart racing.

"So, how can I help?" She grinned, keeping her distance. In fact, she didn't step forward or backward.

"I don't rightly know," he answered, staring at the shiny necklace again.

"Would you perhaps be looking for..." she said, her eyes shifting toward the item of interest. "A Christmas gift for someone special?"

"Yes," he turned to her, speaking softly, and again, "Yes."

"Tell me about her," she asked. "And I'll find something to suit her fancy."

"She is a kind spirit. Kinder than any I've come across. A faith bearing woman, modest, though, sometimes just a little over the top," he answered.

"Faith bearing? Of what faith?"

"Christian,"

"Protestant or Catholic?"

"Uh," he didn't know the answer to that. "Park Street Church?"

"Protestant it is." She smiled, turning. "Right this way."

So, he followed her. It was the first time, in a very, very long time he came to something new, and yet, he cared about nothing more. This was important to him, he felt it. If nothing else would come of his relationship with Jennifer that would be fine. But he wanted her to know how he felt about her, the flickering light or candle she was to him, but one whose flame must never die out. A flame worth protecting, up to, and at the cost of his own life if necessary.

"Ah, here we are," she said, pointing him to an aisle filled with crosses. Some were extravagant, others were not. Some were simple, just like Jennifer was, as extravagant as she pretended to act sometimes, it was not the norm for the core of who she was.

There was one such cross that caught his eye. It hung lightly on a silver chain necklace. The chains large enough to hold inscriptions, of which, meant nothing to him, but following the cross itself, golden gleaming light shimmering from the chandeliers hanging from the ceilings.

"That's the one," he said.

The retail worker smiled, pulled it off the rack, and packed it in a little box, placing it into a marginally larger gift box so no one would know where it came from, or what was inside, for all the emotions he held inside were meant for no one. None other than her. Slithers already knew what was inside. She didn't need a box. Not where she was.

Taking it outside, he put the box in his coat pocket, and his hand held it so no one would take it from him. If anything ever happened to this, that would be the true tragedy of the spirit of Christmas.

Chapter 32 Christmas Party

Status Report:

Black Eagle Company sinks the Oregon Pacific Chinese fleet. The Chinese pilots, low on fuel, fly toward the fleets, shot down by Black Eagle Company's pilots and MG. Some Chinese debris is cast aboard the fleets. The Company's fleet sails southward into California Pacific.

In a pincer attack, Southern California and Oregon Armed Forces with Black Eagle Company flank the remaining infantry and cavalry troops in Northern California. The large company came back from the north and moved southward to the southernmost end of California.

***

Ted pulled up in front of the store. The snowflakes casually floated down, ever so softly, white flakes glimmering the store-light, and Jennifer smiling ear to ear her lips reached, sprinted out from the store, her hand holding a few paper bags, heavy at the bottom. She opened the car, got in her seat, the bags resting on her lap as she pulled the seatbelt over her.

"Hurry. Christmas awaits." She said, clicking in the seatbelt.

"Did you pay?" He asked, putting the car in gear before speeding off.

"Hey, hey, hey!" She turned to him. "We don't talk about that."

"Jennifer," he said.

"Of course, I paid! I'm not a freeloader!" She frowned.

"Sorry, I asked," he laughed.

***

"Lamar," Sakura called out, honking her horn in her truck. "Come on. My ice cream is melting."

Her car was parked outside a small apartment complex, windows tinted ever so lightly, some cracked windows at the side. The door opened, and there Lamar was, dawdling as he always did. He held some plastic bags. He stepped into the truck, pulled himself in, clasped his seatbelt on.

"What'd ya get?" She asked, peering into the bag. She rolled her eyes. *Potato chips.*

"Just chips," he replied.

"Put in the address, will you? I don't want to get lost getting to Sudbury," she said, driving the car into the street as Lamar typed in the address for his phone's GPS.

***

"Jeffrey." Michael said as he knocked repeatedly against the door. "Come on, we'll be late."

Jeffrey heard the pound on his door. "Coming."

The Christmas party, and of all things, gifts to be exchanged. *I don't want anything from you tonight, Ghost. Keep your gifts to yourself.*

He grabbed his holster, strapped it to his side, pulling out his pistol, the safety on, before placing it in his pocket. Can't be caught dead in this surprise, now, could he? After all, Russians were coming, and they were coming soon. Though he couldn't imagine having to be the one to use a weapon during a Christmas party... but just in case.

More knocking.

"Come on, Jeff, we're gonna be late." He heard Michael's voice call out from the other side of the door. Michael appeared to be worried about being on time for once. What changed? "The canned bread isn't going to bake itself."

Canned bread. One of the many keepsakes from Mom. You got the recipe?

He shook his head again. He pulled open a drawer inside his room, and grabbed his Kabar knife, sliding it into his boot. *Just in case.*

He rushed back to the door, opening it. "Mom gave you her recipe?"

"No. I borrowed it without permission nor the intent to return it. Yes, she gave it to me, come on."

***

Samantha was shifting over to the side of the kitchen, scrubbing the plates with her dishcloth. Erin was behind her, setting the table. The table was long enough to fit all of them there. Plates were set down with the silverware beside them, a regular glass for water or a variety of other non-alcoholic beverages. This, Sam knew, was mainly for Sakura. The little kiddie of the group with big dreams and aspirations.

"Sam, check on the turkey, please," she said, opening the white door down the cellar, and then walked down the creaking steps.

Sam nodded as she went over to the oven, opened it. The heat blasted her face. She took two red oven mitts, pulled it out, and set it on the stove top, stabbing it viscerally with the thermometer. She read both thermometers by the thigh bone and the breast, reading one-eighty and one-seventy degrees respectively.

"Erin. It's done. Michael should be here soon," Sam called back.

Erin walked up with several 2-liters. "You didn't bring your carving knife?"

"No, Michael has it. He'll cut it," she replied.

"Sam." She set the drinks on the counter. "You had one job."

There was a knock on the door before she could muster a response.

"Can you get that please?" Erin hurried over into the back of her pantry, rummaging through some things before coming back out with napkins and paper towels.

Sam nodded, pushing the baking sheet to the back of the stove. She wiped her hands before striding briskly down the hall, lightly lit, and the red carpet with yellow engravings framing it. The corner toward the door was a little disheveled. She bent down low.

Another rhythmic knock on the door. Three times.

"In a minute," she called out, bending down to fix the carpet. She patted herself down, smoothing the wrinkles out of her green apron as she reached for the doorknob, turning it.

The door swung open; a cold wind brushed through her. She pulled back, allowing Tim through. "Out of the way," he cried out, holding a large box. Closing the door, she turned back before he ran past her.

"Tim," the tall man wobbled back and forth, the clumsy events coordinator.

"You need a hand?" she inquired.

"Yes, please. I thought you'd never ask." He turned, smiling, placing the box on the ground.

"Huh." She put a hand on her hip. "I was trying to be nice. You didn't need to be a jerk about it."

"Oh, Jennifer's not here, so I figured—"

"You don't know that," she quipped, sneering to the side. "Honestly, I'd expect that kind of behavior from her of all people, not you. Do you treat your clients that way?"

"Of course, not." He took his foggy glasses off, cleaned them with a handkerchief.

"Is that Tim?" Erin called.

"Yes, Erin, it is I," he replied, picking his box back up and leading the way for Sam to follow him back into the kitchen.

"You have a carving knife?" Erin brushed her red hair behind her ear with a smile.

You're not being subtle about this are you?

"Nope. Why in the world would I have one of those," he dropped the box again, opening it with such grandiose in a way she would really only expect from Jennifer.

"You miss Jennifer, don't you?" She asked.

He pulled out a Tupperware filled with chopped potatoes marinating in some ingredients he whipped together. "Yeah, what gave me away?" He turned. "Erin, you have a spare pan? I want to put these in the oven."

"Sure, over there," she jerked her head toward her cabinet, wooden with soft engravings. He hurried over, pulled out the pan, and poured all his potatoes into it. Tim refused to make beans, so no one would ever blame him for spilling the beans ever again. Honestly, she couldn't remember if it was his fault or not, it was too long ago and became a recurring joke between her friends and him. Not that it mattered at all.

Another knock at the door.

I swear. This is going to be like that Jackson film and all the dwarves interrupting a peaceful little halfling.

"I'll get it." Sam rolled her eyes, turned around, and scurried back down the hall.

The clamor of pans and activity came from the kitchen, and Erin laughed giddily at her new crush. Sam skipped over the carpet and opened the door to Michael and Jeffrey with their hair covered in snow. She glanced at Jeff, nothing seemed unusual about him, but she didn't realize he was coming. He was holding a large cardboard box.

She turned to Michael. "You bring the carving knife?"

"Yes." He pulled out a little box.

She turned her gaze back over to Jeff. "What's in the box?"

"Mom's famous canned bread." He smiled, hand shivering in the cold. "So, can we come in, or do you expect us to freeze our balls off?"

"Well, language like that will get you nowhere," she scowled, turning to Michael. "Seriously, teach him some manners, will you? He may be a decade and a half older than you but that's no excuse to have the mouth of a sailor, now, is there?" She shook her head. "Michael, get in here and get to carving the turkey, please, and take the bread. I'll have a moment with Jeffrey alone."

"Out in the cold?" Jeffrey protested.

"Yes, in the cold." She crossed her arms over her chest.

"As you wish," Michael replied, grabbing the box from Jeffrey, and stepping inside, moving along to the kitchen.

Her legs crossed over the ice threshold as Jeffrey frowned, clearly uneasy by this sudden gesture. She wasn't entirely sure if he knew why she was going through such a great length to talk to him, and him alone. But Jeff was the source, unintentionally or not, for Ted's outright hostile behavior. Sure, Ted was the only one of them who swore openly, and rarely. His curses were well meant, and if he decided to curse you out, you had best look in the mirror. And Ted, just the other week called Jeff a 'Mother fucker' out in the open, which was unusual, even for him. Sam closed the door behind her, leaning against it.

"If you're going to—"

"Shut it," she said. She peered behind him, the wind howling, snow dusting off the white glistening surface of the ground. Her blood began to chill, and her arms trembled with the cold. She gazed to the left and to the right, and no other lights from cars were coming their way. She was alone with Jeff, but it would not be long before *he* was to be expected. *Need to keep this brief.* "You should know that Ted will be here."

"I was aware of the possibility, but wh—"

"Now, I don't mean to be rude." She began, "but Jennifer and I went through some very dark places. It was like a hole which I barely understand. Now, I do not, and Jennifer does not, nor does anyone want to see Ted like he was when we found him. I don't know what bad blood you two have with each other, but it is clear to me, he isn't fond of you, and because of that, neither am I. I am certain Jennifer feels the same way. So, stay away from him. Do you understand me?"

"I don't think Michael would appreciate you talking to me this way." He stepped forward, his white misty breath in her face.

"I love Michael. And I love Ted. And I love Jennifer. And Ted was in a dark place so deep, we were nearly swallowed up entirely." She stepped forward, standing tall. "If you do anything tonight that forces me to choose Michael over Ted and Jennifer, I will choose them. And you should know that Ted wouldn't appreciate that."

He stepped back, clearly uncomfortable.

"I know you're not afraid of me. Why would you be? But you're afraid of Ted. Now, let's all be civil tonight. And don't touch or even talk to Ted unless he speaks to you. You understand?"

"Loud and clear," he frowned. "May I come in now?"

"Yes." She opened the door for him to briskly stride along as if nothing happened.

Headlights approached from the road. *That was more time-consuming than I meant it to be.* She peered over, her hands covering the lights from her eyes as a truck parked in the driveway. The Georgia plate was well visible. The doors opened and shut swiftly as Lamar and Sakura jumped out of it. Lamar slipped on the ice, dropping some bags.

"Ah!"

"Careful!" Sam yelled, running over, exhaling white breath, but Sakura was around the other end of the car first, picking this considerably larger man up with relative ease, or that's how Sakura made it look anyway.

"Samantha, can you grab that?" Sakura pointed to the bags in the snow.

"You okay?" She asked, picking up the paper bags and wiped off the snow.

"Yeah, I'm fine. Just an old war wound, as it were," he replied. "I'm fine actually," he turned to Sakura. "You can let me go, you know."

"Oh, right," she stepped away from him.

"Well then," Samantha smiled. "Welcome again to Sudbury, the home of Erin, or as Ted likes to call her, the Gutenberg Press!"

"What's the Gutenberg Press?" Sakura asked, following behind her.

"It's a joke. Her last name's Gutenberg." She opened the door for them.

"Okay, but what is it?"

"It's the world's first printing press," she answered. "Before then, they just had monks with carpal tunnel rewriting everything on new paper and scrolls. There's your useless lesson for the day!"

Sam led them into the kitchen. Michael was chatting up a storm with Tim, laughing away, carving the turkey; Erin was greeting Sakura and Lamar, simultaneously putting together a few bowls for the potato chips they brought, and Jeffrey was cutting the cans open with a *military knife?* And slicing the canned bread before placing them on a cookie sheet, putting them in the oven underneath the potatoes.

Four knocks on the wood door reached her ears again.

I knew this was coming. Just like that movie.

She ran back to the door down the corridor. She opened the door, and Jennifer and Ted grinned at her.

"Hurry, take this," Jennifer said, giving her some bags. "It's the pie that I totally paid for."

"I'm not entirely sure if she's joking or not," he chuckled.

Samantha hoisted the bags from her, allowing them both to come in. She pointed and waved her hand to both to give her their ears. They leaned forward. *Honestly, I didn't expect Ted to understand that.* "Hey, I was unaware, so don't get mad at me, but Jeffrey is here."

"What?" Jennifer exclaimed softly, peering into the kitchen cautiously, and her smirk turned upside down. Her fists were clenched, and when Samantha thought she saw her, gritted her teeth. This was going to be a gritty Christmas party.

Ted immediately retreated his hands into his coat pocket. She knew that gesture all too well. No one else would know, save maybe Jennifer. His wrist trembled in his pocket. With what, she couldn't rightly guess. Anxiety? Fear? Hatred? Truth was, there was so much she didn't know about Jeffrey and Ted together, that it could be anything that would lead to nothing less than a tragedy.

"He came along with Michael, and I literally just found out, so don't get mad," she continued. "Look, I spoke with Jeffrey privately."

"Why would you do that?" Jennifer frowned.

Just like the time from the phone, Jennifer's voice was soft, but harsh, and the sudden reaction to being scolded was not one she was used to. Often, she was the one yelling at truck drivers, not the other way around. But she didn't feel like she understood how to properly read a room anymore, since she got this wrong.

"I told him not to talk to Ted at all unless Ted spoke to him. Now, I've instructed him to stay as far away as possible. Granted, this is a party so that might not at all be doable, but we can try," she looked Ted in the eyes. "Is this okay?"

Jennifer turned to him. "Tedward, it's up to you."

He bowed his head to the ground, panting heavily. Jennifer reached a hand in his pocket, both hands, and wrapped them around his, pulling it out ever so gently. Raising his hand to her chest, softly breathing to match his rhythm.

With the little time they had with him, about a year and a half now, perhaps a little longer since she mustered up the courage to force a meeting with him in Teri Nation. It surprised her that Jennifer knew his bodily rhythms. At least as well as she did anyway.

"Ted," Sam said again. "May I touch your shoulder?"

He turned his eyes toward her, not saying a thing, not nodding or shaking a head. He just stood still as his hands left his pockets. *There's a step. Come on.*

He slowly turned to the door, and Sam touched his shoulder, squeezing it tightly. He didn't jolt, not this time, as if he was at a calm. An unusual calm given the fact that he was about to eat again with an enemy. Though she was certain with the level of hatred that existed between the two, perhaps it was better not knowing. His free hand reached for the door.

No, Sam thought.

The door was pushed, the lock settling in place as it clicked shut. Ted's palm kept it shut as he reached for the regular lock, turning it. He exhaled one last time, before touching the door with his forehead. "It'll have to be."

So, we can spend Christmas together after all.

"Okay, then that's that," Sam said.

"Ted, are you sure?" Jennifer asked as if to grant him permission and the agency to leave, to let it be purely his choice, or if evacuation from the premises was a much better idea. She couldn't force him to stay, she wanted him to. Michael never should have brought Jeff here, and it was Sam's fault for not finding the time to tell him.

"Ted, I'm sorry."

He turned, brightly smiling. This was the fakest smile ever.

"It's quite all right," he said.

No. It isn't. But you're forcing yourself to be here now. You don't have to do this.

He looked into her eyes, stepping forward glancing at her as if to say, 'Yes, I do.'

He forced his way past her and passed his way into the kitchen.

The smell of turkey, gravy and fresh baked bread filled her nose, but she looked down, realizing a fatal error. She didn't like this feeling swelling up inside her chest, making it incredibly difficult to breathe.

"Sam." Jennifer grabbed her shoulder.

She felt a strong grip, stronger than any other time Jennifer's grabbed her before. Turning, twisting her feet abruptly to face her. "Look, Jennifer, sorry, I didn't know he was coming. Honest."

Jennifer exhaled a sigh of disappointment. That's what it was, and a sigh of impending dread, as if something absolutely horrible was going to fall upon them this night. Just the sense of dread, and a tragedy. That is exactly what neither of them wanted. "Just, do whatever you can to keep Jeffrey as far away from him as possible."

"I—"

"Can you do that for me? For Ted, I mean?" She stared in her eyes, glazed over, frowning. Her lips curled downward.

"I will do everything I can," she replied.

"Good, now let's go!" She wiped her eyes and returned a smile to her face.

Ted changed something in you. What is it? She turned, taking Jennifer's hand with the bags, smelling of pies, apple and pecan. Her favorite, personally. This was going to be one Christmas she is certain she won't forget, but was this going to be a Christmas she was going to *want* to forget? Truth was, there was only one way to find out, by moving forward, one step at a time. First the left. And then the right. She entered almost unwillingly into the kitchen.

Dinner was already served, and everyone was seated. Jeffrey and Ted were as far away from one another as humanly possible at this table. The turkey was resting in several different carved slices minus the legs, resting on the pan with the steaming carcass plaguing the stovetop.

Wine was poured. Except for Sakura. They gave her grape juice. She didn't mind, or so it seemed anyway, eagerly taking out her cup, ready to be poured into. She glanced over at Jeffrey, sitting next to Michael, and an open seat next to him. Erin was at one head, and on the other end was Jennifer, next to her, seating Ted, Tim, and Lamar.

"Sam, get over here." Erin ushered her from behind the kitchen counter leading into the dining room, before standing behind her head seat.

Sam scurried, pulling off her apron, neatly folding it on the back of her chair. Erin had a nice smirk on her face. The freckles made her endearing, like the beautiful host she was, and the role she was to play tonight. This was the first time she arranged everything, and even though it was a group effort, her arrangement for this was flawless.

Tim had better be careful, she thought. If she cared enough, she might come after his job. She chuckled softly at the thought. She liked money too much to take a gross pay cut just for that.

"Thank you all for coming." Erin spoke almost like a politician.

Who was missing? Where's John? Sam's eyes scanned the table to meet those whom Erin was making eye contact with when she noticed an empty chair. "Merry Christmas everyone, and I want to thank Sam especially for cooking the turkey and keeping it fresh since November."

The table applauded. Sam did the Jennifer-like thing to do, and stood, pushing the chair, and bowed to everyone at the table, before promptly sitting again.

"Now, before we get started, I'll pray for our meal, and I'll—"

"Why don't you tell us how this is all going to work before we eat?" Michael interrupted.

"Michael," Jennifer shouted from across the table. "You mustn't interrupt our host, it's rude."

"Now, now, Jennifer." Erin waved her hands down to the table as if she was pushing on some invisible box. "He has a point. I will pray, we will eat, and then we'll go into my living room. And then we'll exchange gifts. And eat some of the delicious pie Jennifer and Ted brought."

"Your terms are acceptable." Michael put his hands on the placemat.

"Okay, let's bow our heads."

Samantha bowed her head into her hands, listening intently to the words for which Erin prayed to God. Despite all the anxiety this night had come to bring her, she felt within her a spirit of calm as Erin prayed over the meal, thanking God for the food, the blessings, and even something as simple as travel mercies getting here despite the storm outside, heavily laden with snow, obscuring even the finest of eyes.

"Amen," Erin finished.

Just like all the disorganized mess of a family dinner, plates were passed around the table, being served by one another. Forks reaching over the turkey, bread being passed out, brown bread, with melted butter spread all over it, just like she liked her bread, nice, melted butter.

The table talk started as soon as the plates were re-sorted back to their respective owner, taking apart the turkey, and eating, some talking with their mouths open. Oh dear, Jennifer would never let them hear the end of it. Not that Samantha particularly cared, but she knew Jennifer was very concerned with manners, especially with important group intimate events, however much she broke those same etiquette rules from time and time again. Especially the time she made Tim clean up the water he spat all over her floor.

Amid all the felicity of this fine dinner, she did manage to see Ted, snarling from time to time, at both Sakura and Jeff. It was barely noticeable, but she saw it. She had grown to understand why he hated Jeffrey. She didn't understand one bit why he didn't like Sakura at all. Even that time after apple picking around the campfire, she didn't get it. She came from the university, as almost all her friends did, huddled around Park Street Church.

Sakura's family had military roots dating all the way back to the Japanese Concentration Camps during WWII. Certain characteristics defined people with the elongated argument of nature over nurture, and truth be told, nurturing external stimuli had a way of shaping the natural world. These things considered, she was still a nobody. She had no ties to any of them, but perhaps, since it was known her family's military background was a special reason for him to dislike her. Yet there was one contradiction in all of this. Ted seemed to hate her less than Jeffrey, but almost an unnoticeable amount, and while he hated Lamar, likely for the same reason, his disdain for Lamar was considerably less than either Sakura or Jeffrey. But she couldn't help but wonder if this hatred toward Sakura was justified, she still didn't know enough, but it seemed unfair, whatever the reason.

It was like Ted was Goldilocks, and Sakura, Jeffrey, and Lamar were the three bears. Whatever was within Ted's relationship to these three were the porridge. Only, the bears were at the kitchen table, already returned, and in place of porridge, too hot, too cold, and just right, was steeping right in front of them. One of them was going to serve him part of their porridge tonight, but what was the temperature? *I don't like this bit at all. God, please let nothing happen between either of them tonight. I beg you!*

With her heart rate settling down a bit, the plates and silverware were clattering about on the empty, scraped clean plates, and there was some food on the table. Likely Erin would save that for tomorrow.

"The living room is right there. Christmas carols are playing," Erin said, standing. "I'll be there in a minute; I just need to pack some of this away first."

"I'll help," Tim offered.

"Tim," Sam said as he stood, adjusting his napkin on the table. "Make sure not to spill the beans this time, okay?"

"What beans?" He asked.

"Those beans," Michael cackled.

"Dear, poor Bean. You deserved so much better than Mr. Timothy," Jennifer exclaimed, an authentic smile returned to her face. *Finally.*

The chairs scraped against Erin's beautiful hardwood floors as the rest of them stood, walking into the living room. She heard the clamoring of plates and silverware enter the sink, and the faucet turned on.

She followed the crowd. *Jingle Bells* was playing in the background, and some presents were lying underneath the tree, carefully wrapped, and topped with name tags. The tree was decorated wildly, and Erin spared no expense, wrapped in lots of decorations—some with Santa and his reindeer, angels, other Chrismon's, some snowmen, and of course, tinsel, red, green, and silver lining throughout the tree, and a lot of bright white lights, carefully interwoven in the tree as to not reveal any wires, lighting the tree up like some mystical spectacle for all to see. At the top of the Tree was a brightly lit star, carefully created and crafted to have that crystalline glow.

In the corner of the room, resting underneath a window, decorated with more Christmas lights was a folding table, and a large green bowl and a ladle inside, and some red cups. Erin went hard on the Christmas colors. She walked over, taking a cup, and spooning some eggnog into her cup, sipping the thick beverage which always had its unique flavor. Such a shame it was only around for Christmas, and no other holiday.

If I want eggnog on my birthday, I'm making eggnog!

Jennifer and Ted were walking her way as Michael and Jeffrey were still chatting, this time, building a lovely group of four with Sakura and Lamar. From the many conversations she's had with Michael pertaining to Jeffrey, he wasn't a trusting man, not that this should affect her relationship with him. She reminded herself: Jeffrey isn't who's important, Ted is.

"Ted," she whispered, sipping her nog, and she felt the thick residue on her upper lip, licking it clean. Can't let something like this go to waste. "You okay?"

"Yes," he replied, not letting his façade down. She knew this time, it wasn't for her, or for Jennifer, but for himself, nuzzling back into solitude with people he trusted. She was thankful that she was one of those people. Hard thing, really, trust. It's so easy a thing to come by, to accept, receive and give away, but once someone has sullied that, it becomes a cynical nature, a beast if you will, asking questions as to the motivations for which people place their kindness. But the trust Ted put in them was not of that nature. He questioned it at first over a year and a half ago, but that was then, and this was now.

"Michael," Erin's voice carried over as she wiped her hands dry with a cloth. "You want to be Santa today?"

"Sure thing," he said, walking over to that beautiful pine tree. It looked amazing, and it still smelled of needles. Some people hated the smell, but she loved it. It was a nice reminder of her home up in Vermont filled with so many trees, so many natural scents.

Michael's hand reached underneath the tree for the first gift. "Tim." He said, tossing it as Tim crossed the threshold, and in his Tim-like fashion, fumbled it in his hands as he unwrapped it.

More presents followed. Samantha received a coupon for some coffee from a small coffee shop with some local aromas. Honestly, this was her favorite breakfast place in the morning. Slow paced place with fast service, and the food was not processed nor heavily filled with preservatives. As God intended.

"Thank you so much, whoever you are," she smiled.

"Oh, Jennifer, this one's for you."

Michael tossed a small box over to her direction. Jennifer caught it with grace. She shook the container, and there was a little rattling noise inside. Ted shuddered at that. Clearly it came from him.

Oh God! Jennifer, you didn't break it did you! No! Sam thought.

A knock on the door.

What now? If I hear a knock on that door one more time...

"Must be John. I'll get it," Erin replied, leaving the room.

Jennifer ripped up the paper, and a beautifully crafted box with light silver embroidery around the edges of the box, tied together in a red ribbon. She pulled the ribbon undone, and it floated carefully, gently onto the ground. The gift's container was pulled open.

Jennifer's eyes gleamed with awe. Eyes shimmering with the silver item, carefully interweaving the chains in her fingers, and pulled up a golden cross. She wasted no time putting it on her neck. "Thank you," she said, turning to Ted. "Tedward, this must be you. How can it not. I love it."

"Ted, don't answer that until the end. This isn't how Secret Santa works." Michael pointed at him.

"He's arrived." Erin came in, leading John with an infectious grin on his face.

Samantha peered over to him, who seemed to be eyeing something specific on Jeffrey's side. Samantha peered at the side, and Jeffrey appeared to be reaching for something behind him, as if reaching for something in his back pocket. *Must have forgotten to put a present in the tree.*

Out of the corner of her eye, she saw Ted turning his attention from Jennifer, who in turn followed his gaze, staring right at Sakura. His eyes narrowed, lips frowned, and his fists clenched at his side. "Ted," Sam asked. "What is it?"

"Shit," he replied.

Sam felt something. It was ever so light, almost barely noticeable. It was almost like a small tremor. Her eyes shifted toward the eggnog. Ripples stretching to the edge of the bowl in which it lay. *Oh no!* A whistle, distant, and approaching closer. Closer. Louder. Dropping her cup to cover her ears. The wood in the building cracked, underneath. Fire roared out the kitchen. Her heart pounded. Fast. Flight. Out the window. Glass shattered around her as she tumbled out, rolling into the snow. Splinters shot out from behind her, scratching her face, warm blood dripping down, painting it. She turned.

Erin's house was covered in flames with the roof collapsing. Black smoke sheltered them from the sky, and in the distance, more flames. More whistling. More missiles. The wood on the ground creaked, and she was remiss, to forget her friends inside the house. Ted. By himself, holding up a beam inside a large gash in the wall. Sakura coughed, and Lamar stumbled behind her. Jeff and Michael walked side by side, shielding Erin and Tim. Jennifer, of course, selfless as always, thinking nothing of herself, came out with all their jackets. The beam crumbled, and Ted swiftly jumped behind her, shielding dear Jennifer from the debris.

Calm headed, frowning, eyes angled downward, focused, silent. He snapped his fingers past her. "West! Erin, lead the way!"

"Where to?" She turned her head.

"Anywhere we can get to the sewers."

What?

"I know just the place, but it's far. You think we can make it? It's a five-mile hike."

"We have no choice."

Chapter 33 Disaster

Status Report:

Black Eagle Company's fleet moves south. Pilots refueled and resupplied with bombs and flew ahead. The fleet's large artillery range shot ahead, shooting at the Chinese Naval fleet. The pilots soared through, bombing the waters and the carriers. Distracted, the final Chinese ship was unable to respond before the last ship sank.

The remaining company from the North came in, securing the border, and capturing the last Chinese infantrymen for interrogation.

***

Samantha panted. Her heart felt like it was going to burst out of her chest. Her palms were sweaty, crusted with coagulated blood pasted on her hands, eyes widened, staring down at the ground, the rubble, rocks overlapped with metal fragments of cars, other debris, glass, shattered as it sprawled over the ground, which was little more than tar of a road, unrecognizable had she even known it. Buildings were nothing but shadows of their former glory, broken into, creaking metal before finally crashing down, sending the dirt and ash her way, fogging the vision of what else lay before her.

Her hands trembled at her side, her ripped pants, and her own blood coursed down in steady streams, just getting out of this nightmare, and walking into another one. Oh, this was a new kind of thrill. She sucked the air through her teeth.

It should be cold in December, and she'd dare say, since she lost track of time, she could very well be in January. *Did that much time really pass?*

Yes. It did. There was no denying it. How could she keep track of the time? Surviving day after day, one new Hell after the next, just waiting for God to release her from this. But she was alive. That was an important thing, or so she thought, until Jeffrey and Ted scowled at one another.

The pistol's holster was in view this time, outside Jeffrey's pants, for it appeared, at least to her, he didn't need nor want to conceal it. That was the least of his concerns since he now held a rifle over his shoulder, strapped to his back. Jeffrey's back was against a large slab of concrete. Ted, scowling, but Ted looked unlike himself, grimacing, and in his eyes was rage that he managed to keep hidden, or at least, level. But he made no attempt to hide his ire, face cringing with lines all over, and never mind the blood coalescing on his face.

Ted was coated in it. His hair dripped and crusted, and his face looked painted. His clothes were torn in several different places; the sleeves, the pants, and even the winter boots, shredded. He was armed, but with a rifle of some kind she didn't recognize, a pistol at his opposite side, and a hunting knife by the looks of it, all of which she knew he didn't own. He didn't have it. Clearly picked up from one of the many he killed. Completely discombobulated in her own grief, she didn't recognize it until now. He was wearing a Russian Combat uniform, and everything that came with it.

She now knew, all those words ago when he said to her, "Saul killed his thousands, and David his tens of thousands; I'd be fortunate if my numbers were nearly that low," that this was no exaggeration.

"Sam," Michael put his hand on her shoulder, looking forward, with a blank expression on his face. "Let's turn around, you don't need to see this."

"And what is *this*, Michael?" She turned to him. "I can't. I need to—"

"Is this what you wanted?" Ted shouted at Jeff. "You dumb mother fucker!"

Canine ran in between them. "You two, we don't have time for your pissing contest,"

"No." He pointed at Canine. "No. *You* don't have time. I have all the time in the world. Now get out of my way. Because of him, I now have a bounty on my head the size of the US Treasury. In the middle of this battlefield, I have all the time in the world. It's you who's running out of time, now piss off."

Canine stepped away from the little dispute, retreating to her small unit of eight men. Samantha knew Ted to be vulgar at times of distress and pain, but every expletive was intentional, meaning very well to lay a curse upon Jeffrey.

"Maybe if you didn't—" Jeffrey began, his hand resting at his side, the side with the pistol.

"Didn't what? Didn't what?" Ted interrupted. "If I didn't do anything? Yeah, like that would make a difference." His hands clenched tightly into fists.

Ted. Don't do this. Please.

Samantha turned to Jennifer, who looked on with an irritable expression on her face, also scowling. Of all people, her face was the least scarred, no dirt on it, no blood dripping down it, and even her clothes remained unharmed. These past few weeks were Hell. Must have especially taken a toll on Jennifer, who she left alone to die. But John stayed with her, protecting her. Maybe. Maybe they should have listened to Ted to begin with. *I don't know anymore.*

"I didn't have a choice for what I did. Naka—" Jeff tried to defend himself once more, but Ted wouldn't have it.

"I don't care about her, she's dead. I ensured that." Ted started to choke up. "So, tell me, did you like it? Did you like any of it?"

"No." Jeff's hands reached down, hand around the pistol, swinging it upward.

But Ted was faster. He unfastened his hunting knife, twirling it within his fingers, air whistling. Hurling it through the air, it was like a bullet with dead accuracy, striking Jeff in the arm, and the pistol dropped to the ground. His other arm reached for the knife. Ted bolted, blue veins climbing up his legs, immediately pinning the knife further into his shoulder, twisting it.

"An eye for an eye," Ted said. "When I saw you, in the bathroom, I told you if you did anything that would force me to start over, I'd rip your fucking arms off. Now that you've done just that, I've changed my mind. I have an objective, and I'm not telling you what it is, but I need you for it. So, when all this is over, I'm just going to break every single bone in your body. All two-hundred and six bones. And I'm going to rip your eyelids off, and then, I'm going to march everyone with the last names Clemens off a fucking cliff, and I'm going to make you watch. Just so you know what you put me through and see what you're missing. Welcome to the thrill of not being able to do a damn thing about it!"

Samantha's jaw opened, and her heart skipped a beat, sinking inside her chest, and her hands trembled uncontrollably, her fingers tapping at her side. Slowly, she closed her jaw, and her eyes narrowed down her nose, refocusing her gaze to Jeff. Her heart felt something. At first surprise, and slowly changed to an indescribable hatred.

Jeff wasn't called back to base because they were moving their pieces. Black Eagle stationed him right there, under their noses. She once believed that there was no such thing as bad people. Naïve of her to think so. There were just people who did good things, and people who did bad things, but now, while there may not be such a thing as a good person, she could say now definitively, Jeff was an evil man.

Jeffrey turned his gaze toward Michael. "Do something, Mike. Don't let him do this to me."

Characters:

Adam Sander: Chief Administrator for the Caster's Administrator.

Alexander: Native to London, a silent type, and a representative of the Caster's Administration.

Alexandra: Malcolm's wife.

Andrea: First Lady and wife to President Snells.

Arjun: Head fae Administrator of India.

Blanka: An Administrator from the Czech Republic. Enjoys her fine wine and excursions and wants nothing more than to get back home.

Bridgette: A London native, an administrator serving directly underneath Adam.

Butcher: Ted's friend from Task Force Seven.

Claire: Lead Fae Administrator of France.

Colton: Lead Fae administrator from the American Branch.

Culain: From Ireland, this administrator comes directly from Camelot. He's known for his outbursts.

Daiki: Head Fae Administrator of Japan.

Elias: Head Fae Administrator of Germany.

Emily Gutenberg: Erin's mother (currently undergoing cancer treatment).

Emily Miller: A delta force operator.

Erin Gutenberg: A stockbroker in Boston. She is part of how Jennifer puts it, "The dysfunctional family."

Gernardt: General of the Armies

Gwen Swan: Head Fae Administrator of Alaska. She also serves as Governor of that State.

Hector: Head Administrator of everything South of Rio Grande.

Ilya: A Russian representative for the Caster's Administration. She's made her home in Camelot.

Jack: A torture victim.

Jeff Clemens: An officer of Black Eagle Company. Michael Clemens' brother.

Jennifer Miller: A biological researcher in Boston. A close friend to Ted Anderson, and alone knows his secrets.

John Spadero: Fae administrator who also serves as Congressman in the state of Massachusetts.

Johnson: Secretary of Defense

Lamar Cooper: A former Marine.

Malcolm: Chief Operating Officer of Black Eagle Company.

Michael Clemens: Business developer consultant. Loves to experiment with his cocktails.

Mikhail: Lead Fae Administrator of Eastern Europe. He has a very playful demeanor.

Obi: Head Fae Administrator of Nigeria.

Oliver: Head Fae Administrator of Australia.

President Snells: President of the United States. To the world, he is considered the single man who brokered World Peace.

Rebecca: Archivist of the libraries inside Camelot.

Roach: Another agent from Task Force Seven

Sakura: An orphan and a college student, looking to serve as an officer of the United States of America.

Samantha Harris: A logistical broker in Boston. Friends with a small group of people, and thoroughly enjoys her Tuesdays,

Sarah McCurdy: Disavowed Fae of the Administration.

Slithers: Ted's deceased beloved from Task Force Seven.

Smith: Admiral of the Navies

Ted Anderson: The man with a past best left buried.

Ticker: Another agent from Task Force Seven.

Tim: An events coordinator. A real silent type.

Wang: Head Fae Administrator of China.

Armanis Ar-feinial, in the gritty pits of despair, he comes from: Bridgeton, Maine, a terribly dreadful place. Currently residing in the Greater Boston Area with his family, he studied Criminal Justice, English, and currently dabbles in a little bit of Finance. His unfaltering passion for writing came from his first exposure from the Lord of the Rings, which he drew inspiration from in his first stories, but alas, as all good things come downward into the grimdark pits, adopting tones from Joe Abercrombie. He loves reading, playing games of all kinds, and he is what you call a practicing writaholic. He is personally known for his

witty sarcastic unasked-for remarks.

Excerpt from The Tragedy of Ted Anderson

Chapter 1 Splintered

~My heart was cloven in two. I could do nothing to stop it. Nothing at all. Just one pawn in a grand scheme, and now, I don't even know who the king is anymore.

***

Dashing through the snow.

Sam's legs pushed through the white fluff, thrusting it in the air. Her chest puffed out. The ground trembled beneath every stride, exhaling heavily. Heart pumping. The footsteps were drowned out by the whistling of the air, as large rockets struck around. Several muffled breaths entered her ears from behind, in front, and to either side of her. Continuing to run, her nails dug into her palms, warm blood pressing down her wrists, and her hair stood on ends, creeping up her spine with chills.

"Run!" Ted yelled with exasperated breath. "Keep going. Don't let the noise startle you. Keep running!"

Sam made the mistake of turning her head, mechanically. All of them ran past her, except Ted and Jennifer, who was huffing and puffing beside him. Sam's hands shook. Her fingers like ice. No gloves. No time to grab her coat. Jennifer's fingers seemed even brittle within this weather, for though it was hot, it was still freezing temperatures. Sam felt like left over chicken that hadn't been microwaved long enough. Hot on the outside but freezing internally.

"Sam, get over here!" Michael called, his hand on her shoulder, pushing her ahead.

Sounds of whistles vibrated the earth again, shattering the foundations of the houses, flames burning up the side, melting the shingles of nearby buildings. Splinters of wood littered the snow around. The peace she once knew, was gone, filling her bones, her blood, her soul, slowly pulling at her mind. The houses, once beautiful, were now hovels, with shattered glass, flames inside, and the metal wrenching beneath the weight and a compromised integrity forced these metal structures to collapse in on themselves, pushing smoke around them.

Michael tugged on her again. A face so serious, and yet softly concerned, eyes glimmering orange with the fire's glow. Eyes narrowing in such a way to show his compassion, his gentle characteristics of which, she knew, at least for a moment, it would be okay. All she had to do, was keep telling herself that in the event that one of those lies she would grow to believe. For such times, hope was all she had, all anyone had in times like this; however, ahead was but a murky pond, which was the only path forward, and yet, she knew nothing of the state of affairs on the other side. False hope, but hope, nonetheless.

"This way!" Erin, the redhead called out. Her arms waved as she approached the street heading into downtown Sudbury.

Sam gasped as squealing cars drove by, wreathed in flames, arms out the windows. Blood painted the windshields, before inevitably crashing into a building, already in flames. The store fronts were no better, already caved in, people pouring out of them, shattering through the glass. Smoke, black, filled the air, rose to a cloud, dismal. Screams, screams, all the screaming. All paired together as if this was a horror movie well-rehearsed, but this wasn't a movie. This was reality.

"Sam, we don't have time for this. Move. You're a broker aren't you? Speed! Get moving!" Ted scolded. "Get moving or—"

Another whistle came by. Ted looked up.

"Shit!" He pushed Jennifer out to the ground, who had the sense to get her coat, and she tumbled to the ground, one hand catching her as she fell, snow, snow fluffing in a dust around her. A startled scream escaped her lips.

"Michael!" Jeff squawked.

In her current state, not entirely aware of her surroundings as Sam should have been, she had forgotten about Jeff, Lamar, Tim, and Sakura, running up behind them, as she suddenly found herself running past them, feeling a push, adrenaline rushed to her head. The high-pitched screeching grew louder. Her eyes gaped open, teeth jittering. Falling in the snow, she did; it was soft, almost like a pillow, but warm like a blanket. *Warm?* An explosion by her ear caused fissures in her body, and pushed her aside, rolling, feeling shards of metal scratching her, and her warm blood trickled out of the wounds. She hissed, Michael was beside her, one hand firmly on her forearm as he immediately pulled her up, glancing at her with a watery smile.

She turned her head immediately to Jennifer, who was underneath Ted, who reared his head towards Sam, scowling with gritted teeth. "When I say run, you run!" It was almost like he was a completely different person.

"Erin!" Sakura called, shifting herself ahead of Jeff, stumbling over her own two feet. "Where are the sewers?"

"Downtown. In the center." Erin jittered her teeth, white breath exhaling between those lips. Erin brought her sleeve to her mouth.

Ted brought Jennifer closer with the group, tightly knitted, and while calm, the people inside downtown were in a panic, scurrying about and screaming as the bombs continued to drop. Ted looked closely in the town, studying, so it seemed. Eyes narrowed, back straight, and not the smile that was generally accustomed on his face, but that of a man who was prepared for Hell. Lips curled downwards into a frown as his gaze studied the calamity before them, the calamity that was once just a peaceful town.

Sam never truly saw him like this before. She'd seen him cry, even lash out, sometimes, but almost always kept a calm and happy demeanor, well, most of the time. No. This was a different Ted. One quiet. Cold and calculating. She briefly found herself turning to look at Jeff, who too was calculating. Hard minds. Cold minds. And regardless of the two, Ted and Jeff, hating one another not more than—*How long have we been out in the snow?* She couldn't remember. Could have been minutes or hours, but the sun never rose, so she doubted a day had past, but paying attention more to the black smoke rising overhead, there would be a time where she wouldn't be able to tell the difference from night or day.

And yet it seemed, as she got her thoughts back on track together, Ted and Jeff seemed to not take notice of one another, regardless of their hatred: for once. Though she did notice the pupils in Jeff's eyes scan back over to Ted every now and again, as if expecting Ted to stab him. *But with what?* That was the question.

And then there was Lamar, limping away. This was going to be hard on him most of all. He seemed to have his eyes mainly on Ted, as if to wait for orders from him, and not from someone like Jeff, almost like he didn't trust him. Though whenever Lamar did dare share even a glance at Jeff, his eyes narrowed into a scowl, there was certainly more than even Lamar was letting on.

John on the other hand, still seemed very isolated from the group, his blazer swaying in the wind. He shook his head before walking over, sticking two thumbs in his pocket. "Ted, what's the game plan here? We can't just wait here, now, can we? Out in the open like this, like cattle."

"No, you can't," he sneered at the politician. "Spadero was it, why don't you be the first to jump right in that mess. Sure, some cover of buildings and cars, but the cover in this situation will do more harm than good. Trip over some bars, or deal with shattering glass, or other like fragments as the artillery blows the cover to bits. Give me a minute more—"

"A minute more, and there'll be no cover to hide behind!" Jeff declared, stepping off to the side. Sakura turned to face him. Samantha could tell she was thinking behind that frown, her almond shaped eyes squinted. The newcomer to their little dysfunctional family, as dysfunctional as it gets, especially now, had her hands in fists clenched at her sides. There was a time to talk, but now simply wasn't it.

"Clemens, you little bitch! In case you haven't noticed; artillery is our enemy here. Far away. Do you see any infantry here? Because I sure don't." Ted hot-temperedly replied, and Sam knew all eyes were on him. Hers especially. This was foreign territory to her. She didn't understand the first thing about escaping *this*. But Ted, she knew, was an expert, and he would show her how, regardless of Jeff's perspective. He brought his voice down to a warble. "Unless of course you know something I don't. Do you?"

Jeff frowned, and jerked his head back, pulling on his ear.

"They will bomb this area, until it's flattened. No cover. Then they'll send in the calvary, and infantry before building up their own base of operations here, input a few radio-signal towers to keep them all nice and handy while the rest of the world is scrambling. Then, will any cover found be worth hiding behind?" Ted explained. "Then, and only then will we move."

Samantha turned her gaze towards downtown, and saw many buildings crumbling to the ground, just as he predicted. There still was some though.

"How would you possibly know that?" Jeff still dissented.

"Because I fought the Russians!" Ted growled, snarling and baring teeth at him like a dog. "I know how they think! You'd think the same too, should you have the balls to fight them. Oh wait, you were emasculated, weren't you?"

Jeff hissed, shaking his head.

"Tedward," Jennifer touched his hand softly, interwove their fingers together. "Please. Now might not be the best time nor place for this. Let us get to somewhere safer, yes?"

"I'm sorry," he turned to her immediately. He let out a sigh, and his facial expression changed entirely, and his gaze softened, the skin on his face relaxed, and his posture loosened.

Sam ignored them a moment, gazing past them, and just like he said, the debris, and any semblance of cover was gone, minus the flames themselves. And the whistling stopped. The ground shook, and she assumed bombs were still being dropped elsewhere nearby, but not here. And that was the important thing.

"Okay, you happy now? We can go," Ted pointed to Erin. "Lead the way. Don't look at the ground. You don't have to run; it'll take some time for the infantry to mobilize."

Erin's eyes were wide opened, but she nodded at Ted's request. They all followed Erin through the rubble. Samantha felt Michael's arm around her shoulder as they walked, finally slowed down with the adrenaline rush, and her heart rate slowed down to what she thought it should be. She leaned into his grasp, allowing herself a sense of calm filling her soul. Th nerves in her arms forced them to tremble, and there wasn't anything she could do about it, just let it vent, and the anxiety fill her, the contrast to Michael's warmth and soothing spirit was unwelcomed.

Well, that was until she ignored Ted's advice as they stepped through the town of Sudbury. Glass shimmering, beautifully crimson, and yet, oh so terrifying. The smoke stunk as the smell of burning meat assaulted her nostrils, and oil, spilling on the ground. The glass broke underneath her feet, crunching, scratching at her ears, like the shards of glass that cut into her face. Flames cackled and burned the debris, and signs unrecognizable.

An arm, limp, lifeless. Just merely resting there peacefully on a street sign, covered in soot. Some ash and embers underneath, slowly dying down, and one might have guessed, the snow was hastily melting. Water, with maroon slowly undulating over the ground, into some grates, which wouldn't have been an appropriate place to enter the sewers.

A little boy.

She couldn't take her eyes off him, but she covered her mouth and came to a complete stop. Michael stopped with her and shared the same horrified expression.

He was just a little a boy. Who couldn't have been more than six years old. The body was petrified. His skull was caved in by a brick. Blood dripping down with an open mouth, teeth shattered, and half the jaw was dangling over his chest as it leaned out of the debris of a closet. Eyes were wide opened, bulging like staring at a cat that was run over by its torso.

Footsteps followed right by her. Ted, grabbed a flaming plank of wood, burning in his hands. "I told you not to look down. Go follow Erin. I'll catch up."

Sam hesitated. *Where were his parents?*

"Now! We don't have time for useless sentiments." Ted scolded.

Michael turned her around and they followed at a brisk pace. However, she couldn't help but look at Ted one more time, the plank, burning. Ted looked at the ground and set the boy on fire. The corpse screamed not. But then, why? Why burn him when he's already dead? Then she remembered something, a quote from someone in a book she couldn't recall the name of, 'There, funeral pyre, fuels the fire, fit for a king'.

Some jets soared overhead. Dropping nothing. Just fear, and anxiety as it plagued her heart, but she followed Ted's advice this time. "Don't look down. Don't look down. Whatever you do, don't look down." She kept telling herself, hoping that it would take the images out of her head. The arm, resting in a midst of beauty, and tragedy, and a boy burned, and body broken.

"Here, but I can't get it open," Erin said.

Jeff grabbed some metal pole off the ground and walked to Erin. She felt Ted's breath behind her, and she could tell by the way he was breathing, exasperated, studying what Jeff was doing with the rod. As Sam grew closer, she saw Jeff take the bar of steel, and stab it into the manhole cover, and twisted it. "Cooper, give me a hand." Lamar rushed over with his limp and assisted in removing the manhole cover. The stench coming up from it was somehow worse than the debris of what used to be Sudbury.

One by one, they took steps, slowly going into the dark. No flashlights, no lighters. Just darkness as she heard the puddles and steps of water, rippling underneath them. Ted was the last one in, and he, by hand, returned the manhole cover. The blood in her body went cold, and her hair stood on ends. The footsteps echoed in these dark halls, as well as the dripping of water. She rubbed her hands together, breathing heavily into them, warming the only part of her body she could.

"Need a jacket?" a voice said. She turned, unable to see who it was.

"Yes," Sam shivered.

"Here," it was John Spadero who handed her his own blazer.

"Thu—thank you," she took it, wrapping it around her. It wasn't much, but it would do.

"Jennifer," Tim's annoying voice called out. Annoying. Yes. Welcomed. clearly.

"Yes, Timothy?" her voice carried over like a bell, slowly approaching her.

"Are you okay?"

"That I am. Thank you for asking the most important of questions. Sadly, I don't have any water for you to spit out," her chuckles were ominous here.

"Is this really the time?" Sakura yelped out from the distance.

"You could be dead in fifteen minutes. Maybe your last words will be an ill-timed ass joke," Jeff said, who, based on the distance of his voice, was even further away than Sakura was.

"I'd rather not be dead in fifteen minutes," she rebuked him harshly. "But the singularly most important question that needs answering, is what do we do now?"

"Hmm?" Ted said. Sam could tell he was right next to Jennifer for the sound of his voice was close by, though she couldn't see him. "Give me a minute to think on it."

***

"Fuck!" Culain scowled from underneath the rocks. He pushed the rubble off from him. Sheet metal to his side, and when he looked up, oh what a thrill that was, looking up, seeing the very thing he knew he shouldn't be able to see. *Fucking stars!* The roof was gone!

Hissing through his teeth, he pulled himself up. The hotel was leveled. Completely. Some bodies and limbs were crushed underneath. Found a few fingers, severed, in such a sad state of affairs. He shook his head, and some dust crumbled out of his hair. He took his ear to the sheet metal, listening. The ground trembled, and some cries for help here, screams for some other incomprehensible reason he couldn't discern, as even more annoying, the damn planes soaring overhead, slicing through the air. *I'm not drunk enough for this shit.*

"Culain!" came a warbled voice. He knew it was Ilya. "You alright?"

"Fucking barely. I see the damn stars!" he glowered. "Blanka and Alexander?"

"Here, at least," Blanka spoke, her voice pushed through the rubble. Alexander jumped off to the side.

"Russians invaded in the middle of the night."

Ilya nursed a sprained wrist, wrapping it in some cloth.

"Ilya," Culain turned to her. "Do you know why?"

"I know not," she said to him. "Why would they ruin the holiness of Christmas?"

"You're Russian! You should know," Alexander exclaimed.

"Well, Alex," she shot back sarcastically. "China invaded the West. Russia is invading the East. Those global trade deals were nightmares for everyone involved. This was a natural occurrence."

"China, I understand," Blanka said. Culain listened closely. It was clear none of them knew why the invasions were really happening, and just trying to find the answer that made sense. "But Russia."

"Relations haven't been great with Russia as of late either," Ilya replied coldly.

"But not enough to fucking invade on the quagmire of a superpower."

"We can speculate on all this—"

"No!" Culain interrupted. "We need something."

"Speculation will get us nowhere," Ilya explained. "And we don't have time for this!"

"We're so close to our objective. And then this happens."

"A coincidence is what this is," Ilya pushed back.

"Unless we're made to think that," Blanka suggested as another jet flew overhead.

Culain peered his head around the corner of the sheet metal. Buildings were burning, glass shimmered as it fell out of skyscrapers. The metal wrenching that terribly dreadful noise as the steel buildings collapsed on themselves. People screamed, running disorganized, and the police cruisers, who could forget, trying to act as barricades. The emergency air horn raised as pistols, for whatever reason, aimed at amphibious armed vehicles approaching up the streets. *Why would you think a fucking pistol will do the trick?*

"What are you getting at?" Alexander crossed his arms.

"Think about it," Blanka continued as the screams grew louder, and more agonizing. "China and Russia started moving almost as soon as Spadero became involved."

"Are you accusing Spadero?"

"No. He's loyal, though selfish, to Camelot. We've seen that much out of him. But he did have to get information that none of us had access to. Which means, someone from the American Branch of the military also knows that Camelot is looking for this Ghost."

Made sense, Culain reasoned. But of course, further questions needed answers before they could do anything else. Why send China and Russia? And Russia even delayed.

"As far as any further explanation, just like we all assume, whoever else knows, likely assumes the same thing. Ghost, or Ted as he calls himself, has a link to McCurdy and therefore the Grail. Sending Russia to kill him by collateral damage would be ideal and would sever any lead we have to obtaining that information."

"So, whoever Spadero spoke to was likely behind this. But there's no evidence," Alexander scoffed, shaking his head. "A lot of good that does us, now, Blanka. This was worthless."

"So, great. Someone is trying to kill the target," Culain said. *Grave. So, there's a traitor, and lines of questions will follow, but those ones aren't important right now.* "Ilya, where is Spadero now?"

"He said he was with Ghost and his friends at Sudbury," she answered.

Alexander took out his phone.

"Don't even bother," Ilya said, waving her hand rather passively. "That won't work. Way too much radio activity going on right now." She turned to the rest of them. "So, Sudbury is west towards central Massachusetts. About thirty-ish miles, I think. So, he's not in immediate harm."

"Why don't we just go there and—"

"What did I say about being Irish!" she scolded Culain. "Sudbury is big. Area wise. They sure as hell aren't there now. Probably went south, north maybe, or further west. At this point, we can assume the information I have on their location is outdated, and we have no way to get that information right now. Let's go underground. Let whatever is coming come over us, and we'll think of something else, but I can't think with all this noise."

"Subway tunnels sound nice," Blanka suggested rather sarcastically, unusual for her.

"Yes, I think those tunnels will do nicely. Quiet in comparison, but for much longer, hard to say," Ilya replied. "Culain, why don't you shut down the power in the subways, so we don't need to worry about the trains running us over."

"Fine," he replied, none too happy about the role of which Ilya was taking, but her ability to be soft and sweet, and instantly turn to a dictator if needed was what he loved about her so much. It was such a shame she was barren, for the two of them did want children.

Chapter 2 Failure to Communicate

~Flames of war were all too familiar to me, but to them? We birthed them into it. Years and months came by; guilt eating me alive like a parasite. Until I myself became dead inside.

***

Sergeant Jackson rode shotgun in the Humvee with his unit, already rolling towards the front lines. This wasn't a pretty sight by any stretch of the imagination. His unit wasn't the first ones there, already, he saw evacuation sites, ushering civilians towards the FOB over in Spencer. Large, armored vehicles, being pushed in, as other rangers were sloppily putting together some mines on the field, sandbags, and barricaded themselves inside the shattered windows of the building. Eyes and lasers pointed out.

The field was gutted. Choppers rising up, delivering munitions and other supplies to their little base, eerily fragile, he would call it, and the scent of blood was filling his nostrils, iron, metallic, and most certainly, unwelcomed. His heart pumped as he looked down, his hand trembled as he unlocked the truck, and jumped outside.

"All Units, standby. Amphibious tangos riding up from the coastline," the radio coughed. "Calvary Oscar Mike your position, ETA fifteen mikes."

Just then, planes split the air, thundering above. He looked up, heart pounding, and the whistling of bombs coming down.

"Move! Move! Move!" Ramirez urged as the rest of his company retreated into the buildings.

The bombs struck; some Humvees were shattered. Limbs went limp, swiveling like loose bolts at the joints. The burning fumes of the air assaulted his nostrils with petrol, and the metal, unmistakable scent of flesh scorching. Soon, he was certain, the flies would come buzzing. No man or women survived who were in the Humvees; including the captain of this regiment, who perished without so much as a scream could evacuate from his lips.

The building was empty, but sturdy, could survive another air raid, but that was it. He pushed himself to the edge of one of the windows, aiming down the sights with his holographic sights, scanning the horizon, dark, and dreary night, hearing the heavy engines rolling up toward them. Ramirez was right by his side, not much his senior. Both patiently waiting.

A voice, Ensign Anderson, one of those silent types, but spoke up when needed to, and that need was great. "Who's got the radio?"

"I do," Specialist Cross called from across the other side of the room, voice echoing by the metal walls. Jackson didn't need to look. He recognized their voices, as only true brothers did.

"Call in command," the building shook amidst more bombs being dropped. "We need air support. We don't have fifteen mikes."

"Command, this is Bravo, do you read? Over." Cross called into the radio.

Jackson didn't blink, his finger trembling ever so slightly near the trigger.

The radio coughed, but nothing comprehensible.

"Command, this is Bravo, do you read me? Over."

The radio coughed again. Nothing comprehensible, but almost again, as if they heard their pleas for air support, the bombs stopped dropping at least.

"Command! Do you read me? This is Bravo. Over."

More of the same.

A sudden flash from a building over yonder, the distance was far and high up in a skyscraper.

"Incoming!"

Jackson felt Ramirez's hand push him, hard, collapsing ono the ground. A shell dropped right on their position. The sound was blaring, it rang in his ears, and sand pushed back everywhere, iron shrapnel shattered, and right inside the building, there was a way in. Jackson grimaced as he pulled himself up, peering just around the corner, his rifle aimed down.

Tanks rolled over the ground, breaking apart the concrete underneath their weight. Infantry soldiers coming in from behind them, using them as cover. The gun atop the tank was firing rounds into the building, shaking the foundations underneath.

"Take Cover!" Jackson declared as he pushed himself behind the steel wall. Bullets struck the building. Flesh and blood ripped, by his comrades, falling to the ground, dead. One was dying, but his body was leaning out the window. One ranger, a private, he didn't know, went to retrieve the dead body.

A large sonic boom entered the air, and a flash from one of the larger buildings.

"Sniper!" Jackson couldn't tell who this warning came from, for the tone, the different pitches of them all were drowned out by the chaotic sound of battle, it was almost indiscernible.

The private's head was ripped clean off.

"COMMAND—"

"Don't bother. They can't hear us," Anderson said calmly. "We're on our own." He clicked his tongue, before addressing Jackson. "You get a positive ID on that Cuckoo?"

"Second building. Third floor. Second window to the left," he replied, pointing just around the corner. Anderson looked closely to the building and stepped immediately into cover.

"Jackson, take point. Take Ramirez, Cross, and Tesla with you. Get into that building and take out the bird's nest. We'll draw fire, and pop smoke," Anderson immediately planned.

Not like this can't go wrong at all.

"Radio frequencies, I'm assuming are jammed. Short wave frequencies might still work," he sighed. "It's probably best you assume there won't be radio contact. Fire a green flare when completed. Failure, fire a standard flare just in case."

Anderson positioned himself, and Cross, Ramirez, Tesla, lined up behind Jackson.

"Lay down suppressing fire! Get an RPG on that tank!" Anderson called out.

"Popping smoke!" Ramirez's loud voice screamed in Jackson's ears as he, begrudgingly, sprinted out the hole in the barricade into the smoke, hissing as he hurried into the building, and three lone Rangers with him. He felt his heart skipping a beat, as he recited the Ranger's Creed to himself.

***

Major Barnes forced himself into the situation room. Officers around the board stood at attention as he forced his eyes onto the strategy board, taking note. "At ease." He scowled and turned to the radios. They seemed quiet. Too quiet. He turned to Warrant Officer Tran. "Sitrep."

"The 75th Ranger regiment is deployed to the front lines, holding onto the coastline. Civilians are now evacuated right on the coast, as far as towns in between us and them, they're unfortunately on their own." She replied, her face solemn. "However, there is one concern. They can't hear us."

"What do you mean?" Barnes asked, carefully frowning into her eyes.

"The soldiers on the ground can't hear us. They've called in but won't call in support. We've responded, but they don't answer back, only repeating themselves repeatedly. However, this might be due to a 1-way communication jammer."

"So, we can't talk to them. Shit." He swore under his breath. "Jammer, do we have any sights on this jammer?"

"Negative," Tran replied, before turning back to the board. "But a jammer this efficient would have to be a large one. We have no sights on it. Could be underground. Or on one of their carriers."

"In other words, we don't know where this jammer is, or how large," Barnes replied, scratching his chin.

"As effective as it is, my best guess with the information we have is that it's sophisticated enough to require adequate space, but something small enough that could be hidden," Tran said. "Regardless, we can't really do anything without knowledge that can only be obtained with boots on the ground."

Barnes looked down at the board. Navy vessels were closing in around Boston Harbor, and Army Rangers, while holding strong, would not hold for long. Not without adequate support that he knows he can't send in without being able to communicate outside the zone. What kind of equipment will be required to take down this jammer? *If they could communicate that they've the location we can potentially blow it with JDAMs.*

"We can hear them, correct? No. That will never work. Shit," he looked her in the eye. "What kind of equipment will we need to dismantle it?"

"Difficult to say since I don't know what it is, I need to get in there, but you're out of your mind if you think I'm going in there without help."

I could kill two birds with one stone here, but the risk still far outweighs the reward.

"You remember how to jump?"

"Yes," she chuckled. "Of course, I do. Wasn't very good at it."

"Captain Copply," he turned to a woman, who turned her chair around. "Get the airborne paratroopers on the field, and get them ready to deploy, and debrief them." He turned back to Tran. "I'm sending you in with Delta."

Chapter 3 Fury

~I look at my baby girl. Only it's not her I see anymore, much the same way it's not her father she sees with those innocent orbs in her head. I see them. All. Thirty-two of them. Some burned. Others shot to shit and Roach; I can still feel her knife cutting at my rotator cuff.

***

A large ruckus at his wooden door, glorious it was, except the person knocking on this dreaded door could use some drumming lessons. The nerve. Adam woke up, bolting right up, rubbing his eyes. He shifted over to his bed and pulled on a t-shirt. The knock was louder, and more obnoxious this time as it rapped against his ears.

"I'm coming!" He put on his slippers. One might never know the beauty of sleep or being rested well enough. He swung the door open, and Bridgette, with her hair on ends, tangled, knotted. She had a scowl on her face, creases around her nose, but the scowl spoke not of anger, but of serious concern. One might think World War III was upon them. "What happened to you?"

She brushed her hair over her shoulder, tilting her head as she curled her lips upward. He hated that she did that. It's almost like she knew it bothered him. "Oh, nothing really, just the fact that Russia is bombing the East Coast of the United States as we speak, and heavily focused on Boston, where, you know, our person of interest happens to be."

He could feel the silence of his room expanding. That's not good at all. Won't do. *Mikhail.* He pushed her to the side and sprinted down the hall, and swiftly opened his office, unlocking the door's arcane symbols, turning before the door swung open. He didn't bother shutting the door, but went down to his computer, turning it on, and looked at the news to confirm it. Several articles all more or less saying the same thing with the grim headline, "Boston is France's Normandy,." Oh, yes, indeed. This won't do at all. He turned to his hand receiver, dialed Mikhail's number.

"Administrator Mikhail, away on urgent business. Please leave your name and brief description of the call. I'll call you back within the next three business days."

Shite! "Mikhail, Adam here, call me back when you get this. Immediately!" He touched the receiver as Bridgette entered the room and closed the door behind them. He dialed Colton.

"Administrator Colton, North American Division. I cannot be reached at this time. Please leave your name, and brief description of the reason for your call and I'll be sure to contact you back within the next three business days."

"Colton, Adam here, call me back when you get this. Immediately!" he slammed the phone to the receiver, and drafted a few emails, and looked up to Bridgette. "What can you tell me of the attacks so far."

"It would appear, Adam, that we were so caught up in the theft of the Grail and everything else, we failed to realize America was about to fight a two-front war between China and Russia. China attacked almost immediately, while Mother Russia has just been wading around in the water. The politics around the war in United States has been, well, uneventful with the President missing."

President? How does the President just go missing? More importantly, how do they just go missing and it not make international television? How did I miss this?

"And of course, the West Coast was obliterated by China, after a whole sleuth of politicking by one impressive executive officer of Black Eagle: Ethan Malcolm. Of course, he retook the West Coast, and is pushing China back, and making his way around to fight the East Coast. But, I doubt he'll make it in time before, well, the person of interest, is killed in collateral."

"The President couldn't have just gone missing and unnoticed by the rest of the world," Adam said, leaning back in his chair. Bridgette took her spot before leaning forward on his desk, violently tapping an impatient index finger.

"Do you think this was Sarah's doing?" she inquired.

A fair question as any. "No. This is far too complex for one person to do. Colton had to be behind Snells' disappearance. There's no other explanation as it was kept reasonably on the hush hush, at least until now. I definitely would have noticed that. But that doesn't explain Russia's or China's involvement in this operation. With things as they are now, those two powers converging on America could be considered organic. But then, why on Earth wouldn't Russia just invade on both fronts, instead of coming all the way through the East."

"Shite," Bridgette swore. "As if we didn't have enough unanswerable questions as it was, what's fifteen more, eh?"

"I'll have to wait on Mikhail's callback. Nothing more I can do," he looked up to her and waved a hand. "Would you be a good dear and get me some tea. I have to try to figure out something."

Chapter 4 Into the Fray

~I want to die. That would be a fitting end for someone like me.

***

Ted looked up at the blackness. Ground still shook, but not as severe as it was before. Surrounding towns were probably leveled. Just like he predicted. He was too right when it came to predicting things. He knew it. A curse, it was, more than a blessing. He heard all the other people down here chatting away, and Lamar, the marine, had been sporting off a nice lighter for some light. *Of course, not like I need to see Clemens wretched face down here. That would be too nice.*

Sitting, his butt wet through his pants, and Jennifer's hand rested on his shoulders. A warm soft touch. Alien it was to him. A touch he rarely felt, except in the hands of Slithers. Only she was ever this kind to him. She loved him in a way he felt Jennifer love him. She knew the façade he held up, and accepted the lies, knowing entirely that it was all fake. And none of that seemed to matter to her.

She was, precious to him. More so than, anything else. Slithers, she was precious to him, and the rest of his comrades from Task Force Seven, but they were all dead. But Jennifer, innocent, pulled into this Hell of War; she was still alive. *Going out there is the last thing I want to do. But if it means you live, I'll gladly do it. And get you to the FOB. That's the only solution here.*

"Look!" Sakura said, scolding Lamar with the light beaming her face. "We can't just stay here."

"Look, I know how you feel but—"

"Hey, ROTC-bitch!" Ted screamed from the other side of the room.

"Ted! That's inappropriate!" Erin called to him.

"I don't give a shit. So, ROTC-Bitch, tell me, you're going to school to become an officer. Why don't you go ahead and tell me what it is we should do?" Ted said, feeling Jennifer's hand squeeze his shoulder. She's never seen him like this. In times of war, he remembered, little time for mourning, little time for anything other than the task at hand. There simply was no time for niceties. "Go ahead, I'll *await* your answer."

"We can't stay here; we need to leave!" she stamped her foot in the puddles, the sound of the ripples of the sewage echoed on the walls.

"And go where exactly? Should I give you a roadmap?" Ted noticed Lamar roll his eyes. He knew. Give an officer a map was a sure way to drive a truck into a ditch. "Where do we go from here?"

She hissed. Her fists at her side, clenching tightly.

"Now, let me think." *Clemens is going to be a problem. I need to presume he's going to fuck me over. I could tie him. Could kill him. Would make things easier, but then I have to account for them not listening to me because I just killed someone for, what any reasonable person would perceive as no reason at all. That'll never work. I could send them west, in hopes to get them to the FOB, provided that is, one is currently set up.* "Clemens, do you know something I don't?"

"What?" he asked dismissively. *Trying to avoid me, are you?*

"FOB. Where is it?"

"FOB?" Samantha turned her head to him.

"Forward Operating Base," Ted answered.

"Why would you think I'd know where that was?" Clemens pushed back. "No, I don't."

"Take a guess," Ted scowled, not trusting him. He knew something. But what?

"I couldn't tell you, no idea," Clemens continued with his façade, lips curled upwards in a snarl.

Well, that was pointless.

Ted sighed, his fingers rapidly snapping, resounding off these walls. "Well, let's see then," he scratched his chin as he felt all eyes were on him. "Getting shelled from Russia's navy, combined with heavy barrages of dropped bombs from air crafts, Tupolev Tu 95 by the sounds of it." He heard the jets from above, muffled with the concrete overhead. "Most likely sending in amphibious armor to capture the mainland before sending in the infantry to set up base, and just steamroll right over the sewers, get the drop on us," he chuckled. "That'd be just my luck. Blitzkrieg. Only this time, no sound trenches to hide in. Likely sabotaged Portland's port already. Probably already on their way with some nice heavy calvary. Hell, it would be a great idea to attack Sandy's beach. A nice way to bypass all those pesky islands in three bays.

"Of course, the Rangers would have already been dispatched from this mythical FOB at a location of which no one apparently knows. Probably pushed themselves right into the action. Probably buy civilians just west of Boston another hour or so, well, before they're all blown up to smithereens. And then steam roll right on to the west. Incompetent fools.

"Probably start bombing civilian populations shortly to send the military in disarray as they slowly break ranks and morale, fueled with nothing but a quagmire in which nothing at all makes sense. Navy is probably close, harboring against what little Navy the United States has stationed right here. Terrible business that. Well, sunken navy vessels will be a bitch to avoid. Make it harder for them to anchor nearby. Carriers are probably taking a backseat. Just holding on to those fighter jets and bombers for a last hurrah.

"I'm about thirty miles. Thirty miles is what separates me and the Russian infantry, but no, that's not what's important here. That damned FOB! Where is it? Portland in all likelihood, and then Sandy's beach, in all likelihood, and most certainly Boston. Rangers will get pushed there, and inevitably flanked. Sounds like a reverse Schlieffen plan to me. Oh, shit. They're all gonna die there." His cackles went off the walls, echoing vehemently. He saw everyone in the room, and all, except Jennifer, looked at him like the monster he was.

Sakura made eye contact with him though, and it seemed to him, she was the only one of them who had any balls to talk to him in this state. Well, Jeff never had any balls to begin with. They shriveled up in whatever previous life he was taken from. He might as well be dickless. Or Sakura stole his. Another chuckle. As naïve as she was, guts she was not in short supply. Such is the stuff of legends, that is, should they live long enough.

"You seem talkative," she began. "What—"

"And if I was, it doesn't mean I was talking to you, now does it?" He sneered at her, looking at her body as she immediately came to a halt.

The lights flickering at the glistening sewage on her fists as they clenched, shaking. Sakura bit her lip as if to hide her own emotions, her own anger, of which, Ted was sure he was the cause of. Hearing sporadic ripples and splashes, his gaze turned to Sam, who's hands trembled at her side with shallow breaths.

She heard Ted's words, and they were different, and what was inside him, this new persona of which she'd never been exposed to before, was sarcastic, cold, and calculating. Those eyes were even empty. No smile outside the inappropriately placed laughs and chuckles. Seemed like even he was lost without a clear way to get them anywhere, but the one thing almost everyone universally agreed upon, was they can't stay in the sewers, for sooner or later, the Russians will be rolling right on top of them. The terror of their situation was illustrated through Ted's battle madness; she called it.

She remembered that day when she forced him out to the café, and he barely drank or ate anything. The words he spoke, his comparison to dictators, the ones he illustrated himself. Averting her gaze to Jennifer, a calm, caring face who was right behind him, accepting that whatever Ted decided to do, would be necessary. Of course, her heart pumped faster. Ask Sam to book a truck really cheap, she could do that. Manage her own emotions in the middle of the prospect of being shot at by people that didn't speak her language, from lands foreign and across the sea, that was something else entirely. She'd almost take losing her customer which she spent a full year trying to procure over this. The sad part about this is that she probably already lost it.

Ted had seen war and has had his fair share of battles. He made that clear to her, and to Jennifer, and still, Jennifer didn't seem frightened. The other thing that bothered her, was he spoke of things of which he should have no knowledge on, as if predicting the battle and how it would go should he not intervene. What was in his head?

And then she remembered the singularly most terrifying thing he ever said to her. Her mouth gaped open when he said to her in that café, 'They said that Saul killed his thousands, and David his tens of thousands. I on the other hand would be lucky if my numbers were nearly that low.' Now, she knew he spoke the truth, and briefly wondered precisely how many people he killed. But that wasn't important. Not now. What was important, is should that be true, only *he* alone could guide them to safety. And there wasn't a doubt in her mind that he was thinking how best to do that.

She broke away from Michael, and briskly walked to him. "Ted," she said, he looked up to her, with a soft compassionate face. Another façade maybe? Or perhaps he genuinely cared about her almost as much as he seemed to Jennifer. "What are we going to do?"

"I'm still thinking, Sam. When I know, you'll know," he answered. "It's best to stay here in the sewers for now."

Sam sighed before walking just past him to lean on Jennifer. The silence was getting to her, what passed for silence anyways, and the threat of oncoming doom paired with them doing nothing was not helping her nerves. Feeling helpless, she elected not to say anything, as she looked at her friends, the orange hue of the light of Lamar's lighter lit the walls of the sewer, and she dared not look down at the sewage. Smelling it was bad enough, and then, she realized Jeff too seemed nervous, and his hands seemed a bit busy for her comfort. What was going on in his head? The other such person among them who was no stranger to battle kept moving his head to the walls, and to the ceilings, as if expecting it to collapse.

Jeff frowned as his hand was in his pocket, fingering his sidearm, gazing at Spadero, whose arms were crossed. Spadero was the one person who just didn't fit here. What was he doing with them? What was he after? *As suspicious as all damned politicians. Live cozy lives they do, sending us to do their dirty work, and the world doesn't quite know yet, that they are the real villains behind all of this. Some with action, others inaction. But I need to get to that FOB, and Malcolm. I can't very well contact him from in here. Radio disturbance is going to make that far more difficult without risking the open air and get shot with a stray.*

Ghost said the Russians will have attacked Portland, Boston, and Sandy's Beach. I don't know where that is, I assume South now, but a three-pronged attack here. Why? But if that's the case, the Army will want to be able to supply all three fronts, so they'd need a logistical solution from one spot that could as easily get to all three points. It'd have to far enough to remain out of range of those guns. Worcester?

I'm not going to be able to leave the party without Malcolm's direction.

I see those gears turning now. Don't think I don't notice. Amidst all of what's going outside, you didn't think I'd overlook this. Overlook you? You may be small to me, but the risk of just considering leaving you alive is disastrous, but I can't just kill you. That would complicate things to a degree of which even I can't predict. Shit. I just don't have enough information to make a good call. Ted thought.

Ted turned his face to Lamar. "Marine, how's that leg doing?"

"Ted," Sakura got in front of him. "Whatever it is, I can do it. He has a limp."

"Thanks for the concern, but I'll manage," Lamar looked down, and grinned before turning a more suitable straight face back at Ted. "How can I help?"

"Oh, you really can't help me, but there's refrigerators and pantries that need raiding. Food and water. Go up, bring them down here, and stay put," Ted answered. "I'm going on a scouting trip."

"Are you insane!" Everyone, except Jennifer's, Clemens', and Spadero's voice was raised in protest.

"Look. I don't have enough information. And I don't know where to go. I need the precise location of the FOB before I can attempt to guide you to safety. This is the only way I can get that information. There is no other way." He turned to Lamar. "Do me a favor. I'd rather not be herding cats when I get back. Keep everyone here. Do not leave until I return."

Lamar sighed, "Affirmative."

"And should," his voice dropped low. "I not return, and there are others who come to escort you out, do not go with them, unless they tell you, 'Seven.'"

Mustn't forget this little primitive shit. "Clemens, I know the saying, you are what you eat, but please don't be a dick," Lamar coughed. "Remember the words I said to you?" He glared into his eyes. *Fear. That's right. You don't have Nakamura anymore to hide behind. My chains are gone.* "It would be wise of you to heed them."

Ted moved to the ladder, and the echoes of his feet on the bars filled Spadero's ears as he watched him go up, remove the manhole cover, and Lamar followed behind him. *World War III. How incredibly inconvenient. Almost like every time I'm so close to him, he ends up far away. Not like I can just chase after him. It's almost like someone knows about this that shouldn't, following in my wake, silently mocking me. It isn't anyone here. Can't be, though Clemens, the man who seems to have some bad blood between Ghost, I'm less sure of. And then of course, should this go awry, and everyone but me ends up killed because of it, will raise suspicions from him. Ghost clearly isn't stupid.*

But this group of people here, there's something about some of them, Sam, and Jennifer in particular. This poor fellow Michael and Tim really just seem to be in the background most of the time, as if carefully scheming themselves. But they're not sinister. Clemens might be. His head is thinking, but his lips refuse to move. He knows something. But what? Whatever it is, might not be related to my purpose here, but Ghost is wary of him, so too should I be. But what part are you playing, Jeff Clemens?

Characters

Adam Sander: Chief Administrator for the Caster's Administrator.

Alexander: Native to London, a silent type, and a representative of the Caster's Administration.

Alexandra: Malcolm's wife.

Andrea: First Lady and wife to President Snells.

Arjun: Head fae Administrator of India.

Blanka: An Administrator from the Czech Republic. Enjoys her fine wine and excursions and wants nothing more than to get back home.

Bridgette: A London native, an administrator serving directly underneath Adam.

Butcher: Ted's friend from Task Force Seven.

Claire: Lead Fae Administrator of France.

Colton: Lead Fae administrator from the American Branch.

Culain: From Ireland, this administrator comes directly from Camelot. He's known for his outbursts.

Daiki: Head Fae Administrator of Japan.

Elias: Head Fae Administrator of Germany.

Emily Gutenberg: Erin's mother (currently undergoing cancer treatment).

Emily Miller: A delta force operator.

Erin Gutenberg: A stockbroker in Boston. She is part of how Jennifer puts it, "The dysfunctional family".

Gernardt: General of the Armies

Gwen Swan: Head Fae Administrator of Alaska. She also serves as Governor of that State.

Hector: Head Administrator of everything South of Rio Grande.

Ilya: A Russian representative for the Caster's Administration. She's made her home in Camelot.

Jack: A torture victim.

Jeff Clemens: An officer of Black Eagle Company. Michael Clemens' brother.

Jennifer Miller: A biological researcher in Boston. A close friend to Ted Anderson, and alone knows his secrets.

John Spadero: Fae administrator who also serves as Congressman in the state of Massachusetts.

Johnson: Secretary of Defense

Lamar Cooper: A former Marine.

Malcolm: Chief Operating Officer of Black Eagle Company.

Michael Clemens: Business developer consultant. Loves to experiment with his cocktails.

Mikhail: Lead Fae Administrator of Eastern Europe. He has a very playful demeanor.

Obi: Head Fae Administrator of Nigeria.

Oliver: Head Fae Administrator of Australia.

President Snells: President of the United States. To the world, he is considered the single man who brokered World Peace.

Rebecca: Archivist of the libraries inside Camelot.

Roach: Another agent from Task Force Seven

Sakura: An orphan and a college student, looking to serve as an officer of the United States of America.

Samantha Harris: A logistical broker in Boston. Friends with a small group of people, and thoroughly enjoys her Tuesdays,

Sarah McCurdy: Disavowed Fae of the Administration.

Slithers: Ted's deceased beloved from Task Force Seven.

Smith: Admiral of the Navies

Ted Anderson: The man with a past best left buried.

Ticker: Another agent from Task Force Seven.

Tim: An events coordinator. A real silent type.

Wang: Head Fae Administrator of China.

Don't miss out!

Visit the website below and you can sign up to receive emails whenever Armanis Ar-feinial publishes a new book. There's no charge and no obligation.

https://books2read.com/r/B-A-HSYS-DWXLD

BOOKS 2 READ

Connecting independent readers to independent writers.

Also by Armanis Ar-feinial

Dawn of Forest Black
The Plagued Elf

Dawn of Forest Black Omnibus collection
Dawn of Forest Black
The Dawn of Forest Black

The Holy Grail War
The Hedgehog
The Nihilistic Neverending Nightmare

Standalone
To Tedward
The Hedgehog Dilemma
Lira
No Happy Endings

www.ingramcontent.com/pod-product-compliance
Lightning Source LLC
Chambersburg PA
CBHW032252020726
47495CB00001B/72